The Heir Of Redclyffe

Vintage
Bookworks

The Heir of Redclyffe

Charlotte M. Yonge

United Kingdom
1853

CONTENTS

CHAPTER 1

In such pursuits if wisdom lies,
Who, Laura, can thy taste despise?
– GAY

The drawing-room of Hollywell House was one of the favoured apartments, where a peculiar air of home seems to reside, whether seen in the middle of summer, all its large windows open to the garden, or, as when our story commences, its bright fire and stands of fragrant green-house plants contrasted with the wintry fog and leafless trees of November. There were two persons in the room– a young lady, who sat drawing at the round table, and a youth, lying on a couch near the fire, surrounded with books and newspapers, and a pair of crutches near him. Both looked up with a smile of welcome at the entrance of a tall, fine-looking young man, whom each greeted with 'Good morning, Philip.'

'Good morning, Laura. Good morning, Charles; I am glad you are downstairs again! How are you to-day?'

'No way remarkable, thank you,' was the answer, somewhat wearily given by Charles.

'You walked?' said Laura.

'Yes. Where's my uncle? I called at the post-office, and brought a letter for him. It has the Moorworth post-mark,' he added, producing it.

'Where's that?' said Charles.

'The post-town to Redclyffe; Sir Guy Morville's place.'

'That old Sir Guy! What can he have to do with my father?'

'Did you not know,' said Philip, 'that my uncle is to be guardian to the boy– his grandson?'

'Eh? No, I did not.'

'Yes,' said Philip; 'when old Sir Guy made it an especial point that my father should take the guardianship, he only consented on condition that my uncle should be joined with him; so now my uncle is alone in the trust, and I cannot help thinking something must have happened at Redclyffe. It is certainly not Sir Guy's writing.'

'It must wait, unless your curiosity will carry you out in search of papa,' said Charles; 'he is somewhere about, zealously supplying the place of Jenkins.'

'Really, Philip,' said Laura, 'there is no telling how much good you have done him by convincing him of Jenkins' dishonesty. To say nothing of the benefit of being no longer cheated, the pleasure of having to overlook the farming is untold.'

Philip smiled, and came to the table where she was drawing. 'Do you know this place?' said she, looking up in his face.

'Stylehurst itself! What is it taken from?'

'From this pencil sketch of your sister's, which I found in mamma's scrap book.'

'You are making it very like, only the spire is too slender, and that tree— can't you alter the foliage?— it is an ash.'

'Is it? I took it for an elm.'

'And surely those trees in the foreground should be greener, to throw back the middle distance. That is the peak of South Moor exactly, if it looked further off.'

She began the alterations, while Philip stood watching her progress, a shade of melancholy gathering on his face. Suddenly, a voice called 'Laura! Are you there? Open the door, and you will see.'

On Philip's opening it, in came a tall camellia; the laughing face, and light, shining curls of the bearer peeping through the dark green leaves.

'Thank you! Oh, is it you, Philip? Oh, don't take it. I must bring my own camellia to show Charlie.'

'You make the most of that one flower,' said Charles.

'Only see how many buds!' and she placed it by his sofa. Is it not a perfect blossom, so pure a white, and so regular! And I am so proud of having beaten mamma and all the gardeners, for not another will be out this fortnight; and this is to go to the horticultural show. Sam would hardly trust me to bring it in, though it was my nursing, not his.'

'Now, Amy,' said Philip, when the flower had been duly admired, 'you must let me put it into the window, for you. It is too heavy for you.'

'Oh, take care,' cried Amabel, but too late; for, as he took it from her, the solitary flower struck against Charles's little table, and was broken off.

'O Amy, I am very sorry. What a pity! How did it happen?'

'Never mind,' she answered; 'it will last a long time in water.'

'It was very unlucky— I am very sorry— especially because of the horticultural show.'

'Make all your apologies to Sam,' said Amy, 'his feelings will be more hurt than mine. I dare say my poor flower would have caught cold at the show, and never held up its head again.'

Her tone was gay; but Charles, who saw her face in the glass, betrayed her by saying, 'Winking away a tear, O Amy!'

'I never nursed a dear gazelle!' quoted Amy, with a merry laugh; and before any more could be said, there entered a middle-aged gentleman, short and slight, with a fresh, weather-beaten, good-natured face, gray whiskers, quick eyes, and a hasty, undecided air in look and movement. He greeted Philip heartily, and the letter was given to him.

'Ha! Eh? Let us look. Not old Sir Guy's hand. Eh? What can be the matter? What? Dead! This is a sudden thing.'

'Dead! Who? Sir Guy Morville?'

'Yes, quite suddenly– poor old man.' Then stepping to the door, he opened it, and called, 'Mamma; just step here a minute, will you, mamma?'

The summons was obeyed by a tall, handsome lady, and behind her crept, with doubtful steps, as if she knew not how far to venture, a little girl of eleven, her turned-up nose and shrewd face full of curiosity. She darted up to Amabel; who, though she shook her head, and held up her finger, smiled, and took the little girl's hand, listening meanwhile to the announcement, 'Do you hear this, mamma? Here's a shocking thing! Sir Guy Morville dead, quite suddenly.'

'Indeed! Well, poor man, I suppose no one ever repented or suffered more than he. Who writes?'

'His grandson– poor boy! I can hardly make out his letter.' Holding it half a yard from his eyes, so that all could see a few lines of hasty, irregular writing, in a forcible hand, bearing marks of having been penned under great distress and agitation, he read aloud:–

'"DEAR MR. EDMONSTONE,–

My dear grandfather died at six this morning. He had an attack of apoplexy yesterday evening, and never spoke again, though for a short time he knew me. We hope he suffered little. Markham will make all arrangements. We propose that the funeral should take place on Tuesday; I hope you will be able to come. I would write to my cousin, Philip Morville, if I knew his address; but I depend on you for saying all that ought to be said. Excuse this illegible letter,– I hardly know what I write.

'"Yours, very sincerely,
'"Guy Morville."'

'Poor fellow!' said Philip, 'he writes with a great deal of proper feeling.'

'How very sad for him to be left alone there!' said Mrs. Edmonstone.

'Very sad– very,' said her husband. 'I must start off to him at once– yes, at once. Should you not say so– eh, Philip?'

'Certainly. I think I had better go with you. It would be the correct thing, and I should not like to fail in any token of respect for poor old Sir Guy.'

'Of course– of course,' said Mr. Edmonstone; 'it would be the correct thing. I am sure he was always very civil to us, and you are next heir after this boy.'

Little Charlotte made a sort of jump, lifted her eyebrows, and stared at Amabel.

Philip answered. 'That is not worth a thought; but since he and I are now the only representatives of the two branches of the house of Morville, it shall not be my fault if the enmity is not forgotten.'

'Buried in oblivion would sound more magnanimous,' said Charles; at which Amabel laughed so uncontrollably, that she was forced to hide her head on her little sister's shoulder. Charlotte laughed too, an imprudent proceeding, as it attracted attention. Her father smiled, saying, half-reprovingly– 'So you are there, inquisitive pussy-cat?' And at her mother's question,– 'Charlotte, what business have you here?' She stole back to her lessons, looking very small, without the satisfaction of hearing her mother's compassionate words– 'Poor child!'

'How old is he?' asked Mr. Edmonstone, returning to the former subject.

'He is of the same age as Laura– seventeen and a half,' answered Mrs. Edmonstone. 'Don't you remember my brother saying what a satisfaction it was to see such a noble baby as she was, after such a poor little miserable thing as the one at Redclyffe?'

'He is grown into a fine spirited fellow,' said Philip.

'I suppose we must have him here,' said Mr. Edmonstone. Should you not say so– eh, Philip?'

'Certainly; I should think it very good for him. Indeed, his grandfather's death has happened at a most favourable time for him. The poor old man had such a dread of his going wrong that he kept him– '

'I know– as tight as a drum.'

'With strictness that I should think very bad for a boy of his impatient temper. It would have been a very dangerous experiment to send him at once among the temptations of Oxford, after such discipline and solitude as he has been used to.'

'Don't talk of it,' interrupted Mr. Edmonstone, spreading out his hands in a deprecating manner. 'We must do the best we can with him, for I have got him on my hands till he is five-and-twenty– his grandfather has tied him up till then. If we can keep him out of mischief, well and good; if not, it can't be helped.'

'You have him all to yourself,' said Charles.

'Ay, to my sorrow. If your poor father was alive, Philip, I should be free of all care. I've a pretty deal on my hands,' he proceeded, looking more important than troubled. 'All that great Redclyffe estate is no sinecure, to say nothing of the youth himself. If all the world will come to me, I can't help it. I must go and speak to the men, if I am to be off to Redclyffe tomorrow. Will you come, Philip?'

'I must go back soon, thank you,' replied Philip. 'I must see about my leave; only we should first settle when to set off.'

This arranged, Mr. Edmonstone hurried away, and Charles began by saying, 'Isn't there a ghost at Redclyffe?'

'So it is said,' answered his cousin; 'though I don't think it is certain whose it is. There is a room called Sir Hugh's Chamber, over the gateway, but the honour of naming it is undecided between Hugo de Morville, who murdered Thomas a Becket, and his namesake, the first Baronet, who lived in the time of William of Orange, when the quarrel began with our branch of the family. Do you know the history of it, aunt?'

'It was about some property,' said Mrs Edmonstone, 'though I don't know the rights of it. But the Morvilles were always a fiery, violent race, and the enmity once begun between Sir Hugh and his brother, was kept up, generation after generation, in a most unjustifiable way. Even I can remember when the Morvilles of Redclyffe used to be spoken of in our family like a sort of ogres.'

'Not undeservedly, I should think,' said Philip. 'This poor old man, who is just dead, ran a strange career. Stories of his duels and mad freaks are still extant.'

'Poor man! I believe he went all lengths,' said Mrs. Edmonstone.

'What was the true version of that horrible story about his son?' said Philip. 'Did he strike him?'

'Oh, no! it was bad enough without that.'

'How?' asked Laura.

'He was an only child, and lost his mother early. He was very ill brought up, and was as impetuous and violent as Sir Guy himself, though with much kindliness and generosity. He was only nineteen when he made a runaway marriage with a girl of sixteen, the sister of a violin player, who was at that time in fashion. His father was very much offended, and there was much dreadfully violent conduct on each side. At last, the young man was driven to seek a reconciliation. He brought his wife to Moorworth, and rode to Redclyffe, to have an interview with his father. Unhappily, Sir Guy was giving a dinner to the hunt, and had been drinking. He not only refused to see him, but I am afraid he used shocking language, and said something about bidding him go back to his fiddling brother in-law. The son was waiting in the hall, heard everything, threw himself on his horse, and rushed away in the dark. His forehead struck against the branch of a tree, and he was killed on the spot.'

'The poor wife?' asked Amabel, shuddering.

'She died the next day, when this boy was born.'

'Frightful!' said Philip. 'It might well make a reformation in old Sir Guy.'

'I have heard that nothing could be more awful than the stillness that fell on that wretched party, even before they knew what had happened— before Colonel Harewood, who had been called aside by the servants, could resolve to come and fetch away the father. No wonder Sir Guy was a changed man from that hour.'

'It was then that he sent for my father,' said Philip.

'But what made him think of doing so?'

'You know Colonel Harewood's house at Stylehurst? Many years ago, when the St. Mildred's races used to be so much more in fashion, Sir Guy and Colonel Harewood, and some men of that stamp, took that house amongst them, and used to spend some time there every year, to attend to something about the training of the horses. There were some malpractices of their servants, that did so much harm in the parish, that my brother was obliged to remonstrate. Sir Guy was very angry at first, but behaved better at last than any of the others. I suspect he was struck by my dear brother's bold, uncompromising ways, for he took to him to a certain degree– and my brother could not help being interested in him, there seemed to be so much goodness in his nature. I saw him once, and never did I meet any one who gave me so much the idea of a finished gentleman. When the poor son was about fourteen, he was with a tutor in the neighbourhood, and used to be a good deal at Stylehurst, and, after the unhappy marriage, my brother happened to meet him in London, heard his story, and tried to bring about a reconciliation.'

'Ha!' said Philip; 'did not they come to Stylehurst? I have a dim recollection of somebody very tall, and a lady who sung.'

'Yes; your father asked them to stay there, that he might judge of her, and wrote to Sir Guy that she was a little, gentle, childish thing, capable of being moulded to anything, and representing the mischief of leaving them to such society as that of her brother, who was actually maintaining them. That letter was never answered, but about ten days or a fortnight after this terrible accident, Colonel Harewood wrote to entreat my brother to come to Redclyffe, saying poor Sir Guy had eagerly caught at the mention of his name. Of course he went at once, and he told me that he never, in all his experience as a clergyman, saw any one so completely broken down with grief.'

I found a great many of his letters among my father's papers,' said Philip; 'and it was a very touching one that he wrote to me on my father's death. Those Redclyffe people certainly have great force of character.'

'And was it then he settled his property on my uncle?' said Charles.

'Yes,' said Mrs. Edmonstone. 'My brother did not like his doing so, but he would not be at rest till it was settled. It was in vain to put him in mind of his grandchild, for he would not believe it could live; and, indeed, its life hung on a thread. I remember my brother telling me how he went to Moorworth to see it– for it could not be brought home– in hopes of bringing, back a report that might cheer its grandfather, but how he found it so weak and delicate, that he did not dare to try to make him take interest in it. It was not till the child was two or three years old, that Sir Guy ventured to let himself grow fond of it.'

'Sir Guy was a very striking person,' said Philip; 'I shall not easily forget my visit to Redclyffe four years ago. It was more like a scene in a romance than anything real– the fine old red sandstone house crumbling away in the exposed parts, the arched gateway covered with ivy; the great quadrangle where the sun never shone, and full of echoes; the large hall and black wainscoted rooms, which the candles never would light up. It is a fit place to be haunted.'

'That poor boy alone there!' said Mrs. Edmonstone; 'I am glad you and your uncle are going to him.'

'Tell us about him,' said Laura.

'He was the most incongruous thing there,' said Philip. 'There was a calm, deep melancholy about the old man added to the grand courtesy which showed he had been what old books call a fine gentleman, that made him suit his house as a hermit does his cell, or a knight his castle; but breaking in on this "penseroso" scene, there was Guy– '

'In what way?' asked Laura.

'Always in wild spirits, rushing about, playing antics, provoking the solemn echoes with shouting, whooping, singing, whistling. There was something in that whistle of his that always made me angry.'

'How did this suit old Sir Guy?'

'It was curious to see how Guy could rattle on to him, pour out the whole history of his doings, laughing, rubbing his hands, springing about with animation– all with as little answer as if he had been talking to a statue.'

'Do you mean that Sir Guy did not like it?'

'He did in his own way. There was now and then a glance or a nod, to show that he was attending; but it was such slight encouragement, that any less buoyant spirits must have been checked.'

'Did you like him, on the whole?' asked Laura. 'I hope he has not this tremendous Morville temper? Oh, you don't say so. What a grievous thing.'

'He is a fine fellow,' said Philip; 'but I did not think Sir Guy managed him well. Poor old man, he was quite wrapped up in him, and only thought how to keep him out of harm's way. He would never let him be with other boys, and kept him so fettered by rules, so strictly watched, and so sternly called to account, that I cannot think how any boy could stand it.'

'Yet, you say, he told everything freely to his grandfather,' said Amy.

'Yes,' added her mother, 'I was going to say that, as long as that went on, I should think all safe.

'As I said before,' resumed Philip, 'he has a great deal of frankness, much of the making of a fine character; but he is a thorough Morville. I remember something that will show you his best and worst sides. You know Redclyffe is a beautiful place, with magnificent cliffs overhanging the sea, and fine woods crowning them. On one of the most inaccessible of these crags there was a hawk's nest, about half-way down, so that looking from the top of the precipice, we could see the old birds fly in and out. Well, what does Master Guy do, but go down this headlong descent after the nest. How he escaped alive no one could guess; and his grandfather could not bear to look at the place afterwards— but climb it he did, and came back with two young hawks, buttoned up inside his jacket.'

'There's a regular brick for you!' cried Charles, delighted.

'His heart was set on training these birds. He turned the library upside down in search of books on falconry, and spent every spare moment on them. At last, a servant left some door open, and they escaped. I shall never forget Guy's passion; I am sure I don't exaggerate when I say he was perfectly beside himself with anger.'

'Poor boy!' said Mrs. Edmonstone.

'Served the rascal right,' said Charles.

'Nothing had any effect on him till his grandfather came out, and, at the sight of him, he was tamed in an instant, hung his head, came up to his grandfather, and said— "I am very sorry," Sir Guy answered, "My poor boy!" and there was not another word. I saw Guy no more that day, and all the next he was quiet and subdued. But the most remarkable part of the story is to come. A couple of days afterwards we were walking in the woods, when, at the sound of Guy's whistle, we heard a flapping and rustling, and beheld, tumbling along, with their clipped wings, these two identical hawks, very glad to be caught. They drew themselves up proudly for him to stroke them, and their yellow eyes looked at him with positive affection.'

'Pretty creatures!' said Amabel. 'That is a very nice end to the story.'

'It is not the end,' said Philip. 'I was surprised to see Guy so sober, instead of going into one of his usual raptures. He took them home; but the first thing I heard in the morning was, that he was gone to offer them to a farmer, to keep the birds from his fruit.'

'Did he do it of his own accord?' asked Laura.

'That was just what I wanted to know; but any hint about them brought such a cloud over his face that I thought it would be wanton to irritate him by questions. However, I must be going. Good-bye, Amy, I hope your Camellia will have another blossom before I come back. At least, I shall escape the horticultural meeting.'

'Good-bye,' said Charles. 'Put the feud in your pocket till you can bury it in old Sir Guy's grave, unless you mean to fight it out with his grandson, which would be more romantic and exciting.'

Philip was gone before he could finish. Mrs. Edmonstone looked annoyed, and Laura said, 'Charlie, I wish you would not let your spirits carry you away.'

'I wish I had anything else to carry me away!' was the reply.

'Yes,' said his mother, looking sadly at him. 'Your high spirits are a blessing; but why misuse them? If they are given to support you through pain and confinement, why make mischief with them?'

Charles looked more impatient than abashed, and the compunction seemed chiefly to rest with Amabel.

'Now,' said Mrs. Edmonstone, 'I must go and see after my poor little prisoner.'

'Ah!' said Laura, as she went; 'it was no kindness in you to encourage Charlotte to stay, Amy, when you know how often that inquisitive temper has got her into scrapes.'

'I suppose so,' said Amy, regretfully; 'but I had not the heart to send her away.'

'That is just what Philip says, that you only want bones and sinews in your character to– '

'Come, Laura,' interrupted Charles, 'I won't hear Philip's criticisms of my sister, I had rather she had no bones at all, than that they stuck out and ran into me. There are plenty of angles already in the world, without sharpening hers.'

He possessed himself of Amy's round, plump, childish hand, and spread out over it his still whiter, and very bony fingers, pinching her 'soft pinky cushions,' as he called them, 'not meant for studying anatomy upon.'

'Ah! you two spoil each other sadly,' said Laura, smiling, as she left the room.

'And what do Philip and Laura do to each other?' said Charles.

'Improve each other, I suppose,' said Amabel, in a shy, simple tone, at which Charles laughed heartily.

'I wish I was as sensible as Laura!' said she, presently, with a sigh.

'Never was a more absurd wish,' said Charles, tormenting her hand still more, and pulling her curls; 'unwish it forthwith. Where should I be without silly little Amy? If every one weighed my wit before laughing, I should not often be in disgrace for my high spirits, as they call them.'

'I am so little younger than Laura,' said Amy, still sadly, though smiling.

'Folly,' said Charles; 'you are quite wise enough for your age, while Laura is so prematurely wise, that I am in constant dread that nature will take her revenge by causing her to do something strikingly foolish!'

'Nonsense!' cried Amy, indignantly. 'Laura do anything foolish!'

'What I should enjoy,' proceeded Charles, 'would be to see her over head and ears in love with this hero, and Philip properly jealous.'

'How can you say such things, Charlie?'

'Why? was there ever a beauty who did not fall in love with her father's ward?'

'No; but she ought to live alone with her very old father and horribly grim maiden aunt.'

'Very well, Amy, you shall be the maiden, aunt.' And as Laura returned at that moment, he announced to her that they had been agreeing that no hero ever failed to fall in love with his guardian's beautiful daughter.

'If his guardian had a beautiful daughter,' said Laura, resolved not to be disconcerted.

'Did you ever hear such barefaced fishing for compliments?' said Charles; but Amabel, who did not like her sister to be teased, and was also conscious of having wasted a good deal of time, sat down to practise. Laura returned to her drawing, and Charles, with a yawn, listlessly turned over a newspaper, while his fair delicate features, which would have been handsome but that they were blanched, sharpened, and worn with pain, gradually lost their animated and rather satirical expression, and assumed an air of weariness and discontent.

Charles was at this time nineteen, and for the last ten years had been afflicted with a disease in the hip-joint, which, in spite of the most anxious care, caused him frequent and severe suffering, and had occasioned such a contraction of the limb as to cripple him completely, while his general health was so much affected as to render him an object of constant anxiety. His mother had always been his most devoted and indefatigable nurse, giving up everything for his sake, and watching him night and day. His father attended to his least caprice, and his sisters were, of course, his slaves; so that he was the undisputed sovereign of the whole family.

The two elder girls had been entirely under a governess till a month or two before the opening of our story, when Laura was old enough to be introduced; and the governess departing, the two sisters became Charles's companions in the drawing-room, while Mrs. Edmonstone, who had a peculiar taste and talent for teaching, undertook little Charlotte's lessons herself.

CHAPTER 2

If the ill spirit have so fair a house,
Good things will strive to dwell with't.
– THE TEMPEST

One of the pleasantest rooms at Hollywell was Mrs. Edmonstone's dressing-room— large and bay-windowed, over the drawing-room, having little of the dressing-room but the name, and a toilet-table with a black and gold japanned glass, and curiously shaped boxes to match; her room opened into it on one side, and Charles's on the other; it was a sort of up-stairs parlour, where she taught Charlotte, cast up accounts, spoke to servants, and wrote notes, and where Charles was usually to be found, when unequal to coming down-stairs. It had an air of great snugness, with its large folding-screen, covered with prints and caricatures of ancient date, its book-shelves, its tables, its peculiarly easy arm-chairs, the great invalid sofa, and the grate, which always lighted up better than any other in the house.

In the bright glow of the fire, with the shutters closed and curtains drawn, lay Charles on his couch, one Monday evening, in a gorgeous dressing-gown of a Chinese pattern, all over pagodas, while little Charlotte sat opposite to him, curled up on a footstool. He was not always very civil to Charlotte; she sometimes came into collision with him, for she, too, was a pet, and had a will of her own, and at other times she could bore him; but just now they had a common interest, and he was gracious.

'It is striking six, so they must soon be here. I wish mamma would let me go down; but I must wait till after dinner.'

'Then, Charlotte, as soon as you come in, hold up your hands, and exclaim, "What a guy!" There will be a compliment!'

'No, Charlie; I promised mamma and Laura that you should get me into no more scrapes.'

'Did you? The next promise you make had better depend upon yourself alone.'

'But Amy said I must be quiet, because poor Sir Guy will be too sorrowful to like a racket; and when Amy tells me to be quiet, I know that I must, indeed.'

'Most true,' said Charles, laughing.

'Do you think you shall like Sir Guy?'

'I shall be able to determine,' said Charles, sententiously, 'when I have seen whether he brushes his hair to the right or left.'

'Philip brushes his to the left.'

'Then undoubtedly Sir Guy will brush his to the right.'

'Is there not some horrid story about those Morvilles of Redclyffe?' asked Charlotte. 'I asked Laura, and she told me not to be curious, so I knew there was something in it; and then I asked Amy, and she said it would be no pleasure to me to know.'

'Ah! I would have you prepared.'

'Why, what is it? Oh! dear Charlie! are you really going to tell me?'

'Did you ever hear of a deadly feud?'

'I have read of them in the history of Scotland. They went on hating and killing each other for ever. There was one man who made his enemy's children eat out of a pig-trough, and another who cut off his head.'

'His own?'

'No, his enemy's, and put it on the table, at breakfast, with a piece of bread in its mouth.'

'Very well; whenever Sir Guy serves up Philip's head at breakfast, with a piece of bread in his mouth, let me know.'

Charlotte started up. 'Charles, what do you mean? Such things don't happen now.'

'Nevertheless, there is a deadly feud between the two branches of the house of Morville.'

'But it is very wrong,' said Charlotte, looking frightened.'

'Wrong? Of course it is.'

'Philip won't do anything wrong. But how will they ever get on?'

'Don't you see? It must be our serious endeavour to keep the peace, and prevent occasions of discord.'

'Do you think anything will happen?'

'It is much to be apprehended,' said Charles, solemnly.

At that moment the sound of wheels was heard, and Charlotte flew off to her private post of observation, leaving her brother delighted at having mystified her. She returned on tip-toe. 'Papa and Sir Guy are come, but not Philip; I can't see him anywhere.'

'Ah you have not looked in Sir Guy's great-coat pocket.'

'I wish you would not plague me so! You are not in earnest?'

The pettish inquiring tone was exactly what delighted him. And he continued to tease her in the same style till Laura and Amabel came running in with their report of the stranger.

'He is come!' they cried, with one voice.

'Very gentlemanlike!' said Laura.

'Very pleasant looking,' said Amy. 'Such fine eyes!'

'And so much expression,' said Laura. 'Oh!'

The exclamation, and the start which accompanied it, were caused by hearing her father's voice close to the door, which had been left partly open. 'Here is poor Charles,' it said, 'come in, and see him; get over the first introduction— eh, Guy?' And before he had finished, both he and the guest were in the room, and Charlotte full of mischievous glee at her sister's confusion.

'Well, Charlie, boy, how goes it?' was his father's greeting. 'Better, eh? Sorry not to find you down-stairs; but I have brought Guy to see you.' Then, as Charles sat up and shook hands with Sir Guy, he continued— 'A fine chance for you, as I was telling him, to have a companion always at hand: a fine chance? eh, Charlie?'

'I am not so unreasonable as to expect any one to be always at hand,' said Charles, smiling, as he looked up at the frank, open face, and lustrous hazel eyes turned on him with compassion at the sight of his crippled, helpless figure, and with a bright, cordial promise of kindness.

As he spoke, a pattering sound approached, the door was pushed open, and while Sir Guy exclaimed, 'O, Bustle! Bustle! I am very sorry,' there suddenly appeared a large beautiful spaniel, with a long silky black and white coat, jetty curled ears, tan spots above his intelligent eyes, and tan legs, fringed with silken waves of hair, but crouching and looking beseeching at meeting no welcome, while Sir Guy seemed much distressed at his intrusion.

'O you beauty!' cried Charles. 'Come here, you fine fellow.'

Bustle only looked wistfully at his master, and moved nothing but his feather of a tail.

'Ah! I was afraid you would repent of your kindness,' said Sir Guy to Mr. Edmonstone.

'Not at all, not at all!' was the answer; 'mamma never objects to in-door pets, eh, Amy?'

'A tender subject, papa,' said Laura; 'poor Pepper!'

Amy, ashamed of her disposition to cry at the remembrance of the dear departed rough terrier, bent down to hide her glowing face, and held out her hand to the dog, which at last ventured to advance, still creeping with his body curved till his tail was foremost, looking imploringly at his master, as if to entreat his pardon.

'Are you sure you don't dislike it?' inquired Sir Guy, of Charles.

'I? O no. Here, you fine creature.'

'Come, then, behave like a rational dog, since you are come,' said Sir Guy; and Bustle, resuming the deportment of a spirited and well-bred spaniel, no longer crouched and curled himself into the shape of a comma, but bounded, wagged his tail, thrust his nose into his master's hand and then proceeded to reconnoitre the rest of the company, paying especial attention to Charles, putting his fore-paws on the sofa, and rearing himself up to contemplate him with a grave, polite curiosity, that was very diverting.

'Well, old fellow,' said Charles, 'did you ever see the like of such a dressing-gown? Are you satisfied? Give me your paw, and let us swear an eternal friendship.'

'I am quite glad to see a dog in the house again,' said Laura, and, after a few more compliments, Bustle and his master followed Mr. Edmonstone out of the room.

'One of my father's well-judged proceedings,' murmured Charles. 'That poor fellow had rather have gone a dozen, miles further than have been lugged in here. Really, if papa chooses to inflict such dressing-gowns on me, he should give me notice before he brings men and dogs to make me their laughing-stock!'

'An unlucky moment,' said Laura. 'Will my cheeks ever cool?'

'Perhaps he did not hear,' said Amabel, consolingly.

'You did not ask about Philip?' said Charlotte, with great earnestness.

'He is staying at Thorndale, and then going to St. Mildred's,' said Laura.

'I hope you are relieved,' said her brother; and she looked in doubt whether she ought to laugh.

'And what do you think of Sir Guy?'

'May he only be worthy of his dog!' replied Charles.

'Ah!' said Laura, 'many men are neither worthy of their wives, nor of their dogs.'

'Dr. Henley, I suppose, is the foundation of that aphorism,' said Charles.

'If Margaret Morville could marry him, she could hardly be too worthy,' said Laura. 'Think of throwing away Philip's whole soul!'

'O Laura, she could not lose that,' said Amabel.

Laura looked as if she knew more; but at that moment, both her father and mother entered, the former rubbing his hands, as he always did when much pleased, and sending his voice before him, as he exclaimed, 'Well, Charlie, well, young ladies, is not he a fine fellow– eh?'

'Rather under-sized,' said Charles.

'Eh? He'll grow. He is not eighteen, you know; plenty of time; a very good height; you can't expect every one to be as tall as Philip; but he's a capital fellow. And how have you been?– any pain?'

'Hem– rather,' said Charles, shortly, for he hated answering kind inquiries, when out of humour.

'Ah, that's a pity; I was sorry not to find you in the drawing-room, but I thought you would have liked just to see him,' said Mr. Edmonstone, disappointed, and apologizing.

'I had rather have had some notice of your intention,' said Charles, 'I would have made myself fit to be seen.'

'I am sorry. I thought you would have liked his coming,' said poor Mr. Edmonstone, only half conscious of his offence; 'but I see you are not well this evening.'

Worse and worse, for it was equivalent to openly telling Charles he was out of humour; and seeing, as he did, his mother's motive, he was still further annoyed when she hastily interposed a question about Sir Guy.

'You should only hear them talk about him at Redclyffe,' said Mr Edmonstone. 'No one was ever equal to him, according to them. Every one said the same— clergyman, old Markham, all of them. Such attention to his grandfather, such proper feeling, so good-natured, not a bit of pride— it is my firm belief that he will make up for all his family before him.'

Charles set up his eyebrows sarcastically.

'How does he get on with Philip?' inquired Laura.

'Excellently. Just what could be wished. Philip is delighted with him; and I have been telling Guy all the way home what a capital friend he will be, and he is quite inclined to look up to him.' Charles made an exaggerated gesture of astonishment, unseen by his father. 'I told him to bring his dog. He would have left it, but they seemed so fond of each other, I thought it was a pity to part them, and that I could promise it should be welcome here; eh, mamma?'

'Certainly. I am very glad you brought it.'

'We are to have his horse and man in a little while. A beautiful chestnut— anything to raise his spirits. He is terribly cut up about his grandfather.

It was now time to go down to dinner; and after Charles had made faces of weariness and disgust at all the viands proposed to him by his mother, almost imploring him to like them, and had at last ungraciously given her leave to send what he could not quite say he disliked, he was left to carry on his teasing of Charlotte, and his grumbling over the dinner, for about the space of an hour, when Amabel came back to him, and Charlotte went down.

'Hum!' he exclaimed. 'Another swan of my father's.'

'Did not you like his looks?'

'I saw only an angular hobbetyhoy.'

'But every one at Redclyffe speaks so well of him.'

'As if the same things were not said of every heir to more acres than brains! However, I could have swallowed everything but the disposition to adore Philip. Either it was gammon on his part, or else the work of my father's imagination.'

'For shame, Charlie.'

'Is it within the bounds of probability that he should be willing, at the bidding of his guardian, to adopt as Mentor his very correct and sententious cousin, a poor subaltern, and the next in the entail? Depend upon it, it is a fiction created either by papa's hopes or Philip's self-complacency, or else the unfortunate youth must have been brought very low by strait-lacing and milk-and-water.'

'Mr. Thorndale is willing to look up to Philip,'

'I don't think the Thorndale swan very– very much better than a tame goose,' said Charles, 'but the coalition is not so monstrous in his case, since Philip was a friend of his own picking and choosing, and so his father's adoption did not succeed in repelling him. But that Morville should receive this "young man's companion," on the word of a guardian whom he never set eyes on before, is too incredible– utterly mythical I assure you, Amy. And how did you get on at dinner?'

'Oh, the dog is the most delightful creature I ever saw, so sensible and well-mannered.'

'It was of the man that I asked.'

'He said hardly anything, and sometimes started if papa spoke to him suddenly. He winced as if he could not bear to be called Sir Guy, so papa said we should call him only by his name, if he would do the same by us. I am glad of it, for it seems more friendly, and I am sure he wants to be comforted.'

'Don't waste your compassion, my dear; few men need it less. With his property, those moors to shoot over, his own master, and with health to enjoy it, there are plenty who would change with him for all your pity, my silly little Amy.'

'Surely not, with that horrible ancestry.'

'All very well to plume oneself upon. I rather covet that ghost myself.'

'Well, if you watched his face, I think you would be sorry for him.'

'I am tired of the sound of his name. One fifth of November is enough in the year. Here, find something to read to me among that trumpery.'

Amy read till she was summoned to tea, when she found a conversation going on about Philip, on whose history Sir Guy did not seem fully informed. Philip was the son of Archdeacon Morville, Mrs. Edmonstone's brother, an admirable and superior man, who had been dead about five years. He left three children, Margaret and Fanny, twenty-five and twenty-three years of age, and Philip, just seventeen. The boy was at the head of his school, highly distinguished for application and good conduct; he had attained every honour there open to him, won golden opinions from all concerned with him, and made proof of talents which could not have failed to raise him to the highest university distinctions. He was absent from home at the time of his father's death, which took place after so short an illness, that there had been no time to summon him back to Stylehurst. Very little property was left to be divided among the three; and as soon as Philip perceived how small was the provision for his sisters, he gave up his hopes of university honours, and obtained a commission in the army.

On hearing this, Sir Guy started forward: 'Noble!' he cried, 'and yet what a pity! If my grandfather had but known it– '

'Ah! I was convinced of that,' broke in Mr. Edmonstone, 'and so, I am sure, was Philip himself; but in fact he knew we should never have given our consent, so he acted quite by himself, wrote to Lord Thorndale, and never said a word, even to his sisters, till the thing was done. I never was more surprised in my life.'

'One would almost envy him the opportunity of making such a sacrifice,' said Sir Guy, yet one must lament it.

'It was done in a hasty spirit of independence,' said Mrs. Edmonstone; 'I believe if he had got a fellowship at Oxford, it would have answered much better.'

'And now that poor Fanny is dead, and Margaret married, there is all his expensive education thrown away, and all for nothing,' said Mr. Edmonstone.

'Ah,' said Mrs. Edmonstone, 'he planned for them to go on living at Stylehurst, so that it would still have been his home. It is a great pity, for his talent is thrown away, and he is not fond of his profession.'

'You must not suppose, though, that he is not a practical man,' said Mr. Edmonstone; 'I had rather take his opinion than any one's, especially about a horse, and there is no end to what I hear about his good sense, and the use he is of to the other young men.'

'You should tell about Mr. Thorndale, papa,' said Laura.

'Ah that is a feather in master Philip's cap; besides, he is your neighbour– at least, his father is.'

'I suppose you know Lord Thorndale?' said Mrs. Edmonstone, in explanation.

'I have seen him once at the Quarter Sessions,' said Sir Guy; 'but he lives on the other side of Moorworth, and there was no visiting.'

'Well, this youth, James Thorndale, the second son, was Philip's fag.'

'Philip says he was always licking him!' interposed Charlotte.'

'He kept him out of some scrape or other, continued Mr. Edmonstone. 'Lord Thorndale was very much obliged to him, had him to stay at his house, took pretty much to him altogether. It was through him that Philip applied for his commission, and he has put his son into the same regiment, on purpose to have him under Philip's eye. There he is at Broadstone, as gentlemanlike a youth as I would wish to see. We will have him to dinner some day, and Maurice too– eh, mamma? Maurice– he is a young Irish cousin of my own, a capital fellow at the bottom, but a regular thoroughgoing rattle. That was my doing. I told his father that he could not do better than put him into the — th. Nothing like a steady friend and a good example, I said, and Kilcoran always takes my advice, and I don't think he has been sorry. Maurice has kept much more out of scrapes of late.'

'O papa,' exclaimed Charlotte, 'Maurice has been out riding on a hired horse, racing with Mr. Gordon, and the horse tumbled down at the bottom of East-hill, and broke its knees.'

'That's the way,' said Mr. Edmonstone, 'the instant my back is turned.'

Thereupon the family fell into a discussion of home affairs, and thought little more of their silent guest.

CHAPTER 3

The hues of bliss more brightly glow
Chastised by sober tints of woe.
– GRAY

'What use shall I make of him?' said Charles to himself, as he studied Sir Guy Morville, who sat by the table, with a book in his hand.

He had the unformed look of a growing boy, and was so slender as to appear taller than he really was. He had an air of great activity; and though he sat leaning back, there was no lounging in his attitude, and at the first summons he roused up with an air of alert attention that recalled to mind the eager head of a listening greyhound. He had no pretension to be called handsome; his eyes were his best feature; they were very peculiar, of a light hazel, darker towards the outside of the iris, very brilliant, the whites tinted with blue, and the lashes uncommonly thick and black; the eyebrows were also very dark, and of a sharply-defined angular shape, but the hair was much lighter, loose, soft, and wavy; the natural fairness of the complexion was shown by the whiteness of the upper part of the forehead, though the rest of the face, as well as the small taper hands, were tanned by sunshine and sea-breezes, into a fresh, hardy brown, glowing with red on the cheeks.

'What use shall I make of him?' proceeded Charles's thoughts. 'He won't be worth his salt if he goes on in this way; he has got a graver specimen of literature there than I ever saw Philip himself read on a week-day; he has been puritanized till he is good for nothing; I'll trouble myself no more about him!' He tried to read, but presently looked up again. 'Plague! I can't keep my thoughts off him. That sober look does not sit on that sun-burnt face as if it were native to it; those eyes don't look as if the Redclyffe spirit was extinguished.'

Mrs. Edmonstone came in, and looking round, as if to find some occupation for her guest, at length devised setting him to play at chess with Charles. Charles gave her an amiable look, expressing that neither liked it; but she was pretty well used to doing him good against his will, and trusted to its coming right in time. Charles was a capital chess-player, and seldom found any one who could play well enough to afford him much real sport, but he found Sir Guy more nearly a match than often fell to his lot; it was a bold dashing game, that obliged him to be on his guard, and he was once so taken by surprise as to be absolutely check-mated. His ill-humour evaporated, he was delighted to find an opponent worth playing with, and henceforth there were games almost every morning or evening, though Sir Guy seemed not to care much about them, except for the sake of pleasing him.

When left to himself, Guy spent his time in reading or in walking about the lanes alone. He used to sit in the bay-window of the drawing-room with his book; but sometimes, when they least expected it, the girls would find his quick eyes following them with an air of amused curiosity, as Amabel waited on Charles and her flowers, or Laura drew, wrote letters, and strove to keep down the piles of books and periodicals under which it seemed as if her brother might some day be stifled— a vain task, for he was sure to want immediately whatever she put out of his reach.

Laura and Amabel both played and sung, the former remarkably well, and the first time they had any music after the arrival of Sir Guy, his look of delighted attention struck everyone. He ventured nearer, stood by the piano when they practised, and at last joined in with a few notes of so full and melodious a voice, that Laura turned round in surprise, exclaiming, 'You sing better I than any of us!'

He coloured. 'I beg your pardon,' he said, 'I could not help it; I know nothing of music.'

'Really!' said Laura, smiling incredulously.

'I don't even know the notes.'

'Then you must have a very good ear. Let us try again.'

The sisters were again charmed and surprised, and Guy looked gratified, as people do at the discovery of a faculty which they are particularly glad to possess. It was the first time he appeared to brighten, and Laura and her mother agreed that it would do him good to have plenty of music, and to try to train that fine voice. He was beginning to interest them all greatly by his great helpfulness and kindness to Charles, as he learnt the sort of assistance he required, as well as by the silent grief that showed how much attached he must have been to his grandfather.

On the first Sunday, Mrs. Edmonstone coming into the drawing-room at about half-past five, found him sitting alone by the fire, his dog lying at his feet. As he started up, she asked if he had been here in the dark ever since church-time?

'I have not wanted light,' he answered with a sigh, long, deep, and irrepressible, and as she stirred the fire, the flame revealed to her the traces of tears. She longed to comfort him, and said—

'This Sunday twilight is a quiet time for thinking.'

'Yes,' he said; 'how few Sundays ago— ' and there he paused.

'Ah! you had so little preparation.'

'None. That very morning he had done business with Markham, and had never been more clear and collected.'

'Were you with him when he was taken ill?' asked Mrs. Edmonstone, perceiving that it would be a relief to him to talk.

'No; it was just before dinner. I had been shooting, and went into the library to tell him where I had been. He was well then, for he spoke, but it was getting dark, and I did not see his face. I don't think I was ten minutes dressing, but when I came down, he had sunk back in his chair. I saw it was not sleep– I rang– and when Arnaud came, we knew how it was.' His, voice became low with strong emotion.'

'Did he recover his consciousness?'

'Yes, that was the comfort,' said Guy, eagerly. 'It was after he had been bled that he seemed to wake up. He could not speak or move, but he looked at me– or– I don't know what I should have done.' The last words were almost inaudible from the gush of tears that he vainly struggled to repress, and he was turning away to hide them, when he saw that Mrs. Edmonstone's were flowing fast.

'You had great reason to be attached to him!' said she, as soon as she could speak.

'Indeed, indeed I had.' And after a long silence– 'He was everything to me, everything from the first hour I can recollect. He never let me miss my parents. How he attended to all my pleasures and wishes, how he watched and cared for me, and bore with me, even I can never know.'

He spoke in short half sentences of intense feeling, and Mrs. Edmonstone was much moved by such affection in one said to have been treated with an excess of strictness, much compassionating the lonely boy, who had lost every family tie in one.

'When the first pain of the sudden parting has passed,' said she, 'you will like to remember the affection which you knew how to value.'

'If I had but known!' said Guy; 'but there was I, hasty, reckless, disregarding his comfort, rebelling against– O, what would I not give to have those restraints restored!'

'It is what we all feel in such losses,' said Mrs. Edmonstone. 'There is always much to wish otherwise; but I am sure you can have the happiness of knowing you were his great comfort.'

'It was what I ought to have been.'

She knew that nothing could have been more filial and affectionate than his conduct, and tried to say something of the kind, but he would not listen.

'That is worst of all,' he said; 'and you must not trust what they say of me. They would be sure to praise me, if I was anything short of a brute.'

A silence ensued, while Mrs. Edmonstone was trying to think of some consolation. Suddenly Guy looked up, and spoke eagerly:–

'I want to ask something– a great favour– but you make me venture. You see how I am left alone– you know how little I can trust myself. Will you take me in hand– let me talk to you– and tell me if I am wrong, as freely as if I were Charles? I know it is asking a great deal, but you knew my grandfather, and it is in his name.'

She held out her hand; and with tears answered—

'Indeed I will, if I see any occasion.'

'You will let me trust to you to tell me when I get too vehement? above all, when you see my temper failing? Thank you; you don't know what a relief it is!'

'But you must not call yourself alone. You are one of us now.'

'Yes; since you have made that promise,' said Guy; and for the first time she saw the full beauty of his smile— a sort of sweetness and radiance of which eye and brow partook almost as much as the lips. It alone would have gained her heart.

'I must look on you as a kind of nephew,' she added, kindly. 'I used to hear so much of you from my brother.'

'Oh!' cried Guy, lighting up, 'Archdeacon Morville was always so kind to me. I remember him very well!'

'Ah! I wish— ' there she paused, and added,— tête-à-tête 'it is not right to wish such things— and Philip is very like his father.'

'I am very glad his regiment is so near. I want to know him better.'

'You knew him at Redclyffe, when he was staying there?'

'Yes,' said Guy, his colour rising; 'but I was a boy then, and a very foolish, headstrong one. I am glad to meet him again. What a grand-looking person he is!'

'We are very proud of him,' said Mrs. Edmonstone, smiling. 'I don't think there has been an hour's anxiety about him since he was born.'

The conversation was interrupted by the sound of Charles's crutches slowly crossing the hall. Guy sprang to help him to his sofa, and then, without speaking, hurried up-stairs.

'Mamma, tete-a-tete with the silent one!' exclaimed Charles.

'I will not tell you all I think of him,' said she, leaving the room.

'Hum!' soliloquised Charles. 'That means that my lady mother has adopted him, and thinks I should laugh at her, or straightway set up a dislike to him, knowing my contempt for heroes and hero-worship. It's a treat to have Philip out of the way, and if it was but possible to get out of hearing of his perfection, I should have some peace. If I thought this fellow had one spice of the kind, I'd never trouble my head about him more; and yet I don't believe he has such a pair of hawk's eyes for nothing!'

The hawk's eyes, as Charles called them, shone brighter from that day forth, and their owner began to show more interest in what passed around. Laura was much amused by a little conversation she held with him one day when a party of their younger neighbours were laughing and talking nonsense round Charles's sofa. He was sitting a little way off in silence, and she took advantage of the loud laughing to say:

'You think this is not very satisfactory?' And as he gave a quick glance of inquiry– 'Don't mind saying so. Philip and I often agree that it is a pity spend so much time in laughing at nothing– at such nonsense.'

'It is nonsense?'

'Listen– no don't, it is too silly.'

'Nonsense must be an excellent thing if it makes people so happy,' said Guy thoughtfully. 'Look at them; they are like– not a picture– that has no life– but a dream– or, perhaps a scene in a play.'

'Did you never see anything like it?'

'Oh, no! All the morning calls I ever saw were formal, every one stiff, and speaking by rote, or talking politics. How glad I used to be to get on horseback again! But to see these– why, it is like the shepherd's glimpse at the pixies!– as one reads a new book, or watches what one only half understands– a rook's parliament, or a gathering of sea-fowl on the Shag Rock.'

'A rook's parliament?'

'The people at home call it a rook's parliament when a whole cloud of rooks settle on some bare, wide common, and sit there as if they were consulting, not feeding, only stalking about, with drooping wings, and solemn, black cloaks.'

'You have found a flattering simile,' said Laura, 'as you know that rooks never open their mouths without cause.'

Guy had never heard the riddle, but he caught the pun instantly, and the clear merry sound of his hearty laugh surprised Charles, who instantly noted it as another proof that was some life in him.

Indeed, each day began to make it evident that he had, on the whole, rather a superabundance of animation than otherwise. He was quite confidential with Mrs. Edmonstone, on whom he used to lavish, with boyish eagerness, all that interested him, carrying her the passages in books that pleased him, telling her about Redclyffe's affairs, and giving her his letters from Markham, the steward. His head was full of his horse, Deloraine, which was coming to him under the charge of a groom, and the consultations were endless about the means of transport, Mr. Edmonstone almost as eager about it as he was himself.

He did not so quickly become at home with the younger portion of the family, but his spirits rose every day. He whistled as he walked in the garden, and Bustle, instead of pacing soberly behind him, now capered, nibbled his pockets, and drew him into games of play which Charles and Amabel were charmed to overlook from the dressing-room window. There was Guy leaping, bounding, racing, rolling the dog over, tripping him up, twitching his ears, tickling his feet, catching at his tail, laughing at Bustle's springs, contortions, and harmless open-mouthed attacks, while the dog did little less than laugh too, with his intelligent amber eyes, and black and red mouth. Charles began to find a new interest in his listless life in the attempt to draw Guy out, and make him give one of his merry laughs. In this, however, he failed when his wit consisted in allusions to the novels of the day, of which Guy knew nothing. One morning he underwent a regular examination, ending in–

'Have you read anything?'

'I am afraid I am very ignorant of modern books.'

'Have you read the ancient ones?' asked Laura.

'I've had nothing else to read.'

'Nothing to read but ancient books!' exclaimed Amabel, with a mixture of pity and astonishment.

'Sanchoniathon, Manetho, Berosus, and Ocellus Lucanus!' said Guy, smiling.

'There, Amy,' said Charles, 'if he has the Vicar of Wakefield among his ancient books, you need not pity him.'

'It is like Philip,' said Laura; 'he was brought up on the old standard books, instead of his time being frittered away on the host of idle modern ones.'

'He was free to concentrate his attention on Sir Charles Grandison,' said Charles.

'How could any one do so?' said Guy. 'How could any one have any sympathy with such a piece of self-satisfaction?'

'Who could? Eh, Laura?' said Charles.

'I never read it,' said Laura, suspecting malice.

'What is your opinion of perfect heroes?' continued Charles.

'Here comes one,' whispered Amy to her brother, blushing at her piece of naughtiness, as Philip Morville entered the room.

After the first greetings and inquiries after his sister, whom he had been visiting, Laura told him what they had been saying of the advantage of a scanty range of reading.

'True,' said Philip; 'I have often been struck by finding how ignorant people are, even of Shakspeare; and I believe the blame chiefly rests on the cheap rubbish in which Charlie is nearly walled up there.'

'Ay,' said Charles, 'and who haunts that rubbish at the beginning of every month? I suppose to act as pioneer, though whether any one but Laura heeds his warnings, remains to be proved.'

'Laura does heed?' asked Philip, well pleased.

'I made her read me the part of Dombey that hurts women's feelings most, just to see if she would go on– the part about little Paul– and I declare, I shall think the worse of her ever after— she was so stony hearted, that to this day she does not know whether he is dead or alive.'

'I can't quite say I don't know whether he lived or died,' said Laura, 'for I found Amy in a state that alarmed me, crying in the green-house, and I was very glad to find it was nothing worse than little Paul.'

'I wish you would have read it,' said Amy; and looking shyly at Guy, she added— 'Won't you?'

'Well done, Amy!' said Charles. 'In the very face of the young man's companion!'

'Philip does not really think it wrong,' said Amy.

'No,' said Philip; 'those books open fields of thought, and as their principles are negative, they are not likely to hurt a person well armed with the truth.'

'Meaning,' said Charles, 'that Guy and Laura have your gracious permission to read Dombey.'

'When Laura has a cold or toothache.'

'And I,' said Guy.

'I am not sure about, the expediency for you,' said Philip 'it would be a pity to begin with Dickens, when there is so much of a higher grade equally new to you. I suppose you do not understand Italian?'

'No,' said Guy, abruptly, and his dark eyebrows contracted.

Philip went on. 'If you did, I should not recommend you the translation of "I promessi Sponsi," one of the most beautiful books in any language. You have it in English, I think, Laura.'

Laura fetched it; Guy, with a constrained 'thank you,' was going to take it up rather as if he was putting a force upon himself, when Philip more quickly took the first volume, and eagerly turned over the pages— I can't stand this,' he said, 'where is the original?'

It was soon produced; and Philip, finding the beautiful history of Fra Cristoforo, began to translate it fluently and with an admirable choice of language that silenced Charles's attempts to interrupt and criticise. Soon Guy, who had at first lent only reluctant attention, was entirely absorbed, his eyebrows relaxed, a look of earnest interest succeeded, his countenance softened, and when Fra Cristoforo humbled himself, exchanged forgiveness, and received "il pane del perdono," tears hung on his eyelashes.

The chapter was finished, and with a smothered exclamation of admiration, he joined the others in begging Philip to proceed. The story thus read was very unlike what it had been to Laura and Amy, when they puzzled it out as an Italian lesson, or to Charles, when he carelessly tossed over the translation in search of Don Abbondio's humours; and thus between reading and conversation, the morning passed very agreeably.

At luncheon, Mr. Edmonstone asked Philip to come and spend a day or two at Hollywell, and he accepted the invitation for the next week. 'I will make Thorndale drive me out if you will give him a dinner.'

'Of course, of course,' said Mr. Edmonstone, 'we shall be delighted. We were talking of asking him, a day or two ago; eh, mamma?'

'Thank you,' said Philip; 'a family party is an especial treat to him,' laying a particular stress on the word 'family party,' and looking at his aunt.

At that moment the butler came in, saying, 'Sir Guy's servant is come, and has brought the horse, sir.'

'Deloraine come!' cried Guy, springing up. 'Where?'

'At the door, sir.'

Guy darted out, Mr. Edmonstone following. In another instant, however, Guy put his head into the room again. 'Mrs. Edmonstone, won't you come and see him? Philip, you have not seen Deloraine.'

Off he rushed, and the others were just in time to see the cordial look of honest gladness with which William, the groom, received his young master's greeting, and the delighted recognition between Guy, Bustle, and Deloraine. Guy had no attention for anything else till he had heard how they had prospered on the journey; and then he turned to claim his friend's admiration for the beautiful chestnut, his grandfather's birthday present. The ladies admired with earnestness that compensated for want of knowledge, the gentlemen with greater science and discrimination; indeed, Philip, as a connoisseur, could not but, for the sake of his own reputation, discover something to criticise. Guy's brows drew together again, and his eyes glanced as if he was much inclined to resent the remarks, as attacks at once on Deloraine and on his grandfather; but he said nothing, and presently went to the stable with Mr. Edmonstone, to see about the horse's accommodations. Philip stood in the hall with the ladies.

'So I perceive you have dropped the title already,' observed he to Laura.

'Yes,' said Mrs. Edmonstone, replying for her daughter, 'it seemed to give him pain by reminding him of his loss, and he was so strange and forlorn just at first, that we were glad to do what we could to make him feel himself more at home.'

'Then you get on pretty well now?'

The reply was in chorus with variations— 'Oh, excellently!'

'He is so entertaining,' said Charlotte.

'He sings so beautifully,' said Amabel.

'He is so right-minded,' said Mrs. Edmonstone.

'So very well informed,' said Laura.

Then it all began again.

'He plays chess so well,' said Amy.

'Bustle is such a dear dog,' said Charlotte.

'He is so attentive to Charlie,' said Mrs. Edmonstone, going into the drawing-room to her son.

'Papa says he will make up for the faults of all his ancestors,' said Amabel.

'His music! oh, his music!' said Laura.

'Philip,' said Charlotte, earnestly, 'you really should learn to like him.'

'Learn, impertinent little puss?' said Philip, smiling, 'why should I not like him?'

'I was sure you would try,' said Charlotte, impressively.

'Is it hard?' said Amy. 'But, oh, Philip! you could not help liking his singing.'

'I never heard such a splendid voice,' said Laura; 'so clear and powerful, and yet so wonderfully sweet in the low soft notes. And a very fine ear: he has a real talent for music.'

'Ah! inherited, poor fellow,' said Philip, compassionately.

'Do you pity him for it?' said Amy, smiling.

'Do you forget?' said Philip. 'I would not advise you to make much of this talent in public; it is too much a badge of his descent.'

'Mamma did not think so,' said Amy. 'She thought it a pity he should not learn regularly, with such a talent; so the other day, when Mr. Radford was giving us a lesson, she asked Guy just to sing up and down the scale. I never saw anything so funny as old Mr Radford's surprise, it was almost like the music lesson in "La Figlia del Reggimento"; he started, and looked at Guy, and seemed in a perfect transport, and now Guy is to take regular lessons.

'Indeed.'

'But do you really mean,' said Laura, 'that if your mother had been a musician's daughter, and you had inherited her talent, that you would be ashamed of it.'

'Indeed, Laura,' said Philip, with a smile, 'I am equally far from guessing what I should do if my mother had been anything but what she was, as from guessing what I should do if I had a talent for music.'

Mrs. Edmonstone here called her daughters to get ready for their walk, as she intended to go to East-hill, and they might as well walk with Philip as far as their roads lay together.

Philip and Laura walked on by themselves, a little in advance of the others. Laura was very anxious to arrive at a right understanding of her cousin's opinion of Guy.

'I am sure there is much to like in him,' she said.

'There is; but is it the highest praise to say there is much to like? People are not so cautious when they accept a man in toto.'

'Then, do you not?'

Philip's answer was—

'He who the lion's whelp has nurst,
At home with fostering hand,
Finds it a gentle thing at first,
Obedient to command,'

'Do you think him a lion's whelp?'

'I am afraid I saw the lion just now in his flashing eyes and contracted brow. There is an impatience of advice, a vehemence of manner that I can hardly deem satisfactory. I do not speak from prejudice, for I think highly of his candour, warmth of heart, and desire to do right; but from all I have seen, I should not venture as yet to place much dependence on his steadiness of character or command of temper.'

'He seems to have been very fond of his grandfather, in spite of his severity. He is but just beginning to brighten up a little.'

'Yes; his disposition is very affectionate,– almost a misfortune to one so isolated from family ties. He showed remarkably well at Redclyffe, the other day; boyish of course, and without much self-command, but very amiably. It is very well for him that he is removed from thence, for all the people idolize him to such a degree that they could not fail to spoil him.'

'It would be a great pity if he went wrong.'

'Great, for he has many admirable qualities, but still they are just what persons are too apt to fancy compensation for faults. I never heard that any of his family, except perhaps that unhappy old Hugh, were deficient in frankness and generosity, and therefore these do not satisfy me. Observe, I am not condemning him; I wish to be perfectly just; all I say is, that I do not trust him till I have seen him tried.'

Laura did not answer, she was disappointed; yet there was a justice and guardedness in what Philip said, that made it impossible to gainsay it, and she was pleased with his confidence. She thought how cool and prudent he was, and how grieved she should be if Guy justified his doubts; and so they walked on in such silence as is perhaps the strongest proof of intimacy. She was the first to speak, led to do so by an expression of sadness about her cousin's mouth. 'What are you thinking of, Philip?'

'Of Locksley Hall. There is nonsense, there is affectation in that, Laura, there is scarcely poetry, but there is power, for there is truth.'

'Of Locksley Hall! I thought you were at Stylehurst.'

'So I was, but the one brings the other.'

'I suppose you went to Stylehurst while you were at St. Mildred's? Did Margaret take you there?'

'Margaret? Not she; she is too much engaged with her book-club, and her soirées, and her societies of every sort and kind.'

'How did you get on with the Doctor?'

'I saw as little of him as I could, and was still more convinced that he does not know what conversation is. Hem!' Philip gave a deep sigh. 'No; the only thing to be done at St. Mildred's is to walk across the moors to Stylehurst. It is a strange thing to leave that tumult of gossip, and novelty, and hardness, and to enter on that quiet autumnal old world, with the yellow leaves floating silently down, just as they used to do, and the atmosphere of stillness round the green churchyard.'

'Gossip!' repeated Laura.' Surely not with Margaret?'

'Literary, scientific gossip is worse than gossip in a primary sense, without pretension.'

'I am glad you had Stylehurst to go to. How was the old sexton's wife?'

'Very well; trotting about on her pattens as merrily as ever.'

'Did you go into the garden?'

'Yes; Fanny's ivy has entirely covered the south wall, and the acacia is so tall and spreading, that I longed to have the pruning of it. Old Will keeps everything in its former state.'

They talked on of the old home, till the stern bitter look of regret and censure had faded from his brow, and given way to a softened melancholy expression.

CHAPTER 4

A fig for all dactyls, a fig for all spondees,
A fig for all dunces and dominie grandees.
– SCOTT

'How glad I am!' exclaimed Guy, entering the drawing-room.

'Wherefore?' inquired Charles.

'I thought I was too late, and I am very glad to find no one arrived, and Mr. and Mrs. Edmonstone not come down.'

'But where have you been?'

'I lost my way on the top of the down; I fancied some one told me there was a view of the sea to be had there.'

'And can't you exist without a view of the sea?'

Guy laughed. 'Everything looks so dull– it is as if the view was dead or imprisoned– walled up by wood and hill, and wanting that living ripple, heaving and struggling.'

'And your fine rocks?' said Laura.

'I wish you could see the Shag stone,– a great island mass, sloping on one side, precipitous on the other, with the spray dashing on it. If you see it from ever so far off, there is still that white foam coming and going– a glancing speck, like the light in an eye.'

'Hark! a carriage.'

'The young man and the young man's companion,' said Charles.

'How can you?' said Laura. 'What would any one suppose Mr. Thorndale to be?'

'Not Philip's valet,' said Charles, 'if it is true that no man is a hero to his "valley-de-sham"; whereas, what is not Philip to the Honourable James Thorndale?'

'Philip, Alexander, and Bucephalus into the bargain,' suggested Amy, in her demure, frightened whisper, sending all but Laura into a fit of laughter, the harder to check because the steps of the parties concerned were heard approaching.

Mr. Thorndale was a quiet individual, one of those of whom there is least to be said, so complete a gentleman that it would have been an insult, to call him gentleman-like; agreeable and clever rather than otherwise, good-looking, with a high-bred air about him, so that it always seemed strange that he did not make more impression.

A ring at the front-door almost immediately followed their arrival.

'Encore?' asked Philip, looking at Laura with a sort of displeased surprise.

'Unfortunately, yes,' said Laura, drawing aside.

'One of my uncle's family parties,' said Philip. 'I wish I had not brought Thorndale. Laura, what is to be done to prevent the tittering that always takes place when Amy and those Harpers are together?'

'Some game?' said Laura. He signed approval; but she had time to say no more, for her father and mother came down, and some more guests entered.

It was just such a party that continually grew up at Hollywell, for Mr. Edmonstone was so fond of inviting, that his wife never knew in the morning how many would assemble at her table in the evening. But she was used to it, and too good a manager even to be called so. She liked to see her husband enjoy himself in his good-natured, open-hearted way. The change was good for Charles, and thus it did very well, and there were few houses in the neighbourhood more popular than Hollywell.

The guests this evening were Maurice de Courcy, a wild young Irishman, all noise and nonsense, a great favourite with his cousin, Mr. Edmonstone; two Miss Harpers, daughters of the late clergyman, good-natured, second-rate girls; Dr. Mayerne, Charles's kind old physician, the friend and much-loved counsellor at Hollywell, and the present vicar, Mr. Ross with his daughter Mary.

Mary Ross was the greatest friend that the Miss Edmonstones possessed, though, she being five-and-twenty, they had not arrived at perceiving that they were on the equal terms of youngladyhood.

She had lost her mother early, and had owed a great deal to the kindness of Mrs. Edmonstone, as she grew up among her numerous elder brothers. She had no girlhood; she was a boy till fourteen, and then a woman, and she was scarcely altered since the epoch of that transition, the same in likings, tastes, and duties. 'Papa' was all the world to her, and pleasing him had much the same meaning now as then; her brothers were like playfellows; her delights were still a lesson in Greek from papa, a school-children's feast, a game at play, a new book. It was only a pity other people did not stand still too. 'Papa,' indeed, had never grown sensibly older since the year of her mother's death: but her brothers were whiskered men, with all the cares of the world, and no holidays; the school-girls went out to service, and were as a last year's brood to an old hen; the very children she had fondled were young ladies, as old, to all intents and purposes, as herself, and here were even Laura and Amy Edmonstone fallen into that bad habit of growing up! though little Amy had still much of the kitten in her composition, and could play as well as Charlotte or Mary herself, when they had the garden to themselves.

Mary took great pains to amuse Charles, always walking to see him in the worst weather, when she thought other visitors likely to fall, and chatting with him as if she was the idlest person in the world, though the quantity she did at home and in the parish would be too amazing to be recorded.

Spirited and decided, without superfluous fears and fineries, she had a firm, robust figure, and a rosy, good-natured face, with a manner that, though perfectly feminine, had in it an air of strength and determination.

Hollywell was a hamlet, two miles from the parish church of East-hill, and Mary had thus seen very little of the Edmonstone's guest, having only been introduced to him after church on Sunday. The pleasure on which Charles chiefly reckoned for that evening was the talking him over with her when the ladies came in from the dining-room. The Miss Harpers, with his sisters, gathered round the piano, and Mrs. Edmonstone sat at Charles's feet, while Mary knitted and talked.

'So you get on well with him?'

'He is one of those people who are never in the way, and yet you never can forgot their presence,' said Mrs. Edmonstone.

'His manners are quite the pink of courtesy,' said Mary.

'Like his grandfather's,' said Mrs. Edmonstone; 'that old-school deference and attention is very chivalrous, and sits prettily and quaintly on his high spirits and animation; I hope it will not wear off.'

'A vain hope,' said Charles. 'At present he is like that German myth, Kaspar Hauser, who lived till twenty in a cellar. It is lucky for mamma that, in his green state, he is courtly instead of bearish.'

'Lucky for you, too, Charlie; he spoils you finely.'

'He has the rare perfection of letting me know my own mind. I never knew what it was to have my own way before.'

'Is that your complaint, Charlie? What next?' said Mary.

'So you think I have my way, do you, Mary? That is all envy, you see, and very much misplaced. Could you guess what a conflict it is every time I am helped up that mountain of a staircase, or the slope of my sofa is altered? Last time Philip stayed here, every step cost an argument, till at last, through sheer exhaustion, I left myself a dead weight on his hands, to be carried up by main strength. And after all, he is such a great, strong fellow, that I am afraid he did not mind it; so next time I crutched myself down alone, and I hope that did provoke him.'

'Sir Guy is so kind that I am ashamed,' said Mrs. Edmonstone. 'It seems as if we had brought him for the sole purpose of waiting on Charles.'

'Half his heart is in his horse,' said Charles. 'Never had man such delight in the "brute creation."'

'They have been his chief playfellows,' said Mrs. Edmonstone. 'The chief of his time was spent in wandering in the woods or on the beach, watching them and their ways.'

'I fairly dreamt of that Elysium of his last night,' said Charles: 'a swamp half frozen on a winter's night, full of wild ducks. Here, Charlotte, come and tell Mary the roll of Guy's pets.'

Charlotte began. 'There was the sea-gull, and the hedgehog, and the fox, and the badger, and the jay, and the monkey, that he bought because it was dying, and cured it, only it died the next winter, and a toad, and a raven, and a squirrel, and– '

'That will do, Charlotte.'

'Oh! but Mary has not heard the names of all his dogs. And Mary, he has cured Bustle of hunting my Puss. We held them up to each other, and Puss hissed horribly, but Bustle did not mind it a bit; and the other day, when Charles tried to set him at her, he would not take the least notice.'

'Now, Charlotte,' said Charles, waving his hand, with a provoking mock politeness, 'have the goodness to return to your friends.

Tea over, Laura proposed the game of definitions. 'You know it. Philip,' said she, 'you taught us.'

'Yes I learnt it of your sisters, Thorndale,' said Philip.

'O pray let us have it. It must be charming!' exclaimed Miss Harper, on this recommendation.

'Definitions!' said Charles, contemptuously. 'Dr. Johnson must be the hand for them.'

'They are just the definitions not to be found in Johnson,' said Mr. Thorndale. 'Our standing specimen is adversity, which may be differently explained according to your taste, as "a toad with a precious jewel in its head," or "the test of friendship."'

'The spirit of words,' said Guy, looking eager and interested.

'Well, we'll try,' said Charles, 'though I can't say it sounds to me promising. Come, Maurice, define an Irishman.'

'No, no, don't let us be personal,' said Laura; 'I had thought of the word "happiness". We are each to write a definition on a slip of paper, then compare them.'

The game was carried on with great spirit for more than an hour. It was hard to say, which made most fun, Maurice, Charles, or Guy; the last no longer a spectator, but an active contributor to the sport. When the break-up came, Mary and Amabel were standing over the table together, collecting the scattered papers, and observing that it had been very good fun. 'Some so characteristic,' said Amy, 'such as Maurice's definition of happiness,– a row at Dublin.'

'Some were very deep, though,' said Mary; 'if it is not treason, I should like to make out whose that other was of happiness.'

'You mean this,' said Amy: '"Gleams from a brighter world, too soon eclipsed or forfeited." I thought it was Philip's, but it is Sir Guy's writing. How very sad! I should not like to think so. And he was so merry all the time! This is his, too, I see; this one about riches being the freight for which the traveller is responsible.'

'There is a great deal of character in them,' said Mary. 'I should not have wondered at any of us, penniless people, philosophizing in the fox and grapes style, but, for him, and at his age— '

'He has been brought up so as to make the theory of wisdom come early,' said Philip, who was nearer than she thought.

'Is that intended for disparagement?' she asked quickly.

I think very highly of him; he has a great deal of sense and right feeling,' was Philip's sedate answer; and he turned away to say some last words to Mr. Thorndale.

The Rosses were the last to depart, Mary in cloak and clogs, while Mr. Edmonstone lamented that it was in vain to offer the carriage; and Mary laughed, and thanked, and said the walk home with Papa was the greatest of treats in the frost and star-light.

'Don't I pity you, who always go out to dinner in a carriage!' were her last words to Laura.

'Well, Guy,' said Charlotte, 'how do you like it?'

'Very much, indeed. It was very pleasant.'

'You are getting into the fairy ring,' said Laura, smiling.

'Ay' he said, smiling too; 'but it does not turn to tinsel. Would it if I saw more of it?' and he looked at Mrs. Edmonstone.

'It would be no compliment to ourselves to say so,' she answered.

'I suppose tinsel or gold depends on the using,' said he, thoughtfully; 'there are some lumps of solid gold among those papers, I am sure, one, in particular, about a trifle. May I see that again? I mean—

'Little things
On little wings
Bear little souls to heaven.'

'Oh! that was only a quotation,' said Amy, turning over the definitions again with him, and laughing at some of the most amusing; while, in the mean time, Philip went to help Laura, who was putting some books away in the ante-room.

'Yes, Laura,' he said, 'he has thought, mind, and soul; he is no mere rattle.'

'No indeed. Who could help seeing his superiority over Maurice?'

'If only he does not pervert his gifts, and if it is not all talk. I don't like such excess of openness about his feelings; it is too like talking for talking's sake.'

'Mamma says it in the transparency of youthfulness. You know he has never been at school; so his thoughts come out in security of sympathy, without fear of being laughed at. But it is very late. Good night.'

The frost turned to rain the next morning, and the torrents streamed against the window, seeming to have a kind of attraction for Philip and Guy, who stood watching them.

Guy wondered if the floods would be out at Redclyffe and his cousins were interested by his description of the sudden, angry rush of the mountain streams, eddying fiercely along, bearing with them tree and rock, while the valleys became lakes, and the little mounds islets; and the trees looked strangely out of proportion when only their branches were visible. 'Oh! a great flood is famous fun,' said he.

'Surely,' said Philip, 'I have heard a legend of your being nearly drowned in some flood.

'Yes,' said Guy, 'I had a tolerable ducking.'

'Oh, tell us about it!' said Amy.

'Ay! I have a curiosity to hear a personal experience of drowning,' said Charles. 'Come, begin at the beginning.'

'I was standing watching the tremendous force of the stream, when I saw an unhappy old ram floating along, bleating so piteously, and making such absurd, helpless struggles, that I could not help pulling off my coat and jumping in after him. It was very foolish, for the stream was too strong– I was two years younger then. Moreover, the beast was very heavy, and not at all grateful for any kind intentions, and I found myself sailing off to the sea, with the prospect of a good many rocks before long; but just then an old tree stretched out its friendly arms through the water; it stopped the sheep, and I caught hold of the branches, and managed to scramble up, while my friend got entangled in them with his wool'–

'Omne quum Proteus pecus egit altos
V isere montes,'

quoted Philip.

'Ovium et summa, genus haesit ulmo,'

added Guy.

'Ovium,' exclaimed Philip, with a face of horror. 'Don't you know that O in Ovis is short? Do anything but take liberties with Horace!'

'Get out of the tree first, Guy,' said Charles, 'for at present your history seems likely to end with a long ohone!'

'Well, Triton– not Proteus– came to the rescue at last,' said Guy, laughing; 'I could not stir, and the tree bent so frightfully with the current that I expected every minute we should all go together; so I had nothing for it but to halloo as loud as I could. No one heard but Triton, the old Newfoundland dog, who presently came swimming up, so eager to help, poor fellow, that I thought he would have throttled me, or hurt himself in the branches. I took off my handkerchief and threw it to him, telling him to take it to Arnaud, who I knew would understand it as a signal of distress.'

'Did he? How long had you to wait?'

'I don't know– it seemed long enough before a most welcome boat appeared, with some men in it, and Triton in an agony. They would never have found me but for him, for my voice was gone; indeed the next thing I remember was lying on the grass in the park, and Markham saying, 'Well, sir, if you do wish to throw away your life, let it be for something better worth saving than Farmer Holt's vicious old ram!'

'In the language of the great Mr. Toots,' said Charles 'I am afraid you got very wet.'

'Were you the worse for it?' said Amy.

'Not in the least. I was so glad to hear it was Holt's! for you must know that I had behaved very ill to Farmer Holt. I had been very angry at his beating our old hound, for, as he thought, worrying his sheep; not that Dart ever did, though.

'And was the ram saved?'

'Yes, and next time I saw it, it nearly knocked me down.'

'Would you do it again?' said Philip.

'I don't know.'

'I hope you had a medal from the Humane Society,' said Charles.

'That would have been more proper for Triton.'

'Yours should have been an ovation,' said Charles, cutting the o absurdly short, and looking at Philip.

Laura saw that the spirit of teasing was strong in Charles this morning and suspected that he wanted to stir up what he called the deadly feud, and she hastened to change the conversation by saying, 'You quite impressed Guy with your translation of Fra Cristoforo.'

'Indeed I must thank you for recommending the book,' said Guy; 'how beautiful it is!'

'I am glad you entered into it,' said Philip; 'it has every quality that a fiction ought to have.'

'I never read anything equal to the repentance of the nameless man.'

'Is he your favourite character?' said Philip, looking at him attentively.

'Oh no– of course not– though he is so grand that one thinks most about him, but no one can be cared about as much as Lucia.'

'Lucia! She never struck me as more than a well-painted peasant girl,' said Philip.

'Oh!' cried Guy, indignantly; then, controlling himself, he continued: 'She pretends to no more than she is, but she shows the beauty of goodness in itself in a– a– wonderful way. And think of the power of those words of hers over that gloomy, desperate man.'

'Your sympathy with the Innominato again,' said Philip. Every subject seemed to excite Guy to a dangerous extent, as Laura thought, and she turned to Philip to ask if he would not read to them again.

'I brought this book on purpose,' said Philip. 'I wished to read you a description of that print from Raffaelle— you know it— the Madonna di San Sisto?'

'The one you brought to show us?' said Amy, 'with the two little angels?'

'Yes, here is the description,' and he began to read—

'Dwell on the form of the Child, more than human in grandeur, seated on the arms of the Blessed Virgin as on an august throne. Note the tokens of divine grace, His ardent eyes, what a spirit, what a countenance is His; yet His very resemblance to His mother denotes sufficiently that He is of us and takes care for us. Beneath are two figures adoring, each in their own manner. On one side is a pontiff, on the other a virgin each a most sweet and solemn example, the one of aged, the other of maidenly piety and reverence. Between, are two winged boys, evidently presenting a wonderful pattern of childlike piety. Their eyes, indeed, are not turned towards the Virgin, but both in face and gesture, they show how careless of themselves they are in the presence of God.'

All were struck by the description. Guy did not speak at first, but the solemn expression of his face showed how he felt its power and reverence. Philip asked if they would like to hear more, and Charles assented: Amy worked, Laura went on with her perspective, and Guy sat by her side, making concentric circles with her compasses, or when she wanted them he tormented her parallel ruler, or cut the pencils, never letting his fingers rest except at some high or deep passage, or when some interesting discussion arose. All were surprised when luncheon time arrived; Charles held out his hand for the book; it was given with a slight smile, and he exclaimed' Latin! I thought you were translating. Is it your own property?'

'Yes.'

'Is it very tough? I would read it, if any one would read it with me.'

'Do you mean me?' said Guy; 'I should like it very much, but you have seen how little Latin I know.'

'That is the very thing,' said Charles; 'that Ovis of yours was music; I would have made you a Knight of the Golden Fleece on the spot. Tutors I could get by shoals, but a fellow-dunce is inestimable.'

'It is a bargain, then,' said Guy; 'if Philip has done with the book and will lend it to us.'

The luncheon bell rang, and they all adjourned to the dining-room. Mr. Edmonstone came in when luncheon was nearly over, rejoicing that his letters were done, but then he looked disconsolately from the window, and pitied the weather. 'Nothing for it but billiards. People might say it was nonsense to have a billiard-table in such a house, but for his part he found there was no getting through a wet day without them. Philip must beat him as usual, and Guy might have one of the young ladies to make a fourth.'

'Thank you,' said Guy, 'but I don't play.'

'Not play– eh?' Well, we will teach you in the spinning of a ball, and I'll have my little Amy to help me against you and Philip.'

'No, thank you,' repeated Guy, colouring, 'I am under a promise.'

'Ha! Eh? What? Your grandfather? He could see no harm in such play as this. For nothing, you understand. You did not suppose I meant anything else?'

'O no, of course not,' eagerly replied Guy; 'but it is impossible for me to play, thank you. I have promised never even to look on at a game at billiards.'

'Ah, poor man, he had too much reason.' uttered Mr. Edmonstone to himself, but catching a warning look from his wife, he became suddenly silent. Guy, meanwhile, sat looking lost in sad thoughts, till, rousing himself, he exclaimed, 'Don't let me prevent you.'

Mr. Edmonstone needed but little persuasion, and carried Philip off to the billiard-table in the front hall.

'O, I am so glad!' cried Charlotte, who had, within the last week, learnt Guy's value as a playfellow. 'Now you will never go to those stupid billiards, but I shall have you always, every rainy day. Come and have a real good game at ball on the stairs.'

She already had hold of his hand, and would have dragged him off at once, had he not waited to help Charles back to his sofa; and in the mean time she tried in vain to persuade her more constant playmate, Amabel, to join the game. Poor little Amy regretted the being obliged to refuse, as she listened to the merry sounds and bouncing balls, sighing more than once at having turned into a grown-up young lady; while Philip observed to Laura, who was officiating as billiard-marker, that Guy was still a mere boy.

The fates favoured Amy at last for about half after three, the billiards were interrupted, and Philip, pronouncing the rain to be almost over, invited Guy to take a walk, and they set out in a very gray wet mist, while Charlotte and Amy commenced a vigorous game at battledore and shuttle-cock.

The gray mist had faded into twilight, and twilight into something like night, when Charles was crossing the hall, with the aid of Amy's arm, Charlotte carrying the crutch behind him, and Mrs. Edmonstone helping Laura with her perspective apparatus, all on their way to dress for dinner; the door opened and in came the two Morvilles. Guy, without, even stopping to take off his great coat, ran at once up-stairs, and the next moment the door of his room was shut with a bang that shook the house, and made them all start and look at Philip for explanation.

'Redclyffe temper,' said he, coolly, with a half-smile curling his short upper lip.

'What have you been doing to him?' said Charles.'

'Nothing. At least nothing worthy of such ire. I only entered on the subject of his Oxford life, and advised him to prepare for it, for his education has as yet been a mere farce. He used to go two or three days in the week to one Potts, a self-educated genius— a sort of superior writing-master at the Moorworth commercial school. Of course, though it is no fault of his, poor fellow, he is hardly up to the fifth form, and he must make the most of his time, if he is not to be plucked. I set all this before him as gently as I could, for I knew with whom I had to deal, yet you see how it is.'

'What did he say?' asked Charles.

'He said nothing; so far I give him credit; but he strode on furiously for the last half mile, and this explosion is the finale. I am very sorry for him, poor boy; I beg no further notice may be taken of it. Don't you want an arm, Charlie?'

'No thank you,' answered Charles, with a little surliness.

'You had better. It really is too much for Amy,' said Philip, making a move as if to take possession of him, as he arrived at the foot of the stairs.

'Like the camellia, I suppose,' he replied; and taking his other crutch from Charlotte, he began determinedly to ascend without assistance, resolved to keep Philip a prisoner below him as long as he could, and enjoying the notion of chafing him by the delay. Certainly teasing Philip was a dear delight to Charles, though it was all on trust, as, if he succeeded, his cousin never betrayed his annoyance by look or sign.

About a quarter of an hour after, there was a knock at the dressing-room door. 'Come in,' said Mrs. Edmonstone, looking up from her letter-writing, and Guy made his appearance, looking very downcast.

'I am come,' he said, 'to ask pardon for the disturbance I made just now. I was so foolish as to be irritated at Philip's manner, when he was giving me some good advice, and I am very sorry.'

'What has happened to your lip?' she exclaimed.

He put his handkerchief to it. 'Is it bleeding still? It is a trick of mine to bite my lip when I am vexed. It seems to help to keep down words. There! I have given myself a mark of this hateful outbreak.'

He looked very unhappy, more so, Mrs. Edmonstone thought, than the actual offence required. 'You have only failed in part,' she said. 'It was a victory to keep down words.'

'The feeling is the thing,' said Guy; 'besides, I showed it plainly enough, without speaking.'

'It is not easy to take advice from one so little your elder,' began Mrs. Edmonstone, but he interrupted her. 'It was not the advice. That was very good; I— ' but he spoke with an effort,— 'I am obliged to him. It was— no, I won't say what,' he added, his eyes kindling, then changing in a moment to a sorrowful, resolute tone, 'Yes, but I will, and then I shall make myself thoroughly ashamed. It was his veiled assumption of superiority, his contempt for all I have been taught. Just as if he had not every right to despise me, with his talent and scholarship, after such egregious mistakes as I had made in the morning. I gave him little reason to think highly of my attainments; but let him slight me as much as he pleases, he must not slight those who taught me. It was not Mr. Potts' fault.'

Even the name could not spoil the spirited sound of the speech, and Mrs. Edmonstone was full of sympathy. 'You must remember,' she said, 'that in the eyes of a man brought up at public school, nothing compensates for the want of the regular classical education. I have no doubt it was very provoking.'

'I don't want to be excused, thank you,' said Guy. 'Oh I am grieved; for I thought the worst of my temper had been subdued. After all that has passed– all I felt– I thought it impossible. Is there no hope for– ' He covered his face with his hands, then recovering and turning to Mrs. Edmonstone, he said, 'It is encroaching too much on your kindness to come here and trouble you with my confessions.'

'No, no, indeed,' said she, earnestly. 'Remember how we agreed that you should come to me like one of my own children. And, indeed, I do not see why you need grieve in this despairing way, for you almost overcame the fit of anger; and perhaps you were off your guard because the trial came in an unexpected way?'

'It did, it did,' he said, eagerly; 'I don't, mind being told point blank that I am a dunce, but that Mr. Potts– nay, by implication– my grandfather should be set at nought in that cool– But here I am again!' said he, checking himself in the midst of his vehemence; 'he did not mean that, of course. I have no one to blame but myself.'

'I am sure,' said Mrs. Edmonstone, 'that if you always treat your failings in this way, you must subdue them at last.'

'It is all failing, and resolving, and failing again!' said Guy.

'Yes, but the failures become slighter and less frequent, and the end is victory.'

'The end victory!' repeated Guy, in a musing tone, as he stood leaning against the mantelshelf.

'Yes, to all who persevere and seek for help,' said Mrs Edmonstone; and he raised his eyes and fixed them on her with an earnest look that surprised her, for it was almost as if the hope came home to him as something new. At that moment, however, she was called away, and directly after a voice in the next room exclaimed, 'Are you there, Guy? I want an arm!' while he for the first time perceived that Charles's door was ajar.

Charles thought all this a great fuss about nothing, indeed he was glad to find there was anyone who had no patience with Philip; and in his usual mischievous manner, totally reckless of the fearful evil of interfering with the influence for good which it was to be hoped that Philip might exert over Guy, he spoke thus: 'I begin to think the world must be more docile than I have been disposed to give it credit for. How a certain cousin of ours has escaped numerous delicate hints to mind his own business is to me one of the wonders of the world.'

'No one better deserves that his advice should be followed,' said Guy, with some constraint.

'An additional reason against it,' said Charles. 'Plague on that bell! I meant to have broken through your formalities and had a candid opinion of Don Philip before it rang.'

'Then I am glad of it; I could hardly have given you a candid opinion just at present.'

Charles was vexed; but he consoled himself by thinking that Guy did not yet feel himself out of his leading-strings, and was still on his good behaviour. After such a flash as this there was no fear, but there was that in him which would create mischief and disturbance enough. Charles was well principled at the bottom, and would have shrunk with horror had it been set before him how dangerous might be the effect of destroying the chance of a friendship between Guy and the only person whose guidance was likely to be beneficial to him; but his idle, unoccupied life, and habit of only thinking of things as they concerned his immediate amusement, made him ready to do anything for the sake of opposition to Philip, and enjoy the vague idea of excitement to be derived from anxiety about his father's ward, whom at the same time he regarded with increased liking as he became certain that what he called the Puritan spirit was not native to him.

At dinner-time, Guy was as silent as on his first arrival, and there would have been very little conversation had not the other gentleman talked politics, Philip leading the discussion to bear upon the duties and prospects of landed proprietors, and dwelling on the extent of their opportunities for doing good. He tried to get Guy's attention, by speaking of Redclyffe, of the large circle influenced by the head of the Morville family, and of the hopes entertained by Lord Thorndale that this power would prove a valuable support to the rightful cause. He spoke in vain; the young heir of Redclyffe made answers as brief, absent, and indifferent, as if all this concerned him no more than the Emperor of Morocco, and Philip, mentally pronouncing him sullen, turned to address himself to Laura.

As soon as the ladies had left the dining-room, Guy roused himself, and began by saying to his guardian that he was afraid he was very deficient in classical knowledge; that he found he must work hard before going to Oxford; and asked whether there was any tutor in the neighbourhood to whom he could apply.

Mr. Edmonstone opened his eyes, as much amazed as if Guy had asked if there was any executioner in the neighbourhood who could cut off his head. Philip was no less surprised, but he held his peace, thinking it was well Guy bad sense enough to propose it voluntarily, as he would have suggested it to his uncle as soon as there was an opportunity of doing so in private. As soon as Mr. Edmonstone had recollected himself, and pronounced it to be exceedingly proper, &c., they entered into a discussion on the neighbouring curates, and came at last to a resolution that Philip should see whether Mr. Lascelles, a curate of Broadstone, and an old schoolfellow of his own, would read with Guy a few hours in every week.

After this was settled, Guy looked relieved, though he was not himself all the evening, and sat in his old corner between the plants and the window, where he read a grave book, instead of talking, singing, or finishing his volume of 'Ten Thousand a Year.' Charlotte was all this time ill at ease. She looked from Guy to Philip, from Philip to Guy; she shut her mouth as if she was forming some great resolve, then coloured, and looked confused, rushing into the conversation with something more mal-apropos than usual, as if on purpose to appear at her ease. At last, just before her bed-time, when the tea was coming in, Mrs. Edmonstone engaged with that, Laura reading, Amy clearing Charles's little table, and Philip helping Mr. Edmonstone to unravel the confused accounts of the late cheating bailiff, Guy suddenly found her standing by him, perusing his face with all the power of her great blue eyes. She started as he looked up, and put her face into Amabel's great myrtle as if she would make it appear that she was smelling to it.

'Well, Charlotte?' said he, and the sound of his voice made her speak, but in a frightened, embarrassed whisper.

'Guy— Guy— Oh! I beg your pardon, but I wanted to— '

'Well, what?' said he, kindly.

'I wanted to make sure that you are not angry with Philip. You don't mean to keep up the feud, do you?'

'Feud?— I hope not,' said Guy, too much in earnest to be diverted with her lecture. 'I am very much obliged to him.'

'Are you really?' said Charlotte, her head a little on one side. 'I thought he had been scolding you.'

Scolding was so very inappropriate to Philip's calm, argumentative way of advising, that it became impossible not to laugh.

'Not scolding, then?' said Charlotte. 'You are too nearly grown up for that, but telling you to learn, and being tiresome.'

'I was so foolish as to be provoked at first,' answered Guy; 'but I hope I have thought better of it, and am going to act upon it.'

Charlotte opened her eyes wider than ever, but in the midst of her amazement Mrs. Edmonstone called to Guy to quit his leafy screen and come to tea.

Philip was to return to Broadstone the next day, and as Mrs. Edmonstone had some errands there that would occupy her longer than Charles liked to wait in the carriage, it was settled that Philip should drive her there in the pony phaeton, and Guy accompany them and drive back, thus having an opportunity of seeing Philip's print of the 'Madonna di San Sisto,' returning some calls, and being introduced to Mr. Lascelles, whilst she was shopping. They appointed an hour and place of meeting, and kept to it, after which Mrs. Edmonstone took Guy with her to call on Mrs. Deane, the wife of the colonel.

It was currently believed among the young Edmonstones that Mamma and Mrs. Deane never met without talking over Mr. Morville's good qualities, and the present visit proved no exception. Mrs. Deane, a kind, open-hearted, elderly lady was very fond of Mr. Morville, and proud of him as a credit to the regiment; and she told several traits of his excellent judgment, kindness of heart, and power of leading to the right course. Mrs. Edmonstone listened, and replied with delight; and no less pleasure and admiration were seen reflected in her young friend's radiant face.

Mrs. Edmonstone's first question, as they set out on their homeward drive, was, whether they had seen Mr. Lascelles?

'Yes,' said Guy, 'I am to begin to morrow, and go to him every Monday and Thursday.'

'That is prompt.'

'Ah! I have no time to lose; besides I have been leading too smooth a life with you. I want something unpleasant to keep me in order. Something famously horrid,' repeated he, smacking the whip with a relish, as if he would have applied that if he could have found nothing else.

'You think you live too smoothly at Hollywell,' said Mrs. Edmonstone, hardly able, with all her respect for his good impulses, to help laughing at this strange boy.

'Yes. Happy, thoughtless, vehement; that is what your kindness makes me. Was it not a proof, that I must needs fly out at such a petty provocation?'

'I should not have thought it such a very exciting life; certainly not such as is usually said to lead to thoughtlessness; and we have been even quieter than usual since you came.'

'Ah, you don't know what stuff I am made of,' said Guy, gravely, though smiling; 'your own home party is enough to do me harm; it is so exceedingly pleasant.'

'Pleasant things do not necessarily do harm.'

'Not to you; not to people who are not easily unsettled; but when I go up-stairs, after a talking, merry evening, such as the night before last, I find that I have enjoyed it too much; I am all abroad! I can hardly fix my thoughts, and I don't know what to do, since here I must be, and I can't either be silent, or sit up in my own room.'

'Certainly not,' said she, smiling; 'there are duties of society which you owe even to us dangerous people.'

'No, no: don't misunderstand me. The fault is in myself. If it was not for that, I could learn nothing but good,' said Guy, speaking very eagerly, distressed at her answer.

'I believe I understand you,' said she, marvelling at the serious, ascetic temper, coupled with the very high animal spirits. 'For your comfort, I believe the unsettled feeling you complain of is chiefly the effect of novelty. You have led so very retired a life, that a lively family party is to you what dissipation would be to other people: and, as you must meet with the world some time or other, it is better the first encounter with should be in this comparatively innocent form. Go on watching yourself, and it will do you no harm.'

Yes, but if I find it does me harm? It would be cowardly to run away, and resistance should be from within. Yet, on the other hand, there is the duty of giving up, wrenching oneself from all that has temptation in it.'

'There is nothing,' said Mrs Edmonstone, 'that has no temptation in it; but I should think the rule was plain. If a duty such as that of living among us for the present, and making yourself moderately agreeable, involves temptations, they must be met and battled from within. In the same way, your position in society, with all its duties, could not be laid aside because it is full of trial. Those who do such things are fainthearted, and fail in trust in Him who fixed their station, and finds room for them to deny themselves in the trivial round and common task. It is pleasure involving no duty that should be given up, if we find it liable to lead us astray.'

'I see,' answered Guy, musingly; 'and this reading comes naturally, and is just what I wanted to keep the pleasant things from getting a full hold of me. I ought to have thought of it sooner, instead of dawdling a whole month in idleness. Then all this would not have happened. I hope it will be very tough.'

'You have no great love for Latin and Greek?'

'Oh!' cried Guy, eagerly, 'to be sure I delight in Homer and the Georgics, and plenty more. What splendid things there are in these old fellows! But, I never liked the drudgery part of the affair; and now if I am to be set to work to be accurate, and to get up all the grammar and the Greek roots, it will be horrid enough in all conscience.'

He groaned as deeply as if he had not been congratulating himself just before on the difficulty.

'Who was your tutor?' asked Mrs. Edmonstone.

'Mr. Potts,' said Guy. 'He is a very clever man; he had a common grammar-school education, but he struggled on– taught himself a great deal– and at last thought it great promotion to be a teacher at the Commercial Academy, as they call it, at Moorworth, where Markham's nephews went to school. He is very clever, I assure you, and very patient of the hard, wearing life he must have of it there; and oh! so enjoying a new book, or an afternoon to himself. When I was about eight or nine, I began with him, riding into Moorworth three times in a week; and I have gone on ever since. I am sure he has done the best he could for me; and he made the readings very pleasant by his own enjoyment. If Philip had known the difficulties that man has struggled through, and his beautiful temper, persevering in doing his best and being contented, I am sure he could never have spoken contemptuously of him.'

'I am sure he would not,' said Mrs. Edmonstone; 'all he meant was, that a person without a university education cannot tell what the requirements are to which a man must come up in these days.'

'Ah!' said Guy, laughing, 'how I wished Mr. Potts had been there to have enjoyed listening to Philip and Mr. Lascelles discussing some new Lexicon, digging down for roots of words, and quoting passages of obscure Greek poets at such a rate, that if my eyes had been shut I could have thought them two withered old students in spectacles and snuff-coloured coats.'

'Philip was in his element.' said Mrs. Edmonstone, smiling.

'Really,' proceeded Guy, with animation, 'the more I hear and see of Philip, the more I wonder. What a choice collection of books he has– so many of them school prizes, and how beautifully bound!'

'Ah! that is one of Philip's peculiar ways. With all his prudence and his love of books, I believe he would not buy one unless he had a reasonable prospect of being able to dress it handsomely. Did you see the print?'

'Yes that I did. What glorious loveliness! There is nothing that does it justice but the description in the lecture. Oh I forgot, you have not heard it. You must let me read it to you by and by. Those two little angels, what faces they have. Perfect innocence– one full of reasoning, the other of unreasoning adoration!'

'I see it!' suddenly exclaimed Mrs. Edmonstone; 'I see what you are like in one of your looks, not by any means, in all– it is to the larger of those two angels.'

'Very seldom, I should guess,' said Guy; and sinking his voice, as if he was communicating a most painful fact, he added, 'My real likeness is old Sir Hugh's portrait at home. But what were we saying? Oh! about Philip. How nice those stories were of Mrs. Deane's.'

'She is very fond of him.'

'To have won so much esteem and admiration, already from strangers, with no prejudice in his favour.– It must be entirely his own doing; and well it may! Every time one hears of him, something comes out to make him seem more admirable. You are laughing at me, and I own it is presumptuous to praise; but I did not mean to praise, only to admire.'

'I like very much to hear my nephew praised; I was only smiling at your enthusiastic way.'

'I only wonder I am not more enthusiastic,' said Guy. 'I suppose it is his plain good sense that drives away that sort of feeling, for he is as near heroism in the way of self-sacrifice as a man can be in these days.'

'Poor Philip! if disappointment can make a hero, it has fallen to his share. Ah! Guy, you are brightening and looking like one of my young ladies in hopes of a tale of true love crossed, but it was only love of a sister.'

'The sister for whom he gave up so much?'

'Yes, his sister Margaret. She was eight or nine years older, very handsome, very clever, a good deal like him– a pattern elder sister; indeed, she brought him up in great part after his mother died, and he was devoted to her. I do believe it made the sacrifice of his prospects quite easy to him, to know it was for her sake, that she would live on at Stylehurst, and the change be softened to her. Then came Fanny's illness, and that lead to the marriage with Dr. Henley. It was just what no one could object to; he is a respectable man in full practice, with a large income; but he is much older than she is, not her equal in mind or cultivation, and though I hardly like to say so, not at all a religious man. At any rate, Margaret Morville was one of the last people one could bear to see marry for the sake of an establishment.'

'Could her brother do nothing?'

'He expostulated with all his might; but at nineteen he could do little with a determined sister of twenty-seven; and the very truth and power of his remonstrance must have made it leave a sting. Poor fellow, I believe he suffered terribly– just as he had lost Fanny, too, which he felt very deeply, for she was a very sweet creature, and he was very fond of her. It was like losing both sisters and home at once.'

'Has he not just been staying with Mrs. Henley?'

'Yes. There was never any coolness, as people call it. He is the one thing she loves and is proud of. They always correspond, and he often stays with her; but he owns to disliking the Doctor, and I don't think he has much comfort in Margaret herself, for he always comes back more grave and stern than he went. Her house, with all her good wishes, can be no home to him; and so we try to make Hollywell supply the place of Stylehurst as well as we can.'

'How glad he must be to have you to comfort him!'

'Philip? Oh no. He was always reserved; open to no one but Margaret, not even to his father, and since her marriage he has shut himself up within himself more than ever. It has, at least I think it is this that has given him a severity, an unwillingness to trust, which I believe is often the consequence of a great disappointment either in love or in friendship.'

'Thank you for telling me,' said Guy: 'I shall understand him better, and look up to him more. Oh! it is a cruel thing to find that what one loves is, or has not been, all one thought. What must he not have gone through!'

Mrs. Edmonstone was well pleased to have given so much assistance to Guy's sincere desire to become attached to his cousin, one of the most favourable signs in the character that was winning so much upon her.

CHAPTER 5

A cloud was o'er my childhood's dream,
I sat in solitude;
I know not how– I know not why,
But round my soul all drearily
There was a silent shroud.
– THOUGHTS IN PAST YEARS

Mrs. Edmonstone was anxious to hear Mr. Lascelle's opinion of his pupil, and in time she learnt that he thought Sir Guy had very good abilities, and a fair amount of general information; but that his classical knowledge was far from accurate, and mathematics had been greatly neglected. He had been encouraged to think his work done when he had gathered the general meaning of a passage, or translated it into English verse, spirited and flowing, but often further from the original than he or his tutor could perceive. He had never been taught to work, at least as other boys study, and great application would be requisite to bring his attainments to a level with those of far less clever boys educated at a public school.

Mr. Lascelles told him so at first; but as there were no reflections on his grandfather, or on Mr. Potts, Guy's lip did not suffer, and he only asked how many hours a day he ought to read. 'Three,' said Mr. Lascelles, with a due regard to a probable want of habits of application; but then, remembering how much was undone, he added, that 'it ought to be four or more, if possible.'

'Four it shall be,' said Guy; 'five if I can.'

His whole strength of will was set to accomplish these four hours, taking them before and after breakfast, working hard all the morning till the last hour before luncheon, when he came to read the lectures on poetry with Charles. Here, for the first time, it appeared that Charles had so entirely ceased to consider him as company, as to domineer over him like his own family.

Used as Guy had been to an active out-of-doors life, and now turned back to authors he had read long ago, to fight his way through the construction of their language, not excusing himself one jot of the difficulty, nor turning aside from one mountain over which his own efforts could carry him, he found his work as tough and tedious as he could wish or fear, and by the end of the morning was thoroughly fagged. Then would have been the refreshing time for recreation in that pleasant idling-place, the Hollywell drawing-room. Any other time of day would have suited Charles as well for the reading, but he liked to take the hour at noon, and never perceived that this made all the difference to his friend of a toil or a pleasure. Now and then Guy gave tremendous yawns; and once when Charles told him he was very stupid, proposed a different time; but as Charles objected, he yielded as submissively as the rest of the household were accustomed to do.

To watch Guy was one of Charles's chief amusements, and he rejoiced greatly in the prospect of hearing his history of his first dinner-party. Mr., Mrs. and Miss Edmonstone, and Sir Guy Morville, were invited to dine with Mr. and Mrs. Brownlow. Mr. Edmonstone was delighted as usual with any opportunity of seeing his neighbours; Guy looked as if he did not know whether he liked the notion or not; Laura told him it would be very absurd and stupid, but there would be some good music, and Charles ordered her to say no more, that he might have the account, the next morning, from a fresh and unprejudiced mind.

The next morning's question was, of course, 'How did you like your party?'

'O, it was great fun.' Guy's favourite answer was caught up in the midst, as Laura replied, 'It was just what parties always are.'

'Come, let us have the history. Who handed who in to dinner? I hope Guy had Mrs. Brownlow.'

'Oh no,' said Laura; we had both the honourables.'

'Not Philip!'

'No,' said Guy; 'the fidus Achetes was without his pious Aeneas.'

'Very good, Guy,' said Charles, enjoying the laugh.

'I could not help thinking of it,' said Guy, rather apologising, 'when I was watching Thorndale's manner; it is such an imitation of Philip; looking droller, I think, in his absence, than in his presence. I wonder if he is conscious of it.'

'It does not suit him at all,' said Mrs. Edmonstone; because he has no natural dignity.'

'A man ought to be six foot one, person and mind, to suit with that grand, sedate, gracious way of Philip's,' said Guy.

'There's Guy's measure of Philip's intellect,' said Charles, 'just six foot one inch.'

'As much more than other people's twice his height,' said Guy.

'Who was your neighbour, Laura?' asked Amy.

'Dr. Mayerne; I was very glad of him, to keep off those hunting friends of Mr. Brownlow, who never ask anything but if one has been to the races, and if one likes balls.'

'And how did Mrs. Brownlow behave?' said Charles.

'She is a wonderful woman,' said Mrs. Edmonstone, in her quiet way; and Guy with an expression between drollery and simplicity, said, 'Then there aren't many like her.'

'I hope not,' said Mrs. Edmonstone.

'Is she really a lady?'

'Philip commonly calls her "that woman,"' said Charles. 'He has never got over her one night classing him with his "young man" and myself, as three of the shyest monkeys she ever came across.'

'She won't say so of Maurice,' said Laura, as they recovered the laugh.

'I heard her deluding some young lady by saying he was the eldest son,' said Mrs. Edmonstone.

'Mamma!' cried Amy, 'could she have thought so?'

'I put in a gentle hint on Lord de Courcy's existence, to which she answered, in her quick way, 'O ay, I forgot; but then he is the second, and that's the next thing.'

'If you could but have heard the stories she and Maurice were telling each other!' said Guy. 'He was playing her off, I believe; for whatever she told, he capped it with something more wonderful. Is she really a lady?'

'By birth,' said Mrs. Edmonstone. It is only her high spirits and small judgment that make her so absurd.'

'How loud she is, too!' said Laura. 'What was all that about horses, Guy?'

'She was saying she drove two such spirited horses, that all the grooms were afraid of them; and when she wanted to take out her little boy, Mr. Brownlow said "You may do as you like my dear, but I won't have my son's neck broken, whatever you do with your own." So Maurice answered by declaring he knew a lady who drove not two, but four-in-hand, and when the leaders turned round and looked her in the face, gave a little nod, and said, 'I'm obliged for your civility.'

'Oh! I wish I had heard that,' cried Laura.

'Did you hear her saying she smoked cigars?'

Everyone cried out with horror or laughter.

'Of course, Maurice told a story of a lady who had a cigar case hanging at her chatelaine, and always took one to refresh her after a ball.'

Guy was interrupted by the announcement of his horse, and rode off at once to Mr. Lascelles.

On his return he went straight to the drawing-room, where Mrs. Edmonstone was reading to Charles, and abruptly exclaimed,—

'I told you wrong. She only said she had smoked one cigar.' Then perceiving that he was interrupting, he added, 'I beg your pardon,' and went away.

The next evening, on coming in from a solitary skating, he found the younger party in the drawing-room, Charles entertaining the Miss Harpers with the story of the cigars. He hastily interposed—

'I told you it was but one.'

'Ay, tried one, and went on. She was preparing an order for Havannah.'

'I thought I told you I repeated the conversation incorrectly.'

'If it is not the letter, it is the spirit,' said Charles, vexed at the interference with his sport of amazing the Miss Harpers with outrageous stories of Mrs. Brownlow.

'It is just like her,' said one of them. 'I could believe anything of Mrs. Brownlow.'

'You must not believe this,' said Guy, gently. 'I repeated incorrectly what had better have been forgotten, and I must beg my foolish exaggeration to go no further.'

Charles became sullenly silent; Guy stood thoughtful; and Laura and Amabel could not easily sustain the conversation till the visitors took their leave.

'Here's a pother!' grumbled Charles, as soon as they were gone.

'I beg your pardon for spoiling your story,' said Guy; but it was my fault, so I was obliged to interfere.'

'Bosh!' said Charles. 'Who cares whether she smoked one or twenty? She is Mrs. Brownlow still.'

The point is, what was truth?' said Laura.

'Straining at gnats,' said Charles.

'Little wings?' said Guy, glancing at Amabel.

'Have it your won way,' said Charles, throwing his head back; 'they must be little souls, indeed that stick at such trash.'

Guy's brows were contracted with vexation, but Laura looked up very prettily, saying–

'Never mind him. We must all honour you for doing such an unpleasant thing.'

'You will recommend him favourably to Philip,' growled Charles.

There was no reply, and presently Guy asked whether he would go up to dress? Having no other way of showing his displeasure, he refused, and remained nursing his ill-humour, till he forgot how slight the offence had been, and worked himself into a sort of insane desire– half mischievous, half revengeful– to be as provoking as he could in his turn.

Seldom had he been more contrary, as his old nurse was wont to call it. No one could please him, and Guy was not allowed to do anything for him. Whatever he said was intended to rub on some sore place in Guy's mind. His mother and Laura's signs made him worse, for he had the pleasure of teasing them, also; but Guy endured it all with perfect temper, and he grew more cross at his failure; yet, from force of habit, at bed-time, he found himself on the stairs with Guy's arm supporting him.

'Good night,' said Charles; 'I tried hard to poke up the lion to-night, but I see it won't do.'

This plea of trying experiments was neither absolutely true nor false; but it restored Charles to himself, by saving a confession that he had been out of temper, and enabling him to treat with him wonted indifference the expostulations of father, mother, and Laura.

Now that the idea of 'poking up the lion' had once occurred, it became his great occupation to attempt it. He wanted to see some evidence of the fiery temper, and it was a new sport to try to rouse it; one, too, which had the greater relish, as it kept the rest of the family on thorns.

He would argue against his real opinion, talk against his better sense, take the wrong side, and say much that was very far from his true sentiments. Guy could not understand at first, and was quite confounded at some of the views he espoused, till Laura came to his help, greatly irritating her brother by hints that he was not in earnest. Next time she could speak to Guy alone, she told him he must not take all Charles said literally.

'I thought he could hardly mean it: but why should he talk so?'

'I can't excuse him; I know it is very wrong, and at the expense of truth, and it is very disagreeable of him— I wish he would not; but he always does what he likes, and it is one of his amusements, so we must bear with him, poor fellow.'

From that time Guy seemed to have no trouble in reining in his temper in arguing with Charles, except once, when the lion was fairly roused by something that sounded like a sneer about King Charles I.

His whole face changed, his hazel eye gleamed with light like an eagle's, and he started up, exclaiming—

'You did not mean that?'

'Ask Strafford,' answered Charles, coolly, startled, but satisfied to have found the vulnerable point.

'Ungenerous, unmanly,' said Guy, his voice low, but quivering with indignation; 'ungenerous to reproach him with what he so bitterly repented. Could not his penitence, could not his own blood'— but as he spoke, the gleam of wrath faded, the flush deepened on the cheek, and he left the room.

'Ha!' soliloquized Charles, 'I've done it! I could fancy his wrath something terrific when it was once well up. I didn't know what was coming next; but I believe he has got himself pretty well in hand. It is playing with edge tools; and now I have been favoured with one flash of the Morville eye, I'll let him alone; but it ryled me to be treated as something beneath his anger, like a woman or a child.'

In about ten minutes, Guy came back: 'I am sorry that I was hasty just now,' said he.

'I did not know you had such personal feelings about King Charles.'

'If you would do me a kindness,' proceeded Guy, 'you would just say you did not mean it. I know you do not, but if you would only say so.'

'I am glad you have the wit to see I have too much taste to be a roundhead.'

'Thank you,' said Guy; 'I hope I shall know your jest from your earnest another time. Only if you would oblige me, you would never jest again about King Charles.'

His brow darkened into a stern, grave expression, so entirely in earnest, that Charles, though making no answer, could not do otherwise than feel compliance unavoidable. Charles had never been so entirely conquered, yet, strange to say, he was not, as usual, rendered sullen.

At night, when Guy had taken him to his room, he paused and said— 'You are sure that you have forgiven me?'

'What! You have not forgotten that yet?' said Charles.

'Of course not.'

'I am sorry you bear so much malice,' said Charles, smiling.

'What are you imagining?' cried Guy. 'It was my own part I was remembering, as I must, you know.'

Charles did not choose to betray that he did not see the necessity.

'I thought King Charles's wrongs were rankling. I only spoke as taking liberties with a friend.'

'Yes,' said Guy, thoughtfully, 'it may be foolish, but I do not feel as if one could do so with King Charles. He is too near home; he suffered to much from scoffs and railings; his heart was too tender, his repentance too deep for his friends to add one word even in jest to the heap of reproach. How one would have loved him!' proceeded Guy, wrapped up in his own thoughts,— 'loved him for the gentleness so little accordant with the rude times and the part he had to act— served him with half like a knight's devotion to his lady-love, half like devotion to a saint, as Montrose did—

'Great, good, and just, could I but rate
My grief, and thy too rigid fate,
I'd weep the world in such a strain,
As it should deluge once again.'

'And, oh!' cried he, with sudden vehemence, 'how one would have fought for him!'

'You would!' said Charles. 'I should like to see you and Deloraine charging at the head of Prince Rupert's troopers.'

'I beg your pardon,' said Guy, suddenly recalled, and colouring deeply; 'I believe I forgot where I was, and have treated you to one of my old dreams in my boatings at home. You may quiz me as much as you please tomorrow. Good night.'

'It was a rhapsody!' thought Charles; 'yes it was. I wonder I don't laugh at it; but I was naturally carried along. Fancy that! He did it so naturally; in fact, it was all from the bottom of his heart, and I could not quiz him— no, no more than Montrose himself. He is a strange article! But he keeps one awake, which is more than most people do!'

Guy was indeed likely to keep every one awake just then; for Mr. Edmonstone was going to take him out hunting for the first time, and he was half wild about it. The day came, and half an hour before Mr. Edmonstone was ready, Guy was walking about the hall, checking many an incipient whistle, and telling every one that he was beforehand with the world, for he had read one extra hour yesterday, and had got through the others before breakfast. Laura thought it very true that, as Philip said, he was only a boy, and moralized to Charlotte on his being the same age as herself– very nearly eighteen. Mrs. Edmonstone told Charles it was a treat to see any one so happy, and when he began to chafe at the delay, did her best to beguile the time, but without much success. Guy had ever learned to wait patiently, and had a custom of marching up and down, and listening with his head thrown back, or, as Charles used to call it, 'prancing in the hall.'

If Mrs. Edmonstone's patience was tried by the preparation for the hunt in the morning, it was no less her lot to hear of it in the evening. Guy came home in the highest spirits, pouring out his delight to every one, with animation and power of description giving all he said a charm. The pleasure did not lose by repetition; he was more engrossed by it every time; and no one could be more pleased with his ardour than Mr. Edmonstone, who, proud of him and his riding, gave a sigh to past hopes of poor Charles, and promoted the hunting with far more glee that he had promoted the reading.

The Redclyffe groom, William, whose surname of Robinson was entirely forgotten in the appellation of William of Deloraine, was as proud of Sir Guy as Mr. Edmonstone could be; but made representations to his master that he must not hunt Deloraine two days in the week, and ride him to Broadstone two more. Guy then walked to Broadstone; but William was no better pleased, for he thought the credit of Redclyffe compromised, and punished him by reporting Deloraine not fit to be used next hunting day. Mr. Edmonstone perceived that Guy ought to have another hunter; Philip heard of one for sale, and after due inspection all admired– even William, who had begun by remarking that there might be so many screw-looses about a horse, that a man did not know what to be at with them.

Philip, who was conducting the negotiation, came to dine at Hollywell to settle the particulars. Guy was in a most eager state; and they and Mr. Edmonstone talked so long about horses, that they sent Charles to sleep; his mother began to read, and the two elder girls fell into a low, mysterious confabulation of their own till they were startled by a question from Philip as to what could engross them so deeply.

'It was,' said Laura, 'a banshee story in Eveleen de Courcy's last letter.'

'I never like telling ghost stories to people who don't believe in them,' half whispered Amabel to her sister.

'Do you believe them?' asked Philip, looking full at her.

'Now I won't have little Amy asked the sort of question she most dislikes,' interposed Laura; 'I had rather ask if you laugh at us for thinking many ghost stories inexplicable?'

'Certainly not.'

'The universal belief could hardly be kept up without some grounds,' said Guy.

'That would apply as well to fairies,' said Philip.

'Every one has an unexplained ghost story,' said Amy.

'Yes,' said Philip; 'but I would give something to meet any one whose ghost story did not rest on the testimony of a friend's cousin's cousin, a very strong-minded person.'

'I can't imagine how a person who has seen a ghost could ever speak of it,' said Amy.

'Did you not tell us a story of pixies at Redclyffe?' said Laura.

'O yes; the people there believe in them firmly. Jonas Ledbury heard them laughing one night when he could not get the gate open,' said Guy.

'Ah! You are the authority for ghosts,' said Philip.

'I forgot that,' said Laura: 'I wonder we never asked you about your Redclyffe ghost.'

'You look as if you had seen it yourself,' said Philip.

'You have not?' exclaimed Amy, almost frightened.

'Come, let us have the whole story,' said Philip. 'Was it your own reflection in the glass? was it old sir Hugh? or was it the murderer of Becket? Come, the ladies are both ready to scream at the right moment. Never mind about giving him a cocked-hat, for with whom may you take a liberty, if not with an ancestral ghost of your own?'

Amy could not think how Philip could have gone on all this time; perhaps it was because he was not watching how Guy's colour varied, how he bit his lip; and at last his eyes seemed to grow dark in the middle, and to sparkle with fire, as with a low, deep tone, like distant thunder, conveying a tremendous force of suppressed passion, he exclaimed, 'Beware of trifling—' then breaking off hastened out of the room.

'What's the matter?' asked Mr. Edmonstone, startled from his nap; and his wife looked up anxiously, but returned to her book, as her nephew replied, 'Nothing.'

'How could you Philip?' said Laura.

'I really believe he has seen it!' said Amy, in a startled whisper.

'He has felt it, Amy— the Morville spirit,' said Philip.

'It is a great pity you spoke of putting a cocked hat to it,' said Laura; 'he must have suspected us of telling you what happened about Mrs. Brownlow.'

'And are you going to do it now?' said her sister in a tone of remonstrance.

'I think Philip should hear it!' said Laura; and she proceeded to relate the story. She was glad to see that her cousin was struck with it; he admired this care to maintain strict truth, and even opened a memorandum-book– the sight of which Charles dreaded– and read the following extract: 'Do not think of one falsity as harmless, and another as slight, and another as unintended. Cast them all aside. They may be light and accidental, but they are an ugly soot from the smoke of the pit, for all that; and it is better that our hearts should be swept clean of them, without over care as to which is the largest or blackest.'

Laura and Amy were much pleased; but he went on to regret that such excellent dispositions should be coupled with such vehemence of character and that unhappy temper. Amy was glad that her sister ventured to hint that he might be more cautious in avoiding collisions.

'I am cautious', replied he, quickly and sternly; 'I am not to be told of the necessity of exercising forbearance with this poor boy; but it is impossible to reckon on all the points on which he is sensitive.'

'He is sensitive,' said Laura. 'I don't mean only in temper, but in everything. I wonder if it is part of his musical temperament to be as keenly alive to all around, as his ear is to every note. A bright day, a fine view, is such real happiness to him; he dwells on every beauty of Redclyffe with such affection; and then, when he reads, Charles says it is like going over the story again himself to watch his face act it in that unconscious manner.'

'He makes all the characters so real in talking them over,' said Amy, 'and he does not always know how they will end before they begin.'

'I should think it hardly safe for so excitable a mind to dwell much on the world of fiction,' said Philip.

'Nothing has affected him so much as Sintram,' said Laura. 'I never saw anything like it. He took it up by chance, and stood reading it while all those strange expressions began to flit over his face, and at last he fairly cried over it so much, that he was obliged to fly out of the room. How often he has read it I cannot tell; I believe he has bought one for himself, and it is as if the engraving had a fascination for him; he stands looking at it as if he was in a dream.'

'He is a great mystery,' said Amy.

'All men are mysterious,' said Philip 'but he not more than others, though he may appear so to you, because you have not had much experience, and also because most of the men you have seen have been rounded into uniformity like marbles, their sharp angles rubbed off against each other at school.'

'Would it be better if there were more sharp angles?' said Laura, thus setting on foot a discussion on public schools, on which Philip had, of course, a great deal to say.

Amy's kind little heart was meanwhile grieving for Guy, and longing to see him return, but he did not come till after Philip's departure. He looked pale and mournful, his hair hanging loose and disordered, and her terror was excited lest he might actually have seen his ancestor's ghost, which, in spite of her desire to believe in ghosts, in general, she did not by any means wish to have authenticated. He was surprised and a good deal vexed to find Philip gone, but he said hardly anything, and it was soon bedtime. When Charles took his arm, he exclaimed, on finding his sleeve wet– 'What can you have been doing?'

'Walking up and down under the wall,' replied Guy, with some reluctance.

'What, in the rain?'

'I don't know, perhaps it was.'

Amy, who was just behind, carrying the crutch, dreaded Charles's making any allusion to Sintram's wild locks and evening wanderings, but ever since the outburst about King Charles, the desire to tease and irritate Guy had ceased.

They parted at the dressing-room door, and as Guy bade her good night, he pushed back the damp hair that had fallen across his forehead, saying, 'I am sorry I disturbed your evening. I will tell you the meaning of it another time.'

'He has certainly seen the ghost!' said silly little Amy, as she shut herself into her own room in such a fit of vague 'eerie' fright, that it was not till she had knelt down, and with her face hidden in her hands, said her evening prayer, that she could venture to lift up her head and look into the dark corners of the room.

'Another time!' Her heart throbbed at the promise.

The next afternoon, as she and Laura were fighting with a refractory branch of wisteria which had been torn down by the wind, and refused to return to its place, Guy, who had been with his tutor, came in from the stable-yard, reduced the trailing bough to obedience, and then joined them in their walk. He looked grave, was silent at first, and then spoke abruptly– 'It is due to you to explain my behaviour last night.'

'Amy thinks you must have seen the ghost,' said Laura, trying to be gay.

'Did I frighten you?' said Guy, turning round, full of compunction. 'No, no. I never saw it. I never even heard of its being seen. I am very sorry.'

'I was very silly,' said Amy smiling.

'But,' proceeded Guy, 'when I think of the origin of the ghost story, I cannot laugh, and if Philip knew all– '

'Oh! He does not,' cried Laura; 'he only looks on it as we have always done, as a sort of romantic appendage to Redclyffe. I should think better of a place for being haunted.'

'I used to be proud of it,' said Guy. 'I wanted to make out whether it was old Sir Hugh or the murderer of Becket, who was said to groan and turn the lock of Dark Hugh's chamber. I hunted among old papers, and a horrible story I found. That wretched Sir Hugh,– the same who began the quarrel with your mother's family– he was a courtier of Charles II, as bad or worse than any of that crew– '

'What was the quarrel about?' said Laura.

'He was believed to have either falsified or destroyed his father's will, so as to leave his brother, your ancestor, landless; his brother remonstrated, and he turned him out of doors. The forgery never was proved, but there was little doubt of it. There are traditions of his crimes without number, especially his furious anger and malice. He compelled a poor lady to marry him, though she was in love with another man; then he was jealous; he waylaid his rival, shut him up in the turret chamber, committed him to prison, and bribed Judge Jeffries to sentence him– nay it is even said he carried his wife to see the execution! He was so execrated that he fled the country; he went to Holland, curried favour with William of Orange, brought his wealth to help him, and that is the deserving action which got him the baronetcy! He served in the army a good many years, and came home when he thought his sins would be forgotten. But do you remember those lines?' and Guy repeated them in the low rigid tone, almost of horror, in which he had been telling the story:–

'On some his vigorous judgments light,
In that dread pause 'twixt day and night,
Life's closing twilight hour;
Round some, ere yet they meet their doom,
Is shed the silence of the tomb,
The eternal shadows lower.'

'It was so with him; he lost his senses, and after many actions of mad violence, he ended by hanging himself in the very room where he had imprisoned his victim.'

'Horrible!' said Laura. 'Yet I do not see why, when it is all past, you should feel it so deeply.'

'How should I not feel it?' answered Guy. 'Is it not written that the sins of the fathers shall be visited on the children? You wonder to see me so foolish about Sintram. Well, it is my firm belief that such a curse of sin and death as was on Sintram rests on the descendants of that miserable man.'

The girls were silent, struck with awe and dismay at the fearful reality with which he pronounced the words. At last, Amy whispered, 'But Sintram conquered his doom.'

At the same time Laura gathered her thoughts together, and said, 'This must be an imagination. You have dwelt on it and fostered it till you believe it, but such notions should be driven away or they will work their own fulfilment.'

'Look at the history of the Morvilles, and see if it be an imagination,' said Guy. 'Crime and bloodshed have been the portion of each– each has added weight and darkness to the doom which he had handed on. My own poor father, with his early death, was, perhaps, the happiest!'

Laura saw the idea was too deeply rooted to be treated as a fancy, and she found a better argument. 'The doom of sin and death is on us all, but you should remember that if you are a Morville, you are also a Christian.'

'He does remember it!' said Amy, raising her eyes to his face, and then casting them down, blushing at having understood his countenance, where, in the midst of the gloomy shades, there rested for an instant the gleam which her mother had likened to the expression of Raffaelle's cherub.'

They walked on for some time in silence. At last Laura exclaimed, 'Are you really like the portrait of this unfortunate Sir Hugh?'

Guy made a sign of assent.

'Oh! It must have been taken before he grew wicked,' said Amy; and Laura felt the same conviction, that treacherous revenge could never have existed beneath so open a countenance, with so much of highmindedness, pure faith and contempt of wrong in every glance of the eagle eye, in the frank expansion of the smooth forehead.

They were interrupted by Mr. Edmonstone's hearty voice, bawling across the garden for one of the men. 'O Guy! are you there?' cried he, as soon as he saw him. 'Just what I wanted! Your gun, man! We are going to ferret a rabbit.'

Guy ran off at full speed in search of his gun, whistling to Bustle. Mr. Edmonstone found his man, and the sisters were again alone.

'Poor fellow!' said Laura.

'You will not tell all this to Philip?' said Amy.

'It would show why he was hurt, and it can be no secret.'

'I dare say you are right, but I have a feeling against it. Well, I am glad he had not seen the ghost!'

The two girls had taken their walk, and were just going in, when, looking round, they saw Philip walking fast and determinedly up the approach, and as they turned back to meet him, the first thing he said was, 'Where is Guy?'

'Ferreting rabbits with papa. What is the matter?'

'And where is my aunt?'

Driving out with Charles and Charlotte. What is the matter?'

'Look here. Can you tell me the meaning of this which I found on my table when I came in this morning?'

It was a card of Sir Guy Morville, on the back of which was written in pencil, 'Dear P., I find hunting and reading don't agree, so take no further steps about the horse. Many thanks for your trouble.– G.M.'

'There,' said Philip, 'is the result of brooding all night on his resentment.' 'Oh no!' cried Laura, colouring with eagerness, 'you do not understand him. He could not bear it last night, because, as he has been explaining to us, that old Sir Hugh's story was more shocking than we ever guessed, and he has a fancy that their misfortunes are a family fate, and he could not bear to hear it spoken of lightly.'

'Oh! He has been telling you his own story, has he?'

Laura's colour grew still deeper, 'If you had been there,' she said, 'you would have been convinced. Why will you not believe that he finds hunting interfere with reading?'

'He should have thought of that before,' said Philip.

'Here have I half bought the horse! I have wasted the whole morning on it, and now I have to leave it on the man's hands. I had a dozen times rather take it myself, if I could afford it. Such a bargain as I had made, and such an animal as you will not see twice in your life.'

'It is a great pity,' said Laura. 'He should have known his own mind. I don't like people to give trouble for nothing.'

'Crazy about it last night, and giving it up this morning! A most extraordinary proceeding. No, no, Laura, this is not simple fickleness, it would be too absurd. It is temper, temper, which makes a man punish himself, in hopes of punishing others.

Laura still spoke for Guy, and Amy rejoiced; for if her sister had not taken up the defence of the absent, she must, and she felt too strongly to be willing to speak. It seemed too absurd for one feeling himself under such a doom to wrangle about a horse, yet she was somewhat amused by the conviction that if Guy had really wished to annoy Philip he had certainly succeeded.

There was no coming to an agreement. Laura's sense of justice revolted at the notion of Guy's being guilty of petty spite; while Philip, firm in his preconceived idea of his character, and his own knowledge of mankind, was persuaded that he had imputed the true motive, and was displeased at Laura's attempting to argue the point. He could not wait to see any one else, as he was engaged to dine out, and he set off again at his quick, resolute pace.

'He is very unfair!' exclaimed Amy.

'He did not mean to be so,' said Laura; 'and though he is mistaken in imputing such motives, Guy's conduct has certainly been vexatious.'

They were just turning to go in, when they were interrupted by the return of the carriage; and before Charles had been helped up the steps, their father and Guy came in sight. While Guy went to shut up Bustle, who was too wet for the drawing-room, Mr. Edmonstone came up to the others, kicking away the pebbles before him, and fidgeting with his gloves, as he always did when vexed.

'Here's a pretty go!' said he. 'Here is Guy telling me he won't hunt any more!'

'Not hunt!' cried Mrs. Edmonstone and Charles at once; 'and why?'

'Oh! something about its taking his mind from his reading; but that can't be it– impossible, you know; I'd give ten pounds to know what has vexed him. So keen as he was about it last night, and I vow, one of the best riders in the whole field. Giving up that horse, too– I declare it is a perfect sin! I told him he had gone too far, and he said he had left a note with Philip this morning.'

'Yes,' said Laura; Philip has just been here about it. Guy left a card, saying, hunting and reading would not agree.'

'That is an excuse, depend upon it,' said Mr. Edmonstone. 'Something has nettled him, I am sure. It could not be that Gordon, could it, with his hail-fellow-well-met manner? I thought Guy did not half like it the other day, when he rode up with his "Hollo, Morville!" The Morvilles have a touch of pride of their own; eh, mamma?'

'I should be inclined to believe his own account of himself,' said she.

'I tell you, 'tis utterly against reason,' said Mr. Edmonstone, angrily. 'If he was a fellow like Philip, or James Ross, I could believe it; but he– he make a book-worm! He hates it, like poison, at the bottom of his heart, I'll answer for it; and the worst of it is, the fellow putting forward such a fair reason one can't– being his guardian, and all– say what one thinks of it oneself. Eh, mamma?'

'Not exactly,' said Mrs. Edmonstone, smiling.

'Well, you take him in hand, mamma. I dare say he will tell you the rights of it, and if it is only that Gordon, explain it rightly to him, show him 'tis only the man's way; tell him he treats me so for ever, and would the Lord-Lieutenant if he was in it.'

'For a' that and a' that,' said Charles, as Amy led him into the drawing-room.

'You are sure the reading is the only reason?' said Amy.'

'He's quite absurd enough for it,' said Charles; but 'absurd' was pronounced in a way that made its meaning far from annoying even to Guy's little champion.

Guy came in the next moment, and running lightly up-stairs after Mrs. Edmonstone, found her opening the dressing-room door, and asked if he might come in.

'By all means,' she said; 'I am quite ready for one of our twilight talks.'

'I am afraid I have vexed Mr. Edmonstone,' began Guy; 'and I am very sorry.'

'He was only afraid that something might have occurred to vex you, which you might not like to mention to him,' said Mrs. Edmonstone, hesitating a little.

'Me! What could I have done to make him think so? I am angry with no one but myself. The fact is only this, the hunting is too pleasant; it fills up my head all day and all night; and I don't attend rightly to anything else. If I am out in the morning and try to pay for it at night, it will not do; I can but just keep awake and that's all; the Greek letters all seem to be hunting each other, the simplest things grow difficult, and at last all I can think of, is how near the minute hand of my watch is near to the hour I have set myself. So, for the last fortnight, every construing with Mr. Lascelles has been worse than the last; and as to my Latin verses, they were beyond everything shocking, so you see there is no making the two things agree, and the hunting must wait till I grow steadier, if I ever do. Heigho! It is a great bore to be so stupid, for I thought— But it is of no use to talk of it!'

'Mr. Edmonstone would be a very unreasonable guardian, indeed, to be displeased,' said his friend, smiling. You say you stopped the purchase of the horse. Why so? Could you not keep him till you are more sure of yourself?'

'Do you think I might?' joyously exclaimed Guy. 'I'll write to Philip this minute by the post. Such a splendid creature: it would do you good to see it— such action— such a neck— such spirit. It would be a shame not to secure it. But no— no— ' and he checked himself sorrowfully. 'I have made my mind before that I don't deserve it. If it was here, it would always have to be tried: if I heard the hounds I don't know I should keep from riding after them; whereas, now I can't, for William won't let me take Deloraine. No, I can't trust myself to keep such a horse, and not hunt. It will serve me right to see Mr. Brownlow on it, and he will never miss such a chance!' and the depth of his sigh bore witness to the struggle it cost him.

'I should not like to use anyone as you use yourself,' said Mrs. Edmonstone, looking at him with affectionate anxiety, which seemed suddenly to change the current of his thought, for he exclaimed abruptly—

'Mrs. Edmonstone, can you tell me anything about my mother?'

'I am afraid not,' said she, kindly; 'you know we had so little intercourse with your family, that I heard little but the bare facts.'

'I don't think,' said Guy, leaning on the chimneypiece, 'that I ever thought much about her till I knew you, but lately I have fancied a great deal about what might have been if she had but lived.'

It was not Mrs. Edmonstone's way to say half what she felt, and she went on— 'Poor thing! I believe she was quite a child.'

'Only seventeen when she died,' said Guy.

Mrs. Edmonstone went to a drawer, took out two or three bundles of old letters, and after searching in them by the fire-light, said– 'Ah! here's a little about her; it is in a letter from my sister-in-law, Philip's mother, when they were staying at Stylehurst.'

'Who? My father and mother?' cried Guy eagerly.

'Did you not know they had been there three or four days?'

'No– I know less about them than anybody,' said he, sadly: but as Mrs. Edmonstone waited, doubtful as to whether she might be about to make disclosures for which he was unprepared, he added, hastily– 'I do know the main facts of the story; I was told them last autumn;' and an expression denoting the remembrance of great suffering came over his face; then, pausing a moment, he said– 'I knew Archdeacon Morville had been very kind.'

'He was always interested about your father,' said Mrs. Edmonstone; 'and happening to meet him in London some little time after his marriage, he– he was pleased with the manner in which he was behaving then, thought– thought– ' And here, recollecting that she must not speak ill of old Sir Guy, nor palliate his son's conduct, poor Mrs. Edmonstone got into an inextricable confusion– all the worse because the fierce twisting of a penwiper in Guy's fingers denoted that he was suffering a great trial of patience. She avoided the difficulty thus: 'It is hard to speak of such things when there is so much to be regretted on both sides; but the fact was, my brother thought your father was harshly dealt with at that time. Of course he had done very wrong; but he had been so much neglected and left to himself, that it seemed hardly fair to visit his offence on him as severely as if he had had more advantages. So it ended in their coming to spend a day or two at Stylehurst; and this is the letter my sister-in-law wrote at the time:

'"Our visitors have just left us, and on the whole I am much better pleased than I expected. The little Mrs. Morville is a very pretty creature, and as engaging as long flaxen curls, apple-blossom complexion, blue eyes, and the sweetest of voices can make her; so full of childish glee and playfulness, that no one would stop to think whether she was lady-like any more than you would with a child. She used to go singing like a bird about the house as soon as the first strangeness wore off, which was after her first game of play with Fanny and Little Philip. She made them very fond of her, as indeed she would make every one who spent a day or two in the same house with her. I could almost defy Sir Guy not to be reconciled after one sight of her sweet sunny face. She is all affection and gentleness, and with tolerable training anything might be made of her; but she is so young in mind and manners, that one cannot even think of blaming her for her elopement, for she had no mother, no education but in music; and her brother seems to have forced it on, thrown her in Mr. Morville's way, and worked on his excitable temperament, until he hurried them into marriage. Poor little girl, I suppose she little guesses what she has done; but it was very pleasant to see how devotedly attached he seemed to her; and there was something beautiful in the softening of his impetuous tones when he said, 'Marianne;' and her pride in him was very pretty, like a child playing at matronly airs."'

Guy gave a long, heavy sigh, brushed away a tear, and after a long silence, said, 'Is that all?'

'All that I like to read to you. Indeed, there is no more about her; and it would be of no use to read all the reports that were going about.– Ah! here,' said Mrs. Edmonstone, looking into another letter, 'she speaks of your father as a very fine young man, with most generous impulses,'– but here again she was obliged to stop, for the next sentence spoke of 'a noble character ruined by mismanagement.' 'She never saw them again,' continued Mrs. Edmonstone; 'Mr. Dixon, your mother's brother, had great influence with your father, and made matters worse– so much worse, that my brother did not feel himself justified in having any more to do with them.'

'Ah! he went to America,' said Guy; 'I don't know any more about him except that he came to the funeral and stood with his arms folded, not choosing to shake hands with my poor grandfather.' After another silence he said, 'Will you read that again?' and when he had heard it, he sat shading his brow with his hand, as if to bring the fair, girlish picture fully before his mind, while Mrs. Edmonstone sought in vain among her letters for one which did not speak of the fiery passions ignited on either side, in terms too strong to be fit for his ears.

When next he spoke it was to repeat that he had not been informed of the history of his parents till within the last few months. He had, of course, known the manner of their death, but had only lately become aware of the circumstances attending it.

The truth was that Guy had grown up peculiarly shielded from evil, but ignorant of the cause of the almost morbid solicitude with which he was regarded by his grandfather. He was a very happy, joyous boy, leading an active, enterprising life, though so lonely as to occasion greater dreaminess and thoughtfulness than usual at such an early age. He was devotedly attached to his grandfather, looking on him as the first and best of human beings, and silencing the belief that Sir Hugh Morville had entailed a doom of crime and sorrow on the family, by a reference to him, as one who had been always good and prosperous.

When, however, Guy had reached an age at which he must encounter the influences which had proved so baneful to others of his family, his grandfather thought it time to give him the warning of his own history.

The sins, which the repentance of years had made more odious in the eyes of the old man, were narrated; the idleness and insubordination at first, then the reckless pursuit of pleasure, the craving for excitement, the defiance of rule and authority, till folly had become vice, and vice had led to crime.

He had fought no fewer than three duels, and only one had been bloodless. His misery after the first had well-nigh led to a reform; but time had dulled its acuteness– it had been lost in fresh scenes of excitement– and at the next offence rage had swept away such recollections. Indeed, so far had he lost the natural generosity of his character, that his remorse had been comparatively slight for the last, which was the worst of all, since he had forced the quarrel on his victim, Captain Wellwood, whose death had left a wife and children almost destitute. His first awakening to a sense of what his course had been, was when he beheld his only child, in the prime of youth, carried lifeless across his threshold, and attributed his death to his own intemperance and violence. That hour made Sir Guy Morville an old and a broken-hearted man; and he repented as vigorously as he had sinned.

From the moment he dared to hope that his son's orphan would be spared, he had been devoted to him, but still mournfully, envying and pitying his innocence as something that could not last.

He saw bright blossoms put forth, as the boy grew older; but they were not yet fruits, and he did not dare to believe they ever would be. The strength of will which had, in his own case, been the slave of his passions, had been turned inward to subdue the passions themselves, but this was only the beginning– the trial was not yet come. He could hope his grandson might repent, but this was the best that he dared to think possible. He could not believe that a Morville could pass unscathed through the world, or that his sins would not be visited on the head of his only descendant; and the tone of his narration was throughout such as might almost have made the foreboding cause its own accomplishment.

The effect was beyond what he had expected; for a soul deeply dyed in guilt, even though loathing its own stains, had not the power of conceiving how foul was the aspect of vice, to one hitherto guarded from its contemplation, and living in a world of pure, lofty day-dreams. The boy sat the whole time without a word, his face bent down and hidden by his clasped hands, only now and then unable to repress a start or shudder at some fresh disclosure; and when it was ended, he stood up, gazed round, and walked uncertainly, as if he did not know where he was. His next impulse was to throw himself on his knee beside his grandfather, and caress him as he used to when a child. The 'good-night' was spoken, and Guy was shut into his room, with his overwhelming emotions.

His grandfather a blood-stained, remorseful man! The doom was complete, himself heir to the curse of Sir Hugh, and fated to run the same career; and as he knew full well, with the tendency to the family character strong within him, the germs of these hateful passions ready to take root downwards and bear fruit upwards, with the very countenance of Sir Hugh, and the same darkening, kindling eyes, of which traditions had preserved the remembrance.

He was crushed for awhile. The consciousness of strength not his own, of the still small voice that could subdue the fire, the earthquake, and the whirlwind, was slow in coming to him; and when it came, he, like his grandfather, had hope rather of final repentance than of keeping himself unstained.

His mind had not recovered the shock when his grandfather died,– died in faith and fear, with good hope of accepted repentance, but unable to convey the assurance of such hope to his grandson. Grief for the only parent he had ever known, and the sensation of being completely alone in the world, were joined to a vague impression of horror at the suddenness of the stroke, and it was long before the influence of Hollywell, or the elasticity of his own youthfulness, could rouse him from his depression.

Even then it was almost against his will that he returned to enjoyment, unable to avoid being amused, but feeling as if joy was not meant for him, and as if those around were walking 'in a world of light,' where he could scarcely hope to tread a few uncertain steps. In this despondency was Guy's chief danger, as it was likely to make him deem a struggle with temptation fruitless, while his high spirits and powers of keen enjoyment increased the peril of recklessness in the reaction.

It was Mrs. Edmonstone who first spoke with him cheerfully of a successful conflict with evil, and made him perceive that his temptations were but such as is common to man. She had given him a clue to discover when and how to trust himself to enjoy; the story of Sintram had stirred him deeply, and this very day, Amy's words, seemingly unheeded and unheard, had brought home to him the hope and encouragement of that marvellous tale.

They had helped him in standing, looking steadfastly upwards, and treading down not merely evil, but the first token of coming evil, regardless of the bruises he might inflict on himself. Well for him if he was constant.

Such was Guy's inner life; his outward life, frank and joyous, has been shown, and the two flowed on like a stream, pure as crystal, but into which the eye cannot penetrate from its depth. The surface would be sometimes obscured by cloud or shade, and reveal the sombre wells beneath; but more often the sunshine would penetrate the inmost recesses, and make them glance and sparkle, showing themselves as clear and limpid as the surface itself.

CHAPTER 6

Can piety the discord heal,
Or stanch the death-feud's enmity?
— Scott

It must not be supposed that such a history of Guy's mind was expressed by himself, or understood by Mrs. Edmonstone; but she saw enough to guess at his character, perceive the sort of guidance he needed, and be doubly interested in him. Much did she wish he could have such a friend as her brother would have been, and hope that nothing would prevent a friendship with her nephew.

The present question about the horse was, she thought, unfortunate, since, though Guy had exercised great self-denial, it was no wonder Philip was annoyed. Mr. Edmonstone's vexation was soon over. As soon as she had persuaded him that there had been no offence, he strove to say with a good grace, that it was very proper, and told Guy he would be a thorough book-worm and tremendous scholar, which Guy took as an excellent joke.

Philip had made up his mind to be forbearing, and to say no more about it. Laura thought this a pity, as they could thus never come to an understanding; but when she hinted it, he wore such a dignified air of not being offended, that she was much ashamed of having tried to direct one so much better able to judge. On his side Guy had no idea the trouble he had caused; so, after bestowing his thanks in a gay, off-hand way, which Philip thought the worst feature of the case, he did his best to bring Hecuba back into his mind, drive the hunters out of it, and appease the much-aggrieved William of Deloraine.

When all William's manoeuvres resulted in his master's not hunting at all, he was persuaded it was Mr. Edmonstone's fault, compassionated Sir Guy with all his heart, and could only solace himself by taking Deloraine to exercise where he was most likely to meet the hounds. He further chose to demonstrate that he was not Mr. Edmonstone's servant, by disregarding some of his stable regulations; but as soon as this came to his master's knowledge, a few words were spoken so sharp and stern, that William never attempted to disobey again.

It seemed as if it was the perception that so much was kept back by a strong force, that made Guy's least token of displeasure so formidable. A village boy, whom he caught misusing a poor dog, was found a few minutes after, by Mr. Ross, in a state of terror that was positively ludicrous, though it did not appear that Sir Guy had said or done much to alarm him; it was only the light in his eyes, and the strength of repressed indignation in his short broken words that had made the impression.

It appeared as if the force of his anger might be fearful, if once it broke forth without control; yet at the same time he had a gentleness and attention, alike to small and great, which, with his high spirit and good nature, his very sweet voice and pleasant smile, made him a peculiarly winning and engaging person; and few who saw him could help being interested in him.

No wonder he had become in the eyes of the Edmonstones almost a part of their family. Mrs. Edmonstone had assumed a motherly control over him, to which he submitted with a sort of affectionate gratitude.

One day Philip remarked, that he never saw any one so restless as Guy, who could neither talk nor listen without playing with something. Scissors, pencil, paper-knife, or anything that came in his way, was sure to be twisted or tormented; or if nothing else was at hand, he opened and shut his own knife so as to put all the spectators in fear for his fingers.

'Yes,' said Laura, 'I saw how it tortured your eyebrows all the time you were translating Schiller to us. I wondered you were not put out.'

'I consider that to be put out— by which you mean to have the intellect at the mercy of another's folly— is beneath a reasonable creature,' said Philip; 'but that I was annoyed, I do not deny. It is a token of a restless, ill-regulated mind.'

'Restless, perhaps,' said Mrs. Edmonstone 'but not necessarily ill-regulated. I should think it rather a sign that he had no one to tell him of the tricks which mothers generally nip in the bud.'

'I was going to say that I think he fidgets less,' said Laura; 'but I think his chief contortions of the scissors have been when Philip has been here.'

'They have, I believe,' said her mother, I was thinking of giving him a hint.'

'Well, aunt, you are a tamer of savage beasts if you venture on such a subject,' said Philip.

'Do you dare me?' she asked, smiling.

'Why, I don't suppose he would do more than give you one of his lightning glances: but that, I think, is more than you desire.'

'Considerably,' said Mrs. Edmonstone; 'for his sake as much as my own.'

'But,' said Laura, 'mamma has nearly cured him of pawing like a horse in the hall when he is kept waiting. He said he knew it was impatience, and begged her to tell him how to cure it. So she treated him as an old fairy might, and advised him in a grave, mysterious way, always to go and play the "Harmonious Blacksmith," when he found himself getting into "a taking", just as if it was a charm. And he always does it most dutifully.'

'It has a very good effect,' said Mrs. Edmonstone; 'for it is apt to act as a summons to the other party, as well as a sedative to him.'

'I must say I am curious to see what you will devise this time,' said Philip; 'since you can't set him to play on the piano; and very few can bear to be told of a trick of the kind.'

In the course of that evening, Philip caused the great atlas to be brought out in order to make investigations on the local habitation of a certain Khan of Kipchack, who existed somewhere in the dark ages. Then he came to Marco Polo, and Sir John Mandeville; and Guy, who knew both the books in the library at Redclyffe, grew very eager in talking them over, and tracing their adventures— then to the Genoese merchants, where Guy confessed himself perfectly ignorant. Andrea Doria was the only Genoese he ever heard of; but he hunted out with great interest all the localities of their numerous settlements. Then came modern Italy, and its fallen palaces; then the contrast between the republican merchant and aristocratic lord of the soil; then the corn laws; and then, and not till then, did Philip glance at his aunt, to show her Guy balancing a Venetian weight on as few of his fingers as could support it.

'Guy,' said she, smiling, 'does that unfortunate glass inspire you with any arguments in favour of the Venetians?'

Guy put it down at once, and Philip proceeded to improved methods of farming, to enable landlords to meet the exigencies of the times. Guy had got hold of Mr. Edmonstone's spectacle-case, and was putting its spring to a hard trial. Mrs. Edmonstone doubted whether to interfere again; she knew this was not the sort of thing that tried his temper, yet she particularly disliked playing him off, as it were for Philip's amusement, and quite as much letting him go on, and lower himself in her nephew's estimation. The spectacle-case settled the matter— a crack was heard, it refused to snap at all; and Guy, much discomfited, made many apologies.

Amy laughed; Philip was much too well-bred to do anything but curl his lip unconsciously. Mrs. Edmonstone waited till he was gone, then, when she was wishing Guy 'good-night' at Charles's door, she said,—

'The spectacle-case forestalled me in giving you a lecture on sparing our nerves. Don't look so very full of compunction— it is only a trick which your mother would have stopped at five years old, and which you can soon stop for yourself.'

'Thank you, I will!' said Guy; 'I hardly knew I did it, but I am very sorry it has teased you.'

Thenceforward it was curious to see how he put down and pushed away all he had once begun to touch and torture. Mrs. Edmonstone said it was self command in no common degree; and Philip allowed that to cure so inveterate a habit required considerable strength of will.

'However,' he said, 'I always gave the Morvilles credit for an iron resolution. Yes, Amy, you may laugh; but if a man is not resolute in a little, he will never be resolute in great matters.'

'And Guy has been resolute the right way this time,' said Laura.

'May he always be the same,' said Philip.

Philip had undertaken, on his way back to Broadstone, to conduct Charlotte to East-hill, where she was to spend the day with a little niece of Mary Ross. She presently came down, her bonnet-strings tied in a most resolute-looking bow, and her little figure drawn up so as to look as womanly is possible for her first walk alone with Philip. She wished the party at home 'goodbye;' and as Amy and Laura stood watching her, they could not help laughing to see her tripping feet striving to keep step, her blue veil discreetly composed and her little head turned up, as if she was trying hard to be on equal terms with the tall cousin, who meanwhile looked graciously down from his height, patronising her like a very small child. After some space, Amy began to wonder what they could talk about, or whether they would talk at all; but Laura said there was no fear of Charlotte's tongue ever being still, and Charles rejoined,—

'Don't you know that Philip considers it due to himself that his audience should never be without conversation suited to their capacity?'

'Nonsense, Charlie!'

'Nay, I give him credit for doing it as well as it is in nature of things for it to be done. The strongest proof I know of his being a superior man, is the way he adapts himself to his company. He lays down the law to us, because he knows we are all born to be his admirers; he calls Thorndale his dear fellow and conducts him like a Mentor; but you may observe how different he is with other people— Mr. Ross, for instance. It is not showing off; it is just what the pattern hero should be with the pattern clergyman. At a dinner party he is quite in his place; contents himself with leaving an impression on his neighbour that Mr. Morville is at home on every subject; and that he is the right thing with his brother officers is sufficiently proved, since not even Maurice either hates or quizzes him.'

'Well, Charlie,' said Laura, well pleased, I am glad you are convinced at last.'

'Do you think I ever wanted to be convinced that we were created for no other end than to applaud Philip? I was fulfilling the object of our existence by enlarging on a remark of Guy's, that nothing struck him more than the way in which Philip could adapt his conversation to the hearers. So the hint was not lost on me; and I came to the conclusion that it was a far greater proof of his sense than all the maxims he lavishes on us.'

'I wonder Guy was the person to make the remark,' said Laura; 'for it is strange that those two never appear to the best advantage together.'

'Oh, Laura, that would be the very reason,' said Amy.

'The very reason?' said Charles. Draw out your meaning, Miss.'

'Yes,' said Amy, colouring, 'If Guy— if a generous person, I mean— were vexed with another sometimes, it would be the very reason he would make the most of all his goodness.'

'Heigh-ho!' yawned Charles. What o'clock is it? I wonder when Guy is ever coming back from that Lascelles.'

'Your wonder need not last long,' said Laura; 'for I see him riding into the stable yard.'

In a few minutes he had entered; and, on being asked if he had met Philip and Charlotte, and how they were getting on, he replied,— 'A good deal like the print of Dignity and Impudence,' at the same time throwing back his shoulders, and composing his countenance to imitate Philip's lofty deportment and sedate expression, and the next moment putting his head on one side with a sharp little nod, and giving a certain espiegle glance of the eye, and knowing twist of one corner of the mouth, just like Charlotte.

'By the by,' added he, 'would Philip have been a clergyman if he had gone to Oxford?'

'I don't know; I don't think it was settled,' said Laura, 'Why?'

'I could never fancy him one' said Guy. 'He would not have been what he is now if he had gone to Oxford,' said Charles. 'He would have lived with men of the same powers and pursuits with himself, and have found his level.'

'And that would have been a very high one,' said Guy.

'It would; but there would be all the difference there is between a feudal prince and an Eastern despot. He would know what it is to live with his match.'

'But you don't attempt to call him conceited!' cried Guy, with a sort of consternation.

'He is far above that; far too grand,' said Amy.

'I should as soon think of calling Jupiter conceited,' said Charles; and Laura did not know how far to be gratified, or otherwise.

Charles had not over-estimated Philip's readiness of self adaptation. Charlotte had been very happy with him, talking over the "Lady of the Lake", which she had just read, and being enlightened, partly to her satisfaction, partly to her disappointment, as to how much was historical. He listened good-naturedly to a fit of rapture, and threw in a few, not too many, discreet words of guidance to the true principles of taste; and next told her about an island, in a pond at Stylehurst, which had been by turns Ellen's isle and Robinson Crusoe's. It was at this point in the conversation that Guy came in sight, riding slowly, his reins on his horse's neck, whistling a slow, melancholy tune, his eyes fixed on the sky, and so lost in musings, that he did not perceive them till Philip arrested him by calling out, 'That is a very bad plan. No horse is to be trusted in that way, especially such a spirited one.'

Guy started, and gathered up his reins, owning it was foolish.

'You look only half disenchanted yet,' said Philip. 'Has Lascelles put you into what my father's old gardener used to call a stud?'

'Nothing so worthy of a stud,' said Guy, smiling and colouring a little. 'I was only dreaming over a picture of ruin—

'The steed is vanish'd from the stall,
No serf is seen in Hassan's hall,
The lonely spider's thin grey pall
Waves, slowly widening o'er the wall.'

'Byron!' exclaimed Philip. 'I hope you are not dwelling on him?'

'Only a volume I found in my room.'

'Oh, the "Giaour"!' said Philip. 'Well, there is no great damage done; but it is bad food for excitable minds. Don't let it get hold of you.'

'Very well;' and there was a cloud, but it cleared in a moment, and, with a few gay words to both, he rode off at a quick pace.

'Foolish fellow!' muttered Philip, looking after him.

After some space of silence, Charlotte began in a very grave tone—

'Philip.'

'Well?'

'Philip.'

Another 'Well!' and another long pause.

'Philip, I don't know whether you'll be angry with me.'

'Certainly not,' said Philip, marvelling at what was coming.

'Guy says he does not want to keep up the feud, and I wish you would not.'

'What do you mean?'

'The deadly feud!' said Charlotte.

'What nonsense is this?' said Philip.

'Surely— Oh Philip, there always was a deadly feud between our ancestors, and the Redclyffe Morvilles, and it was very wrong, and ought not to be kept up now.'

'It is not I that keep it up.'

'Is it not?' said Charlotte. 'But I am sure you don't like Guy. And I can't think why not, unless it is the deadly feud, for we are all so fond of him. Laura says it is a different house since he came.'

'Hum!' said Philip. 'Charlotte, you did well to make me promise not to be angry with you, by which, I presume, you mean displeased. I should like to know what put this notion into your head.'

'Charlie told me,' almost whispered Charlotte, hanging down her head. 'And— and— '

'And what? I can't hear.'

Charlotte was a good deal frightened; but either from firmness, or from the female propensity to have the last word, or it might be the spirit of mischief, she got out– 'You have made me quite sure of it yourself.'

She was so alarmed at having said this, that had it not been undignified, she would have run quite away, and never stopped till she came to East-hill. Matters were not mended when Philip said authoritatively, and as if he was not in the least bit annoyed (which was the more vexatious), 'What do you mean, Charlotte?'

She had a great mind to cry, by way of getting out of the scrape; but having begun as a counsellor and peacemaker, it would never do to be babyish; and on his repeating the question, she said, in a tone which she could not prevent from being lachrymose, 'You make Guy almost angry, you tease him, and when people praise him, you answer as if it would not last! And it is very unfair of you,' concluded she, with almost a sob.

'Charlotte,' replied Philip, much more kindly than she thought she deserved, after the reproach that seemed to her so dreadfully naughty, 'you may dismiss all fear of deadly feud, whatever you may mean by it. Charles has been playing tricks on you. You know, my little cousin, that I am a Christian, and we live in the nineteenth century.'

Charlotte felt as if annihilated at the aspect of her own folly. He resumed– 'You misunderstood me. I do think Guy very agreeable. He is very attentive to Charles, very kind to you, and so attractive, that I don't wonder you like him. But those who are older than you see that he has faults, and we wish to set him on his guard against them. It may be painful to ourselves, and irritating to him, but depend upon it, it is the proof of friendship. Are you satisfied, my little cousin?'

She could only say humbly, 'I beg your pardon.'

'You need not ask pardon. Since you had the notion, it was right to speak, as it was to me, one of your own family. When you are older, you need never fear to speak out in the right place. I am glad you have so much of the right sort of feminine courage, though in this case you might have ventured to trust to me.'

So ended Charlotte's anxieties respecting the deadly feud, and she had now to make up her mind to the loss of her playfellow, who was to go to Oxford at Easter, when he would be just eighteen, his birthday being the 28th of March. Both her playmates were going, Bustle as well as Guy, and it was at first proposed that Deloraine should go too, but Guy bethought himself that Oxford would be a place of temptation for William; and not choosing to trust the horse to any one else, resolved to leave both at Hollywell.

His grandfather had left an allowance for Guy, until his coming of age, such as might leave no room for extravagance, and which even Philip pronounced to be hardly sufficient for a young man in his position. 'You know,' said Mr. Edmonstone, in his hesitating, good-natured way, 'if ever you have occasion sometimes for a little— a little more— you need only apply to me. Don't be afraid, anything rather than run into debt. You know me, and 'tis your own.'

'This shall do,' said Guy, in the same tone as he had fixed his hours of study.

Each of the family made Guy a birthday present, as an outfit for Oxford; Mr. Edmonstone gave him a set of studs, Mrs. Edmonstone a Christian Year, Amabel copied some of his favourite songs, Laura made a drawing of Sintram, Charlotte worked a kettle-holder, with what was called by courtesy a likeness of Bustle. Charles gave nothing, professing that he would do nothing to encourage his departure.

'You don't know what a bore it is to lose the one bit of quicksilver in the house!' said he, yawning. 'I shall only drag on my existence till you come back.'

'You, Charles, the maker of fun!' said Guy, amazed.

'It is a case of flint and steel,' said Charles; 'but be it owing to who it will, we have been alive since you came here. You have taken care to be remembered. We have been studying you, or laughing at you, or wondering what absurdity was to come next.'

'I am very sorry— that is, if you are serious. I hoped at least I appeared like other people.'

'I'll tell you what you appear like. Just what I would be if I was a free man.'

'Never say that, Charlie!'

'Nay, wait a bit. I would never be so foolish. I would never give my sunny mornings to Euripides; I would not let the best hunter in the county go when I had wherewithal to pay for him.'

'You would not have such an ill-conditioned self to keep in rule.'

'After all,' continued Charles, yawning, 'it is no great compliment to say I am sorry you are going. If you were an Ethiopian serenader, you would be a loss to me. It is something to see anything beyond this old drawing-room, and the same faces doing the same things every day. Laura poking over her drawing, and meditating upon the last entry in Philip's memorandum-book, and Amy at her flowers or some nonsense or other, and Charlotte and the elders all the same, and a lot of stupid people dropping in and a lot of stupid books to read, all just alike. I can tell what they are like without looking in!' Charles yawned again, sighed, and moved wearily. 'Now, there came some life and freshness with you. You talk of Redclyffe, and your brute creation there, not like a book, and still less like a commonplace man; you are innocent and unsophisticated, and take new points of view; you are something to interest oneself about; your coming in is something to look forward to; you make the singing not such mere milk-and-water, your reading the Praelectiones is an additional landmark to time; besides the mutton of to-day succeeding the beef of yesterday. Heigh-ho! I'll tell you what, Guy. Though I may carry it off with a high hand, 'tis no joke to be a helpless log all the best years of a man's life,– nay, for my whole life,– for at the very best of the contingencies the doctors are always flattering me with, I should make but a wretched crippling affair of it. And if that is the best hope they give me, you may guess it is likely to be a pretty deal worse. Hope? I've been hoping these ten years, and much good has it done me. I say, Guy,' he proceeded, in a tone of extreme bitterness, though with a sort of smile, 'the only wonder is that I don't hate the very sight of you! There are times when I feel as if I could bite some men,– that Tomfool Maurice de Courcy, for instance, when I hear him rattling on, and think– '

'I know I have often talked thoughtlessly, I have feared afterwards I might have given you pain.'

'No, no, you never have; you have carried me along with you. I like nothing better than to hear of your ridings, and shootings, and boatings. It is a sort of life.'

Charles had never till now alluded seriously to his infirmity before Guy, and the changing countenance of his auditor showed him to be much affected, as he stood leaning over the end of the sofa, with his speaking eyes earnestly fixed on Charles, who went on:

'And now you are going to Oxford. You will take your place among the men of your day. You will hear and be heard of. You will be somebody. And I!– I know I have what they call talent– I could be something. They think me an idle dog; but where's the good of doing anything? I only know if I was not– not condemned to– to this– this life,' (had it not been for a sort of involuntary respect to the gentle compassion of the softened hazel eyes regarding him so kindly, he would have used the violent expletive that trembled on his lip;) 'if I was not chained down here, Master Philip should not stand alone as the paragon of the family. I've as much mother wit as he.'

'That you have,' said Guy. 'How fast you see the sense of a passage. You could excel very much if you only tried.'

'Tried?' And what am I to gain by it?'

'I don't know that one ought to let talents rust,' said Guy, thoughtfully; 'I suppose it is one's duty not; and surely it is a pity to give up those readings.'

'I shall not get such another fellow dunce as you,' said Charles, 'as I told you when we began, and it would be a mere farce to do it alone. I could not make myself, if I would.'

'Can't you make yourself do what you please?' said Guy, as if it was the simplest thing in the world.

'Not a bit, if the other half of me does not like it. I forget it, or put it off, and it comes to nothing. I do declare, though, I would get something to break my mind on, merely as a medical precaution, just to freshen myself up, if I could find any one to do it with. No, nothing in the shape of a tutor, against that I protest.'

'Your sisters,' suggested Guy.

'Hum'! Laura is too intellectual already, and I don't mean to poach on Philip's manor; and if I made little Amy cease to be silly, I should do away with all the comfort I have left me in life. I don't know, though, if she swallowed learning after Mary Ross's pattern, that it need do her much harm.'

Amy came into the room at the moment. 'Amy, here is Guy advising me to take you to read something awfully wise every day, something that will make you as dry as a stick, and as blue– '

'As a gentianella,' said Guy.

'I should not mind being like a gentianella,' said Amy. 'But what dreadful thing were you setting him to do?'

'To make you read all the folios in my uncle's old library,' said Charles. 'All that Margaret has in keeping against Philip has a house of his own.'

'Sancho somebody, and all you talked of when first you came?' said Amy.

'We were talking of the hour's reading that Charlie and I have had together lately,' said Guy.

'I was thinking how Charlie would miss that hour,' said Amy; 'and we shall be very sorry not to have you to listen to.'

'Well, then, Amy, suppose you read with me?'

'Oh, Charlie, thank you! Should you really like it?' cried Amy, colouring with delight. 'I have always thought it would be so very delightful if you would read with me, as James Ross used with Mary, only I was afraid of tiring you with my stupidity. Oh, thank you!'

So it was settled, and Charles declared that he put himself on honour to give a good account of their doings to Guy, that being the only way of making himself steady to his resolution; but he was perfectly determined not to let Philip know anything about the practice he had adopted, since he would by no means allow him to guess that he was following his advice.

Charles had certainly grown very fond of Guy, in spite of his propensity to admire Philip, satisfying himself by maintaining that, after all, Guy only tried to esteem his cousin because he thought it a point of duty, just as children think it right to admire the good boy in a story book; but that he was secretly fretted and chafed by his perfection. No one could deny that there were often occasions when little misunderstandings would arise, and that, but for Philip's coolness and Guy's readiness to apologise they might often have gone further; but at the same time no one could regret these things more than Guy himself, and he was willing and desirous to seek Philip's advice and assistance when needed. In especial, he listened earnestly to the counsel which was bestowed on him about Oxford: and Mrs. Edmonstone was convinced that no one could have more anxiety to do right and avoid temptation. She had many talks with him in her dressing-room, promising to write to him, as did also Charles; and he left Hollywell with universal regrets, most loudly expressed by Charlotte, who would not be comforted without a lock of Bustle's hair, which she would have worn round her neck if she had not been afraid that Laura would tell Philip.

'He goes with excellent intentions,' said Philip, as they watched him from the door.

'I do hope he will do well,' said Mrs. Edmonstone.

'I wish he may,' said Philip; 'the agreeableness of his whole character makes one more anxious. It is very dangerous. His name, his wealth, his sociable, gay disposition, that very attractive manner, all are so many perils, and he has not that natural pleasure in study that would be of itself a preservative from temptation. However, he is honestly anxious to do right, and has excellent principles. I only fear his temper and his want of steadiness. Poor boy, I hope he may do well!'

CHAPTER 7

— Pray, good shepherd, what
Fair swain is this that dances with your daughter?
He sings several times faster than you'll tell money;
he utters them as he had eaten ballads, and all men's
ears grow to his tunes.
— WINTER'S TALE

It was a glorious day in June, the sky of pure deep dazzling blue, the sunshine glowing with brightness, but with cheerful freshness in the air that took away all sultriness, the sun tending westward in his long day's career, and casting welcome shadows from the tall firs and horse-chestnuts that shaded the lawn. A long rank of haymakers— men and women— proceeded with their rakes, the white shirt-sleeves, straw bonnets, and ruddy faces, radiant in the bath of sunshine, while in the shady end of the field were idler haymakers among the fragrant piles, Charles half lying on the grass, with his back against a tall haycock; Mrs. Edmonstone sitting on another, book in hand; Laura sketching the busy scene, the sun glancing through the chequered shade on her glossy curls; Philip stretched out at full length, hat and neck-tie off, luxuriating in the cool repose after a dusty walk from Broadstone; and a little way off, Amabel and Charlotte pretending to make hay, but really building nests with it, throwing it at each other, and playing as heartily as the heat would allow.

They talked and laughed, the rest were too hot, too busy, or too sleepy for conversation, even Philip being tired into enjoying the "dolce far niente"; and they basked in the fresh breezy heat and perfumy hay with only now and then a word, till a cold, black, damp nose was suddenly thrust into Charles's face, a red tongue began licking him; and at the same moment Charlotte, screaming 'There he is!' raced headlong across the swarths of hay, to meet Guy, who had just ridden into the field. He threw Deloraine's rein to one of the haymakers, and came bounding to meet her, just in time to pick her up as she put her foot into a hidden hole, and fell prostrate.

In another moment he was in the midst of the whole party, who crowded round and welcomed him as if he had been a boy returning from his first half-year's schooling; and never did little school-boy look more holiday-like than he, with all the sunshine of that June day reflected, as it were, in his glittering eyes and glowing face, while Bustle escaping from Charles's caressing arm, danced round, wagging his tail in ecstasy, and claiming his share of the welcome. Then Guy was on the ground by Charles, rejoicing to find him out there, and then, some dropping into their former nests on the hay, some standing round, they talked fast and eagerly in a confusion of sound that did not subside for the first ten minutes so as to allow anything to be clearly heard. The first distinct sentence was Charlotte's 'Bustle, darling old fellow, you are handsomer than ever!'

'What a delicious day!' next exclaimed Guy, following Philip's example, by throwing off hat and neck-tie.

'A spontaneous tribute to the beauty of the day,' said Charles.

'Really it is so ultra-splendid as to deserve notice!' said Philip, throwing himself completely back, and looking up.

'One cannot help revelling in that deep blue!' said Laura.

'Tomorrow'll be the happiest time of all the glad new year,' hummed Guy.

'Ah you will teach us all now,' said Laura, 'after your grand singing lessons.'

'Do you know what is in store for you, Guy?' said Amy. 'Oh! haven't you heard about Lady Kilcoran's ball?'

'You are to go, Guy,' said Charlotte. 'I am glad I am not. I hate dancing.'

'And I know as much about it as Bustle,' said Guy, catching the dog by his forepaws, and causing him to perform an uncouth dance.

'Never mind, they will soon teach you,' said Mrs. Edmonstone.

'Must I really go?'

'He begins to think it serious,' said Charles.

'Is Philip going?' exclaimed Guy, looking as if he was taken by surprise.

'He is going to say something about dancing being a healthful recreation for young people,' said Charles.

'You'll be disappointed,' said Philip. 'It is much too hot to moralize.'

'Apollo unbends his bow,' exclaimed Charles. 'The captain yields the field.'

'Ah! Captain Morville, I ought to have congratulated you,' said Guy. 'I must come to Broadstone early enough to see you on parade.'

'Come to Broadstone! You aren't still bound to Mr. Lascelles,' said Charles.

'If he has time for me,' said Guy. 'I am too far behind the rest of the world to afford to be idle this vacation.'

'That's right, Guy,' exclaimed Philip, sitting up, and looking full of approval. 'With so much perseverance, you must get on at last. How did you do in collections?'

'Tolerably, thank you.'

'You must be able to enter into the thing now,' proceeded Philip. 'What are you reading?'

'Thucydides.'

'Have you come to Pericles' oration? I must show you some notes that I have on that. Don't you get into the spirit of it now?'

'Up-hill work still,' answered Guy, disentangling some cinders from the silky curls of Bustle's ear.

'Which do you like best— that or the ball?' asked Charles.

'The hay-field best of all,' said Guy, releasing Bustle, and blinding him with a heap of hay.

'Of course!' said Charlotte, 'who would not like hay-making better than that stupid ball?'

'Poor Charlotte!' said Mrs. Edmonstone; commiseration which irritated Charlotte into standing up and protesting,

'Mamma, you know I don't want to go.'

'No more do I, Charlotte,' said her brother, in a mock consoling tone. 'You and I know what is good for us, and despise sublunary vanities.'

'But you will go, Guy,' said Laura; 'Philip is really going.'

'In spite of Lord Kilcoran's folly in going to such an expense as either taking Allonby or giving the ball,' said Charles.

'I don't think it is my business to bring Lord Kilcoran to a sense of his folly,' said Philip. 'I made all my protests to Maurice when first he started the notion, but if his father chose to take the matter up, it is no concern of mine.'

'You will understand, Guy,' said Charles, 'that this ball is specially got up by Maurice for Laura's benefit.'

'Believe as little as you please of that speech, Guy,' said Laura; 'the truth is that Lord Kilcoran is very good-natured, and Eveleen was very much shocked to hear that Amy had never been to any ball, and I to only one, and so it ended in their giving one.'

'When is it to be?'

'On Thursday week,' said Amy. 'I wonder if you will think Eveleen as pretty as we do!'

'She is Laura's great friend, is not she?'

'I like her very much; I have known her all my life, and she has much more depth than those would think who only know her manner.' And Laura looked pleadingly at Philip as she spoke.

'Are there any others of the family at home?' said Guy.

'The two younger girls, Mabel and Helen, and the little boys,' said Amy. 'Lord de Courcy is in Ireland, and all the others are away.'

'Lord de Courcy is the wisest man of the family, and sets his face against absenteeism,' said Philip, 'so he is never visible here.'

'But you aren't going to despise it, I hope, Guy,' said Amy, earnestly; 'it will be so delightful! And what fun we shall have in teaching you to dance!'

Guy stretched himself, and gave a quaint grunt.

'Never mind, Guy,' said Philip, 'very little is required. You may easily pass in the crowd. I never learnt.'

'Your ear will guide you,' said Laura.

'And no one can stay at home, since Mary Ross is going,' said Amy. 'Eveleen was always so fond of her, that she came and forced a promise from her by telling her she should come with mamma, and have no trouble.'

'You have not seen Allonby,' said Laura. 'There are such Vandykes, and among them, such a King Charles!'

'Is not that the picture,' said Charles, 'before which Amy– '

'O don't, Charlie!'

'Was found dissolved in tears?'

'I could not help it,' murmured Amy, blushing crimson.

'There is all Charles's fate in his face,' said Philip,– 'earnest, melancholy, beautiful! It would stir the feelings– were it an unknown portrait. No, Amy, you need not be ashamed of your tears.'

But Amy turned away, doubly ashamed.

'I hope it is not in the ball-room,' said Guy.

'No said Laura, 'it is in the library.'

Charlotte, whose absence had become perceptible from the general quietness, here ran up with two envelopes, which she put into Guy's hands. One contained Lady Kilcoran's genuine card of invitation for Sir Guy Morville, the other Charlotte had scribbled in haste for Mr. Bustle.

This put an end to all rationality. Guy rose with a growl and a roar, and hunted her over half the field, till she was caught, and came back out of breath and screaming, 'We never had such a haymaking!'

'So I think the haymakers will say!' answered her mother, rising to go indoors. 'What ruin of haycocks!'

'Oh, I'll set all that to rights,' said Guy, seizing a hay-fork.

'Stop, stop, take care!' cried Charles. 'I don't want to be built up in the rick, and by and by, when my disconsolate family have had all the ponds dragged for me, Deloraine will be heard to complain that they give him very odd animal food.'

'Who could resist such a piteous appeal!' said Guy, helping him to rise, and conducting him to his wheeled chair. The others followed, and when, shortly after, Laura looked out at her window, she saw Guy, with his coat off, toiling like a real haymaker, to build up the cocks in all their neat fairness and height, whistling meantime the 'Queen of the May,' and now and then singing a line. She watched the old cowman come up, touching his hat, and looking less cross than usual; she saw Guy's ready greeting, and perceived they were comparing the forks and rakes, the pooks and cocks of their counties; and, finally, she beheld her father ride into the field, and Guy spring to meet him.

No one could have so returned to what was in effect a home, unless his time had been properly spent; and, in fact, all that Mr. Edmonstone or Philip could hear of him, was so satisfactory, that Philip pronounced that the first stage of the trial had been passed irreproachably, and Laura felt and looked delighted at this sanction to the high estimation in which she held him.

His own account of himself to Mrs. Edmonstone would not have been equally satisfactory if she had not had something else to check it with. It was given by degrees, and at many different times, chiefly as they walked round the garden in the twilight of the summer evenings, talking over the many subjects mentioned in the letters which had passed constantly. It seemed as if there were very few to whom Guy would ever give his confidence; but that once bestowed, it was with hardly any reserve, and that was his great relief and satisfaction to pour out his whole mind, where he was sure of sympathy.

To her, then, he confided how much provoked he was with himself, his 'first term,' he said, 'having only shown him what an intolerable fool he had to keep in order.' By his account, he could do nothing 'without turning his own head, except study, and that stupefied it.' 'Never was there a more idle fellow; he could work himself for a given time, but his sense would not second him; and was it not most absurd in him to take so little pleasure in what was his duty, and enjoy only what was bad for him?'

He had tried boating, but it had distracted him from his work; so he had been obliged to give it up, and had done so in a hasty vehement manner, which had caused offence, and for which he blamed himself. It had been the same with other things, till he had left himself no regular recreation but walking and music. 'The last,' he said, 'might engross him in the same way; but he thought (here he hesitated a little) there were higher ends for music, which made it come under Mrs. Edmonstone's rule, of a thing to be used guardedly, not disused.' He had resumed light reading, too, which he had nearly discontinued before he went to Oxford. 'One wants something,' he said, 'by way of refreshment, where there is no sea nor rock to look at, and no Laura and Amy to talk to.'

He had made one friend, a scholar of his own college, of the name of Wellwood. This name had been his attraction; Guy was bent on friendship with him; if, as he tried to make him out to be, he was the son of that Captain Wellwood whose death had weighed so heavily on his grandfather's conscience, feeling almost as if it were his duty to ask forgiveness in his grandfather's name, yet scarcely knowing how to venture on advances to one to whom his name had such associations. However, they had gradually drawn together, and at length entered on the subject, and Guy then found he was the nephew, not the son of Captain Wellwood; indeed, his former belief was founded on a miscalculation, as the duel had taken place twenty-eight years ago. He now heard all his grandfather had wished to know of the family. There were two unmarried daughters, and their cousin spoke in the highest terms of their self-devoted life, promising what Guy much wished, that they should hear what deep repentance had followed the crime which had made them fatherless. He was to be a clergyman, and Guy admired him extremely, saying, however, that he was so shy and retiring, it was hard to know him well.

From not having been at school, and from other causes, Guy had made few acquaintance; indeed, he amused Mrs. Edmonstone by fearing he had been morose. She was ready to tell him he was an ingenious self-tormentor; but she saw that the struggle to do right was the main spring of the happiness that beamed round him, in spite of his self-reproach, heart-felt as it was. She doubted whether persons more contented with themselves were as truly joyous, and was convinced that, while thus combating lesser temptations, the very shadow of what are generally alone considered as real temptations would hardly come near him.

If it had not been for these talks, and now and then a thoughtful look, she would have believed him one of the most light-hearted and merriest of beings. He was more full of glee and high spirits than she had ever seen him; he seemed to fill the whole house with mirth, and keep every one alive by his fun and frolic, as blithe and untiring as Maurice de Courcy himself, though not so wild.

Very pleasant were those summer days– reading, walking, music, gardening. Did not they all work like very labourers at the new arbour in the midst of the laurels, where Charles might sit and see the spires of Broadstone? Work they did, indeed! Charles looking on from his wheeled chair, laughing to see Guy sawing as if for his living and Amy hammering gallantly, and Laura weaving osiers, and Charlotte flying about with messages.

One day, they were startled by an exclamation from Charles. 'Ah, ha! Paddy, is that you?' and beheld the tall figure of a girl, advancing with a rapid, springing step, holding up her riding habit with one hand, with the other whisking her coral-handled whip. There was something distinguished in her air, and her features, though less fine than Laura's, were very pretty, by the help of laughing dark blue eyes, and very black hair, under her broad hat and little waving feather. She threatened Charles with her whip, calling out– 'Aunt Edmonstone said I should find you here. What is the fun now?'

'Arbour building,' said Charles; 'don't you see the head carpenter!'

'Sir Guy?' whispered she to Laura, looking up at him, where he was mounted on the roof, thatching it with reed, the sunshine full on his glowing face and white shirt sleeves.

'Here!' said Charles, as Guy swung himself down with a bound, his face much redder than sun and work had already made it, 'here's another wild Irisher for you.'

'Sir Guy Morville– Lady Eveleen de Courcy,' began Laura; but Lady Eveleen cut her short, frankly holding out her hand, and saying, 'You are almost a cousin, you know. Oh, don't leave off. Do give me something to do. That hammer, Amy, pray– Laura, don't you remember how dearly I always loved hammering?'

'How did you come?' said Laura.

'With papa– 'tis his visit to Sir Guy. 'No, don't go,' as Guy began to look for his coat; 'he is only impending. He is gone on to Broadstone, but he dropped me here, and will pick me up on his way back. Can't you give me something to do on the top of that ladder? I should like it mightily; it looks so cool and airy.'

'How can you, Eva?' whispered Laura, reprovingly; but Lady Eveleen only shook her head at her, and declaring she saw a dangerous nail sticking out, began to hammer it in with such good will, that Charles stopped his ears, and told her it was worse than her tongue. 'Go on about the ball, do.'

'Oh,' said she earnestly, 'do you think there is any hope of Captain Morville's coming?'

'Oh yes,' said Laura.

'I am so glad! That is what papa is gone to Broadstone about. Maurice said he had given him such a lecture, that he would not be the one to think of asking him, and papa must do it himself; for if he sets his face against it, it will spoil it all.'

'You may make your mind easy,' said Charles, 'the captain is lenient, and looks on the ball as a mere development of Irish nature. He has been consoling Guy on the difficulties of dancing.'

'Can't you dance?' said Lady Eveleen, looking at him with compassion.

'Such is my melancholy ignorance,' said Guy.

'We have been talking of teaching him,' said Laura.

'Talk! will that do it?' cried Lady Eveleen, springing up. 'We will begin this moment. Come out on the lawn. Here, Charles,' wheeling him along, 'No, thank you, I like it,' as Guy was going to help her. 'There, Charles, be fiddler go on, tum-tum, tee! that'll do. Amy, Laura, be ladies. I'm the other gentleman,' and she stuck on her hat in military style, giving it a cock. She actually set them quadrilling in spite of adverse circumstances, dancing better, in her habit, than most people without one, till Lord Kilcoran arrived.

While he was making his visit, she walked a little apart, arm-in-arm with Laura. 'I like him very much,' she said; 'he looks up to anything. I had heard so much of his steadiness, that it is a great relief to my mind to see him so unlike his cousin.'

'Eveleen!'

'No disparagement to the captain, only I am so dreadfully afraid of him. I am sure he thinks me such an unmitigated goose. Now, doesn't he?'

'If you would but take the right way to make him think otherwise, dear Eva, and show the sense you really have.'

'That is just what my fear of him won't let me do. I would not for the world let him guess it, so there is nothing for it but sauciness to cover one's weakness. I can't be sensible with those that won't give me credit for it. But you'll mind and teach Sir Guy to dance; he has so much spring in him, he deserves to be an Irishman.'

In compliance with this injunction, there used to be a clearance every evening; Charles turned into the bay window out of the way, Mrs. Edmonstone at the piano, and the rest figuring away, the partnerless one, called 'puss in the corner', being generally Amabel, while Charlotte, disdaining them all the time, used to try to make them imitate her dancing-master's graces, causing her father to perform such caricatures of them, as to overpower all with laughing.

Mr. Edmonstone was half Irish. His mother, Lady Mabel Edmonstone, had never thoroughly taken root in England, and on his marriage, had gone with her daughter to live near her old home in Ireland. The present Earl of Kilcoran was her nephew, and a very close intercourse had always been kept up between the families, Mr. and Mrs. Edmonstone being adopted by their younger cousins as uncle and aunt, and always so called.

The house at Allonby was in such confusion, that the family there expected to dine nowhere on the day of the ball, and the Hollywell party thought it prudent to secure their dinner at home, with Philip and Mary Ross, who were to go with them.

By special desire, Philip wore his uniform; and while the sisters were dressing Charlotte gave him a thorough examination, which led to a talk between him and Mary on accoutrements and weapons in general; but while deep in some points of chivalrous armour, Mary's waist was pinched by two mischievous hands, and a little fluttering white figure danced around her.

'O Amy! what do you want with me?'

'Come and be trimmed up,' said Amy.

'I thought you told me I was to have no trouble. I am dressed,' said Mary, looking complacently at her full folds of white muslin.

'No more you shall; but you promised to do as you were told.' And Amy fluttered away with her.

'Do you remember,' said Philip, 'the comparison of Rose Flammock dragging off her father, to a little carved cherub trying to uplift a solid monumental hero?'

'O, I must tell Mary!' cried Charlotte; but Philip stopped her, with orders not to be a silly child.

'It is a pity Amy should not have her share,' said Charles.

'The comparison to a Dutch cherub?' asked Guy.

'She is more after the pattern of the little things on little wings, in your blotting-book,' said Charles; 'certain lines in the predicament of the cherubs of painters— heads "et proeterea nihil".'

'O Guy, do you write verses? cried Charlotte.

'Some nonsense,' muttered Guy, out of countenance; 'I thought I had made away with that rubbish; where is it?'

'In the blotting-book in my room,' said Charles. 'I must explain that the book is my property, and was put into your room when mamma was beautifying it for you, as new and strange company. On its return to me, at your departure, I discovered a great accession of blots and sailing vessels, beside the aforesaid little things.'

'I shall resume my own property,' said Guy, departing in haste.

Charlotte ran after him, to beg for a sight of it; and Philip asked Charles what it was like.

'A romantic incident,' said Charles, 'just fit for a novel. A Petrarch leaving his poems about in blotting-books.'

Charles used the word Petrarch to stand for a poet, not thinking what lady's name he suggested; and he was surprised at the severity of Philip's tone as he inquired, 'Do you mean anything, or do you not?'

Perceiving with delight that he had perplexed and teased, he rejoiced in keeping up the mystery:

'Eh? is it a tender subject with you, too?'

Philip rose, and standing over him, said, in a low but impressive tone:

'I cannot tell whether you are trifling or not; but you are no boy now, and can surely see that this is no subject to be played with. If you are concealing anything you have discovered, you have a great deal to answer for. I can hardly imagine anything more unfortunate than that he should become attached to either of your sisters.'

'Et pourquoi?' asked Charles, coolly.

'I see,' said Philip, retreating to his chair, and speaking with great composure, 'I did you injustice by speaking seriously.' Then, as his uncle came into the room, he asked some indifferent question, without betraying a shade of annoyance.

Charles meanwhile congratulated himself on his valour in keeping his counsel, in spite of so tall a man in scarlet; but he was much nettled at the last speech, for if a real attachment to his sister had been in question, he would never have trifled about it. Keenly alive to his cousin's injustice, he rejoiced in having provoked and mystified the impassable, though he little knew the storm he had raised beneath that serene exterior of perfect self-command.

The carriages were announced, and Mr. Edmonstone began to call the ladies, adding tenfold to the confusion in the dressing-room. There was

Laura being completed by the lady's maid, Amabel embellishing Mary, Mrs. Edmonstone with her arm loaded with shawls, Charlotte flourishing about. Poor Mary– it was much against her will– but she had no heart to refuse the wreath of geraniums that Amy's own hands had woven for her; and there she sat, passive as a doll, though in despair at their all waiting for her. For Laura's toilette was finished, and every one began dressing her at once; while Charlotte, to make it better, screamed over the balusters that all were ready but Mary. Sir Guy was heard playing the 'Harmonious Blacksmith,' and Captain Morville's step was heard, fast and firm. At last, when a long chain was put round her neck, she cried out, 'I have submitted to everything so far; I can bear no more!' jumped up, caught hold of her shawl, and was putting it on, when there was a general outcry that they must exhibit themselves to Charles.

They all ran down, and Amy, flying up to her brother, made a splendid sweeping curtsey, and twirled round in a pirouette.

'Got up, regardless of expense!' cried Charles; 'display yourselves.'

The young ladies ranged themselves in imitation of the book of fashions. The sisters were in white, with wreaths of starry jessamine. It was particularly becoming to Laura's bella-donna lily complexion, rich brown curls, and classical features, and her brother exclaimed:

'Laura is exactly like Apollo playing the lyre, outside mamma's old manuscript book of music.'

'Has not Amy made beautiful wreaths?' said Laura. 'She stripped the tree, and Guy had to fetch the ladder, to gather the sprays on the top of the wall.'

'Do you see your bit of myrtle, Guy,' said Amy, pointing to it, on Laura's head, 'that you tried to persuade me would pass for jessamine?'

'Ah! it should have been all myrtle,' said Guy.

Philip leant meantime against the door. Laura only once glanced towards him, thinking all this too trifling for him, and never imagining the intense interest with which he gave a meaning to each word and look.

'Well done, Mary!' cried Charles, 'they have furbished you up handsomely.'

Mary made a face, and said she should wonder who was the fashionable young lady she should meet in the pier-glasses at Allonby. Then Mr. Edmonstone hurried them away, and they arrived in due time.

The saloon at Allonby was a beautiful room, one end opening into a conservatory, full of coloured lamps, fresh green leaves, and hot-house plants. There they found as yet only the home party, the good-natured, merry Lord Kilcoran, his quiet English wife, who had bad health, and looked hardly equal to the confusion of the evening; Maurice, and two younger boys; Eveleen, and her two little sisters, Mabel and Helen.

'This makes it hard on Charlotte,' thought Amy, while the two girls dragged her off to show her the lamps in the conservatory; and the rest attacked Mrs. Edmonstone for not having brought Charlotte, reproaching her with hardness of heart of which they had never believed her capable– Lady Eveleen, in especial, talking with that exaggeration of her ordinary manner which her dread of Captain Morville made her assume. Little he recked of her; he was absorbed in observing how far Laura's conduct coincided with Charles's hints. On the first opportunity, he asked her to dance, and was satisfied with her pleased acquiescence; but the next moment Guy came up, and in an eager manner made the same request.

'I am engaged,' said she, with a bright, proud glance at Philip; and Guy pursued Amabel into the conservatory, where he met with better success. Mr. Edmonstone gallantly asked Mary if he was too old a partner, and was soon dancing with the step and spring that had once made him the best dancer in the county.

Mrs. Edmonstone watched her flock, proud and pleased, thinking how well they looked and that, in especial, she had never been sensible how much Laura's and Philip's good looks excelled the rest of the world. They were much alike in the remarkable symmetry both of figure and feature, the colour of the deep blue eye, and fairness of complexion.

'It is curious,' thought Mrs. Edmonstone, 'that, so very handsome as Philip is, it is never the first thing remarked about him, just as his height never is observed till he is compared with other people. The fact is, that his superior sense carries off a degree of beauty which would be a misfortune to most men. It is that sedate expression and distinguished air that make the impression. How happy Laura looks, how gracefully she moves. No, it is not being foolish to think no one equal to Laura. My other pair!' and she smiled much more; 'you happy young things, I would not wish to see anything pleasanter than your merry faces. Little Amy looks almost as pretty as Laura, now she is lighted up by blush and smile, and her dancing is very nice, it is just like her laughing, so quiet, and yet so full of glee. I don't think she is less graceful than her sister, but the complete enjoyment strikes one more. And as to enjoyment– there are those bright eyes of her partner's perfectly sparkling with delight; he looks as if it was a world of enchantment to him. Never had any one a greater capacity for happiness than Guy.'

Mrs. Edmonstone might well retain her opinion when, after the quadrille, Guy came to tell her that he had never seen anything so delightful; and he entertained Mary Ross with his fresh, joyous pleasure, through the next dance.

'Laura,' whispered Eveleen, 'I've one ambition. Do you guess it? Don't tell him; but if he would, I should have a better opinion of myself ever after.

I'm afraid he'll depreciate me to his friend; and really with Mr. Thorndale, I was no more foolish than a ball requires.'

Lady Eveleen hoped in vain. Captain Morville danced with little Lady Helen, a child of eleven, who was enchanted at having so tall a partner; then, after standing still for some time, chose his cousin Amabel.

'You are a good partner and neighbour,' said he, giving her his arm, 'you don't want young lady talk.'

'Should you not have asked Mary? She has been sitting down this long time.'

'Do you think she cares for such a sport as dancing?'

Amy made no answer.

'You have been well off. You were dancing with Thorndale just now.'

'Yes. It was refreshing to have an old acquaintance among so many strangers. And he is so delighted with Eveleen; but what is more, Philip, that Mr. Vernon, who is dancing with Laura, told Maurice he thought her the prettiest and most elegant person here.'

'Laura might have higher praise,' said Philip, 'for hers is beauty of countenance even more than of feature. If only— '

'If?' said Amy.

'Look round, Amy, and you will see many a face which speaks of intellect wasted, or, if cultivated, turned aside from its true purpose, like the double blossom, which bears leaves alone.'

'Ah! you forget you are talking to silly little Amy. I can't see all that. I had rather think people as happy and good as they look.'

'Keep your child-like temper as long as you can— all your life,' perhaps, for this is one of the points where it is folly to be wise.'

'Then you only meant things in general? Nothing about Laura?'

'Things in general,' repeated Philip; 'bright promises blighted or thrown away— '

But he spoke absently, and his eye was following Laura. Amy thought he was thinking of his sister, and was sorry for him. He spoke no more, but she did not regret it, for she could not moralize in such a scene, and the sight and the dancing were pleasure enough.

Guy, in the meantime, had met an Oxford acquaintance, who introduced him to his sisters— pretty girls— whose father Mr. Edmonstone knew, but who was rather out of the Hollywell visiting distance. They fell into conversation quickly, and the Miss Alstons asked him with some interest, 'Which was the pretty Miss Edmonstone?' Guy looked for the sisters, as if to make up his mind, for the fact was, that when he first knew Laura and Amy, the idea of criticising beauty had not entered his mind, and to compare them was quite a new notion. 'Nay,' said he at last, 'if you cannot discover for yourselves when they are both before your eyes, I will do nothing so invidious as to say which is the pretty one. I'll tell which is the eldest and which the youngest, but the rest you must decide for yourself.'

'I should like to know them,' said Miss Alston. 'Oh! they are both very nice-looking girls.'

'There, that is Laura– Miss Edmonstone,' said Guy, 'that tall young lady, with the beautiful hair and jessamine wreath.'

He spoke as if he was proud of her, and had a property in her. The tone did not escape Philip, who at that moment was close to them, with Amy on his arm; and, knowing the Alstons slightly, stopped and spoke, and introduced his cousin, Miss Amabel Edmonstone. At the same time Guy took one of the Miss Alstons away to get some tea.

'So you knew my cousin at Oxford?' said Philip, to the brother.

'Yes, slightly. What an amusing fellow he is!'

'There is something very bright, very unlike other people about him,' said Miss Alston.

'How does he get on? Is he liked?'

'Why, yes, I should say so, on the whole; but it is rather as my sister says, he is not like other people.'

'In what respect?'

'Oh I can hardly tell. He is a very pleasant person, but he ought to have been at school. He is a man of crotchets.'

'Hard-working?'

'Very; he makes everything give way to that. He is a capital companion when he is to be had, but he lives very much to himself. He is a man of one friend, and I don't see much of him.'

Another dance began, Mr. Alston went to look for his partner, Philip and Amy moved on in search of ice. 'Hum!' said Philip to himself, causing Amy to gaze up at him, but he was musing too intently for her to venture on a remark. She was thinking that she did not wonder that strangers deemed Guy crotchety, since he was so difficult to understand; and then she considered whether to take him to see King Charles, in the library, and concluded that she would wait, for she felt as if the martyr king's face would look on her too gravely to suit her present tone.

Philip helped her to ice, and brought her back to her mother's neighbourhood without many more words. He then stood thoughtful for some time, entered into conversation with one of the elder gentlemen, and, when that was interrupted, turned to talk to his aunt.

Lady Eveleen and her two cousins were for a moment together. 'What is the matter, Eva?' said Amy, seeing a sort of dissatisfaction on her bright face.

'The roc's egg?' said Laura, smiling. 'The queen of the evening can't be content– '

'No; you are the queen, if the one thing can make you so— the one thing wanting to me.'

'How absurd you are, Eva— when you say you are so afraid of him, too.'

'That is the very reason. I should get a better opinion of myself! Besides, there is nobody else so handsome. I declare I'll make a bold attempt.'

'Oh! you don't think of such a thing,' cried Laura, very much shocked.

'Never fear,' said Eveleen, 'faint heart, you know.' And with a nod, a flourish, of her bouquet, and an arch smile at her cousin's horror, she moved on, and presently they heard her exclaiming, gaily, 'Captain Morville, I really must scold you. You are setting a shocking example of laziness! Aunt Edmonstone, how can you encourage such proceedings! Indolence is the parent of vice, you know.'

Philip smiled just as much as the occasion required, and answered, 'I beg your pardon, I had forgotten my duty. I'll attend to my business better in future.' And turning to a small, shy damsel, who seldom met with a partner, he asked her to dance. Eveleen came back to Laura with a droll disappointed gesture. 'Insult to injury,' said she, disconsolately.

'Of course,' said Amy, 'he could not have thought you wanted to dance with him, or you would not have gone to stir him up.'

'Well, then, he was very obtuse.'

'Besides, you are engaged.'

'O yes, to Mr. Thorndale! But who would be content with the squire when the knight disdains her?'

Mr. Thorndale came to claim Eveleen at that moment. It was the second time she had danced with him, and it did not pass unobserved by Philip, nor the long walk up and down after the dance was over. At length his friend came up to him and said something warm in admiration of her. 'She is very Irish,' was Philip's answer, with a cold smile, and Mr. Thorndale stood uncomfortable under the disapprobation, attracted by Eveleen's beauty and grace, yet so unused to trust his own judgment apart from 'Morville's,' as to be in an instant doubtful whether he really admired or not.

'You have not been dancing with her?' he said, presently.

'No: she attracts too many to need the attention of a nobody like myself.'

That 'too many,' seeming to confound him with the vulgar herd, made Mr. Thorndale heartily ashamed of having been pleased with her.

Philip was easy about him for the present, satisfied that admiration had been checked, which, if it had been allowed to grow into an attachment, would have been very undesirable.

The suspicions Charles had excited were so full in Philip's mind, however, that he could not as easily set it at rest respecting his cousin. Guy had three times asked her to dance, but each time she had been engaged. At last, just as the clock struck the hour at which the carriage had been ordered, he came up, and impetuously claimed her. 'One quadrille we must have, Laura, if you are not tired?'

'No! Oh, no! I could dance till this time to-morrow.'

'We ought to be going,' said Mrs. Edmonstone.

'O pray, Mrs. Edmonstone, this one more,' cried Guy, eagerly. 'Laura owes me this one.'

'Yes, this one more, mamma,' said Laura, and they went off together, while Philip remained, in a reverie, till requested by his aunt to see if the carriage was ready.

The dance was over, the carriage was waiting, but Guy and Laura did not appear till, after two or three minutes spent in wonder and inquiries, they came quietly walking back from the library, where they had been looking at King Charles.

All the way home the four ladies in the carriage never ceased laughing and talking. The three gentlemen in theirs acted diversely. Mr. Edmonstone went to sleep, Philip sat in silent thought, Guy whistled and hummed the tunes, and moved his foot very much as if he was still dancing.

They met for a moment, and parted again in the hall at Hollywell, where the daylight was striving to get in through the closed shutters. Philip went on to Broadstone, Guy said he could not go to bed by daylight, called Bustle, and went to the river to bathe, and the rest crept upstairs to their rooms. And so ended Lord Kilcoran's ball.

CHAPTER 8

Like Alexander, I will reign,
And I will reign alone,
My thoughts shall ever more disdain
A rival near my throne.
But I must rule and govern still,
And always give the law,
And have each subject at my will,
And all to stand in awe.
– MONTROSE.

One very hot afternoon, shortly after the ball, Captain Morville walked to Hollywell, accelerating his pace under the influence of anxious reflections.

He could not determine whether Charles had spoken in jest; but in spite of Guy's extreme youth, he feared there was ground for the suspicion excited by the hint, and was persuaded that such an attachment could produce nothing but unhappiness to his cousin, considering how little confidence could be placed in Guy. He perceived that there was much to inspire affection— attractive qualities, amiable disposition, the talent for music, and now this recently discovered power of versifying, all were in Guy's favour, besides the ancient name and long ancestry, which conferred a romantic interest, and caused even Philip to look up to him with a feudal feeling as head of the family. There was also the familiar intercourse to increase the danger; and Philip, as he reflected on these things, trembled for Laura, and felt himself her only protector; for his uncle was nobody, Mrs. Edmonstone was infatuated, and Charles would not listen to reason. To make everything worse, he had that morning heard that there was to be a grand inspection of the regiment, and a presentation of colours; Colonel Deane was very anxious; and it was plain that in the interval the officers would be allowed little leisure. The whole affair was to end with a ball, which would lead to a repetition of what had already disturbed him.

Thus meditating, Philip, heated and dusty, walked into the smooth green enclosure of Hollywell. Everything, save the dancing clouds of insect youth which whirled in his face, was drooping in the heat. The house— every door and window opened— seemed gasping for breath; the cows sought refuge in the shade; the pony drooped its head drowsily; the leaves hung wearily; the flowers were faint and thirsty; and Bustle was stretched on the stone steps, mouth open, tongue out, only his tail now and then moving, till he put back his ears and crested his head to greet the arrival. Philip heard the sounds that had caused the motion of the sympathizing tail— the rich tones of Guy's voice. Stepping over the dog, he entered, and heard more clearly—

'Two loving hearts may sever,
For sorrow fails them never.'

And then another voice—

'Who knows not love in sorrow's night,
He knows not love in light.'

In the drawing-room, cool and comfortable in the green shade of the Venetian blinds of the bay window, stood Laura, leaning on the piano, close to Guy, who sat on the music-stool, looking thoroughly at home in his brown shooting-coat, and loosely-tied handkerchief.

Any one but Philip would have been out of temper, but he shook hands as cordially as usual, and would not even be the first to remark on the heat.

Laura told him he looked hot and tired, and invited him to come out to the others, and cool himself on the lawn. She went for her parasol, Guy ran for her camp stool, and Philip, going to the piano, read what they had been singing. The lines were in Laura's writing, corrected, here and there, in Guy's hand.

BE STEADFAST.

Two loving hearts may sever,
Yet love shall fail them never.
Love brightest beams in sorrow's night,
Love is of life the light.

Two loving hearts may sever,
Yet hope shall fail them never.
Hope is a star in sorrow's night,
Forget-me-not of light.

Two loving hearts may sever,
Yet faith may fail them never.
Trust on through sorrow's night,
Faith is of love and hope the light.

Two loving hearts may sever,
For sorrow fails them never.
Who knows not love in sorrow's night,
He knows not love in light.

Philip was by no means pleased. However, it was in anything but a sentimental manner that Guy, looking over him, said, 'For sever, read, be separated, but "a" wouldn't rhyme.'

'I translated it into prose, and Guy made it verse,' said Laura; 'I hope you approve of our performance.'

'It is that thing of Helmine von Chezy, "Beharre", is it not?' said Philip, particularly civil, because he was so much annoyed. 'You have rendered the spirit very well', but you have sacrificed a good deal to your double rhymes.'

'Yes; those last lines are not troubled with any equality of feet,' said Guy; 'but the repetition is half the beauty. It put me in mind of those lines of Burns—

"Had we never loved so kindly,
Had we never loved so blindly,
Never met and never parted,
We had ne'er been broken hearted;"

but there is a trust in these that is more touching than that despair.'

'Yes; the despair is ready, to wish the love had never been,' said Laura. 'It does not see the star of trust. Why did you use that word "trust" only once, Guy?'

'I did not want to lose the three— faith, hope, love,— faith keeping the other two alive.'

'My doubt was whether it was right to have that analogy.'

'Surely,' said Guy, eagerly, 'that analogy must be the best part of earthly love.'

Here Charlotte came to see if Guy and Laura meant to sing all the afternoon; and they went out. They found the others in the arbour, and Charlotte's histories of its construction, gave Philip little satisfaction. They next proceeded to talk over the ball.

'Ah!' said Philip, 'balls are the fashion just now. What do you say, Amy, [he was more inclined to patronize her than any one else] to the gaieties we are going to provide for you?'

'You! Are you going to have your new colours? Oh! you are not going to give us a ball?'

'Well! that is fun!' cried Guy. 'What glory Maurice de Courcy must be in!'

'He is gone to Allonby,' said Philip, 'to announce it; saying, he must persuade his father to put off their going to Brighton. Do you think he will succeed?'

'Hardly,' said Laura; 'poor Lady Kilcoran was so knocked up by their ball, that she is the more in want of sea air. Oh, mamma, Eva must come and stay here.'

'That she must,' said Mrs. Edmonstone; 'that will make it easy. She is the only one who will care about the ball.'

Philip was obliged to conceal his vexation, and to answer the many eager questions about the arrangements. He stayed to dinner, and as the others went in-doors to dress, he lingered near Charlotte, assuming, with some difficulty, an air of indifference, and said– 'Well, Charlotte, did you tease Guy into showing you those verses?'

'Oh yes,' said Charlotte, with what the French call "un air capable".'

'Well, what were they?'

'That I mustn't tell. They were very pretty; but I've promised.'

'Promised what?'

'Never to say anything about them. He made it a condition with me, and I assure you, I am to be trusted.'

'Right,' said Philip; 'I'll ask no more.'

'It would be of no use,' said Charlotte, shaking her head, as if she wished he would prove her further.

Philip was in hopes of being able to speak to Laura after dinner, but his uncle wanted him to come and look over the plans of an estate adjoining Redclyffe, which there was some idea of purchasing. Such an employment would in general have been congenial; but on this occasion, it was only by a strong force that he could chain his attention, for Guy was pacing the terrace with Laura and Amabel, and as they passed and repassed the window, he now and then caught sounds of repeating poetry.

In this Guy excelled. He did not read aloud well; he was too rapid, and eyes and thoughts were apt to travel still faster than the lips, thus producing a confusion; but no one could recite better when a passage had taken strong hold of his imagination, and he gave it the full effect of the modulations of his fine voice, conveying in its inflections the impressions which stirred him profoundly. He was just now enchanted with his first reading of 'Thalaba,' where he found all manner of deep meanings, to which the sisters listened with wonder and delight. He repeated, in a low, awful, thrilling tone, that made Amy shudder, the lines in the seventh book, ending with–

"Who comes from the bridal chamber!
It is Azrael, angel of death."'

'You have not been so taken up with any book since Sintram.' said Laura.

'It is like Sintram,' he replied.

'Like it?'

'So it seems to me. A strife with the powers of darkness; the victory, forgiveness, resignation, death.

"Thou know'st the secret wishes of my heart,
Do with me as thou wilt, thy will is best."'

'I wish you would not speak as if you were Thalaba yourself,' said Amy, 'you bring the whole Domdaniel round us.'

'I am afraid he is going to believe himself Thalaba as well as Sintram,' said Laura. 'But you know Southey did not see all this himself, and did not understand it when it was pointed out.'

'Don't tell us that,' said Amy.

'Nay; I think there is something striking in it,' said Guy then, with a sudden transition, 'but is not this ball famous?'

And their talk was of balls and reviews till nine o'clock, when they were summoned to tea.

On the whole, Philip returned to Broadstone by no means comforted.

Never had he known so much difficulty in attending with patience to his duties as in the course of the next fortnight. They became a greater durance, as he at length looked his feelings full in the face, and became aware of their true nature.

He perceived that the loss of Laura would darken his whole existence; yet he thought that, were he only secure of her happiness, he could have resigned her in silence. Guy was, however, one of the last men in the world whom he could bear to see in possession of her; and probably she was allowing herself to be entangled, if not in heart, at least in manner. If so, she should not be unwarned. He had been her guide from childhood, and he would not fail her now.

Three days before the review, he succeeded in finding time for a walk to Hollywell, not fully decided on the part he should act, though resolved on making some remonstrance. He was crossing a stile, about a mile and a half from Hollywell, when he saw a lady sitting on the stump of a tree, sketching, and found that fate had been so propitious as to send Laura thither alone. The rest had gone to gather mushrooms on a down, and had left her sketching the view of the spires of Broadstone, in the cleft between the high green hills. She was very glad to see him, and held up her purple and olive washes to be criticised; but he did not pay much attention to them. He was almost confused at the sudden manner in which the opportunity for speaking had presented itself.

'It is a long time since I have seen you,' said he, at last.

'An unheard-of time.'

'Still longer since we have had any conversation.'

'I was just thinking so. Not since that hot hay-making, when Guy came home. Indeed, we have had so much amusement lately that I have hardly had time for thought. Guy says we are all growing dissipated.'

'Ah! your German, and dancing, and music, do not agree with thought.'

'Poor music!' said Laura, smiling. 'But I am ready for a lecture; I have been feeling more like a butterfly than I like.'

'I know you think me unjust about music, and I freely confess that I cannot estimate the pleasure it affords, but I doubt whether it is a safe pleasure. It forms common ground for persons who would otherwise have little in common, and leads to intimacies which occasion results never looked for.'

'Yes,' said Laura, receiving it as a general maxim.

'Laura, you complain of feeling like a butterfly. Is not that a sign that you were made for better things?'

'But what can I do? I try to read early and at night, but I can't prevent the fun and gaiety; and, indeed, I don't think I would. It is innocent, and we never had such a pleasant summer. Charlie is so— so much more equable, and mamma is more easy about him, and I can't help thinking it does them all good, though I do feel idle.'

'It is innocent, it is right for a little while,' said Philip; 'but your dissatisfaction proves that you are superior to such things. Laura, what I fear is, that this summer holiday may entangle you, and so fix your fate as to render your life no holiday. O Laura take care; know what you are doing!'

'What am I doing?' asked Laura, with an alarmed look of ingenuous surprise.

Never had it been so hard to maintain his composure as now, when her simplicity forced him to come to plainer terms. 'I must speak,' he continued, 'because no one else will. Have you reflected whither this may tend? This music, this versifying, this admitting a stranger so unreservedly into your pursuits?'

She understood now, and hung her head. He would have given worlds to judge of the face hidden by her bonnet; but as she did not reply, he spoke on, his agitation becoming so strong, that the struggle was perceptible in the forced calmness of his tone. 'I would not say a word if he were worthy, but Laura— Laura, I have seen Locksley Hall acted once; do not let me see it again in a way which— which would give me infinitely more pain.'

The faltering of his voice, so resolutely subdued, touched, her extremely, and a thrill of exquisite pleasure glanced through her, on hearing confirmed what she had long felt, that she had taken Margaret's place— nay, as she now learnt, that she was even more precious to him. She only thought of reassuring him.

'No, you need never fear that. He has no such thought, I am sure.' She blushed deeply, but looked in his face. 'He treats us both alike, besides, he is so young.'

'The mischief is not done,' said Philip, trying to resume his usual tone; 'I only meant to speak in time. You might let your manner go too far; you might even allow your affections to be involved without knowing it, if you were not on your guard.'

'Never!' said Laura. 'Oh, no; I could never dream of that with Guy. I like Guy very much; I think better of him than you do; but oh no; he could never be my first and best; I could never care for him in that way. How could you think so, Philip?'

'Laura, I cannot but look on you with what may seem over-solicitude. Since I lost Fanny, and worse than lost Margaret, you have been my home;

my first, my most precious interest. O Laura!' and he did not even attempt to conceal the trembling and tenderness of his voice, 'could I bear to lose you, to see you thrown away or changed– you, dearest, best of all?'

Laura did not turn away her head this time, but raising her beautiful face, glowing with such a look as had never beamed there before, while tears rose to her eyes, she said, 'Don't speak of my changing towards you. I never could; for if there is anything to care for in me, it is you that have taught it to me.'

If ever face plainly told another that he was her first and best, Laura's did so now. Away went misgivings, and he looked at her in happiness too great for speech, at least, he could not speak till he had mastered his emotion, but his countenance was sufficient reply. Even then, in the midst of this flood of ecstasy, came the thought, 'What have I done?'

He had gone further than he had ever intended. It was a positive avowal of love; and what would ensue? Cessation of intercourse with her, endless vexations, the displeasure of her family, loss of influence, contempt, and from Mr. Edmonstone, for the pretensions of a penniless soldier. His joy was too great to be damped, but it was rendered cautious. 'Laura, my own!' (what delight the words gave her,) 'you have made me very happy. We know each other now, and trust each other for ever.'

'O yes, yes; nothing can alter what has grown up with us.'

'It is for ever!' repeated Philip. 'But, Laura, let us be content with our own knowledge of what we are to each other. Do not let us call in others to see our happiness.'

Laura looked surprised, for she always considered any communication about his private feelings too sacred to be repeated, and wondered he should think the injunction necessary. 'I never can bear to talk about the best kinds of happiness,' said she; 'but oh!' and she sprang up, 'here they come.'

Poor Mrs. Edmonstone, as she walked back from her mushroom-field, she little guessed that words had been spoken which would give the colouring to her daughter's whole life– she little guessed that her much-loved and esteemed nephew had betrayed her confidence! As she and the girls came up, Philip advanced to meet them, that Laura might have a few moments to recover, while with an effort he kept himself from appearing absent in the conversation that ensued. It was brief, for having answered some questions with regard to the doings on the important day, he said, that since he had met them he would not come on to Hollywell, and bade them farewell, giving Laura a pressure of the hand which renewed the glow on her face.

He walked back, trying to look through the dazzling haze of joy so as to see his situation clearly. It was impossible for him not to perceive that there had been an absolute declaration of affection, and that he had established a private understanding with his cousin. It was not, however, an engagement, nor did he at present desire to make it so. It was impossible for him as yet to marry, and he was content to wait without a promise, since that could not add to his entire reliance on Laura. He could not bear to be rejected by her parents: he knew his poverty would be the sole ground of objection, and he was not asking her to share it. He believed sincerely that a long, lingering attachment to himself would be more for her good than a marriage with one who would have been a high prize for worldly aims, and was satisfied that by winning her heart he had taken the only sure means of securing her from becoming attached to Guy, while secrecy was the only way of preserving his intercourse with her on the same footing, and exerting his influence over the family.

It was calmly reflected, for Philip's love was tranquil, though deep and steady, and the rather sought to preserve Laura as she was than to make her anything more; and this very calmness contributed to his self-deception on this first occasion that he had ever actually swerved from the path of right.

With an uncomfortable sensation, he met Guy riding home from his tutor, entirely unsuspicious. He stopped and talked of the preparations at Broadstone, where he had been over the ground with Maurice de Courcy, and had heard the band.

'What did you think of it? said Philip, absently.

'They should keep better time! Really, Philip, there is one fellow with a bugle that ought to be flogged every day of his life!' said Guy, making a droll, excruciated face.

How a few words can change the whole current of ideas. The band was connected with Philip, therefore he could not bear to hear it found fault with, and adduced some one's opinion that the man in question was one of the best of their musicians.

Guy could not help shrugging his shoulders, as he laughed, and said,—'Then I shall be obliged to take to my heels if I meet the rest. Good-bye.'

'How conceited they have made that boy about his fine ear,' thought Philip. 'I wonder he is not ashamed to parade his music, considering whence it is derived.'

CHAPTER 9

A h! county Guy, the hour is nigh,
The sun has left the lea,
The orange flower perfumes the bower,
The breeze is on the sea.
The lark, his lay, who thrilled all day,
Sits hushed, his partner nigh,
Breeze, bird, and flower, confess the hour,
But where is county Guy?
– SCOTT

How was it meantime with Laura? The others were laughing and talking round her, but all seemed lost in the transcendent beam that had shone out on her. To be told by Philip that she was all to him that he had always been to her! This one idea pervaded her– too glorious, too happy for utterance, almost for distinct thought. The softening of his voice, and the look with which he had regarded her, recurred again and again, startling her with a sudden surprise of joy almost as at the first moment. Of the future Laura thought not. Never had a promise of love been made with less knowledge of what it amounted to: it seemed merely an expression of sentiments that she had never been without; for had she not always looked up to Philip more than any other living creature, and gloried in being his favourite cousin? Ever since the time when he explained to her the plates in the Encyclopaedia, and made her read 'Joyce's Scientific Dialogues,' when Amy took fright at the first page. That this might lead further did not occur to her; she was eighteen, she had no experience, not even in novels, she did not know what she had done; and above all, she had so leant to surrender her opinions to Philip, and to believe him always right, that she would never have dreamt of questioning wherever he might choose to lead her. Even the caution of secrecy did not alarm her, though she wondered that he thought it required, safe as his confidence always was with her. Mrs. Edmonstone had been so much occupied by Charles's illness, as to have been unable to attend to her daughters in their girlish days; and in the governess's time the habit had been disused of flying at once to her with every joy or grief. Laura's thoughts were not easy of access, and Philip had long been all in all to her. She was too ignorant of life to perceive that it was her duty to make this conversation known; or, more truly, she did not awaken her mind to consider that anything could be wrong that Philip desired.

On coming home, she ran up to her own room, and sitting by the open window, gave herself up to that delicious dream of new-found joy.

There she still sat when Amy came in, opening the door softly, and treading lightly and airily as she entered, bringing two or three roses of different tints.

'Laura! not begun to dress?'

'Is it time?'

'Shall I answer you according to what Philip calls my note of time, and tell you the pimpernels are closed, and the tigridias dropping their leaves? It would be a proper answer for you; you look as if you were in Fairy Land.'

'Is papa come home?'

'Long ago! and Guy too. Why, where could you have been, not to have heard Guy and Eveleen singing the Irish melodies?'

'In a trance,' said Laura, starting up, and laughing, with a slight degree of constraint, which caused Amy, who was helping her to dress, to exclaim, 'Has anything happened, Laura?'

'What should have happened?'

'I can't guess, unless the fairies in the great ring on Ashendown came to visit you when we were gone. But seriously, dear Laura, are you sure you are not tired? Is nothing the matter?'

'Nothing at all, thank you. I was only thinking over the talk I had with Philip.'

'Oh!'

Amy never thought of entering into Philip's talks with Laura, and was perfectly satisfied.

By this time Laura was herself again, come back to common life, and resolved to watch over her intercourse with Guy; since, though she was convinced that all was safe at present, she had Philip's word for it that there might be danger in continuing the pleasant freedom of their behaviour.

Nothing could be more reassuring than Guy's demeanour. His head seemed entirely full of the Thursday, and of a plan of his own for enabling Charles to go to the review. It had darted into his head while he was going over the ground with Maurice. It was so long since Charles had thought it possible to attempt any amusement away from home, and former experiments had been so unsuccessful, that it had never even occurred to him to think of it; but he caught at the idea with great delight and eagerness. Mrs. Edmonstone seemed not to know what to say; she had much rather that it had not been proposed; yet it was very kind of Guy, and Charles was so anxious about it that she knew not how to oppose him.

She could not bear to have Charles in a crowd, helpless as he was; and she had an unpleasing remembrance of the last occasion when they had taken him to a flower-show, where they had lost, first Mr. Edmonstone, next the carriage, and lastly, Amy and Charlotte– all had been frightened, and Charles laid up for three days from the fatigue.

Answers, however, met each objection. Charles was much stronger; Guy's arm would be ready for him; Guy would find the carriage. Philip would be there to help, besides Maurice; and whenever Charles was tired, Guy would take him home at once, without spoiling any one's pleasure.

'Except your own,' said Mrs. Edmonstone.

'Thank you; but this would be so delightful.'

'Ah!' said Charles, 'it would be as great a triumph as the dog's that caught the hare with the clog round his neck– the dog's, I mean.'

'If you will but trust me with him,' said Guy, turning on her all the pleading eloquence of his eyes, 'you know he can get in and out of the pony-carriage quite easily.'

'As well as walk across the room,' said Charles.

'I would drive him in it, and tell William to ride in and be at hand to hold the pony or take it out; and the tent is so near, that you could get to the breakfast, unless the review had been enough for you. I paced the distance to make sure, and it is no further than from the garden-door to the cherry-tree.'

'That is nothing,' said Charles.

'And William shall be in waiting to bring the pony the instant you are ready, and we can go home independently of every one else.'

'I thought,' interposed Mrs. Edmonstone, 'that you were to go to the mess-dinner– what is to become of that?'

'O,' said Charles, 'that will be simply a bore, and he may rejoice to be excused from going the whole hog.'

'To be sure, I had rather dine in peace at home.'

Mrs. Edmonstone was not happy, but she had great confidence in Guy; and her only real scruple was, that she did not think it fair to occupy him entirely with attendance on her son. She referred it to papa, which, as every one knew, was the same as yielding the point, and consoled herself by the certainty that to prevent it would be a great disappointment to both the youths. Laura was convinced that to achieve the adventure of Charles at the review, was at present at least a matter of far more prominence with Guy than anything relating to herself.

All but Laura and her mother were wild about the weather, especially on Wednesday, when there was an attempt at a thunder storm. Nothing was studied but the sky; and the conversation consisted of prognostications, reports of rises and falls of the glass, of the way weather-cocks were turning, or about to turn, of swallows flying high or low, red sunsets, and halos round the moon, until at last Guy, bursting into a merry laugh, begged Mrs. Edmonstone's pardon for being such a nuisance, and made a vow, and kept it, that be the weather what it might, he would say not another word about it that evening; it deserved to be neglected, for he had not been able to settle to anything all day.

He might have said for many days before; for since the last ball, and still more since Lady Eveleen had been at Hollywell, it had been one round of merriment and amusement. Scrambling walks, tea-drinkings out of doors, dances among themselves, or with the addition of the Harpers, were the order of the day. Amy, Eveleen, and Guy, could hardly come into the room without dancing, and the piano was said to acknowledge nothing but waltzes, polkas, and now and then an Irish jig, for the special benefit of Mr. Edmonstone's ears. The morning was almost as much spent in mirth as the afternoon, for the dawdlings after breakfast, and before luncheon, had a great tendency to spread out and meet, there was new music and singing to be practised, or preparations made for evening's diversion, or councils to be held, which Laura's absence could not break up, though it often made Amy feel how much less idle and frivolous Laura was than herself. Eveleen said the same, but she was visiting, and it was a time to be idle; and Mr. Lascelles seemed to be of the same opinion with regard to his pupil; for, when Guy was vexed at not having done as much work as usual, he only laughed at him for expecting to be able to go to balls, and spend a summer of gaiety, while he studied as much as at Oxford.

Thursday morning was all that heart could wish, the air cooled by the thunder, and the clouds looking as if raining was foreign to their nature. Mr. and Mrs. Edmonstone, their daughters, and Lady Eveleen, were packed inside and outside the great carriage, while Guy, carefully settling Charles in the low phaeton, putting in all that any one recommended, from an air-cushion to an umbrella, flourished his whip, and drove off with an air of exultation and delight.

Everything went off to admiration. No one was more amused than Charles. The scene was so perfectly new and delightful to one accustomed to such a monotonous life, that the very sight of people was a novelty. Nowhere was there so much laughing and talking as in that little carriage, and whenever Mrs. Edmonstone's anxious eye fell upon it, she always saw Charles sitting upright, with a face so full of eager interest as to banish all thought of fatigue. Happy, indeed, he was. He enjoyed the surprise of his acquaintance at meeting him; he enjoyed Dr. Mayerne's laugh and congratulation; he enjoyed seeing how foolish Philip thought him, nodding to his mother and sisters, laughing at the dreadful faces Guy could not help making at any particularly discordant note of the offensive bugle; and his capabilities rising with his spirits, he did all that the others did, walked further than he had done for years, was lifted up steps without knowing how, sat out the whole breakfast, talked to all the world, and well earned the being thoroughly tired, as he certainly was when Guy put him into the carriage and drove him home, and still more so when Guy all but carried him up stairs, and laid him on the sofa in the dressing-room.

However, his mother announced that it would have been so unnatural if he had not been fatigued, that she should have been more anxious, and leaving him to repose, they all, except Mr. Edmonstone, who had stayed to dine at the mess, sat down to dinner.

Amy came down dressed just as the carriage had been announced, and found Laura and Eveleen standing by the table, arranging their bouquets, while Guy, in the dark, behind the piano, was playing– not, as usual, in such cases, the Harmonious Blacksmith, but a chant.

'Is mamma ready?' asked Laura.

'Nearly,' said Amy, 'but I wish she was not obliged to go! I am sure she cannot bear to leave Charlie.'

'I hope she is not going on my account,' said Eveleen.

'No, said Laura, 'we must go; it would so frighten papa if we did not come. Besides, there is nothing to be uneasy about with Charles.'

'O no,' said Amy; 'she says so, only she is always anxious, and she is afraid he is too restless to go to sleep.'

'We must get home as fast as we can; if you don't mind, Eva,' said Laura, remembering how her last dance with Guy had delayed them.

'Can I do any good to Charlie?' said Guy, ceasing his music. I don't mean to go.'

'Not go!' cried the girls in consternation.

'He is joking!' said Eveleen. 'But, I declare!' added she, advancing towards him, 'he is not dressed! Come, nonsense, this is carrying it too far; you'll make us all too late, and then I'll set Maurice at you.'

'I am afraid it is no joke,' said Guy, smiling.

'You must go. It will never do for you to stay away,' said Laura, decidedly.

'Are you tired? Aren't you well?' asked Amy.

'Quite well, thank you, but I am sure I had better not.'

Laura thought she had better not seem anxious to take him, so she left the task of persuasion, to the others, and Amy went on.

'Neither Mamma nor Charlie could bear to think you stayed because of him.'

'I don't, I assure you, Amy. I meant it before. I have been gradually finding out that it must come to this.'

'Oh, you think it a matter of right and wrong! But you don't think balls wrong?'

'Oh no; only they won't do for such an absurd person as I am. The last turned my head for a week, and I am much too unsteady for this.'

'Well, if you think it a matter of duty, it can't be helped,' said Amy sorrowfully; 'but I am very sorry.'

'Thank you,' said Guy, thinking it compassion, not regret; 'but I shall do very well. I shall be all the happier to-morrow for a quiet hour at my Greek, and you'll tell me all the fun.'

'You liked it so much!' said Amy; 'but you have made up your mind and I ought not to tease you.'

'That's right Amy; he does it on purpose to be teased,' said Eveleen, 'and I never knew anybody so provoking. Mind, Sir Guy, if you make us all too late, you shan't have the ghost of a quadrille with me.'

'I shall console myself by quadrilling with Andromache,' said Guy.

'Come, no nonsense– off to dress directly! How can you have the conscience to stand there when the carriage is at the door?'

'I shall have great pleasure in handing you in when you are ready.'

'Laura– Amy! Does he really mean it?'

'I am afraid he does,' said Amy.

Eveleen let herself fall on the sofa as if fainting. 'Oh,' she said, 'take him away! Let me never see the face of him again! I'm perfectly overcome! All my teaching thrown away!'

'I am sorry for you,' said Guy, laughing.

'And how do you mean to face Maurice?'

'Tell him his first bugle has so distracted me that I can't answer for the consequences if I come to-night.

'Mrs. Edmonstone came in, saying,–

'Come, I have kept you waiting shamefully, but I have been consoling myself by thinking you must be well entertained, as I heard no Harmonious Blacksmith. Papa will be wondering where we are.'

'Oh, mamma! Guy won't go.'

'Guy! is anything the matter?'

'Nothing, thank you, only idleness.'

'This will never do. You really must go, Guy.'

'Indeed! I think not. Pray don't order me, Mrs. Edmonstone.'

'What o'clock is it, Amy? Past ten! Papa will be in despair! What is to be done? How long do you take to dress, Guy?'

'Not under an hour,' said Guy, smiling.

'Nonsense! But if there was time I should certainly send you. Self-discipline may be carried too far, Guy. But now it can't be helped– I don't know how to keep papa waiting any longer. Laura, what shall I do?'

'Let me go to Charles,' answered Guy. 'Perhaps I can read him to sleep.'

'Thank you; but don't talk, or he will be too excited. Reading would be the very thing! It will be a pretty story to tell every one who asks for you that I have left you to nurse my son!'

'No, for no such good reason,' said Guy; 'only because I am a great fool.'

'Well, Sir Guy, I am glad you can say one sensible word,' said Lady Eveleen.

'Too true, I assure you,' he answered, as he handed her in. 'Good night! You will keep the quadrille for me till I am rational.'

He handed the others in, and shut the door. Mrs. Edmonstone, ruffled out of her composure, exclaimed,–

'Well, this is provoking!'

'Every one will be vexed,' said Laura.

'It will be so stupid,' said Amy.

'I give him up,' said Eveleen. 'I once had hopes of him.'

'If it was not for papa, I really would turn back this moment and fetch him,' cried Mrs. Edmonstone, starting forward. 'I'm sure it will give offence. I wish I had not consented.'

'He can't be made to see that his presence is of importance to any living creature,' said Laura.

'What is the reason of this whim?' said Eveleen.

'No, Eveleen, it is not whim,' said Laura; 'it is because he thinks dissipation makes him idle.'

'Then if he is idle I wonder what the rest of the world is!' said Eveleen. 'I am sure we all ought to stay at home too.'

'I think so,' said Amy. 'I know I shall feel all night as if I was wrong to be there.'

'I am angry,' said Mrs. Edmonstone; 'and yet I believe it is a great sacrifice.'

'Yes, mamma; after all our looking forward to it,' said Amy. 'Oh! yes,' and her voice lost its piteous tone, 'it is a real sacrifice.'

'If he was not a mere boy, I should say a lover's quarrel was at the bottom of it,' said Eveleen. 'Depend upon it, Laura, it is all your fault. You only danced once with him at our ball, and all this week you have played for us, as if it was on purpose to cut him.'

Laura was glad of the darkness, and her mother, who had a particular dislike to jokes of this sort, went on,– 'If it were only ourselves I should not care, but there are so many who will fancy it caprice, or worse.'

'The only comfort is,' said Amy, 'that it is Charlie's gain.'

'I hope they will not talk,' said Mrs. Edmonstone. 'But Charlie will never hold his tongue. He will grow excited, and not sleep all night.'

Poor Mrs. Edmonstone! her trials did not end here, for when she replied to her husband's inquiry for Guy, Mr. Edmonstone said offence had already been taken at his absence from the dinner; he would not have had this happen for fifty pounds; she ought not to have suffered it; but it was all her nonsense about Charles, and as to not being late, she should have waited till midnight rather than not have brought him. In short, he said as much more than he meant, as a man in a pet is apt to say, and nevertheless Mrs. Edmonstone had to look as amiable and smiling as if nothing was the matter.

The least untruthful answer she could frame to the inquiries for Sir Guy Morville was, that young men were apt to be lazy about balls, and this sufficed for good-natured Mrs. Deane, but Maurice poured out many exclamations about his ill-behaviour, and Philip contented himself with the mere fact of his not being there, and made no remark.

Laura turned her eyes anxiously on Philip. They had not met since the important conversation on Ashen-down, and she found herself looking with more pride than ever at his tall, noble figure, as if he was more her own; but the calmness of feeling was gone. She could not meet his eye, nor see him turn towards her without a start and tremor for which she could not render herself a reason, and her heart beat so much that it was at once a relief and a disappointment that she was obliged to accept her other cousin as her first partner. Philip had already asked Lady Eveleen, for he neither wished to appear too eager in claiming Laura, nor to let his friend think he had any dislike to the Irish girl.

Eveleen was much pleased to have him for her partner, and told herself she would be on her good behaviour. It was a polka, and there was not much talk, which, perhaps, was all the better for her. She admired the review, and the luncheon, and spoke of Charles without any sauciness, and Philip was condescending and agreeable.

'I must indulge myself in abusing that stupid cousin of yours!' said she. Did you ever know a man of such wonderful crotchets?'

'This is a very unexpected one,' said Philip.

'It came like a thunder clap. I thought till the last moment he was joking, for he likes dancing so much; he was the life of our ball, and how could any one suppose he would fly off at the last moment?'

'He seems rather to enjoy doing things suddenly.'

'I tell Laura she has affronted him,' said Eveleen, laughing. 'She has been always busy of late when we have wanted her; and I assure her his pride has been piqued. Don't you think that is an explanation, Captain Morville?'

It was Captain Morvilles belief, but he would not say so.

'Isn't Laura looking lovely?' Eveleen went on. 'I am sure she is the beauty of the night!' She was pleased to see Captain Morville's attention gained. 'She is even better dressed than at our ball— those Venetian pins suit the form of her head so well. Her beauty is better than almost any one's, because she has so much countenance.'

'True,' said Philip.

'How proud Maurice looks of having her on his arm. Does not he? Poor Maurice! he is desperately in love with her!'

'As is shown by his pining melancholy.'

Eveleen laughed with her clear hearty laugh. 'I see you know what we mean by being desperately in love! No,' she added more gravely, 'I am very glad it is only that kind of desperation. One could not think of Maurice and Laura together. He does not know the best part of Laura.'

Eveleen was highly flattered by Captain Morville conducting her a second time round the room, instead of at once restoring her to her aunt.

He secured Laura next, and leading her away from her own party, said, 'Laura, have you been overdoing it?'

'It is not that,' said Laura, wishing she could keep from blushing.

'It is the only motive that could excuse his extraordinary behaviour.'

'Surely you know he says that he is growing unsettled. It is part of his rule of self discipline.'

'Absurd!– exaggerated!– incredible! This is the same story as there was about the horse. It is either caprice or temper, and I am convinced that some change in your manner– nay, I say unconscious, and am far from blaming you– is the cause. Why else did he devote himself to Charles, and leave you all on my uncle's hands in the crowd?'

'We could shift for ourselves much better than Charlie.'

'This confirms my belief that my warning was not mistimed. I wish it could have been done without decidedly mortifying him and rousing his temper, because I am sorry others should be slighted; but if he takes your drawing back so much to heart, it shows that it was time you should do so.'

'If I thought I had!'

'It was visible to others– to another, I should say.'

'O, that is only Eveleen's nonsense! The only difference I am conscious of having made, was keeping more up-stairs, and not trying to persuade him to come here to-night.'

'I have no doubt it was this that turned the scale, He only waited for persuasion, and you acted very wisely in not flattering his self-love.'

'Did I?– I did not know it.'

'A woman's instinct is often better than reasoning, Laura; to do the right thing without knowing why. But come, I suppose we must play our part in the pageant of the night.'

For that evening Laura, contrary to the evidence of her senses, was persuaded by her own lover that Guy was falling in love with her; and after musing all through the dance, she said, 'What do you think of the scheme that has been started for my going to Ireland with papa?'

'Your going to Ireland?'

'Yes; you know none of us, except papa, have seen grandmamma since Charles began to be ill, and there is some talk of his taking me with him when he goes this summer.'

'I knew he was going, but I thought it was not to be till later in the year– not till after the long vacation.'

'So he intended, but he finds he must be at home before the end of October, and it would suit him best to go in August.'

'Then what becomes of Guy?'

'He stays at Hollywell. It will be much better for Charles to have him there while papa is away. I thought when the plan was first mentioned I should be sorry, except that it is quite right to go to grandmamma; but if it is so, about Guy, this absence would be a good thing– it would make a break, and I could begin again on different terms.'

'Wisely judged, Laura. Yes, on that account it would be very desirable, though it will be a great loss to me, and I can hardly hope to be so near you on your return.'

'Ah! yes, so I feared!' sighed Laura.

'But we must give up something; and for Guy's own sake, poor fellow, it will be better to make a break, as you say. It will save him pain by and by.'

'I dare say papa will consult you about when his journey is to be. His only doubt was whether it would do to leave Guy so long alone, and if you say it would be safe, it would decide him at once.'

'I see little chance of mischief. Guy has few temptations here, and a strong sense of honour; besides, I shall be at hand. Taking all things into consideration, Laura, I think that, whatever the sacrifice to ourselves, it is expedient to recommend his going at once, and your accompanying him.'

All the remainder of the evening Philip was occupied with attentions to the rest of the world, but Laura's eyes followed him everywhere, and though she neither expected nor desired him to bestow more time on her, she underwent a strange restlessness and impatience of feeling. Her numerous partners teased her by hindering her from watching him moving about the room, catching his tones, and guessing what he was talking of;– not that she wanted to meet his eye, for she did not like to blush, nor did she think it pleased him to see her do so, for he either looked away immediately or conveyed a glance which she understood as monitory. She kept better note of his countenance than of her own partner's.

Mr. Thorndale, meanwhile, kept aloof from Lady Eveleen de Courcy, but Captain Morville perceived that his eyes were often turned towards her, and well knew it was principle, and not inclination, that held him at a distance. He did indeed once ask her to dance, but she was engaged, and he did not ask her to reserve a future dance for him, but contented himself with little Amy.

Amy was doing her best to enjoy herself, because she thought it ungrateful not to receive pleasure from those who wished to give it, but to her it wanted the zest and animation of Lady Kilcoran's ball. Besides, she knew she had been as idle as Guy, or still more so, and she thought it wrong she should have pleasure while he was doing penance. It was on her mind, and damped her spirits, and though she smiled, and talked, and admired, and danced lightly and gaily, there was a sensation of weariness throughout, and no one but Eveleen was sorry when Mrs. Edmonstone sent Maurice to see for the carriage.

Philip was one of the gentlemen who came to shawl them. As he put Laura's cloak round her shoulders he was able to whisper, 'Take care; you must be cautious— self-command.'

Laura, though blushing and shrinking the moment before was braced by his words and tone to attempt all he wished. She looked up in what she meant to be an indifferent manner, and made some observation in a careless tone— anything rather than let Philip think her silly. After what he had said, was she not bound more than ever to exert herself to the utmost, that he might not be disappointed in her? She loved him only the better for what others might have deemed a stern coldness of manner, for it made the contrast of his real warmth of affection more precious. She mused over it, as much as her companions' conversation would allow, on the road home. They arrived, Mrs. Edmonstone peeped into Charles's room, announced that he was quietly asleep, and they all bade each other good night, or good morning, and parted.

CHAPTER 10

Leonora. Yet often with respect he speaks of thee.
Tasso. Thou meanest with forbearance, prudent, subtle,
'Tis that annoys me, for he knows to use
Language so smooth and so conditional,
That seeming praise from him is actual blame.
– GOETHE'S Tasso

When the Hollywell party met at breakfast, Charles showed himself by no means the worse for his yesterday's experiment. He said he had gone to sleep in reasonable time, lulled by some poetry, he knew not what, of which Guy's voice had made very pretty music, and he was now full of talk about the amusement he had enjoyed yesterday, which seemed likely to afford food for conversation for many a week to come. After all the care Guy had taken of him, Mrs. Edmonstone could not find it in her heart to scold, and her husband, having spent his vexation upon her, had none left to bestow on the real culprit. So when Guy, with his bright morning face, and his hair hanging shining and wet round it, opened the dining-room door, on his return from bathing in the river, Mr. Edmonstone's salutation only conveyed that humorous anger that no one cares for.

'Good morning to you, Sir Guy Morville! I wonder what you have to say for yourself.'

'Nothing,' said Guy, smiling; then, as he took his place by Mrs. Edmonstone, 'I hope you are not tired after your hard day's work?'

'Not at all, thank you.'

'Amy, can you tell me the name of this flower?'

'Oh! have you really found the arrow-head? How beautiful! Where did you get it? I didn't know it grew in our river.'

'There is plenty of it in that reedy place beyond the turn. I thought it looked like something out of the common way.'

'Yes! What a purple eye it has! I must draw it. O, thank you.'

'And, Charlotte, Bustle has found you a moorhen's nest.'

'How delightful! Is it where I can go and see the dear little things?'

'It is rather a swamp; but I have been putting down stepping-stones for you, and I dare say I can jump you across. It was that which made me so late, for which I ought to have asked pardon,' said he to Mrs. Edmonstone, with his look of courtesy.

Never did man look less like an offended lover, or like a morose self-tormentor.

'There are others later,' said Mrs. Edmonstone, looking at Lady Eveleen's empty chair.

'So you think that is all you have to ask pardon for,' said Mr. Edmonstone. 'I advise you to study your apologies, for you are in pretty tolerable disgrace.'

'Indeed, I am very sorry,' said Guy, with such a change of countenance that Mr. Edmonstone's good nature could not bear to see it.

'Oh, 'tis no concern of mine! It would be going rather the wrong way, indeed, for you to be begging my pardon for all the care you've been taking of Charlie; but you had better consider what you have to say for yourself before you show your face at Broadstone.'

'No?' said Guy, puzzled for a moment, but quickly looking relieved, and laughing, 'What! Broadstone in despair for want of me?'

'And we perfectly exhausted with answering questions as to what was become of Sir Guy.'

'Dreadful,' said Guy, now laughing heartily, in the persuasion that it was all a joke.

'O, Lady Eveleen, good morning; you are come in good time to give me the story of the ball, for no one else tells me one word about it.'

'Because you don't deserve it,' said she. 'I hope you have repented by this time.'

'If you want to make me repent, you should give me a very alluring description.'

'I shan't say one word about it; I shall send you to Coventry, as Maurice and all the regiment mean to do,' said Eveleen, turning away from him with a very droll arch manner of offended dignity.

'Hear, hear! Eveleen send any one to Coventry!' cried Charles. 'See what the regiment say to you.'

'Ay, when I am sent to Coventry?'

'O, Paddy, Paddy!' cried Charles, and there was a general laugh.

'Laura seems to be doing it in good earnest without announcing it,' added Charles, when the laugh was over, 'which is the worst sign of all.'

'Nonsense, Charles,' said Laura, hastily; then afraid she had owned to annoyance, she blushed and was angry with herself for blushing.

'Well, Laura, do tell me who your partners were?'

Very provoking, thought Laura, that I cannot say what is so perfectly natural and ordinary, without my foolish cheeks tingling. He may think it is because he is speaking to me. So she hurried on: 'Maurice first, then Philip,' and then showed, what Amy and Eveleen thought, strange oblivion of the rest of her partners.

They proceeded into the history of the ball; and Guy thought no more of his offences till the following day, when he went to Broadstone. Coming back, he found the drawing-room full of visitors, and was obliged to sit down and join in the conversation; but Mrs. Edmonstone saw he was inwardly chafing, as he betrayed by his inability to remain still, the twitchings of his forehead and lip, and a tripping and stumbling of the words on his tongue. She was sure he wanted to talk to her, and longed to get rid of Mrs. Brownlow; but the door was no sooner shut on the visitors, than Mr. Edmonstone came in, with a long letter for her to read and comment upon. Guy took himself out of the way of the consultation, and began to hurry up and down the terrace, until, seeing Amabel crossing the field towards the little gate into the garden, he went to open it for her.

She looked up at him, and exclaimed— 'Is anything the matter?'

'Nothing to signify,' he said; 'I was only waiting for your mother. I have got into a mess, that is all.'

'I am sorry,' began Amy, there resting in the doubt whether she might inquire further, and intending not to burthen him with her company, any longer than till she reached the house door; but Guy went on,—

'No, you have no occasion to be sorry; it is all my own fault; at least, if I was clear how it is my fault, I should not mind it so much. It is that ball. I am sure I had not the least notion any one would care whether I was there or not.'

'I am sure we missed you very much.'

'You are all so kind; beside, I belong in a manner you; but what could it signify to any one else? And here I find that I have vexed every one.'

'Ah!' said Amy, 'mamma said she was afraid it would give offence.'

'I ought to have attended to her. It was a fit of self-will in managing myself,' said Guy, murmuring low, as if trying to find the real indictment; 'yet I thought it a positive duty; wrong every way.'

'What has happened?' said Amy, turning back with him, though she had reached the door.

'Why, the first person I met was Mr. Gordon; and he spoke like your father, half in joke, and I thought entirely so; he said something about all the world being in such a rage, that I was a bold man to venture into Broadstone. Then, while I was at Mr. Lascelles', in came Dr. Mayerne. 'We missed you at the dinner,' he said; 'and I hear you shirked the ball, too.' I told him how it was, and he said he was glad that was all, and advised me to go and call on Colonel Deane and explain. I thought that the best way— indeed, I meant it before, and was walking to his lodgings when Maurice de Courcy met me. 'Ha!' he cries out, 'Morville! I thought at least you would have been laid up for a month with the typhus fever! As a friend, I advise you to go home and catch something, for it is the only excuse that will serve you. I am not quite sure that it will not be high treason for me to be seen speaking to you.' I tried to get at the rights of it, but he is such a harum-scarum fellow there was no succeeding. Next I met Thorndale, who only bowed and passed on the other side of the street— sign enough how it was with Philip; so I thought it best to go at once to the Captain, and get a rational account of what was the matter.'

'Did you?' said Amy, who, though concerned and rather alarmed, had been smiling at the humorous and expressive tones with which he could not help giving effect to his narration.

'Yes. Philip was at home, and very– very– '

'Gracious?' suggested Amy, as he hesitated for a word.

'Just so. Only the vexatious thing was, that we never could succeed in coming to an understanding. He was ready to forgive; but I could not disabuse him of an idea– where he picked it up I cannot guess– that I had stayed away out of pique. He would not even tell me what he thought had affronted me, though I asked him over and over again to be only straightforward; he declared I knew.'

'How excessively provoking!' cried Amy. 'You cannot guess what he meant?'

'Not the least in the world. I have not the most distant suspicion. It was of no use to declare I was not offended with any one; he only looked in that way of his, as if he knew much better than I did myself, and told me he could make allowances.'

'Worse than all! How horrid of him.'

'No, don't spoil me. No doubt he thinks he has grounds, and my irritation was unjustifiable. Yes, I got into my old way. He cautioned me, and nearly made me mad! I never was nearer coming to a regular outbreak. Always the same! Fool that I am.'

'Now, Guy, that is always your way; when other people are provoking, you abuse yourself. I am sure Philip was so, with his calm assertion of being right.'

'The more provoking, the more trial for me.'

'But you endured it. You say it was only nearly an outbreak. You parted friends? I am sure of that.'

'Yes, it would have been rather too bad not to do that.'

'Then why do you scold yourself, when you really had the victory?'

'The victory will be if the inward feeling as well as the outward token is ever subdued.'

'O, that must be in time, of course. Only let me hear how you got on with Colonel Deane.'

'He was very good-natured, and would have laughed it off, but Philip went with me, and looked grand, and begged in a solemn way that no more might be said. I could have got on better alone; but Philip was very kind, or, as you say, gracious.'

'And provoking,' added Amy, 'only I believe you do not like me to say so.'

'It is more agreeable to hear you call him so at this moment than is good for me. I have no right to complain, since I gave the offence.'

'The offence?'

'The absenting myself.'

'Oh! that you did because you thought it right.'

'I want to be clear that it was right.'

'What do you mean?' cried she, astonished. 'It was a great piece of self-denial, and I only felt it wrong not to be doing the same.'

'Nay, how should such creatures as you need the same discipline as I?'

She exclaimed to herself how far from his equal she was— how weak, idle, and self-pleasing she felt herself to be; but she could not say so— the words would not come; and she only drooped her little head, humbled by his treating her as better than himself.

He proceeded:—

'Something wrong I have done, and I want the clue. Was it self-will in choosing discipline contrary to your mother's judgment? Yet she could not know all. I thought it her kindness in not liking me to lose the pleasure. Besides, one must act for oneself, and this was only my own personal amusement.'

'Yes,' said Amy, timidly hesitating.

'Well?' said he, with the gentle, deferential tone that contrasted with his hasty, vehement self-accusations. 'Well?' and he waited, though not so as to hurry or frighten her, but to encourage, by showing her words had weight.

'I was thinking of one thing,' said Amy; 'is it not sometimes right to consider whether we ought to disappoint people who want us to be pleased?'

'There it is, I believe,' said Guy, stopping and considering, then going on with a better satisfied air, 'that is a real rule. Not to be so bent on myself as to sacrifice other people's feelings to what seems best for me. But I don't see whose pleasure I interfered with.'

Amy could have answered, 'Mine;' but the maidenly feeling checked her again, and she said, 'We all thought you would like it.'

'And I had no right to sacrifice your pleasure! I see, I see. The pleasure of giving pleasure to others is so much the best there is on earth, that one ought to be passive rather than interfere with it.'

'Yes,' said Amy, 'just as I have seen Mary Ross let herself be swung till she was giddy, rather than disappoint Charlotte and Helen, who thought she liked it.'

'If one could get to look at everything with as much indifference as the swinging! But it is all selfishness. It is as easy to be selfish for one's own good as for one's own pleasure; and I dare say, the first is as bad as the other.'

'I was thinking of something else,' said Amy. 'I should think it more like the holly tree in Southey. Don't you know it? The young leaves are sharp and prickly, because they have so much to defend themselves from, but as the tree grows older, it leaves off the spears, after it has won the victory.'

'Very kind of you, and very pretty, Amy,' said he, smiling; 'but, in the meantime, it is surely wrong to be more prickly than is unavoidable, and there is the perplexity. Selfish! selfish! selfish! Oneself the first object. That is the root.'

'Guy, if it is not impertinent to ask, I do wish you would tell me one thing. Why did you think it wrong to go to that ball?' said Amy, timidly.

'I don't know that I thought it wrong to go to that individual ball,' said Guy; 'but my notion was, that altogether I was getting into a rattling idle way, never doing my proper quantity of work, or doing it properly, and talking a lot of nonsense sometimes. I thought, last Sunday, it was time to make a short turn somewhere and bring myself up. I could not, or did not get out of the pleasant talks as Laura does, so I thought giving up this ball would punish me at once, and set me on a new tack of behaving like a reasonable creature.'

'Don't call yourself too many names, or you won't be civil to us. We all, except Laura, have been quite as bad.'

'Yes; but you had not so much to do.'

'We ought,' said Amy; 'but I meant to be reasonable when Eveleen is gone.'

Perhaps I ought to have waited till then, but I don't know. Lady Eveleen is so amusing that it leads to farther dawdling, and it would not do to wait to resist the temptation till it is out of the way.'

As he spoke, they saw Mrs. Edmonstone coming out, and went to meet her. Guy told her his trouble, detailing it more calmly than before he had found out his mistake. She agreed with him that this had been in forgetting that his attending the ball did not concern only himself, but he then returned to say that he could not see what difference it made, except to their own immediate circle.

'If it was not you, Guy, who made that speech, I should call it fishing for a compliment. You forget that rank and station make people sought after.'

'I suppose there is something in that,' said Guy, thoughtfully; 'at any rate, it is no bad thing to think so, it is so humiliating.'

'That is not the way most people would take it.'

'No? Does not it prevent one from taking any attention as paid to one's real self? The real flattering thing would be to be made as much of as Philip is, for one's own merits, and not for the handle to one's name.'

'Yes, I think so,' said Amy.

'Well, then,' as if he wished to gather the whole conversation into one resolve, the point is to consider whether abstaining from innocent things that may be dangerous to oneself mortifies other people. If so, the vexing them is a certain wrong, whereas the mischief of taking the pleasure is only a possible contingency. But then one must take it out of oneself some other way, or it becomes an excuse for self-indulgence.'

'Hardly with you,' said Mrs. Edmonstone, smiling.

'Because I had rather go at it at once, and forget all about other people. You must teach me consideration, Mrs. Edmonstone, and in the meantime will you tell me what you think I had better do about this scrape?'

'Let it alone,' said Mrs. Edmonstone. 'You have begged every one's pardon, and it had better be forgotten as fast as possible. They have made more fuss already than it is worth. Don't torment yourself about it any more; for, if you have made a mistake, it is on the right side; and on the first opportunity, I'll go and call on Mrs. Deane, and see if she is very implacable.'

The dressing-bell rang, and Amy ran up-stairs, stopping at Laura's door, to ask how she prospered in the drive she had been taking with Charles and Eveleen.

Amy told her of Guy's trouble, and oh! awkward question, inquired if she could guess what it could be that Philip imagined that Guy had been offended at.

'Can't he guess?' said poor Laura, to gain time, and brushing her hair over her face.

'No, he has no idea, though Philip protested that he knew, and would not tell him. Philip must have been most tiresome.'

'What? Has Guy been complaining?'

'No, only angry with himself for being vexed. I can't think how Philip can go on so!'

'Hush! hush, Amy, you know nothing about it. He has reasons— '

'I know,' said Amy, indignantly; 'but what right has he to go on mistrusting? If people are to be judged by their deeds, no one is so good as Guy, and it is too bad to reckon up against him all his ancestors have done. It is wolf and lamb, indeed.'

'He does not!' cried Laura. 'He never is unjust! How can you say so, Amy?'

'Then why does he impute motives, and not straightforwardly tell what he means?'

'It is impossible in this case,' said Laura.

'Do you know what it is?'

'Yes,' said Laura, perfectly truthful, and feeling herself in a dreadful predicament.

'And you can't tell me?'

'I don't think I can.'

'Nor Guy?'

'Not for worlds,' cried Laura, in horror.

'Can't you get Philip to tell him?'

'Oh no, no! I can't explain it, Amy; and all that can be done is to let it die away as fast as possible. It is only the rout about it that is of consequence.'

'It is very odd,' said Amy, 'but I must dress,' and away she ran, much puzzled, but with no desire to look into Philip's secrets.

Laura rested her head on her hand, sighed, and wondered why it was so hard to answer. She almost wished she had said Philip had been advising her to discourage any attachment on Guy's part; but then Amy might have laughed, and asked why. No! no! Philip's confidence was in her keeping, and cost her what it might, she would be faithful to the trust.

There was now a change. The evenings were merry, but the mornings were occupied. Guy went off to his room, as he used to do last winter; Laura commenced some complicated perspective, or read a German book with a great deal of dictionary; Amy had a book of history, and practised her music diligently; even Charles read more to himself, and resumed the study with Guy and Amy; Lady Eveleen joined in every one's pursuits, enjoyed them, and lamented to Laura that it was impossible to be rational at her own home.

Laura tried to persuade her that there was no need that she should be on the level of the society round her, and it ended in her spending an hour in diligent study every morning, promising to continue it when she went home, while Laura made such sensible comments that Eveleen admired her more than ever; and she, knowing that some were second-hand from Philip, others arising from his suggestions, gave him all the homage paid to herself, as a tribute to him who reigned over her whole being.

Yet she was far from happy. Her reserve towards Guy made her feel stiff and guarded; she had a craving for Philip's presence, with a dread of showing it, which made her uncomfortable. She wondered he had not been at Hollywell since the bail, for he must know that she was going to Ireland in a fortnight, and was not likely to return till his regiment had left Broadstone.

An interval passed long enough for her not to be alone in her surprise at his absenting himself before he at length made his appearance, just before luncheon, so as to miss the unconstrained morning hours he used so much to enjoy. He found Guy, Charles, and Amy, deep in Butler's Analogy.

'Are you making poor little Amy read that?' said he.

'Bravo!' cried Charles; 'he is so disappointed that it is not Pickwick that he does not know what else to say.'

'I don't suppose I take much in,' said Amy; 'but I like to be told what it means.'

'Don't imagine I can do that,' said Guy.

'I never spent much time over it,' said Philip; 'but I should think you were out of your depth.'

'Very well,' said Charles; 'we will return to Dickens to oblige you.'

'It is your pleasure to wrest my words,' replied Philip, in his own calm manner, though he actually felt hurt, which he had never done before. His complacency was less secure, so that there was more need for self-assertion.

'Where are the rest?' he asked.

'Laura and Eveleen are making a dictation lesson agreeable to Charlotte,' said Amy; 'I found Eva making mistakes on purpose.'

'How much longer does she stay?'

'Till Tuesday. Lord Kilcoran is coming to fetch her.'

Charlotte entered, and immediately ran up-stairs to announce her cousin's arrival. Laura was glad of this previous notice, and hoped her blush and tremor were not observed. It was a struggle, through luncheon time, to keep her colour and confusion within bounds; but she succeeded better than she fancied she did, and Philip gave her as much help as he could, by not looking at her. Seeing that he dreaded nothing so much as her exciting suspicion, she was at once braced and alarmed.

Her father was very glad to see him, and reproached him for making himself a stranger, while her sisters counted up the days of his absence.

'There was the time, to be sure, when we met you on Ashen-down, but that was a regular cheat. Laura had you all to herself.'

Laura bent down to feed Bustle, and Philip felt his colour deepening.

Mr. Edmonstone went on to ask him to come and stay at Hollywell for a week, vowing he would take no refusal. 'A week was out of the question, said Philip; 'but he could come for two nights.' Amabel hinted that there was to be a dinner-party on Thursday, thinking it fair to give him warning of what he disliked, but he immediately chose that very day. Again he disconcerted all expectations, when it was time to go out. Mrs. Edmonstone and Charles were going to drive, the young ladies and Guy to walk, but Philip disposed himself to accompany his uncle in a survey of the wheat.

Laura perceived that he would not risk taking another walk with her when they might be observed. It showed implicit trust to leave her to his rival; but she was sorry to find that caution must put an end to the freedom of their intercourse, and would have stayed at home, but that Eveleen was so wild and unguarded that Mrs. Edmonstone did not like her to be without Laura as a check on her, especially when Guy was of the party. There was some comfort in that warm pressure of her hand when she bade Philip good-bye, and on that she lived for a long time. He stood at the window watching them till they were out of sight, then moved towards his aunt, who with her bonnet on, was writing an invitation for Thursday, to Mr. Thorndale.

'I was thinking,' said he, in a low voice, 'if it would not be as well, if you liked, to ask Thorndale here for those two days.'

'If you think so,' returned Mrs. Edmonstone, looking at him more inquiringly than he could well bear.

'You know how he enjoys being here, and I owe them all so much kindness.'

'Certainly; I will speak to your uncle,' said she, going in search of him. She presently returned, saying they should be very glad to see Mr. Thorndale, asking him at the same time, in her kind tones of interest, after an old servant for whom he had been spending much thought and pains. The kindness cut him to the heart, for it evidently arose from a perception that he was ill at ease, and his conscience smote him. He answered shortly, and was glad when the carriage came; he lifted Charles into it, and stood with folded arms as they drove away.

'The air is stormy,' said Charles, looking back at him.'

'You thought so, too?' said Mrs. Edmonstone, eagerly.

'You did!'

'I have wondered for some time past.'

'It was very decided to-day– that long absence– and there was no provoking him to be sententious. His bringing his young man might be only to keep him in due subjection; but his choosing the day of the party, and above all, not walking with the young ladies.'

'It not like himself,' said Mrs. Edmonstone, in a leading tone.

'Either the sweet youth is in love, or in the course of some strange transformation.'

'In love!' she exclaimed. 'Have you any reason for thinking so?'

'Only as a solution of phenomena; but you look as if I had hit on the truth.'

'I hope it is no such thing; yet– '

'Yet?' repeated Charles, seriously. 'I think he has discovered the danger.'

'The danger of falling in love with Laura? Well, it would be odd if he was not satisfied with his own work. But he must know how preposterous that would be.'

'And you think that would prevent it?' said his mother, smiling. 'He is just the man to plume himself on making his judgment conquer his inclination, setting novels at defiance. How magnanimously he would resolve to stifle a hopeless attachment!'

'That is exactly what I think he is doing. I think he has found out the state of his feelings, and is doing all in his power to check them by avoiding her, especially in tete-a-tetes, and an unconstrained family party. I am nearly convinced that is his reason for bringing Mr. Thorndale, and fixing on the day of the dinner. Poor fellow, it must cost him a great deal, and I long to tell him how I thank him.'

'Hm! I don't think it unlikely,' said Charles. 'It agrees with what happened the evening of the Kilcoran ball, when he was ready to eat me up for saying something he fancied was a hint of a liking of Guy's for Laura. It was a wild mistake, for something I said about Petrarch, forgetting that Petrarch suggested Laura; but it put him out to a degree, and he made all manner of denunciations on the horror of Guy's falling in love with her. Now, as far as I see, Guy is much more in love with you, or with Deloraine, and the idea argues far more that the Captain himself is touched.'

'Depend upon it, Charlie, it was this that led to his detecting the true state of the case. Ever since that he has kept away. It is noble!'

'And what do you think about Laura?'

'Poor child! I doubt if it was well to allow so much intimacy; yet I don't see how it could have been helped.'

'So you think she is in for it? I hope not; but she has not been herself of late.'

'I think she misses what she has been used to from him, and thinks him estranged, but I trust it goes no further. I see she is out of spirits; I wish I could help her, dear girl, but the worst of all would be to let her guess the real name and meaning of all this, so I can't venture to say a word.'

'She is very innocent of novels,' said Charles, 'and that is well. It would be an unlucky business to have our poor beauty either sitting 'like Patience on a monument', or 'cockit up on a baggage-waggon.' But that will never be. Philip is not the man to have a wife in barracks. He would have her like his books, in morocco, or not at all.'

'He would never involve her in discomforts. He may be entirely trusted, and as long as he goes on as he has begun, there is no harm done; Laura will cheer up, will only consider him as her cousin and friend, and never know he has felt more for her.'

'Her going to Ireland is very fortunate.'

'It has made me still more glad that the plan should take place at once.'

'And you say "nothing to nobody"?'

'Of course not. We must not let him guess we have observed anything; there is no need to make your father uncomfortable, and such things need not dawn on Amy's imagination.'

It may be wondered at that Mrs. Edmonstone should confide such a subject to her son, but she knew that in a case really affecting his sister, and thus introduced, his silence was secure. In fact, confidence was the only way to prevent the shrewd, unscrupulous raillery which would have caused great distress, and perhaps led to the very disclosure to be deprecated. Of late, too, there had been such a decrease of petulance in Charles, as justified her in trusting him, and lastly, it must be observed that she was one of those open-hearted people who cannot make a discovery nor endure an anxiety without imparting it. Her tact, indeed, led her to make a prudent choice of confidants, and in this case her son was by far the best, though she had spoken without premeditation. Her nature would never have allowed her to act as her daughter was doing; she would have been without the strength to conceal her feelings, especially when deprived of the safety-valve of free intercourse with their object.

The visit took place as arranged, and very uncomfortable it was to all who looked deeper than the surface. In the first place, Philip found there the last person he wished his friend to meet— Lady Eveleen, who had been persuaded to stay for the dinner-party; but Mr. Thorndale was, as Charles would have said, on his good behaviour, and, ashamed of the fascination her manners exercised over him, was resolved to resist it, answered her gay remarks with brief sentences and stiff smiles, and consorted chiefly with the gentlemen.

Laura was grave and silent, trying to appear unconscious, and only succeeding in being visibly constrained. Philip was anxious and stern in his attempts to appear unconcerned, and even Guy was not quite as bright and free as usual, being puzzled as to how far he was forgiven about the ball.

Amabel could not think what had come to every one, and tried in vain to make them sociable. In the evening they had recourse to a game, said to be for Charlotte's amusement, but in reality to obviate some of the stiffness and constraint; yet even this led to awkward situations. Each person was to set down his or her favourite character in history and fiction, flower, virtue, and time at which to have lived, and these were all to be appropriated to the writers. The first read was—

'Lily of the valley— truth— Joan of Arc— Padre Cristoforo— the present time.'

'Amy!' exclaimed Guy.

'I see you are right,' said Charles; 'but tell me your grounds!'

'Padre Cristoforo,' was the answer.

'Fancy little Amy choosing Joan of Arc,' said Eveleen, 'she who is afraid of a tolerable sized grasshopper.'

'I should like to have been Joan's sister, and heard her tell about her visions,' said Amy.

'You would have taught her to believe them,' said Philip.

'Taught her!' cried Guy. 'Surely you take the high view of her.'

'I think,' said Philip, 'that she is a much injured person, as much by her friends as her enemies; but I don't pretend to enter either enthusiastically or philosophically into her character.'

What was it that made Guy's brow contract, as he began to strip the feather of a pen, till, recollecting himself, he threw it from him with a dash, betraying some irritation, and folded his hands.

'Lavender,' read Charlotte.

'What should make any one choose that?' cried Eveleen.

'I know!' said Mrs. Edmonstone, looking up. 'I shall never forget the tufts of lavender round the kitchen garden at Stylehurst.'

Philip smiled. Charlotte proceeded, and Charles saw Laura's colour deepening as she bent over her work.

'"Lavender– steadfastness– Strafford– Cordelia in 'King Lear'– the late war." How funny!' cried Charlotte. 'For hear the next: "Honeysuckle– steadfastness– Lord Strafford– Cordelia– the present time." Why, Laura, you must have copied it from Philip's.'

Laura neither looked nor spoke. Philip could hardly command his countenance as Eveleen laughed, and told him he was much flattered by those becoming blushes. But here Charles broke in,– 'Come, make haste, Charlotte, don't be all night about it;' and as Charlotte paused, as if to make some dangerous remark, he caught the paper, and read the next himself. Nothing so startled Philip as this desire to cover their confusion. Laura was only sensible of the relief of having attention drawn from her by the laugh that followed.

'A shamrock– Captain Rock– the tailor that was "blue moulded for want of a bating"– Pat Riotism– the time of Malachy with the collar of gold.'

'Eva!' cried Charlotte.

'Nonsense,' said Eveleen; 'I am glad I know your tastes, Charles. They do you honour.'

'More than yours do, if these are yours,' said Charles, reading them contemptuously; 'Rose– generosity– Charles Edward– Catherine Seyton– the civil wars.'

'You had better not have disowned Charlie's, Lady Eveleen,' said Guy.

'Nay do you think I would put up with such a set as these?' retorted Charles; 'I am not fallen so low as the essence of young ladyism.'

'What can you find to say against them?' said Eveleen.

'Nothing,' said Charles, 'No one ever can find anything to say for or against young ladies' tastes.'

'You seem to be rather in the case of the tailor yourself,' said Guy, 'ready to do battle, if you could but get any opposition.'

'Only tell me,' said Amy, 'how you could wish to live in the civil wars?'

'O, because they would be so entertaining.'

'There's Paddy, genuine Paddy at last!' exclaimed Charles. 'Depend upon it, the conventional young lady won't do, Eva.'

After much more discussion, and one or two more papers, came Guy's– the last. 'Heather– Truth– King Charles– Sir Galahad– the present time.'

'Sir how much? exclaimed Charles.

'Don't you know him?' said Guy. 'Sir Galahad– the Knight of the Siege Perilous– who won the Saint Greal.'

'What language is that?' said Charles.

'What! Don't you know the Morte d'Arthur! I thought every one did! Don't you, Philip!'

'I once looked into it. It is very curious, in classical English; but it is a book no one could read through.'

'Oh!' cried Guy, indignantly; then, 'but you only looked into it. If you had lived with its two fat volumes, you could not help delighting in it. It was my boating-book for at least three summers.'

'That accounts for it,' said Philip; 'a book so studied in boyhood acquires a charm apart from its actual merits.'

'But it has actual merits. The depth, the mystery, the allegory– the beautiful characters of some of the knights.'

'You look through the medium of your imagination,' said Philip; but you must pardon others for seeing a great sameness of character and adventure, and for disapproving of the strange mixture of religion and romance.'

'You've never read it,' said Guy, striving to speak patiently.

'A cursory view is sufficient to show whether a book will repay the time spent in reading it.'

'A cursory view enable one to judge better than making it your study? Eh, Philip?' said Charles.

'It is no paradox. The actual merits are better seen by an unprejudiced stranger than by an old friend who lends them graces of his own devising.'

Charles laughed: Guy pushed back his chair, and went to look out at the window. Perhaps Philip enjoyed thus chafing his temper; for after all he had said to Laura, it was satisfactory to see his opinion justified, so that he might not feel himself unfair. It relieved his uneasiness lest his understanding with Laura should be observed. It had been in great peril that evening, for as the girls went up to bed, Eveleen gaily said, 'Why, Laura, have you quarrelled with Captain Morville?'

'How can you say such things, Eva? Good night.' And Laura escaped into her own room.

'What's the meaning of it, Amy?' pursued Eveleen.

'Only a stranger makes us more formal,' said Amy.

'What an innocent you are! It is of no use to talk to you!' said Eveleen, running away.

'No; but Eva,' said Amy, pursuing her, 'don't go off with a wrong fancy. Charles has teased Laura so much about Philip, that of course it makes her shy of him before strangers; and it would never have done to laugh about their choosing the same things when Mr. Thorndale was there.'

'I must be satisfied, I suppose. I know that is what you think, for you could not say any other.'

'But what do you think?' said Amy, puzzled.

'I won't tell you, little innocence— it would only shock you.'

'Nothing you really thought about Laura could shock me,' said Amy; 'I don't mean what you might say in play.'

'Well, then, shall you think me in play or earnest when I say that I think Laura likes Philip very much?'

'In play' said Amy; 'for you know that if we had not got our own Charlie to show us what a brother is, we should think of Philip as just the same as a brother.'

'A brother! You are pretending to be more simple than you really are, Amy! Don't you know what I mean?'

'O,' said Amy, her cheeks lighting up, 'that must be only play, for he has never asked her.'

'Ah, but suppose she was in the state just ready to be asked?'

'No, that could never be, for he could never ask her,'

'Why not, little Amy?'

'Because we are cousins, and everything,' said Amy, confused. 'Don't talk any more about it, Eva; for though I know it is all play, I don't like it, and mamma, would not wish me to talk of such things. And don't you laugh about it, dear Eva, pray; for it only makes every one uncomfortable. Pray!'

Amy had a very persuasive way of saying 'pray,' and Eveleen thought she must yield to it. Besides, she respected Laura and Captain Morville too much to resolve to laugh at them, whatever she might do when her fear of the Captain made her saucy.

Mrs. Edmonstone thought it best on all accounts to sit in the drawing-room the next morning; but she need not have taken so much pains to chaperon her young ladies, for the gentlemen did not come near them.

Laura was more at ease in manner, though very far from happy, for she was restlessly eager for a talk with Philip; while he was resolved not to seek a private interview, sure that it would excite suspicion, and willing to lose the consciousness of his underhand proceedings.

This was the day of the dinner-party, and Laura's heart leaped as she calculated that it must fall to Philip's lot to hand her in to dinner. She was not mistaken, he did give her his arm; and they found themselves most favourably placed, for Philip's other neighbour was Mrs. Brownlow, talking at a great rate to Mr. de Courcy, and on Laura's side was the rather deaf Mr. Hayley, who had quite enough to do to talk to Miss Brownlow. Charles was not at table, and not one suspicious eye could rest on them, yet it was not till the second course was in progress that he said anything which the whole world might not have heard. Something had passed about Canterbury, and its distance from Hollywell.

'I can be here often,' said Philip.

'I am glad.'

'If you can only be guarded,– and I think you are becoming so.'

'Is this a time to speak of– ? Oh, don't!'

'It is the only time. No one is attending, and I have something to say to you.'

Overpowering her dire confusion, in obedience to him, she looked at the epergne, and listened.

'You have acted prudently. You have checked– ' and he indicated Guy– 'without producing more than moderate annoyance. You have only to guard your self-possession.'

'It is very foolish,' she murmured.

'Ordinary women say so, and rest contented with the folly. You can do better things.'

There was a thrill of joy at finding him conversing with her as his 'own;' it overcame her embarrassment and alarm, and wishes he would not choose such a time for speaking.'

'How shall I?' said she.

'Employ yourself. Employ and strengthen your mind!'

'How shall I, and without you?'

'Find something to prevent you from dwelling on the future. That drawing is dreamy work, employing the fingers and leaving the mind free.'

'I have been trying to read, but I cannot fix my mind.'

'Suppose you take what will demand attention. Mathematics, algebra. I will send you my first book of algebra, and it will help you to work down many useless dreams and anxieties.'

'Thank you; pray do; I shall be very glad of it.'

'You will find it give a power and stability to your mind, and no longer have to complain of frivolous occupation.'

'I don't feel frivolous now,' said Laura, sadly; 'I don't know why it is that everything is so altered, I am really happier, but my light heart is gone.'

'You have but now learnt the full powers of your soul, Laura, you have left the world of childhood, with the gay feelings which have no depth.'

'I have what is better,' she whispered.

'You have, indeed. But those feelings must be regulated, and strengthening the intellect strengthens the governing power.'

Philip, with all his sense, was mystifying himself, because he was departing from right, the only true 'good sense.' His right judgment in all things was becoming obscured, so he talked metaphysical jargon, instead of plain practical truth, and thought he was teaching Laura to strengthen her powers of mind, instead of giving way to dreams, when he was only leading her to stifle meditation, and thus securing her complete submission to himself.

She was happier after this conversation, and better able to pay attention to the guests, nor did she feel guilty when obliged to play and sing in the evening– for she knew he must own that she could do no otherwise.

Lady Eveleen gave, however, its brilliancy to the party. She had something wonderfully winning and fascinating about her, and Philip owned to himself that it took no small resolution on the part of Mr. Thorndale to keep so steadily aloof from the party in the bay window, where she was reigning like a queen, and inspiring gaiety like a fairy. She made Guy sing with her; it was the first time he had ever sung, except among themselves, as Mrs. Edmonstone had never known whether he would like to be asked; but Eveleen refused to sing some of the Irish melodies unless he would join her, and without making any difficulty he did so. Mrs. Brownlow professed to be electrified, and Eveleen declaring that she knew she sung like a peacock, told Mrs. Brownlow that the thing to hear was Sir Guy singing glees with Laura and Amy. Of course, they were obliged to sing. Mrs. Brownlow was delighted; and as she had considerable knowledge of music, they all grew eager and Philip thought it very foolish of Guy to allow so much of his talent and enthusiasm to display themselves.

When all the people were gone, and the home party had wished each other good-night, Philip lingered in the drawing-room to finish a letter. Guy, after helping Charles up-stairs, came down a few moments after, to fetch something which he had forgotten. Philip looked up,– 'You contributed greatly to the entertainment this evening,' he said.

Guy coloured, not quite sure that this was not said sarcastically, and provoked with himself for being vexed.

'You think one devoid of the sixth sense has no right to speak,' said Philip.

'I can't expect all to think it, as I do, one of the best things in this world or out of it,' said Guy, speaking quickly.

'I know it is so felt by those who understand its secrets,' said Philip. 'I would not depreciate it; so you may hear me patiently, Guy. I only meant to warn you, that it is often the means of bringing persons into undesirable intimacies, from which they cannot disentangle themselves as easily as they enter them.'

A flush crossed Guy's cheek, but it passed, and he simply said– 'I suppose it may. Good-night.'

Philip looked after him, and pondered on what it was that had annoyed him– manner, words, or advice. He ascribed it to Guy's unwillingness to be advised, since he had observed that his counsel was apt to irritate him, though his good sense often led him to follow it. In the present case, Philip thought Mrs. Brownlow and her society by no means desirable for a youth like Guy; and he was quite right.

Philip and his friend went the next morning; and in the afternoon Laura received the book of algebra– a very original first gift from a lover. It came openly, with a full understanding that she was to use it by his recommendation; her mother and brother both thought they understood the motive, which one thought very wise, and the other very characteristic.

Lord Kilcoran and Lady Eveleen also departed. Eveleen very sorry to go, though a little comforted by the prospect of seeing Laura so soon in Ireland, where she would set her going in all kinds of 'rationalities– reading, and school teaching, and everything else.'

'Ay,' said Charles, when all were out of hearing but his mother; 'and I shrewdly suspect the comfort would be still greater if it was Sir Guy Morville who was coming.'

'It would be no bad thing,' said his mother: 'Eveleen is a nice creature with great capabilities.'

'Capabilities! but will they ever come to anything?'

'In a few years,' said Mrs. Edmonstone; 'and he is a mere boy at present, so there is plenty of time for both to develop themselves.'

'Most true, madame mere; but it remains to be proved whether the liking for Sir Guy, which has taken hold of my lady Eveleen, is strong enough to withstand all the coquetting with young Irishmen, and all the idling at Kilcoran.'

'I hope she has something better to be relied on than the liking for Sir Guy.'

'You may well do so, for I think he has no notion of throwing off his allegiance to you– his first and only love. He liked very well to make fun with Eva; but he regarded her rather as a siren, who drew him off from his Latin and Greek.'

'Yes; I am ashamed of myself for such a fit of match-making! Forget it, Charlie, as fast as you can.'

CHAPTER 11

This warld's wealth, when I think o't,
Its pride, and a' the lave o't,
Fie, fie on silly coward man,
That he should be the slave o't.
— BURNS

In another week Mr. Edmonstone and his eldest daughter were to depart on their Irish journey. Laura, besides the natural pain in leaving home, was sorry to be no longer near Philip, especially as it was not likely that he would be still at Broadstone on their return; yet she was so restless and dissatisfied, that any change was welcome, and the fear of betraying herself almost took away the pleasure of his presence.

He met them at the railway station at Broadstone, where Mr. Edmonstone, finding himself much too early, recollected something he had forgotten in the town, and left his daughter to walk up and down the platform under Philip's charge. They felt it a precious interval, but both were out of spirits, and could hardly profit by it.

'You will be gone long before we come back,' said Laura.

'In a fortnight or three weeks, probably.'

'But you will still be able to come to Hollywell now and then?'

'I hope so. It is all the pleasure I can look for. We shall never see such a summer again.'

'Oh, it has been a memorable one!'

'Memorable! Yes. It has given me an assurance that compensates for all I have lost; yet it has made me feel, more than ever before, how poverty withers a man's hopes.'

'O Philip, I always thought your poverty a great, noble thing!'

'You thought like a generous-tempered girl who has known nothing of its effects.'

'And do you know that Guy says the thing to be proud of is of holding the place you do, without the aid of rank or riches.'

'I would not have it otherwise— I would not for worlds that my father had acted otherwise,' said Philip. 'You understand that, Laura.'

'Of course I do.'

'But when you speak— when Guy speaks of my holding the place I do, you little know what it is to feel that powers of usefulness are wasted— to know I have the means of working my way to honour and distinction, such as you would rejoice in Laura, to have it all within, yet feel it thrown away. Locksley Hall, again— "every door is barred with gold, and opens but to golden keys."'

'I wish there was anything to be done,' said Laura.

'It is my profession that is the bar to everything. I have sold the best years of my life, and for what? To see my sister degrade herself by that marriage.'

'That is the real grief,' said Laura.

'But for that, I should never have cast a look back on what I relinquished. However, why do I talk of these things, these vain regrets? They only occurred because my welfare does not concern myself alone— and here's your father.'

Mr. Edmonstone returned, out of breath, in too much bustle remark his daughter's blushes. Even when the train was moving off, he still had his head out at the window, calling to Philip that they should expect a visit from him as soon as ever they returned. Such cordiality gave Philip a pang; and in bitterness of spirit he walked back to the barracks. On the way he met Mrs. Deane who wanted to consult him about inviting his cousin, Sir Guy to a dinner-party she intended to give next week. 'Such an agreeable, sensible youth, and we feel we owe him some attention, he took so much pains to make apologies about the ball.'

'I dare say he will be very happy to come.'

'We will write at once. He is a very fine young man, without a shade of vanity or nonsense.'

'Yes; he has very pleasant, unaffected manners.'

'I am sure he will do credit to his estate. It is a very handsome fortune, is it not?'

'It is a very large property.'

'I am glad of it; I have no doubt we shall see him one of the first men of his time.'

These words brought into contrast in Philip's mind the difference between Guy's position and his own. The mere possession of wealth was winning for Guy, at an age when his merits could only be negative, that estimation which his own tried character had scarcely achieved, placing him not merely on a level with himself, but in a situation where happiness and influence came unbidden. His own talents, attainments, and equal, if not superior claims, to gentle blood, could not procure him what seemed to lie at Guy's feet. His own ability and Laura's heart alone were what wealth could not affect; yet when he thought how the want of it wasted the one, and injured the hopes of the other, he recurred to certain visions of his sister Margaret's, in days gone by, of what he was to do as Sir Philip, lord of Redclyffe. He was speculating on what would have happened had Guy died in his sickly infancy, when, suddenly recollecting himself, he turned his mind to other objects.

Guy was not much charmed with Mrs. Deane's invitation. He said he knew he must go to make up for his rudeness about the ball; but he grumbled enough to make Mrs. Edmonstone laugh at him for being so stupid as to want to stay hum-drum in the chimney corner. No doubt it was very pleasant there. There was that peculiar snugness which belongs to a remnant of a large party, when each member of it feels bound to prevent the rest from being dull. Guy devoted himself to Charles more than ever, and in the fear that he might miss the late variety of amusement, exerted even more of his powers of entertainment than Lady Eveleen had called forth.

There were grave readings in the mornings, and long walks in the afternoons, when he dragged Charles, in his chair, into many a place he had never expected to see again, and enabled him to accompany his mother and sisters in many a delightful expedition. In the evening there was music, or light reading, especially poetry, as this was encouraged by Mrs. Edmonstone, in the idea that it was better that so excitable and enthusiastic a person as Guy should have his objects of admiration tested by Charles's love of ridicule.

Mr. Edmonstone had left to Guy the office of keeping the 1st of September, one which he greatly relished. Indeed, when he thought of his own deserted manors, he was heard to exclaim, in commiseration for the neglect, 'Poor partridges!' The Hollywell shooting was certainly not like that at Redclyffe, where he could hardly walk out of his own grounds, whereas here he had to bear in mind so many boundaries, that Philip was expecting to have to help him out of some direful scrape. He had generally walked over the whole extent, and assured himself that the birds were very wild, and Bustle the best of dogs, before breakfast, so as to be ready for all the occupations of the day. He could scarcely be grateful when the neighbours, thinking it must be very dull for him to be left alone with Mrs. Edmonstone and her crippled son, used to ask him to shoot or dine. He always lamented at first, and ended by enjoying himself.

One night, he came home, in such a state of eagerness, that he must needs tell his good news; and, finding no one in the drawing-room, he ran up-stairs, opened Charles's door, and exclaimed– 'There's to be a concert at Broadstone!' Then perceiving that Charles was fast asleep, he retreated noiselessly, reserving his rejoicings till morning, when it appeared that Charles had heard, but had woven the announcement into a dream.

This concert filled Guy's head. His only grief was that it was to be in the evening, so that Charles could not go to it; and his wonder was not repressed at finding that Philip did not mean to favour it with his presence, since Guy would suffice for squire to Mrs. Edmonstone and her daughters.

In fact, Philip was somewhat annoyed by the perpetual conversation about the concert, and on the day on which it was to take place resolved on making a long expedition to visit the ruins of an old abbey, far out of all reports of it. As he was setting out, he was greeted, in a very loud voice, by Mr. Gordon.

'Hollo, Morville! how are you? So you have great doings to-night, I hear!' and he had only just forced himself from him, when he was again accosted, this time in a hasty, embarrassed manner,–

'I beg your pardon, sir, but the ties of relationship– '

He drew himself up as if he was on parade, faced round, and replied with an emphatic 'Sir!' as he behold a thin, foreign-looking man, in a somewhat flashy style of dress, who, bowing low, repeated breathlessly,–

'I beg your pardon– Sir Guy Morville, I believe!'

'Captain Morville, sir!'

'I beg your pardon– I mistook. A thousand pardons,' and he retreated; while Philip, after a moment's wonder, pursued his walk.

The Hollywell party entered Broadstone in a very different temper, and greatly did they enjoy the concert, both for themselves and for each other. In the midst of it, while Amy was intent on the Italian words of a song, Guy touched her hand, and pointed to a line in the programme–

Solo on the violin.... MR. S. B. DIXON.

She looked up in his face with an expression full of inquiry; but it was no time for speaking, and she only saw how the colour mantled on his cheek when the violinist appeared, and how he looked down the whole time of the performance, only now and then venturing a furtive though earnest glance.

He did not say anything till they were seated in the carriage, and then astonished Mrs. Edmonstone by exclaiming–

'It must be my uncle!– I am sure it must. I'll ride to Broadstone the first thing to-morrow, and find him out.'

'Your uncle!' exclaimed Mrs. Edmonstone. 'I never thought of that.'

S. B. Dixon,' said Guy. 'I know his name is Sebastian. It cannot be any one else. You know he went to America. How curious it is! I suppose there is no fear of his being gone before I can come in to-morrow.'

'I should think not. Those musical people keep late hours.'

'I would go before breakfast. Perhaps it would be best to go to old Redford, he will know all about him; or to the music-shop. I am so glad! It is the very thing I always wished.'

'Did you?' said Mrs. Edmonstone to herself. 'I can't say every one would be of your mind; but I can't help liking you the better for it. I wish the man had kept further off. I wish Mr. Edmonstone was at home. I hope no harm will come of it. I wonder what I ought to do. Shall I caution him? No; I don't think I can spoil his happiness– and perhaps the man may be improved. He is his nearest relation, and I have no right to interfere. His own good sense will protect him– but I wish Mr. Edmonstone was at home.'

She therefore did not check his expressions of delight, nor object to his going to Broadstone early the next morning. He had just dismounted before the inn-yard, when a boy put a note into his hand, and he was so absorbed in its contents, that he did not perceive Philip till after two greetings had passed unheard. When at length he was recalled, he started, and exclaimed, rapturously, as he put the note into his cousin's hand,

'See here— it is himself!'

'Who?'

'My uncle. My poor mother's own brother.'

'Sebastian Bach Dixon,' read Philip. 'Ha! it was he who took me for you yesterday.'

'I saw him at the concert— I was sure it could be no other. I came in on purpose to find him, and here he is waiting for me. Is not it a happy chance?'

'Happy!' echoed Philip, in a far different tone.

'How I have longed for this— for any one who could remember and tell me of her— of my mother— my poor, dear young mother! And her own brother! I have been thinking of it all night, and he knows I am here, and is as eager as myself. He is waiting for me,' ended Guy, hurrying off.

'Stop!' said Philip, gravely. 'Think before acting. I seriously advise you to have nothing to do with this man, at least personally. Let me see him, and learn what he wants.'

'He wants me,' impatiently answered Guy. 'You are not his nephew.'

'Thank heaven!' thought Philip. 'Do you imagine your relationship is the sole cause of his seeking you?'

'I don't know— I don't care!' cried Guy, with vehemence. 'I will not listen to suspicions of my mother's brother.'

'It is more than suspicion. Hear me calmly. I speak for your good. I know this man's influence was fatal to your father. I know he did all in his power to widen the breach with your grandfather.'

'That was eighteen years ago,' said Guy, walking on, biting his lip in a fiery fit of impatience.

'You will not hear. Remember, that his position and associates render him no fit companion for you. Nay, listen patiently. You cannot help the relationship. I would not have you do otherwise than assist him. Let him not complain of neglect, but be on your guard. He will either seriously injure you, or be a burden for life.'

'I have heard you so far— I can hear no more,' said Guy, no longer restraining his impetuosity. 'He is my uncle, that I know, I care for nothing else. Position— nonsense! what has that to do with it? I will not be set against him.'

He strode off; but in a few moments turned back, overtook Philip, said— 'Thank you for your advice. I beg your pardon for my hastiness. You mean kindly, but I must see my uncle.' And, without waiting for an answer, he was gone.

In short space he was in the little parlour of the music-shop, shaking hands with his uncle, and exclaiming,–

'I am so glad! I hoped it was you!'

'It is very noble-hearted! I might have known it would be so with the son of my dearest sister and of my generous friend!' cried Mr. Dixon, with eagerness that had a theatrical air, though it was genuine feeling that filled his eyes with tears.

'I saw your name last night' continued Guy. 'I would have tried to speak to you at once, but I was obliged to stay with Mrs. Edmonstone, as I was the only gentleman with her.'

'Ah! I thought it possible you might not be able to follow the dictate of your own heart; but this is a fortunate conjuncture, in the absence of your guardian.'

Guy recollected Philip's remonstrance, and it crossed him whether his guardian might be of the same mind; but he felt confident in having told all to Mrs. Edmonstone.

'How did you know I was here?' he asked.

'I learnt it in a most gratifying way. Mr. Redford, without knowing our connection– for on that I will always be silent– mentioned that the finest tenor he had ever known, in an amateur, belonged to his pupil, Sir Guy Morville. You can imagine my feelings at finding you so near, and learning that you had inherited your dear mother's talent and taste.'

The conversation was long, for there was much to hear. Mr. Dixon had kept up a correspondence at long intervals with Markham, from whom he heard that his sister's child survived, and was kindly treated by his grandfather; and inquiring again on the death of old Sir Guy, learnt that he was gone to live with his guardian, whose name, and residence Markham had not thought fit to divulge. He had been much rejoiced to hear his name from the music-master, and he went on to tell how he had been misled by the name of Morville into addressing the captain, who had a good deal of general resemblance to Guy's father, a fine tall young man, of the same upright, proud deportment. He supposed he was the son of the Archdeacon, and remembering how strongly his own proceedings had been discountenanced at Stylehurst, had been much disconcerted, and deeming the encounter a bad omen, had used more caution in his advances to his nephew. It was from sincere affection that he sought his acquaintance, though very doubtful as to the reception he might meet, and was both delighted and surprised at such unembarrassed, open-hearted affection.

The uncle and nephew were not made to understand each other. Sebastian Dixon was a man of little education, and when, in early youth, his talents had placed him high in his own line, he had led a careless, extravagant life. Though an evil friend, and fatal counsellor, he had been truly attached to Guy's father, and the secret engagement, and runaway marriage with his beautiful sister, had been the romance of his life, promoted by him with no selfish end. He was a proud and passionate man, and resenting Sir Guy's refusal to receive his sister as a daughter, almost as much as Sir Guy was incensed at the marriage, had led his brother-in-law to act in a manner which cut off the hope of reconciliation, and obliged Archdeacon Morville to give up his cause. He had gloried in supporting his sister and her husband, and enabling them to set the old baronet at defiance. But young Morville's territorial pride could not brook that he should be maintained, and especially that his child, the heir of Redclyffe, should be born while he was living at the expense of a musician. This feeling, aided by a yearning for home, and a secret love for his father, mastered his resentment; he took his resolution, quarrelled with Dixon, and carried off his wife, bent with desperation on forcing his father into receiving her.

Sebastian had not surmounted his anger at this step when he learnt its fatal consequences. Ever since that time, nothing had prospered with him: he had married and sunk himself lower, and though he had an excellent engagement, the days were past when he was the fashion, and his gains and his triumphs were not what they had been. He had a long list of disappointments and jealousies with which to entertain Guy, who, on his side, though resolved to like him, and dreading to be too refined to be friends with his relations, could not feel as thoroughly pleased as he intended to have been.

Music was, however, a subject on which they could meet with equal enthusiasm, and by means of this, together with the aid of his own imagination, Guy contrived to be very happy. He stayed with his uncle as long as he could, and promised to spend a day with him in London, on his way to Oxford, in October.

The next morning, when Philip knew that Guy would be with his tutor, he walked to Hollywell, came straight up to his aunt's dressing-room, asked her to send Charlotte down to practise, and, seating himself opposite to her, began—

'What do you mean to do about this unfortunate rencontre?'

'Do you mean Guy and his uncle? He is very much pleased, poor boy! I like his entire freedom from false shame.'

'A little true shame would be hardly misplaced about such a connection.'

'It is not his fault, and I hope it will not be his misfortune,' said Mrs. Edmonstone.

'That it will certainly be,' replied Philip, 'if we are not on our guard; and, indeed, if we are, there is little to be done with one so wilful. I might as well have interfered with the course of a whirlwind.'

'No, no, Philip; he is too candid to be wilful.'

'I cannot be of your opinion, when I have seen him rushing into this acquaintance in spite of the warnings he must have had here— to say nothing of myself.'

'Nay, there I must defend him, though you will think me very unwise; I could not feel that I ought to withhold him from taking some notice of so near a relation.'

Philip did think her so unwise, that he could only reply, gravely—

'We must hope it may produce no evil effects.'

'How?' she exclaimed, much alarmed. 'Have you heard anything against him?'

'You remember, of course, that Guy's father was regularly the victim of this Dixon.'

'Yes, yes; but he has had enough to sober him. Do you know nothing more?' said Mrs. Edmonstone, growing nervously anxious lest she had been doing wrong in her husband's absence.

'I have been inquiring about him from old Redford, and I should judge him to be a most dangerous companion; as, indeed, I could have told from his whole air, which is completely that of a roué.'

'You have seen him, then?'

'Yes. He paid me the compliment of taking me for Sir Guy, and of course made off in dismay when he discovered on whom he had fallen. I have seldom seen a less creditable-looking individual.'

'But what did Mr. Redford say? Did he know of the connection?'

'No; I am happy to say he did not. The fellow has decency enough not to boast of that. Well, Redford did not know much of him personally: he said he had once been much thought of, and had considerable talent and execution, but taste changes, or he has lost something, so that, though he stands tolerably high in his profession, he is not a leader. So much for his musical reputation. As to his character, he is one of those people who are called no one's enemy but their own, exactly the introduction Guy has hitherto happily wanted to every sort of mischief.'

'I think,' said Mrs. Edmonstone, trying to console herself, 'that Guy is too much afraid of small faults to be invited by larger evils. While he punishes himself for an idle word, he is not likely to go wrong in greater matters.'

'Not at present.'

'Is the man in debt or difficulties? Guy heard nothing of that, and I thought it a good sign.'

'I don't suppose he is. He ought not, for he has a fixed salary, besides what he gets by playing at concerts when it is not the London season. The wasting money on a spendthrift relation would be a far less evil than what I apprehend.'

'I wish I knew what to do! It is very unlucky that your uncle is from home.'

'Very.'

Mrs. Edmonstone was frightened by the sense of responsibility, and was only anxious to catch hold of something to direct her.

'What would you have me do?' she asked, hopelessly.

'Speak seriously to Guy. He must attend to you: he cannot fly out with a woman as he does with me. Show him the evils that must result from such an intimacy. If Dixon was in distress, I would not say a word, for he would be bound to assist him but as it is, the acquaintance can serve no purpose but degrading Guy, and showing him the way to evil. Above all, make a point of his giving up visiting him in London. That is the sure road to evil. A youth of his age, under the conduct of a worn-out roué, connected with the theatres! I can hardly imagine anything more mischievous.'

'Yes, yes; I will speak to him,' said Mrs. Edmonstone, perfectly appalled.

She promised, but she found the fulfilment difficult, in her dislike of vexing Guy, her fear of saying what was wrong, and a doubt whether the appearance of persecuting Mr. Dixon was not the very way to prevent Guy's own good sense from finding out his true character, so she waited, hoping Mr. Edmonstone might return before Guy went to Oxford, or that he might write decisively.

Mrs. Edmonstone might have known her husband better than to expect him to write decisively when he had neither herself nor Philip at his elbow. The same post had brought him a letter from Guy, mentioning his meeting with his uncle, and frankly explaining his plans for London; another from Philip, calling on him to use all his authority to prevent this intercourse, and a third from his wife. Bewildered between them, he took them to his sister, who, being as puzzle-headed as himself, and only hearing his involved history of the affair, confused him still more; so he wrote to Philip, saying he was sorry the fellow had turned up, but he would guard against him. He told Guy he was sorry to say that his uncle used to be a sad scamp, and he must take care, or it would be his poor father's story over again; and to Mrs. Edmonstone he wrote that it was very odd that everything always did go wrong when he was away.

He thought these letters a great achievement, but his wife's perplexity was not materially relieved.

After considering a good while, she at length spoke to Guy; but it was not at a happy time, for Philip, despairing of her, had just taken on himself to remonstrate, and had angered him to the verge of an outbreak.

Mrs. Edmonstone, as mildly as she could, urged on him that such intercourse could bring him little satisfaction, and might be very inconvenient; that his uncle was in no distress, and did not require assistance; and that it was too probable that in seeking him out he might meet with persons who might unsettle his principles,– in short, that he had much better give up the visit to London.

'This is Philip's advice,' said Guy.

'It is; but– '

Guy looked impatient, and she paused.

'You must forgive me,' he said, 'if I follow my own judgment. If Mr. Edmonstone chose to lay his commands on me, I suppose I must submit; but I cannot see that I am bound to obey Philip.'

'Not to obey, certainly; but his advice– '

'He is prejudiced and unjust,' said Guy.

'I don't believe that my uncle would attempt to lead me into bad company; and surely you would not have me neglect or look coldly on one who was so much attached to my parents. If he is not a gentleman, and is looked down on by the world, it is not for his sister's son to make him conscious of it.'

'I like your feelings, Guy; I can say nothing against it, but that I am much afraid your uncle is not highly principled.'

'You have only Philip's account of him.'

'You are resolved?'

'Yes. I do not like not to take your advice, but I do believe this is my duty. I do not think my determination is made in self-will,' said Guy, thoughtfully; 'I cannot think that I ought to neglect my uncle, because I happen to have been born in a different station, which is all I have heard proved against him,' he added, smiling. 'You will forgive me, will you not, for not following your advice? for really and truly, if you will let me say so, I think you would not have given it if Philip had not been talking to you.'

Mrs. Edmonstone confessed, with a smile, that perhaps it was so; but said she trusted much to Philip's knowledge of the world. Guy agreed to this; though still declaring Philip had no right to set him against his uncle, and there the discussion ended.

Guy went to London. Philip thought him very wilful, and his aunt very weak; and Mr. Edmonstone, on coming home, said it could not be helped, and he wished to hear no more about the matter.

CHAPTER 12

Her playful smile, her buoyance wild,
Bespeak the gentle, mirthful child;
But in her forehead's broad expanse,
Her chastened tones, her thoughtful glance,
Is mingled, with the child's light glee,
The modest maiden's dignity.

One summer's day, two years after the ball and review, Mary Ross and her father were finishing their early dinner, when she said,—

'If you don't want me this afternoon, papa, I think I shall walk to Hollywell. You know Eveleen de Courcy is there.'

'No, I did not. What has brought her?'

'As Charles expresses it, she has over-polked herself in London, and is sent here for quiet and country air. I want to call on her, and to ask Sir Guy to give me some idea as to the singing the children should practise for the school-feast?'

'Then you think Sir Guy will come to the feast?'

'I reckon on him to conceal all the deficiencies in the children's singing.'

'He won't desert you, as he did Mrs. Brownlow?'

'O papa! you surely did not think him to blame in that affair?'

'Honestly, Mary, if I thought about the matter at all, I thought it a pity he should go so much to the Brownlows.'

'I believe I could tell you the history, if you thought it worth while; and though it may be gossip, I should like you to do justice to Sir Guy.'

'Very well; though I don't think there is much danger of my doing otherwise. I only wondered he should become intimate there at all.'

'I believe Mrs. Edmonstone thinks it right he should see as much of the world as possible, and not be always at home in their own set.'

'Fair and proper.'

'You know she has shown him all the people she could,— had Eveleen staying there, and the Miss Nortons, and hunted him out to parties, when he had rather have been at home.'

'I thought he was fond of society. I remember your telling me how amused you were with his enjoyment of his first ball.'

'Ah! he was two years younger then, and all was new. He seems to me too deep and sensitive not to find more pain than pleasure in commonplace society. I have sometimes seen that he cannot speak either lightly or harshly of what he disapproves, and people don't understand him. I was once sitting next him, when there was some talking going on about an elopement; he did not laugh, looked almost distressed, and at last said in a very low voice, to me, "I wish people would not laugh about such things."'

'He is an extraordinary mixture of gaiety of heart, and seriousness.'

'Well, when Mrs. Brownlow had her nieces with her, and was giving those musical parties, his voice made him valuable; and Mrs. Edmonstone told him he ought to go to them. I believe he liked it at first, but he found there was no end to it; it took up a great deal of time, and was a style of thing altogether that was not desirable. Mrs Edmonstone thought at first his reluctance was only shyness and stay-at-home nonsense, that ought to be overcome; but when she had been there, and saw how Mrs. Brownlow beset him, and the unpleasant fuss they made about his singing, she quite came round to his mind, and was very sorry she had exposed him to so much that was disagreeable.'

'Well, Mary, I am glad to hear your account. My impression arose from something Philip Morville said.'

'Captain Morville never can approve of anything Sir Guy does! It is not like Charles.'

'How improved Charles Edmonstone is. He has lost that spirit of repining and sarcasm, and lives as if he had an object.'

'Yes; he employs himself now, and teaches Amy to do the same. You know, after the governess went, we were afraid little Amy would never do anything but wait on Charles, and idle in her pretty gentle way; but when he turned to better things so did she, and her mind has been growing all this time. Perhaps you don't see it, for she has not lost her likeness to a kitten, and looks all demure silence with the elders, but she takes in what the wise say.'

'She is a very good little thing; and I dare say will not be the worse for growing up slowly.'

'Those two sisters are specimens of fast and slow growth. Laura has always seemed to be so much more than one year older than Amy, especially of late. She is more like five-and-twenty than twenty. I wonder if she overworks herself. But how we have lingered over our dinner!'

By half-past three, Mary was entering a copse which led into Mr. Edmonstone's field, when she heard gay tones, and a snatch of one of the sweetest of old songs,—

Weep no more, lady; lady, weep no more,
Thy sorrow is in vain;
For violets pluck'd, the sweetest showers
Will ne'er make grow again.

A merry, clear laugh followed, and a turn in the path showed her Guy, Amy, and Charlotte, busy over a sturdy stock of eglantine. Guy, little changed in these two years,— not much taller, and more agile than robust,—

was lopping vigorously with his great pruning-knife, Amabel nursing a bundle of drooping rose branches, Charlotte, her bonnet in a garland of wild sweet-brier, holding the matting and continually getting entangled in the long thorny wreaths.

'And here comes the "friar of orders gray," to tell you so,' exclaimed Guy, as Mary, in her gray dress, came on them.

'Oh, that is right, dear good friar,' cried Amy.

'We are so busy,' said Charlotte; 'Guy has made Mr. Markham send all these choice buds from Redclyffe.'

'Not from the park,' said Guy, 'we don't deal much in gardening; but Markham is a great florist, and these are his bounties.'

'And are you cutting that beautiful wild rose to pieces?'

'Is it not a pity?' said Amy. 'We have used up all the stocks in the garden, and this is to be transplanted in the autumn.'

'She has been consoling it all the time by telling it it is for its good,' said Guy; 'cutting off wild shoots, and putting in better things.'

'I never said anything so pretty; and, after all, I don't know that the grand roses will be equal to these purple shoots and blushing buds with long whiskers.'

'So Sir Guy was singing about the violets plucked to comfort you. But you must not leave off, I want to see how you do it. I am gardener enough to like to look on.'

'We have only two more to put in.'

Knife and fingers were busy, and Mary admired the dexterity with which the slit was made in the green bark, well armed with firm red thorns, and the tiny scarlet gem inserted, and bound with cotton and matting. At the least critical parts of the work, she asked after the rest of the party, and was answered that papa had driven Charles out in the pony carriage, and that Laura and Eveleen were sitting on the lawn, reading and working with mamma. Eveleen was better, but not strong, or equal to much exertion in the heat. Mary went on to speak of her school feast and ask her questions.

'O Guy, you must not go before that!' cried Charlotte.

'Are you going away?'

'He is very naughty, indeed,' said Charlotte. 'He is going, I don't know where all, to be stupid, and read mathematics.'

'A true bill, I am sorry to say,' said Guy; 'I am to join a reading-party for the latter part of the vacation.'

'I hope not before Thursday week, though we are not asking you to anything worth staying for.'

'Oh, surely you need not go before that!' said Amy, 'need you?'

'No; I believe I may stay till Friday, and I should delight in the feast, thank you, Miss Ross,– I want to study such things. A bit more matting, Amy, if you please. There, I think that will do.'

'Excellently. Here is its name. See how neatly Charlie has printed it, Mary. Is it not odd, that he prints so well when he writes so badly?'

'"The Seven Sisters." There, fair sisterhood, grow and thrive, till I come to transplant you in the autumn. Are there any more?'

'No, that is the last. Now, Mary, let us come to mamma.'

Guy waited to clear the path of the numerous trailing briery branches, and the others walked on, Amy telling how sorry they were to lose Guy's vacation, but that he thought he could not give time enough to his studies here, and had settled, at Oxford, to make one of a reading-party, under the tutorship of his friend, Mr. Wellwood.

'Where do they go?'

'It is not settled. Guy wished it to be the sea-side; but Philip has been recommending a farmhouse in Stylehurst parish, rather nearer St. Mildred's Wells than Stylehurst, but quite out in the moor, and an immense way from both.'

'Do you think it will be the place?'

'Yes; Guy thinks it would suit Mr. Wellwood, because he has friends at St. Mildred's, so he gave his vote for it. He expects to hear how it is settled to-day or to-morrow.'

Coming out on the lawn, they found the three ladies sitting under the acacia, with their books and work. Laura did, indeed, look older than her real age, as much above twenty as Amy looked under nineteen. She was prettier than ever; her complexion exquisite in delicacy, her fine figure and the perfect outline of her features more developed; but the change from girl to woman had passed over her, and set its stamp on the anxious blue eye, and almost oppressed brow. Mary thought it would be hard to define where was that difference. It was not want of bloom, for of that Laura had more than any of the others, fresh, healthy, and bright, while Amy was always rather pale, and Lady Eveleen was positively wan and faded by London and late hours; nor was it loss of animation, for Laura talked and laughed with interest and eagerness; nor was it thought, for little Amy, when at rest, wore a meditative, pensive countenance; but there was something either added or taken away, which made it appear that the serenity and carelessness of early youth had fled from her, and the air of the cares of life had come over her.

Mary told her plans,– Church service at four, followed by a tea-drinking in the fields; tea in the garden for the company, and play for the school children and all who liked to join them. Every one likes such festivals, which have the recommendation of permitting all to do as they please, bringing friends together in perfect ease and freedom, with an object that raises them above the rank of mere gatherings for the pleasure of rich neighbours.

Mrs. Edmonstone gladly made the engagement and Lady Eveleen promised to be quite well, and to teach the children all manner of new games, though she greatly despised the dullness of English children, and had many droll stories of the stupidity of Laura's pupils, communicated to her, with perhaps a little exaggeration, by Charles, and still further embellished by herself, for the purpose of exciting Charlotte's indignation.

Mary proceeded to her consultation about the singing, and was conducted by Guy and Amy to the piano, and when her ears could not be indoctrinated by their best efforts, they more than half engaged to walk to East-hill, and have a conversation with the new school-master, whom Mary pitied for having fallen on people so unable to appreciate his musical training as herself and her father. The whole party walked back with her as far as the shade lasted; and at the end of the next field she turned, saw them standing round the stile, thought what happy people they were, and then resumed her wonder whither Laura's youthfulness had flown.

The situation of Philip and Laura had not changed. His regiment had never been at any great distance from Hollywell, and he often came, venturing more as Laura learnt to see him with less trepidation. He seldom or never was alone with her; but his influence was as strong as ever, and look, word, and gesture, which she alone could understand, told her what she was to him, and revealed his thoughts. To him she was devoted, all her doings were with a view to please him, and deserve his affection; he was her world, and sole object. Indeed, she was sometimes startled by perceiving that tenderly as she loved her own family, all were subordinate to him. She had long since known the true name of her feelings for him; she could not tell when or how the certainty had come, but she was conscious that it was love that they had acknowledged for one another and that she only lived in the light of his love. Still she did not realize the evil of concealment; it was so deep a sensation of her innermost heart, that she never could imagine revealing it to any living creature, and she had besides so surrendered her judgment to her idol, that no thought could ever cross her that he had enjoined what was wrong. Her heart and soul were his alone, and she left the future to him without an independent desire or reflection. All the embarrassments and discomforts which her secret occasioned her were met willingly for his sake, and these were not a few, though time had given her more self-command, or, perhaps, more properly speaking, had hardened her.

She always had a dread of tete-a-tetes and conversations over novels, and these were apt to be unavoidable when Eveleen was at Hollywell. The twilight wanderings on the terrace were a daily habit, and Eveleen almost always paired with her. On this evening in particular, Laura was made very uncomfortable by Eveleen's declaring that it was positively impossible and unnatural that the good heroine of some novel should have concealed her engagement from her parents. Laura could not help saying that there might be many excuses; then afraid that she was exciting suspicion, changed the subject in great haste, and tried to make Eveleen come indoors, telling her she would tire herself to death, and vexed by her cousin's protestations that the fresh cool air did her good. Besides, Eveleen was looking with attentive eyes at another pair who were slowly walking up and down the shady walk that bordered the grass-plot, and now and then standing still to enjoy the subdued silence of the summer evening, and the few distant sounds that marked the perfect lull.

'How calm— how beautiful!' murmured Amabel.

'It only wants the low solemn surge and ripple of the tide, and its dash on the rocks,' said Guy. 'If ever there was music, it is there; but it makes one think what the ear must be that can take in the whole of those harmonics.'

'How I should like to hear it!'

'And see it. O Amy! to show you the sunny sea,— the sense of breadth and vastness in that pale clear horizon line, and the infinite number of fields of light between you and it,— and the free feelings as you stand on some high crag, the wind blowing in your face across half the globe, and the waves dashing far below! I am growing quite thirsty for the sea.'

'You know, papa said something about your taking your reading-party to Redclyffe.'

'True, but I don't think Markham would like it, and it would put old Mrs. Drew into no end of a fuss.'

'Not like to have you?'

'O yes, I should be all very well; but if they heard I was bringing three or four men with me, they would think them regular wild beasts. They would be in an awful fright. Besides, it is so long since I have been at home, that I don't altogether fancy going there till I settle there for good.'

'Ah! it will be sad going there at first.'

'And it has not been my duty yet.'

'But you will be glad when you get there?'

'Sha'n't I? I wonder if any one has been to shoot the rabbits on the shag rock. They must have quite overrun it by this time. But I don't like the notion of the first day. There is not only the great change, but a stranger at the vicarage.'

'Do you know anything about the new clergyman? I believe Mrs. Ashford is a connection of Lady Thorndale's?'

'Yes; Thorndale calls them pattern people, and I have no doubt they will do great good in the parish. I am sure we want some enlightenment, for we are a most primitive race, and something beyond Jenny Robinson's dame school would do us no harm.'

Here Mr. Edmonstone called from the window that they must come in.

Mrs. Edmonstone thought deeply that night. She had not forgotten her notion that Eveleen was attracted by Guy's manners, and had been curious to see what would happen when Eveleen was sent to Hollywell for country air.

She had a very good opinion of Lady Eveleen. Since the former visit, she had shown more spirit of improvement, and laid aside many little follies; she had put herself under Laura's guidance, and tamed down into what gave the promise of a sensible woman, more than anything that had hitherto been observed in her; and little addicted to match-making as Mrs. Edmonstone was, she could not help thinking that Eva was almost worthy of her dear Guy (she never could expect to find anyone she should think quite worthy of him, he was too like one of her own children for that), and on the other hand, how delighted Lord and Lady Kilcoran would be. It was a very pretty castle in the air; but in the midst of it, the notion suddenly darted into Mrs. Edmonstone's head, that while she was thinking of it, it was Amy, not Eveleen, who was constantly with Guy. Reading and music, roses, botany, and walks on the terrace! She looked back, and it was still the same. Last Easter vacation, how they used to study the stars in the evening, to linger in the greenhouse in the morning nursing the geraniums, and to practise singing over the school-room piano; how, in a long walk, they always paired together; and how they seemed to share every pursuit or pleasure.

Now Mrs. Edmonstone was extremely fond of Guy, and trusted him entirely; but she thought she ought to consider how far this should be allowed. Feeling that he ought to see more of the world, she had sent him as much as she could into society, but it had only made him cling closer to home. Still he was but twenty, it was only a country neighbourhood, and there was much more for him to see before he could fairly be supposed to know his own mind. She knew he would act honourably; but she had a horror of letting him entangle himself with her daughter before he was fairly able to judge of his own feelings. Or, if this was only behaving with a brother's freedom and confidence, Mrs. Edmonstone felt it was not safe for her poor little Amy, who might learn so to depend on him as to miss him grievously when this intimacy ceased, as it must when he settled at his own home. It would be right, while it was still time, to make her remember that they were not brother and sister, and by checking their present happy, careless, confidential intercourse, to save her from the chill which seemed to have been cast on Laura. Mrs. Edmonstone was the more anxious, because she deeply regretted not having been sufficiently watchful in Laura's case, and perhaps she felt an unacknowledged conviction that if there was real love on Guy's part, it would not be hurt by a little reserve on Amy's. Yet to have to speak to her little innocent daughter on such a matter disturbed her so much, that she could hardly have set about it, if Amy had not, at that very moment, knocked at her door.

'My dear, what has kept you up so late?'

'We have been sitting in Eveleen's room, mamma, hearing about her London life; and then we began to settle our plans for to-morrow, and I came to ask what you think of them. You know Guy has promised to go and hear the East-hill singing, and we were proposing, if you did not mind it, to take the pony-carriage and the donkey, and go in the morning to East-hill, have luncheon, and get Mary to go with us to the top of the great down, where we have never been. Guy has been wanting us, for a long time past, to go and see the view, and saying there is a track quite smooth enough to drive Charlie to the top.'

Amy wondered at her mother's look of hesitation. In fact, the scheme was so accordant with their usual habits that it was impossible to find any objection; yet it all hinged on Guy, and the appointment at East-hill might lead to a great many more.

'Do you wish us to do anything else, mamma? We don't care about it.'

'No, my dear,' said Mrs. Edmonstone, 'I see no reason against it. But— ' and she felt as if she was making a desperate plunge, 'there is something I want to say to you.'

Amy stood ready to hear, but Mrs. Edmonstone paused. Another effort, and she spoke:—

'Amy, my dear, I don't wish to find fault, but I thought of advising you to take care. About Guy— '

The very brilliant pink which instantly overspread Amy's face made her mother think her warning more expedient.

'You have been spending a great deal of time with him of late, very sensibly and pleasantly, I know; I don't blame you at all, my dear, so you need not look distressed. I only want you to be careful. You know, though we call him cousin, he is scarcely a relation at all.'

'O mamma, don't go on,' said poor little Amy, hurriedly; 'indeed I am very sorry!'

For Amy understood that it was imputed to her that she had been forward and unmaidenly. Mrs. Edmonstone saw her extreme distress, and, grieved at the pain she had inflicted, tried to reassure her as much as might be safe.

'Indeed, my dear, you have done nothing amiss. I only intended to tell you to be cautious for fear you should get into a way of going on which might not look well. Don't make any great difference, I only meant that there should not be quite so much singing and gardening alone with him, or walking in the garden in the evening. You can manage to draw back a little, so as to keep more with me or with Laura, and I think that will be the best way.'

Every word, no matter what, increased the burning of poor Amy's cheeks. A broad accusation of flirting would have been less distressing to many girls than this mild and delicate warning was to one of such shrinking modesty and maidenly feeling. She had a sort of consciousness that she enjoyed partaking in his pursuits, and this made her sense of confusion and shame overwhelming. What had she been thoughtlessly doing? She could not speak, she could not look. Her mother put her arm round her, and Amy hid her head on her shoulder, and held her fast. Mrs. Edmonstone kissed and caressed the little fluttering bird, then saying, 'Good night, my own dear child,' unloosed her embrace.

'Good night, dear mamma,' whispered Amy. 'I am very sorry.'

'You need not be sorry, my dear, only be careful. Good night.' And it would be hard to say whether the mother or the daughter had the hottest cheeks.

Poor little Amy! what was her dismay as she asked herself, again and again, what she had been doing and what she was to do? The last was plain,— she knew what was right, and do it she must. There would be an end of much that was pleasant, and a fresh glow came over her as she owned how very, very pleasant; but if it was not quite the thing,— if mamma did not approve, so it must be. True, all her doings received their zest from Guy,— her heart bounded at the very sound of his whistle, she always heard his words through all the din of a whole party,— nothing was complete without him, nothing good without his without his approval,— but so much the more shame for her. It was a kind of seeking him which was of all things the most shocking. So there should be an end of it,— never mind the rest! Amy knelt down, and prayed that she might keep her resolution.

She did not know how much of her severity towards herself was learned from the example that had been two years before her. Nor did she think whether the seeking had been mutual; she imagined it all her own doing, and did not guess that she would give pain to Guy by withdrawing herself from him.

The morning gave vigour to her resolution, and when Laura came to ask what mamma thought of their project, Amy looked confused— said she did not know— she believed it would not do. But just then in came her mother, to say she had been considering of the expedition, and meant to join it herself. Amy understood, blushed, and was silently grateful.

When Laura wanted to alter her demeanour towards Guy, being perfectly cool, and not in the least conscious, she had acted with great judgment, seen exactly what to do, and what to leave undone, so as to keep up appearances.

But it was not so with Amy. She was afraid of herself, and was in extremes. She would not come down till the last moment, that there might be no talking in the window. She hardly spoke at breakfast-time, and adhered closely to Laura and Eveleen when they wandered in the garden. Presently Charles looked out from the dressing-room window, calling,–

'Amy, Guy is ready to read.'

'I can't come. Read without me,' she answered, hoping Charlie would not be vexed, and feeling her face light up again.

The hour for the expedition came, and Amy set off walking with Laura, because Guy was with Mrs. Edmonstone; but presently, after holding open a gate for Charlotte, who was on the donkey, he came up to the sisters, and joined in the conversation. Amy saw something in the hedge– a foxglove, she believed– it would have done as well if it had been a nettle– she stopped to gather it, hoping to fall behind them, but they waited for her. She grew silent, but Guy appealed to her. She ran on to Charlotte and her donkey, but at the next gate Guy had joined company again. At last she put herself under her mother's wing, and by keeping with her did pretty well all the time she was at East-hill. But when they went on, she was riding the donkey, and it, as donkeys always are, was resolved on keeping a-head of the walkers, so that as Guy kept by her side, it was a more absolute tete-a-tete than ever.

At the top of the hill they found a fine view, rich and extensive, broad woods, fields waving with silvery barley, trim meadows, fair hazy blue distance, and a dim line of sea beyond. This, as Amy knew, was Guy's delight, and further, what she would not tell herself, was that he chiefly cared for showing it to her. It was so natural to call him to admire everything beautiful, and ask if it was equal to Redclyffe, that she found herself already turning to him to participate in his pleasure, as he pointed out all that was to be seen; but she recollected, blushed, and left her mother to speak. He had much to show. There was a hanging wood on one side of the hill, whence he had brought her more than one botanical prize, and she must now visit their native haunts. It was too great a scramble for Mrs. Edmonstone, with all her good will; Eveleen was to be kept still, and not to tire herself; Laura did not care for botany, nor love brambles, and Amy was obliged to stand and look into the wood, saying, 'No, thank you, I don't think I can,' and then run back to Mary and Charles; while Charlotte was loudly calling out that it was delightful fun, and that she was very stupid. In another minute Guy had overtaken her, and in his gentle, persuasive voice, was telling her it was very easy, and she must come and see the bird's-nest orchises. She would have liked it above all things, but she thought it very kind of Guy not to seem angry when she said, 'No, thank you.'

Mary, after what she had seen yesterday, could not guess at the real reason, or she would have come with her; but she thought Amy was tired, and would rather not. Poor Amy was tired, very tired, before the walk was over, but her weary looks made it worse, for Guy offered her his arm. 'No thank you,' she said, 'I am getting on very well;' and she trudged on resolutely, for her mother was in the carriage, and to lag behind the others would surely make him keep with her.

Mrs. Edmonstone was very sorry for her fatigue, but Amy found it a good excuse for not wandering in the garden, or joining in the music. It had been a very uncomfortable day; she hoped she had done right; at any rate, she had the peaceful conviction of having tried to do so.

The next day, Amy was steady to her resolution. No reading with the two youths, though Charles scolded her; sitting in her room till Guy was gone out, going indoors as soon as she heard him return, and in the evening staying with Charles when her sisters and cousins went out; but this did not answer, for Guy came and sat by them. She moved away as soon as possible, but the more inclined she was to linger, the more she thought she ought to go; so murmuring something about looking for Laura, she threw on her scarf, and sprung to the window. Her muslin caught on the bolt, she turned, Guy was already disentangling it, and she met his eye. It was full of anxious, pleading inquiry, which to her seemed upbraiding, and, not knowing what to do, she exclaimed, hurriedly, 'Thank you; no harm done!' and darted into the garden, frightened to feel her face glowing and her heart throbbing. She could not help looking back to see if he was following. No, he was not attempting it; he was leaning against the window, and on she hastened, the perception dawning on her that she was hurting him; he might think her rude, unkind, capricious, he who had always been so kind to her, and when he was going away so soon. 'But it is right; it must be done,' said little Amy to herself, standing still, now that she was out of sight. 'If I was wrong before, I must bear it now, and he will see the rights of it sooner or later. The worst of all would be my not doing the very most right to please any body. Besides he can't really care for missing silly little Amy when he has mamma and Charlie. And he is going away, so it will be easier to begin right when he comes back. Be that as it may, it must be done. I'll get Charlie to tell me what he was saying about the painted glass.'

CHAPTER 13

Oh, thou child of many prayers!
Life hath quicksands— life hath snares—
Care and age come unawares.

Like the swell of some sweet tune,
Morning rises into noon,
May glides onward into June.
— Longfellow

'What is the matter with Amy? What makes her so odd?' asked Charles, as his mother came to wish him good night.

'Poor little dear! don't take any notice,' was all the answer he received; and seeing that he was to be told no more, he held his peace.

Laura understood without being told. She, too, had thought Guy and Amy were a great deal together, and combining various observations, she perceived that her mother must have given Amy a caution. She therefore set herself, like a good sister, to shelter Amy as much as she could, save her from awkward situations, and, above all, to prevent her altered manner from being remarked. This was the less difficult, as Eveleen was subdued and languid, and more inclined to lie on the sofa and read than to look out for mirth.

As to poor little Amy, her task was in one way become less hard, for Guy had ceased to haunt her, and seemed to make it his business to avoid all that could cause her embarrassment; but in another way it hurt her much more, for she now saw the pain she was causing. If obliged to do anything for her, he would give a look as if to ask pardon, and then her rebellious heart would so throb with joy as to cause her dismay at having let herself fall into so hateful a habit as wishing to attract attention. What a struggle it was not to obey the impulse of turning to him for the smile with which he would greet anything in conversation that interested them both, and how wrong she thought it not to be more consoled when she saw him talking to Eveleen, or to any of the others, as if he was doing very well without her. This did not often happen; he was evidently out of spirits, and thoughtful, and Amy was afraid some storm might be gathering respecting Mr. Sebastian Dixon, about whom there always seemed to be some uncomfortable mystery.

Mrs. Edmonstone saw everything, and said nothing. She was very sorry for them both, but she could not interfere, and could only hope she had done right, and protected Amy as far as she was able. She was vexed now and then to see Eveleen give knowing smiles and significant glances, feared that she guessed what was going on, and wondered whether to give her a hint not to add to Amy's confusion; but her great dislike to enter on such a subject prevailed, and she left things to take their course, thinking that, for once, Guy's departure would be a relief.

The approach of anything in the shape of a party of pleasure was one of the best cures for Eveleen's ailments, and the evening before Mary's tea-drinking, she was in high spirits, laughing and talking a great deal, and addressing herself chiefly to Guy. He exerted himself to answer, but it did not come with life and spirit, his countenance did not light up, and at last Eveleen said, 'Ah! I see I am a dreadful bore. I'll go away, and leave you to repose.'

'Lady Eveleen!' he exclaimed, in consternation; 'what have I been doing— what have I been thinking of?'

'Nay, that is best known to yourself, though I think perhaps I could divine,' said she, with that archness and grace that always seemed to remove the unfavourable impression that her proceedings might have given. 'Shall I?'

'No, no,' he answered, colouring crimson, and then trying to laugh off his confusion, and find some answer, but without success; and Eveleen, perceiving her aunt's eyes were upon her, suddenly recollected that she had gone quite as far as decorum allowed, and made as masterly a retreat as the circumstances permitted.

'Well, I have always thought a "penny for your thoughts" the boldest offer in the world, and now it is proved.'

This scene made Mrs. Edmonstone doubly annoyed, the next morning, at waking with a disabling headache, which made it quite impossible for her to attempt going to Mary Ross's fete. With great sincerity, Amy entreated to be allowed to remain at home, but she thought it would only be making the change more remarkable; she did not wish Mary to be disappointed; among so many ladies, Amy could easily avoid getting into difficulties; while Laura would, she trusted, be able to keep Eveleen in order.

The day was sunny, and all went off to admiration. The gentlemen presided over the cricket, and the ladies over 'blind man's buff' and 'thread my needle;' but perhaps Mary was a little disappointed that, though she had Sir Guy's bodily presence, the peculiar blitheness and animation which he usually shed around him were missing. He sung at church, he filled tiny cups from huge pitchers of tea, he picked up and pacified a screaming child that had tumbled off a gate— he was as good-natured and useful as possible, but he was not his joyous and brilliant self.

Amy devoted herself to the smallest fry, played assiduously for three quarters of an hour with a fat, grave boy of three, who stood about a yard-and-a-half from her, solemnly throwing a ball into her lap, and never catching it again, took charge of many caps and bonnets, and walked about with Louisa Harper, a companion whom no one envied her.

In conclusion, the sky clouded over, it became chilly, and a shower began to fall. Laura pursued Eveleen, and Amy hunted up Charlotte from the utmost parts of the field, where she was the very centre of 'winding up the clock,' and sorely against her will, dragged her off the wet grass. About sixty yards from the house, Guy met them with an umbrella, which, without speaking, he gave to Charlotte. Amy said, 'Thank you,' and again came that look. Charlotte rattled on, and hung back to talk to Guy, so that Amy could not hasten on without leaving her shelterless. It may be believed that she had the conversation to herself. At the door they met Mary and her father, going to dismiss their flock, who had taken refuge in a cart-shed at the other end of the field. Guy asked if he could be of any use; Mr. Ross said no, and Mary begged Amy and Charlotte to go up to her room, and change their wet shoes.

There, Amy would fain have stayed, flushed and agitated as those looks made her; but Charlotte was in wild spirits, delighted at having been caught in the rain, and obliged to wear shoes a mile too large, and eager to go and share the fun in the drawing-room. There, in the twilight, they found a mass of young ladies herded together, making a confused sound of laughter, and giggling, while at the other end of the room, Amy could just see Guy sitting alone in a dark corner.

Charlotte's tongue was soon the loudest in the medley, to which Amy did not at first attend, till she heard Charlotte saying—

'Ah! you should hear Guy sing that.'

'What?' she whispered to Eveleen.

'"The Land of the Leal,"' was the answer.

'I wish he would sing it now,' said Ellen Harper.

'This darkness would be just the time for music,' said Eveleen; 'it is quite a witching time.'

'Why don't you ask him?' said Ellen. 'Come, Charlotte, there's a good girl, go and ask him.'

'Shall I?' said Charlotte, whispering and giggling with an affectation of shyness.

'No, no, Charlotte,' said Laura.

'No! why not?' said Eveleen. 'Don't be afraid, Charlotte.'

'He is so grave,' said Charlotte.

Eveleen had been growing wilder and less guarded all day, and now, partly liking to tease and surprise the others, and partly emboldened by the darkness, she answered,—

'It will do him all manner of good. Here, Charlotte, I'll tell you how to make him. Tell him Amy wants him to do it.'

'Ay! tell him so,' cried Ellen, and they laughed in a manner that overpowered Amy with horror and shyness. She sprung to seize Charlotte, and stop her; she could not speak, but Louisa Harper caught her arm, and Laura's grave orders were drowned in a universal titter, and suppressed exclamation,– 'Go, Charlotte, go; we will never forgive you if you don't!'

'Stop!' Amy struggled to cry, breaking from Louisa, and springing up in a sort of agony. Guy, who had such a horror of singing anything deep in pathos or religious feeling to mixed or unfit auditors, asked to do so in her name! 'Stop! oh, Charlotte!' It was too late; Charlotte, thoughtless with merriment, amused at vexing Laura, set up with applause, and confident in Guy's good nature, had come to him, and was saying,– 'Oh, Guy! Amy wants you to come and sing us the "Land of the Leal."'

Amy saw him start up. What, did he think of her? Oh, what! He stepped towards them. The silly girls cowered as if they had roused a lion. His voice was not loud– it was almost as gentle as usual; but it quivered, as if it was hard to keep it so, and, as well as she could see, his face was rigid and stern as iron. 'Did you wish it?' he said, addressing himself to her, as if she was the only person present.

Her breath was almost gone. 'Oh! I beg your pardon,' she faltered. She could not exculpate herself, she saw it looked like an idle, almost like an indecorous trick, unkind, everything abhorrent to her and to him, especially in the present state of things. His eyes were on her, his head bent towards her; he waited for an answer. 'I beg your pardon,' was all she could say.

There was– yes, there was– one of those fearful flashes of his kindling eye. She felt as if she was shrinking to nothing; she heard him say, in a low, hoarse tone, 'I am afraid I cannot;' then Mr. Ross, Mary, lights came in; there was a bustle and confusion, and when next she was clearly conscious, Laura was ordering the carriage.

When it came, there was an inquiry for Sir Guy.

'He is gone home,' said Mr. Ross. 'I met him in the passage, and wished him good night.'

Mr. Ross did not add what he afterwards told his daughter, that Guy seemed not to know whether it was raining or not; that he had put an umbrella into his hand, and seen him march off at full speed, through the pouring rain, with it under his arm.

The ladies entered the carriage. Amy leant back in her corner, Laura forbore to scold either Eveleen or Charlotte till she could have them separately; Eveleen was silent, because she was dismayed at the effect she had produced, and Charlotte, because she knew there was a scolding impending over her.

They found no one in the drawing-room but Mr. Edmonstone and Charles, who said they had heard the door open, and Guy run up-stairs, but they supposed he was wet through, as he had not made his appearance. It was very inhospitable in the girls not to have made room for him in the carriage.

Amy went to see how her mother was, longing to tell her whole trouble, but found her asleep, and was obliged to leave it till the morrow. Poor child, she slept very little, but she would not go to her mother before breakfast, lest she should provoke the headache into staying another day. Guy was going by the train at twelve o'clock, and she was resolved that something should be done; so, as soon as her father had wished Guy goodbye, and ridden off to his justice meeting, she entreated her mother to come into the dressing-room, and hear what she had to say.

'Oh, mamma! the most dreadful thing has happened!' and, hiding her face, she told her story, ending with a burst of weeping as she said how Guy was displeased. 'And well he might be! That after all that has vexed him this week, I should tease him with such a trick. Oh, mamma, what must he think?'

'My dear, there was a good deal of silliness; but you need not treat it as if it was so very shocking.'

'Oh, but it hurt him! He was angry, and now I know how it is, he is angry with himself for being angry. Oh, how foolish I have been! What shall I do?'

'Perhaps we can let him know it was not your fault,' said Mrs. Edmonstone, thinking it might be very salutary for Charlotte to send her to confess.

'Do you think so?' cried Amy, eagerly. 'Oh! that would make it all comfortable. Only it was partly mine, for not keeping Charlotte in better order, and we must not throw it all on her and Eveleen. You think we may tell him?'

'I think he ought not to be allowed to fancy you let your name be so used.'

A message came for Mrs. Edmonstone, and while she was attending to it, Amy hastened away, fully believing that her mother had authorized her to go and explain it to Guy, and ask his pardon. It was what she thought the natural thing to do, and she was soon by his side, as she saw him pacing, with folded arms, under the wall.

Much had lately been passing in Guy's mind. He had gone on floating on the sunny stream of life at Hollywell, too happy to observe its especial charm till the change in Amy's manner cast a sudden gloom over all. Not till then did he understand his own feelings, and recognize in her the being he had dreamt of. Amy was what made Hollywell precious to him. Sternly as he was wont to treat his impulses, he did not look on his affection as an earthborn fancy, liable to draw him from higher things, and, therefore, to be combated; he deemed her rather a guide and guard whose love might arm him, soothe him, and encourage him. Yet he had little hope, for he did not do justice to his powers of inspiring affection; no one could distrust his temper and his character as much as he did himself, and with his ancestry and the doom he believed attached to his race, with his own youth and untried principles, with his undesirable connections, and the reserve he was obliged to exercise regarding them, he considered himself as objectionable a person as could well be found, as yet untouched by any positive crime, and he respected the Edmonstones too much to suppose that these disadvantages could be counterbalanced for a moment by his position; indeed, he interpreted Amy's coolness by supposing that there was a desire to discourage his attentions. No poor tutor or penniless cousin ever felt he was doing a more desperate thing in confessing an attachment, than did Sir Guy Morville when he determined that all should be told, at the risk of losing her for ever, and closing against himself the doors of his happy home. It was not right and fair by her parents, he thought, so to regard their daughter, and live in the same house with his sentiments unavowed, and as to Amy herself, if his feelings had reached such a pitch of sensitiveness that he must needs behave like an angry lion, because her name had been dragged into an idle joke, it was high time it should be explained, unpropitious as the moment might be for declaring his attachment, when he had manifested such a temper as any woman might dread. Thus he made up his mind that, come of it what might, he would not leave Hollywell that day till the truth was told. Just as he was turning to find Mrs. Edmonstone and 'put his fate to the touch,' a little figure stood beside him, and Amy's own sweet, low tones were saying, imploringly,–

'Guy, I wanted to tell you how sorry I am you were so teased last night.'

'Don't think of it!' said he, taken extremely by surprise

'It was our fault, I could not stop it; I should have kept Charlotte in better order, but they would not let her hear me. I knew it was what you dislike particularly, and I was very sorry.'

'You– I was– I was. But no matter now. Amy,' he added earnestly, 'may I ask you to walk on with me a little way? I must say something to you.'

Was this what 'mamma' objected to? Oh no! Amy felt she must stay now, and, in truth, she was glad it was right, though her heart beat fast, fast, faster, as Guy, pulling down a long, trailing branch of Noisette rose, and twisting it in his hand, paused for a few moments, then spoke collectedly, and without hesitation, though with the tremulousness of subdued agitation, looking the while not at her, but straight before him.

'You ought to be told why your words and looks have such effect on me as to make me behave as I did last night. Shame on me for such conduct! I know its evil, and how preposterous it must make what I have to tell you. I don't know now long it has been, but almost ever since I came here, a feeling has been growing up in me towards you, such as I can never have for any one else.'

The flame rushed into Amy's cheeks, and no one could have told what she felt, as he paused again, and then went on speaking more quickly, as if his emotion was less under control.

'If ever there is to be happiness for me on earth, it must be through you; as you, for the last three years, have been all my brightness here. What I feel for you is beyond all power of telling you, Amy! But I know full well all there is against me— I know I am untried, and how can I dare to ask one born to brightness and happiness to share the doom of my family?'

Amy's impulse was that anything shared with him would be welcome; but the strength of the feeling stifled the power of expression, and she could not utter a word.

'It seems selfish even to dream of it,' he proceeded, 'yet I must,— I cannot help it. To feel that I had your love to keep me safe, to know that you watched for me, prayed for me, were my own, my Verena,— oh Amy! it would be more joy than I have ever dared to hope for. But mind,' he added, after another brief pause, 'I would not even ask you to answer me now, far less to bind yourself, even if— if it were possible. I know my trial is not come; and were I to render myself, by positive act, unworthy even to think of you, it would be too dreadful to have entangled you, and made you unhappy. No. I speak now, because I ought not to remain here with such feelings unknown to your father and mother.'

At that moment, close on the other side of the box-tree clump, were heard the wheels of Charles's garden-chair, and Charlotte's voice talking to him, as he made his morning tour round the garden. Amy flew off, like a little bird to its nest, and never stopped till, breathless and crimson, she darted into the dressing room, threw herself on her knees, and with her face hidden in her mother's lap, exclaimed in panting, half-smothered, whispers, which needed all Mrs. Edmonstone's intuition to make them intelligible,—

'O mamma, mamma, he says— he says he loves me!'

Perhaps Mrs. Edmonstone was not so very much surprised; but she had no time to do more than raise and kiss the burning face, and see, at a moment's glance, how bright was the gleam of frightened joy, in the downcast eye and troubled smile; when two knocks, given rapidly, were heard, and almost at the same moment the door opened, and Guy stood before her, his face no less glowing than that which Amy buried again on her mother's knee.

'Come in, Guy,' said Mrs. Edmonstone, as he stood doubtful for a moment at the door, and there was a sweet smile of proud, joyful affection on her face, conveying even more encouragement than her tone. Amy raised her head, and moved as if to leave the room.

'Don't go,' he said, earnestly, 'unless you wish it.'

Amy did not wish it, especially now that she had her mother to save her confusion, and she sat on a footstool, holding her mother's hand, looking up to Guy, whenever she felt bold enough, and hanging down her head when he said what showed how much more highly he prized her than silly little Amy could deserve.

'You know what I am come to say,' he began, standing by the mantel-shelf, as was his wont in his conferences with Mrs. Edmonstone; and he repeated the same in substance as he had said to Amy in the garden, though with less calmness and coherence, and far more warmth of expression, as if, now that she was protected by her mother's presence, he exercised less force in self-restraint.

Never was anyone happier than was Mrs. Edmonstone; loving Guy so heartily, seeing the beauty of his character in each word, rejoicing that such affection should be bestowed on her little Amy, exulting in her having won such a heart, and touched and gratified by the free confidence with which both had at once hastened to pour out all to her, not merely as a duty, but in the full ebullition of their warm young love. The only difficulty was to bring herself to speak with prudence becoming her position, whilst she was sympathizing with them as ardently as if she was not older than both of them put together. When Guy spoke of himself as unproved, and undeserving of trust, it was all she could do to keep from declaring there was no one whom she thought so safe.

'While you go on as you have begun, Guy?'

'If you tell me to hope! Oh, Mrs. Edmonstone, is it wrong that an earthly incentive to persevere should have power which sometimes seems greater than the true one?'

'There is the best and strongest ground of all for trusting you,' said she. 'If you spoke keeping right only for Amy's sake, then I might fear; but when she is second, there is confidence indeed.'

'If speaking were all!' said Guy.

'There is one thing I ought to say,' she proceeded; 'you know you are very young, and though— though I don't know that I can say so in my own person, a prudent woman would say, that you have seen so little of the world, that you may easily meet a person you would like better than such a quiet little dull thing as your guardian's daughter.'

The look that he cast on Amy was worth seeing, and then, with a smile, he answered—

'I am glad you don't say it in your own person.'

'It is very bold and presumptuous in me to say anything at all in papa's absence' said Mrs. Edmonstone, smiling; 'but I am sure he will think in the same way, that things ought to remain as they are, and that it is our duty not to allow you to be, or to feel otherwise than entirely at liberty.'

'I dare say it may be right in you,' said Guy, grudgingly. 'However, I must not complain. It is too much that you should not reject me altogether.'

To all three that space was as bright a gleam of sunshine as ever embellished life, so short as to be free from a single care, a perfectly serenely happy present, the more joyous from having been preceded by vexations, each of the two young things learning that there was love where it was most precious. Guy especially, isolated and lonely as he stood in life, with his fear and mistrust of himself, was now not only allowed to love, and assured beyond his hopes that Amy returned his affection, but found himself thus welcomed by the mother, and gathered into the family where his warm feelings had taken up their abode, while he believed himself regarded only as a guest and a stranger.

They talked on, with happy silences between, Guy standing all the time with his branch of roses in his hand, and Amy looking up to him, and trying to realize it, and to understand why she was so very, very happy.

No one thought of time till Charlotte rushed in like a whirlwind, crying–

'Oh, here you are! We could not think what had become of you. There has Deloraine been at the door these ten minutes, and Charlie sent me to find you, for he says if you are too late for Mrs. Henley's dinner, she will write such an account of you to Philip as you will never get over.'

Very little of this was heard, there was only the instinctive consternation of being too late. They started up, Guy threw down his roses, caught Amy's hand and pressed it, while she bent down her head, hiding the renewed blush; he dashed out of the room, and up to his own, while Mrs. Edmonstone and Charlotte hurried down. In another second, he was back again, and once more Amy felt the pressure of his hand on hers–

'Good-bye!' he said; and she whispered another 'Good-bye!' the only words she had spoken.

One moment more he lingered,–

'My Verena!' said he; but the hurrying sounds in the hall warned him– he sprang down to the drawing-room. Even Charles was on the alert, standing, leaning against the table, and looking eager; but Guy had not time to let him speak, he only shook hands, and wished good-bye, with a sort of vehement agitated cordiality, concealed by his haste.

'Where's Amy?' cried Charlotte. 'Amy! Is not she coming to wish him good-bye?'

He said something, of which 'up-stairs' was the only audible word; held Mrs. Edmonstone's hand fast, while she said, in a low voice– 'You shall hear from papa to-morrow,' then sprung on his horse, and looked up. Amy was at the window, he saw her head bending forward, under its veil of curls, in the midst of the roses round the lattice; their eyes met once more, he gave one beamy smile, then rode off at full speed, with Bustle racing after him, while Amy threw herself on her knees by her bed, and with hands clasped over her face, prayed that she might be thankful enough, and never be unworthy of him.

Every one wanted to get rid of every one else except Mrs. Edmonstone; for all but Charlotte guessed at the state of the case, and even she perceived that something was going on. Lady Eveleen was in a state of great curiosity; but she had mercy, she knew that they must tell each other before it came to her turn, and very good-naturedly she invited Charlotte to come into the garden with her, and kept her out of the way by a full account of her last fancy ball, given with so much spirit and humour that Charlotte could not help attending.

Charles and Laura gained little by this kind manoeuvre, for their mother was gone up again to Amy, and they could only make a few conjectures. Charles nursed his right hand, and asked Laura how hers felt? She looked up from her work, to which she had begun to apply herself diligently, and gazed at him inquiringly, as if to see whether he intended anything.

'For my part,' he added, 'I certainly thought he meant to carry off the hands of some of the family.'

'I suppose we shall soon hear it explained,' said Laura, quietly.

'Soon! If I had an many available legs as you, would I wait for other people's soon?'

'I should think she had rather be left to mamma,' said Laura, going on with her work.

'Then you do think there is something in it?' said Charles, peering up in her face; but he saw he was teasing her, recollected that she had long seemed out of spirits, and forbore to say any more. He was, however, too impatient to remain longer quiet, and presently Laura saw him adjusting his crutches.

'O Charlie! I am sure it will only be troublesome.'

'I am going to my own room,' said Charles, hopping off. 'I presume you don't wish to forbid that.'

His room had a door into the dressing-room, so that it was an excellent place for discovering all from which they did not wish to exclude him, and he did not believe he should be unwelcome; for though he might pretend it was all fun and curiosity, he heartily loved his little Amy.

The tap of his crutches, and the slow motion with which he raised himself from step to step, was heard, and Amy, who was leaning against her mother, started up, exclaiming—

'O mamma, here comes Charlie! May I tell him? I am sure I can't meet him without.'

'I suspect he has guessed it already,' said Mrs. Edmonstone, going to open the door, just as he reached the head of the stairs, and then leaving them.

'Well, Amy,' said he, looking full at her carnation cheeks, 'are you prepared to see me turn lead-coloured, and fall into convulsions, like the sister with the spine complaint?'

'O Charlie! You know it. But how?'

Amy was helping him to the sofa, laid him down, and sat by him on the old footstool; he put his arm round her neck, and she rested her head on his shoulder.

'Well, Amy,' I give you joy, my small woman,' said he, talking the more nonsense because of the fullness in his throat; 'and I hope you give me credit for amazing self-denial in so doing.'

'O Charlie— dear Charlie!' and she kissed him, she could not blush more, poor little thing, for she had already reached her utmost capability of redness— 'it is no such thing.'

'No such thing? What has turned you into a turkey-cock all at once or what made him nearly squeeze off my unfortunate fingers? No such thing, indeed!'

'I mean— I mean, it is not that. We are so very young, and I am so silly.'

'Is that his reason?'

'You must make me so much better and wiser. Oh, if I could but be good enough!'

For that matter, I don't think any one else would be good enough to take care of such a silly little thing. But what is the that, that it is, or is not?'

'Nothing now, only when we are older. At least, you know papa has not heard it.'

'Provided my father gives his consent, as the Irish young lady added to all her responses through the marriage service. But tell me all— all you like, I mean— for you will have lovers' secrets now, Amy.'

Mrs. Edmonstone had, meantime, gone down to Laura. Poor Laura, as soon as her brother had left the room, she allowed the fixed composure of her face to relax into a restless, harassed, almost miserable expression, and walked up and down with agitated steps.

'O wealth, wealth!'— her lips formed the words, without uttering them— 'what cruel differences it makes! All smooth here! Young, not to be trusted, with strange reserves, discreditable connections,— that family,— that fearful temper, showing itself even to her! All will be overlooked! Papa will be delighted, I know he will! And how is it with us? Proved, noble, superior, owned as such by all, as Philip is, yet, for that want of hateful money, he would be spurned. And, for this— for this— the love that has grown up with our lives must be crushed down and hidden— our life is wearing out in wearying self-watching!'

The lock of the door turned, and Laura had resumed her ordinary expression before it opened, and her mother came in: but there was anything but calmness beneath, for the pang of self-reproach had come– 'Was it thus that she prepared to hear these tidings of her sister?'

'Well, Laura,' began Mrs. Edmonstone, with the eager smile of one bringing delightful news, and sure of sympathy.

'It is so, then?' said Laura. 'Dear, dear, little Amy! I hope– ' and her eyes filled with tears; but she had learnt to dread any outbreak of feeling, conquered it in a minute, and said–

'What has happened? How does it stand?'

'It stands, at least as far as I can say without papa, as the dear Guy very rightly and wisely wished it to stand. There is no positive engagement, they are both too young; but he thought it was not right to remain here without letting us know his sentiments towards her.'

A pang shot through Laura; but it was but for a moment. Guy might doubt where Philip need never do so. Her mother went on,–

'Their frankness and confidence are most beautiful. We know dear little Amy could not help it; but there was something very sweet, very noble, in his way of telling all.'

Another pang for Laura. But no! it was only poverty that was to blame. Philip would speak as plainly if his prospects were as fair.

'Oh, I hope it will do well,' said she.

'It must,– it will!' cried Mrs. Edmonstone, giving way to her joyful enthusiasm of affection. 'It is nonsense to doubt, knowing him as we do. There is not a man in the world with whom I could be so happy to trust her.'

Laura could not hear Guy set above all men in the world, and she remembered Philip's warning to her, two years ago.

'There is much that is very good and very delightful about him,' she said, hesitatingly.

'You are thinking of the Morville temper,' said her mother; 'but I am not afraid of it. A naturally hot temper, controlled like his by strong religious principle, is far safer than a cool easy one, without the principle.'

Laura thought this going too far, but she felt some compensation due to Guy, and acknowledged how strongly he was actuated by principle. However– and it was well for her– they could not talk long, for Eveleen and Charlotte were approaching, and she hastily asked what was to be done about telling Eva, who could not fail to guess something.

'We must tell her, and make her promise absolute secrecy,' said Mrs. Edmonstone. 'I will speak to her myself; but I must wait till I have seen papa. There is no doubt of what he will say, but we have been taking quite liberties enough in his absence.'

Laura did not see her sister till luncheon, when Amy came down, with a glow on her cheeks that made her so much prettier than usual, that Charles wished Guy could have seen her. She said little, and ran up again as soon as she could. Laura followed her; and the two sisters threw their arms fondly round each other, and kissed repeatedly.

'Mamma has told you? said Amy. 'Oh, it has made me so very happy; and every one is so kind.'

'Dear, dear Amy!'

'I'm only afraid– '

'He has begun so well– '

'Oh, nonsense! You cannot think I could be so foolish as to be afraid for him! Oh no! But if he should take me for more than I am worth. O Laura, Laura! What shall I do to be as good and sensible as you! I must not be silly little Amy any more.'

'Perhaps he likes you best as you are?'

'I don't mean cleverness: I can't help that,– and he knows how stupid I am,– but I am afraid he thinks there is more worth in me. Don't you know, he has a sort of sunshine in his eyes and mind, that makes all he cares about seem to him brighter and better than it really is. I am afraid he is only dressing me up with that sunshine.'

'It must be strange sunshine that you want to make you better and brighter than you are,' said Laura, kissing her.

'I'll tell you what it is,' said Amy folding her hands, and standing with her face raised, 'it won't do now, as you told me once, to have no bones in my character. I must learn to be steady and strong, if I can; for if this is to be, he will depend on me, I don't mean, to advise him, for he knows better than anybody, but to be– you know what– if vexation, or trouble was to come! And Laura, think if he was to depend on me, and I was to fail! Oh, do help me to have firmness and self-command, like you!'

'It was a long time ago that we talked of your wanting bones.'

'Yes, before he came; but I never forget it.'

Laura was obliged to go out with Eveleen. All went their different ways; and Amy had the garden to herself to cool her cheeks in. But this was a vain operation, for a fresh access of burning was brought on while Laura was helping her to dress for dinner, when her father's quick step sounded in the passage. He knocked at her door, and as she opened it, he kissed her on each cheek; and throwing his arm round her, exclaimed,–

'Well, Miss Amy, you have made a fine morning's work of it! A pretty thing, for young ladies to be accepting offers while papa is out of the way. Eh, Laura?'

Amy knew this was a manifestation of extreme delight; but it was not very pleasant to Laura.

'So you have made a conquest!' proceeded Mr. Edmonstone; 'and I heartily wish you joy of it, my dear. He is as amiable and good-natured a youth as I would wish to see; and I should say the same if he had not a shilling in the world.'

Laura's heart bounded; but she knew, whatever her father might fancy, the reality would be very different if Guy were as poor as Philip.

'I shall write to him this very evening,' he continued, 'and tell him, if he has the bad taste to like such a silly little white thing, I am not the man to stand in his way. Eh, Amy? Shall I tell him so?'

'Tell him what you please, dear papa.'

'Eh? What I please? Suppose I say we can't spare our little one, and he may go about his business?'

'I'm not afraid of you, papa.'

'Come, she's a good little thing– sha'n't be teased. Eh, Laura? what do you think of it, our beauty, to see your younger sister impertinent enough to set up a lover, while your pink cheeks are left in the lurch?'

Laura not being wont to make playful repartees, her silence passed unnoticed. Her feelings were mixed; but perhaps the predominant one was satisfaction that it was not for her pink cheeks that she was valued.

It had occurred to Mrs. Edmonstone that it was a curious thing, after her attempt at scheming for Eveleen, to have to announce to her that Guy was attached to her own daughter; nay, after the willingness Eveleen had manifested to be gratified with any attention Guy showed her, it seemed doubtful for a moment whether the intelligence would be pleasing to her. However, Eveleen was just the girl to like men better than women, and never to be so happy as when on the verge of flirting; it would probably have been the same with any other youth that came in her, way, and Guy might fully be acquitted of doing more than paying her the civilities which were requisite from him to any young lady visitor. He had, two years ago, when a mere boy, idled, laughed, and made fun with her, but his fear of trifling away his time had made him draw back, before he had involved himself in what might have led to anything further; and during the present visit, no one could doubt that he was preoccupied with Amy. At any rate, it was right that Eveleen should know the truth, in confidence, if only to prevent her from talking of any surmises she might have.

Mrs. Edmonstone was set at ease in a moment. Eveleen was enchanted, danced round and round the room, declared they would be the most charming couple in the world; she had seen it all along; she was so delighted they had come to an understanding at last, poor things, they were so miserable all last week; and she must take credit to herself for having done it all. Was not her aunt very much obliged to her?

'My dear Eva,' exclaimed Mrs. Edmonstone, into whose mind the notion never entered that any one could boast of such a proceeding as hers last night; but the truth was that Eveleen, feeling slightly culpable, was delighted that all had turned out so well, and resolved to carry it off with a high hand.

'To be sure! Poor little Amy! when she looked ready to sink into the earth, she little knew her obligations to me! Was not it the cleverest thing in the world? It was just the touch they wanted– the very thing!'

'My dear, I am glad I know that you are sometimes given to talking nonsense,' said Mrs. Edmonstone, laughing.

'And you won't believe me serious? You won't be grateful to me for my lucky hit' said Eveleen, looking comically injured. 'Oh auntie, that is very hard, when I shall believe to my dying day that I did it!'

'Why, Eva, if I thought it had been done by design, I should find it very hard to forgive you for it at all, rather hard even to accept Guy, so you had better not try to disturb my belief that it was only that spirit of mischief that makes you now and then a little mad.'

'Oh dear! what a desperate scolding you must have given poor little Charlotte!' exclaimed Eveleen, quaintly.

Mrs. Edmonstone could not help laughing as she confessed that she had altogether forgotten Charlotte.

'Then you will. You'll go on forgetting her,' cried Eveleen. 'She only did what she was told, and did not know the malice of it. There, you're relenting! There's a good aunt! And now, if you won't be grateful, as any other mamma in the world would have been, and as I calculated on, when I pretended to have been a prudent, designing woman, instead of a wild mischievous monkey at least you'll forgive me enough to invite me to the wedding. Oh! what a beauty of a wedding it will be! I'd come from Kilcoran all the way on my bare knees to see it. And you'll let me be bridesmaid, and have a ball after it?'

'There is no saying what I may do, if you'll only be a good girl, and hold your tongue. I don't want to prevent your telling anything to your mamma, of course, but pray don't let it go any further. Don't let Maurice hear it, I have especial reasons for wishing it should not be known. You know it is not even an engagement, and nothing must be done which can make Guy feel in the least bound?'

Eveleen promised, and Mrs. Edmonstone knew that she had sense and proper feeling enough for her promise to deserve trust.

CHAPTER 14

For falsehood now doth flow,
And subject faith doth ebbe,
Which would not be, if reason ruled,
Or wisdom weav'd the webbe.

The daughter of debate,
That eke discord doth sowe,
Shal reape no gaine where former rule
Hath taught stil peace to growe.
– QUEEN ELIZABETH

'ATHENAEUM TERRACE,
ST MILDRED'S,
August 4th,

'MY DEAR PHILIP,– Thank you for returning the books, which were brought safely by Sir Guy. I am sorry you do not agree in my estimate of them. I should have thought your strong sense would have made you perceive that reasoning upon fact, and granting nothing without tangible proof, were the best remedy for a dreamy romantic tendency to the weakness and credulity which are in the present day termed poetry and faith. It is curious to observe how these vague theories reduce themselves to the absurd when brought into practice. There are two Miss Wellwoods here, daughters of that unfortunate man who fell in a duel with old Sir Guy Morville, who seem to make it their business to become the general subject of animadversion, taking pauper children into their house, where they educate them in a way to unfit them for their station, and teach them to observe a sort of monastic rule, preaching the poor people in the hospital to death, visiting the poor at all sorts of strange hours. Dr Henley actually found one of them, at twelve o'clock at night, in a miserable lodging-house, filled with the worst description of inmates. Quite young women, too, and with no mother or elder person to direct them; but it is the fashion among the attendants at the new chapel to admire them. This subject has diverted me from what I intended to say with respect to the young baronet. Your description agrees with all I have hitherto seen, though I own I expected a Redclyffe Morville to have more of the "heros de roman", or rather of the grand tragic cast of figure, as, if I remember right, was the case with this youth's father, a much finer and handsomer young man. Sir Guy is certainly gentlemanlike, and has that sort of agreeability which depends on high animal spirits. I should think him clever, but superficial; and with his mania for music, he can hardly fail to be merely an accomplished man. In spite of all you said of the Redclyffe temper, I was hardly prepared to find it so ready to flash forth on the most inexplicable provocations. It is like walking on a volcano. I have seen him two or three times draw himself up, bite his lip, and answer with an effort and a sharpness that shows how thin a crust covers the burning lava; but I acknowledge that he has been very civil and attentive, and speaks most properly of what he owes to you. I only hope he will not be hurt by the possession of so large a property so early in life, and I have an idea that our good aunt at Hollywell has done a good deal to raise his opinion of himself. We shall, of course, show him every civility in our power, and give him the advantage of intellectual society at our house. His letters are directed to this place, as you know South Moor Farm is out of the cognizance of the post. They seem to keep up a brisk correspondence with him from Hollywell. Few guardians' letters are, I should guess, honoured with such deepening colour as his while reading one from my uncle. He tells me he has been calling at Stylehurst; it is a pity, for his sake, that Colonel Harewood is at home, for the society of those sons is by no means advisable for him. I can hardly expect to offer him what is likely to be as agreeable to him as the conversation and amusements of Edward and Tom Harewood, who are sure to be at home for the St. Mildred's races. I hear Tom has been getting into fresh scrapes at Cambridge.

'Your affectionate sister,

'MARGARET HENLEY.'

'ATHENAEUM TERRACE.
ST. MILDRED'S,

Sept. 6th.

'MY DEAR PHILIP,— No one can have a greater dislike than myself to what is called mischief-making; therefore I leave it entirely to you to make what use you please of the following facts, which have fallen under my notice. Sir Guy Morville has been several times at St. Mildred's, in company with Tom Harewood, and more than once alone with some strange questionable-looking people; and not many days ago, my maid met him coming out of a house in one of the low streets, which it is hard to assign a motive for his visiting. This, however, might be accident, and I should never have thought of mentioning it, but for a circumstance that occurred this morning. I had occasion to visit Grey's Bank, and while waiting in conversation with Mr. Grey, a person came in whom I knew to be a notorious gambler, and offered a cheque to be changed. As it lay on the counter, my eye was caught by the signature. It was my uncle's. I looked again, and could not be mistaken. It was a draft for £30 on Drummond, dated the 12th of August, to Sir Guy Morville, signed C. Edmonstone, and endorsed in Sir Guy's own writing, with the name of John White. In order that I might be certain that I was doing the poor young man no injustice, I outstayed the man, and asked who he was, when Mr. Grey confirmed me in my belief that it was one Jack White, a jockeying sort of man who attends all the races in the country, and makes his livelihood by betting and gambling. And now, my dear brother, make what use of this fact you think fit, though I fear there is little hope of rescuing the poor youth from the fatal habits which are hereditary in his family, and must be strong indeed not to have been eradicated by such careful training as you say he has received. I leave it entirely to you, trusting in your excellent judgment, and only hoping you will not bring my name forward. Grieving much at having to be the first to communicate such unpleasant tidings, which will occasion so much vexation at Hollywell.'

'Your affectionate sister,
'MARGARET HENLEY.'

Captain Morville was alone when he received the latter of these letters. At first, a look divided between irony and melancholy passed over his face, as he read his sister's preface and her hearsay evidence, but, as he went farther, his upper lip curled, and a sudden gleam, as of exultation in a verified prophecy, lighted his eye, shading off quickly, however, and giving place to an iron expression of rigidity and sternness, the compressed mouth, coldly-fixed eye, and sedate brow, composed into a grave severity that might have served for an impersonation of stern justice. He looked through the letter a second time, folded it up, put it in his pocket, and went about his usual affairs; but the expression did not leave his face all day; and the next morning he took a day-ticket by the railway to Broadstone, where, as it was the day of the petty sessions, he had little doubt of meeting Mr. Edmonstone. Accordingly, he had not walked far down the High Street, before he saw his uncle standing on the step of the post-office, opening a letter he had just received.

'Ha! Philip, what brings you here? The very man I wanted. Coming to Hollywell?'

'No, thank you, I go back this evening,' said Philip, and, as he spoke, he saw that the letter which Mr. Edmonstone held, and twisted with a hasty, nervous movement, was in Guy's writing.

'Well, I am glad you are here, at any rate. Here is the most extraordinary thing! What possesses the boy I cannot guess. Here's Guy writing to me for– What do you think? To send him a thousand pounds!'

'Hem!' said Philip in an expressive tone; yet, as if he was not very much amazed; 'no explanation, I suppose?'

'No, none at all. Here, see what he says yourself. No! Yes, you may,' added Mr. Edmonstone, with a rapid glance at the end of the letter,– a movement, first to retain it, and then following his first impulse, with an unintelligible murmuring.

Philip read,–

'SOUTH MOOR, SEPT. 7th.

'MY DEAR MR. EDMONSTONE,– You will be surprised at the request I have to make you, after my resolution not to exceed my allowance. However, this is not for my own expenses, and it will not occur again. I should be much obliged to you to let me have £1000, in what manner you please, only I should be glad if it were soon. I am sorry I am not at liberty to tell you what I want it for, but I trust to your kindness. Tell Charlie I will write to him in a day or two, but, between our work, and walking to St. Mildred's for the letters, which we cannot help doing every day, the time for writing is short. Another month, however, and what a holiday it will be! Tell Amy she ought to be here to see the purple of the hills in the early morning; it almost makes up for having no sea. The races have been making St. Mildred's very gay; indeed, we laugh at Wellwood for having brought us here, by way of a quiet place. I never was in the way of so much dissipation in my life.

'Yours very affectionately,
'GUY MORVILLE.'

'Well, what do you think of it? What would you do in my place– eh, Philip! What can he want of it, eh?' said Mr. Edmonstone, tormenting his riding-whip, and looking up to study his nephew's face, which, with stern gravity in every feature, was bent over the letter, as if to weigh every line. 'Eh, Philip?' repeated Mr. Edmonstone, several times, without obtaining an answer.

'This is no place for discussion,' at last said Philip, deliberately returning the letter. 'Come into the reading-room. We shall find no one there at this hour. Here we are.'

'Well– well– well,' began Mr. Edmonstone, fretted by his coolness to the extreme of impatience, 'what do you think of it? He can't be after any mischief; 'tis not in the boy; when– when he is all but– Pooh! what am I saying? Well, what do you think?'

'I am afraid it confirms but too strongly a report which I received yesterday.'

'From your sister? Does she know anything about it?'

'Yes, from my sister. But I was very unwilling to mention it, because she particularly requests that her name may not be used. I came here to see whether you had heard of Guy lately, so as to judge whether it was needful to speak of it. This convinces me; but I must beg, in the first instance, that you will not mention her, not even to my aunt.'

'Well, yes; very well. I promise. Only let me hear.'

'Young Harewood has, I fear, led him into bad company. There can now be no doubt that he has been gambling.'

Philip was not prepared for the effect of these words. His uncle started up, exclaiming– 'Gambling! Impossible! Some confounded slander! I don't believe one word of it! I won't hear such things said of him,' he repeated, stammering with passion, and walking violently about the room. This did not last long; there was something in the unmoved way in which Philip waited till he had patience to listen, which gradually mastered him; his angry manner subsided, and, sitting down, he continued the argument, in a would-be-composed voice.

'It is utterly impossible! Remember, he thinks himself bound not so much as to touch a billiard cue.'

'I could have thought it impossible, but for what I have seen of the way in which promises are eluded by persons too strictly bound,' said Philip. 'The moral force of principle is the only efficient pledge.'

'Principle! I should like to see who has better principles than Guy!' cried Mr. Edmonstone. 'You have said so yourself, fifty times, and your aunt has said so, and Charles. I could as soon suspect myself.' He was growing vehement, but again Philip's imperturbability repressed his violence, and he asked, 'Well, what evidence have you? Mind, I am not going to believe it without the strongest. I don't know that I would believe my own eyes against him.'

'It is very sad to find such confidence misplaced,' said Philip. 'Most sincerely do I wish this could be proved to be a mistake; but this extraordinary request corroborates my sister's letter too fully.'

'Let me hear,' said Mr. Edmonstone feebly. Philip produced his letter, without reading the whole of it; for he could not bear the appearance of gossip and prying, and would not expose his sister; so he pieced it out with his own words, and made it sound far less discreditable to her. It was quite enough for Mr. Edmonstone; the accuracy of the details seemed to strike him dumb; and there was a long silence, which he broke by saying, with a deep sigh,–

'Who could have thought it? Poor little Amy!'

'Amy?' exclaimed Philip.

'Why, ay. I did not mean to have said anything of it, I am sure; but they did it among them,' said Mr. Edmonstone, growing ashamed, under Philip's eye, as of a dreadful piece of imprudence. 'I was out of the way at the time, but I could not refuse my consent, you know, as things stood then.'

'Do you mean to say that Amy is engaged to him?'

'Why, no– not exactly engaged, only on trial, you understand, to see if he will be steady. I was at Broadstone; 'twas mamma settled it all. Poor little thing, she is very much in love with him, I do believe, but there's an end of everything now.'

'It is very fortunate this has been discovered in time,' said Philip. 'Instead of pitying her, I should rejoice in her escape.'

'Yes,' said Mr. Edmonstone, ruefully. 'Who could have thought it?'

'I am afraid the mischief is of long standing,' proceeded Philip, resolved, since he saw his uncle so grieved, to press him strongly, thinking that to save Amy from such a marriage was an additional motive. 'He could hardly have arrived at losing as much as a thousand pounds, all at once, in this month at St. Mildred's. Depend upon it, that painful as it may be at present, there is great reason, on her account, to rejoice in the discovery. You say he has never before applied, to you for money?'

'Not a farthing beyond his allowance, except this unlucky thirty pounds, for his additional expense of the tutor and the lodging.'

'You remember, however, that he has always seemed short of money, never appeared able to afford himself any little extra expense. You have noticed it, I know. You remember, too, how unsatisfactory his reserve about his proceedings in London has been, and how he has persisted in delaying there, in spite of all warnings. The work, no doubt, began there, under the guidance of his uncle; and now the St. Mildred's races and Tom Harewood have continued it.'

'I wish he had never set foot in the place!'

'Nay; for Amy's sake, the exposure is an advantage, if not for his own. The course must have been long since begun; but he contrived to avoid what could lead to inquiry, till he has at length involved himself in some desperate scrape. You see, he especially desires to have the money soon, and he never even attempts to say you would approve of the object.

'Yes; he has the grace not to say that.'

'Altogether, it is worse than I could have thought possible,' said Philip. I could have believed him unstable and thoughtless; but the concealment, and the attempting to gain poor Amy's affections in the midst of such a course—'

'Ay, ay!' cried Mr. Edmonstone, now fully provoked; 'there is the monstrous part. He thought I was going to give up my poor little girl to a gambler, did he? but he shall soon see what I think of him,— riches, Redclyffe, title, and all!'

'I knew that would be your feeling.'

'Feel! Yes; and he shall feel it, too. So, Sir Guy, you thought you had an old fool of a guardian, did you, whom you could blind as you pleased? but you shall soon see the difference!'

'Better begin cautiously,' suggested Philip. 'Remember his unfortunate temper, and write coolly.'

'Coolly? You may talk of coolness; but 'tis enough to make one's blood boil to be served in such a way. With the face to be sending her messages in the very same letter! That is a pass beyond me, to stand coolly to see my daughter so treated.'

'I would only give him the opportunity of saying what he can for himself. He may have some explanation.'

'I'll admit of no explanation! Passing himself off for steadiness itself; daring to think of my daughter, and all the time going on in this fashion! I hate underhand ways! I'll have no explanation. He may give up all thoughts of her. I'll write and tell him so before I'm a day older; nay, before I stir from this room. My little Amy, indeed!'

Philip put no obstacles in the way of this proposal, for he knew that his uncle's displeasure, though hot at first, was apt to evaporate in exclamations; and he thought it likely that his good nature, his partiality for his ward, his dislike to causing pain to his daughter, and, above all, his wife's blind confidence in Guy, would, when once at home, so overpower his present indignation as to prevent the salutary strictness which was the only hope of reclaiming Guy. Beside, a letter written under Philip's inspection was likely to be more guarded, as well as more forcible, than an unassisted composition of his own, as was, indeed, pretty well proved by the commencement of his first attempt.

'My dear Guy,— I am more surprised than I could have expected at your application.'

Philip read this aloud, so as to mark its absurdity, and he began again.

'I am greatly astonished, as well as concerned, at your application, which confirms the unpleasant reports— '

'Why say anything of reports?' said Philip. 'Reports are nothing. A man is not forced to defend himself from reports.'

'Yes,— hum— ha,— the accounts I have received. No. You say there is not to be a word of Mrs. Henley.'

'Not a word that can lead her to be suspected.'

'Confirms– confirms– ' sighed Mr. Edmonstone.

'Don't write as if you went on hearsay evidence. Speak of proofs– irrefragable proofs– and then you convict him at once, without power of eluding you.'

So Mr. Edmonstone proceeded to write, that the application confirmed the irrefragable proofs, then laughed at himself, and helplessly begged Philip to give him a start. It now stood thus:–

'Your letter of this morning has caused me more concern than surprise, as it unhappily only adds confirmation to the intelligence already in my possession; that either from want of resolution to withstand the seductions of designing persons, or by the impetuosity and instability of your own character, you have been led into the ruinous and degrading practice of gambling; and that from hence proceed the difficulties that occasion your application to me for money. I am deeply grieved at thus finding that neither the principles which have hitherto seemed to guide you, nor the pledges which you used to hold sacred, nor, I may add, the feelings you have so recently expressed towards a member of my family, have been sufficient to preserve you from yielding to a temptation which could never be presented to the mind of any one whose time was properly occupied in the business of his education.'

'Is that all I am to say about her,' exclaimed Mr. Edmonstone, 'after the atrocious way the fellow has treated her in?'

'Since it is, happily, no engagement, I cannot see how you can, with propriety, assume that it is one, by speaking of breaking it off. Besides, give him no ground for complaint, or he will take refuge in believing himself ill-used. Ask him if he can disprove it, and when he cannot, it will be time enough to act further. But wait– wait, sir,' as the pen was moving over the paper, impatient to dash forward. 'You have not told him yet of what you accuse him.'

Philip meditated a few moments, then produced another sentence.

'I have no means of judging how long you have been following this unhappy course; I had rather believe it is of recent adoption, but I do not know how to reconcile this idea with the magnitude of your demand, unless your downward progress has been more rapid than usual in such beginnings. It would, I fear, be quite vain for me to urge upon you all the arguments and reasons that ought to have been present to your mind, and prevented you from taking the first fatal step. I can only entreat you to pause, and consider the ruin and degradation to which this hateful vice almost invariably conducts its victims, and consistently with my duty as your guardian, everything in my power shall be done to extricate you from the embarrassments in which you have involved yourself. But, in the first place,

I make it a point that you treat me with perfect confidence, and make a full, unequivocal statement of your proceedings; above all, that you explain the circumstances, occasioning your request for this large sum. Remember, I say, complete candour on your part will afford the only means of rescuing you from difficulties, or of in any degree restoring you to my good opinion.'

So far the letter had proceeded slowly, for Philip was careful and deliberate in composition, and while he was weighing his words, Mr. Edmonstone rushed on with something unfit to stand, so as to have to begin over again. At last, the town clock struck five; Philip started, declaring that if he was not at the station in five minutes, he should lose the train; engaged to come to Hollywell on the day an answer might be expected, and hastened away, satisfied by having seen two sheets nearly filled, and having said there was nothing more but to sign, seal, and send it.

Mr. Edmonstone had, however, a page of note-paper more, and it was with a sensation of relief that he wrote,—

'I wish, from the bottom of my heart, that you could clear yourself. If a dozen men had sworn it till they were black in the face, I would not have believed it of you that you could serve us in such a manner, after the way you have been treated at home, and to dare to think of my daughter with such things on your mind. I could never have believed it, but for the proofs Philip has brought; and I am sure he is as sorry as myself. Only tell the whole truth, and I will do my best to get you out of the scrape. Though all else must be at an end between us, I am your guardian still, and I will not be harsh with you.'

He posted his letter, climbed up his tall horse, and rode home, rather heavy-hearted; but his wrath burning out as he left Broadstone behind him. He saw his little Amy gay and lively, and could not bear to sadden her; so he persuaded himself that there was no need to mention the suspicions till he had heard what Guy had to say for himself. Accordingly, he told no one but his wife; and she, who thought Guy as unlikely to gamble as Amy herself, had not the least doubt that he would be able to clear himself, and agreed that it was much better to keep silence for the present.

CHAPTER 15

'Tis not unknown to you, Antonio,
How much I have disabled mine estate,
By something showing a more swelling port
Than my faint means would grant continuance.
— Merchant of Venice

St. Mildred's was a fashionable summer resort, which the virtues of a mineral spring, and the reputation of Dr. Henley, had contributed to raise to a high degree of prosperity. It stood at the foot of a magnificent range of beautifully formed hills, where the crescents and villas, white and smart, showed their own insignificance beneath the purple peaks that rose high above them.

About ten miles distant, across the hills, was Stylehurst, the parish of the late Archdeacon Morville, and the native place of Philip and his sister Margaret. It was an extensive parish, including a wide tract of the hilly country; and in a farm-house in the midst of the moorland, midway between St. Mildred's and the village of Stylehurst, had Mr. Wellwood fixed himself with his three pupils.

Guy's first visit was of course to Mrs. Henley, and she was, on her side, prepared by her brother to patronize him as Philip would have done in her place. Her patronage was valuable in her own circle; her connections were good; the Archdeacon's name was greatly respected; she had a handsome and well-regulated establishment, and this, together with talents which, having no family, she had cultivated more than most women have time to do, made her a person of considerable distinction at St. Mildred's. She was, in fact, the leading lady of the place— the manager of the book-club, in the chair at all the charitable committees, and the principal person in society, giving literary parties, with a degree of exclusiveness that made admission to them a privilege.

She was a very fine woman, handsomer at two-and-thirty than in her early bloom; her height little less than that of her tall brother, and her manner and air had something very distinguished. The first time Guy saw her, he was strongly reminded both of Philip and of Mrs. Edmonstone, but not pleasingly. She seemed to be her aunt, without the softness and motherly affection, coupled with the touch of naivete that gave Mrs. Edmonstone her freshness, and loveableness; and her likeness to her brother included that decided, self-reliant air, which became him well enough, but which did not sit as appropriately on a woman.

Guy soon discovered another resemblance— for the old, unaccountable impatience of Philip's conversation, and relief in escaping from it, haunted him before he had been a quarter of an hour in Mrs. Henley's drawing-room. She asked after the Hollywell party; she had not seen her cousins since her marriage, and happily for his feelings, passed over Laura and Amy as if they were nonentities; but they were all too near his heart for him to be able with patience to hear 'poor Charles's' temper regretted, and still less the half-sarcastic, half-compassionate tone in which she implied that her aunt spoilt him dreadfully, and showed how cheap she hold both Mr. and Mrs. Edmonstone.

Two years ago, Guy could not have kept down his irritation; but now he was master of himself sufficiently to give a calm, courteous reply, so conveying his own respect for them, that Mrs. Henley was almost disconcerted.

Stylehurst had great interest for Guy, both for the sake of Archdeacon Morville's kindness, and as the home which Philip regarded with affection, that seemed the one softening touch in his character. So Guy visited the handsome church, studied the grave-yard, and gathered the traditions of the place from the old sexton's wife, who rejoiced in finding an auditor for her long stories of the good Archdeacon, Miss Fanny, and Mr. Philip. She shook her head, saying times were changed, and 'Miss Morville that was, never came neist the place.'

The squire, Colonel Harewood, was an old friend of his grandfather's, and therefore was to be called on. He had never been wise, and had been dissipated chiefly from vacancy of mind; he was now growing old, and led a quieter life, and though Guy did not find him a very entertaining companion, he accepted, his civilities, readily, for his grandfather's sake. When his sons came home, Guy recognized in them the description of men he was wont to shun at Oxford, as much from distaste as from principle; but though he did not absolutely avoid them, he saw little of them, being very busy, and having pleasant companions in his fellow pupils. It was a very merry party at South Moor, and Guy's high spirits made him the life of everything.

The first time Mr. Wellwood went to call on his cousins at St. Mildred's, the daughters of that officer who had fallen by the hand of old Sir Guy, he began repeating, for the twentieth time, what an excellent fellow Morville was; then said he should not have troubled them with any of his pupils, but Morville would esteem their receiving him as an act of forgiveness, and besides, he wished them to know one whom he valued so highly. Guy thus found himself admitted into an entirely new region. There were two sisters, together in everything. Jane, the younger, was a kind-hearted, commonplace person, who would never have looked beyond the ordinary range of duties and charities; but Elizabeth was one of those who rise up, from time to time, as burning and shining lights. It was not spending a quiet, easy life, making her charities secondary to her comforts, but devoting time, strength, and goods; not merely giving away what she could spare, but actually sharing all with the poor, reserving nothing for the future. She not only taught the young, and visited the distressed, but she gathered orphans into her house, and nursed the sick day and night. Neither the means nor the strength of the two sisters could ever have been supposed equal to what they were known to have achieved. It seemed as if the power grew with the occasion, and as if they had some help which could not fail them. Guy venerated them more and more, and many a long letter about them was written to Mrs. Edmonstone for Amy to read. There is certainly a 'tyrannous hate' in the world for unusual goodness, which is a rebuke to it, and there was a strong party against the sisters. At the head of it was Mrs. Henley, who had originally been displeased at their preferring the direction of the clergyman to that of the ladies' committee, though the secret cause of her dislike was, perhaps, that Elizabeth Wellwood was just what Margaret Morville might have been. So she blamed them, not, indeed for their charity, but for slight peculiarities which might well have been lost in the brightness of the works of mercy. She spoke as with her father's authority, though, if she had been differently disposed, she might have remembered that his system and principles were the same as theirs, and that, had he been alive, he would probably have fully approved of their proceedings. Archdeacon Morville's name was of great weight, and justified many persons, in their own opinion, in the opposition made to Miss Wellwood, impeding her usefulness, and subjecting her to endless petty calumnies.

These made Guy very angry. He knew enough of the Archdeacon through Mrs. Edmonstone, and the opinions held by Philip, to think his daughter was ascribing to him what he had never held but, be that as it might, Guy could not bear to hear good evil spoken of, and his indignation was stirred as he heard these spiteful reports uttered by people who sat at home at ease, against one whose daily life was only too exalted for their imitation. His brow contracted, his eye kindled, his lip was bitten, and now and then, when he trusted himself to reply, it was with a keen, sharp power of rebuke that made people look round, astonished to hear such forcible words from one so young. Mrs. Henley was afraid of him, without knowing it; she thought she was sparing the Morville temper when she avoided the subject, but as she stood in awe of no one else, except her brother, she disliked him accordingly.

One evening Guy had been dining at Dr. Henley's, and was setting out, enjoying his escape from Mrs. Henley and her friends, and rejoicing in the prospect of a five miles' walk over the hills by moonlight. He had only gone the length of two streets, when he saw a dark figure at a little distance from him, and a voice which he had little expected to hear, called out,—

'Sir Guy himself! No one else could whistle that Swedish air so correctly!'

'My uncle!' exclaimed Guy. 'I did not know that you were here!'

Mr. Dixon laughed, said something about a fortunate rencontre, and began an account about a concert somewhere or other, mixed up with something about his wife and child, all so rambling and confused, that Guy, beginning to suspect he had been drinking, was only anxious to get rid of him, asked where he lodged, and talked of coming to see him in the morning. He soon found, however, that this had not been the case, at least not to any great extent. Dixon was only nervous and excited, either about something he had done, or some request he had to make, and he went on walking by his nephew's side, talking in a strange, desultory way of open, generous-hearted fellows overlooking a little indiscretion, and of Guy's riches, which he seemed to think inexhaustible.

'If there is anything that you want me to do for you, tell me plainly what it is,' said Guy, at last.

Mr. Dixon began to overwhelm him with thanks, but he cut them short. 'I promise nothing. Let me hear what you want, and I can judge whether I can do it.'

Sebastian broke out into exclamations at the words 'if I can,' as if he thought everything in the power of the heir of Redclyffe.

'Have I not told you,' said Guy, 'that for the present I have very little command of money? Hush! no more of that,' he added, sternly, cutting off an imprecation which his uncle was commencing on those who kept him so short.

'And you are content to bear it? Did you never hear of ways and means? If you were to say but one word of borrowing, they would go down on their knees to you, and offer you every farthing you have to keep you in their own hands.'

'I am quite satisfied,' said Guy, coldly.

'The greater fool are you!' was on Dixon's lips, but he did not utter it, because he wanted to propitiate him; and after some more circumlocution, Guy succeeded in discovering that he had been gambling, and had lost an amount which, unless he could obtain immediate assistance, would become known, and lead to the loss of his character and situation. Guy stood and considered. He had an impulse, but he did not think it a safe one, and resolved to give himself time.

'I do not say that I cannot help you,' he answered, 'but I must have time to consider.'

'Time! would you see me ruined while you are considering?'

'I suppose this must be paid immediately. Where do you lodge?'

Mr. Dixon told him the street and number.

'You shall hear from me to-morrow morning. I cannot trust my present thoughts. Good night!'

Mr. Dixon would fain have guessed whether the present thoughts were favourable, but all his hope in his extremity was in his nephew; it might be fatal to push him too far, and, with a certain trust in his good-nature, Sebastian allowed him to walk away without further remonstrance.

Guy knew his own impetuous nature too well to venture to act on impulse in a doubtful case. He had now first to consider what he was able to do, and secondly what he would do; and this was not as clear to his mind as in the earlier days of his acquaintance with his uncle.

Their intercourse had never been on a comfortable footing. It would perhaps have been better if Philip's advice had been followed, and no connection kept up. Guy had once begged for some definite rule, since there was always vexation when he was known to have been with his uncle, and yet Mr. Edmonstone would never absolutely say he ought not to see him. As long as his guardian permitted it, or rather winked at it, Guy did not think it necessary to attend to Philip's marked disapproval. Part of it was well founded, but part was dislike to all that might be considered as vulgar, and part was absolute injustice to Sebastian Dixon, there was everything that could offend in his line of argument, and in the very circumstance of his interfering; and Guy had a continual struggle, in which he was not always successful, to avoid showing the affront he had taken, and to reason down his subsequent indignation. The ever-recurring irritation which Philip's conversation was apt to cause him, made him avoid it as far as he could, and retreat in haste from the subjects on which they were most apt to disagree, and so his manner had assumed an air of reserve, and almost of distrust, with his cousin, that was very unlike its usual winning openness.

This had been one unfortunate effect of his intercourse with his uncle, and another was a certain vague, dissatisfied feeling which his silence, and Philip's insinuations respecting the days he spent in London, left on Mr. Edmonstone's mind, and which gained strength from their recurrence. The days were, indeed, not many; it was only that in coming from and going to Oxford, he slept a night at an hotel in London (for his uncle never would take him to his lodgings, never even would tell him where they were, but always gave his address at the place of his engagement), was conducted by him to some concert in the evening, and had him to breakfast in the morning. He could not think there was any harm in this; he explained all he had done to Mr. Edmonstone the first time, but nothing was gained by it: his visits to London continued to be treated as something to be excused or overlooked— as something not quite correct.

He would almost have been ready to discontinue them, but that he saw that his uncle regarded him with affection, and he could not bear the thought of giving up a poor relation for the sake of the opinion of his rich friends. These meetings were the one pure pleasure to which Sebastian looked, recalling to him the happier days of his youth, and of his friendship with Guy's father; and when Guy perceived how he valued them, it would have seemed a piece of cruel neglect to gratify himself by giving the time to Hollywell.

Early in the course of their acquaintance, the importunity of a creditor revealed that, in spite of his handsome salary, Sebastian Dixon was often in considerable distress for money. In process of time, Guy discovered that at the time his uncle had been supporting his sister and her husband in all the luxury he thought befitted their rank, he had contracted considerable debts, and he had only been able to return to England on condition of paying so much a-year to his creditors. This left him very little on which to maintain his family, but still his pride made him bent on concealing his difficulties, and it was not without a struggle that he would at first consent to receive assistance from his nephew.

Guy resolved that these debts, which he considered as in fact his father's own, should be paid as soon as he had the command of his property; but, in the meantime, he thought himself bound to send his uncle all the help in his power, and when once the effort of accepting it at all was over, Dixon's expectations extended far beyond his power. His allowance was not large, and the constant requests for a few pounds to meet some pressing occasion were more than he could well meet. They kept him actually a great deal poorer than men without a tenth part of his fortune, and at the end of the term he would look back with surprise at having been able to pay his way; but still he contrived neither to exceed his allowance, nor to get into debt. This was, indeed, only done by a rigid self-denial of little luxuries such as most young men look on nearly as necessaries; but he had never been brought up to think self-indulgence a consequence of riches, he did not care what was said of him, he had no expensive tastes, for he did not seek after society, so that he was not ill-prepared for such a course, and only thought of it as an assistance in abstaining from the time-wasting that might have tempted him if he had had plenty of money to spend.

The only thing that concerned him was a growing doubt lest he might be feeding extravagance instead of doing good; and the more he disliked himself for the suspicion, the more it would return. There was no doubt much distress, the children were sickly; several of them died; the doctor's bills, and other expenses, pressed heavily, and Guy blamed himself for having doubted. Yet, again, he could not conceal from himself traces that his uncle was careless and imprudent. He had once, indeed, in a violent fit of self-reproach, confessed as much, allowed that what ought to have been spent in the maintenance of his family, had gone in gambling, but immediately after, he had been seized with a fit of terror, and implored Guy to guard the secret, since, if once it came to the knowledge of his creditors, it would be all over with him. Concealment of his present difficulties was therefore no less necessary than assistance in paying the sum he owed. Indeed, as far as Guy was able to understand his confused statement, what he wanted was at once to pay a part of his debt, before he could go on to a place where he was engaged to perform, and where he would earn enough to make up the rest.

Guy had intended to have sent for Deloraine, but had since given up the idea, in order to be able to help forward some plans of Miss Wellwood's, and resigning this project would enable him to place thirty pounds at his uncle's disposal, leaving him just enough to pay his expenses at South Moor, and carry him back to Hollywell. It was sorely against his inclination that, instead of helping a charity, his savings should go to pay gaming debts, and his five-miles walk was spent in self-debate on the right and wrong of the matter, and questions what should be done for the future– for he was beginning to awaken to the sense of his responsibility, and feared lest he might be encouraging vice.

Very early next morning Guy put his head into his tutor's room, announced that he must walk into St. Mildred's on business, but should be back by eleven at the latest, ran down-stairs, called Bustle, and made interest with the farmer's wife for a hunch of dry bread and a cup of new milk.

Then rejoicing that he had made up his mind, though not light-hearted enough to whistle, he walked across the moorland, through the white morning mist, curling on the sides of the hills in fantastic forms, and now and then catching his lengthened shadow, so as to make him smile by reminding him of the spectre of the Brocken.

Not without difficulty, he found a back street, and a little shop, where a slovenly maid was sweeping the steps, and the shutters were not yet taken down. He asked if Mr. Dixon lodged there. 'Yes,' the woman said, staring in amazement that such a gentleman could be there at that time in the morning, asking for Mr. Dixon.

'Is he at home?'

'Yes, sir but he is not up yet. He was very late last night. Did you want to speak to him? I'll tell Mrs. Dixon.'

'Is Mrs. Dixon here? Then tell her Sir Guy Morville would be glad to speak to her.'

The maid curtseyed, hurried off, and returned with a message from Mrs. Dixon to desire he would walk in. She conducted him through a dark passage, and up a still darker stair, into a dingy little parlour, with a carpet of red and green stripes, a horsehair sofa, a grate covered with cut paper, and a general perfume of brandy and cigars. There were some preparations for breakfast, but no one was in the room but a little girl, about seven years old, dressed in shabby-genteel mourning.

She was pale and sickly-looking, but her eyes were of a lovely deep blue, with a very sweet expression, and a profusion of thick flaxen curls hung round her neck and shoulders. She said in a soft, little, shy voice,—

'Mamma says she will be here directly, if you will excuse her a moment.'

Having made this formal speech, the little thing was creeping off on tiptoe, so as to escape before the maid shut the door, but Guy held out his hand, sat down so as to be on a level with her, and said,—

'Don't go, my little maid. Won't you come and speak to your cousin Guy?'

Children never failed to be attracted, whether by the winning beauty of his smile, or the sweetness of the voice in which he spoke to anything small or weak, and the little girl willingly came up to him, and put her hand into his. He stroked her thick, silky curls, and asked her name.

'Marianne,' she answered.

It was his mother's name, and this little creature had more resemblance to his tenderly-cherished vision of his young mother than any description Dixon could have given. He drew her closer to him, took the other small, cold hand, and asked her how she liked St. Mildred's.

'Oh! much better than London. There are flowers!' and she proudly exhibited a cup holding some ragged robins, dead nettles, and other common flowers which a country child would have held cheap. He admired and gained more of her confidence, so that she had begun to chatter away quite freely about 'the high, high hills that reached up to the sky, and the pretty stones,' till the door opened, and Mrs. Dixon and Bustle made their entrance.

Marianne was so much afraid of the dog, Guy so eager to console, and her mother to scold her, and protest that it should not be turned out, that there was nothing but confusion, until Guy had shown her that Bustle was no dangerous wild beast, induced her to accept his offered paw, and lay a timid finger on his smooth, black head, after which the transition was short to dog and child sitting lovingly together on the floor, Marianne stroking his ears, and admiring him with a sort of silent ecstasy.

Mrs. Dixon was a great, coarse, vulgar woman, and Guy perceived why his uncle had been so averse to taking him to his home, and how he must have felt the contrast between such a wife and his beautiful sister. She had a sort of broad sense, and absence of pretension, but her manner of talking was by no means pleasant, as she querulously accused her husband of being the cause of all their misfortunes, not even restrained by the presence of her child from entering into a full account of his offences.

Mrs. Dixon said she should not say a word, she should not care if it was not for the child, but she could not see her wronged by her own father, and not complain; poor little dear! she was the last, and she supposed she should not keep her long.

It then appeared that on her husband's obtaining an engagement for a series of concerts at the chief county town, Mrs. Dixon had insisted on coming with him to St. Mildred's in the hope that country air might benefit Marianne, who, in a confined lodging in London, was pining and dwindling as her brothers and sisters had done before her. Sebastian, who liked to escape from his wife's grumbling and rigid supervision, and looked forward to amusement in his own way at the races, had grudgingly allowed her to come, and, as she described it, had been reluctant to go to even so slight an expense in the hope of saving his child's life. She had watched him as closely as she could; but he had made his escape, and the consequences Guy already knew.

If anything could have made it worse, it was finding that after parting last night, he had returned, tried to retrieve his luck, had involved himself further, had been drinking more; and at the very hour when his nephew was getting up to see what could be done for him, had come home in a state, which made it by no means likely that he would be presentable, if his wife called him, as she offered to do.

Guy much preferred arranging with her what was to be done on the present emergency. She was disappointed at finding thirty pounds was all the help he could give; but she was an energetic woman, full of resources, and saw her way, with this assistance, through the present difficulty. The great point was to keep the gambling propensities out of sight of the creditors; and as long as this was done, she had hope. Dixon would go the next morning to the town where the musical meeting was to be held, and there he would be with his employers, where he had a character to preserve, so that she was in no fear of another outbreak.

It ended, therefore, in his leaving with her Mr. Edmonstone's draft, securing its destination by endorsing it to the person who was to receive it; and wishing her good morning, after a few more kind words to little Marianne, who had sat playing with Bustle all the time, sidling continually nearer and nearer to her new cousin, her eyes bent down, and no expression on her face which could enable him to guess how far she listened to or comprehended the conversation so unfit for her ear. When he rose to go, and stooped to kiss her, she looked wistfully in his face, and held up a small sparkling bit of spar, the most precious of all her hoards, gleaned from the roadsides of St. Mildred's.

'What, child, do you want to give it to Sir Guy?' said her mother. 'He does not want such trumpery, my dear, though you make such a work with it.'

'Did you mean to give it to me, my dear?' said Guy, as the child hung her head, and, crimsoned with blushes, could scarcely whisper her timid 'Yes.'

He praised it, and let her put it in his waistcoat pocket, and promised he would always keep it; and kissed her again, and left her a happy child, confident in his promise of always keeping it, though her mother augured that he would throw it over the next hedge.

He was at South Moor by eleven o'clock, in time for his morning's business, and made up for the troubles of the last few hours by a long talk with Mr. Wellwood in the afternoon, while the other two pupils were gone to the races, for which he was not inclined, after his two ten-mile walks.

The conversation was chiefly on Church prospects in general, and in particular on Miss Wellwood and her plans; how they had by degrees enlarged and developed as the sin, and misery, and ignorance around had forced themselves more plainly on her notice, and her means had increased and grown under her hand in the very distribution. Other schemes were dawning on her mind, of which the foremost was the foundation of a sort of school and hospital united, under the charge of herself, her sister, and several other ladies, who were desirous of joining her, as a sisterhood. But at present it was hoping against hope, for there were no funds with which to make a commencement. All this was told at unawares, drawn forth by different questions and remarks, till Guy inquired how much it would take to give them a start?'

'It is impossible to say. Anything, I suppose, between one thousand and twenty. But, by the bye, this design of Elizabeth's is an absolute secret. If you had not almost guessed it, I should never have said one word to you about it. You are a particularly dangerous man, with your connection with Mrs. Henley. You must take special good care nothing of it reaches her.'

Guy's first impression was, that he was the last person to mention it to Mrs. Henley; but when he remembered how often her brother was at Hollywell, he perceived that there might be a train for carrying the report back again to her, and recognized the absolute necessity of silence.

He said nothing at the time, but a bright scheme came into his head, resulting in the request for a thousand pounds, which caused so much astonishment. He thought himself rather shabby to have named no more, and was afraid it was an offering that cost him nothing; but he much enjoyed devising beforehand the letter with which he would place the money at the disposal of Miss Wellwood's hospital.

CHAPTER 16

Yet burns the sun on high beyond the cloud;
Each in his southern cave,
The warm winds linger, but to be allowed
One breathing o'er the wave,
One flight across the unquiet sky;
Swift as a vane may turn on high,
The smile of heaven comes on.
So waits the Lord behind the veil,
His light on frenzied cheek, or pale,
To shed when the dark hour is gone.
– LYRA INNOCENTIUM

On the afternoon on which Guy expected an answer from Mr. Edmonstone, he walked with his fellow pupil, Harry Graham, to see if there were any letters from him at Dr. Henley's.

The servant said Mrs. Henley was at home, and asked them to come in and take their letters. These were lying on a marble table, in the hall; and while the man looked in the drawing-room for his mistress, and sent one of the maids up-stairs in quest of her, Guy hastily took up one, bearing his address, in the well-known hand of Mr. Edmonstone.

Young Graham, who had taken up a newspaper, was startled by Guy's loud, sudden exclamation,– '

'Ha! What on earth does this mean?'

And looking up, saw his face of a burning, glowing red, the features almost convulsed, the large veins in the forehead and temples swollen with the blood that rushed through them, and if ever his eyes flashed with the dark lightning of Sir Hugh's, it was then.

'Morville! What's the matter?'

'Intolerable!– insulting! Me? What does he mean?' continued Guy, his passion kindling more and more. 'Proofs? I should like to see them! The man is crazy! I to confess! Ha!' as he came towards the end, 'I see it,– I see it. It is Philip, is it, that I have to thank. Meddling coxcomb! I'll make him repent it,' added he, with a grim fierceness of determination. Slandering me to them! And that,'– looking at the words with regard to Amy,– 'that passes all. He shall see what it is to insult me!'

'What is it? Your guardian out of humour?' asked his companion.

'My guardian is a mere weak fool. I don't blame him,– he can't help it; but to see him made a tool of! He twists him round his finger, abuses his weakness to insult– to accuse. But he shall give me an account!'

Guy's voice had grown lower and more husky; but though the sound sunk, the force of passion rather increased than diminished; it was like the low distant sweep of the tempest as it whirls away, preparing to return with yet more tremendous might. His colour, too, had faded to paleness, but the veins were still swollen, purple, and throbbing, and there was a stillness about him that made his wrath more than fierce, intense, almost appalling.

Harry Graham was dumb with astonishment; but while Guy spoke, Mrs. Henley had come down, and was standing before them, beginning a greeting. The blood rushed back into Guy's cheeks, and, controlling his voice with powerful effort, he said,–

'I have had an insulting– an unpleasant letter,' he added, catching himself up. 'You must excuse me;' and he was gone.

'What has happened?' exclaimed Mrs. Henley, though, from her brother's letter, as well as from her observations during a long and purposely slow progress, along a railed gallery overhanging the hall, and down a winding staircase, she knew pretty well the whole history of his anger.

'I don't know,' said young Graham. 'Some absurd, person interfering between him and his guardian. I should be sorry to be him to fall in his way just now. It must be something properly bad. I never saw a man in such a rage. I think I had better go after him, and see what he has done with himself.'

'You don't think,' said Mrs. Henley, detaining him, 'that his guardian could have been finding fault with him with reason?'

'Who? Morville? His guardian must have a sharp eye for picking holes, if he can find any in Morville. Not a steadier fellow going,– only too much so.'

'Ah!' thought Mrs. Henley, 'these young men always hang together;' and she let him escape without further question. But, when he emerged from the house, Guy was already out of sight, and he could not succeed in finding him.

Guy had burst out of the house, feeling as if nothing could relieve him but free air and rapid motion; and on he hurried, fast, faster, conscious alone of the wild, furious tumult of rage and indignation against the maligner of his innocence, who was knowingly ruining him with all that was dearest to him, insulting him by reproaches on his breaking a most sacred, unblemished word, and, what Guy felt scarcely less keenly, forcing kind-hearted Mr. Edmonstone into a persecution so foreign to his nature. The agony of suffering such an accusation, and from such a quarter,– the violent storm of indignation and pride,– wild, undefined ideas of a heavy reckoning,– above all, the dreary thought of Amy denied to him for ever,– all these swept over him, and swayed him by turns, with the dreadful intensity belonging to a nature formed for violent passions, which had broken down, in the sudden shock, all the barriers imposed on them by a long course of self-restraint.

On he rushed, reckless whither he went, or what he did, driven forward by the wild impulse of passion, far over moor and hill, up and down, till at last, exhausted at once by the tumult within, and by the violent bodily exertion, a stillness– a suspension of thought and sensation– ensued; and when this passed, he found himself seated on a rock which crowned the summit of one of the hills, his handkerchief loosened, his waistcoat open, his hat thrown off, his temples burning and throbbing with a feeling of distraction, and the agitated beatings of his heart almost stifling his panting breath.

'Yes,' he muttered to himself, 'a heavy account shall he pay me for this crowning stroke of a long course of slander and ill-will! Have I not seen it? Has not he hated me from the first, misconstrued every word and deed, though I have tried, striven earnestly, to be his friend,– borne, as not another soul would have done, with his impertinent interference and intolerable patronizing airs! But he has seen the last of it! anything but this might be forgiven; but sowing dissension between me and the Edmonstones– maligning me there. Never! Knowing, too, as he seems to do, how I stand, it is the very ecstasy of malice! Ay! this very night it shall be exposed, and he shall be taught to beware– made to know with whom he has to deal.'

Guy uttered this last with teeth clenched, in an excess of deep, vengeful ire. Never had Morville of the whole line felt more deadly fierceness than held sway over him, as he contemplated his revenge, looked forward with a dire complacency to the punishment he would wreak, not for this offence alone, but for a long course of enmity. He sat, absorbed in the plan of vengeance, perfectly still, for his physical exhaustion was complete; but as the pulsations of his heart grew less wild, his purpose became sterner and more fixed. He devised its execution, planned his sudden journey, saw himself bursting on Philip early next morning, summoning him to answer for his falsehoods. The impulse to action seemed to restore his power over his senses. He looked round, to see where he was, raising his head from his hands.

The sun was setting opposite to him, in a flood of gold,– a ruddy ball, surrounded with its pomp of clouds, on the dazzling sweep of horizon. That sight recalled him not only to himself, but to his true and better self; the good angel so close to him for the twenty years of his life, had been driven aloof but for a moment, and now, either that, or a still higher and holier power, made the setting sun bring to his mind, almost to his ear, the words,–

Let not the sun go down upon your wrath,

Neither give place to the devil.

Guy had what some would call a vivid imagination, others a lively faith. He shuddered, then, his elbows on his knees, and his hands clasped over his brow, he sat, bending forward, with his eyes closed, wrought up in a fearful struggle; while it was to him as if he saw the hereditary demon of the Morvilles watching by his side, to take full possession of him as a rightful prey, unless the battle was fought and won before that red orb had passed out of sight. Yes, the besetting fiend of his family— the spirit of defiance and resentment— that was driving him, even now, while realizing its presence, to disregard all thoughts save of the revenge for which he could barter everything— every hope once precious to him.

It was horror at such wickedness that first checked him, and brought him back to the combat. His was not a temper that was satisfied with half measures. He locked his hands more rigidly together, vowing to compel himself, ere he left the spot, to forgive his enemy— forgive him candidly— forgive him, so as never again to have to say, 'I forgive him!' He did not try to think, for reflection only lashed up his sense of the wrong: but, as if there was power in the words alone, he forced his lips to repeat,—

'Forgive us our trespasses, as we forgive them that trespass against us.'

Coldly and hardly were they spoken at first; again he pronounced them, again, again,— each time the tone was softer, each time they came more from the heart. At last the remembrance of greater wrongs, and worse revilings came upon him, his eyes filled with tears, the most subduing and healing of all thoughts— that of the great Example— became present to him; the foe was driven back.

Still he kept his hands over his face. The tempter was not yet defeated without hope. It was not enough to give up his first intention (no great sacrifice, as he perceived, now that he had time to think how Philip would be certain to treat a challenge), it was not enough to wish no ill to his cousin, to intend no evil measure, he must pardon from the bottom of his heart, regard him candidly, and not magnify his injuries.

He sat long, in deep thought, his head bent down, and his countenance stern with inward conflict. It was the hardest part of the whole battle, for the Morville disposition was as vindictive as passionate; but, at last, he recovered clearness of vision. His request might well appear unreasonable, and possibly excite suspicion, and, for the rest, it was doing a man of honour, like Philip, flagrant injustice to suspect him of originating slanders. He was, of course, under a mistake, had acted, not perhaps kindly, but as he thought, rightly and judiciously, in making his suspicions known. If he had caused his uncle to write provokingly, every one knew that was his way, he might very properly wish, under his belief, to save Amabel; and though the manner might have been otherwise, the proceeding itself admitted complete justification. Indeed, when Guy recollected the frenzy of his rage, and his own murderous impulse, he was shocked to think that he had ever sought the love of that pure and gentle creature, as if it had been a cruel and profane linking of innocence to evil. He was appalled at the power of his fury, he had not known he was capable of it, for his boyish passion, even when unrestrained, had never equalled this, in all the strength of early manhood.

He looked up, and saw that the last remnant of the sun's disk was just disappearing beneath the horizon. The victory was won!

But Guy's feeling was not the rejoicing of the conquest, it was more the relief which is felt by a little child, weary of its fit of naughtiness, when its tearful face is raised, mournful yet happy, in having won true repentance, and it says, 'I am sorry now.'

He rose, looked at his watch, wondered to find it so late; gazed round, and considered his bearings, perceiving, with a sense of shame, how far he had wandered; then retraced his steps slowly and wearily, and did not reach South Moor till long after dark.

CHAPTER 17

My blood hath been too cold and temperate,
Unapt to stir at these indignities;
But you have found me.
– KING HENRY IV

Philip, according to promise, appeared at Hollywell, and a volume of awful justice seemed written on his brow. Charles, though ignorant of its cause, perceived this at a glance, and greeted him thus:–

'Enter Don Philip II, the Duke of Alva, alguazils, corregidors, and executioners.'

'Is anything the matter, Philip?' said Amy; a question which took him by surprise, as he could not believe her in ignorance. He was sorry for her, and answered gravely,–

'Nothing is amiss with me, thank you, Amy,'

She knew he meant that he would tell no more, and would have thought no more about it, but that she saw her mother was very uneasy.

'Did you ask whether there were any letters at the post?' said Charles. 'Guy is using us shamefully– practising self-denial on us, I suppose. Is there no letter from him?'

'There is,' said Philip, reluctantly.

'Well, where is it?'

'It is to your father.'

'Oh!' said Charles, with a disappointed air. 'Are you sure? Depend on it, you overlooked my M. He has owed me a letter this fortnight. Let me see.'

'It is for my uncle,' repeated Philip, as if to put an end to the subject.

'Then he has been so stupid as to forget my second name. Come, give it me. I shall have it sooner or later.'

'I assure you, Charles, it is not for you.'

'Would not any one suppose he had been reading it?' exclaimed Charles.

'Did you know Mary Ross was gone to stay with her brother John?' broke in Mrs. Edmonstone, in a nervous, hurried manner.

'No is she?' replied Philip.

'Yes; his wife is ill.'

The universal feeling was that something was amiss, and mamma was in the secret. Amy looked wistfully at her, but Mrs. Edmonstone only gazed at the window, and so they continued for some minutes, while an uninteresting exchange of question and answer was kept up between her and her nephew until at length the dressing-bell rang, and cleared the room. Mrs. Edmonstone lingered till her son and daughters were gone, and said,–

'You have heard from St. Mildred's?'

'Yes,' said Philip, as if he was as little inclined to be communicative to her as to his cousins.

'From Guy, or from Margaret?'

'From Margaret.'

'But you say there is a letter from him?'

'Yes, for my uncle.'

'Does she say nothing more satisfactory?' asked his aunt, her anxiety tortured by his composure. 'Has she learnt no more?'

'Nothing more of his proceedings. I see Amy knows nothing of the matter?'

'No; her papa thought there was no need to distress her till we had seen whether he could explain.'

'Poor little thing!' said Philip; 'I am very sorry for her.

Mrs. Edmonstone did not choose to discuss her daughter's affairs with him, and she turned the conversation to ask if Margaret said much of Guy.

'She writes to tell the spirit in which he received my uncle's letter. It is only the Morville temper, again, and, of course, whatever you may think of that on Amy's account, I should never regard it, as concerns myself, as other than his misfortune. I hope he may be able to explain the rest.'

'Ah! there comes your uncle!' and Mr. Edmonstone entered.

'How d'ye do, Philip? Brought better news, eh?'

'Here is a letter to speak for itself.'

'Eh? From Guy? Give it me. What does he say? Let me see. Here, mamma, read it; your eyes are best.'

Mrs. Edmonstone read as follows:–

'MY DEAR MR. EDMONSTONE,– Your letter surprised and grieved me very much. I cannot guess what proofs Philip may think he has, of what I never did, and, therefore, I cannot refute them otherwise than by declaring that I never gamed in my life. Tell me what they are, and I will answer them. As to a full confession, I could of course tell you of much in which I have done wrongly, though not in the way which he supposes. On that head, I have nothing to confess. I am sorry I am prevented from satisfying you about the £1000, but I am bound in honour not to mention the purpose for which I wanted it. I am sure you could never believe I could have said what I did to Mrs. Edmonstone if I had begun on a course which I detest from the bottom of my heart. Thank you very much for the kindness of the latter part of your letter. I do not know how I could have borne it, if it had ended as it began. I hope you will soon send me these proofs of Philip's. Ever your affectionate, 'G. M.'

Not a little surprised was Philip to find that he was known to be Guy's accuser; but the conclusion revealed that his style had betrayed him, and that Mr. Edmonstone had finished with some mention of him, and he resolved that henceforth he would never leave a letter of his own dictation till he had seen it signed and sealed.

'Well!' cried Mr. Edmonstone, joyfully beating his own hand with his glove, 'that is all right. I knew it would be so. He can't even guess what we are at. I am glad we did not tease poor little Amy. Eh, mamma?— eh, Philip?' the last eh being uttered much more doubtfully, and less triumphantly than the first.

'I wonder you think it right,' said Philip.

'What more would you have?' said Mr. Edmonstone, hastily.

'Confidence.'

'Eh? Oh, ay, he says he can't tell— bound in honour.'

'It is easy to write off-hand, and say I cannot satisfy you, I am bound in honour; but that is not what most persons would think a full justification, especially considering the terms on which you stand.'

'Why, yes, he might have said more. It would have been safe enough with me.'

'It is his usual course of mystery, reserve, and defiance.'

'The fact is,' said Mr. Edmonstone, turning away, 'that it is a very proper letter; right sense, proper feeling— and if he never gamed in his life, what would you have more?'

'There are different ways of understanding such a denial as this,' said Philip. 'See, he says not in the way in which I suppose.' He held up his hand authoritatively, as his aunt was about to interpose. 'It was against gaming that his vow was made. I never thought he had played, but he never says he has not betted.'

'He would never be guilty of a subterfuge!' exclaimed Mr. Edmonstone, indignantly.

'I should not have thought so, without the evidence of the payment of the cheque, my uncle had just given him, to this gambling fellow,' said Philip; 'yet it is only the natural consequence of the habit of eluding inquiry into his visits to London.'

'I can't see any reason for so harsh an accusation,' said she.

'I should hardly want more reason than his own words. He refuses to answer the question on which my uncle's good opinion depends; he owns he has been to blame, and thus retracts his full denial. In my opinion, his letter says nothing so plainly as, "While I can stand fair with you I do not wish to break with you."'

'He will not find that quite so easy.' cried Mr. Edmonstone. 'I am no fool to be hoodwinked, especially where my little Amy is concerned. I'll see all plain and straight before he says another word of her. But you see what comes of their settling it while I was out of the way.'

Mrs. Edmonstone was grieved to see him so hurt at this. It could not have been helped, and if all had been smooth, he never would have thought of it again; but it served to keep up his dignity in his own eyes, and, as he fancied, to defend him from Philip's censure, and he therefore made the most of it, which so pained her that she did not venture to continue her championship of Guy.

'Well, well,' said Mr. Edmonstone, 'the question is what to do next– eh, Philip?' I wish he would have spoken openly. I hate mysteries. I'll write and tell him this won't do; he must be explicit– eh, Philip?'

'We will talk it over by and by,' said Philip.

His aunt understood that it was to be in her absence, and left the room, fearing it would be impossible to prevent Amy from being distressed, though she had no doubt that Guy would be able to prove his innocence of the charges. She found Amy waiting for her in her room.

'Don't, ring, mamma, dear. I'll fasten your dress,' said she; then pausing– 'Oh! mamma, I don't know whether I ought to ask, but if you would only tell me if there is nothing gone wrong.'

'I don't believe there is anything really wrong, my dear,' said Mrs. Edmonstone, kissing her, as she saw how her colour first deepened and then faded.

'Oh! no,' said she.

'But there is some mystery about his money-matters, which has vexed your papa.'

'And what has Philip to do with it?'

'I cannot quite tell, my dear. I believe Margaret Henley has heard something, but I do not know the whole.'

'Did you see his letter, mamma? said Amy, in a low, trembling voice.

'Yes, it is just like himself, and absolutely denies the accusations.'

Amy did not say 'then they are false,' but she held up her head.

'Then papa is satisfied?' she said.

'I have no doubt all will be made clear in time,' said her mother; 'but there is still something unexplained, and I am afraid things may not go smoothly just now. I am very sorry, my little Amy, that such a cloud should have come over you, she added, smoothing fondly the long, soft hair, sad at heart to see the cares and griefs of womanhood gathering over her child's bright, young life.

'I said I must learn to bear things!' murmured Amy to herself. 'Only,' and the tears filled her eyes, and she spoke with almost childish simplicity of manner, 'I can't bear them to vex him. I wish Philip would let papa settle it alone. Guy will be angry, and grieved afterwards.'

They were interrupted by the dinner-bell, but Amy ran into her own room for one moment.

'I said I would learn to bear,' said she to herself, 'or I shall never be fit for him. Yes, I will, even though it is the thinking he is unhappy. He said I must be his Verena; I know what that means; I ought not to be uneasy, for he will bear it beautifully, and say he is glad of it afterwards. And I will try not to seem cross to Philip.'

Mr. Edmonstone was fidgety and ill at ease, found fault with the dinner, and was pettish with his wife. Mrs. Edmonstone set Philip off upon politics, which lasted till the ladies could escape into the drawing-room. In another minute Philip brought in Charles, set him down, and departed. Amy, who was standing by the window, resting her forehead against the glass, and gazing into the darkness, turned round hastily, and left the room, but in passing her brother, she put her hand into his, and received a kind pressure. Her mother followed her, and the other three all began to wonder. Charles said he had regularly been turned out of the dining-room by Philip, who announced that he wanted to speak to his uncle, and carried him off.

They conjectured, and were indignant at each other's conjectures, till their mother returned, and gave them as much information as she could; but this only made them very anxious. Charles was certain that Mrs. Henley had laid a cockatrice egg, and Philip was hatching it; and Laura could not trust herself to defend Philip, lest she should do it too vehemently. They could all agree in desire to know the truth, in hope that Guy was not culpable, and, above all, in feeling for Amy; but by tacit consent they were silent on the three shades of opinion in their minds. Laura was confident that Philip was acting for the best; Mrs. Edmonstone thought he might be mistaken in his premises, but desirous of Guy's real good; and Charles, though sure he would allege nothing which he did not believe to be true, also thought him ready to draw the worst conclusions from small grounds, and to take pleasure in driving Mr. Edmonstone to the most rigorous measures.

Philip, meanwhile, was trying to practise great moderation and forbearance, not bringing forward at first what was most likely to incense Mr. Edmonstone, and without appearance of animosity in his cool, guarded speech. There was no design in this, he meant only to be just; yet anything less cool would have had far less effect.

When he shut the dining-room door, he found his uncle wavering, touched by the sight of his little Amy, returning to his first favourable view of Guy's letter, ready to overlook everything, accept the justification, and receive his ward on the same footing as before, though he was at the same time ashamed that Philip should see him relent, and desirous of keeping up his character for firmness, little guessing how his nephew felt his power over him, and knew that he could wield him at will.

Perceiving and pitying his feebleness, and sincerely believing strong measures the only rescue for Amy, the only hope for Guy, Philip found himself obliged to work on him by the production of another letter from his sister. He would rather, if possible, have kept this back, so much did his honourable feeling recoil from what had the air of slander and mischief-making; but he regarded firmness on his uncle's part as the only chance for Guy or for his cousin, and was resolved not to let him swerve from strict justice.

Mrs. Henley had written immediately after Guy's outburst in her house, and, taking it for granted that her brother would receive a challenge, she wrote in the utmost alarm, urging him to remember how precious he was to her, and not to depart from his own principles.

'You would not be so mad as to fight him, eh?' said Mr. Edmonstone, anxiously. 'You know better– besides, for poor Amy's sake.'

'For the sake of right,' replied Philip, 'no. I have reassured my sister. I have told her that, let the boy do what he will, he shall never make me guilty of his death.'

'You have heard from him, then?'

'No; I suppose a night's reflection convinced him that he had no rational grounds for violent proceedings, and he had sense enough not to expose himself to such an answer as I should have given. What caused his wrath to be directed towards me especially, I cannot tell, nor can my sister,' said Philip, looking full at his uncle; 'but I seem to have come in for a full share of it.'

He proceeded to read the description of Guy's passion, and the expressions he had used. Violent as it had been, it did not lose in Mrs. Henley's colouring; and what made the effect worse was that she had omitted to say she had overheard his language, so that it appeared as if he had been unrestrained even by gentlemanly feeling, and had thus spoken of her brother and uncle in her presence.

Mr. Edmonstone was resentful now, really displeased, and wounded to the quick. The point on which he was especially sensitive was his reputation for sense and judgment; and that Guy, who had shown him so much respect and affection, whom he had treated with invariable kindness, and received into his family like a son, that he should thus speak of him shocked him extremely. He was too much overcome even to break out into exclamations at first, he only drank off his glass of wine hastily, and said, 'I would never have thought it!'

With these words, all desire for forbearance and toleration departed. If Guy could speak thus of him, he was ready to believe any accusation, to think him deceitful from the first, to say he had been trifling with Amy, to imagine him a confirmed reprobate, and cast him off entirely. Philip had some difficulty to restrain him from being too violent; and to keep him to the matter in hand, he defended Guy from the exaggerations of his imagination in a manner which appeared highly noble, considering how Guy had spoken of him. Before they parted that night, another letter had been written, which stood thus,—

'DEAR SIR GUY,— Since you refuse the confidence which I have a right to demand, since you elude the explanation I asked, and indulge yourself in speaking in disrespectful terms of me and my family, I have every reason to suppose that you have no desire to continue on the same footing as heretofore at Hollywell. As your guardian, I repeat that I consider myself bound to keep a vigilant watch over your conduct, and, if possible, to recover you from the unhappy course in which you have involved yourself: but all other intercourse between you and this family must cease. 'Your horse shall be sent to Redclyffe to-morrow.

'Yours faithfully,
'C. EDMONSTONE.'

This letter was more harsh than Philip wished; but Mr. Edmonstone would hardly be prevailed on to consent to enter on no further reproaches. He insisted on banishing Deloraine, as well as on the mention of Guy's disrespect, both against his nephew's opinion; but it was necessary to let him have his own way on these points, and Philip thought himself fortunate in getting a letter written which was in any degree rational and moderate.

They had been so busy, and Mr. Edmonstone so excited, that Philip thought it best to accept the offer of tea being sent them in the dining-room, and it was not till nearly midnight that their conference broke up, when Mr. Edmonstone found his wife sitting up by the dressing-room fire, having shut Charles's door, sorely against his will.

'There,' began Mr. Edmonstone, 'you may tell Amy she may give him up, and a lucky escape she has had. But this is what comes of settling matters in my absence.' So he proceeded with the narration, mixing the facts undistinguishably with his own surmises, and overwhelming his wife with dismay. If a quarter of this was true, defence of Guy was out of the question; and it was still more impossible to wish Amy's attachment to him to continue; and though much was incredible, it was no time to say so. She could only hope morning would soften her husband's anger, and make matters explicable.

Morning failed to bring her comfort. Mr. Edmonstone repeated that Amy must be ordered to give up all thoughts of Guy, and she perceived that the words ascribed to him stood on evidence which could not be doubted. She could believe he might have spoken them in the first shock of an unjust imputation, and she thought he might have been drawn into some scrape to serve a friend; but she could never suppose him capable of all Mr. Edmonstone imagined.

The first attempt to plead his cause, however, brought on her an angry reply; for Philip, by a hint, that she never saw a fault in Guy, had put it into his uncle's head that she would try to lead him, and made him particularly inaccessible to her influence.

There was no help for it, then; poor little Amy must hear the worst; and it was not long before Mrs. Edmonstone found her waiting in the dressing-room. Between obedience to her husband, her conviction of Guy's innocence, and her tenderness to her daughter, Mrs. Edmonstone had a hard task, and she could scarcely check her tears as Amy nestled up for her morning kiss.

'O mamma! what is it?'

'Dearest, I told you a cloud was coming. Try to bear it. Your papa is not satisfied with Guy's answer, and it seems he spoke some hasty words of papa and Philip; they have displeased papa very much, and, my dear child, you must try to bear it, he has written to tell Guy he must not think any more of you.'

'He has spoken hasty words of papa!' repeated Amy, as if she had not heard the rest. 'How sorry he must be!'

As she spoke, Charles's door was pushed open, and in he came, half dressed, scrambling on, with but one crutch, to the chair near which she stood, with drooping head and clasped hands.

'Never mind, little Amy, he said; 'I'll lay my life 'tis only some monstrous figment of Mrs. Henley's. Trust my word, it will right itself; it is only a rock to keep true love from running too smooth. Come, don't cry, as her tears began to flow fast, 'I only meant to cheer you up.'

'I am afraid, Charlie, said his mother, putting a force on her own feeling, 'it is not the best or kindest way to do her good by telling her to dwell on hopes of him.'

'Mamma one of Philip's faction!' exclaimed Charles.

'Of no faction at all, Charles, but I am afraid it is a bad case;' and Mrs. Edmonstone related what she knew; glad to address herself to any one but Amy, who stood still, meanwhile, her hands folded on the back of her brother's chair.

Charles loudly protested that the charges were absurd and preposterous, and would be proved so in no time. He would finish dressing instantly, go to speak to his father, and show him the sense of the thing. Amy heard and hoped, and his mother, who had great confidence in his clear sight, was so cheered as almost to expect that today's post might carry a conciliatory letter.

Meantime, Laura and Philip met in the breakfast-room, and in answer to her anxious inquiry, he had given her an account of Guy, which, though harsh enough, was far more comprehensible than what the rest had been able to gather.

She was inexpressibly shocked, 'My poor dear little Amy!' she exclaimed. 'O Philip, now I see all you thought to save me from!'

'It is an unhappy business that it ever was permitted!'

'Poor little dear! She was so happy, so very happy and sweet in her humility and her love. Do you know, Philip, I was almost jealous for a moment that all should be so easy for them; and I blamed poverty; but oh! there are worse things than poverty!'

He did not speak, but his dark blue eye softened with the tender look known only to her; and it was one of the precious moments for which she lived. She was happy till the rest came down, and then a heavy cloud seemed to hang on them at breakfast time.

'Charles, who found anxiety on Guy's account more exciting, though considerably less agreeable, than he had once expected, would not go away with the womankind; but as soon as the door was shut, exclaimed,

'Now then, Philip, let me know the true grounds of your persecution.'

It was not a conciliating commencement. His father was offended, and poured out a confused torrent of Guy's imagined misdeeds, while Philip explained and modified his exaggerations.

'So the fact is,' said Charles, at length, 'that Guy has asked for his own money, and when in lieu of it he received a letter full of unjust charges, he declared Philip was a meddling coxcomb. I advise you not to justify his opinion.'

Philip disdained to reply, and after a few more of Mr. Edmonstone's exclamations Charles proceeded,

'This is the great sum total.'

'No,' said Philip; 'I have proof of his gambling.'

'What is it?'

'I have shown it to your father, and he is satisfied.'

'Is it not proof enough that he is lost to all sense of propriety, that he should go and speak in that fashion of us, and to Philip's own sister?' cried Mr. Edmonstone. 'What would you have more?'

'That little epithet applied to Captain Morville is hardly, to my mind, proof sufficient that a man is capable of every vice,' said Charles, who, in the pleasure of galling his cousin, did not perceive the harm he did his friend's cause, by recalling the affront which his father, at least, felt most deeply. Mr. Edmonstone grew angry with him for disregarding the insulting term applied to himself; and Charles, who, though improved in many points, still sometimes showed the effects of early habits of disrespect to his father, answered hastily, that no one could wonder at Guy's resenting such suspicions; he deserved no blame at all, and would have been a blockhead to bear it tamely.

This was more than Charles meant, but his temper was fairly roused, and he said much more than was right or judicious, so that his advocacy only injured the cause. He had many representations to make on the injustice of condemning Guy unheard, of not even laying before him the proofs on which the charges were founded, and on the danger of actually driving him into mischief, by shutting the doors of Hollywell against him. 'If you wanted to make him all you say he is, you are taking the very best means.'

Quite true; but Charles had made his father too angry to pay attention. This stormy discussion continued for nearly two hours, with no effect save inflaming the minds of all parties. At last Mr. Edmonstone was called away; and Charles, rising, declared he should go at that moment, and write to tell Guy that there was one person at least still in his senses.

'You will do as you please,' said Philip.

'Thank you for the permission,' said Charles, proudly.

'It is not to me that your submission is due,' said Philip.

'I'll tell you what, Philip, I submit to my own father readily, but I do not submit to Captain Morville's instrument.'

'We have had enough of unbecoming retorts for one day,' said Philip, quietly, and offering his arm.

Much as Charles disliked it, he was in too great haste not to accept it; and perceiving that there were visitors in the drawing-room, he desired to go up-stairs.

'People who always come when they are not wanted!' he muttered, as he went up, pettish with them as with everything else.

'I do not think you in a fit mood to be advised, Charles,' said Philip; 'but to free my own conscience, let me say this. Take care how you promote this unfortunate attachment.'

'Take care what you say!' exclaimed Charles, flushing with anger, as he threw himself forward, with an impatient movement, trusting to his crutch rather than retain his cousin's arm; but the crutch slipped, he missed his grasp at the balusters, and would have fallen to the bottom of the flight if Philip had not been close behind. Stretching out his foot, he made a barrier, receiving Charles's weight against his breast, and then, taking him in his arms, carried him up the rest of the way as easily as if he had been a child. The noise brought Amy out of the dressing-room, much frightened, though she did not speak till Charles was deposited on the sofa, and assured them he was not in the least hurt, but he would hardly thank his cousin for having so dexterously saved him; and Philip, relieved from the fear of his being injured, viewed the adventure as a mere ebullition of ill-temper, and went away.

'A fine helpless log am I,' exclaimed Charles, as he found himself alone with Amy. 'A pretty thing for me to talk of being of any use, when I can't so much as show my anger at an impertinence about my own sister, without being beholden for not breaking my neck to the very piece of presumption that uttered it.'

'Oh, don't speak so' began Amy; and at that moment Philip was close to them, set down the crutch that had been dropped, and went without speaking.

'I don't care who hears,' said Charles; 'I say there is no greater misery in this world than to have the spirit of a man and the limbs of a cripple. I know if I was good for anything, things would not long be in this state. I should be at St. Mildred's by this time, at the bottom of the whole story, and Philip would be taught to eat his words in no time, and make as few wry faces as suited his dignity. But what is the use of talking? This sofa'— and he struck his fist against it— 'is my prison, and I am a miserable cripple, and it is mere madness in me to think of being attended to.'

'O Charlie!' cried Amy, caressingly, and much distressed, 'don't talk so. Indeed, I can't bear it! You know it is not so.'

'Do I? Have not I been talking myself hoarse, showing up their injustice, saying all a man could say to bring them to reason, and not an inch could I move them. I do believe Philip has driven my father stark mad with these abominable stories of his sister's, which I verily believe she invented herself.'

'O no, she could not. Don't say so.'

'What! Are you going to believe them, too?'

'Never!'

'It is that which drives me beyond all patience,' proceeded Charles, 'to see Philip lay hold of my father, and twist him about as he chooses, and set every one down with his authority.'

'Philip soon goes abroad,' said Amy, who could not at the moment say anything more charitable.

'Ay! there is the hope. My father will return to his natural state provided they don't drive Guy, in the meantime, to do something desperate.'

'No, they won't,' whispered Amy.

'Well, give me the blotting-book. I'll write to him this moment, and tell him we are not all the tools of Philip's malice.'

Amy gave the materials to her brother, and then turning away, busied herself in silence as best she might, in the employment her mother had recommended her, of sorting some garden-seeds for the cottagers. After an interval, Charles said,

'Well, Amy, what shall I say to him for you?'

There was a little silence, and presently Amy whispered, 'I don't think I ought.'

'What?' asked Charles, not catching her very low tones, as she sat behind him, with her head bent down.

'I don't think it would be right,' she repeated, more steadily.

'Not right for you to say you don't think him a villain?'

'Papa said I was to have no– 'and there her voice was stopped with tears.

'This is absurd, Amy,' said Charles; 'when it all was approved at first, and now my father is acting on a wrong impression; what harm can there be in it? Every one would do so.'

'I am sure he would not think it right,' faltered Amy.

'He? You'll never have any more to say to him, if you don't take care what you are about.'

'I can't help it,' said Amy, in a broken voice. 'It is not right.'

'Nonsense! folly!' said Charles. 'You are as bad as the rest. When they are persecuting, and slandering, and acting in the most outrageous way against him, and you know one word of yours would carry him through all, you won't say it, to save him from distraction, and from doing all my father fancies he has done. Then I believe you don't care a rush for him, and never want to see him again, and believe the whole monstrous farrago. I vow I'll say so.'

'O Charles, you are very cruel!' said Amy, with an irrepressible burst of weeping.

'Then, if you don't believe it, why can't you send one word to comfort him?'

She wept in silence for some moments; at last she said,–

'It would not comfort him to think me disobedient. He will trust me without, and he will know what you think. You are very kind, dear Charlie; but don't persuade me any more, for I can't bear it. I am going away now; but don't fancy I am angry, only I don't think I can sit by while you write that letter.'

Poor little Amy, she seldom knew worse pain than at that moment, when she was obliged to go away to put it out of her power to follow the promptings of her heart to send the few kind words which might prove that nothing could shake her love and trust.

A fresh trial awaited her when she looked from her own window. She saw Deloraine led out, his chestnut neck glossy in the sun and William prepared for a journey, and the other servants shaking hands, and bidding him good-bye. She saw him ride off, and could hardly help flying back to her brother to exclaim, 'O Charlie, they have sent Deloraine away!' while the longing to send one kind greeting became more earnest than ever; but she withstood it, and throwing herself on the bed, exclaimed,–

'He will never come back– never, never!' and gave way, unrestrainedly, to a fit of weeping; nor was it till this had spent itself that she could collect her thoughts.

She was sitting on the side of her bed trying to compose herself, when Laura, came in.

'My own Amy– my poor, dearest,– I am very sorry!'

'Thank you, dear Laura,' and Amy gladly rested her aching head on her shoulder.

'I wish I knew what to do for you!' proceeded Laura. 'You cannot, cease to think about him, and yet you ought.'

'If I ought, I suppose I can,' said Amy in a voice exhausted with crying.

'That's right, darling. You will not be weak, and pine for one who is not worthy.'

'Not worthy, Laura?' said Amy, withdrawing her arm, and holding up her head.

'Ah! my poor Amy, we thought– '

'Yes; and it is so still. I know it is so. I know he did not do it.'

'Then what do you think of Margaret and Philip?'

'There is some mistake.'

And how can you defend what he said of papa?'

'I don't,' said Amy, hiding her face. 'That is the worst; but I am sure it was only a moment's passion, and that he must be very unhappy about it now. I don't think papa would mind it, at least not long, if it was not for this other dreadful misapprehension. O, Laura! why cannot something be done to clear it up?'

'Everything will be done,' said Laura. Papa has written to Mr. Wellwood, and Philip means to go and make inquiries at Oxford and St. Mildred's.'

'When?' asked Amy.

'Not till term begins. You know he is to have a fortnight's leave before the regiment goes to Ireland.'

'Oh, I hope it will come right then. People must come to an understanding when they meet; it is so different from writing.'

'He will do everything to set things on a right footing. You may be confident of that, Amy, for your sake as much as anything else.'

'I can't think why he should know I have anything to do with it,' said Amy, blushing. 'I had much rather he did not.'

'Surely, Amy, you think he can be trusted with your secret; and there is no one who can take more care for you. You must look on him as one of ourselves.'

Amy made no answer, and Laura, was annoyed.

'You are vexed with him for having told this to papa; but that is not reasonable of you, Amy; your better sense must tell you that it is the only truly kind course, both towards Guy and yourself.'

It was said in Philip's manner, which perhaps made it harder to bear; and Amy could scarcely answer,—

'He means it for the best.'

'You would not have had him be silent?'

'I don't know,' said Amy, sadly. 'No; he should have done something, but he might have done it more kindly.'

Laura endeavoured to persuade her that nothing could have been more kind and judicious, and Amy sat dejectedly owning the good intention, and soothed by the affection of her family; with the bitter suffering of her heart unallayed, with all her fond tender feelings torn at the thought of what Guy must be enduring, and with the pain of knowing it was her father's work. She had one comfort, in the certainty that Guy would bear it nobly. She was happy to find her confidence confirmed by her mother and Charles; and one thing she thought she need not give up, though she might no longer think of him as her lover, she might be his Verena still, whether he knew it or not. It could not be wrong to remember any one in her prayers, and to ask that he might not be led into temptation, but have strength to abide patiently. That helped her to feel that he was in the hands of One to whom the secrets of all hearts are known; and a line of poetry seemed to be whispered in her ears, in his own sweet tones,—

Wait, and the cloud shall roll away.

So, after the first day, she went on pretty well. She was indeed silent and grave, and no longer the sunbeam of Hollywell; but she took her share in what was passing, and a common observer would hardly have remarked the submissive melancholy of her manner. Her father was very affectionate, and often called her his jewel of good girls; but he was too much afraid of women's tears to talk to her about Guy, he left that to her mother: and Mrs. Edmonstone, having seen her submit to her father's will, was unwilling to say more.

She doubted whether it was judicious to encourage her in dwelling on Guy; for, even supposing his character clear, they had offended him deeply, and released him from any engagement to her, so that there was nothing to prevent him from forming an attachment elsewhere. Mrs. Edmonstone did not think he would; but it was better to say nothing about him, lest she should not speak prudently, and only keep up the subject in Amy's mind.

Charles stormed and wrangled, told Mr. Edmonstone 'he was breaking his daughter's heart, that was all;' and talked of unfairness and injustice, till Mr. Edmonstone vowed it was beyond all bearing, that his own son should call him a tyrant, and accused Guy of destroying all peace in his family.

The replies to the letters came; some thought them satisfactory, and the others wondered that they thought so. Mr. Wellwood gave the highest character of his pupil, and could not imagine how any irregularities could be laid to his charge; but when asked in plain terms how he disposed of his time, could only answer in general, that he had friends and engagements of his own at St. Mildred's and its neighbourhood, and had been several times at Mrs. Henley's and at Colonel Harewood's. The latter place, unfortunately, was the very object of Philip's suspicions; and thus the letter was anything but an exculpation.

Guy wrote to Charles in the fulness of his heart, expressing gratitude for his confidence and sympathy. He again begged for the supposed evidence of his misconduct, declaring he could explain it, whatever it might be, and proceeded to utter deep regrets for his hasty expressions.

'I do not know what I may have said,' he wrote; 'I have no doubt it was unpardonable, for I am sure my feelings were so, and that I deserve whatever I have brought on myself. I can only submit to Mr. Edmonstone's sentence, and trust that time will bring to his knowledge that I am innocent of what I am accused of. He has every right to be displeased with me.

Charles pronounced this to be only Guy's way of abusing himself; but his father saw in it a disguised admission of guilt. It was thought, also, to be bad sign that Guy intended to remain at South Moor till the end of the vacation, though Charles argued that he must be somewhere; and if they wished to keep him out of mischief, why exile him from Hollywell! He would hardly listen to his mother's representation, that on Amy's account it would not be right to have him there till the mystery was cleared up.

He tried to stir his father up to go and see Guy at St. Mildred's, and investigate matters for himself; but, though Mr. Edmonstone would have liked the appearance of being important, this failed, because Philip declared it to be unadvisable, knowing that it would be no investigation at all, and that his uncle would be talked over directly. Next, Charles would have persuaded Philip himself to go, but the arrangements about his leave did not make this convenient; and it was put off till he should pay his farewell visit to his sister, in October. Lastly, Charles wrote to Mrs. Henley, entreating her to give him some information about this mysterious evidence which was wanting, but her reply was a complete 'set down' for interference in a matter with which he had no concern.

He was very angry. In fact, the post seldom came in without occasioning a fresh dispute, which only had the effect of keeping up the heat of Mr. Edmonstone's displeasure, and making the whole house uncomfortable.

Fretfulness and ill-humour seemed to have taken possession of Charles and his father. Such a state of things had not prevailed since Guy's arrival: Hollywell was hardly like the same house; Mrs. Edmonstone and Laura could do nothing without being grumbled at or scolded by one or other of the gentlemen; even Amy now and then came in for a little petulance on her father's part, and Charles could not always forgive her for saying in her mournful, submissive tome,– 'It is of no use to talk about it!'

CHAPTER 18

This just decree alone I know,
Man must be disciplined by woe,
To me, whate'er of good or ill
The future brings, since come it will,
I'll bow my spirit, and be still.
– AESCHYLUS, (Anstice's Translation.)

Guy, in the meantime, was enduring the storm in loneliness, for he was unwilling to explain the cause of his trouble to his companions. The only occasion of the suspicions, which he could think of, was his request for the sum of money; and this he could not mention to Mr. Wellwood, nor was he inclined to make confidants of his other companions, though pleasant, right-minded youths.

He had only announced that he had had a letter which had grieved him considerably, but of which he could not mention the contents; and as Harry Graham, who knew something of the Broadstone neighbourhood, had picked up a report that Sir Guy Morville was to marry Lady Eveleen de Courcy, there was an idea among the party that there was some trouble in the way of his attachment. He had once before been made, by some joke, to colour and look conscious; and now this protected him from inconvenient questions, and accounted for his depression. He was like what he had been on first coming to Hollywell– grave and silent, falling into reveries when others were talking, and much given to long, lonely wanderings. Accustomed as he had been in boyhood to a solitary life in beautiful scenery, there was something in a fine landscape that was to him like a friend and companion; and he sometimes felt that it would have been worse if he had been in a dull, uniform country, instead of among mountain peaks and broad wooded valleys. Working hard, too, helped him not a little, and conic sections served him almost as well as they served Laura.

A more real help was the neighbourhood of Stylehurst. On the first Sunday after receiving Mr. Edmonstone's letter, he went to church there, instead of with the others, to St. Mildred's. They thought it was for the sake of the solitary walk; but he had other reasons for the preference. In the first place it was a Communion Sunday, and in the next, he could feel more kindly towards Philip there, and he knew he needed all that could strengthen such a disposition.

Many a question did he ask himself, to certify whether he wilfully entertained malice or hatred, or any uncharitableness. It was a long, difficult examination; but at its close, he felt convinced that, if such passions knocked at the door of his heart, it was not at his own summons, and that he drove them away without listening to them. And surely he might approach to gain the best aid in that battle, especially as he was certain of his strong and deep repentance for his fit of passion, and longing earnestly for the pledge of forgiveness.

The pardon and peace he sought came to him, and in such sort that the comfort of that day, when fresh from the first shock, and waiting in suspense for some new blow, was such as never to be forgotten. They linked themselves with the grave shade of the clustered gray columns, and the angel heads on roof of that old church; with the long grass and tall yellow mullens among its churchyard graves, and with the tints of the elm-trees that closed it in, their leaves in masses either of green or yellow, and opening here and there to show the purple hills beyond.

He wandered in the churchyard between the services. All enmity to Philip was absent now; and he felt as if it would hardly return when he stood by the graves of the Archdeacon and of the two Frances Morvilles, and thought what that spot was to his cousin. There were a few flowers planted round Mrs. Morville's grave, but they showed that they had long been neglected, and no such signs of care marked her daughter Fanny's. And when Guy further thought of Mrs. Henley, and recollected how Philip had sacrificed all his cherished prospects and hopes of distinction, and embraced an irksome profession, for the sake of these two sisters, he did not find it difficult to excuse the sternness, severity, and distrust which were an evidence how acutely a warm heart had suffered.

Though he suffered cruelly from being cut off from Amy, yet his reverence for her helped him to submit. He had always felt as if she was too far above him; and though he had, beyond his hopes, been allowed to aspire to the thought of her, it was on trial, and his failure, his return to his old evil passions, had sunk him beneath her. He shuddered to think of her being united to anything so unlike herself, and which might cause her so much misery; it was wretchedness to think that even now she might be suffering for him; and yet not for worlds would he have lost the belief that she was so feeling, or the remembrance of the looks which had shone on him so sweetly and timidly as she sat at her mother's feet; though that remembrance was only another form of misery. But Amy would be tranquil, pure and good, whatever became of him, and he should always be able to think of her, looking like one of those peaceful spirits, with bending head, folded hands, and a star on its brow, in the "Paradiso" of Flaxman. Her serenity would be untouched; and though she might be lost to him, he could still be content while he could look up at it through his turbid life. Better she were lost to him than that her peace should be injured.

He still, of course, earnestly longed to prove his innocence, though his hopes lessened, for as long as the evidence was withheld, he had no chance.

After writing as strongly as he could, he could do no more, except watch for something that might unravel the mystery; and Charles's warm sympathy and readiness to assist him were a great comfort.

He had not seen his uncle again; perhaps Sebastian was ashamed to meet him after their last encounter, and was still absent on his engagement; but the wife and child were still at St. Mildred's, and one afternoon, when Guy had rather unwillingly gone thither with Mr. Wellwood, he saw Mrs. Dixon sitting on one of the benches which were placed on the paths cut out on the side of the hill, looking very smart and smiling, among several persons of her own class.

To be ashamed to recognise her was a weakness beneath him; he spoke to her, and was leaving her, pluming herself on his notice, when he saw little Marianne's blue eyes fixed wistfully upon him, and held out his hand to her. She ran up to him joyfully, and he led her a few steps from her mother's party. 'Well, little one, how are you? I have your piece of spar quite safe. Have you said how d'ye do to Bustle?'

'Bustle! Bustle!' called the soft voice but it needed a whistle from his master to bring him to be caressed by the little girl.

'Have you been taking any more pleasant walks?'

'Oh yes. We have been all round these pretty paths. And I should like to go to the top of this great high hill, and see all round; but mamma says she has got a bone in her leg, and cannot go.'

'Do you think mamma would give you leave to go up with me? Should you like it?'

She coloured all over; too happy even to thank him.

'Then,' said Guy to his tutor, 'I will meet you here when you have done your business in the town, in an hour or so. Poor little thing, she has not many pleasures.'

Mrs. Dixon made no difficulty, and was so profuse in thanks that Guy got out of her way as fast as he could, and was soon on the soft thymy grass of the hill-side, the little girl frisking about him in great delight, playing with Bustle, and chattering merrily.

Little Marianne was a delicate child, and her frolic did not last long. As the ascent became steeper, her breath grew shorter, and she toiled on in a resolute uncomplaining manner after his long, vigorous steps, till he looked round, and seeing her panting far behind, turned to help her, lead her, and carry her, till the top was achieved, and the little girl stood on the topmost stone, gazing round at the broad sunny landscape, with the soft green meadows, the harvest fields, the woods in their gorgeous autumn raiment, and the moorland on the other side, with its other peaks and cairns, brown with withered bracken, and shadowed in moving patches by the floating clouds. The exhilarating wind brought a colour into her pale cheeks, and her flossy curls were blowing over her face.

He watched her in silence, pleased and curious to observe how beautiful a scene struck the childish eye of the little Londoner. The first thing she said, after three or four minutes' contemplation— a long time for such a child— was, 'Oh! I never saw anything so pretty!' then presently after, 'Oh! I wish little brother Felix was here!'

'This is a pleasant place to think about your little brother,' said Guy, kindly; and she looked up in his face, and exclaimed, 'Oh! do you know about Felix?'

'You shall tell me' said Guy. 'Here, sit on my knee, and rest after your scramble.'

'Mamma never lets me talk of Felix, because it makes her cry,' said Marianne; but I wish it sometimes.'

Her little heart was soon open. It appeared that Felix was the last who had died, the nearest in age to Marianne, and her favourite playfellow. She told of some of their sports in their London home, speaking of them with eagerness and fondness that showed what joys they had been, though to Guy they seemed but the very proof of dreariness and dinginess. She talked of walks to school, when Felix would tell what he would do when he was a man, and how he took care of her at the crossings, and how rude boys used to drive them, and how they would look in at the shop windows and settle what they would buy if they were rich. Then she talked of his being ill— ill so very long; how he sat in his little chair, and could not play, and then always lay in bed, and she liked to sit by him, there; but at last he died, and they carried him away in a great black coffin, and he would never come back again. But it was so dull now, there was no one to play with her.

Though the little girl did not cry, she looked very mournful, and Guy tried to comfort her, but she did not understand him. 'Going to heaven' only conveyed to her a notion of death and separation, and this phrase, together with a vague idea who had made her, and that she ought to be good, seemed to be the extent of the poor child's religious knowledge. She hardly ever had been at church and though she had read one or two Bible stories, it seemed to have been from their having been used as lessons at school. She had a dim notion that good people read the Bible, and there was one on the little table at home, with the shell-turkey-cock standing upon it, and mamma read it when Felix died; but it was a big book, and the shell-turkey-cock always stood upon it; in short, it seemed only connected with mamma's tears, and the loss of her brother.

Guy was very much shocked, and so deep in thought that he could hardly talk to the child in their progress down the hill; but she was just so tired as to be inclined to silence, and quite happy clinging to his hand, till he delivered her over to her mother at the foot of the hill, and went to join his tutor, at the place appointed.

'Wellwood,' said he, breaking silence, when they had walked about half way back to the farm, 'do you think your cousin would do me a great kindness? You saw that child? Well, if the parents consent, it would be the greatest charity on earth if Miss Wellwood would receive her into her school.'

'On what terms? What sort of an education is she to have?'

'The chief thing she wants is to be taught Christianity, poor child; the rest Miss Wellwood may settle. She is my first cousin. I don't know whether you are acquainted with our family history?' and he went on to explain as much as was needful. It ended in a resolution that if Miss Wellwood would undertake the charge, the proposal should be made to Mrs. Dixon.

It was a way of assisting his relations likely to do real good, and on the other hand, he would be able, under colour of the payment for the child, to further Miss Wellwood's schemes, and give her the interest of the thousand pounds, until his five and twentieth year might put his property in his own power.

Miss Wellwood readily consented, much pleased with the simplicity and absence of false shame he showed in the whole transaction, and very anxious for the good of a child in a class so difficult to reach. He next went to Mrs. Dixon, expecting more difficulty with her, but he found none. She thought it better Marianne should live at St. Mildred's than die in London, and was ready to catch at the prospect of her being fitted for a governess. Indeed, she was so strongly persuaded that the rich cousin might make Marianne's fortune, that she would have been very unwilling to interfere with the fancy he had taken for her.

Little Marianne was divided between fear of leaving mamma and liking for St. Mildred's, but her first interview with Miss Wellwood, and Miss Jane's showing her a little white bed, quite turned the scale in their favour. Before the time came for Guy's return to Oxford, he had seen her settled, heard her own account of her happy life, and had listened to Miss Jane Wellwood's delight in her sweet temper and good disposition.

Those thousand pounds; Guy considered again and again whether he could explain their destination, and whether this would clear him. It seemed to him only a minor charge, and besides his repugnance to mention such a design, he saw too many obstacles in his way. Captain Morville and his sister were the very persons from whom Miss Wellwood's project was to be kept secret. Besides, what would be gained? It was evident that Guy's own assertions were doubted, and he could bring no confirmation of them; he had never spoken of his intention to his tutor, and Mr. Wellwood could, therefore, say nothing in his favour. If Mr. Edmonstone alone had been concerned, or if this had been the only accusation, Guy might have tried to explain it; but with Philip he knew it would be useless, and therefore would not enter on the subject. He could only wait patiently.

CHAPTER 19

Most delicately, hour by hour,
He canvassed human mysteries,
And stood aloof from other minds.
Himself unto himself he sold,
Upon himself, himself did feed,
Quiet, dispassionate, and cold,
With chiselled features clear and sleek.
– TENNYSON

Guy had been about a week at Oxford, when one evening, as he was sitting alone in his rooms, he received an unexpected visit from Captain Morville. He was glad, for he thought a personal interview would remove all misconstructions, and held out his hand cordially, saying:–

'You here, Philip! When did you come?'

'Half an hour ago. I am on my way to spend a week with the Thorndales. I go on to-morrow to my sister's.'

While speaking, Philip was surveying the apartment, for he held that a man's room is generally an indication of his disposition, and assuredly there was a great deal of character in his own, with the scrupulous neatness and fastidious taste of its arrangements. Here, he thought, he could not fail to see traces of his cousin's habits, but he was obliged to confess to himself that there was very little to guide him. The furniture was strictly as its former occupant had left it, only rather the worse for wear, and far from being in order. The chairs were so heaped with books and papers, that Guy had to make a clearance of one before his visitor could sit down, but there was nothing else to complain of, not even a trace of cigars; but knowing him to be a great reader and lover of accomplishments, Philip wondered that the only decorations were Laura's drawing of Sintram, and a little print of Redclyffe, and the books were chiefly such as were wanted for his studies, the few others having for the most part the air of old library books, as if he had sent for them from Redclyffe. Was this another proof that he had some way of frittering away his money with nothing to show for it? A Sophocles and a lexicon were open before him on the table, and a blotting-book, which he closed, but not before Philip had caught sight of what looked like verses.

Neither did his countenance answer Philip's expectations. It had not his usual bright lively expression; there was a sadness which made him smile like a gleam on a showery day, instead of constant sunshine; but there was neither embarrassment nor defiance, and the gleam-like smile was there, as with a frank, confiding tone, he said,–

'This is very kind of you, to come and see what you can do for me.'

Philip was by no means prepared to be thus met half-way, but he thought Guy wanted to secure him as an intercessor, and hardened himself into righteous severity.

'No one can be more willing to help you than I, but you must, in the first place, help yourself.'

Instantly the sedate measured tone made Guy's heart and head throb with impatience, awakening all the former memories so hardly battled down; but with the impulse of anger came the thought, 'Here it is again! If I don't keep it down now, I am undone! The enemy will seize me again!' He forced himself not to interrupt, while Philip went calmly on.

'While you are not open, nothing can be done.'

'My only wish, my only desire, is to be open,' said Guy, speaking fast and low, and repressing the feeling, which, nevertheless, affected his voice; 'but the opportunity of explanation has never been given me.'

'You need complain of that no longer. I am here to convey to my uncle any explanation you may wish to address to him. I will do my best to induce him to attend to it favourably, but he is deeply offended and hurt by what has passed.'

'I know– I know,' said Guy, colouring deeply, and all irritation disappearing from voice and manner; 'I know there is no excuse for me. I can only repeat that I am heartily sorry for whatever I may have said, either of him or of you.'

'Of course,' returned Philip, 'I should never think of resenting what you may have said in a moment of irritation, especially as you express regret for it. Consider it as entirely overlooked on my part.'

Guy was nearly choked in uttering a 'Thank you,' which did not sound, after all, much like acceptance of forgiveness.

'Now to the real matter at issue,' said Philip: 'the application for the money, which so amazed Mr. Edmonstone.'

'I do not see that it is the point,' said Guy, 'I wanted it for a scheme of my own: he did not think fit to let me have it, so there is an end of the matter.'

'Mr Edmonstone does not think so. He wishes to be convinced that you have not spent it beforehand.'

'What would you have beyond my word and honour that I have not?' exclaimed Guy.

Far be it from me to say that he doubts it,' said Philip; and as at those words the flash of the Morville eye darted lightning, he expected that the next moment, 'Do you?' would be thundered forth, and he could not, with truth, answer 'No;' but it was one of his maxims that a man need never be forced into an open quarrel, and he tranquilly continued– 'but it is better not to depend entirely on assertion. Why do you not bring him full proofs of your good intention, and thus restore yourself to his confidence?'

'I have said that I am bound not to mention the purpose.'

'Unfortunate!' said Philip; then, while Guy bit his lip till it bled, the pain really a relief, by giving some vent to his anger at the implied doubt, he went on,– 'If it is impossible to clear this up, the next advice I would give is, that you should show what your expenditure has been; lay your accounts before him, and let them justify you.'

Most people would have resented this as an impertinent proposal, were it only that doing so would have served to conceal the awkward fact that the accounts had not been kept at all. Guy had never been taught to regard exactness in this respect as a duty, had no natural taste for precision, and did not feel responsible to any person; nor if he had kept any, could he have shown them, without exposing his uncle. To refuse, would, however, be a subterfuge, and after a moment, he made an effort, and confessed he had none to show, though he knew Philip would despise him for it as a fool, and probably take it as positive evidence against him.

It would have been more bearable if Philip would but have said 'How foolish,' instead of drily repeating 'Unfortunate!'

After a pause, during which Guy was not sufficiently master of himself to speak, Philip added– 'Then this matter of the thousand pounds is to be passed over? You have no explanation to offer?'

'No:' and again he paused. 'When my word is not accepted, I have no more to say. But this is not the point. What I would know is, what are the calumnies that accuse me of having gamed? If you really wish to do me a service, you will give me an opportunity of answering these precious proofs.'

'I will' answered Philip; who could venture on doing so himself, though, for his sister's sake, it was unsafe to trust Mr. Edmonstone, with whom what was not an absolute secret was not a secret at all. 'My uncle knows that a thirty pound cheque of his, in your name, was paid by you to a notorious gamester.'

Guy did not shrink, as he simply answered– 'It is true.'

'Yet you have neither played, nor betted, nor done anything that could come under the definition of gambling?'

'No.'

'Then why this payment?'

'I cannot explain that. I know appearances are against me,' replied Guy steadily, and with less irritation than he had hitherto shown. I once thought my simple word would have sufficed, but, since it seems that will not do, I will not again make what you call assertions.'

'In fact, while you profess a desire to be open and sincere, a mystery appears at every turn. What would you have us do?'

'As you think fit,' he answered proudly.

Philip had been used to feel men's wills and characters bend and give way beneath his superior force of mind. They might, like Charles, chafe and rage, but his calmness always gave him the ascendant almost without exertion, and few people had ever come into contact with him without a certain submission of will or opinion. With Guy alone it was not so; he had been sensible of it once or twice before; he had no mastery, and could no more bend that spirit than a bar of steel. This he could not bear, for it obliged him to be continually making efforts to preserve his own sense of superiority.

'Since this is your ultimatum,' he said– 'since you deny your confidence, and refuse any reply to these charges, you have no right to complain of suspicion. I shall do my best, both as your true friend, and as acting with your guardian's authority, to discover all that may lead to the elucidation of the mystery. In the first place, I am desired to make every inquiry here as to your conduct and expenditure. I hope they will prove satisfactory.'

'I am very much obliged to you,' answered Guy, his voice stern and dignified, and the smile that curled his lip was like Philip's own.

Philip was positively annoyed, and desirous to say something to put him down, but he had not committed himself by any vehemence, and Philip was too cool and wise to compromise his own dignity, so he rose to go, saying, 'Good night! I am sorry I cannot induce you to act in the only way that can right you.'

'Good night!' replied Guy, in the same dignified manner in which he had spoken ever since his passion had been surmounted.

They parted, each feeling that matters were just where they were before. Philip went back to his inn, moralizing on the pride and perverseness which made it impossible to make any impression on a Redclyffe Morville, whom not even the fear of detection could lead to submission.

Next morning, while Philip was hastily breakfasting, the door opened, and Guy entered, pale and disturbed, as if he had been awake all night.

'Philip!' said he, in his frank, natural voice, 'I don't think we parted last night as your good intentions deserved.'

'O, ho!' thought Philip; 'the fear of an investigation has brought him to reason;' and he said, 'Well, I am very glad you see things in a truer light this morning;' then asked if he had breakfasted. He had; and his cousin added,

'Have you anything to say on the matter we discussed last night?'

'No. I can only repeat that I am not guilty, and wait for time to show my innocence. I only came to see you once more, that I might feel we parted friends.'

'I shall always hope to be a true friend.'

'I did not come here for altercation,' said Guy (an answer rather to the spirit than the words), 'so I will say no more. If you wish to see me again, you will find me in my rooms. Good-bye.'

Philip was puzzled. He wondered whether Guy had come wishing to propitiate him, but had found pride indomitable at the last moment; or whether he had been showing himself too severely just to admit entreaty. He would be able to judge better after he had made his inquiries, and he proceeded with them at once. He met with no such replies as he expected. Every one spoke of Sir Guy Morville in high terms, as strict in his habits of application, and irreproachable in conduct. He was generally liked, and some regret was expressed that he lived in so secluded a manner, forming so few intimacies; but no one seemed to think it possible that anything wrong could be imputed to him. Philip could even perceive that there was some surprise that such inquiries should be made at all, especially by so young a man as himself. Mr. Wellwood, the person whom he most wished to see, was not at Oxford, but was at home preparing for his ordination.

Nor could Philip get nearer to the solution of the mystery when he went to the tradesmen, who were evidently as much surprised as the tutors, and said he always paid in ready money. Captain Morville felt like a lawyer whose case is breaking down, no discoveries made, nothing done; but he was not one whit convinced of his cousin's innocence, thinking the college authorities blind and careless, and the tradesmen combined to conceal their extortions, or else that the mischief had been done at St. Mildred's. He was particularly provoked when he remembered Guy's invitation to him to come to his rooms, knowing, as he must have done, what would be the result of his inquiry.

Philip was conscious that it would have been kind to have gone to say that, so far, he had found nothing amiss, but he did not like giving Guy this passing triumph. It made no difference in his real opinion; and why renew a useless discussion? He persuaded himself that he had left himself no time, and should miss the train, and hastened off to the station, where he had to wait a quarter of an hour, consoling himself with reflecting—

'After all, though I might have gone to him, it would have been useless. He is obstinate, and occasions of irritating his unfortunate temper are above all to be avoided.'

One short year after, what would not Philip have given for that quarter of an hour!

By six o'clock he was at St. Mildred's, greeted with delight by his sister, and with cordiality by Dr. Henley. They were both proud of him, and every tender feeling his sister had was for Philip, her pet, and her pupil in his childhood, and her most valued companion and counsellor through her early womanhood.

She had a picked dinner-party to meet him, for she knew the doctor's conversation was not exactly the thing to entertain him through a whole evening, and the guests might well think they had never seen a handsomer or more clever brother and sister than Mrs. Henley and Captain Morville. The old county families, if they did wonder at her marriage, were always glad to meet her brother, and it was a great pleasure to him to see old friends.

Only once did his sister, in the course of the evening, make him feel the difference of their sentiments, and that was about Miss Wellwood. Philip defended her warmly; and when he heard that there was a plan getting up for excluding her from the hospital, he expressed strong disapprobation at the time; and after the guests were gone, spoke upon the subject with his sister and her husband. The doctor entered into no party questions, and had only been stirred up to the opposition by his wife; he owned that the Miss Wellwoods had done a great deal of good, and made the nurses do their duty better than he had ever known, and was quite ready to withdraw his opposition. Mrs. Henley argued about opinions, but Philip was a match for her in her own line; and the end of it was, that though she would not allow herself to be convinced, and shook her head at her brother's way of thinking, he knew he had prevailed, and that Miss Wellwood would be unmolested.

There was not another person in the world to whom Margaret would have yielded; and it served to restore him to the sense of universal dominion which had been a little shaken by his conversation with Guy.

'Sir Guy was a great deal with the Wellwoods,' said Mrs. Henley.

'Was he, indeed?'

'O, you need not think of that. It would be too absurd. The youngest must be twice his age.'

'I was not thinking of any such thing,' said Philip, smiling, as he thought of the very different course Guy's affections had taken.

'I did hear he was to marry Lady Eveleen de Courcy. Is there anything in that report?'

'No; certainly not.'

'I should pity the woman who married him, after the specimen I saw of his temper.'

'Poor boy!' said Philip.

'Lady Eveleen has been a great deal at Hollywell, has she not? I rather wondered my aunt should like to have her there, considering all things.'

'What things, sister?'

'Considering what a catch he would be for one of the Edmonstone girls.'

'I thought you had just been pitying the woman who should marry him. Perhaps my aunt had Lady Eveleen there to act as a screen for her own daughters.'

'That our good-natured aunt should have acted with such ultra-prudence!' said Margaret, laughing at his grave ironical tone. 'Lady Eveleen is very pretty, is she not? A mere beauty, I believe?'

'Just so; she is much admired; but Guy is certainly not inclined to fall in love with her.'

'I should have thought him the very man to fall in love young, like his father. Do you think there is any chance for either of the Edmonstones? Laura's beauty he spoke of, but it was not in a very lover-like way. Do you admire Laura so much?'

'She is very pretty.'

'And little Amy?'

'She is a mere child, and will hardly ever be anything more; but she is a very good little amiable thing.'

'I wish poor Charles's temper was improved.'

'So do I; but it is very far from improvement at present, in consequence of his zeal for Guy. Guy has been very attentive and good natured to him, and has quite won his heart; so that I should positively honour him for his championship if it was not in great degree out of opposition to his father and myself. To-morrow, Margaret, you must give me some guide to the most probable quarters for learning anything respecting this poor boy's follies.'

Mrs. Henley did her best in that way, and Philip followed up his inquiries with great ardour, but still unsuccessfully. Jack White, the hero of the draft, was not at St. Mildred's, nor likely to be heard of again till the next races; and whether Sir Guy had been on the race-ground at all was a doubtful point. Next, Philip walked to Stylehurst, to call on Colonel Harewood, and see if he could learn anything in conversation with him; but the Colonel did not seem to know anything, and his sons were not at home. Young Morville was, he thought, a spirited lad, very good natured; he had been out shooting once or twice with Tom, and had a very fine spaniel. If he had been at the races, the Colonel did not know it; he had some thoughts of asking him to join their party, but had been prevented.

This was no reason, thought Philip, why Guy might not have been with Tom Harewood without the Colonel's knowledge. Tom was just the man to lead him amongst those who were given to betting; he might have been drawn in, and, perhaps, he had given some pledge of payment when he was of age, or, possibly, obtained an immediate supply of money from the old steward at Redclyffe, who was devotedly attached to him. If so, Philip trusted to be able to detect it from the accounts; on the other supposition, there was no hope of discovery.

The conversation with Colonel Harewood kept him so late that he had no time for going, as usual, to his old haunts, at Stylehurst; nor did he feel inclined just then to revive the saddening reflections they excited. He spent the evening in talking over books with his sister, and the next day proceeded on his journey to Thorndale Park.

This was one of the places where he was always the most welcome, ever since he had been a school-boy, received in a way especially flattering, considering that the friendship was entirely owing to the uncompromising good sense and real kindness with which he had kept in order the follies of his former fag.

Charles might laugh, and call them the young man and young man's companion, and Guy more classically term them the pious Aeneas and his fidus Achates, but it was a friendship that did honour to both; and the value that the Thorndales set upon Captain Morville was not misplaced, and scarcely over-rated. Not particularly clever themselves, they the more highly appreciated his endowments, and were proud that James had been able to make such a friend, for they knew, as well as the rest of the world, that Captain Morville was far from seeking the acquaintance for the sake of their situation in life, but that it was from real liking and esteem. How far this esteem was gained by the deference the whole family paid to his opinion, was another question; at any rate, the courting was from them.

The Miss Thorndales deemed Captain Morville the supreme authority in drawing, literature, and ecclesiastical architecture; and whenever a person came in their way who was thought handsome, always pronounced that he was not by any means equal to James's friend. Lady Thorndale delighted to talk over James with him, and thank him for his kindness; and Lord Thorndale, rather a pompous man himself, liked his somewhat stately manners, and talked politics with him, sincerely wishing he was his neighbour at Redclyffe, and calculating how much good he would do there. Philip listened with interest to accounts of how the Thorndale and Morville influence had always divided the borough of Moorworth, and, if united, might dispose of it at will, and returned evasive answers to questions what the young heir of Redclyffe might be likely to do.

James Thorndale drove his friend to Redclyffe, as Philip had authority from Mr. Edmonstone to transact any business that might be required with Markham, the steward; and, as has been said before, he expected to discover in the accounts something that might explain why Guy had ceased to press for the thousand pounds. However, he could find nothing amiss in them, though– bearing in mind that it is less easy to detect the loss of a score of sheep than of one– he subjected them to a scrutiny which seemed by no means agreeable to the gruff old grumbling steward. He also walked about the park, saw to the marking of certain trees that were injuring each other; and finding that there was a misunderstanding between Markham and the new rector, Mr. Ashford, about certain parish matters, where the clergyman was certainly right, he bore down Markham's opposition with Mr. Edmonstone's weight, and felt he was doing good service.

He paused at the gate, and looked back at the wide domain and fine old house. He pitied them, and the simple-hearted, honest tenantry, for being the heritage of such a family, and the possession of one so likely to misuse them, instead of training them into the means of conferring benefits on them, on his country. What would not Philip himself do if those lands were his,– just what was needed to give his talents free scope? and what would it be to see his beautiful Laura their mistress?

CHAPTER 20

The longing for ignoble things,
The strife for triumph more than truth,
The hardening of the heart, that brings
Irreverence for the dreams of youth.
– LONGFELLOW

After his week at Thorndale Park, Captain Morville returned to make his farewell visit at Hollywell, before joining his regiment at Cork, whence it was to sail for the Mediterranean. He reckoned much on this visit, for not even Laura herself could fathom the depth of his affection for her, strengthening in the recesses where he so sternly concealed it, and viewing her ever as more faultless since she had been his own. While she was his noble, strong-minded, generous, fond Laura, he could bear with his disappointment in his sister, with the loss of his home, and with the trials that had made him a grave, severe man. She had proved the strength of her mind by the self-command he had taught her, and for which he was especially grateful to her, as it made him safer and more unconstrained, able to venture on more demonstration than in those early days when every look had made her blush and tremble.

Mr. Edmonstone brought the carriage to fetch him from the station, and quickly began,–

'I suppose, as you have not written, you have found nothing out?'

'Nothing.'

'And you could do nothing with him. Eh?'

'No; I could not get a word of explanation, nor break through the fence of pride and reserve. I must do him the justice to say that he bears the best of characters at Oxford; and if there were any debts I could not get at them from the tradesmen.'

'Well, well, say no more about it; he is an ungrateful young dog, and I am sick of it. I only wish I could wash my hands of him altogether. It was mere folly to expect any of that set could ever come to good. There's everything going wrong all at once now; poor little Amy breaking her heart after him, and, worse than all, there's poor Charlie laid up again,' said Mr. Edmonstone, one of the most affectionate people in the world; but his maundering mood making him speak of Charles's illness as if he only regarded it as an additional provocation for himself.

'Charles ill!' exclaimed Philip.

'Yes; another, of those formations in the joint. I hoped and trusted that was all over now; but he is as bad as ever,– has not been able to move for a week, and goodness knows when he will again.'

'Indeed! I am very sorry. Is there as much pain as before?'

'Oh, yes. He has not slept a wink these four nights. Mayerne talks of opium; but he says he won't have it till he has seen you, he is so anxious about this unlucky business. If anything could persuade me to have Guy back again it would be that this eternal fretting after him is so bad for poor Charlie.'

'It is on Amy's account that it is impossible to have him here,' said Philip.

'Ay! He shall never set eyes on Amy again unless all this is cleared up, which it never will be, as I desire mamma to tell her. By the bye, Philip, Amy said something of your having a slip with Charles on the stairs.'

There was very nearly an accident; but I believed he was not hurt. I hope it has nothing to do with this illness?'

'He says it was all his own fault,' said Mr. Edmonstone, 'and that he should have been actually down but for you.'

'But is it really thought it can have caused this attack?'

'I can hardly suppose so; but Thompson fancies there may have been some jar. However, don't distress yourself; I dare say it would have come on all the same.'

Philip did not like to be forgiven by Mr. Edmonstone, and there was something very annoying in having this mischance connected with his name, though without his fault; nor did he wish Charles to have the kind of advantage over him that might be derived from seeming to pass over his share in the misfortune.

When they arrived at Hollywell, it was twilight, but no one was in the drawing-room, generally so cheerful at that time of day; the fire had lately been smothered with coals, and looked gloomy and desolate. Mr. Edmonstone left Philip there, and ran up to see how Charles was, and soon after Laura came in, sprang to his side, and held his hand in both hers.

'You bring no good news?' said she, sadly, as she read the answer in his face. 'O! how I wish you had. It would be such a comfort now. You have heard about poor Charlie?'

'Yes; and very sorry I am. But, Laura, is it really thought that accident could have occasioned it?'

'Dr. Mayerne does not think so, only Mr. Thompson talked of remote causes, when Amy mentioned it. I don't believe it did any harm, and Charlie himself says you saved him from falling down-stairs.'

Philip had begun to give Laura his version of the accident, as he had already done to her father, when Mrs. Edmonstone came down, looking harassed and anxious. She told her nephew that Charles was very desirous to see him, and sent him up at once.

There was a fire in the dressing-room, and the door was open into the little room, which was only lighted by a lamp on a small table, where Amy was sitting at work. After shaking hands, she went away, leaving him alone with Charles, who lay in his narrow bed against the wall, fixed in one position, his forehead contracted with pain, his eyelids red and heavy from sleeplessness, his eyes very quick and eager, and his hands and arms thrown restlessly outside the coverings.

'I am very sorry to find you here,' said Philip, coming up to him, and taking, rather than receiving, his hot, limp hand. 'Is the pain very bad?'

'That is a matter of course,' said Charles, in a sharp, quick manner, his voice full of suffering. 'I want to hear what you have been doing at Oxford and St. Mildred's.'

'I am sorry I do not bring the tidings you wish.'

'I did not expect you would. I know you too well; but I want to hear what you have been doing– what he said,' answered Charles, in short, impatient sentences.

'It can be of no use, Charlie. You are not in a state to enter on agitating subjects.'

'I tell you I will hear all,' returned Charles, with increased asperity. 'I know you will say nothing to his advantage that you can help, but still I know you will speak what you think the truth, and I want to judge for myself.'

'You speak as if I was not acting for his good.'

'Palaver!' cried Charles, fully sensible of the advantage his illness gave him. 'I want the facts. Begin at the beginning. Sit down– there's a chair by you. Now tell me, where did you find him?'

Philip could not set Charles down in his present state, and was obliged to submit to a cross-examination, in which he showed no abatement of his natural acuteness, and, unsparing as he always was, laid himself under no restraint at all. Philip was compelled to give a full history of his researches; and if he had afforded no triumph to Guy, Charles revenged him.

'Pray, what did Guy say when he heard the result of this fine voyage of discovery?'

'I did not see him again.'

'Not see him! not tell him he was so far justified!'

'I had no time– at least I thought not. It would have been useless, for while these mysteries continue, my opinion is unchanged, and there was no benefit in renewing vain disputes.'

'Say no more!' exclaimed Charles. 'You have said all I expected, and more too. I gave you credit for domineering and prejudice, now I see it is malignity.'

As he spoke, Laura entered from the dressing-room, and stood aghast at the words, and then looked imploringly at her cousin. Dr. Mayerne was following her, and Charles called out,–

'Now, doctor, give me as much opium as you please. I only want to be stupefied till the world has turned round, and then you may wake me.'

Philip shook hands with Dr. Mayerne, and, without betraying a shade of annoyance, wished Charles good night; but Charles had drawn the coverings over his head, and would not hear him.

'Poor fellow!' said Philip to Laura, when they were out of the room. 'He is a very generous partisan, and excitement and suffering make him carry his zeal to excess.'

'I knew you could not be angry with him.'

'I could not be angry at this time at far more provocation given by any one belonging to you, Laura.'

Laura's heart had that sensation which the French call "se serrer", as she heard him allude to the long separation to which there seemed no limit; but they could say no more.

'Amy,' said Charles, when she returned to him after dinner, 'I am more than ever convinced that things will right themselves. I never saw prejudice more at fault.'

'Did he tell you all about it?'

'I worked out of him all I could, and it is my belief Guy had the best of it. I only wonder he did not horsewhip Philip round the quadrangle. I wish he had.'

'Oh, no, no! But he controlled himself?'

'If he had not we should have heard of it fast enough;' and Charles told what he had been able to gather, while she sat divided between joy and pain.

Philip saw very little more of Charles. He used to come to ask him how he was once a day, but never received any encouragement to lengthen his visit. These gatherings in the diseased joint were always excessively painful, and were very long in coming to the worst, as well as afterwards in healing; and through the week of Philip's stay at Hollywell, Charles was either in a state of great suffering, or else heavy and confused with opiates. His mother's whole time and thoughts were absorbed in him; she attended to him day and night, and could hardly spare a moment for anything else. Indeed, with all her affection and anxiety for the young lovers, Charles was so entirely her engrossing object, that her first feeling of disappointment at the failure of Philip's journey of investigation was because it would grieve Charlie. She could not think about Guy just then, and for Amy there was nothing for it but patience; and, good little creature, it was very nice to see her put her own troubles aside, and be so cheerful a nurse to her brother. She was almost always in his room, for he liked to have her there, and she could not conquer a certain shrinking from Philip.

Laura had once pleaded hard and earnestly for Guy with Philip, but all in vain; she was only taught to think the case more hopeless than before. Laura was a very kind nurse and sister, but she could better be spared than her mother and Amy, so that it generally fell to her lot to be down-stairs, making the drawing-room habitable. Dr. Mayerne, whenever Charles was ill, used to be more at Hollywell than at his own house, and there were few days that he did not dine there. When Amy was out of the way, Philip used to entertain them with long accounts of Redclyffe, how fine a place it was, how far the estate reached on the Moorworth road, of its capacities for improvement, wastes of moorland to be enclosed or planted, magnificent timber needing nothing but thinning. He spoke of the number of tenantry, and the manorial rights, and the influence in both town and county, which, in years gone by, had been proved to the utmost in many a fierce struggle with the house of Thorndale. Sir Guy Morville might be one of the first men in England if he were not wanting to himself. Mr. Edmonstone enjoyed such talk, for it made him revel in the sense of his own magnanimity in refusing his daughter to the owner of all this; and Laura sometimes thought how Philip would have graced such a position, yet how much greater it was to rest entirely on his own merits.

'Ah, my fine fellow!' muttered Dr. Mayerne to himself one day, when Philip and his uncle had left the room, just after a discourse of this kind, 'I see you have not forgotten you are the next heir.'

Laura coloured with indignation, exclaimed, 'Oh!' then checked herself, as if such an aspersion was not worthy of her taking the trouble to refute it.

'Ah! Miss Edmonstone, I did not know you were there.'

'Yes, you were talking to yourself, just as if you were at home,' said Charlotte, who was specially pert to the old doctor, because she knew herself to be a great pet. 'You were telling some home truths to make Laura angry.'

'Well, he would make a very good use of it if he had it,' said the doctor.

'Now you'll make me angry,' said Charlotte; 'and you have not mended matters with Laura. She thinks nothing short of four-syllabled words good enough for Philip.'

'Hush! nonsense, Charlotte!' said Laura, much annoyed.

'There Charlotte, she is avenging herself on you because she can't scold me' said the doctor, pretending to whisper.

'Charlotte is only growing more wild than ever for want of mamma,' said Laura, trying to laugh it off, but there was so much annoyance evident about her, that Dr. Mayerne said,—

'Seriously, I must apologize for my unlucky soliloquy; not that I thought I was saying much harm, for I did not by any means say or think the Captain wished Sir Guy any ill, and few men who stood next in succession to such a property would be likely to forget it.'

'Yes, but Philip is not like other men,' said Charlotte, who, at fourteen, had caught much of her brother's power of repartee, and could be quite as provoking, when unrestrained by any one whom she cared to obey.

Laura felt it was more for her dignity not to notice this, and replied, with an effort for a laugh,—

'It must be your guilty conscience that sets you apologizing, for you said no harm, as you observe.'

'Yes,' said Dr. Mayerne, good-humouredly. 'He does very well without it, and no doubt he would be one of the first men in the country if he had it; but it is in very good hands now, on the whole. I don't think, even if the lad has been tempted into a little folly just now, that he can ever go very far wrong.'

'No, indeed,' said Charlotte; 'but Charlie and I don't believe he has done anything wrong.'

She spoke in a little surly decided tone, as if her opinion put an end to the matter, and Philip's return closed the discussion.

Divided as the party were between up-stairs and down-stairs, and in the absence of Charles's shrewd observation, Philip and Laura had more opportunity of intercourse than usual, and now that his departure would put an end to suspicion, they ventured on more openly seeking each other. It never could be the perfect freedom that they had enjoyed before the avowal of their sentiments, but they had many brief conversations, giving Laura feverish, but exquisite, delight at each renewal of his rare expressions of tenderness.

'What are you going to do to-day?' he asked, on the last morning before he was to leave Hollywell. 'I must see you alone before I go.'

She looked down, and he kept his eyes fixed on her rather sternly, for he had never before made a clandestine appointment, and he did not like feeling ashamed of it. At last she said,—

'I go to East-hill School this afternoon. I shall come away at half-past three.'

Mary Ross was still absent; her six nephews and nieces having taken advantage of her visit to have the measles, not like reasonable children, all at once, so as to be one trouble, but one after the other, so as to keep Aunt Mary with them as long as possible; and Mr. Ross did not know what would have become of the female department of his parish but for Laura, who worked at school-keeping indefatigably.

Laura had some difficulty in shaking off Charlotte's company this afternoon, and was obliged to make the most of the probability of rain, and the dreadful dirt of the roads. Indeed, she represented it as so formidable, that Mrs. Edmonstone, who had hardly time to look out of window, much less to go out of doors, strongly advised her to stay at home herself; and Charlotte grew all the more eager for the fun. Luckily, however, for Laura, Dr. Mayerne came in, laughing at the reports of the weather; and as he was wanted to prescribe for a poor old man in an opposite direction, he took Charlotte with him to show the way, and she was much better pleased to have him for a companion than the grave Laura.

Philip, in the meantime, had walked all the way to Broadstone, timing his return exactly, that he might meet Laura as she came out of the school, and feel as if it had been by chance. It was a gray, misty November day, and the leaves of the elm-trees came floating round them, yellow and damp.

'You have had a wet walk,' said Laura, as they met.

'It is not quite raining,' he answered; and they proceeded for some minutes in silence, until he said,– 'It is time we should come to an understanding.'

She looked at him in alarm, and his voice was immediately gentler; indeed, at times it was almost inaudible from his strong emotion. 'I believe that no affection has ever been stronger or truer than ours.'

'Has been!' repeated Laura, in a wondering, bewildered voice.

'And is, if you are satisfied to leave things as they are.'

'I must be, if you are.'

'I will not say I am satisfied with what must be, as I am situated; but I felt it due to you to set the true state of the case before you. Few would venture their love as I do mine with you, bound in reality, though not formally, with no promise sought or given; yet I am not more assured that I stand here than I am that our love is for ever.'

'I am sure it is!' she repeated fervently. 'O Philip, there never was a time I did not love you: and since that day on Ashen Down, I have loved you with my whole heart. I am sometimes afraid it has left no proper room for the rest, when I find how much more I think of your going away than of poor Charles.'

'Yes,' he said, 'you have understood me as none but you would have done, through coldness and reserve, apparently, even towards yourself, and when to others I have seemed grave and severe beyond my years. You have never doubted, you have recognized the warmth within; you have trusted your happiness to me, and it shall be safe in my keeping, for, Laura, it is all mine.'

'There is only one thing,' said Laura, timidly; 'would it not be better if mamma knew?'

'Laura, I have considered that, but remember you are not bound; I have never asked you to bind yourself. You might marry to-morrow, and I should have no right to complain. There is nothing to prevent you.'

She exclaimed, as if with pain.

'True,' he answered; 'you could not, and that certainty suffices me. I ask no more without your parents' consent; but it would be giving them and you useless distress and perplexity to ask it now. They would object to my poverty, and we should gain nothing; for I would never be so selfish as to wish to expose you to such a life as that of the wife of a poor officer; and an open engagement could not add to our confidence in each other. We must be content to wait for my promotion. By that time'– he smiled gravely– 'our attachment will have lasted so many years as to give it a claim to respect.'

'It is no new thing.'

'No newer than our lives; but remember, my Laura, that you are but twenty.'

'You have made me feel much older,' sighed Laura, 'not that I would be a thoughtless child again. That cannot last long, not even for poor little Amy'

'No one would wish to part with the deeper feelings of elder years to regain the carelessness of childhood, even to be exempted from the suffering that has brought them.'

'No, indeed.'

'For instance, these two years have scarcely been a time of great happiness to you.'

'Sometimes,' whispered Laura, 'sometimes beyond all words, but often dreary and oppressive.'

'Heaven knows how unwillingly I have rendered it so. Rather than dim the brightness of your life, I would have repressed my own sentiments for ever.'

'But, then, where would have been my brightness?'

'I would, I say, but for a peril to you. I see my fears were unfounded. You were safe; but in my desire to guard you from what has come on poor Amy, my feelings, though not wont to overpower me, carried me further than I intended.'

'Did they?'

'Do not suppose I regret it. No, no, Laura; those were the most precious moments in my life, when I drew from you those words and looks which have been blessed in remembrance ever since; and doubly, knowing, as I do, that you also prize that day.'

'Yes– yes;– '

'In the midst of much that was adverse, and with a necessity for a trust and self-control of which scarce a woman but yourself would have been capable, you have endured nobly– '

'I could bear anything, if you were not going so far away,'

'You will bear that too, Laura, and bravely. It will not be for ever.'

'How long do you think?'

'I cannot tell. Several years may pass before I have my promotion. It may be that I shall not see that cheek in its fresh bloom again, but I shall find the same Laura that I left, the same in love, and strength, and trust.'

'Ah; I shall grow faded and gray, and you will be a sun-burnt old soldier,' said Laura, smiling, and looking, half sadly, half proudly, up to his noble features; 'but hearts don't change like faces!'

After they came near the house, they walked up and down the lane for a long time, for Philip avoided a less public path, in order to keep up his delusion that he was doing nothing in an underhand way. It grew dark, and the fog thickened, straightening Laura's auburn ringlets, and hanging in dew-drops on Philip's rough coat, but little recked they; it was such an hour as they had never enjoyed before. Philip had never so laid himself open, or assured her so earnestly of the force of his affection; and her thrills of ecstasy overcame the desolate expectation of his departure, and made her sensible of strength to bear seven, ten, twenty years of loneliness and apparent neglect. She knew him, and he would never fail her.

Yet, when at last they went in-doors, and Amy followed her to her room, wondering to find her so wet, and so late, who could have seen the two sisters without reading greater peace and serenity in the face of the younger.

Philip felt an elder brother's interest for poor little Amy. He did not see much of her; but he compassionated her as a victim to her mother's imprudence, hoping she would soon be weaned from her attachment. He thought her a good, patient little thing, so soft and gentle as probably not to have the strength and depth that would make the love incurable; and the better he liked her, the more unfit he thought her for Guy. It would have been uniting a dove and a tiger; and his only fear was, that when he was no longer at hand, Mr. Edmonstone's weak good-nature might be prevailed on to sacrifice her. He did his best for her protection, by making his uncle express a resolution never to admit Guy into his family again, unless the accusation of gambling was completely disproved.

The last morning came, and Philip went to take leave of Charles. Poor Charles was feebler by this time, and too much subdued by pain and languor to receive him as at first, but the spirit was the same; and when Philip wished him good-bye, saying he hoped soon to hear he was better, he returned for answer,

'Good-bye, Philip, I hope soon to hear you are better. I had rather have my hip than your mind.'

He was in no condition to be answered, and Philip repeated his good-bye, little thinking how they were to meet again.

The others were assembled in the hall. His aunt's eyes were full of tears, for she loved him dearly, her brother's only son, early left motherless, whom she had regarded like her own child, and who had so nobly fulfilled all the fondest hopes. All his overbearing ways and uncalled-for interference were forgotten, and her voice gave way as she embraced him, saying,

'God bless you, Philip, wherever you may be. We shall miss you very much!'

Little Amy's hand was put into his, and he squeezed it kindly; but she could hardly speak her 'good-bye,' for the tears that came, because she was grieved not to feel more sorry that her highly-esteemed cousin, so kind and condescending to her, was going away for so very long a time.

'Good-bye, Philip,' said Charlotte; 'I shall be quite grown up by the time you come home.'

'Don't make such uncivil auguries, Puss,' said her father; but Philip heard her not, for he was holding Laura's hand in a grasp that seemed as if it never would unclose.

CHAPTER 21

I will sing, for I am sad,
For many my misdeeds;
It is my sadness makes me glad,
For love for sorrow pleads.
– WILLIAMS.

After his last interview with Philip, Guy returned to his rooms to force himself into occupation till his cousin should come to acknowledge that here, at least, there was nothing amiss. He trusted that when it was proved all was right in this quarter, the prejudice with regard to the other might be diminished, though his hopes were lower since he had found out the real grounds of the accusation, reflecting that he should never be able to explain without betraying his uncle.

He waited in vain. The hour passed at which Philip's coming was possible; Guy was disappointed, but looked for a letter; but post after post failed to bring him one. Perhaps Philip would write from Hollywell, or else Mr. Edmonstone would write, or at least he was sure that Charles would write– Charles, whose confidence and sympathy, expressed in almost daily letters, had been such a comfort. But not a line came. He reviewed in memory his last letter to Charles, wondering whether it could have offended him; but it did not seem possible; he thought over all that Philip could have learnt in his visit, to see if it could by any means have been turned to his disadvantage. But he knew he had done nothing to which blame could be attached; he had never infringed the rules of college discipline; and though still backward, and unlikely to distinguish himself, he believed that was the worst likely to have been said of him. He only wished his true character was as good as what would be reported of him.

As he thought and wondered, he grew more and more restless and unhappy. He could imagine no reason for the silence, unless Mr. Edmonstone had absolutely forbidden any intercourse, and it did not seem probable that he would issue any commands in a manner to bind a grown-up son, more especially as there had been no attempt at communication with Amy. It was terrible thus, without warning, to be cut off from her, and all besides that he loved. As long as Charles wrote, he fancied her sitting by, perhaps sealing the letter, and he could even tell by the kind of paper and envelope, whether they were sitting in the dressing-room or down-stairs; but now there was nothing, no assurance of sympathy, no word of kindness; they might all have given him up; those unhappy words were like a barrier, cutting him off for ever from the happiness of which he had once had a glimpse. Was the Redclyffe doom of sin and sorrow really closing in upon him?

If it had not been for chapel and study, he hardly knew how he should have got through that term; but as the end of it approached, a feverish impatience seized on him whenever the post came in, for a letter, if only to tell him not to come to Hollywell. None came, and he saw nothing for it but to go to Redclyffe; and if he dreaded seeing it in its altered state when his spirits were high and unbroken, how did he shrink from it now! He did, however, make up his mind, for he felt that his reluctance almost wronged his own beloved home. Harry Graham wanted to persuade him to come and spend Christmas at his home, with his lively family, but Guy felt as if gaiety was not for him, even if he could enjoy it. He did not wish to drown his present feelings, and steadily, though gratefully, refused this as well as one or two other friendly invitations.

After lingering in vain till the last day of term, he wrote to desire that his own room and the library might be made ready for him, and that 'something' might be sent to meet him at Moorworth.

Railroads had come a step nearer, even to his remote corner of the world, in the course of the last three years; but there was still thirty miles of coach beyond, and these lay through a part of the country he had never seen before. It was for the most part bleak, dreary moor, such as, under the cold gray wintry sky, presented nothing to rouse him from his musings on the welcome he might have been at that very moment receiving at Hollywell.

A sudden, dip in the high ground made it necessary for the coach to put on the drag, and thus it slowly entered a village, which attracted attention from its wretched appearance. The cottages, of the rough stone of the country, were little better than hovels; slates were torn off, windows broken. Wild-looking uncombed women, in garments of universal dirt colour, stood at the doors; ragged children ran and shrieked after the coach, the church had a hole in the roof, and stood tottering in spite of rude repairs; the churchyard was trodden down by cattle, and the whole place only resembled the pictures of Irish dilapidation.

'What miserable place is this?' asked a passenger. 'Yes, that's what all gentlemen ask,' replied the coachman; 'and well you may. There's not a more noted place for thieves and vagabonds. They call it Coombe Prior.'

Guy well knew the name, though he had never been there. It was a distant offset of his own property, and a horrible sense of responsibility for all the crime and misery there came over him.

'Is there no one to look; after it?' continued the traveller. 'No squire, no clergyman?'

'A fox-hunting parson,' answered the coachman; 'who lives half-a-dozen miles off, and gallops over for the service.'

Guy knew that the last presentation had been sold in the days of his grandfather's extravagance, and beheld another effect of ancestral sin.

'Do you know who is the owner of the place?'

'Yes, sir; 'tis Sir Guy Morville. You have heard tell of the old Sir Guy Morville, for he made a deal of noise in the world.'

'What! The noted– '

'I ought not to allow you to finish your sentence,' said Guy, very courteously, 'without telling you that I am his grandson.'

'I beg your pardon!' exclaimed the traveller.

'Nay,' said Guy, with a smile; 'I only thought it was fair to tell you.'

'Sir Guy himself!' said the coachman, turning round, and touching his hat, anxious to do the honours of his coach. 'I have not seen you on this road before, sir, for I never forget a face; I hope you'll often be this way.'

After a few more civilities, Guy was at liberty to attend to the fresh influx of sad musings on thoughtless waste affecting not only the destiny of the individual himself, but whole generations besides. How many souls might it not have ruined? 'These sheep, what had they done!' His grandfather had repented, but who was to preach repentance unto these? He did not wonder now that his own hopes of happiness had been blighted; he only marvelled that a bright present or future had ever been his–

While souls were wandering far and wide,
And curses swarmed on every side.

The traveller was, meanwhile, observing the heir of Redclyffe, possessor of wealth and wide lands. Little did he guess how that bright-eyed youth looked upon his riches.

Miles were passed in one long melancholy musing, till Guy was roused by the sight of familiar scenes, and found himself rattling over the stones of the little borough of Moorworth, with the gray, large-windowed, old-fashioned houses, on each side, looking at him with friendly eyes. There, behind those limes cut out in arches, was the commercial school, where he had spent many an hour in construing with patient Mr. Potts; and though he had now a juster appreciation of his old master's erudition, which he had once thought so vast, he recollected with veneration his long and patient submission to an irksome, uncongenial life. Rumbling on, the coach was in the square market-place, the odd-looking octagon market-house in the middle, and the inn– the respectable old 'George'– with its long rank of stables and out-buildings forming one side. It was at this inn that Guy had been born, and the mistress having been the first person who had him in her arms, considered herself privileged to have a great affection for him, and had delighted in the greetings he always exchanged with her when he put up his pony at her stable, and went to his tutor.

There was a certainty of welcome here that cheered him, as he swung himself from the roof of the coach, lifted Bustle down, and called out to the barmaid that he hoped Mrs. Lavers was well.

The next moment Mrs. Lavers was at the door herself, with her broad, good-humoured face, close cap, bright shawl, and black gown, just as Guy always recollected, and might, if he could, have recollected, when he was born. If she had any more guests she neither saw nor cared for them; her welcome was all for him; and he could not but smile and look cheerful, if only that he might not disappoint her, feeling, in very truth, cheered and gratified by her cordiality. If he was in a hurry, he would not show it; and he allowed her to seat him in her own peculiar abode, behind the glass-cases of tongue and cold chicken, told her he came from Oxford, admired her good fire, and warmed his hands over it, before he even asked if the 'something' had arrived which was to take him home. It was coming to the door at the moment, and proved to be Mr. Markham's tall, high-wheeled gig, drawn by the old white-faced chestnut, and driven by Markham himself– a short, sturdy, brown-red, honest-faced old man, with frosted hair and whiskers, an air more of a yeoman than of a lawyer; and though not precisely gentlemanlike, yet not ungentlemanlike, as there was no pretension about him.

Guy darted out to meet him, and was warmly shaken by the hand, though the meeting was gruff.

'So, Sir Guy! how d'ye do? I wonder what brings you here on such short notice? Good morning, Mrs. Lavers. Bad roads this winter.'

'Good morning, Mr. Markham. It is a treat, indeed, to have Sir Guy here once more; so grown, too.'

'Grown– hum!' said Markham, surveying him; 'I don't see it. He'll never be as tall as his father. Have you got your things, Sir Guy? Ay, that's the way,– care for nothing but the dog. Gone on by the coach, most likely.'

They might have been, for aught Guy knew to the contrary, but Boots had been more attentive, and they were right. Mrs. Lavers begged he would walk in, and warm himself; but Markham answered,–

'What do you say, Sir Guy? The road is shocking, and it will be as dark as a pit by the time we get home.'

'Very well; we won't keep old Whiteface standing,' said Guy. 'Good-bye, Mrs. Lavers thank you. I shall see you again before long.'

Before Markham had finished a short private growl on the shocking state of the Moorworth pavement, and a protest that somebody should be called over the coals, Guy began,– '

'What a horrible place Coombe Prior is!'

'I only know I wish you had more such tenants as Todd,' was Markham's answer. 'Pays his rent to a day, and improves his land.'

'But what sort of man is he?'

'A capital farmer. A regular screw, I believe; but that is no concern of mine.'

'There are all the cottages tumbling down.'

'Ay? Are they? I shouldn't wonder, for they are all in his lease; and he would not lay out an unproductive farthing. And a precious bad lot they are there, too! There were actually three of them poaching in Cliffstone hanger this autumn; but we have them in jail. A pretty pass of impudence to be coming that distance to poach.'

Guy used to be kindled into great wrath by the most distant hint of poachers; but now he cared for men, not for game; and instead of asking, as Markham expected, the particulars of their apprehension, continued—

'The clergyman is that Halroyd, is he not?'

'Yes; every one knows what he is. I declare it went against me to take his offer for the living; but it could not be helped. Money must be had; but there! least said, soonest mended.'

'We must mend it,' said Guy, so decidedly, that Markham looked at him with surprise.

'I don't see what's to be done till Halroyd dies; and then you may give the living to whom you please. He lives so hard he can't last long, that is one comfort.'

Guy sighed and pondered; and presently Markham resumed the conversation.

'And what has brought you home at a moment's notice? You might as well have written two or three days before, at least.'

'I was waiting in hopes of going to Hollywell,' said Guy sorrowfully.

'Well, and what is the matter? You have not been quarrelling with your guardian, I hope and trust! Going the old way, after all!' exclaimed Markham, not in his usual gruff, grumbling note, but with real anxiety, and almost mournfulness.

'He took up some unjust suspicion of me. I could not bear it patiently, and said something that has offended him.'

'Oh, Sir Guy! hot and fiery as ever. I always told you that hasty temper would be the ruin of you.'

'Too true!' said Guy, so dejectedly, that the old man instantly grew kinder, and was displeased with Mr. Edmonstone.

'What could he have taken into his head to suspect you of?'

'Of gaming at St. Mildred's.'

'You have not?'

'Never!'

'Then why does not he believe you?'

'He thinks he has proof against me. I can't guess how he discovered it; but I was obliged to pay some money to a gambling sort of man, and he thinks I lost it.'

'Then why don't you show him your accounts?'

'For one reason— because I have kept none.'

As if it was an immense relief to his mind, Markham launched out into a discourse on the extreme folly, imprudence, and all other evils of such carelessness. He was so glad to find this was the worst, that his lecture lasted for two miles and a half, during which Guy, though attentive at first, had ample space for all the thrills of recognition at each well-known spot.

There was the long green-wooded valley between the hills where he had shot his first woodcock; there was the great stone on which he had broken his best knife in a fit of geological research; there was the pool where he used to skate; there the sudden break in the lulls that gave the first view of the sea. He could not help springing up at the sight— pale, leaden, and misty as it was; and though Markham forthwith rebuked him for not listening, his heart was still beating as at the first sight of a dear old friend, when that peep was far behind. More black heaths, with stacks of peat and withered ferns. Guy was straining his eyes far off in the darkness to look for the smoke of the old keeper's cottage chimney, and could with difficulty refrain from interrupting Markham to ask after the old man.

Another long hill, and then began a descent into a rich valley, beautiful fields of young wheat, reddish soil, full of fatness, large spreading trees with noble limbs, cottages, and cottage gardens, very unlike poor Coombe Prior; Markham's house— a perfect little snuggery covered all over with choice climbing plants, the smart plastered doctor's house, the Morville Arms, looking honest and venerable, the church, with its disproportionately high tower, the parsonage rather hidden behind it; and, on the opposite side of the road, the park-wall and the gate, where old Sarah stood, in an ecstasy of curtsies.

Guy jumped out to meet her, and to spare Whiteface; for there was a sharp, steep bit of hill, rising from the lodge, trying to horses, in spite of the road being cut out in long spirals. On he ran, leaving the road to Markham, straight up the high, steep, slippery green slope. He came in sight at the great dark-red sandstone pile of building; but he passed it, and ran on to where the ground rose on one side of it still more abruptly, and at the highest point was suddenly broken away and cut off into a perpendicular crag, descending in some parts sheer down to the sea, in others a little broken, and giving space for the growth of stunted brushwood. He stood at the highest point, where the precipice was most abrupt. The sea was dashing far beneath; the ripple, dash, and roar were in his ears once more; the wind— such wind as only blows over the sea— was breathing on his face; the broad, free horizon far before him; the field of waves, in gray and brown shade indeed, but still his own beloved waves; the bay, shut in with rocks, and with Black Shag Island and its train of rocks projecting far out to the west, and almost immediately beneath him, to the left, the little steep street of the fishing part of the village, nestled into the cove, which was formed by the mouth of a little mountain-stream, and the dozen boats it could muster rocking on the water.

Guy stood and looked as if he could never cease looking, or enjoying the sea air and salt breeze. It was real pleasure at first, for there were his home, his friends, and though there was a throb and tightness of heart at thinking how all was changed but such as this, and how all must change; how he had talked with Amy of this very thing, and had longed to have her standing beside him there; yet there was more of soothing than suffering in the sensation.

So many thoughts rushed through his mind, that he fancied he had stood there a long time, when he turned and hastened down again, but he had been so rapid as to meet Markham before the servants had had time to miss him.

The servants were indeed few. There was, alas! William of Deloraine, waiting to hold Whiteface; there was Arnaud, an old Swiss, first courier and then butler to old Sir Guy; there was Mrs. Drew, the housekeeper, also a very old servant; and these were all; but their welcome was of the heartiest, in feeling, if not in demonstration as the gig went with an echoing, thundering sound under the deep archway that led into the paved quadrangle; round which the house was built, that court where, as Philip had truly averred, the sun hardly ever shone, so high were the walls on each side.

Up the stone steps into the spacious dark hall, and into the large, gloomy library, partially lighted by a great wood fire, replying to Mrs. Drew's questions about his dinner and his room, and asking Markham to stay and dine with him, Guy at length found himself at home, in the very room where he had spent every evening of his boyhood, with the same green leather arm-chair, in the very place where his grandfather used to sit.

Markham consented to dine with him, and the evening was spent in talking over the news of Redclyffe. Markham spoke with much bitterness of the way in which Captain Morville had taken upon him; his looking into the accounts, though any one was welcome to examine them, was, he thought, scarcely becoming in so young a man— the heir-at-law, too.

'He can't help doing minutely whatever he undertakes,' said Guy. If you had him here, you would never have to scold him like me.'

'Heaven forbid!' said Markham, hastily. 'I know the same place would not hold him and me long.'

'You have told me nothing of our new vicar. How do you get on with him?'

'None the better for that same Captain Morville,' replied Markham, plunging forthwith into his list of grievances, respecting which he was waging a petty warfare, in the belief that he was standing up for his master's rights.

Mr. Bernard, the former clergyman, had been a quiet, old-fashioned man, very kind-hearted, but not at all active, and things had gone on in a sleepy, droning, matter-of-fact way, which Markham being used to, thought exactly what ought to be. Now, Mr. Ashford was an energetic person, desirous to do his utmost for the parish, and whatever he did was an offence to Markham, from the daily service, to the objecting to the men going out fishing on Sunday. He opposed every innovation with all his might, and Captain Morville's interference, which had borne Markham down with Mr. Edmonstone's authority, had only made him more determined not to bate an inch. He growled every time Guy was inclined to believe Mr. Ashford in the right, and brought out some fresh complaint. The grand controversy was at present about the school. There was a dame's school in the cove or fishing part of the parish, maintained at the expense of the estate, in a small cottage far from the church, and Mr. and Mrs. Ashford had fixed their eyes on a house in the village, and so near the church as to be very convenient for a Sunday School. It only wanted to be floored, and to have a partition taken down, but to this Markham would not consent, treating it as a monstrous proposal to take away the school from old Jenny Robinson.

'I suppose Mr. Ashford meant to pension her off?' said Guy.

'He did say something about it; but who is to do it, I should like to know?'

'We are, I suppose.'

'Pay two schoolmistresses mistresses at once! One for doing nothing! A pretty tolerable proposal for Mr. Ashford to be making?'

'I don't see why. Of course it is my business!'

'Besides, I don't see that she is not as fit to keep school as ever she was.'

'That may well be,' said Guy, smiling. 'We never used to be noted for our learning.'

'Don't you be for bringing new lights into the parish, Sir Guy, or we shall never have any more peace.'

'I shall see about old Jenny,' answered Guy. 'As to the house, that must be done directly. Her cottage is not fit to keep school in.'

Grunt, grunt; but though a very unbending viceroy, a must from the reigning baronet had a potent effect on Markham, whether it was for good or evil. He might grumble, but he never disobeyed, and the boy he was used to scold and order had found that Morville intonation of the must, which took away all idea of resistance. He still, however remonstrated.

'As you please, Sir Guy, but we shall have the deer frightened, and the plantations cut to pieces, if the boys from the Cove are to be crossing the park.'

'I'll be answerable for all the damage. If they are once properly spoken to, they will be on honour to behave well. I have seen a little of what a village school ought to be at East-hill, and I should like to see Redclyffe like it.'

Grunt again; and Guy found that to make Markham amiable, he must inquire after all his nephews and nieces.

All the evening he had much to occupy him, and the dreaded sense of solitude and bereavement did not come on till he had parted with Markham, and stood alone before the fire in the large, gloomy room, where the light of the lamp seemed absorbed in the darkness of the distant corners, and where he had scarcely been since the moment when he found his grandfather senseless in that very chair. How different had that room once been in his eyes, when his happy spirits defied every association of gloom, and the bookshelves, the carved chairs, the heavy dark-green curtains and deep windows were connected with merry freaks, earnest researches, delightful achievements or discoveries! How long ago that time seemed! and how changed was he!

There was a certain tendency to melancholy in Guy's mind. High spirits, prosperity, and self-discipline, had kept it from developing itself until the beginning of his troubles, but since that time it had been gradually gaining ground, and this was a time of great suffering, as he stood alone in his forefathers' house, and felt himself, in his early youth, a doomed man, destined to bear the penalty of their crimes in the ruin of his dearest hopes, as if his heirloom of misery had but waited to seize on him till the very moment when it would give him the most to endure.

'But bear it, I must and will!' said he, lifting his head from the carved chimney-piece, where he had been resting it. 'I have been in will a murderer myself, and what right have I to repine like the Israelites, with their self-justifying proverb? No; let me be thankful that I was not given up even then, but have been able to repent, and do a little better next time. It will be a blessing as yet ungranted to any of us, if indeed I should bear to the full the doom of sorrow, so that it may be vouchsafed me only to avoid actual guilt. Yes, Amy, your words are still with me— "Sintram conquered his doom,"— and it was by following death! Welcome, then, whatever may be in store for me, were it even a long, cheerless life without you, Amy. There is another world!'

With the energy of freshened resolution, he lighted his candle, and walked, with echoing steps, up the black oak staircase, along the broad gallery, up another flight, down another passage, to his own room. He had expressly written 'his own room,' and confirmed it on his arrival, or Mrs.

Drew would have lodged him as she thought more suitably for the master of the house. Nothing had been done to alter its old familiar aspect, except lighting a fire, which he had never seen there before. There were all his boyish treasures, his bows and arrows, his collection of birds' wings, his wonderful weapons and contrivances, from his fire-balloon down to the wren's-egg, all just as he left them, their good condition attesting the care that Mrs. Drew had taken for his sake.

He renewed his acquaintance with them with a sort of regretful affection and superiority; but there was a refreshment in these old memories which aided the new feeling of life imparted to him by his resolution to bear. Nor had he only to bear, he had also to do; and before the late hour at which he fell asleep, he had made up his mind what was the first step to be taken about Coombe Priory, and had remembered with rejoicing that whereas he had regretted leaving the chapel at college which had so comforted and helped him, there was now daily service at Redclyffe Church. The last thing in his mind, before reflection was lost in sleep, was this stanza—

Gales from Heaven, if so He will,
Sweeter melodies may wake
On the lowly mountain rill
Than the meeting waters make.
Who hath the Father and the Son,
May be left, but not alone.

CHAPTER 22

And when the solemn deep church-bell
Entreats the soul to pray,
The midnight phantoms feel the spell,
The shadows sweep away.

Down the broad Vale of Tears afar,
The spectral camp is fled;
Faith shineth as a morning star,
Our ghastly fears are dead.
– LONGFELLOW

Mr. Ashford was a connection of Lady Thorndale's, and it was about a year since the living of Redclyffe had been presented to him. Mr. and Mrs. Ashford were of course anxious to learn all they could about their young squire, on whom the welfare of the parish depended, even more than in most cases, as the whole was his property. Their expectations were not raised by Mr. Markham's strenuous opposition to all their projects, and his constant appeals to the name of 'Sir Guy'; but, on the other hand, they were pleased by the strong feeling of affection that all the villagers manifested for their landlord.

The inhabitants of Redclyffe were a primitive race, almost all related to each other, rough and ignorant, and with a very strong feudal feeling for 'Sir Guy,' who was king, state, supreme authority, in their eyes; and Mrs. Ashford further found that 'Master Morville,' as the old women called him in his individual character, was regarded by them with great personal affection.

On the occasion when Captain Morville came to Redclyffe, and left James Thorndale to spend a couple of hours at the parsonage, they interrogated the latter anxiously on his acquaintance with Sir Guy. He had not the least idea of creating prejudice, indeed, he liked him as a companion, but he saw everything through the medium of his friend, and spoke something to this effect: He was very agreeable; they would like his manners; he was tolerably clever, but not to be named in the same day with his cousin for abilities, far less in appearance. Very pleasant, generally liked, decidedly a taking man; but there was some cloud over him just now– debts, probably. Morville had been obliged to go to Oxford about it; but Mr. Thorndale did not profess to understand it, as of course Morville said as little of it as he could. Thereupon all began to admire the aforesaid Morville, already known by report, and whose fine countenance and sensible conversation confirmed all that had been said of him.

And as, after his interference, Mr. Markham's opposition became surly, as well as sturdy, and Sir Guy's name was sure to stand arrayed against them whichever way they turned, the younger part of the family learnt to regard him somewhat in the light of an enemy, and their elders awaited his majority with more of fear than of hope.

'Mamma!' cried Edward Ashford, rushing in, so as to bring the first news to his mother, who had not been to the early service, 'I do believe Sir Guy is come!'

'Sir Guy was at church!' shouted Robert, almost at the same moment.

Mr. Ashford confirmed the intelligence.

'I saw him speaking, after church, to some of the old men, so afterwards I went to ask old John Barton, and found him with tears in his eyes, positively trembling with delight, for he said he never thought to have heard his cheery voice again, and that he was coming down by and by to see the last letter from Ben, at sea.'

'That is very nice! Shall you call?'

'Yes. Even if he is only here for a day or two, it will be better to have made the acquaintance.'

Mr. Ashford went to the Park at two in the afternoon, and did not return till near four.

'Well,' said he, 'it is as James Thorndale says, there is something very prepossessing about him.'

'Have you been there all this time?'

'Yes. He was not at home; so I left my card, and was coming away, when I met him at the turn leading to the Cove. He need not have seen me unless he had liked, but he came up in a good-natured cordial way, and thanked me for coming to call.'

'Is he like his cousin?'

'Not in the least; not nearly so tall or so handsome, but with a very pleasant face, and seeming made up of activity, very slight, as if he was all bone and sinew. He said he was going to see the Christmas ox at the farm, and asked me to come with him. Presently we came to a high gate, locked up. He was over it in an instant, begged me to wait while he ran on to the farm for the key, and was back in a second with it.'

'Did he enter on any of the disputed subjects!'

'He began himself about the school, saying the house should be altered directly; and talked over the whole matter very satisfactorily; undertook himself to speak to Jenny Robinson; and was very glad to hear you meant her still to keep the infants at the Cove; so I hope that matter is in a right train.'

'If Mr. Markham will but let him.'

'O, he is king or more here! We met Markham at the farm; and the first thing, after looking at the cattle, Sir Guy found some planks lying about, and said they were the very thing for flooring the school. Markham mentioned some barn they were intended for, but Sir Guy said the school must be attended to at once, and went with us to look at it. That was what kept me so long, measuring and calculating; and I hope it may be begun in a week.'

'This is delightful! What more could we wish?'

'I don't think he will give trouble in parish matters, and in personal intercourse he will be sure to be most agreeable. I wish I knew there was nothing amiss. It seems strange for him to come here for the vacation, instead of going to his guardian's, as usual, and altogether he had an air of sadness and depression, not like a youth, especially such an active one. I am afraid something is wrong; those engaging people are often unstable. One thing I forgot to tell you. We were walking through that belt of trees on the east side of the hill, when he suddenly called out to ask how came the old ash-tree to be marked. Markham answered in his gruff way, it was not his doing, but the Captain's. He turned crimson, and began some angry exclamation, but as Markham was going on to tell something else about it, he stopped him short, saying, 'Never mind! I dare say it's all right. I don't want to hear any more!' And I don't think he spoke much again till we got into the village. I am afraid there is some misunderstanding between the cousins.'

'Or more likely Mr. Markham is teaching him some jealousy of his heir. We could not expect two Captain Morvilles in one family, and I am glad it is no worse.'

All that the Ashfords further saw of their young baronet made an impression in his favour; every difficulty raised by the steward disappeared; their plans were forwarded, and they heard of little but his good-nature to the poor people; but still they did not know how far to trust these appearances, and did not yet venture to form an opinion on him, or enter into intimacy.

'So the singers will not come to us on Christmas Eve, because they say they must go to the Park,' said Edward, rather savagely.

'I was thinking,' said Mrs. Ashford, 'how forlorn it will be for that poor youth to spend his Christmas-day alone in that great house. Don't you think we might ask him to dinner?'

Before Mr. Ashford could answer, the boys made such an uproar at the proposal of bringing a stranger to spoil their Christmas, that their parents gave up the idea.

It was that Christmas-day that Guy especially dreaded, as recalling so many contrasts both with those passed here and at Hollywell. Since his return, he had been exerting himself to attend to what he felt to be his duty, going about among his people, arranging for their good or pleasure, and spending a good deal of time over his studies. He had written to Mr. Ross, to ask his advice about Coombe Prior, and had set Markham, much against his will, to remonstrate with Farmer Todd about the repairs; but though there was a sort of satisfaction in doing these things— though the attachment of his dependants soothed him, and brought a new sense of the relation between himself and them— though views of usefulness were on each side opening before him— yet there was a dreariness about everything; he was weary even while he undertook and planned energetically; each new project reminding him that there was no Amy to plan with him. He could not sufficiently care for them.

Still more dreary was his return to his old haunts, and to the scenery which he loved so devotedly— the blue sea and purple hills, which had been like comrades and playfellows, before he had known what it was to have living companions. They used to be everything to him, and he had scarcely a wish beyond; afterwards his dreams had been of longing affection for them, and latterly the idea of seeing Amy love them and admire them had been connected with every vision of them; and now the sight of the reality did but recall the sense that their charm had departed; they could no longer suffice to him as of old; and their presence brought back to him, with fresh pangs of disappointment, the thought of lost happiness and ruined hopes, as if Amy alone could restore their value.

The depression of his spirits inclined him to dwell at present more on the melancholy history of his parents than on anything else. He had hitherto only heard the brief narration of his grandfather, when he could ask no questions; but he now obtained full particulars from Markham, who, when he found him bent on hearing all, related everything, perhaps intending it as a warning against the passions which, when once called into force, he dreaded to find equally ungovernable in his present master.

Mr. Morville had been his great pride and glory, and, in fact, had been so left to his care, as to have been regarded like a son of his own. He had loved him, if possible, better than Guy, because he had been more his own; he had chosen his school, and given him all the reproofs which had ever been bestowed on him with his good in view, and how he had grieved for him was never known to man. It was the first time he had ever talked it over, and he described, with strong, deep feeling, the noble face and bearing of the dark-eyed, gallant-looking stripling, his generosity and high spirit tainted and ruined by his wild temper and impatience of restraint. There seemed to have been a great sweetness of disposition, excellent impulses, and so strong a love of his father, in spite of early neglect and present resentment, as showed what he might have been with only tolerable training, which gave Guy's idea of him more individuality than it had ever had before, and made him better understand what his unhappy grandfather's remorse had been. Guy doubted for a moment whether it had not been selfish to make Markham narrate the history of the time when he had suffered so much; and Markham, when he had been led into telling it, and saw the deepening sadness on his young master's countenance, wished it had not been told, and ended by saying it was of no use to stir up what was better forgotten.

He would have regretted the telling it still more if he had known how Guy acted it all over in his solitude; picturing his father standing an outcast at the door of his own home, yielding his pride and resentment for the sake of his wife, ready to do anything, yearning for reconciliation, longing to tread once more the friendly, familiar hall, and meeting only the angry repulse and cruel taunt! He imagined the headlong passion, the despair, the dashing on his horse in whirlwind-like swiftness, then the blow— the fall— the awful stillness of the form carried back to his father's house, and laid on that table a dead man! Fierce wrath— then another world! Guy worked himself up in imagining the horror of the scene, till it was almost as if he had been an actor in it.

Yet he had never cared so much for the thought of his father as for his mother. His yearning for her which he had felt in early days at Hollywell, had returned in double force, as he now fancied that she would have been here to comfort him, and to share his grief, to be a Mrs. Edmonstone, whose love no fault and no offence could ever cancel.

He rode to Moorworth, and made Mrs. Lavers tell him all she remembered. She was nothing loath, and related how she had been surprised by Mr. Morville arriving with his fair, shrinking young wife, and how she had rejoiced in his coming home again. She described Mrs. Morville with beautiful blue eyes and flaxen hair, looking pale and delicate, and with clinging caressing ways like a little child afraid to be left.

'Poor thing!' said Mrs. Lavers, wiping her eyes; 'when he was going, she clung about him, and cried, and was so timid about being left, that at last he called me, and begged me to stay with her, and take care of her. It was very pretty to see how gentle and soft he was to her, sharp and hasty as he was with most; and she would not let him go, coaxing him not to stay away long; till at last he put her on the sofa, saying, "There, there, Marianne, that will do. Only be a good child, and I'll come for you." I never forget those words, for they were the last I ever heard him speak.'

'Well?'

'Poor dear! she cried heartily at first; but after a time she cheered up, and quite made friends with me. I remember she told me which were Mr. Morville's favourite songs, and sang little scraps of them.'

'Can you remember what they were?' eagerly exclaimed Guy.

'Law, no, air; I never had no head for music. And she laughed about her journey to Scotland, and got into spirits, only she could not bear I should go out of the room; and after a time she grew very anxious for him to come back. I made her some tea, and tried to get her to bed, but she would not go, though she seemed very tired; for she said Mr. Morville would come to take her to Redclyffe, and she wanted to hear all about the great house, listening for him all the time, and I trying to quiet her, and telling her the longer he stayed the better chance there was. Then came a call for me, and down-stairs I found everything in confusion; the news had come– I never knew how. I had not had time to hear it rightly myself, when there was a terrible cry from up-stairs. Poor thing! whether she thought he was come, or whether her mind misgave her, she had come after me to the head of the stairs, and heard what they were saying. I don't believe she ever rightly knew what had happened, for before I could get to her she had fainted; and she was very ill from that moment.'

'And it was the next day she died!' said Guy, looking up, after a long silence. 'Did she– could she take any notice of me?'

'No, sir; she lived but half an hour, or hardly that, after you were born.' I told her it was a son; but she was not able to hear or mind me, and sank away, fainting like. I fancied I heard her say something like "Mr. Morville," but I don't know; and her breath was very soon gone. Poor dear!' added Mrs. Lavers, wiping away her tears. 'I grieved for her as if she had been my own child; but then I thought of her waking up to hear he was dead. I little thought then, Sir Guy, that I should ever see you stand there,– strong and well grown. I almost thought you were dead already when I sent for Mr. Harrison to baptize you.'

'Was it you that did so?' said Guy, his face, mournful before, lighting up in a sudden beam of gratitude. 'Then I have to thank you for more than all the world besides.'

'Law, sir!' said Mrs. Lavers, smiling, and looking pleased, though as if but half entering into his meaning. 'Yes, it was in that very china bowl; I have kept it choice ever since, and never let it be used for anything. I thought it was making very bold, but the doctor and all thought you could not live, and Mr. Harrison might judge. I was very glad just before he came that Mr. Markham came from Redclyffe. He had not been able to leave poor Sir Guy before.'

Guy soon after set out on his homeward ride. His yearning to hear of his mother had been satisfied; but though he could still love the fair, sweet vision summoned up by her name, he was less disposed to feel that it had been hard upon him that she died. It was not Amy. In spite of his tender compassion and affection, he knew that he had not lost a Verena in her. None could occupy that place save Amy; and his mind, from custom, reverted to Amy as still his own, thrilled like a freshly-touched wound, and tried to realize the solace that even yet she might be praying for him.

It was dreariness and despondency by day, and he struggled with it by energy and occupation; but it was something even worse in the evening, in the dark, solitary library, where the very size of the room gave an additional sense of loneliness; and in the silence he could hear, through the closed shutters, the distant plash and surge of the tide,– a sound, of which, in former years, he had never been sensible. There, evening after evening, he sat,– his attention roaming from his employment to feed on his sad reflections.

One evening he went to the large dark dining-room, unlocked the door, which echoed far through the house, and found his way through the packed-up furniture to a picture against the wall, to which he held up his light. It was a portrait by Lely, a half-length of a young man, one hand on his sword, the other holding his plumed hat. His dark chestnut hair fell on each side of a bright youthful face, full of life and health, and with eyes which, even in painting, showed what their vividness must have been. The countenance was full of spirit and joy; but the mouth was more hard and stern than suited the rest; and there was something in the strong, determined grasp of the sword, which made it seem as if the hand might be a characteristic portrait. In the corner of the picture was the name– 'Hugo Morville. AEt. 2O, 1671.'

Guy stood holding up his light, and looking fixedly at it for a considerable time. Strange thoughts passed through his mind as the pictured eyes seemed to gaze piercingly down into his own. When he turned away, he muttered aloud,–

'He, too, would have said– "Is thy servant a dog, that he should do this?"'

It seemed to him as if he had once been in a happier, better world, with the future dawning brightly on him; but as if that once yielding to the passions inherited from that wretched man, had brought on him the doom of misery. He had opened the door to the powers of evil, and must bear the penalty.

These feelings might partly arise from its having been only now that, had all been well, he could have been with Amabel; so that it seemed as if he had never hitherto appreciated the loss. He had at first comforted himself by thinking it was better to be without her than to cause her distress; but now he found how hard it was to miss her– his bright angel. Darkness was closing on him; a tedious, aimless life spread out before him; a despair of doing good haunted him, and with it a sense of something like the presence of an evil spirit, triumphing in his having once put himself within its grasp.

It was well for Guy that he was naturally active, and had acquired power over his own mind. He would not allow himself to brood over these thoughts by day, and in the evening he busied himself as much as possible with his studies, or in going over with Markham matters that would be useful to him to know when he came to the management of his property. Yet still these thoughts would thicken on him, in spite of himself, every evening when he sat alone in the library.

The late hours of Christmas Eve was the time when he had most to suffer. The day had been gloomy and snowy, and he had spent it almost entirely in solitude, with no companion or diversion to restore the tone of his mind, when he had tried it with hard study. He tried to read, but it would not do; and he was reduced to sit looking at the fire, recalling this time last year, when he had been cutting holly, helping the sisters to deck the house, and in the evening enjoying a merry Christmas party, full of blitheness and glee, where there were, of course, special recollections of Amabel.

As usual, he dwelt on the contrast, mused on the estrangement of Mrs. Edmonstone, and tormented himself about Charles's silence, till he fell into the more melancholy train of thought of the destiny of his race.

Far better for him to bear all alone than to bring on Amy grief and horror, such as had fallen on his own mother, but it was much to bear that loneliness and desolation for a lifetime. The brow was contracted, and the lip drawn into a resolute expression of keeping down suffering, like that of a man enduring acute bodily pain; as Guy was not yielding, he was telling himself— telling the tempter, who would have made him give up the struggle— that it was only for a life, and that it was shame and ingratitude to be faint-hearted, on the very night when he ought to be rejoicing that One had come to ruin the power of the foe, and set him free. But where was his rejoicing? Was he cheered,— was he comforted? Was not the lone, blank despondency that had settled on him more heavily than ever, a token that he was shut out from all that was good,— nay, that in former years there had been no true joy in him, only enjoyment of temporal pleasure? Had his best days of happiness been, then, nothing but hollowness and self-deception?

At that moment the sound of a Christmas carol came faintly on his ear. It was one of those tunes which, when the village choir were the only musicians he knew, he had thought, unrivalled; and now, even to his tutored, delicate ear, softened as it was by distance, and endeared by association, it was full of refreshing, soothing harmony. He undrew the curtain, opened the shutter, and looked into the court, where he saw some figures standing. As soon as the light shone from the window, the carol was resumed, and the familiar tones were louder and harsher, but he loved them, with all their rudeness and dissonance, and throwing up the window, called the singers by name, asking why they stood out in the snow, instead of coming into the hall, as usual.

The oldest of the set came to the window to answer,— so old a man that his voice was cracked, and his performance did more harm than good in the psalms at church.

'You see, Sir Guy,' said he, 'there was some of us thought you might not like to have us coming and singing like old times, 'cause 'tis not all as it used to be here with you. Yet we didn't like not to come at all, when you had been away so long, so we settled just to begin, and see whether you took any notice.'

'Thank you. It was a very kind thought, James,' said Guy, touched by the rough delicacy of feeling manifested by these poor men; 'I had rather hear the carols than anything. Come to the front door; I'll let you in.'

'Thank you, sir,' with a most grateful touch of the hat; and Guy hastened to set things in order, preferring the carols to everything at that moment, even though disabused of his pristine admiration for James Robinson's fiddle, and for Harry Ray's grand shake. A long space was spent in listening, and a still longer in the endeavour to show what Mr. Ashford meant by suggesting some improvements which they were regarding with dislike and suspicion, till they found Sir Guy was of the same mind. In fact, when he had sung a verse or two to illustrate his meaning, the opinion of the choir was, that, with equal advantages, Sir Guy might sing quite as well as Harry Ray.

It was the first time he had heard his own voice, except at church, since the earlier days of St. Mildred's, but as he went up the long stairs and galleries to bed, he found himself still singing. It was,

Who lives forlorn,
On God's own word doth rest,
His path is bright
With heavenly light,
His lot among the blest.

He wondered, and remembered finding music for it with Amy's help. He sighed heavily, but the anguish of feeling, the sense of being in the power of evil, had insensibly left him, and though sad and oppressed, the unchangeable joy and hope of Christmas were shedding a beam on him.

They were not gone when he awoke, and rose to a solitary breakfast without one Christmas greeting. The light of the other life was beginning to shine out, and make him see how to do and to bear, with that hope before him. The hope was becoming less vague; the resolution, though not more firm, yet less desponding, that he would go on to grapple with temptation, and work steadfastly; and with that hope before him, he now felt that even a lifetime without Amy would be endurable.

The power of rejoicing came more fully at church, and the service entered into his soul as it never had done before. It had never been such happiness, though repentance and mournful feelings were ever present with him; nor was his 'Verena' absent from his mind. He walked about between the services, saw the poor people dining in their holly-decked houses, exchanging Christmas wishes with them, and gave his old, beautiful, bright smile as he received demonstrations of their attachment, or beheld their enjoyment. He went home in the dark, allowed Mrs. Drew to have her own way, and serve him and Bustle with a dinner sufficient for a dozen people, and was shut up for the solitary Christmas evening which he had so much dreaded, and which would have been esteemed a misfortune even by those who had no sad thoughts to occupy them.

Yet when the clock struck eleven he was surprised, and owned that it had been more than not being unhappy. The dark fiends of remorse and despair had not once assaulted him, yet it had not been by force of employment that they had been averted. He had read and written a little, but very little, and the time had chiefly been spent in a sort of day-dream, though not of a return to Hollywell, nor of what Redclyffe might be with Amy. It had been of a darkened and lonely course, yet, in another sense, neither dark nor lonely, of a cheerless home and round of duties, with a true home beyond; and still it had been a happy, refreshing dream, and he began the next morning with the fresh brightened spirit of a man who felt that such an evening was sent him to reinvigorate his energies, and fit him for the immediate duties that lay before him.

On the breakfast-table was what he had not seen for a long time– a letter directed to him. It was from Mr. Ross, in answer to his question about Coombe Prior, entering readily into the subject, and advising him to write to the Bishop, altogether with a tone of friendly interest which, especially as coming from one so near Hollywell, was a great pleasure, a real Christmas treat. There was the wonted wish of the season– a happy Christmas– which he took gratefully, and lastly there was a mention that Charles Edmonstone was better, the suffering over, though he was not yet allowed to move.

It was a new light that Charles's silence had been occasioned by illness, and his immediate resolution was to write at once to Mr. Ross, to beg for further particulars. In the meantime, the perception that there had been no estrangement was such a ray as can hardly be imagined without knowing the despondency it had enlivened. The truth was, perhaps, that the tone of mind was recovering, and after having fixed himself in his resolution to endure, he was able to receive comfort and refreshment from without as well as from within.

He set to work to write at once to the Bishop, as Mr. Ross advised. He said he could not bear to lose time, and therefore wrote at once. He should be of age on the 28th of March, and he hoped then to be able to arrange for a stipend for a curate, if the Bishop approved, and would kindly enter into communication on the appointment with Mr. Halroyd, the incumbent. After considering his letter a little while, and wishing he was sufficiently intimate with Mr. Ashford to ask him if it would do, he wrote another to Mr. Ross, to inquire after Charles; then he worked for an hour at mathematics, till a message came from the gamekeeper to ask whether he would go out shooting, whereat Bustle, evidently understanding, jumped about, and wagged his tail so imploringly, that Guy could not resist, so he threw his books upon the top of the great pile on the sofa, and, glad that at least he could gratify dog and man, he sent word that he should be ready in five minutes.

He could not help enjoying the ecstasy of all the dogs, and, indeed he was surprised to find himself fully alive to the delight of forcing his way through a furze-brake, hearing the ice in the peaty bogs crackle beneath his feet; getting a good shot, bringing down his bird, finding snipe, and diving into the depths of the long, winding valleys and dingles, with the icicle-hung banks of their streamlets. He came home through the village at about half-past three o'clock, sending the keeper to leave some of his game at the parsonage, while he went himself to see how the work was getting on at the school. Mr. and Mrs. Ashford and the boys were come on the same errand, in spite of the cloud of dust rising from the newly-demolished lath-and-plaster partition. The boys looked with longing eyes at the gun in his hand, and the half-frozen compound of black and red mud on his gaiters; but they were shy, and their enmity added to their shyness, so that even when he shook hands with them, and spoke good-naturedly, they did not get beyond a monosyllable.

Mr. and Mrs. Ashford, feeling some compunction for having left him to his solitude so long, asked him to dinner for one of the ensuing days, with some idea of getting some one to meet him, and named six o'clock.

'Won't that put you out? Don't you always dine early?' said he. 'If you would let me, I should like to join you at your tea-time.'

'If you will endure a host of children,' said Mr. Ashford, 'I should like it of all things,' said Guy. 'I want to make acquaintance very much,' and he put his hand on Robert's shoulder. 'Besides, I want to talk to you about the singing, and how we are to get rid of that fiddle without breaking James Robinson's heart.'

The appointment was made, and Guy went home to his hasty dinner, his Greek, and a little refreshing return afterwards to the books which had been the delight of younger days. There was no renewal of the burthen of despair that had so long haunted his evenings. Employments thickened on his hands as the days passed on. There was further correspondence about Coombe Prior and the curate, and consultations with Markham about farmer Todd, who was as obstinate and troublesome as possible. Guy made Markham come to Coombe Prior with him, examine and calculate about the cottages, and fairly take up the subject, though without much apparent chance of coming to any satisfactory result. A letter came from Mr. Ross, telling him even more than he had ventured to hope, for it brought a message from Charles himself. Charles had been delighted to hear of him, and had begged that he might be told how very sorry he had been not to write; and how incapable he had been, and still was; but that he hoped Guy would write to him, and believe him in the same mind. Mr. Ross added an account of Charles's illness, saying the suffering had been more severe than usual, and had totally disabled him for many weeks; that they had since called in a London surgeon, who had given him hope that he might be better now than ever before, but had prescribed absolute rest for at least six weeks longer, so that Charles was now flat on his back all day, beginning to be able to be amused, and very cheerful and patient.

The pleasure of entering into communication with Hollywell again, and knowing that Charles at least would be glad to hear from him, was so exquisite, that he was almost surprised, considering that in essentials he was where he was before, and even Charles could not be Amy.

CHAPTER 23

They hadna sailed a league, a league,
A league, but barely three,
When the lift grew dark, and the wind grew loud,
And gurly grew the sea.
– SIR PATRICK SPENS.– (Old Ballad.)

Guy's evening with the Ashfords threw down many of the barriers in the way of intimacy. He soon made friends with the children, beginning with the two years old baby, and ending with gaining even the shy and sturdy Robin, who could not hold out any longer, when it appeared that Sir Guy could tell him the best place for finding sea-urchins, the present objects of his affections.

'But we should have to go through the park,' said Edward, disconsolately, when Guy had described the locality.

'Well, why not?'

'We must not go into the park!' cried the children, in chorus.

'Not go into the park!' exclaimed Guy, looking at Mrs. Ashford, in amazement; then, as it flashed on him that it was his part to give leave, he added,– 'I did not know I was such a dog in the manger. I thought all the parish walked naturally in the park. I don't know what else it is good for. If Markham will lock it up, I must tell him to give you a key.'

The boys were to come the next day– to be shown the way to the bay of urchins, and thenceforth they became his constant followers to such a degree, that their parents feared they were very troublesome, but he assured them to the contrary; and no mother in the world could have found it in her heart to keep them away from so much happiness. There was continually a rushing home with a joyous outcry,– 'Mamma! Sir Guy gave me a ride on his horse!' 'Mamma! Sir Guy helped us to the top of that great rock!' 'Oh, papa! Sir Guy says we may come out shooting with him to-morrow, if you will let us!' 'Mamma! papa! look! Do you see? I shot this rabbit my own self with Sir Guy's gun!' 'Papa! papa! Sir Guy showed us his boat, and he says he will take us out to the Shag Rock, if you will give us leave!'

This was beyond what papa, still further beyond what mamma, could like, since the sea was often very rough in parts near the Shag; there were a good many sunken rocks, and boys, water, and rocks, did not appear by any means a safe conjunction, so Mrs. Ashford put the matter off for the present by the unseasonableness of the weather; and Mr. Ashford asked one or two of the fishermen how far they thought landing on the Shag a prudent attempt.

They did not profess to have often tried, they always avoided those rocks; but it could hardly be very dangerous, they said, for when Sir Guy was a boy, he used to be about there for ever, at first with an old boatman, and afterwards alone in his little boat. They had often wondered he was trusted there; but if any one knew the rocks, he did.

Still, Mrs. Ashford could not make up her mind to like the idea, and the boys came to Sir Guy in a state of great discomposure.

'Never mind' he said, 'perhaps we shall manage it in the summer. We will get your father to go out with us himself; and, in the meantime, who likes to come with me after the rabbits in Cliffstone Copse? Farmer Holt will thank Robin for killing a dozen or so, for he makes grievous complaints of them.'

Guy conducted the boys out of sight of the sea, and, to console them, gave them so much more use of the gun than usual, that it might be considered as a wonder that he escaped being shot. Yet it did not prevent a few sighs being spent on the boating.

'Can't you forget it?' said Guy, smiling. 'You have no loss, after all, for we are likely to have no boating weather this long time. Hark! don't you hear the ground-swell?'

'What's that?' said the boys, standing still to listen to the distant surge, like a continuous low moan, or roar, far, far away, though there was no wind, and the sea was calm.

'It is the sound that comes before stormy weather,' said Guy. 'It is as if the sea was gathering up its forces for the tempest.'

'But what?– how? Tell me what it really is,' said Robin.

'I suppose it is the wind on the sea before it has reached us,' said Guy. 'How solemn it is!'

Too solemn for the boys, who began all manner of antics and noises, by way of silencing the impression of awfulness. Guy laughed, and joined in their fun; but as soon as they were gone home, he stood in silence for a long time, listening to the sound, and recalling the mysterious dreams and fancies with which it was connected in his boyhood, and which he had never wished thus to drive away.

The storm he had predicted came on; and by the evening of the following day, sea and wind were thundering, in their might, against the foot of the crags. Guy looked from the window, the last thing at night, and saw the stars twinkling overhead, with that extreme brilliancy which is often seen in the intervals of fitful storms, and which suggested thoughts that sent him to sleep in a vague, soothing dream.

He was wakened by one tremendous continued roar of sea, wind, and thunder combined. Such was the darkness, that he could not see the form of the window, till a sheet of pale blue lightning brought it fully out for the moment. He sat up, and listened to the 'glorious voice' that followed it, thought what an awful night at sea, and remembered when he used to fancy it would be the height of felicity to have a shipwreck at Redclyffe, and shocked Mrs. Bernard by inhuman wishes that a ship would only come and be wrecked. How often had he watched, through sounds like these, for a minute gun! Nay, he had once actually called up poor Arnaud in the middle of the night for an imaginary signal. Redclyffe Bay was a very dangerous one; a fine place for a wreck, with its precipitous crags, its single safe landing-place, and the great Shag Stone, on the eastern side, with a whole progeny of nearly sunken rocks, dreaded in rough weather by the fishermen themselves; but it was out of the ordinary track of vessels, and there were only a few traditions of terrible wrecks long before his time.

It seemed as if he had worked up his fancy again, for the sound of a gun was for a moment in his ear. It was lost in the rush of hail against the window, and the moaning of the wind round the old house; but presently it returned too surely to be imaginary. He sprang to the window, and the broad, flickering glare of lightning revealed the black cliff and pale sea-line; then all was dark and still, while the storm was holding its breath for the thunder-burst which in a few more seconds rolled overhead, shaking door and window throughout the house. As the awful sound died away, in a moment's lull, came the gun again. He threw up the window, and as the blast of wind and rain swept howling into the room, it brought another report.

To close the window, light his candle, throw on his clothes, and hasten down-stairs, was the work of a very few seconds. Luckily, the key of the boat-house was lying on the table in the hall, where he had left it, after showing the boat to the Ashford boys; he seized it, caught up the pocket telescope, put on a rough coat, and proceeded to undo the endless fastenings of the hall-door, a very patience-trying occupation; and, when completed, the gusts that were eddying round the house, ready to force their way in everywhere, took advantage of the first opening to blow out his candle.

However, they had in one way done good service, for the shower had been as brief as it was violent, and the inky cloud was drifting away furiously towards the east, leaving the moon visible, near her setting, and allowing her white cold light to shine forth, contrasting with the distant sheets of pale lightning, growing fainter and fainter.

Guy ran across the court, round to the west side of the house, and struggled up the slope in the face of the wind, which almost swept him down again; and when at length he had gained the summit, came rushing against him with such force that he could hardly stand. He did, however, keep his ground, and gazed out over the sea. The swell was fearful; marked by the silver light on one side, where it caught the moonbeams, and the black shade on the other, ever alternating, so that the eye could, not fix on them for a moment; the spray leapt high in its whiteness, and the Shag stood up hard, bold, and black. The waves thundered, bursting on the cliff and, high as he stood, the spray dashed almost blinding in his face, while the wind howled round him, as if gathering its might for the very purpose of wrenching him from the cliff; but he stood firm, and looked out again, to discern clearly what he thought he had seen. It was the mast of a vessel, seen plainly against the light silvery distance of sea on the reef west of the Shag. It was in a slanting direction, and did not move; he could not doubt that the ship had struck on the dangerous rocks at the entrance of the bay; and as his eyes became more accustomed to the unusual light, and made out what objects were or were not familiar, he could perceive the ship herself. He looked with the glass, but could see no one on board, nor were any boats in sight; but observing some of the lesser rocks, he beheld some moving figures on them. Help!– instant help!– was his thought; and he looked towards the Cove. Lights were in the cottage windows, and a few sounds came up to him, as if the fishing population were astir.

He hastened to the side of the cliff, which was partly clothed with brushwood. There was a descent– it could hardly be called a path– which no one ventured to attempt but himself and a few of the boldest birds'-nesting boys of the village; but he could lose no time, and scrambling, leaping, swinging himself by the branches, he reached the foot of the cliff in safety, and in five minutes more was on the little quay at the end of the steep street of the Cove.

The quay was crowded with the fisher-people, and there was a strange confusion of voices; some saying all was lost; some that the crew had got to the rock; others, that some one ought to put off and help them; others, that a boat would never live in such a sea; and an old telescope was in great requisition.

Ben Robinson, a tall, hardy young man, of five-and-twenty, wild, reckless, high-spirited and full of mischief and adventure, was standing on a pile at the extreme verge above the foaming water, daring the others to go with him to the rescue; and, though Jonas Ledbury, a feeble old man, was declaring, in a piteous tone, it was a sin and a shame to let so many poor creatures be lost in sight, without one man stirring to help them; yet all stood irresolute, watching the white breakers dashing on the Shag, and the high waves that swelled and rolled between.

'Do you know where the crew are?' exclaimed Guy, shouting as loud as he could, for the noise of the winds and waves was tremendous.

'There, sir, on the flat black stone,' said the fortunate possessor of the telescope. 'Some ten or eleven of them, I fancy, all huddled together.'

'Ay, ay!' said old Ledbury. 'Poor creatures! there they be; and what is to be done, I can't say! I never saw a boat in such a sea, since the night poor Jack, my brother, was lost, and Will Ray with him.'

'I see them,' said Guy, who had in the meantime looked through his glass. 'How soon is high water?'

It was an important question, for the rocks round the Shag were covered before full tide, even when the water was still. There was a looking up at the moon, and then Guy and the fishermen simultaneously exclaimed, that it would be in three hours; which gave scarcely an hour to spare.

Without another word, Guy sprang from the quay to the boat-house, unlocked it, and, by example, showed that the largest boat was to be brought out. The men helped him vigorously, and it stood on the narrow pebbly beach, the only safe landing-place in the whole bay; he threw into it a coil of rope, and called out in his clear commanding voice– 'Five to go with me!'

Hanging back was at an end. They were brave men, who had wanted nothing but a leader, and with Sir Guy at their head, were ready for anything. Not five, but five-and-twenty were at his command; and even in the hurry of the moment, a strong, affectionate feeling filled his eyes with tears as he saw these poor fellows ready to trust their lives in his hands.

'Thank you– thank you!' he exclaimed. 'Not all, though; you, Ben Robinson, Harry Ray, Charles Ray, Ben Ledbury, Wat Green.'

They were all young men, without families, such as could best be spared; and each, as his name was called, answered, 'Here, Sir Guy!' and came forward with a resolute satisfied air.

'It would be best to have a second boat,' said Guy. 'Mr. Brown,' to the owner of the telescope, 'will you lend yours? 'tis the strongest and lightest. Thank you. Martin had best steer it, he knows the rocks;' and he went on to name the rest of the crew; but at the last there was a moment's pause, as if he doubted.

A tall athletic young fisherman took advantage of it to press forward.

'Please your honour, Sir Guy, may not I go?'

'Better not, Jem,' answered Guy. 'Remember,' in a lower voice, 'your mother has no one but you. Here!' he called, cheerfully, 'Jack Horn, you pull a good oar! Now, then, are we ready?'

'All ready,– yes, sir!'

The boat was launched, not without great difficulty, in the face of such a sea. The men stoutly took their oars, casting a look forward at the rocks, then at the quay, and on the face of their young steersman. Little they guessed the intense emotion that swelled in his breast as he took the helm, to save life or to lose it; enjoying the enterprise, yet with the thought that his lot might be early death; glad it was right thus to venture, earnest to save those who had freely trusted to him, and rapidly, though most earnestly, recalling his own repentance. All this was in his mind, though nothing was on his face but cheerful resolution.

Night though it was, tidings of the wreck had reached the upper part of the village; and Mr. Ashford, putting his head out of his window to learn the cause of the sounds in the street, was informed by many voices that a ship was on the Shag reef, and that all were lost. To hasten to the Cove to learn the truth, and see if any assistance could yet be afforded, was his instant thought; and he had not taken many steps before he was overtaken by a square, sturdy figure, wrapped in an immense great-coat.

'So, Mr. Markham, you are on your way to see about this wreck.'

'Why, ay,' said Markham, roughly, though not with the repellent manner usual with him towards Mr. Ashford, 'I must be there, or that boy will be in the thickest of it. Wherever is mischief, there is he. I only wonder he has not broken his neck long ago.'

'By mischief, you mean danger?'

'Yes. I hope he has not heard of this wreck, for if he has, no power on earth would keep him back from it.'

Comparing the reports they had heard, the clergyman and steward walked on, Markham's anxiety actually making him friendly. They reached the top of the steep street of the Cove; but though there was a good view of the sea from thence, they could distinguish nothing, for another cloud was rising, and had obscured the moon. They were soon on the quay, now still more crowded, and heard the exclamations of those who were striving to keep their eyes on the boats.

'There's one!' 'No!' 'Yes, 'tis!' 'That's Sir Guy's!'

'Sir Guy!' exclaimed Markham. 'You don't mean he is gone? Then I am too late! What could you be thinking of, you old fool, Jonas, to let that boy go? You'll never see him again, I can tell you. Mercy! Here comes another squall! There's an end of it, then!'

Markham seemed to derive some relief from railing at the fishermen, singly and collectively, while Mr. Ashford tried to learn the real facts, and gather opinions as to the chance of safety. The old fishermen held that there was frightful risk, though the attempt was far from hopeless; they said the young men were all good at their oars, Sir Guy knew the rocks very well, and the chief fear was, that he might not know how to steer in such a sea; but they had seen that, though daring, he was not rash. They listened submissively to Mr. Markham, but communicated in an under-tone to the vicar, how vain it would have been to attempt to restrain Sir Guy.

'Why, sir,' said old James Robinson, 'he spoke just like the captain of a man-of-war, and for all Mr. Markham says, I don't believe he'd have been able to gainsay him.'

'Your son is gone with him?'

'Ay, sir; and I would not say one word to stop him. I know Sir Guy won't run him into risk for nothing; and I hope, please God, if Ben comes back safe, it may be the steadying of him.'

''Twas he that volunteered to go before Sir Guy came, they say?'

'Yes, sir,' said the old man, with a pleased yet melancholy look. 'Ben's brave enough; but there's the difference. He'd have done it for the lark, and to dare the rest; but Sir Guy does it with thought, and because it is right. I wish it may be the steadying of Ben!'

The shower rushed over them again, shorter and less violent than the former one, but driving in most of the crowd, and only leaving on the quay the vicar, the steward, and a few of the most anxious fishermen. They could see nothing; for the dark slanting line of rain swept over the waves, joining together the sea and thick low cloud; and the roaring of the sea and moaning of the wind were fearful. No one spoke, till at last the black edges of the Shag loomed clearer, the moon began to glance through the skirts of the cloud, and the heaving and tossing of the sea, became more discernible.

'There!– there!' shouted young Jem, the widow's son.

'The boats?'

'One!'

'Where?– where?– for heaven's sake! That's nothing!' cried Markham.

'Yes– yes! I see both,' said Jem. 'The glass! Where's Mr. Brown's glass!'

Markham was trying to fix his own, but neither hand nor eye were steady enough; he muttered,– 'Hang the glass!' and paced up and down in uncontrollable anxiety. Mr. Ashford turned with him, trying to speak consolingly, and entirely liking the old man. Markham was not ungrateful, but he was almost in despair.

'It is the same over again!' said he. 'He is the age his father was, though Mr. Morville never was such as he– never– how should he? He is the last of them– the best– he would have been– he was. Would to heaven I were with him, that, if he is lost, we might all go together.'

'There, sir,' called Jem, who, being forbidden to do anything but watch, did so earnestly; 'they be as far now as opposite West Cove. Don't you see them, in that light place?'

The moon had by this time gone down, but the first great light of dawn was beginning to fall on the tall Shag, and show its fissures and dark shades, instead of leaving it one hard, unbroken mass. Now and then Jem thought he saw the boats; but never so distinctly as to convince the watchers that they had not been swamped among the huge waves that tumbled and foamed in that dangerous tract.

Mr. Ashford had borrowed Markham's telescope, and was looking towards the rock, where the shipwrecked crew had taken refuge.

'There is some one out of the boat, climbing on the rocks. Can you make him out, Jem?'

'I see– I see,' said Mr. Brown; 'there are two of them. They are climbing along the lee-side of the long ridge of rocks.'

'Ay, ay,' said old Ledbury; 'they can't get in a boat close to the flat rocks, they must take out a line. Bold fellows!'

'Where are the boats?' asked Mr. Ashford.

'I can tell that,' said Ledbury; 'they must have got under the lee of the lesser Shag. There's a ring there that Sir Guy had put in to moor his boat to. They'll be made fast there, and those two must be taking the rope along that ledge, so as for the poor fellows on the rock to have a hold of, as they creep along to where the boats are.'

'Those broken rocks!' said Mr. Ashford. 'Can there be a footing, and in such a sea?'

'Can you give a guess who they be, sir?' asked Robinson, earnestly. 'If you'd only let Jem have a look, maybe he could guess.'

Markham's glass was at his service.

'Hullo! what a sea! I see them now. That's Ben going last– I know his red cap. And the first– why, 'tis Sir Guy himself!'

'Don't be such a fool, Jem' cried Markham, angrily. 'Sir Guy knows better. Give me the glass.'

But when it was restored, Markham went on spying in silence, while Brown, keeping fast possession of his own telescope, communicated his observations.

'Ay, I see them. Where are they? He's climbing now. There's a breaker just there, will wash them off, as sure as they're alive! I don't see 'em. Yes, I do– there's Redcap! There's something stirring on the rock!'

So they watched till, after an interval, in which the boats disappeared behind the rocks, they were seen advancing over the waters again– one– yes– both, and loaded. They came fast, they were in sight of all, growing larger each moment, mounting on the crest of the huge rolling waves, then plunged in the trough so long as to seem as if they were lost, then rising– rising high as mountains. Over the roaring waters came at length the sound of voices, a cheer, pitched in a different key from the thunder of wind and wave; they almost fancied they knew the voice that led the shout. Such a cheer as rose in answer, from all the Redclyffe villagers, densely crowded on quay, and beach, and every corner of standing ground!

The sun was just up, his beams gilded the crests of the leaping waves, and the spray danced up, white and gay, round the tall rocks, whose shadow was reflected in deep green, broken by the ever-moving swell. The Shag and its attendant rocks, and the broken vessel, were bathed in the clear morning light; the sky was of a beautiful blue, with magnificent masses of dark cloud, the edges, where touched by the sunbeams, of a pearly white; and across the bay, tracing behind them glittering streams of light, came up the two boats with their freight of rescued lives. Martin's boat was the first to touch the landing-place.

'All saved,' he said; 'all owing to him,' pointing back to Sir Guy.

There was no time for questions; the wan, drenched sailors had to be helped on shore, and the boat hauled up out of the way. In the meantime, Guy, as he steered in past the quay, smiled and nodded to Mr. Ashford and Markham, and renewed the call, 'All safe!' Mr. Ashford thought that he had never seen anything brighter than his face– the eyes radiant in the morning sun, the damp hair hanging round it, and life, energy, and promptitude in every feature and movement.

The boat came in, the sailors were assisted out, partly by their rescuers, partly by the spectators. Guy stood up, and, with one foot on the seat, supported on his knee and against his arm a little boy, round whom his great-coat was wrapped.

'Here, Jem!' he shouted, to his rejected volunteer, who had been very active in bringing in the boat, 'here's something for you to do. This poor little fellow has got a broken arm. Will you ask your mother to take him in? She's the best nurse in the parish. And send up for Mr. Gregson.'

Jem received the boy as tenderly as he was given; and, with one bound, Guy was by the side of his two friends. Mr. Ashford shook hands with heartfelt gratulation; Markham exclaimed,–

'There, Sir Guy, after the old fashion! Never was man so mad in this world! I've done talking! You'll never be content till you have got your death. As if no one could do anything without you.'

'Was it you who carried out the line on the rock?' said Mr. Ashford.

'Ben Robinson and I. I had often been there, after sea anemones and weeds, and I had a rope round me, so don't be angry, Markham.'

'I have no more to say,' answered Markham, almost surly. 'I might as well talk to a sea-gull at once. As if you had any right to throw away your life!'

'I enjoyed it too much to have anything to say for myself,' said Guy; 'besides, we must see after these poor men. There were two or three nearly drowned. Is no one gone for Mr. Gregson?'

Mr. Gregson, the doctor, was already present, and no one who had any authority could do anything but attend to the disposal of the shipwrecked crew. Mr. Ashford went one way, Markham another, Guy a third; but, between one cottage and another, Mr. Ashford learnt some particulars. The crew had been found on a flat rock and the fishermen had at first thought all their perils in vain, for it was impossible to bring the boats up, on account of the rocks, which ran out in a long reef. Sir Guy, who knew the place, steered to the sheltered spot where he had been used to make fast his own little boat, and undertook to make his way from thence to the rock where the crew had taken refuge, carrying a rope to serve as a kind of hand-rail, when fastened from one rock to the other. Ben insisted on sharing his peril, and they had crept along the slippery, broken reefs, lashed by the surge, for such a distance, that the fishermen shuddered as they spoke of the danger of being torn off by the force of the waves, and dashed against the rocks. Nothing else could have saved the crew. They had hardly accomplished the passage through the rising tide, even with the aid of the rope and the guidance of Sir Guy and Ben, and, before the boats had gone half a mile on their return, the surge was tumbling furiously over the stones where they had been found.

The sailors were safely disposed of, in bed, or by the fireside, the fishers vying in services to them. Mr. Ashford went to the cottage of Charity Ledbury, Jem's mother, to inquire for the boy with the broken arm. As he entered the empty kitchen, the opposite door of the stairs was opened, and Guy appeared, stepping softly, and speaking low.

'Poor little fellow!' he said; 'he is just going to sleep. He bore it famously!'

'The setting his arm?'

'Yes. He was quite sensible, and very patient, and that old Charity Ledbury is a capital old woman. She and Jem are delighted to have him, and will nurse him excellently. How are all the others? Has that poor man come to his senses?'

'Yes. I saw him safe in bed at old Robinson's. The captain is at the Browns'.'

'I wonder what time of day it is?'

'Past eight. Ah! there is the bell beginning. I was thinking of going to tell Master Ray we are not too much excited to remember church-going this morning; but I am glad he has found it out only ten minutes too late. I must make haste. Good-bye!'

'May not I come, too, or am I too strange a figure?' said Guy, looking at his dress, thrown on in haste, and saturated with sea-water.

'May you?' said Mr. Ashford, smiling. 'Is it wise, with all your wet things?'

'I am not given to colds,' answered Guy, and they walked on quickly for some minutes; after which he said, in a low voice and hurried manner,— 'would you make some mention of it in the Thanksgiving?'

'Of course I will' said Mr. Ashford, with much emotion. 'The danger must have been great.'

'It was,' said Guy, as if the strong feeling would show itself. 'It was most merciful. That little boat felt like a toy at the will of the winds and waves, till one recollected who held the storm in His hand.'

He spoke very simply, as if he could not help it, with his eye fixed on the clear eastern sky, and with a tone of grave awe and thankfulness which greatly struck Mr. Ashford, from the complete absence of self-consciousness, or from any attempt either to magnify or depreciate his sense of the danger.

'You thought the storm a more dangerous time than your expedition on the rock?'

'It was not. The fishermen, who were used to such things, did not think much of it; but I am glad to have been out on such a night, if only for the magnificent sensation it gives to realize one's own powerlessness and His might. As for the rock, there was something to do to look to one's footing, and cling on; no time to think.'

'It was a desperate thing!'

'Not so bad as it looked. One step at a time is all one wants, you know, and that there always was. But what a fine fellow Ben Robinson is! He behaved like a regular hero— it was the thorough contempt and love of danger one reads of. There must be a great deal of good in him, if one only knew how to get hold of it.'

'Look there!' was Mr. Ashford's answer, as he turned his head at the church wicket; and, at a short distance behind, Guy saw Ben himself walking up the path, with his thankful, happy father, a sight that had not been seen for months, nay, for years.

'Ay,' he said, 'such a night as this, and such a good old man as the father, could not fail to bring out all the good in a man.'

'Yes,' thought Mr. Ashford, 'such a night, under such a leader! The sight of so much courage based on that foundation is what may best touch and save that man.'

After church, Guy walked fast away; Mr. Ashford went home, made a long breakfast, having the whole story to tell, and was on to the scene of action again, where he found the master, quite restored, and was presently joined by Markham. Of Sir Guy, there was no news, except that Jem Ledbury said he had looked in after church to know how the cabin boy was going on, and the master, understanding that he had been the leader in the rescue, was very anxious to thank him, and walked up to the house with Markham and Mr. Ashford.

Markham conducted them straight to the library, the door of which was open. He crossed the room, smiled, and made a sign to Mr. Ashford, who looked in some surprise and amusement. It has been already said that the room was so spacious that the inhabited part looked like a little encampment by the fire, though the round table was large, and the green leather sofa and arm chair were cumbrous.

However, old Sir Guy's arm-chair was never used by his grandson; Markham might sit there, and Bustle did sometimes, but Guy always used one of the unpretending, unluxurious chairs, which were the staple of the room. This, however, was vacant, and on the table before it stood the remains of breakfast, a loaf reduced to half its dimensions, an empty plate and coffee-cup. The fire was burnt down to a single log, and on the sofa, on all the various books with which it was strewed, lay Guy, in anything but a comfortable position, his head on a great dictionary, fairly overcome with sleep, his very thick, black eyelashes resting on his fresh, bright cheek, and the relaxation of the grave expression of his features making him look even younger than he really was. He was so sound asleep that it was not till some movement of Markham's that he awoke, and started up, exclaiming,–

'What a horrid shame! I am very sorry!'

'Sorry! what for?' said Markham. 'I am glad, at any rate, you have been wise enough to change your things, and eat some breakfast.'

'I meant to have done so much,' said Guy; 'but sea-wind makes one so sleepy!' Then, perceiving the captain, he came forward, hoping he was quite recovered.

The captain stood mystified, for he could not believe this slim youth could be the Sir Guy of whose name he had heard so much, and, after answering the inquiry, he began,–

'If I could have the honour of seeing Sir Guy– '

'Well?' said Guy.

'I beg your pardon, sir!' said the captain, while they all laughed, 'I did not guess you could be so young a gentleman. I am sure, sir, 'tis what any man might be proud of having done, and– I never saw anything like it!' he added, with a fresh start, 'and it will do you honour everywhere. All our lives are owing to you, sir.'

Guy did not cut him short, though very glad when it was over. He felt he should not, in the captain's place, like to have his thanks shortened, and besides, if ever there was happiness or exultation, it was in the glistening eyes of old Markham, the first time he had ever been able to be justly proud of one of the family, whom he loved with so much faithfulness and devotion.

CHAPTER 24

Is there a word, or jest, or game,
But time encrusteth round
With sad associate thoughts the same?
– ELIZABETH BARRETT BROWNING.

Among the persons who spent a forlorn autumn was Mr. Ross, though his troubles were not quite of the same description as those of his young parishioners. He missed his daughter very much; all his household affairs got out of order; the school-girls were naughty, and neither he, nor Miss Edmonstone, nor the mistress, could discover the culprits; their inquiries produced nothing but a wild confusion of mutual accusations, where the truth was undistinguishable. The cook never could find anything to make broth of, Mr. Ross could, never lay his hands on the books he wanted for himself or anybody else; and, lastly, none of his shirts ever had their buttons on.

Mary, meanwhile, had to remain through a whole course of measles, then to greet the arrival of a new nephew, and to attend his christening: but she had made a vow that she would be at home by Christmas, and she kept it.

Mr. Ross had the satisfaction of fetching her home from the station the day before Christmas Eve, and of seeing her opposite to him, on her own side of the table, in the evening, putting on the buttons, and considering it an especial favour and kindness, for which to be for ever grateful, that he had written all his Christmas sermons beforehand, so as to have a whole evening clear before her. He was never a great letter-writer, and Mary had a great deal to hear, for all that had come to her were the main facts, with very few details.

'I have had very few letters, even from Hollywell,' said she. 'I suppose it is on account of Charles's illness. You think him really better?'

'Yes, much better. I forgot to tell you, you are wanted for their Christmas party to-morrow night.'

'Oh! he is well enough for them not to put it off! Is he able to be out of bed?'

'No, he lies perfectly flat, and looks very thin. It has been a very severe illness. I don't think I ever knew him suffer so much; but, at the same time, I never knew him behave so well, or show so much patience, and consideration for other people, I was the more surprised, because at first he seemed to have relapsed into all the ways he thought he had shaken off; he was so irritable and fretful, that poor Mrs. Edmonstone looked worn out; but it seems to have been only the beginning of the illness; it was very different after he was laid up.'

'Has he had you to see him?'

'Yes, he asked for it, which he never did before, and Amabel reads to him every morning. There is certainly much more that is satisfactory about those young Edmonstones than there once seemed reason to expect.'

'And now tell me about Sir Guy. What is the matter? Why does he not come home this winter!'

'I cannot tell you the rights of it, Mary. Mr. Edmonstone is very much offended about something he is reported to have said, and suspects him of having been in mischief at St. Mildred's; but I am not at all persuaded that it is not one of Mr. Edmonstone's affronts.'

'Where is he?'

'At Redclyffe. I have a letter from him which I am going to answer to-night. I shall tell the Edmonstones about it, for I cannot believe that, if he had been guilty of anything very wrong, his mind would be occupied in this manner;' and he gave Mary the letter.

'Oh, no!' exclaimed Mary, as she read. 'I am sure he cannot be in any mischief. What an admirable person he is! I am very sorry this cloud has arisen! I was thinking last summer how happy they all were together.'

'Either this or Charles's illness has cast a gloom over the whole house. The girls are both grown much graver.'

'Amy graver?' said Mary, quickly.

'I think so. At least she did not seem to cheer up as I should have expected when her brother grew better. She looks as if she had been nursing him too closely, and yet I see her walking a good deal.'

'Poor little Amy!' said Mary, and she asked no more questions, but was anxious to make her own observations.

She did not see the Edmonstones till the next evening, as the day was wet, and she only received a little note telling her that one carriage would be sent to fetch her and Mr. Ross. The whole of the family, except Charles, were in the drawing-room, but Mary looked chiefly at Amy. She was in white, with holly in her hair, and did not look sorrowful; but she was paler and thinner than last summer, and though she spoke, smiled, and laughed when she ought, it was without the gay, childish freedom of former times. She was a small, pale, quiet girl now, not a merry, caressing kitten. Mary recollected what she had been in the wood last summer, and was sure it was more than Charles's illness that had altered her; yet still Amy had not Laura's harassed look.

Mary had not much talk with Amy, for it was a large party, with a good many young ladies and children, and Amy had a great deal of work in the way of amusing them. She had a wearied look, and was evidently exerting herself to the utmost.

'You look tired,' said Mary, kindly.

'No, it is only stupidity,' said Amy, smiling rather sadly. 'We can't be entertaining without Charlie.'

'It has been a melancholy winter,' began Mary, but she was surprised, for Amy's face and neck coloured in a moment; then, recovering herself, with some hesitation, she said,–

'Oh! but Charlie is much better, and that is a great comfort. I am glad you are come home, Mary.'

'We are going to have some magic music,' was said at the other end of the room. 'Who will play?'

'Little Amy!' said Mr. Edmonstone. 'Where is she? She always does it to admiration. Amy, come and be a performer.'

Amy rose, and came forward, but the colour had flushed into her cheeks again, and the recollection occurred to Mary, that her fame as a performer, in that way, arose from the very amusing manner in which she and Sir Guy had conducted the game last year. At the same moment her mother met her, and whispered,–

'Had you rather not, my dear?'

'I can do it, mamma, thank you– never mind.'

'I should like to send you up to Charlie– he has been so long alone.'

'Oh! thank you, dear mamma,' with a look of relief.

'Here is Charlotte wild to be a musician,' said Mrs. Edmonstone. 'Perhaps you will see how she can manage; for I think Charles must want a visit from his little nurse.'

Amy moved quietly away, and entered Charles's room, full of warm gratitude for the kindness which was always seeking how to spare her.

Charles was asleep, and throwing a shawl round her, she sat down in the dim light of the lamp, relieved by the stillness, only broken by now and then a louder note of the music down-stairs. It was very comfortable, after all that buzz of talk, and the jokes that seemed so nonsensical and tiresome. There were but two people who could manage to make a party entertaining, and that was the reason it was so different last year. Then Amy wondered if she was the only person who felt sick at heart and dreary; but she only wondered for a moment– she murmured half aloud to herself, 'I said I never would think of him except at my prayers! Here I am doing it again, and on Christmas night. I won't hide my eyes and moan over my broken reed; for Christmas is come, and the circles of song are widening round! Glory! good will, peace on earth! How he sang it last year, the last thing, when the people were gone, before we went up to bed. But I am breaking my resolution again. I must do something.'

She took up a book of sacred poetry, and began to learn a piece which she already nearly knew; but the light was bad, and it was dreamy work; and probably she was half asleep, for her thoughts wandered off to Sintram and the castle on the Mondenfelsen, which seemed to her like what she had pictured the Redclyffe crags, and the castle itself was connected in her imagination with the deep, echoing porch, while Guy's own voice seemed to be chanting–

Who lives forlorn,
On God's own word doth rest;
His path is bright
With heavenly light,
His lot among the blest.

'Are you there, Amy?' said Charles, waking. 'What are you staying here for? Don't they want you?'

'Mamma was so kind as to send me up.'

'I am glad you are come, for I have something to tell you. Mr. Ross has been up to see me, you know, and he has a letter from Guy.'

Amy's heart beat fast, and, with eyes fixed on the ground, she listened as Charles continued to give an account of Guy's letter about Coombe Prior. 'Mr. Ross is quite satisfied about him, Amy,' he concluded. 'I wish you could have heard the decided way in which he said, "He will live it down."'

Amy's answer was to stoop down and kiss her brother's forehead.

Another week brought Guy's renewal of the correspondence.

'Amy, here is something for you to read,' said Charles, holding up the letter as she came into the room.

She knew the writing. 'Wait one moment, Charlie, dear;' and she ran out of the room, found her mother fortunately alone, and said, averting her face,– 'Mamma, dear, do you think I ought to let Charlie show me that letter?'

Mrs. Edmonstone took hold of her hand, and drew her round so as to look into the face through its veiling curls. The hand shook, and the face was in a glow of eagerness. 'Yes, dearest!' said she, for she could not help it; and then, as Amy ran back again, she asked herself whether it was foolish, and bad for her sweet little daughter, then declared to herself that it must– it should– it would come right.

There was not a word of Amy in the letter, but it, or something else, made her more bright and cheerful than she had been for some time past. It seemed as if the lengthening days of January were bringing renewed comfort with them, when Charles, who ever since October had been confined to bed, was able to wear the Chinese dressing-gown, be lifted to a couch, and wheeled into the dressing-room, still prostrate, but much enjoying the change of scene, which he called coming into the world.

These were the events at quiet Hollywell, while Redclyffe was still engrossed with the shipwreck, which seemed to have come on purpose to enliven and occupy this solitary winter. It perplexed the Ashfords about their baronet more than ever. Mr. Ashford said that no one whose conscience was not clear could have confronted danger as he had done; and yet the certainty that he was under a cloud, and the sadness, so inconsistent with his age and temperament still puzzled them. Mrs. Ashford thought she had made a discovery. The second day after the wreck, the whole crew, except the little cabin-boy, were going to set off to the nearest sea-port; and the evening preceding their departure, they were to meet their rescuers, the fishermen, at a supper in the great servants' hall at the park. Edward and Robert were in great glory, bringing in huge branches of evergreens to embellish the clean, cold place; and Mr. and Mrs. Ashford and Grace were to come to see the entertainment, after having some coffee in the library.

Guy prepared it for his company by tumbling his books headlong from the sofa to a more remote ottoman, sticking a bit of holly on the mantel-shelf, putting out his beloved old friend, Strutt's 'Sports and Pastimes,' to amuse Grace, and making up an immense fire; and then, looking round, thought the room was uncommonly comfortable; but the first thing that struck Mrs. Ashford, when, with face beaming welcome, he ushered her in from the great hall, was how forlorn rooms looked that had not a woman to inhabit them.

The supper went off with great eclat. Arnaud at the head of the table carved with foreign courtesies, contrasted with the downright bluff way of the sailors. As soon as Sir Guy brought Mrs. Ashford to look in on them, old James Robinson proposed his health, with hopes he would soon come and live among them for good, and Jonas Ledbury added another wish, that 'Lady Morville' might soon be there too. At these words, an expression of pain came upon Guy's face; his lips were rigidly pressed together; he turned hastily away, and paced up and down before he could command his countenance. All were so busy cheering, that no one heeded his change of demeanour save Mrs. Ashford; and though, when he returned to the place where he had been standing, his complexion was deepened, his lip quivered, and his voice trembled in returning thanks, Mr. Ashford only saw the emotion naturally excited by his people's attachment.

The lady understood it better; and when she talked it over with her husband in the evening, they were convinced the cause of his trouble must be some unfortunate attachment, which he might think it his duty to overcome; and having settled this, they became very fond of him, and anxious to make Redclyffe agreeable to him.

Captain and crew departed; the little boy was better, and his hosts, Charity and Jem Ledbury, only wished to keep him for ever; the sensation at Redclyffe was subsiding, when one morning Markham came, in a state of extreme satisfaction and importance, to exhibit the county paper, with a full account of the gallant conduct of the youthful baronet. Two or three days after, on coming home from a ride to Coombe Prior, Guy found Lord Thorndale's card, and heard from Arnaud that 'my lord had made particular inquiries how long he would be in the country, and had been to the cliff to see where the wreck was.'

Markham likewise attached great importance to this visit, and went off into a long story about his influence, and the representation of Moorworth, or even of the county. As soon as Guy knew what he was talking about, he exclaimed, 'Oh, I hope all that is not coming on me yet! Till I can manage Todd and Coombe Prior, I am sure I am not fit to manage the country!'

A few mornings after, he found on the table an envelope, which he studied, as if playing with his eagerness. It had an East-hill post-mark, and a general air of Hollywell writing, but it was not in the hand of either of the gentlemen, nor was the tail of the y such as Mrs. Edmonstone was wont to make. It had even a resemblance to Amabel's own writing that startled him. He opened it at last, and within found the hand he could not doubt– Charles's, namely– much more crooked than usual, and the words shortened and blotted:–

'DEAR G.,– I ought not to do this, but I must; I have tyrannized over Charlotte, and obtained the wherewithal. Write me a full account of your gallant conduct. I saw it first in A.'s face. It has done you great good with my father. I will write more when I can. I can't get on now. 'C. M. E.'

He might well say he had first seen it in his sister's face. She had brought him the paper, and was looking for something he wanted her to read to him, when 'Redclyffe Bay' met her eye, and then came the whole at one delightful glance. He saw the heightened colour, the exquisite smile, the tear-drop on the eyelash.

'Amy! what have you there?'

She pointed to the place, gave the paper into his hand, and burst into tears, the gush of triumphant feeling. Not one was shed because she was divided from the hero of the shipwreck; they were pure unselfish tears of joy, exultation, and thankfulness. Charles read the history, and she listened in silence; then looked it over again with him, and betrayed how thoroughly she had been taught the whole geography of Redclyffe Bay. The next person who came in was Charlotte; and as soon as she understood what occupied them, she went into an ecstasy, and flew away with the paper, rushing with it straight into her father's room, where she broke into the middle of his letter-writing, by reading it in a voice of triumph.

Mr. Edmonstone was delighted. He was just the person who would be far more taken with an exploit of this kind, such as would make a figure in the world, than by steady perseverance in well-doing, and his heart was won directly. His wrath at the hasty words had long been diminishing, and now was absolutely lost in his admiration. 'Fine fellow! noble fellow!' he said. 'He is the bravest boy I ever heard of, but I knew what was in him from the first. I wish from my heart there was not this cloud over him. I am sure the whole story has not a word of truth in it, but he won't say a word to clear himself, or else we would have him here again to-morrow.'

This was the first time Mr. Edmonstone had expressed anything of real desire to recall Guy, and it was what Charles meant in his letter.

The tyranny over Charlotte was exercised while the rest were at dinner, and they were alone together. They talked over the adventure for the tenth time that day, and Charles grew so excited that he vowed that he must at once write to Guy, ordered her to give him the materials, and when she hesitated, forced her into it, by declaring that he should get up and reach the things himself, which would be a great deal worse. She wanted to write from his dictation, but he would not consent, thinking that his mother might not consider it proper, and he began vigorously; but though long used to writing in a recumbent posture, he found himself less capable now than he had expected, and went on soliloquizing thus: 'What a pen you've given me, Charlotte. There goes a blot! Here, another dip, will you! and take up that with the blotting paper before it becomes more like a spider.'

'Won't you make a fresh beginning?'

'No, that has cost me too much already. I've got no more command over my fingers. Here we go into the further corner of the paper. Well! C. M. E. There 'tis— do it up, will you? If he can read it he'll be lucky. How my arms ache!'

'I hope it has not hurt you, Charlie; but I am sure he will be very glad of it. Oh! I am glad you said that about Amy.'

'Who told you to read it, Puss?'

'I could not help it, 'tis so large.'

'I believe I didn't ought to have said it. Don't tell her I did,' said Charles; 'but I couldn't for the life of me— or what is more to the purpose, for the trouble of it— help putting it. He is too true a knight not to hear that his lady, not exactly smiled, but cried.'

'He is a true knight,' said Charlotte, emphatically, as with her best pen, and with infinite satisfaction, she indited the 'Sir Guy Morville, Bart., Redclyffe Park, Moorworth,' only wishing she could lengthen out the words infinitely.

'Do you remember, Charlie, how we sat here the first evening he came, and you took me in about the deadly feud?'

'It was no take-in,' said Charles; 'only the feud is all on one side.'

'Oh, dear! it has been such a stupid winter without Guy,' sighed Charlotte; 'if this won't make papa forgive him, I don't know what will.'

'I wish it would, with all my heart,' said Charles; 'but logically, if you understand the word, Charlotte, it does not make much difference to the accusation. It would not exactly be received as exculpatory evidence in a court of justice.'

'You don't believe the horrid stories?'

'I believe that Guy has gamed quite as much as I have myself; but I want to see him cleared beyond the power of Philip to gainsay or disbelieve it. I should like to have such a force of proof as would annihilate Philip, and if I was anything but what I am, I would have it. If you could but lend me a leg for two days, Charlotte.'

'I wish I could.'

'One thing shall be done,' proceeded Charles: 'my father shall go and meet him in person when he comes of age. Now Don Philip is out of the way, I trust I can bring that about.'

'If he would but come here!'

'No, that must not be, as mamma says, till there is some explanation; but if I was but in my usual state, I would go with papa and meet him in London. I wonder if there is any chance of it. The 28th of March– ten weeks off! If I can but get hold of those trusty crutches of mine by that time I'll do, and I'll do, and I'll do. We will bring back Amy's knight with flying colours.'

'Oh how happy we should be!'

'If I only knew what sort of sense that Markham of his may have, I would give him a hint, and set him to ferret out at St. Mildred's. Or shall I get Dr. Mayerne to order me there for change of air?'

So schemed Charles; while Guy, on his side, busied himself at Redclyffe as usual; took care and thought for the cabin-boy– returned Lord Thorndale's call without finding him at home– saw the school finished, and opened– and became more intimate with the Ashfords.

He said he should not come home at Easter, as he should be very busy reading for his degree; and as his birthday this year fell in Holy Week, there could be no rejoicings; besides, as he was not to have his property in his own hands till he was five-and-twenty, it would make no difference to the people. The Ashfords agreed they had rather he was safe at home for the vacation, and were somewhat anxious when he spoke of coming home to settle, after he had taken his degree.

For his own part he was glad the season would prevent any rejoicings, for he was in no frame of mind to enter into them and his birthday had been so sad a day for his grandfather, that he had no associations of pleasure connected with it.

Markham understood the feeling, liked it, and shared it, only saying that they would have their day of rejoicing when he married. Guy could not answer, and the old steward remarked the look of pain.

'Sir Guy,' said he, 'is it that which is wrong with you? Don't be angry with an old man for asking the question, but I only would hope and trust you are not getting into any scrape.'

'Thank you, Markham,' said Guy, after an effort; 'I cannot tell you about it. I will only set you at rest by saying it is nothing you could think I ought to be ashamed of.'

'Then why– what has come between? What could man or woman object to in you?' said Markham, regarding him proudly.

'These unhappy suspicions,' said Guy.

I can't make it out,' said Markham. 'You must have been doing something foolish to give rise to them.'

Guy told nearly what he had said on the first day of his return, but nothing could be done towards clearing up the mystery, and he returned to Oxford as usual.

March commenced, and Charles, though no longer absolutely recumbent, and able to write letters again, could not yet attempt to use his crutches, so that all his designs vanished, except that of persuading his father to go to London to meet Guy and Markham there, and transact the business consequent on his ward's attaining his majority. He trusted much to Guy's personal influence, and said to his father, 'You know no one has seen him yet but Philip, and he would tell things to you that he might not to him.'

It was an argument that delighted Mr. Edmonstone.

'Of course I have more weight and experience, and– and poor Guy is very fond of us. Eh, Charlie?'

So Charles wrote to make an appointment for Guy to meet his guardian and Markham in London on Easter Tuesday. 'If you will clear up the gambling story,' he wrote, 'all may yet be well.'

Guy sighed as he laid aside the letter. 'All in vain, kind Charlie,' said he to himself, 'vain as are my attempts to keep my poor uncle from sinking himself further! Is it fair, though,' continued he, with vehemence, 'that the happiness of at least one life should be sacrificed to hide one step in the ruin of a man who will not let himself be saved? Is it not a waste of self-devotion? Have I any right to sacrifice hers? Ought I not rather'– and a flash of joy came over him– 'to make my uncle give me back my promise of concealment? I can make it up to him. It cannot injure him, since only the Edmonstones will know it! But'– and he pressed his lips firmly together– 'is this the spirit I have been struggling for this whole winter? Did I not see that patient waiting and yielding is fit penance for my violence. It would be ungenerous. I will wait and bear, contented that Heaven knows my innocence at least in this. For her, when at my best I dreaded that my love might bring sorrow on her– how much more now, when I have seen my doom face to face, and when the first step towards her would be what I cannot openly and absolutely declare to be right? That would be the very means of bringing the suffering on her, and I should deserve it.'

Guy quitted these thoughts to write to Markham to make the appointment, finishing his letter with a request that Markham would stop at St. Mildred's on his way to London, and pay Miss Wellwood, the lady with whom his uncle's daughter was placed, for her quarter's board. 'I hope this will not be a very troublesome request,' wrote Guy; 'but I know you had rather I did it in this way, than disobey your maxims, as to not sending money by the post.'

The time before the day of meeting was spent in strengthening himself against the pain it would be to refuse his confidence to Mr. Edmonstone, and thus to throw away the last chance of reconciliation, and of Amy. This would be the bitterest pang of all— to see them ready to receive him, and he forced to reject their kindness.

So passed the preceding week, and with it his twenty-first birthday, spent very differently from the way in which it would ordinarily be passed by a youth in his position. It went by in hard study and sad musings, in bracing himself to a resolution that would cost him all he held dear, and, as the only means of so bracing himself, in trying to fix his gaze more steadily beyond the earth.

Easter day steadied the gaze once more for him, and as the past week had nerved him in the spirit of self-sacrifice, the feast day brought him true unchanging joy, shining out of sadness, and enlightening the path that would lead him to keep his resolution to the utmost, and endure the want of earthly hope.

CHAPTER 25

Already in thy spirit thus divine,
Whatever weal or woe betide,
Be that high sense of duty still thy guide,
And all good powers will aid a soul like thine.
– SOUTHEY

'Now for it!' thought Guy, as he dismissed his cab, and was shown upstairs in the hotel. 'Give me the strength to withstand!'

The door was opened, and he beheld Mr. Edmonstone, Markham, and another– it surely was Sebastian Dixon! All sprung up to receive him; and Mr. Edmonstone, seizing him by both hands, exclaimed–

'Here he is himself! Guy, my boy, my dear boy, you are the most generous fellow in the world! You have been used abominably. I wish my two hands had been cut off before I was persuaded to write that letter, but it is all right now. Forget and forgive– eh, Guy? You'll come home with me, and we will write this very day for Deloraine.'

Guy was almost giddy with surprise. He held one of Mr. Edmonstone's hands, and pressed it hard; his other hand he passed over his eyes, as if in a dream. 'All right?' he repeated.

'All right!' said Mr. Edmonstone. 'I know where your money went, and I honour you for it, and there stands the man who told me the whole story. I said, from the first, it was a confounded slander. It was all owing to the little girl.'

Guy turned his face in amazement towards his uncle, who was only waiting to explain. 'Never till this morning had I the least suspicion that I had been the means of bringing you under any imputation. How could you keep me in ignorance?'

'You have told– '

'Of the cheque,' broke in Mr. Edmonstone, 'and of all the rest, and of your providing for the little girl. How could you do it with that pittance of an allowance of yours? And Master Philip saying you never had any money! No wonder, indeed!'

'If I had known you were pinching yourself,' said Dixon, 'my mind would have revolted– '

'Let me understand it,' said Guy, grasping the back of a chair. 'Tell me, Markham. Is it really so? Am I cleared? Has Mr. Edmonstone a right to be satisfied?'

'Yes, Sir Guy,' was Markham's direct answer. 'Mr. Dixon has accounted for your disposal of the thirty pound cheque, and there is an end of the matter.'

Guy drew a long breath, and the convulsive grasp of his fingers relaxed.

'I cannot thank you enough!' said he to his uncle; then to Mr. Edmonstone, 'how is Charles?'

'Better– much better, you shall see him to-morrow– eh, Guy?'

'But I cannot explain about the one thousand pounds.'

'Never mind– you never had it, so you can't have misspent it. That's neither here nor there.'

'And you forgive my language respecting you?'

'Nonsense about that! If you never said anything worse than that Philip was a meddling coxcomb, you haven't much to repent of; and I am sure I was ten old fools when I let him bore me into writing that letter.'

'No, no; you did right under your belief; and circumstances were strong against me. And is it clear? Are we where we were before?'

'We are– we are in everything, only we know better what you are worth, Guy. Shake hands once more. There's an end of all misunderstanding and vexation, and we shall be all right at home again!'

The shake was a mighty one. Guy shaded his face for a moment or two, and then said–

'It is too much. I don't understand it. How did you know this matter wanted explanation?' said he, turning to his uncle.

'I learnt it from Mr. Markham, and you will do me the justice to believe, that I was greatly shocked to find that your generosity– '

'The truth of the matter is this,' said Markham. 'You sent me to Miss Wellwood's, at St. Mildred's. The principal was not within, and while waiting for her to make the payment, I got into conversation with her sister, Miss Jane. She told me that the child, Mr. Dixon's daughter, was always talking of your kindness, especially of a morning at St. Mildred's, when you helped him in some difficulty. I thought this threw some light on the matter, found out Mr. Dixon this morning, and you see the result.'

'I do, indeed,' said Guy; 'I wish I could attempt to thank you all.'

'Thanks enough for me to see you look like yourself,' said Markham. 'Did you think I was going to sit still and leave you in the mess you had got yourself into, with your irregularity about keeping your accounts?'

'And to you,' said Guy, looking at his uncle, as if it was especially pleasant to be obliged to him. 'You never can guess what I owe to you!'

'Nay, I deserve no thanks at all,' said Sebastian, 'since I was the means of bringing the imputation on you; and I am sure it is enough for a wretch like me, not to have brought only misery wherever I turn– to have done something to repair the evil I have caused. Oh, could I but bring back your father to what he was when first I saw him as you are now!'

He was getting into one of those violent fits of self-reproach, at once genuine and theatrical, of which Guy had a sort of horror, and it was well Mr. Edmonstone broke in, like comedy into tragedy.

'Come, what's past can't be helped, and I have no end of work to be done, so there's speechifying enough for once. Mr. Dixon, you must not be going. Sit down and look over the newspaper, while we sign these papers. You must dine with us, and drink your nephew's health, though it is not his real birthday.'

Guy was much pleased that Mr. Edmonstone should have given this invitation, as well as with the consideration Markham had shown for Dixon in his narration. Mr. Dixon, who had learnt to consider parents and guardians as foes and tyrants, stammered and looked confused and enraptured; but it appeared that he could not stay, for he had a professional engagement. He gave them an exhortation to come to the concert where he was employed, and grew so ardent in his description of it, that Guy could have wished to go; but his companions were in haste to say there was far too much to do. And the next moment Guy told himself, that Mr. Edmonstone's good-natured face and joyous 'eh, Guy?' were more to him than any music he could hear nearer than Hollywell.

He went down-stairs with his uncle, who all the way raved about the music, satisfied to find ears that could comprehend, and was too full of it even to attend or respond to the parting thanks, for his last words were something about a magnificent counter-tenor.

Guy walked up slowly, trying to gather his thoughts: but when it came back to him that Amy was his again, his brain seemed to reel with ecstasy, and it would have taken far more time than he could spare to recall his sober senses, so he opened the door, to convince himself at least of Mr. Edmonstone's presence, and was received with another shake of the hand.

'So here you are again. I was afraid he was carrying you off to his concert after all! I believe you have half a mind for it. Do you like to stay in London for the next? Eh, Guy?' and it was good to hear Mr. Edmonstone's hearty laugh, as he patted his ward on the shoulder, saw his blushing, smiling shake of the head, and gave a knowing look, which let in a fresh light on Markham, and luckily was unseen by Guy.

'Well,' continued Mr. Edmonstone, 'the man is more gentlemanlike than I expected. A good sort of fellow at the bottom, I dare say. He was pretty considerably shocked to find he had brought you into such a scrape.'

'He is very generous,' said Guy. 'Oh, there is much of a noble character in him.'

'Noble! humph!' put in Markham. 'He has gone down-hill fast enough, since I used to see him in your father's time; but I am glad he had the decency not to be the undoing of you.'

'His feeling is his great point,' said Guy, 'when you can once get at it. I wish— ' But breaking off short, 'I can't make it out. What did little Marianne tell you? Or was it Miss Wellwood?'

'It was first the youngest sister,' said Markham. 'I sat there talking to her some little time; she said you had been very kind to the family, and the child was very grateful to you— was always talking of some morning when you and your dog came, and helped her mother. Her father had been out all night, and her mother was crying, she said, and declaring he would be sent to prison, till you came and helped them.'

'Yes, that's it,' said Guy.

'Well, I remembered what you had told me of the mystery of the draft, and guessed that this might be the clue to it. I begged to see the child, and in she came, the very image of your mother, and a sharp little thing that knew what she meant, but had not much idea of the shame, poor child, about her father. She told me the story of his coming home in the morning, and her mother being in great distress, and saying they were ruined, till you came and talked to her mother, and gave her something. I asked if it was money, and she said it was paper. I showed her a draft, and she knew it was like that. So then I made her tell me where to find her father, whom I used to know in old times, and had to write to, now and then. I hunted him up, and a creditable figure he was, to be sure; but I got the truth out of him at last, and when he heard you had got into disgrace on his account, he raved like a tragedy hero, and swore he would come and tell your guardian the whole story. I put him into a cab for fear he should repent, and he had just got to the end of it when you came in.'

'It is of no use to thank you again, Markham!'

'Why, I have been getting your family out of scrapes these forty years or thereabouts,' said Markham; "tis all I am good for; and if they had been no worse than this one it would be better for all of us. But time is getting on, and there is enough to do.'

To the accounts they went at once. There was a good deal to be settled; and though Guy had as yet no legal power, according to his grandfather's will, he was of course consulted about everything. He was glad that, since he could not be alone to bring himself to the realization of his newly-recovered happiness, he should have this sobering and engrossing occupation. There he sat, coolly discussing leases and repairs, and only now and then allowing himself a sort of glimpse at the treasury of joy awaiting him whenever he had time to dwell on it. The Coombe Prior matters were set in a better train, the preliminary arrangements about the curacy were made, and Guy had hopes it would be his friend Mr. Wellwood's title for Orders.

There was no time to write to Hollywell, or rather Mr. Edmonstone forgot to do so till it was too late, and then consoled himself by observing that it did not signify if his family were taken by surprise, since joy killed no one.

His family were by no means of opinion that it did not signify when the next morning's post brought them no letter. Mrs Edmonstone and Charles had hoped much, and Amy did not know how much she hoped until the melancholy words, 'no letter,' passed from one to the other.

To make it worse, by some of those mismanagements of Mr. Edmonstone's which used to run counter to his wife's arrangements, a dinner-party had been fixed for this identical Wednesday, and the prospect was agreeable to no one, especially when the four o'clock train did not bring Mr. Edmonstone, who, therefore, was not to be expected till seven, when all the world would be arrived.

Laura helped Amy to dress, put the flowers in her hair, kissed her, and told her it was a trying day; and Amy sighed wearily, thanked her, and went down with arms twined in hers, whispering, 'If I could help being so foolish as to let myself have a little hope!'

Laura thought the case so hopeless, that she was sorry Amy could not cease from the foolishness, and did not answer. Amy sat down at the foot of the sofa, whither Charles was now carried down every day, and without venturing to look at him, worked at her netting. A carriage— her colour came and went, but it was only some of the guests; another— the Brownlows. Amy was speaking to Miss Brownlow when she heard more greetings; she looked up, caught by the arm of the sofa, and looked again. Her father was pouring out apologies and welcomes, and her mother was shaking hands with Guy.

Was it a dream? She shut her eyes, then looked again. He was close to her by this time, she felt his fingers close on her white glove for one moment, but she only heard his voice in the earnest 'How are you, Charlie?' Her father came to her, gave her first his usual kiss of greeting, then, not letting her go, looked at her for a moment, and, as if he could not help it, kissed her on both cheeks, and said, 'How d'ye do, my little Amy?' in a voice that meant unutterable things. All the room was swimming round; there was nothing for it but to run away, and she ran, but from the ante-room she heard the call outside, 'Sir Guy's bag to his room,' and she could not rush out among the servants. At that moment, however, she spied Mary Ross and her father; she darted up to them, said something incoherent about Mary's bonnet, and took her up to her own room.

'Amy, my dear, you look wild. What has come to you?'

'Papa is come home, and— ' the rest failed, and Amy was as red as the camellia in her hair.

'And?' repeated Mary, 'and the mystery is explained?'

'Oh! I don't know; they are only just come, and I was so silly, I ran away,— I did not know what to do.'

'They are come, are they?' thought Mary. 'My little Amy, I see it all.'

She made the taking off her bonnet and the settling her lace as elaborate an operation as she could, and Amy flitted about as if she did not by any means know what she was doing. A springy, running step was heard on the stairs and in the passage, and Mary, though she could not see her little friend's face, perceived her neck turn red for a moment, after which Amy took her arm, pressed it affectionately, and they went down.

Mrs. Edmonstone was very glad to see Amabel looking tolerably natural. 'Mamma' was of course burning to hear all, but she was so confident that the essentials were safe, that her present care was to see how her two young lovers would be able to comport themselves, and to be on her guard against attending to them more than to her guests.

Amy, after passing by Charles, and getting a squeeze from his ever-sympathizing hand, put herself away behind Mary, while Laura talked to every one, hoping to show that there was some self-possession in the family. Guy reappeared, but, after one glance to see if Amy was present, he did not look at her again, but went and leant over the lower end of Charles's sofa, just as he used to do; and Charles lay gazing at him, and entirely forgetting what he had been trying to say just before to Mrs. Brownlow, professing to have come from London that morning, and making the absent mistakes likely to be attributed to the lovers themselves.

Mr. Edmonstone came, and dinner followed. As Mrs. Edmonstone paired off her company, she considered what to do with her new arrival.

'If you had come two hours ago,' said she, within herself, 'I would have let you be at home. Now you must be a great man, and be content with me. It will be better for Amy.'

Accordingly Guy was between her and Mrs. Gresham. She did not try to speak to him, and was amused by his fitful attempts at making conversation with Mrs. Gresham, when it struck him that he ought to be taking notice of her. Amy (very fortunately, in her own opinion) was out of sight of him, on the same side of the table, next to Mr. Ross, who, like his daughter, guessed enough about the state of things to let her alone.

Charles was enjoying all manner of delightful conjectures with Charlotte, till the ladies returned to the drawing-room, and then he said as much as he dared to Mary Ross, far more than she had gained from Laura, who, as they came out of the dining-room, had said,—

'Don't ask me any questions, for I know nothing at all about it.'

Amy was talked to by Mrs. Gresham about club-books, and new flowers, to which she was by this time able to attend very well, satisfied that his happiness had returned, and content to wait till the good time for knowing how. She could even be composed when the gentlemen came in, Guy talking to Mr. Ross about Coombe Prior, and then going to Charles; but presently she saw no more, for a request for music was made, and she was obliged to go and play a duet with Laura. She did not dislike this, but there followed a persecution for some singing. Laura would have spared her, but could not; and while she was turning over the book to try to find something that was not impossible to begin, and Laura whispering encouragingly, 'This— try this— your part is almost nothing; or can't you do this?' another hand turned over the leaves, as if perfectly at home in them, and, without speaking, as if it was natural for him to spare Amy, found a song which they had often sung together, where she might join as much or as little as she chose, under cover of his voice. She had not a thought or sensation beyond the joy of hearing it again, and she stood, motionless, as if in a trance. When it was over, he said to Laura, 'I beg your pardon for making such bad work. I am so much out of practice.'

Mrs. Brownlow was seen advancing on them; Amy retreated, leaving Guy and Laura to fulfil all that was required of them, which they did with a very good grace, and Laura's old familiar feeling began to revive, so much that she whispered while he was finding the place, 'Don't you dislike all this excessively?'

'It does as well as anything else, thank you,' was the answer. 'I can do it better than talking.'

At last they were released, and the world was going away. Mary could not help whispering to Mrs. Edmonstone, 'How glad you must be to get rid of us!' and, as Mrs. Edmonstone answered with a smile, she ventured further to say,— 'How beautifully Amy has behaved!'

Little Amy, as soon as she had heard the last carriage roll off, wished every one good night, shook hands with Guy, holding up the lighted candle between him and her face as a veil, and ran away to her own room. The others remained in a sort of embarrassed silence, Mr. Edmonstone rubbing his hands; Laura lighted the candles, Charlotte asked after Bustle, and was answered that he was at Oxford, and Charles, laying hold of the side of the sofa, pulled himself by it into a sitting posture.

'Shall I help you?' said Guy.

'Thank you, but I am not ready yet; besides, I am an actual log now, and am carried as such, so it is of no use to wait for me. Mamma shall have the first turn, and I won't even leave my door open.'

'Yes, yes, yes; go and have it out with mamma, next best to Amy herself, as she is run away— eh, Guy?' said Mr. Edmonstone.

Guy and Mrs. Edmonstone had not hitherto trusted themselves to speak to each other, but they looked and smiled; then, wishing the rest good night, they disappeared. Then there was a simultaneous outbreak of 'Well?'

'All right!' said Mr. Edmonstone. 'Every word was untrue. He is the noblest fellow in the world, as I knew all the time, and I was an old fool for listening to a pack of stories against him.'

'Hurrah!' cried Charles, drumming on the back of his sofa. 'Let us hear how the truth came out, and what it was.'

'It was that Dixon. There has he been helping that man for ever, sending his child to school, giving him sums upon sums, paying his gaming debts with that cheque!'

'Oh, oh!' cried Charles.

'Yes that was it! The child told Markham of it, and Markham brought the father to tell me. It puts me in a rage to think of the monstrous stories Philip has made me believe!'

'I was sure of it!' cried Charles. 'I knew it would come out that he had only been so much better than other people that nobody could believe it. Cleared! cleared! Why, Charlotte, Mr. Ready-to-halt will be for footing it cleverly enough!' as she was wildly curvetting round him.

'I was always sure,' said Mr. Edmonstone. 'I knew it was not in him to go wrong. It was only Philip, who would persuade me black was white.'

'I never believed one word of it,' said Charles; 'still less after I saw Philip's animosity.'

'"Les absens ont toujours tort,"' interrupted Laura; then, afraid of saying too much, she added,– 'Come, Charlotte, it is very late.'

'And I shall be the first to tell Amy!' cried Charlotte. 'Good night, papa!– good night, Charlie!'

She rushed up-stairs, afraid of being forestalled. Laura lingered, putting some books away in the ante-room, trying to overcome the weary pain at her heart. She did not know how to be confident. Her father's judgment was worthless in her eyes, and Philip had predicted that Amy would be sacrificed after all. To see them happy made her sigh at the distance of her own hopes, and worse than all was self-reproach for unkindness in not rejoicing with the rest, in spite of her real affection for Guy himself. When she thought of him, she could not believe him guilty; when she thought of Philip's belief, she could not suppose him innocent, and she pitied her sister for enjoying a delusive happiness. With effort, however, she went to her room, and, finding her a little overpowered by Charlotte's tumultuous joy, saw that peace and solitude were best for her till she could have more certain intelligence, and, after very tender good-nights, carried off Charlotte.

It would be hard to describe Mrs. Edmonstone's emotion, as she preceded Guy to the dressing-room, and sat down, looking up to him as he stood in his old place by the fire. She thought he did not look well, though it might be only that the sun-burnt colour had given place to his natural fairness; his eyes, though bright as ever, did not dance and sparkle; a graver expression sat on his brow; and although he still looked very young, a change there certainly was, which made him man instead of boy— a look of having suffered, and conquered suffering. She felt even more motherly affection for him now than when he last stood there in the full tide of his first outburst of his love for her daughter, and her heart was almost too full for speech; but he seemed to be waiting for her, and at last she said,— 'I am very glad to have you here again.'

He smiled a little, then said, 'May I tell you all about it?'

'Sit down here. I want very much to hear it. I am sure you have gone through a good deal.'

I have, indeed,' said he, simply and gravely; and there was a silence, while she was certain that, whatever he might have endured, he did not feel it to have been in vain.

'But it is at an end,' said she. 'I have scarcely seen Mr. Edmonstone, but he tells me he is perfectly satisfied.'

'He is so kind as to be satisfied, though you know I still cannot explain about the large sum I asked him for.'

'We will trust you,' said Mrs. Edmonstone, smiling, 'but I am very anxious to hear how you came to an understanding.'

Guy went over the story in detail, and very much affected she was to hear how entirely unfounded had been the suspicion, and how thankful he was for Mr. Edmonstone's forgiveness.

'You had rather to forgive us!' said she.

'You forget how ill I behaved,' said Guy, colouring. 'If you knew the madness of those first moments of provocation, you would think that the penance of a lifetime, instead of only one winter, would scarce have been sufficient.'

'You would not say, as Charles does, that the suspicion justified your anger?'

'No, indeed!' He paused, and spoke again. 'Thank Heaven, it did not last long; but the insight it gave me into the unsubdued evil about me was a fearful thing.'

'But you conquered it. They were the unguarded exclamations of the first shock. Your whole conduct since, especially the interview with Philip, has shown that your anger has not been abiding, and that you have learnt to subdue it.'

'It could not abide, for there was no just cause of offence. Of course such a dreadful outburst warned me to be on my guard; and you know the very sight of Philip is a warning that there is danger in that way! I mean,' said

Guy, becoming conscious that he had been very severe, 'I mean that I know of old that I am apt to be worried by his manner, and that ought to make me doubly cautious.'

Mrs. Edmonstone was struck by the soberer manner in which he spoke of his faults. He was as ready to take full blame, but without the vehemence which he used to expend in raving at himself instead of at the offender. It seemed as if he had brought himself to the tone he used to desire so earnestly.

'I am very glad to be able to explain all to Philip,' he said.

'I will write as soon as possible. Oh, Mrs. Edmonstone! if you knew what it is to be brought back to such unhoped-for happiness, to sit here once more, with you,'– his voice trembled, and the tears were in her eyes,– 'to have seen her, to have all overlooked, and return to all I hoped last year. I want to look at you all, to believe that it is true,' he finished, smiling.

'You both behaved very well this evening,' said she, laughing, because she could do so better than anything else at that moment.

'You both!' murmured Guy to himself.

'Ah! little Amy has been very good this winter.'

He answered her with a beautiful expression of his eyes, was silent a little while, and suddenly exclaimed, in a candid, expostulating tone, 'But now, seriously, don't you think it a very bad thing for her?'

'My dear Guy,' said she, scarcely repressing a disposition to laugh, 'I told you last summer what I thought of it, and you must settle the rest with Amy to-morrow. I hear the drawing-room bell, which is a sign I must send you to bed. Good night!'

'Good night!' repeated Guy, as he held her hand. 'It is so long since I have had any one to wish me good night! Good night, mamma!'

She pressed his hand, then as he ran down to lend a helping hand in carrying Charles, she, the tears in her eyes, crossed the passage to see how it was with her little Amy, and to set her at rest for the night. Amy's candle was out, and she was in bed, lying full in the light of the Easter moon, which poured in glorious whiteness through her window. She started up as the door opened. 'Oh, mamma! how kind of you to come!'

'I can only stay a moment, my dear; your papa is coming up; but I must just tell you that I have been having such a nice talk with dear Guy. He has behaved beautifully, and papa is quite satisfied. Now, darling, I hope you will not lie awake all night, or you won't be fit to talk to him to-morrow.'

Amy sat up in bed, and put her arms round her mother's neck. 'Then he is happy again,' she whispered. 'I should like to hear all.'

'He shall tell you himself to-morrow, my dear. Now, good night! you have been a very good child. Now, go to sleep, my dear one.'

Amy lay down obediently. 'Thank you for coming to tell me, dear mamma,' she said. 'I am very glad; good night.'

She shut her eyes, and there was something in the sweet, obedient, placid look of her face, as the white moonlight shone upon it, that made her mother pause and gaze again with the feeling, only tenderer, left by a beautiful poem. Amy looked up to see why she delayed; she gave her another kiss, and left her in the moonlight.

Little Amy's instinct was to believe the best and do as she was bidden, and there was a quietness and confidence in the tone of her mind which gave a sort of serenity of its own even to suspense. A thankful, happy sensation that all was well, mamma said so, and Guy was there, had taken possession of her, and she did not agitate herself to know how or why, for mamma, had told her to put herself to sleep; so she thought of all the most thanksgiving verses of her store of poetry, and before the moon had passed away from her window, Amabel Edmonstone was wrapped in a sleep dreamless and tranquil as an infant's.

CHAPTER 26

Hence, bashful cunning,
And prompt me, plain and holy innocence.
I am your wife if you will marry me.
– TEMPEST

Amabel awoke to such a sense of relief and repose that she scarcely liked to ask herself the cause, lest it might ruffle her complete peace. Those words 'all right,' seemed to be enough to assure her that the cloud was gone.

Her mother came in, told her one or two of the main facts, and took her down under her wing, only stopping by the way for a greeting to Charles, who could not rise till after breakfast. He held her fast, and gazed up in her face, but she coloured so deeply, cast down her eyes, and looked so meek and submissive, that he let her go, and said nothing.

The breakfast party were for the most part quiet, silent, and happy. Even Charlotte was hushed by the subdued feeling of the rest, and Mr. Edmonstone's hilarity, though replied to in turn by each, failed to wake them into mirth. Guy ran up and down-stairs continually, to wait upon Charles; and thus the conversation was always interrupted as fast as it began, so that the only fact that came out was the cause of the lateness of their arrival yesterday. Mr. Edmonstone had taken it for granted that Guy, like Philip, would watch for the right time, and warn him, while Guy, being excessively impatient, had been so much afraid of letting himself fidget, as to have suffered the right moment to pass, and then borne all the blame.

'How you must have wanted to play the Harmonious Blacksmith,' said Charlotte.

'I caught myself going through the motions twice,' said Guy.

Mrs. Edmonstone said to herself that he might contest the palm of temper with Amy even; the difference being, that hers was naturally sweet, his a hasty one, so governed that the result was the same. When breakfast was over, as they were rising, Guy made two steps towards Amabel, at whom he had hitherto scarcely looked, and said, very low, in his straightforward way: 'Can I speak to you a little while?'

Amy's face glowed as she moved towards him, and her mother said something about the drawing-room, where the next moment she found herself. She did not use any little restless arts to play with her embarrassment; she did not torment the flowers or the chimney ornaments, nor even her own rings, she stood with her hands folded and her head a little bent down, like a pendant blossom, ready to listen to whatever might be said to her.

He did not speak at first, but moved uneasily about. At last he came nearer, and began speaking fast and nervously.

'Amabel, I want you to consider— you really ought to think whether this is not a very bad thing for you.'

The drooping head was raised, the downcast lids lifted up, and the blue eyes fixed on him with a look at once confiding and wondering. He proceeded—

'I have brought you nothing but unhappiness already. So far as you have taken any interest in me, it could cause you only pain, and the more I think of it, the more unfit it seems that one so formed for light, and joy, and innocent mirth, should have anything to do with the darkness that is round me. Think well of it. I feel as if I had done a selfish thing by you, and now, you know, you are not bound. You are quite free! No one knows anything about it, or if they did, the blame would rest entirely with me. I would take care it should. So, Amy, think, and think well, before you risk your happiness.'

'As to that,' replied Amy, in a soft, low voice, with such a look of truth in her clear eyes, 'I must care for whatever happens to you, and I had rather it was with you, than without you,' she said, casting them down again.

'My Amy!— my own!— my Verena!'— and he held fast one of her hands, as they sat together on the sofa— 'I had a feeling that so it might be through the very worst, yet I can hardly believe it now.'

'Guy,' said Amy, looking up, with the gentle resolution that had lately grown on her, 'you must not take me for more than I am worth, and I should like to tell you fairly. I did not speak last time, because it was all so strange and so delightful, and I had no time to think, because I was so confused. But that is a long time ago, and this has been a very sad winter, and I have thought a great deal. I know, and you know, too, that I am a foolish little thing; I have been silly little Amy always; you and Charlie have helped me to all the sense I have, and I don't think I could ever be a clever, strong-minded woman, such as one admires.'

'Heaven forbid!' ejaculated Guy; moved, perhaps, by a certain remembrance of St. Mildred's.

'But,' continued Amy, 'I believe I do really wish to be good, and I know you have helped me to wish it much more, and I have been trying to learn to bear things, and so'— out came something, very like a sunny smile, though some tears followed— 'so if you do like such a silly little thing, it can't be helped, and we will try to make the best of her. Only don't say any more about my being happier without you, for one thing I am very sure of, Guy, I had rather bear anything with you, than know you were bearing it alone. I am only afraid of being foolish and weak, and making things worse for you.'

'So much worse! But still,' he added, 'speak as you may, my Amy, I cannot, must not, feel that I have a right to think of you as my own, till you have heard all. You ought to know what my temper is before you risk yourself in its power. Amy, my first thought towards Philip was nothing short of murder.'

She raised her eyes, and saw how far entirely he meant what he said.

'The first— not the second,' she murmured.

'Yes, the second— the third. There was a moment when I could have given my soul for my revenge!'

'Only a moment!'

'Only a moment, thank Heaven! and I have not done quite so badly since. I hope I have not suffered quite in vain; but if that shock could overthrow all my wonted guards, it might, though I pray Heaven it may not, it might happen again.'

'I think you conquered yourself then, and that you will again,' said Amy.

'And suppose I was ever to be mad enough to be angry with you?'

Amy smiled outright here. 'Of course, I should deserve it; but I think the trouble would be the comforting you afterwards. Mamma said'— she added, after a long silence, during which Guy's feeling would not let him speak— 'mamma said, and I think, that you are much safer and better with such a quick temper as yours, because you are always struggling and fighting with it, on the real true religious ground, than a person more even tempered by nature, but not so much in earnest in doing right.'

'Yes, if I did not believe myself to be in earnest about that, I could never dare to speak to you at all.'

'We will help each other,' said Amy; 'you have always helped me, long before we knew we cared for each other!'

'And, Amy, if you knew how the thought of you helped me last winter, even when I thought I had forfeited you for ever.'

Their talk only ceased when, at one o'clock, Mrs. Edmonstone, who had pronounced in the dressing-room that three hours was enough for them at once, came in, and asked Guy to go and help to carry Charles down-stairs.

He went, and Amy nestled up to her mother, raising her face to be kissed.

'It is very nice!' she whispered; and then arranged her brother's sofa, as she heard his progress down-stairs beginning. He was so light and thin as to be very easily carried, and was brought in between Guy and one of the servants. When he was settled on the sofa, he began thus,— 'There was a grand opportunity lost last winter. I was continually rehearsing the scene, and thinking what waste it was to go through such a variety of torture without the dignity of danger. If I could but have got up ever so small an alarm, I would have conjured my father to send for Guy, entreated pathetically that the reconciliation might be effected, and have drawn my last breath clasping their hands, thus! The curtain falls!'

He made a feint of joining their hands, put his head back, and shut his eyes with an air and a grace that put Charlotte into an ecstasy, and made even Amy laugh, as she quitted the room, blushing.

'But if it had been your last breath,' said Charlotte, 'you would not have been much the wiser.'

'I would have come to life again in time to enjoy the "coup de theatre". I had some thoughts of trying an overdose of opium; but I thought Dr. Mayerne would have found me out. I tell you, because it is fair I should have the credit; for, Guy, if you knew what she was to me all the winter, you would perceive my superhuman generosity in not receiving you as my greatest enemy.'

'I shall soon cease to be surprised at any superhuman generosity,' said Guy. 'But how thin you are, Charlie; you are a very feather to carry; I had no notion it had been such a severe business.'

'Most uncommon!' said Charles, shaking his head, with a mock solemnity.

'It was the worst of all,' said Mrs. Edmonstone, 'six weeks of constant pain.'

'How very sorry Philip must have been!' exclaimed Guy.

'Philip?' said Charlotte.

'Why, was it not owing to him? Surely, your father told me so. Did not he let you fall on the stairs?'

'My dear father!' exclaimed Charles, laughing; 'every disaster that happens for the next twelvemonth will be imputed to Philip.'

'How was it, then?' said Guy.

'The fact was this,' said Charles; 'it was in the thick of the persecution of you, and I was obliged to let Philip drag me upstairs, because I was in a hurry. He took the opportunity of giving me some impertinent advice which I could not stand. I let go his arm, forgetting what a dependent mortal I am, and down I should assuredly have gone, if he had not caught me, and carried me off, as a fox does a goose, so it was his fault, as one may say, in a moral, though not in a physical sense.'

'Then,' said his mother, 'you do think your illness was owing to that accident?'

'I suppose the damage was brewing, and that the shake brought it into an active state. There's a medical opinion for you!'

'Well, I never knew what you thought of it before,' said Mrs. Edmonstone.

'Why, when I had a condor to pick on Guy's account with Philip, I was not going to pick a crow on my own,' said Charles. 'Oh! is luncheon ready; and you all going? I never see anybody now. I want the story of the shipwreck, though, of course, Ben What's-his-name was the hero, and Sir Guy Morville not a bit of it.'

Laura wanted to walk to East Hill, and the other young people agreed to go thither, too.

'It will be nice to go to church there to-day' said Amy, in a half-whisper, heard only by Guy, and answered by a look that showed how well he understood and sympathized.

'Another thing,' said Amy, colouring a good deal; 'shall you mind my telling Mary? I behaved so oddly last night, and she was so kind to me that I think I ought.'

Mary had seen enough last night to be very curious to-day, though hardly expecting her curiosity to be gratified. However, as she was putting on her bonnet for church, she looked out of her window, and saw the four coming across the fields from Hollywell. Guy and Amy did not walk into the village arm-in-arm; but, as they came under the church porch, Guy, unseen by all held out his hand, sought hers, and, for one moment, pressed it fervently. Amy knew he felt this like their betrothal.

After the service, they stood talking with Mr. Ross and Mary, for some little time. Amy held apart, and Mary saw how it was. As they were about to turn homewards, Amy said quickly, 'Come and walk a little way home with me.'

She went on with Mary before the rest, and when out of sight of them all, said, 'Mary!' and then stopped short.

'I guess something, Amy,' said Mary.

'Don't tell any one but Mr. Ross.'

'Then I have guessed right. My dear little Amy, I am very glad! So that was the reason you flew out of the room last evening, and looked so bright and glowing!'

'It was so good of you to ask no questions!'

'I don't think I need ask any now, Amy; for I see in your face how right and happy it all is.'

'I can't tell you all, Mary, but I must one thing,– that the whole terrible story arose from his helping a person in distress. I like you to know that.'

'Papa was always sure that he had not been to blame,' said Mary.

'Yes; so Charlie told me, and that is the reason I wanted you to know.'

'Then, Amy, something of this had begun last summer?'

'Yes; but not as it is now. I did not half know what it was then.'

'Poor dear little Amy,' said Mary; 'what a very sad winter it must have been for you!'

'Oh, very!' said Amy; 'but it was worse for him, because he was quite alone; and here every one was so kind to me. Mamma and Laura, and poor Charlie, through all his illness and pain, he was so very kind. And do you know, Mary, now it is all over, I am very glad of this dismal time; for I think that it has taught me how to bear things better.'

She looked very happy. Yet it struck Mary that it was strange to hear that the first thought of a newly-betrothed maiden was how to brace herself in endurance. She wondered, however, whether it was not a more truly happy and safe frame than that of most girls, looking forward to a life of unclouded happiness, such as could never be realized. At least, so it struck Mary, though she owned to herself that her experience of lovers was limited.

Mary walked with Amy almost to the borders of Hollywell garden; and when the rest came up with them, though no word passed, there was a great deal of congratulation in her warm shake of Guy's hand, and no lack of reply in his proud smile and reddening cheek. Charlotte could not help turning and going back with her a little way, to say, 'Are not you delighted, Mary? Is not Amy the dearest thing in the world? And you don't know, for it is a secret, and I know it, how very noble Guy has been, while they would suspect him.'

'I am very, very glad, indeed! It is everything delightful.'

'I never was so happy in my life,' said Charlotte; 'nor Charlie, either. Only think of having Guy for our brother; and he is going to send for Bustle to-morrow.'

Mary laughed, and parted with Charlotte, speculating on the cause of Laura's graver looks. Were they caused by the fear of losing her sister, or by a want of confidence in Guy?

That evening, how happy was the party at Hollywell, when Charles put Guy through a cross-examination on the shipwreck, from the first puff of wind to the last drop of rain; and Guy submitted very patiently, since he was allowed the solace of praising his Redclyffe fishermen.

Indeed, this time was full of tranquil, serene happiness. It was like the lovely weather only to be met with in the spring, and then but rarely, when the sky is cloudless, and intensely blue,– the sunshine one glow of clearness without burning,– not a breath of wind checks the silent growth of the expanding buds of light exquisite green. Such days as these shone on Guy and Amabel, looking little to the future, or if they did so at all, with a grave, peaceful awe, reposing in the present, and resuming old habits,– singing, reading, gardening, walking as of old, and that intercourse with each other that was so much more than ever before.

It was more, but it was not quite the same; for Guy was a very chivalrous lover; the polish and courtesy that sat so well on his frank, truthful manners, were even more remarkable in his courtship. His ways with Amy had less of easy familiarity than in the time of their brother-and-sister-like intimacy, so that a stranger might have imagined her wooed, not won. It was as if he hardly dared to believe that she could really be his own, and treated her with a sort of reverential love and gentleness, while she looked up to him with ever-increasing honour. She was better able to understand him now than in her more childish days last summer; and she did not merely see, as before, that she was looking at the upper surface of a mystery. He had, at the same time, grown in character, his excitability and over-sensitiveness seemed to have been smoothed away, and to have given place to a calmness of tone, that was by no means impassibility.

When alone with Amy, he was generally very grave, often silent and meditative, or else their talk was deep and serious; and even with the family he was less merry and more thoughtful than of old, though very bright and animated, and showing full, free affection to them all, as entirely accepted and owned as one of them.

So, indeed, he was. Mr. Edmonstone, with his intense delight in lovers, patronized them, and made commonplace jokes, which they soon learnt to bear without much discomposure. Mrs. Edmonstone was all that her constant appellation of 'mamma' betokened, delighting in Guy's having learnt to call her so. Charles enjoyed the restoration of his friend, the sight of Amy's happiness, and the victory over Philip, and was growing better every day. Charlotte was supremely happy, watching the first love affair ever conducted in her sight, and little less so in the return of Bustle, who resumed his old habits as regularly as if he had only left Hollywell yesterday.

Laura alone was unhappy. She did not understand her own feelings; but sad at heart she was; with only one who could sympathize with her, and he far away, and the current of feeling setting against him. She could not conceal her depression, and was obliged to allow it to be attributed to the grief that one sister must feel in parting with another; and as her compassion for her little Amy, coupled with her dread of her latent jealousy, made her particularly tender and affectionate, it gave even more probability to the supposition. This made Guy, who felt as if he was committing a robbery on them all, particularly kind to her, as if he wished to atone for the injury of taking away her sister; and his kindness gave her additional pain at entertaining such hard thoughts of him.

How false she felt when she was pitied! and how she hated the congratulations, of which she had the full share! She thought, however, that she should be able to rejoice when she had heard Philip's opinion; and how delightful it would be for him to declare himself satisfied with Guy's exculpation.

CHAPTER 27

I forgave thee all the blame,
I could not forgive the praise.
– TENNYSON

'If ever there was a meddlesome coxcomb on this earth!' Such was the exclamation that greeted the ears of Guy as he supported Charles into the breakfast-room; and, at the same time, Mr. Edmonstone tossed a letter into Guy's plate, saying,–

'There's something for you to read.'

Guy began; his lips were tightly pressed together; his brows made one black line across his forehead, and his eye sparkled even through his bent-down eyelashes; but this lasted only a few moments; the forehead smoothed, again, and there was a kind of deliberate restraint and force upon himself, which had so much power, that no one spoke till he had finished, folded it up with a sort of extra care, and returned it, only saying,

'You should not show one such letters, Mr. Edmonstone.'

'Does not it beat everything?' cried Mr. Edmonstone. 'If that is not impertinence, I should like to know what is! But he has played my Lord Paramount rather too long, as I can tell him! I ask his consent, forsooth! Probation, indeed! You might marry her to-morrow, and welcome. There, give it to mamma. See if she does not say the same. Mere spite and malice all along.'

Poor Laura! would no one refute such cruel injustice? Yes, Guy spoke, eagerly,–

'No no; that it never was. He was quite right under his belief.'

'Don't tell me! Not a word in his favour will I hear!' stormed on Mr. Edmonstone. 'Mere envy and ill-will.'

'I always told him so,' said Charles. 'Pure malignity!'

'Nonsense, Charlie!' said Guy, sharply; 'there is no such thing about him.'

'Come, Guy; I can't stand this,' said Mr. Edmonstone. 'I won't have him defended; I never thought to be so deceived; but you all worshipped the boy as if every word that came out of his mouth was Gospel truth, and you've set him up till he would not condescend to take an advice of his own father, who little thought what an upstart sprig he was rearing; but I tell him he has come to the wrong shop for domineering– eh, mamma?'

'Well!' cried Mrs. Edmonstone, who had read till near the end with tolerable equanimity; this really is too bad!'

'Mamma and all!' thought poor Laura, while her mother continued,– 'It is wilful prejudice, to say the least,– I never could have believed him capable of it!'

Charles next had the letter, and was commenting on it in a style of mingled sarcasm and fury; while Laura longed to see it justify itself, as she was sure it would.

'Read it, all of you— every bit,' said Mr. Edmonstone, 'that you may see this paragon of yours!'

'I had rather not,' said Amy, shrinking as it came towards her.

'I should like you to do so, if you don't dislike it very much,' said Guy.

She read in silence; and then came the turn of Laura, who marvelled at the general injustice as she read.

'CORK, April 8th.

'MY DEAR UNCLE,— I am much obliged to you for the communication of your intention with regard to Amabel; but, indeed, I must say I am a good deal surprised that you should have so hastily resolved on so important a step, and have been satisfied with so incomplete an explanation of circumstances which appeared to you, as well as to myself, to show that Guy's character was yet quite unsettled, and his conduct such as to create considerable apprehension that he was habitually extremely imprudent, to say the least of it, in the management of his own affairs. How much more unfit, therefore, to have the happiness of another intrusted to him? I believe— indeed, I understood you to have declared to me that you were resolved never to allow the engagement to be renewed, unless he should, with the deference which is only due to you as his guardian, consent to clear up the mystery with which he has thought fit to invest all his pecuniary transactions, and this, it appears, he refuses, as he persists in denying all explanation of his demand for that large sum of money. As to the cheque, which certainly was applied to discreditable uses, though I will not suffer myself to suppose that Guy was in collusion with his uncle, yet it is not at all improbable that Dixon, not being a very scrupulous person, may, on hearing of the difficulties in which his nephew has been placed, come forward to relieve him from his embarrassment, in the hope of further profit, by thus establishing a claim on his gratitude. In fact, this proof of secretly renewed intercourse with Dixon rather tends to increase the presumption that there is something wrong. I am not writing this in the expectation that the connection should be entirely broken off, for that, indeed, would be out of the question as things stand at present, but for my little cousin's sake, as well as his own, I entreat of you to pause. They are both extremely young— so young, that if there was no other ground, many persons would think it advisable to wait a few years; and why not wait until the time fixed by his grandfather for his coming into possession of his property? If the character of his attachment to Amabel is firm and true, the probation may be of infinite service to him, as keeping before him, during the most critical period of his life, a powerful motive for restraining the natural impetuosity of his disposition; while, on the other hand, if this should prove to have been a mere passing fancy for the first young lady into whose society he has been thrown on terms of easy familiar intercourse, you will then have the satisfaction of reflecting that your care and caution have preserved your daughter from a life of misery. My opinion has never altered respecting him, that he is brave and generous, with good feelings and impulses, manners peculiarly attractive, and altogether a character calculated to inspire affection, but impetuous and unsteady, easily led into temptation, yet obstinate in reserve, and his temper of unchecked violence. I wish him happiness of every kind; and, as you well know, would, do my utmost for his welfare; but my affection for your whole family, and my own conscientious conviction, make me feel it my duty to offer this remonstrance, which I hope will be regarded as by no means the result of any ill-will, but simply of a sincere desire for the good of all parties, such as can only be evinced by plain speaking.

'Yours affectionately,
'P. MORVILLE.'

All the time Laura was reading, Guy was defending Philip against the exaggerated abuse that Mr. Edmonstone and Charles were pouring out, till at last, Mrs. Edmonstone, getting out of patience, said,—

'My dear Guy, if we did not know you so well, we should almost accuse you of affectation.'

'Then I shall go away,' said Guy, laughing as he rose. 'Can you come out with me?' said he, in a lower tone, leaning over the back of Amy's chair.

'No; wait a bit,' interposed Mr. Edmonstone; 'don't take her out, or you won't be to be found, anywhere, and I want to speak to you before I write my letter, and go to the Union Meeting. I want to tell Master Philip, on the spot, that the day is fixed, and we snap our fingers at him and his probation. Wait till twenty-five! I dare say!'

At 'I want to speak to you,' the ladies had made the first move towards departure, but they were not out of hearing at the conclusion. Guy looked after Amy, but she would not look round, and Charles lay twisting Bustle's curls round his fingers, and smiling to himself at the manner in which the letter was working by contraries. The overthrow of Philip's influence was a great triumph for him, apart from the way in which it affected his friend and his sister.

Mr. Edmonstone was disappointed that Guy would not set about fixing the day, in time for him to announce it in a letter to be written in the course of an hour. Guy said he had not begun on the subject with Amy, and it would never do to hurry her. Indeed, it was a new light to himself that Mr. Edmonstone would like it to take place so soon.

'Pray, when did you think it was to be?' said Mr. Edmonstone. 'Upon my word, I never in all my days saw a lover like you, Guy!'

'I was too happy to think about the future; besides, I did not know whether you had sufficient confidence in me.'

'Confidence, nonsense! I tell you if I had a dozen daughters, I would trust them all to you.'

Guy smiled, and was infected by Charles's burst of laughing, but Mr. Edmonstone went on unheeding– 'I have the most absolute confidence in you! I am going to write to Philip this minute, to tell him he has played three-tailed Bashaw rather too long. I shall tell him it is to be very soon, at any rate; and that if he wishes to see how I value his pragmatical advice, he may come and dance at the wedding. I declare, your mamma and that colonel of his have perfectly spoilt him with their flattery! I knew what would come of it; you all would make a prodigy of him, till he is so puffed up, that he entirely forgets who he is!'

'Not I' said Charles; 'that can't be laid to my door.'

'But I'll write him such a letter this instant as shall make him remember what he is, and show him who he has to deal with. Eh, Charlie?'

'Don't you think,' said Guy, preparing to go, 'that it might be better to wait a day or two, till we see our way clearer, and are a little cooler?'

'I tell you, Guy, there is no one that puts me out of patience now, but yourself. You are as bad as Philip himself. Cool? I am coolness itself, all but what's proper spirit for a man to show when his family is affronted, and himself dictated to, by a meddling young jackanapes. I'll serve him out properly!'

A message called him away. Guy stood looking perplexed and sorrowful.

'Never mind,' said Charles, 'I'll take care the letter is moderate. Besides, it is only Philip, and he knows that letter-writing is not his forte.'

'I am afraid things will be said in irritation, which you will both regret. There are justice and reason in the letter.'

'There shall be more in the answer, as you will see.'

'No, I will not see. It is Mr. Edmonstone's concern, not mine. I am the last person who should have anything to do with it.'

'Just what the individual in question would not have said.'

'Would you do one thing to oblige me, Charlie?'

'Anything but not speaking my mind to, or of, the captain.'

'That is the very thing, unluckily. Try to get the answer put off till to-morrow, and that will give time to look at this letter candidly.'

'All the candour in the world will not make me think otherwise than that he is disappointed at being no longer able to make us the puppets of his malevolence. Don't answer, or if you do, tell me what you say in favour of that delicate insinuation of his.'

Guy made a step towards the window, and a step back again. ''Tis not fair to ask such questions,' he replied, after a moment. 'It is throwing oil on the fire. I was trying to forget it. He neither knows my uncle nor the circumstances.'

'Well, I am glad there is a point on which you can't even pretend to stand up for him, or I should have thought you crazed with Quixotism. But I am keeping you when you want to be off to Amy. Never mind Mr. Ready-to-halt; I shall wait till my father comes back. If you want the letter put off you had better give some hopes of– Oh! he is gone, and disinterested advice it is of mine, for what is to become of me without Amy remains to be proved. Laura, poor thing, looks like Patience on a monument. I wonder whether Philip's disgrace has anything to do with it. Hum! If mamma's old idea was right, the captain has been more like moth and candle than consistent with his prudence, unless he thought it "a toute epreuve". I wonder what came to pass last autumn, when I was ill, and mamma's head full of me. He may not intend it, and she may not know it, but I would by no means answer for Cupid's being guiltless of that harassed look she has had ever since that ball-going summer. Oh! there go that pretty study, Amy and her true knight. As to Guy, he is more incomprehensible than ever; yet there is no avoiding obeying him, on the principle on which that child in the "Moorland cottage" said she should obey Don Quixote.'

So when his father came in, Charles wiled him into deferring the letter till the next day, by giving him an indistinct hope that some notion when the marriage would be, might be arrived at by that time. He consented the more readily, because he was in haste to investigate a complaint that had just been made of the union doctor; but his last words to his wife and son before he went, were– 'Of course, they must marry directly, there is nothing on earth to wait for. Live at Redclyffe alone? Not to be thought of. No, I'll see little Amy my Lady Morville, before Philip goes abroad, if only to show him I am not a man to be dictated to.'

Mrs. Edmonstone sighed; but when he was gone, she agreed with Charles that there was nothing to wait for, and that it would be better for Guy to take his wife at once with him, when he settled at Redclyffe. So it must be whenever Amy could make up her mind to it; and thereupon they made plans for future meetings, Charles announcing that the Prince of the Black

Isles would become locomotive, and Charlotte forming grand designs upon Shag Island.

In the meantime, Guy and Amy were walking in the path through the wood, where he began: 'I would not have asked you to do anything so unpleasant as reading that letter, but I thought you ought to consider of it.'

'It was just like himself! How could he?' said Amy, indignantly.

'I wonder whether he will ever see his own harshness?' said Guy. 'It is very strange, that with all his excellence and real kindness, there should be some distortion in his view of all that concerns me. I cannot understand it.'

'You must let me call it prejudice, Guy, in spite of your protest. It is a relief to say something against him.'

'Amy, don't be venomous!' said Guy, in a playful tone of reproach.

'Yes; but you know it is not me whom he has been abusing.'

'Well,' said Guy, musingly, 'I suppose it is right there should be this cloud, or it would be too bright for earth. It has been one of my chief wishes to have things straight with Philip, ever since the time he stayed at Redclyffe as a boy. I saw his superiority then; but it fretted me, and I never could make a companion of him. Ever since, I have looked to his approval as one of the best things to be won. It shows his ascendancy of character; yet, do what I will, the mist has gone on thickening between us; and with reason, for I have never been able to give him the confidence he required, and his conduct about my uncle has so tried my patience, that I never have been quite sure whether I ought to avoid him or not.'

'And now you are the only person who will speak for him. I don't wonder papa is provoked with you,' said she, pretending to be wilful. 'I only hope you don't want to make me do the same. I could bear anything better than his old saying about your attractive manners and good impulses, and his opinion that has never altered. O Guy, he is the most provoking person in all the world. Don't try to make me admire him, nor be sorry for him.'

'Not when you remember how he was looked on here? and how, without doing anything worthy of blame, nay, from his acting unsparingly, as he thought right, every one has turned against him? even mamma, who used to be so fond of him?'

'Not Laura.'

'No, not Laura, and I am thankful to her for it; for all this makes me feel as if I had supplanted him.'

'Yes, yes, yes, it is like you; but don't ask me to feel that yet,' said Amy, with tears in her eyes,' or I shall be obliged to tell you what you won't like to hear, about his tone of triumph that terrible time last year. It was so very different, I don't think I could ever forgive him, if it had not made me so miserable too.'

Guy pressed her arm. 'Yes; but he thought himself right. He meant to do the kindest thing by you,' said he, so entirely without effort, that no one could doubt it came straight from his heart. 'So he thinks still, Amy; there is fairness, justice, good sense in his letter, and we must not blind our eyes to it, though there is injustice, at least, harshness. I did fail egregiously in my first trial.'

'Fail!'

'In temper.'

'Oh!'

'And, Amy, I wanted to ask what you think about the four years he speaks of. Do you think, as he says, my habits might be more fixed, and altogether you might have more confidence?'

'I don't look on you quite as he does now,' said Amy, with a very pretty smile. 'Do you think his opinion of you will ever alter?'

'But what do you think? Is there not some reason in what he says?'

'The only use I can see is, that perhaps I should be wiser at twenty-four, and fitter to take care of such a great house; but then you have been always helping me to grow wiser, and I am not much afraid but that you will be patient with me. Indeed, Guy, I don't know whether it is a thing I ought to say,' she added, blushing, 'but I think it would be dismal for you to go and live all alone at Redclyffe.'

'Honestly, Amy,' replied he, after a little pause, 'if you feel so, and your father approves, I don't think it will be better to wait. I know your presence is a safeguard, and if the right motives did not suffice to keep me straight, and I was only apparently so from hopes of you, why then I should be so utterly good for nothing at the bottom, if not on the surface, that you had better have nothing to say to me.'

Amy laughed incredulously.

'That being settled,' proceeded Guy, 'did you hear what your father said as you left the breakfast-room?'

She coloured all over, and there was silence. 'What did you answer?' said she, at length.

'I said, whatever happened, you must not be taken by surprise in having to decide quickly. Do you wish to have time to think? I'll go in and leave you to consider, if you like.'

'I only want to know what you wish,' said Amy, not parting with his arm.

'I had rather you did just as suits you best. Of course, you know what my wish must be.'

Amy walked on a little way in silence. 'Very well,' said she, presently, 'I think you and mamma had better settle it. The worst'— she had tears in her eyes— 'the going away— mamma— Charlie— all that will be as bad at one time as at another.' The tears flowed faster. 'It had better be as you all like best.'

'O Amy! I wonder at myself for daring to ask you to exchange your bright cheerful home for my gloomy old house.'

'No, your home,' said Amy, softly.

'I used to wonder why it was called gloomy; but it will be so no more when you are there. Yet there is a shadow hanging over it, which makes it sometimes seem too strange that you and it should be brought together.'

'I have read somewhere that there is no real gloom but what people raise for themselves.'

'True. Gloom is in sin, not sorrow. Yes, there would be no comfort if I were not sure that if aught of grief or pain should come to you through me, it will not, cannot really hurt you, my Amy.'

'No, unless by my own fault, and you will help me to meet it. Hark! was that a nightingale?'

'Yes, the first! How beautiful! There– don't you see it? Look on that hazel, you may see its throat moving. Well!' when they had listened for a long time,– 'after all, that creature and the sea will hardly let one speak of gloom, even in this world, to say nothing of other things.

'The sea! I am glad I have never seen it, because now you will show it to me for the first time.'

'You will never, can never imagine it, Amy! and he sung,–

'With all tones of waters blending,
Glorious is the breaking deep,
Glorious, beauteous, without ending,
Songs of ocean never sleep.'

A silence followed, only broken by the notes of the birds, and presently by the strokes of the great clock. Guy looked at his watch.

'Eleven, Amy! I must go to my reading, or you will have to be very much ashamed of me.'

For, after the first few days, Guy had returned to study regularly every day. He said it was a matter of necessity, not at all of merit, for though he did not mean to try for honours, Amy must not marry a plucked man. His whole career at Oxford had been such a struggle with the disadvantages of his education, that all his diligence had, he thought, hardly raised him to a level with his contemporaries. Moreover, courtship was not the best preparation for the schools, so that though he knew he had done his best, he expected no more than to pass respectably, and told Amy it was very good of her to be contented with a dunce, whereat she laughed merrily. But she knew him too well to try to keep him lingering in the April sunshine, and in they went, Guy to his Greek, and Amy to her mother. Charlotte's lessons had been in abeyance, or turned over to Laura of late, and Mrs.

Edmonstone and her dressing-room were always ready for the confidences of the family, who sought her there in turn— all but one, and that the one whose need was the sorest.

Amy and her mother comforted themselves with a good quiet cry, that was not exactly sorrowful, and came to the conclusion that Guy was the most considerate person in the world, and they would do whatever best suited him and papa. So, when Mr. Edmonstone came home, he was rewarded for putting off the letter by finding every one willing to let the marriage take place whenever he pleased. There were various conferences in the dressing-room, and Guy and Amy both had burning faces when they came down to dinner. Laura beheld them with a throbbing heart, while she mechanically talked to Dr. Mayerne, as if nothing was going on. She was glad there was no singing that evening, for she felt incapable of joining; and when at night Charles and his father talked of sitting up to write to Philip, the misery was such that she had no relief till she had shut herself in her room, to bear or to crush the suffering as best she might.

She was still sitting helpless in her wretchedness when Amy knocked at the door, and came in glowing with blushes and smiles, though her eyelashes were dewy with tears.

'Laura, dearest! if you would not be so very unhappy! I wish I knew what to do for you.'

Laura laid her head on her shoulder, and cried. It was a great comfort, little as Amy could understand her trouble. Amy kissed her, soothed her caressingly, cried too, and said, in broken sentences, how often they would be together, and how comfortable it was that Charlie was so much better, and Charlotte quite a companion.

'Then you have fixed the day?' whispered Laura, at last.

'The Tuesday in Whitsun-week,' returned Amy, resting her forehead on Laura's shoulder. 'They all thought it right.'

Laura flung her arms round her, and wept too much to speak.

'Dear, dear Laura!' said Amy, after a time, 'it is very kind of you, but— '

'Oh, Amy! you don't know. You must not think so much better of me than I deserve. It is not only— No, I would not be so selfish, if but— but— ' Never had her self-command so given way.

'Ah! you are unhappy about Philip,' said Amy; and Laura, alarmed lest she might have betrayed him, started, and tried to recover herself; but she saw Amy was quite unsuspicious, and the relief from this fright helped her through what her sister was saying,— 'Yes, you, who were so fond of him, must be vexed at this unkindness on his part.'

'I am sure it is his real wish for your good,' murmured Laura.

'I dare say!' said Amy, with displeasure. Then changing her tone, 'I beg your pardon, dear Laura, but I don't think I can quite bear to hear any one but Guy defend him.'

'It is very generous.'

'Oh, is not it, Laura? and he says he is so grieved to see us turned against Philip, after being so fond of him; he says it makes him feel as if he had supplanted him, and that he is quite thankful to you for taking his part still.'

'How shall I bear it?' sighed Laura, to herself.

'I wonder whether he will come?' said Amy, thoughtfully.

'He will,' said Laura.

'You think so?' said Amy. 'Well, Guy would be glad. Yes. O Laura, if Philip would learn to do Guy justice, I don't think there would be any more to wish!'

'He will in time,' said Laura. 'He is too generous not to be won by such generosity as Guy's; and when all this is forgotten, and all these accusations have been lived down, he will be the warmest of friends.'

'Yes,' said Amy, as if she wished to be convinced; 'but if he would only leave off saying his opinion has never altered, I think I could bring myself to look on him as Guy wants me to do. Good night! dear Laura, and don't be unhappy. Oh! one thing I must tell you; Guy made Charles promise to do all he could not to let it be a hasty letter. Now, good night!'

Poor Laura, she knew not whether gratitude to Guy was not one of her most painful sensations. She wished much to know what had been said in the letter; but only one sentence transpired, and that was, that Mr. Edmonstone had never heard it was necessary to apply to a nephew for consent to a daughter's marriage. It seemed as if it must have been as cutting as Charles could make it; but Laura trusted to Philip's knowledge of the family, and desire for their good, to make him forgive it, and the expectation of seeing him again at the wedding, cheered her. Indeed, a hope of still greater consequences began to rise in her mind, after Charles one day said to her, 'I think you ought to be much obliged to Guy. This morning, he suddenly exclaimed, "I say, Charlie, I wish you would take care Amy's fortune is not settled on her so that it can't be got rid of." I asked how he meant to make ducks and drakes of it; and he explained, that if either of you two did not happen to marry for money, like Amy, it might do you no harm.'

'We are very much obliged to him,' said Laura, more earnestly than Charles had expected. 'Do you know what it is, Charlie?'

'Oh! you want to calculate the amount of your obligation! Somewhere about five thousand pounds, I believe.'

Charles watched Laura, and the former idea recurred, as he wondered whether there was any particular meaning in her inquiry.

Meaning, indeed, there was. Laura knew nothing about the value of money; she did not know what Philip had of his own; how far five, or even ten, thousand would go in enabling them to marry, or whether it was available in her father's lifetime; but she thought this prospect might smooth the way to the avowal of their attachment, as effectually as his promotion; she reckoned on relief from the weary oppression of secrecy, and fully expected that it would all be told in the favourable juncture, when her parents were full of satisfaction in Amy's marriage. Gratitude to Guy would put an end to all doubt, dislike, and prejudice, and Philip would receive him as a brother.

These hopes supported Laura, and enabled her to take part with more appearance of interest in the consultations and arrangements for the marriage, which were carried on speedily, as the time was short, and Mr. Edmonstone's ideas were on a grand scale. It seemed as if he meant to invite all the world, and there were no limits to his views of breakfast, carriages, and splendours. His wife let him run on without contradiction, leaving the plans either to evaporate or condense, as time might prove best. Guy took Amy out walking, and asked what she thought of it.

'Do you dislike it very much?' she said.

'I can hardly tell. Of course, as a general rule, the less parade and nonsense the better; but if your father wishes it, and if people do find enjoyment in that way, it seems hard they should not have all they can out of it.'

'Oh, yes; the school children and poor people,' said Amy.

'How happy the Ashford children will be, feasting the poor people at Redclyffe! Old Jonas Ledbury will be in high glory.'

'To be sure it does not seem like merit to feast one's poor neighbours rather than the rich. It is so much pleasanter.'

'However, since the poor will be feasted, I don't think the rich ones will do us much harm.'

'I am sure I shall know very little about them,' said Amy.

'The realities are so great to us, that they will swallow up the accessories. There must be the church, and all that; and for the rest, Amy, I don't think I shall find out whether you wear lace or grogram.'

'There's encouragement for me!' said Amy, laughing. 'However, what I mean is, that I don't care about it, if I am not obliged to attend, and give my mind, to those kind of things just then, and that mamma will take care of.'

'Is it not a great trouble for her? I forgot that. It was selfish; for we slip out of the fuss, and it all falls on her.'

'Yes,' said Amy; 'but don't you think it would tease her more to have to persuade papa out of what he likes, and alter every little matter? That would be worry, the rest only exertion; and, do you know, I think,' said she, with a rising tear, 'that it will be better for her, to keep her from thinking about losing me.'

'I see. Very well, we will take the finery quietly. Only one thing, Amy, we will not be put out of,– we will not miss the full holy-day service.'

'Oh, yes; that will be the comfort.'

'One other thing, Amy. You know I have hardly a friend of my own; but there is one person I should like to ask,– Markham. He has been so kind, and so much attached to me; he loved my father so devotedly, and suffered so much at his death, that it is a pity he should not be made happy; and very happy he will be.'

'And there is one person I should like to ask, Guy, if mamma thinks we can do it. I am sure little Marianne ought to be one of my bridesmaids. Charlotte would take care of her, and it would be very nice to have her.'

CHAPTER 28

But no kind influence deign they shower,
Till pride be quelled and love be free.
– SCOTT

Kilcoran was about twenty miles from Cork, and Captain Morville was engaged to go and spend a day or two there. Maurice de Courcy drove him thither, wishing all the way for some other companion, since no one ever ventured to smoke a cigar in the proximity of 'Morville'; and, besides, Maurice's conversational powers were obliged to be entirely bestowed on his horse and dog, for the captain, instead of, as usual, devoting himself to suit his talk to his audience, was wrapped in the deepest meditation, now and then taking out a letter and referring to it.

This letter was the reply jointly compounded by Mr. Edmonstone and Charles, and the subject of his consideration was, whether he should accept the invitation to the wedding. Charles had taken care fully to explain how the truth respecting the cheque had come out, and Philip could no longer suspect that it had been a fabrication of Dixon's; but while Guy persisted in denial of any answer about the thousand pounds, he thought the renewal of the engagement extremely imprudent. He was very sorry for poor little Amy, for her comfort and happiness were, he thought, placed in the utmost jeopardy, with such a hot temper, under the most favourable circumstances; and there was the further peril, that when the novelty of the life with her at Redclyffe had passed off, Guy might seek for excitement in the dissipation to which his uncle had probably already introduced him. In the four years' probation, he saw the only hope of steadying Guy, or of saving Amy, and he was much concerned at the rejection of his advice, entirely for their sakes, for he could not condescend to be affronted at the scornful, satirical tone towards himself, in which Charles's little spitefulness was so fully apparent.

The wedding was a regular sacrifice, and Amabel was nothing but a victim; but an invitation to Hollywell had a charm for him that he scarcely could resist. To see Laura again, after having parted, as he thought, for so many years, delighted him in anticipation; and it would manifest his real interest in his young cousins, and show that he was superior to taking offence at the folly of Charles or his father.

These were his first thoughts and inclinations; his second were, that it was contrary to his principles to sanction so foolish and hasty a marriage by his presence; that he should thus be affording a triumph to Guy, and to one who would use it less moderately– to Charles. It would be more worthy of himself, more consistent with his whole course of conduct, to refuse his presence, instead of going amongst them when they were all infatuated, and unable to listen to sober counsel. If he stayed away now, when Guy should have justified his opinion, they would all own how wisely he had acted, and would see the true dignity which had refused, unlike common minds, to let his complaisance draw him into giving any sanction to what he so strongly disapproved. Laura, too, would pass through this trying time better if she was not distracted by watching him; she would understand the cause of his absence, and he could trust her to love and comprehend him at a distance, better than he could trust her to hear the marriage-service in his presence without betraying herself. Nor did he wish to hear her again plead for the confession of their engagement; and, supposing any misadventure should lead to its betrayal, what could be more unpleasant than for it to be revealed at such a time, when Charles would so turn it against him, that all his influence and usefulness would be for ever at an end?

Love drew him one way, and consistency another. Captain Morville had never been so much in the condition of Mahomet's coffin in his life; and he grew more angry with his uncle, Charles, and Guy, for having put him in so unpleasant a predicament. So the self-debate lasted all the way to Kilcoran and he only had two comforts— one, that he had sent the follower who was always amenable to good advice, safe out of the way of Lady Eveleen, to spend his leave of absence at Thorndale— the other, that Maurice de Courcy was, as yet, ignorant of the Hollywell news, and did not torment him by talking about it.

This satisfaction, however, lasted no longer than till their arrival at Kilcoran; for, the instant they entered the drawing-room, Lady Eveleen exclaimed, 'O Maurice, I have been so longing for you to come! Captain Morville, I hope you have not told him, for I can't flatter myself to be beforehand with you, now at least.'

'He has told me nothing,' said Maurice; 'indeed, such bad company has seldom been seen as he has been all the way.'

'You don't mean that you don't know it? How delightful! O, mamma! think of knowing something Captain Morville does not!'

'I am afraid I cannot flatter you so far,' said Philip, knowing this was no place for allowing his real opinion to be guessed.

'Then you do know?' said Lady Kilcoran, sleepily; 'I am sure it is a subject of great rejoicing.'

'But what is it, Eva? Make haste and tell,' said Maurice.

'No; you must guess!'

'Why, you would not be in such a way about it if it was not a wedding.'

'Right, Maurice; now, who is it?'

'One of the Edmonstones, I suppose. 'Tis Laura?'

'Wrong!'

'What, not Laura! I thought she would have been off first. Somebody's got no taste, then, for Laura is the prettiest girl I know.'

'Ah! your heart has escaped breaking this time, Maurice. It is that little puss, Amy, that has made a great conquest. Now guess.'

'Oh! young Morville, of course. But what possessed him to take Amy, and leave Laura?'

'Perhaps Laura was not to be had. Men are so self-sufficient, that they always think they may pick and choose. Is it not so, Captain Morville? I like Sir Guy better than most men, but Laura is too good for any one I know. If I could make a perfect hero, I would at once, only Charles would tell me all the perfect heroes in books are bores. How long have you known of it, Captain Morville?'

'For the last ten days.'

'And you never mentioned it?'

'I did not know whether they intended to publish it.'

'Now, Captain Morville, I hope to make some progress in your good opinion. Of course, you believe I can't keep a secret; but what do you think of my having known it ever since last summer, and held my tongue all that time?'

'A great effort, indeed,' said Philip, smiling. 'It would have been greater, I suppose, if the engagement had been positive, not conditional.'

'Oh! every one knew what it must come to. No one could have the least fear of Sir Guy. Yes; I saw it all. I gave my little aid, and I am sure I have a right to be bridesmaid, as I am to be. Oh! won't it be charming? It is to be the grandest wedding that ever was seen. It is to be on Whit-Tuesday; and papa is going to take me and Aunt Charlotte; for old Aunt Mabel says Aunt Charlotte must go. There are to be six bridesmaids, and a great party at the breakfast; everything as splendid as possible; and I made Mrs. Edmonstone promise from the first that we should have a ball. You must go, Maurice.'

'I shall be on the high seas!'

'Oh yes, that is horrid! But you don't sail with the regiment, I think, Captain Morville. You surely go?'

'I am not certain,' said Philip; especially disgusted by hearing of the splendour, and thinking that he had supposed Guy would have had more sense; and it showed how silly Amy really was, since she was evidently only anxious to enjoy the full paraphernalia of a bride.

'Not certain!' exclaimed Maurice and Eveleen, in a breath.

'I am not sure that I shall have time. You know I have been intending to make a walking tour through Switzerland before joining at Corfu.'

'And you really would prefer going by yourself– "apart, unfriended, melancholy, slow."'

'Very slow, indeed,' said Maurice.

'A wedding is a confused melancholy affair,' said Philip. 'You know I am no dancing man, Lady Eveleen; one individual like myself can make little difference to persons engrossed with their own affairs; I can wish my cousins well from a distance as well as at hand; and though they have been kind enough to ask me, I think that while their house is overflowing with guests of more mark, my room will be preferred to my company.'

'Then you do not mean to go?' said Lady Kilcoran. 'I do not,' she continued, 'for my health is never equal to so much excitement, and it would only be giving poor Mrs. Edmonstone additional trouble to have to attend to me.'

'So you really mean to stay away?' said Eveleen.

'I have not entirely decided.'

'At any rate you must go and tell old Aunt Mabel all about them,' said Eveleen. 'She is so delighted. You will be quite worshipped, at the cottage, for the very name of Morville. I spend whole hours in discoursing on Sir Guy's perfections.'

Philip could not refuse; but his feelings towards Guy were not warmed by the work he had to go through, when conducted to the cottage, where lived old Lady Mabel Edmonstone and her daughter, and there required to dilate on Guy's excellence. He was not wanted to speak of any of the points where his conscience would not let him give a favourable report; it was quite enough for him to tell of Guy's agreeable manners and musical talents, and to describe the beauty and extent of Redclyffe. Lady Mabel and Miss Edmonstone were transported; and the more Philip saw of the light and superficial way in which the marriage was considered, the more unwilling he became to confound himself with such people by eagerness to be present at it, and to join in the festivities. Yet he exercised great forbearance in not allowing one word of his disapproval or misgivings to escape him; no censure was uttered, and Lady Eveleen herself could not make out whether he rejoiced or not. He was grave and philosophical, superior to nonsensical mirth, that was all that she saw; and he made himself very agreeable throughout his visit, by taking condescending interest in all that was going on, and especially to Lady Eveleen, by showing that he thought her worthy of rational converse.

He made himself useful, as usual. Lord Kilcoran wanted a tutor for his two youngest boys, and it had been proposed to send them to Mr. Wellwood, at his curacy at Coombe Prior. He wished to know what Captain Morville thought of the plan; and Philip, thinking that Mr. Wellwood had been very inattentive to Guy's proceedings at St. Mildred's, though he would not blame him, considered it very fortunate that he had a different plan to recommend. One of the officers of his regiment had lately had staying with him a brother who had just left Oxford, and was looking out for a tutorship, a very clever and agreeable young man, whom he liked particularly, and he strongly advised Lord Kilcoran to keep his sons under his own eye, and place them under the care of this gentleman. His advice, especially when enforced by his presence, was almost sure to prevail, and thus it was in the present case.

The upshot of his visit was, that he thought worse and worse of the sense of the whole Edmonstone connection,– considered that it would be of no use for him to go to Hollywell,– adhered to his second resolution, and wrote to his uncle a calm and lofty letter, free from all token of offence, expressing every wish for the happiness of Guy and Amabel, and thanking his uncle for the invitation, which, however, he thought it best to decline, much as he regretted losing the opportunity of seeing Hollywell and its inhabitants again. His regiment would sail for Corfu either in May or June; but he intended, himself, to travel on foot through Germany and Italy, and would write again before quitting Ireland.

'So,' said Charles, 'there were at the marriage the Picanninies, and the Joblillies, and the Garryulies, but not the grand Panjandrum himself.'

'Nor the little round button at top!' rejoined Charlotte.

'Well, it's his own look out,' said Mr. Edmonstone. 'It is of a piece with all the rest.'

'I am sure we don't want him,' said Charlotte.

'Not in this humour,' said her mother.

Amy said nothing; and if she did not allow herself to avow that his absence was a relief, it was because she saw it was a grief and disappointment to Guy.

Laura was, of course, very much mortified,– almost beyond the power of concealment. She thought he would have come for the sake of seeing her, and she had reckoned so much on this meeting that it was double vexation. He did not know what he was missing by not coming; and she could not inform him, for writing to him was impossible, without the underhand dealings to which they would never, either of them, have recourse. So much for herself; and his perseverance in disapproval, in spite of renewed explanation, made her more anxious and sorry on Amy's account. Very mournful were poor Laura's sensations; but there was no remedy but to try to bewilder and drive them away in the bustle of preparation.

Guy had to go and take his degree, and then return to make his own preparations at Redclyffe. Amy begged him, as she knew he would like, to leave things alone as much as possible; for she could not bear old places to be pulled to pieces to suit new-comers; and she should like to find it just as he had been used to it.

He smiled, and said, 'It should only be made habitable.' She must have a morning-room, about which he would consult Mrs. Ashford: and he would choose her piano himself. The great drawing-room had never been unpacked since his grandmother's time, so that must be in repair; and, as for a garden, they would lay it out together. There could not be much done; for though they did not talk of it publicly, lest they should shock Mr. Edmonstone, they meant to go home directly after their marriage.

To Oxford, then, went Guy; his second letter announced that he had done tolerably well on his examination; and it came round to the Edmonstones, that it was a great pity he had not gone up for honours, as he would certainly have distinguished himself.

Redclyffe was, of course, in a state of great excitement at the news that Sir Guy was going to be married. Markham was very grand with the letter that announced it, and could find nothing to grumble about but that the lad was very young, and it was lucky it was no worse.

Mrs. Ashford was glad it was so good a connection, and obtained all the intelligence she could from James Thorndale, who spoke warmly of the Hollywell family in general; and, in particular, said that the young ladies looked after schools and poor people,– that Miss Edmonstone was very handsome and clever– a very superior person; but as to Miss Amabel, he did not know that there was anything to say about her. She was just like other young ladies, and very attentive to her invalid brother.

Markham's enmity to Mr. Ashford had subsided at the bidding of his master; and he informed him one day, with great cordiality, that Sir Guy would be at home the next. He was to sleep that night at Coombe Prior, and ride to Redclyffe in the morning; and, to the great delight of the boys, it was at the parsonage door that he dismounted.

Mrs. Ashford looked up in his bright face, and saw no more of the shade that had perplexed her last winter. His cheeks were deeper red as she warmly shook hands with him; and then the children sprung upon him for their old games,– the boys claiming his promise, with all their might, to take them out to the Shag. She wondered when she should venture to talk to him about Miss Amabel. He next went to find Markham, and met him before he reached his house. Markham was too happy not to grant and grumble more than ever.

'Well, Sir Guy; so here you are! You've lost no time about it, however. A fine pair of young housekeepers, and a pretty example of early marriages for the parish!'

Guy laughed. 'You must come and see the example, Markham. I have a message from Mr. and Mrs. Edmonstone, to ask you to come to Hollywell at Whitsuntide.'

Grunt! 'You are making a fool of me, Sir Guy. What's a plain old man like me to do among all your lords and ladies, and finery and flummery? I'll do no such thing.'

'Not to oblige me?'

'Oblige you? Nonsense! Much you'll care for me!'

'Nay, Markham, you must not stay away. You, my oldest and best friend,– my only home friend. I owe all my present happiness to you, and it would really be a great disappointment to me if you did not come. She wishes it, too.'

'Well, Sir Guy,' and the grunt was of softer tone, 'if you do choose to make a fool of me, I can't help it. You must have your own way; though you might have found a friend that would do you more credit.'

'Then I may say that you will come?'

'Say I am very much obliged to Mr. and Mrs. Edmonstone for their invitation. It is very handsome of them.'

'Then you will have the settlements ready by that time. You must, Markham.'

'I'll see about it.'

'And the house must be ready to come home to at once.'

'You don't know what you are talking of, Sir Guy!' exclaimed Markham, at once aghast and angry.

'Yes, I do. We don't intend to turn the house upside down with new furniture.'

'You may talk as you please, Sir Guy, but I know what's what; and it is mere nonsense to talk of bringing a lady to a house in this condition. A pretty notion you have of what is fit for your bride! I hope she knows what sort of care you mean to take of her!'

'She will be satisfied,' said Guy. 'She particularly wishes not to have everything disarranged, I only must have two rooms furnished for her.'

'But the place wants painting from head to foot, and the roof is in such a state– '

'The roof? That's serious!'

'Serious; I believe so. You'll have it about your ears in no time, if you don't look sharp.'

'I'll look this minute,' said Guy, jumping up. 'Will you come with me?'

Up he went, climbing about in the forest of ancient timbers, where he could not but be convinced that there was more reason than he could wish in what Markham said, and that his roof was in no condition to bring his bride to. Indeed it was probable that it had never been thoroughly repaired since the time of old Sir Hugh, for the Morvilles had not been wont to lay out money on what did not make a display. Guy was in dismay, he sent for the builder from Moorworth; calculated times and costs; but, do what he would, he could not persuade himself that when once the workmen were in Redclyffe, they would be out again before the autumn.

Guy was very busy during the fortnight he spent at home. There were the builder and his plans, and Markham and the marriage settlements, and there were orders to be given about the furniture. He came to Mrs. Ashford about this, conducted her to the park, and begged her to be so kind as to be his counsellor, and to superintend the arrangement. He showed her what was to be Amy's morning-room— now bare and empty, but with the advantages of a window looking south, upon the green wooded slope of the park, with a view of the church tower, and of the moors, which were of very fine form. He owned himself to be profoundly ignorant about upholstery matters, and his ideas of furniture seemed to consist in prints for the walls, a piano, a bookcase, and a couch for Charles.

'You have heard about Charles?' said he, raising his bright face from the list of needful articles which he was writing, using the window-seat as a table.

'Not much,' said Mrs. Ashford. 'Is he entirely confined to the sofa?'

'He cannot move without crutches; but no one could guess what he is without seeing him. He is so patient, his spirits never flag; and it is beautiful to see how considerate he is, and what interest he takes in all the things he never can share, poor fellow. I don't know what Hollywell would be without Charlie! I wonder how soon he will be able to come here! Hardly this year, I am afraid, for things must be comfortable for him, and I shall never get them so without Amy, and then it will be autumn. Well, what next? Oh, you said window-curtains. Some blue sort of stuff, I suppose, like the drawing-room ones at Hollywell. What's the name of it?'

In fact, Mrs. Ashford was much of his opinion, that he never would make things comfortable without Amy, though he gave his best attention to the inquiries that were continually made of him; and where he had an idea, carried it out to the utmost. He knew much better what he was about in the arrangements for Coombe Prior, where he had installed his friend, Mr. Wellwood, and set on foot many plans for improvements, giving them as much attention as if he had nothing else to occupy his mind. Both the curate and Markham were surprised that he did not leave these details till his return home; but he answered,—

'Better do things while we may. The thought of this unhappy place is enough to poison everything; and I don't think I could rest without knowing that the utmost was being done for it.'

He was very happy making arrangements for a village feast on the wedding-day. The Ashfords asked if he would not put it off till his return, and preside himself.

'It won't hurt them to have one first. Let them make sure of all the fun they can,' he answered; and the sentiment was greatly applauded by Edward and Robert, who followed him about more than ever, and grew so fond of him, that it made them very angry to be reminded of the spirit of defiance in which their acquaintance had begun. Nevertheless they seemed to be preparing the same spirit for his wife, for when their mother told them they must not expect to monopolize him thus when he was married, they declared, that they did not want a Lady Morville at all, and could not think why he was so stupid as to want a wife.

Their father predicted that he would never have time to fulfil his old engagement of taking them out to the Shag Rock, but the prediction was not verified, for he rowed both them and Mr. Ashford thither one fine May afternoon, showed them all they wanted to see, and let them scramble to their heart's content. He laughed at their hoard of scraps of the wood of the wreck, which they said their mamma had desired them to fetch for her.

So many avocations came upon Guy at once,– so many of the neighbours came to call on him,– such varieties of people wanted to speak to him,– the boys followed him so constantly,– and he had so many invitations from Mr. Wellwood and the Ashfords, that he never had any time for himself, except what must be spent in writing to Amabel. There was a feeling upon him, that he must have time to commune with himself, and rest from this turmoil of occupation, in the solitude of which Redclyffe had hitherto been so full. He wanted to be alone with his old home, and take leave of it, and of the feelings of his boyhood, before beginning on this new era of his life; but whenever he set out for a solitary walk, before he could even get to the top of the crag, either Markham marched up to talk over some important question,– a farmer waylaid him to make some request,– some cottager met him, to tell of a grievance,– Mr. Wellwood rode over,– or the Ashford boys rushed up, and followed like his shadow.

At length, on Ascension day, the last before he was to leave Redclyffe, with a determination that he would escape for once from his pursuers, he walked to the Cove as soon as he returned from morning service, launched his little boat and pushed off into the rippling whispering waters. It was a resumption of the ways of his boyhood; it seemed like a holiday to have left all these cares behind him, just as it used to be when all his lessons were prepared, and he had leave to disport himself, by land or water, the whole afternoon, provided he did not go out beyond the Shag Rock. He took up his sculls and rowed merrily, singing and whistling to keep time with their dash, the return to the old pleasure quite enough at first, the salt breeze, the dashing waves, the motion of the boat. So he went on till he had come as far as his former boundary, then he turned and gazed back on the precipitous rocks, cleft with deep fissures, marbled with veins of different shades of red, and tufted here and therewith clumps of samphire, grass, and a little brushwood, bright with the early green of spring. The white foam and spray were leaping against their base, and roaring in their hollows; the tract of wavelets between glittered in light, or heaved green under the shadow of the passing clouds; the sea-birds floated smoothly in sweeping undulating lines,

As though life's only call and care
Were graceful motion;

the hawks poised themselves high in air near the rocks. The Cove lay in sunshine, its rough stone chimneys and rude slate roofs overgrown with moss and fern, rising rapidly, one above the other, in the fast descending hollow, through which a little stream rushed to the sea,– more quietly than its brother, which, at some space distant, fell sheer down over the crag in a white line of foam, brawling with a tone of its own, distinguishable among all the voices of the sea contending with the rocks. Above the village, in the space where the outline of two hills met and crossed, rose the pinnacled tower of the village church, the unusual height of which was explained by the old custom of lighting a beacon-fire on its summit, to serve as a guide to the boats at sea. Still higher, apparently on the very brow of the beetling crag that frowned above, stood the old Gothic hall, crumbling and lofty, a fit eyrie for the eagles of Morville. The sunshine was indeed full upon it; but it served to show how many of the dark windows were without the lining of blinds and curtains, that alone gives the look of life and habitation to a house. How crumbled by sea-wind were the old walls, and the aspect altogether full of a dreary haughtiness, suiting with the whole of the stories connected with its name, from the time when it was said the very dogs crouched and fled from the presence of the sacrilegious murderer of the Archbishop, to the evening when the heir of the line lay stretched a corpse before his father's gate.

Guy sat resting on his oars, gazing at the scene, full of happiness, yet with a sense that it might be too bright to last, as if it scarcely befitted one like himself. The bliss before him, though it was surely a beam from heaven, was so much above him, that he hardly dared to believe it real: like a child repeating, 'Is it my own, my very own?' and pausing before it will venture to grasp at a prize beyond its hopes. He feared to trust himself fully, lest it should carry him away from his self-discipline, and dazzle him too much to let him keep his gaze on the light beyond; and he rejoiced in this time of quiet, to enable him to strive for power over his mind, to prevent himself from losing in gladness the balance he had gained in adversity.

It was such a check as he might have wished for, to look at that grim old castle, recollect who he was, and think of the frail tenure of all earthly joy, especially for one of the house of Morville. Could that abode ever be a home for a creature like Amy, with the bright innocent mirth that seemed too soft and sweet ever to be overshadowed by gloom and sorrow? Perhaps she might be early taken from him in the undimmed beauty of her happiness and innocence, and he might have to struggle through a long lonely life with only the remembrance of a short-lived joy to lighten it; and when he reflected that this was only a melancholy fancy, the answer came from within, that there was nothing peculiar to him in the perception that earthly happiness was fleeting. It was best that so it should be, and that he should rest in the trust that brightened on him through all,– that neither life nor death, sorrow nor pain, could separate, for ever, him and his Amy.

And he looked up into the deep blue sky overhead, murmuring to himself, 'In heart and mind thither ascend, and with Him continually dwell,' and gazed long and intently as he rocked on the green waters, till he again spoke to himself,– 'Why stand ye here gazing up into heaven?' then pulled vigorously back to the shore, leaving a shining wake far behind him.

CHAPTER 29

Hark, how the birds do sing,
And woods do ring!
All creatures have their joy, and man hath his;
Yet if we rightly measure,
Man's joy and pleasure
Rather hereafter than in present is:

Not that he may not here
Taste of the cheer,
But as birds drink and straight lift up the head,
So must he sip and think
Of better drink
He may attain to after he is dead.
– HERBERT

Guy returned to Hollywell on the Friday, there to spend a quiet week with them all, for it was a special delight to Amy that Hollywell and her family were as precious to him for their own sakes as for hers. It was said that it was to be a quiet week– but with all the best efforts of Mrs. Edmonstone and Laura to preserve quiet, there was an amount, of confusion that would have been very disturbing, but for Amy's propensity never to be ruffled or fluttered.

What was to be done in the honeymoon was the question for consideration. Guy and Amy would have liked to make a tour among the English cathedrals, pay a visit at Hollywell, and then go home and live in a corner of the house till the rest was ready; for Amy could not see why she should take up so much more room than old Sir Guy, and Guy declared he could not see that happiness was a reason for going pleasure-hunting; but Charles pronounced this very stupid, and Mr. Edmonstone thought a journey on the Continent was the only proper thing for them to do. Mrs. Edmonstone wished Amy to see a little of the world. Amy was known to have always desired to see Switzerland; it occurred to Guy that it would be a capital opportunity of taking Arnaud to see the relations he had been talking for the last twenty years of visiting, and so they acquiesced; for as Guy said, when they talked it over together, it did not seem to him to come under the denomination of pleasure-hunting, since they had not devised it for themselves; they had no house to go to; they should do Arnaud a service, and perhaps they should meet Philip.

'That will not be pleasure-hunting, certainly,' said Amy; then, remembering that he could not bear to hear Philip under-rated, she added,

'I mean, unless you could convince him, and then it would be more than pleasure.'

'It would be my first of unattained wishes,' said Guy. 'Then we will enjoy the journey.'

'No fear on that score,'

'And for fear we should get too much into the stream of enjoyment, as people abroad forget home-duties, let us stick to some fixed time for coming back.'

'You said Redclyffe would be ready by Michaelmas.'

'I have told the builder it must be. So, Amy, as far as it depends on ourselves, we are determined to be at home by Michaelmas.'

All seemed surprised to find the time for the wedding so near at hand. Charles's spirits began to flag, Amy was a greater loss to him than to anybody else; she could never again be to him what she had been, and unable as he was to take part in the general bustle and occupation, he had more time for feeling this, much more than his mother and Laura, who were employed all day. He and Guy were exemplary in their civilities to each other in not engrossing Amy, and one who had only known him three years ago, when he was all exaction and selfishness, could have hardly believed him to be the same person who was now only striving to avoid giving pain, by showing how much it cost him to yield up his sister. He could contrive to be merry, but the difficulty was to be cheerful; he could make them all laugh in spite of themselves, but when alone with Amy, or when hearing her devolve on her sisters the services she had been wont to perform for him, it was almost more than he could endure; but then he dreaded setting Amy off into one of her silent crying-fits, for which the only remedy was the planning a grand visit to Redclyffe, and talking overall the facilities of railroads and carriages.

The last day had come, and a long strange one it was; not exactly joyful to any, and very sad to some, though Amy, with her sweet pensive face, seemed to have a serenity of her own that soothed them whenever they looked at her. Charlotte, though inclined to be wild and flighty, was checked and subdued in her presence; Laura could not be entirely wretched about her; Charles lay and looked at her without speaking; her father never met her without kissing her on each side of her face, and calling her his little jewel; her mother— but who could describe Mrs. Edmonstone on that day, so full of the present pain, contending with the unselfish gladness.

Guy kept out of the way, thinking Amy ought to be left to them. He sat in his own room a good while, afterwards rode to Broadstone, in coming home made a long visit to Mr. Ross; and when he returned, he found Charles in his wheeled chair on the lawn, with Amy sitting on the grass by his side. He sat down by her and there followed a long silence,— one of those pauses full of meaning.

'When shall we three meet again?' at length said Charles, in a would-be lively tone.

'And where?' said Amy.

'Here,' said Charles; 'you will come here to tell your adventures, and take up Bustle.'

'I hope so,' said Guy. 'We could not help it. The telling you about it will be a treat to look forward to all the time.'

'Yes; your sight-seeing is a public benefit. You have seen many a thing for me.'

'That is the pleasure of seeing and hearing, the thing that is not fleeting,' said Guy.

'The unselfish part, you mean,' said Charles; and mused again, till Guy, starting up, exclaimed—

'There are the people!' as a carriage came in view in the lane. 'Shall I wheel you home, Charlie?'

'Yes, do.'

Guy leant over the back, and pushed him along; and as he did so murmured in a low tremulous tone, 'Wherever or whenever we may be destined to meet, Charlie, or if never again, I must thank you for a great part of my happiness here— for a great deal of kindness and sympathy.'

Charles looked straight before him, and answered— 'The kindness was all on your part. I had nothing to give in return but ill-temper and exactions. But, Guy, you must not think I have not felt all you have done for me. You have made a new man of me, instead of a wretched stick, laughing at my misery, to persuade myself and others that I did not feel it. I hope you are proud of it.'

'As if I had anything to do with it!'

'Hadn't, you, that's all! I know what you won't deny, at any rate— what a capital man-of-all-work you have been to me, when I had no right to ask it, as now we have,' he added, smiling, because Amy was looking at him, but not making a very successful matter of the smile. 'When you come back, you'll see me treat you as indeed "a man and a brother."'

This talk retarded them a little, and they did not reach the house till the guests were arriving. The first sight that met the eyes of Aunt Charlotte and Lady Eveleen as they entered, was, in the frame of the open window, Guy's light agile figure, assisting Charles up the step, his brilliant hazel eyes and glowing healthy complexion contrasting with Charles's pale, fair, delicate face, and features sharpened and refined by suffering. Amy, her deep blushes and downcast eyes almost hidden by her glossy curls, stood just behind, carrying her brother's crutch.

'There they are,' cried Miss Edmonstone, springing forward from her brother and his wife, and throwing her arms round Amy in a warm embrace.

'My dear, dear little niece, I congratulate you with all my heart, and that I do.'

'I'll spare your hot cheeks, Amy dearest!' whispered Eveleen, as Amy passed to her embrace, while Aunt Charlotte hastily kissed Charles, and proceeded— 'I don't wait for an introduction;' and vehemently shook hands with Guy.

'Ay, did I say a word too much in his praise?' said Mr. Edmonstone. 'Isn't he all out as fine a fellow as I told you?'

Guy was glad to turn away to shake hands with Lord Kilcoran, and the next moment he drew Amy out of the group eagerly talking round Charles's sofa, and holding her hand, led her up to a sturdy, ruddy-brown, elderly man, who had come in at the same time, but after the first reception had no share in the family greetings. 'You know him, already,' said Guy; and Amy held out her hand, saying—

'Yes, I am sure I do.'

Markham was taken by surprise, he gave a most satisfied grunt, and shook hands as heartily as if she had been his favourite niece.

'And the little girl?' said Amy.

'O yes.— I picked her up at St. Mildred's: one of the servants took charge of her in the hall.'

'I'll fetch her,' cried Charlotte, as Amy was turning to the door, and the next moment she led in little Marianne Dixon, clinging to her hand. Amy kissed her, and held her fast in her arms, and Marianne looked up, consoled in her bewilderment, by the greeting of her dear old friend, Sir Guy.

Mr. Edmonstone patted her head; and when the others had spoken kindly to her, Charlotte, under whose especial charge Guy and Amy had placed her, carried her off to the regions up-stairs.

The rest of the evening was hurry and confusion. Mrs. Edmonstone was very busy, and glad to be so, as she must otherwise have given way; and there was Aunt Charlotte to be talked to, whom they had not seen since Charles's illness. She was a short, bustling, active person, with a joyous face, inexhaustible good-humour, a considerable touch of Irish, and referring everything to her mother,— her one thought. Everything was to be told to her, and the only drawback to her complete pleasure was the anxiety lest she should be missed at home.

Mrs. Edmonstone was occupied with her, telling her the history of the engagement, and praising Guy; Amy went up as soon as dinner was over, to take leave of old nurse, and to see little Marianne; and Eveleen sat between Laura and Charlotte, asking many eager questions, which were not all convenient to answer.

Why Sir Guy had not been at home at Christmas was a query to which it seemed as if she should never gain a reply; for that Charles had been ill, and

Guy at Redclyffe, was no real answer; and finding she should not be told, she wisely held her tongue. Again she made an awkward inquiry–

'Now tell me, is Captain Morville pleased about this or not?'

Laura would have been silent, trusting to Eveleen's propensity for talking, for bringing her to some speech that it might be easier to answer, but Charlotte exclaimed, 'What has he been saying about it?'

'Saying? O nothing. But why does not he come?'

'You have seen him more lately than we have,' said Laura.

'That is an evasion,' said Eveleen; 'as if you did not know more of his mind than I could ever get at, if I saw him every day of my life.'

'He is provoking, that is all,' answered Charlotte. 'I am sure we don't want him; but Laura and Guy will both of them take his part.'

A call came at that moment,– the box of white gloves was come, and Laura must come and count them. She would fain have taken Charlotte with her; but neither Charlotte nor Eveleen appeared disposed to move, and she was obliged to leave them. Eva had already guessed that there was more chance of hearing the facts from Charlotte, and presently she knew a good deal. Charlotte had some prudence, but she thought she might tell her own cousin what half the neighbourhood knew– that Philip had suspected Guy falsely, and had made papa very angry with him, that the engagement had been broken off, and Guy had been banished, while all the time he was behaving most gloriously. Now it was all explained; but in spite of the fullest certainty, Philip would not be convinced, and wanted them to have waited five years.

Eveleen agreed with Charlotte that this was a great deal too bad, admired Guy, and pitied Amy to her heart's content.

'So, he was banished, regularly banished!' said she. 'However of course Amy never gave him up.'

'Oh, she never mistrusted him one minute.'

'And while he had her fast, it was little he would care for the rest.'

'Yes, if he had known it, but she could not tell him.'

Eveleen looked arch.

'But I am sure she did not,' said Charlotte, rather angrily.

'You know nothing about it, my dear.'

'Yes, but I do; for mamma said to Charlie how beautifully she did behave, and he too,– never attempting any intercourse.'

'Very good of you to believe it.'

'I am sure of it, certain sure,' said Charlotte. 'How could you venture to think they would either of them do anything wrong?'

'I did not say they would.'

'What, not to write to each other when papa had forbidden it, and do it in secret, too?'

'My dear, don't look so innocently irate. Goodness has nothing to do with it, it would be only a moderate constancy. You know nothing at all of lovers.'

'If I know nothing of lovers, I know a great deal of Amy and Guy, and I am quite sure that nothing on earth would tempt them to do anything in secret that they were forbidden.'

'Wait till you are in love, and you'll change your mind.'

'I never mean to be in love,' said Charlotte indignantly. Eveleen laughed the more, Charlotte grew more angry and uncomfortable at the tone of the conversation, and was heartily glad that it was broken off by the entrance of the gentlemen. Guy helped Charles to the sofa, and then turned away to continue his endless talk on Redclyffe business with Markham. Charlotte flew up to the sofa, seized an interval when no one was in hearing, and kneeling down to bring her face on a level with her brother's whispered–
'Charlie, Eva won't believe but that Guy and Amy kept up some intercourse last winter.'

'I can't help it, Charlotte.'

'When I tell her they did not, she only laughs at me. Do tell her they did not.'

'I have too much self-respect to lay myself open to ridicule.'

'Charlie, you don't think it possible yourself?' exclaimed Charlotte, in consternation.

'Possible– no indeed.'

'She will say it is not wrong, and that I know nothing of lovers.'

'You should have told her that ours are not commonplace lovers, but far beyond her small experience.'

'I wish I had! Tell her so, Charlie; she will believe you.'

'I sha'n't say one word about it.'

'Why not?'

'Because she is not worthy. If she can't appreciate them, I would let her alone. I once thought better of Eva, but it is very bad company she keeps when she is not here.'

Charles, however, was not sorry when Eveleen came to sit by him, for a bantering conversation with her was the occupation of which he was moat capable. Amy, returning, came and sat in her old place beside him, with her hand in his, and her quiet eyes fixed on the ground.

The last evening for many weeks that she would thus sit with him,– the last that she would ever be a part of his home. She had already ceased to belong entirely to him; she who had always been the most precious to him, except his mother.

Only his mother could have been a greater loss,– he could not dwell on the anticipation; and still holding her hand, he roused himself to listen, and answer gaily to Eveleen's description of the tutor, Mr. Fielder, 'a thorough gentleman, very clever and agreeable, who had read all the books in the world; the ugliest, yes, without exaggeration, the most quaintly ugly man living,– little, and looking just as if he was made of gutta percha, Eveleen said, 'always moving by jerks,– so Maurice advised the boys not to put him near the fire, lest he should melt.'

'Only when he gives them some formidable lesson, and they want to melt his heart,' said Charles, talking at random, in hopes of saying something laughable.

'Then his eyes– 'tis not exactly a squint, but a cast there is, and one set of eyelashes are black and the other light, and that gives him just the air of a little frightful terrier of Maurice's named Venus, with a black spot over one eye. The boys never call him anything but Venus.'

'And you encourage them in respect for their tutor?'

'Oh, he holds his own at lessons, I trow; but he pretends to have such a horror of us wild Irish, and to wonder not to find us eating potatoes with our fingers, and that I don't wear a petticoat over my head instead of a bonnet, in what he calls the classical Carthaginian Celto-Hibernian fashion.'

'Dear me,' said Charlotte, 'no wonder Philip recommended him.'

'O, I assure you he has the gift, no one else but Captain Morville talks near as well.'

So talked on Eveleen, and Charles answered her as much in her own fashion as he could, and when at last the evening came to an end, every one felt relieved.

Laura lingered long in Amy's room, perceiving that hitherto she had known only half the value of her sister her sweet sister. It would be worse than ever now, when left with the others, all so much less sympathizing, all saying sharp things of Philip, none to cling to her with those winsome ways that had been unnoted till the time when they were no more to console her, and she felt them to have been the only charm that had softened her late dreary desolation.

So full was her heart, that she must have told Amy all her grief but for the part that Philip had acted towards Guy, and her doubts of Guy would not allow her the consolation of dwelling on Amy's happiness, which cheered the rest. She could only hang about her in speechless grief, and caress her fondly, while Amy cried, and tried to comfort her, till her mother came to wish her good night.

Mrs. Edmonstone did not stay long, because she wished Amy, if possible to rest.

'Mamma' said Amy, as she received her last kiss, 'I can't think why I am not more unhappy.'

'It is all as it should be,' said Mrs. Edmonstone.

Amabel slept, and awakened to the knowledge that it was her wedding-day. She was not to appear at the first breakfast, but she came to meet Charles in the dressing-room; and as they sat together on the sofa, where she had watched and amused so many of his hours of helplessness, he clasped round her arm his gift,– a bracelet of his mother's hair. His fingers trembled and his eyes were hazy, but he would not let her help him. Her thanks were obliged to be all kisses, no words would come but 'Charlie; Charlie! how could I ever have promised to leave you?'

'Nonsense! who ever dreamt that my sisters were to be three monkeys tied to a dog?'

It was impossible not to smile, though it was but for a moment,– Charles's mirth was melancholy.

'And, dear Charlie, you will not miss me so very much; do pray let Charlotte wait upon you.'

'After the first, perhaps, I may not hate her. Oh, Amy, I little knew what I was doing when I tried to get him back again for you. I was sawing off the bough I was sitting on. But there! I will not flatter you, you've had enough to turn that head of yours. Stand up, and let me take a survey. Very pretty, I declare,– you do my education credit. There, if it will be for your peace, I'll do my best to wear on without you. I've wanted a brother all my life, and you are giving me the very one I would have picked out of a thousand– the only one I could forgive for presuming to steal you, Amy. Here he is. Come in,' he added, as Guy knocked at his door, to offer to help him down-stairs.

Guy hardly spoke, and Amy could not look in his face. It was late, and he took down Charles at once. After this, she had very little quiet, every one was buzzing about her, and putting the last touches to her dress; at last, just as she was quite finished, Charlotte exclaimed, 'Oh, there is Guy's step; may I call him in to have one look?'

Mrs. Edmonstone did not say no; and Charlotte, opening the dressing-room door, called to him. He stood opposite to Amy for some moments, then said, with a smile, 'I was wrong about the grogram. I would not for anything see you look otherwise than you do.'

It seemed to Mrs. Edmonstone and Laura that these words made them lose sight of the details of lace and silk that had been occupying them, so that they only saw the radiance, purity, and innocence of Amy's bridal appearance. No more was said, for Mr. Edmonstone ran up to call Guy, who was to drive Charles in the pony-carriage.

Amabel, of course, went with her parents. Poor child! her tears flowed freely on the way, and Mr. Edmonstone, now that it had really come to the point of parting with his little Amy, was very much overcome, while his wife, hardly refraining from tears, could only hold her daughter's hand very close.

The regular morning service was a great comfort, by restoring their tranquillity, and by the time it was ended, Amabel's countenance had settled into its own calm expression of trust and serenity. She scarcely even trembled when her father led her forward; her hand did not shake, and her voice, though very low, was firm and audible, while Guy's deep, sweet tones had a sort of thrill and quiver of intense feeling.

No one could help observing that Laura was the most agitated person present; she trembled so much that she was obliged to lean on Charlotte, and her tears gave the infection to the other bridesmaids— all but Mary Ross, who could never cry when other people did, and little Marianne, who did nothing but look and wonder.

Mary was feeling a great deal, both of compassion for the bereaved family and of affectionate admiring joy for the young pair who knelt before the altar. It was a showery day, with gleams of vivid sunshine, and one of these suddenly broke forth, casting a stream of colour from a martyr's figure in the south window, so as to shed a golden glory on the wave of brown hair over Guy's forehead, then passing on and tinting the bride's white veil with a deep glowing shade of crimson and purple.

Either that golden light, or the expression of the face on which it beamed, made Mary think of the lines—

> Where is the brow to wear in mortal's sight,
> The crown of pure angelic light?

Charles stood with his head leaning against a pillar as if he could not bear to look up; Mr. Edmonstone was restless and almost sobbing; Mrs. Edmonstone alone collected, though much flushed and somewhat trembling, while the only person apparently free from excitement was the little bride, as there she knelt, her hand clasped in his, her head bent down, her modest, steadfast face looking as if she was only conscious of the vow she exchanged, the blessing she received, and was, as it were, lifted out of herself.

It was over now. The feast, in its fullest sense, was held, and the richest of blessings had been called down on them.

The procession came out of the vestry in full order, and very pretty it was; the bride and bridegroom in the fresh bright graciousness of their extreme youth, and the six bridesmaids following; Laura and Lady Eveleen, two strikingly handsome and elegant girls; Charlotte, with the pretty little fair Marianne; Mary Ross, and Grace Harper. The village people who stood round might well say that such a sight as that was worth coming twenty miles to see.

The first care, after the bridal pair had driven off, was to put Charles into his pony-carriage. Charlotte, who had just pinned on his favour, begged to drive him, for she meant to make him her especial charge, and to succeed to all Amy's rights. Mrs. Edmonstone asked whether Laura would not prefer going with him, but she hastily answered,

'No, thank you, let Charlotte;' for with her troubled feelings, she could better answer talking girls than parry the remarks of her shrewd, observant brother.

Some one said it would rain, but Charlotte still pleaded earnestly.

'Come, then, puss,' said Charles, rallying his spirits, 'only don't upset me, or it will spoil their tour.'

Charlotte drove off with elaborate care,– then came a deep sigh, and she exclaimed, 'Well! he is our brother, and all is safe.'

'Yes,' said Charles; 'no more fears for them.'

'Had you any? I am very glad if you had.'

'Why?'

'Because it was so like a book. I had a sort of feeling, all the time, that Philip would come in quite grand and terrible.'

'As if he must act Ogre. I am not sure that I had not something of the same notion,– that he might appear suddenly, and forbid the banns, entirely for Amy's sake, and as the greatest kindness to her.'

'Oh!'

'However, he can't separate them now; let him do his worst, and while Amy is Guy's wife, I don't think we shall easily be made to quarrel. I am glad the knot is tied, for I had a fatality notion that the feud was so strong, that it was nearly a case of the mountains bending and the streams ascending, ere she was to be our foeman's bride.'

'No,' said Charlotte, 'it ought to be like that story of Rosaura and her kindred, don't you remember? The fate would not be appeased by the marriage, till Count Julius had saved the life of one of the hostile race. That would be it,– perhaps they will meet abroad, and Guy will do it.'

'That won't do. Philip will never endanger his precious life, nor ever forgive Guy the obligation. Well, I suppose there never was a prettier wedding– how silly of me to say so, I shall be sick of hearing it before night.'

'I do wish all these people were gone; I did not know it would be so horrid. I should like to shut myself up and cry, and think what I could ever do to wait on you. Indeed, Charlie, I know I never can be like Amy but if you– '

'Be anything but sentimental; I don't want to make a fool of myself' said Charles, with a smile and tone as if he was keeping sorrow at bay. 'Depend upon it if we were left to ourselves this evening, we should be so desperately savage that we should quarrel furiously, and there would be no Amy to set us to rights.'

'How Aunt Charlotte did cry! What a funny little woman she is.'

'Yes, I see now who you take after, puss. You'll be just like her when you are her age.'

'So I mean to be,— I mean to stay and take care of you all my life, as she does of grandmamma.'

'You do, do you?'

'Yes. I never mean to marry, it is so disagreeable. O dear! But how lovely dear Amy did look.'

'Here's the rain!' exclaimed Charles, as some large drops began to fall in good time to prevent them from being either savage or sentimental, though at the expense of Charlotte's pink and white; for they had no umbrella, and she would not accept a share of Charles's carriage-cloak. She laughed, and drove on fast through the short cut, and arrived at the house-door, just as the pelting hail was over, having battered her thin sleeves, and made her white bonnet look very deplorable. The first thing they saw was Guy, with Bustle close to him, for Bustle had found out that something was going on that concerned his master, and followed him about more assiduously than ever, as if sensible of the decree, that he was to be left behind to Charlotte's care.

'Charlotte, how wet you are.'

'Never mind, Charlie is not.' She sprung out, holding his hand, and felt as if she could never forget that moment when her new brother first kissed her brow.

'Where's Amy?'

'Here!' and while Guy lifted Charles out, Charlotte was clasped in her sister's arms.

'Are you wet, Charlie?'

'No, Charlotte would not be wise, and made me keep the cloak to myself.'

'You are wet through, poor child; come up at once, and change,' said Amy, flying nimbly up the stairs,— up even to Charlotte's own room, the old nursery, and there she was unfastening the drenched finery.

'O Amy, don't do all this. Let me ring.'

'No, the servants are either not come home or are too busy. Charles won't want me, he has Guy. Can I find your white frock?'

'Oh, but Amy— let me see!' Charlotte made prisoner the left hand, and looked up with an arch smile at the face where she had called up a blush. 'Lady Morville must not begin by being lady's-maid.'

'Let me— let me, Charlotte, dear, I sha'n't be able to do anything for you this long time.' Amy's voice trembled, and Charlotte held her fast to kiss her again.

'We must make haste,' said Amy, recovering herself. 'There are the carriages.'

While the frock was being fastened, Charlotte looked into the Prayer-book Amy had laid down. There was the name, Amabel Frances Morville, and the date.

'Has he just written it?' said Charlotte.

'Yes; when we came home.'

'O Amy! dear, dear Amy; I don't know whether I am glad or sorry!'

'I believe I am both,' said Amy.

At that moment Mrs. Edmonstone and Laura hastened in. Then was the time for broken words, tears and smiles, as Amy leant against her mother, who locked her in a close embrace, and gazed on her in a sort of trance, at once of maternal pride and of pain, at giving up her cherished nestling. Poor Laura! how bitter were her tears, and how forced her smiles,– far unlike the rest!

No one would care to hear the details of the breakfast, and the splendours of the cake; how Charlotte recovered her spirits while distributing the favours: and Lady Eveleen set up a flirtation with Markham, and forced him into wearing one, though he protested, with many a grunt, that she was making a queer fool of him; how often Charles was obliged to hear it had been a pretty wedding; and how well Lord Kilcoran made his speech proposing the health of Sir Guy and Lady Morville. All the time, Laura was active and useful,– feeling as if she was acting a play, sustaining the character of Miss Edmonstone, the bridesmaid at her sister's happy marriage; while the true Laura, Philip's Laura, was lonely, dejected, wretched; half fearing for her sister, half jealous of her happiness, forced into pageantry with an aching heart,– with only one wish, that it was over, and that she might be again alone with her burden.

She was glad when her mother rose, and the ladies moved into the drawing-room,– glad to escape from Eveleen's quick eye, and to avoid Mary's clear sense,– glad to talk to comparative strangers,– glad of the occupation of going to prepare Amabel for her journey. This lasted a long time,– there was so much to be said, and hearts were so full, and Amy over again explained to Charlotte how to perform all the little services to Charles which she relinquished; while her mother had so many affectionate last words, and every now and then stopped short to look at her little daughter, saying, she did not know if it was not a dream.

At length Amabel was dressed in her purple and white shot silk, her muslin mantle, and white bonnet. Mrs. Edmonstone left her and Laura to have a few words together, and went to the dressing-room. There she found Guy, leaning on the mantelshelf, as he used to do when he brought his troubles to her. He started as she entered.

'Ought I not to be here? he said. 'I could not help coming once more. This room has always been the kernel of my home, my happiness here.'

'Indeed, it has been a very great pleasure to have you here.'

'You have been very kind to me,' he proceeded, in a low, reflecting tone. 'You have helped me very much, very often; even when– Do you remember the day I begged you to keep me in order, as if I were Charles? I did not think then– '

He was silent; and Mrs. Edmonstone little able to find words, smiling, tried to say,– 'I little thought how truly and how gladly I should be able to call you my son;' and ended by giving him a mother's kiss.

'I wish I could tell you half,' said Guy,– 'half what I feel for the kindness that made a home to one who had no right to any. Coming as a stranger, I found– '

'We found one to love with all our hearts,' said Mrs. Edmonstone. 'I have often looked back, and seen that you brought a brightness to us all– especially to poor Charles. Yes, it dates from your coming; and I can only wish and trust, Guy, that the same brightness will rest on your own home.'

'There must be brightness where she is,' said Guy.

'I need not tell you to take care of her,' said Mrs. Edmonstone, smiling. 'I think I can trust you; but I feel rather as I did when first I sent her and Laura to a party of pleasure by themselves.'

Laura at this moment, came in. Alone with Amy, she could not speak, she could only cry; and fearful of distressing her sister, she came away; but here, with Guy, it was worse, for it was unkind not to speak one warm word to him. Yet what could she say! He spoke first–

'Laura, you must get up your looks again, now this turmoil is over. Don't do too much mathematics, and wear yourself down to a shadow.'

Laura gave her sad, forced smile.

'Will you do one thing for me, Laura? I should like to have one of your perspective views of the inside of the church. Would it be too troublesome to do?'

'Oh, no; I shall be very glad.'

'Don't set about it till you quite like it, and have plenty of time. Thank you. I shall think it is a proof that you can forgive me for all the pain I am causing you. I am very sorry.

'You are so very kind,' said Laura, bursting into tears; and, as her mother was gone, she could not help adding, 'but don't try to comfort me, Guy; don't blame yourself,– 'tisn't only that,– but I am so very, very unhappy.'

'Amy told me you were grieved for Philip. I wish I could help it, Laura. I want to try to meet him in Switzerland, and, if we can, perhaps it may be set right. At any rate he will be glad to know you see the rights of it.'

Laura wept still more; but she could never again lose the sisterly feeling those kind words had awakened. If Philip had but known what he missed!

Charlotte ran in. 'Oh, I am glad to find you here, Guy; I wanted to put you in mind of your promise. You must write me the first letter you sign "Your affectionate brother!"'

'I won't forget, Charlotte.'

'Guy! Where's Guy?' called Mr. Edmonstone. 'The rain's going off. You must come down, both of you, or you'll be too late.'

Mrs. Edmonstone hastened to call Amabel. Those moments that she had been alone, Amabel had been kneeling in an earnest supplication that all might be forgiven that she had done amiss in the home of her childhood, that the blessings might be sealed on her and her husband, and that she might go forth from her father's house in strength sent from above. Her mother summoned her; she rose, came calmly forth, met Guy at the head of the stairs, put her arm in his, and they went down.

Charles was on the sofa in the ante-room, talking fast, and striving for high spirits.

'Amy, woman, you do us credit! Well, write soon, and don't break your heart for want of me.'

There was a confusion of good-byes, and then all came out to the hall door; even Charles, with Charlotte's arm. One more of those fast-locked embraces between the brother and sister, and Mr. Edmonstone put Amabel into the carriage.

'Good-bye, good-bye, my own dearest little one! Bless you, bless you! and may you be as happy as a Mayflower! Guy, goodbye. I've given you the best I had to give,– and 'tis you that are welcome to her. Take care what you do with her, for she's a precious little jewel! Good-bye, my boy!'

Guy's face and grasping hand were the reply. As he was about to spring into the carriage, he turned again. 'Charlotte, I have shut Bustle up in my room. Will you let him out in half an hour? I've explained it all to him, and he will be very good. Good-bye.'

'I'll take care of him. I'll mention him in every letter.'

'And, Markham, mind, if our house is not ready by Michaelmas, we shall be obliged to come and stay with you.'

Grunt!

Lastly, as if he could not help it, Guy dashed up the step once more, pressed Charles's hand, and said, 'God bless you, Charlie!'

In an instant he was beside Amabel, and they drove off,– Amabel leaning forward, and gazing wistfully at her mother and Charles, till she was startled by a long cluster of laburnums, their yellow bloom bent down and heavy with wet, so that the ends dashed against her bonnet, and the crystal drops fell on her lap.

'Why, Amy, the Hollywell flowers are weeping for the loss of you!

She gave a sweet, sunny smile through her tears. At that moment they came beyond the thick embowering shrubs, while full before them was the dark receding cloud, on which the sunbeams were painting a wide-spanned rainbow. The semicircle was perfect, and full before them, like an arch of triumph under which they were to pass.

'How beautiful!' broke from them both.

'Guy,' said the bride, after a few minutes had faded the rainbow, and turned them from its sight, 'shall I tell you what I was thinking? I was thinking, that if there is a doom on us, I am not afraid, if it will only bring a rainbow.'

'The rainbow will come after, if not with it,' said Guy.

CHAPTER 30

She's a winsome wee thing,
She's a handsome wee thing,
She's a bonnie wee thing,
This sweet wee wifie of mine.
– BURNS

'Look here, Amy,' said Guy, pointing to a name in the traveller's book at Altdorf.

'Captain Morville!' she exclaimed, 'July 14th. That was only the day before yesterday.'

'I wonder whether we shall overtake him! Do you know what was this gentleman's route?' inquired Guy, in French that was daily becoming more producible.

The gentleman having come on foot, with nothing but his knapsack, had not made much sensation. There was a vague idea that he had gone on to the St. Gothard; but the guide who was likely to know, was not forthcoming, and all Guy's inquiries only resulted in, 'I dare say we shall hear of him elsewhere.'

To tell the truth, Amabel was not much disappointed, and she could see, though he said nothing, that Guy was not very sorry. These two months had been so very happy, there had been such full enjoyment, such freedom from care and vexation, or aught that could for a moment ruffle the stream of delight. Scenery, cathedrals music, paintings, historical association, had in turn given unceasing interest and pleasure; and, above all, Amabel had been growing more and more into the depths of her husband's mind, and entering into the grave, noble thoughts inspired by the scenes they were visiting. It had been a sort of ideal happiness, so exquisite, that she could hardly believe it real. A taste of society, which they had at Munich, though very pleasant, had only made them more glad to be alone together again; any companion would have been an interruption, and Philip, so intimate, yet with his carping, persecuting spirit towards Guy, was one of the last persons she could wish to meet; but knowing that this was by no means a disposition Guy wished to encourage, she held her peace.

For the present, no more was said about Philip; and they proceeded to Interlachen, where they spent a day or two, while Arnaud was with his relations; and they visited the two beautiful lakes of Thun and Brientz. On first coming among mountains, Amabel had been greatly afraid of the precipices, and had been very much alarmed at the way in which Guy clambered about, with a sureness of foot and steadiness of head acquired long ago on the crags of Redclyffe, and on which the guides were always complimenting him; but from seeing him always come down safe, and from having been enticed by him to several heights, which had at first seemed to her most dizzy and dangerous, she had gradually laid aside her fears, and even become slightly, very slightly, adventurous herself.

One beautiful evening, they were wandering on the side of the Beatenberg, in the little narrow paths traced by the tread of the goats and their herdsmen. Amabel sat down to try to sketch the outline of the white-capped Jung Frau and her attendant mountains, wishing she could draw as well as Laura, but intending her outline to aid in describing the scene to those whose eyes she longed to have with her. While she was drawing, Guy began to climb higher, and was soon out of sight, though she still heard him whistling. The mountains were not easy to draw, or rather she grew discontented with her black lines and white paper, compared with the dazzling snow against the blue sky, tinged by the roseate tints of the setting sun, and the dark fissures on the rocky sides, still blacker from the contrast.

She put up her sketching materials, and began to gather some of the delightful treasury of mountain flowers. A gentle slope of grass was close to her, and on it grew, at some little distance from her, a tuft of deep purple, the beautiful Alpine saxifrage, which she well knew by description. She went to gather it, but the turf was slippery, and when once descending, she could not stop herself; and what was the horror of finding herself half slipping, half running down a slope, which became steeper every moment, till it was suddenly broken off into a sheer precipice! She screamed, and grasped with both hands at some low bushes, that grew under a rock at the side of the treacherous turf. She caught a branch, and found herself supported, by clinging to it with her hands, while she rested on the slope, now so nearly perpendicular, that to lose her hold would send her instantly down the precipice. Her whole weight seemed to depend on that slender bough, and those little hands that clenched it convulsively,– her feet felt in vain for some hold. 'Guy! Guy!' she shrieked again. Oh, where was he? His whistle ceased,– he heard her,– he called,

'Here!'

'Oh, help me!' she answered. But with that moment's joy came the horror, he could not help her– he would only fall himself. 'Take care! don't come on the grass!' she cried. She must let go the branch in a short, time then a slip, the precipice,– and what would become of him? Those moments were hours.

'I am coming– hold fast!' She heard his voice above her, very near. To find him so close made the agony of dread and of prayer even more intense. To be lost, with her husband scarcely a step from her! Yet how could he stand on the slippery turf, and so as to be steady enough to raise her up?

'Now, then!' he said, speaking from the rock under which the brushwood grew, 'I cannot reach you unless you raise up your hand to me– your left hand– straight up. Let go. Now!'

It was a fearful moment. Amabel could not see him, and felt as if relinquishing her grasp of the tree was certain destruction. The instinct of self-preservation had been making her cling desperately with that left hand, especially as it held by the thicker part of the bough. But the habit of implicit confidence and obedience was stronger still; she did not hesitate, and tightening her hold with the other hand, she unclasped the left and stretched it upwards.

Joy unspeakable to feel his fingers close over her wrist, like iron, even while the bush to which she had trusted was detaching itself, almost uprooted by her weight! If she had waited a second she would have been lost, but her confidence had been her safety. A moment or two more, and with closed eyes she was leaning against him; his arm was round her, and he guided her steps, till, breathless, she found herself on the broad well-trodden path, out of sight of the precipice.

'Thank heaven!' he said, in a very low voice, as he stood still. 'Thank God! my Amy, I have you still.'

She looked up and saw how pale he was, though his voice had been so steady throughout. She leant on his breast, and rested her head on his shoulder again in silence, for her heart was too full of awe and thankfulness for words, even had she not been without breath or power to speak, and needing his support in her giddiness and trembling.

More than a minute passed thus. Then, beginning to recover, she looked up to him again, and said, 'Oh, it was dreadful! I did not think you could have saved me.'

'I thought so too for a moment!' said Guy, in a stifled voice. 'You are better now? You are not hurt? are you sure?'

'Quite sure! I did not fall, you know, only slipped. No, I have nothing the matter with me, thank you.'

She tried to stand alone, but the trembling returned. He made her sit down, and she rested against him, while he still made her assure him that she was unhurt. 'Yes, quite unhurt– quite well; only this wrist is a little strained, and no wonder. Oh, I am sure it was Providence that made those bushes grow just there!'

'How did it happen?'

'It was my fault. I went after a flower; my foot slipped on the turf, and I could not stop myself. I thought I should have run right down the precipice.'

She shut her eyes and shuddered again. 'It was frightful!' he said, holding her fast. 'It was a great mercy, indeed. Thank heaven, it is over! You are not giddy now.'

'Oh, no; not at all!'

'And your wrist?'

'Oh, that's nothing. I only told you to show you what was the worst,' said Amy, smiling with recovered playfulness, the most re-assuring of all.

'What flower was it?'

'A piece of purple saxifrage. I thought there was no danger, for it did not seem steep at first.'

'No, it was not your fault. You had better not move just yet; sit still a little while.'

'O Guy, where are you going?'

'Only for your sketching tools and my stick. I shall not be gone an instant. Sit still and recover.'

In a few seconds he came back with her basket, and in it a few of the flowers.

'Oh, I am sorry,' she said, coming to meet him; 'I wish I had told you I did not care for them. Why did you?'

'I did not put myself in any peril about them. I had my trusty staff, you know.'

'I am glad I did not guess what you were doing. I thought it so impossible, that I did not think of begging you not. I shall keep them always. It is a good thing for us to be put in mind how frail all our joy is.'

'All?' asked Guy, scarcely as if replying to her, while, though his arm pressed hers, his eye was on the blue sky, as he answered himself, 'Your joy no man taketh from you.'

Amabel was much impressed, as she thought what it would have been for him if his little wife bad been snatched from him so suddenly and frightfully. His return– his meeting her mother– his desolate home and solitary life. She could almost have wept for him. Yet, at the moment of relief from the fear of such misery, he could thus speak. He could look onward to the joy beyond, even while his cheek was still blanched with the horror and anguish of the apprehension; and how great they had been was shown by the broken words he uttered in his sleep, for several nights afterwards, while by day he was always watching and cautioning her. Assuredly his dependence on the joy that could not be lost did not make her doubt his tenderness; it only made her feel how far behind him she was, for would it have been the same with her, had the danger been his?

In a couple of days they arrived at the beautiful Lugano, and, as usual, their first walk was to the post-office, but disappointment awaited them. There had been some letters addressed to the name of Morville, but the Signor Inglese had left orders that such should be forwarded to Como. Amabel, in her best Italian, strove hard to explain the difference between the captain and Sir Guy, the Cavaliere Guido, as she translated him, who stood by looking much amused by the perplexities of his lady's construing; while the post-master, though very polite and sorry for the Signora's disappointment, stuck to the address being Morville, poste restante.

'There is one good thing,' said the cavaliere, as they walked away, 'we can find the captain now. I'll write and ask him– shall I say to meet us at Varenna or at Bellagio?'

'Whichever suits him best, I should think. It can't make much difference to us.'

'Your voice has a disconsolate cadence,' said Guy, looking at her with a smile.

'I did not mean it,' she answered; 'I have not a word to say against it. It is quite right, and I am sure I don't wish to do otherwise.'

'Only it is the first drawback in our real day-dream.'

'Just so, and that is all,' said Amy; 'I am glad you feel the same, not that I want you to change your mind.'

'Don't you remember our resolution against mere pleasure-hunting? That adventure at Interlachen seemed to be meant to bring us up short just as we were getting into that line.'

'You think we were?'

'I was, at least; for I know it was a satisfaction not to find a letter, to say Redclyffe was ready for us.'

'I had rather it was Redclyffe than Philip.'

'To be sure, I would not change my own dancing leaping waves for this clear blue looking-glass of a lake, or even those white peaks. I want you to make friends with those waves, Amy. But it is a more real matter to make friends with Philip, the one wish of my life. Not that I exactly expect to clear matters up, but if some move is not made now, when it may, we shall stand aloof for life, and there will be the feud where it was before.'

'It is quite right,' said Amy; 'I dare say that, meeting so far from home, he will be glad to see us, and to hear the Hollywell news. I little thought last autumn where I should meet him again.'

On the second evening from that time, Philip Morville was walking, hot and dusty, between the high stone walls bordering the road, and shutting out the beautiful view of the lake, at the entrance of Ballagio, meditating on the note he had received from Guy, and intending to be magnanimous, and overlook former offences for Amabel's sake. He would show that he considered the marriage to have cleared off old scores, and that as long as she was happy, poor little thing, her husband should be borne with, though not to the extent of the spoiling the Edmonstones gave him.

Thus reflecting, he entered the town, and walked on in search of the hotel. He presently found himself on a terrace, looking out on the deep blue lake, there divided by the promontory of Bellagio, into two branches, the magnificent mountain forms rising opposite to him. A little boat was crossing, and as it neared the landing-place, he saw that it contained a gentleman and lady, English– probably his cousins themselves. They looked up, and in another moment had waved their recognition. Gestures and faces were strangely familiar, like a bit of Hollywell transplanted into that Italian scene. He hastened to the landing-place, and was met by a hearty greeting from Guy, who seemed full of eagerness to claim their closer relationship, and ready to be congratulated.

'How d'ye do, Philip? I am glad we have caught you at last. Here she is.'

If he had wished to annoy Philip, he could hardly have done so more effectually than by behaving as if nothing was amiss, and disconcerting his preparations for a reconciliation. But the captain's ordinary manner was calculated to cover all such feelings; and as he shook hands, he felt much kindness for Amabel, as an unconscious victim, whose very smiles were melancholy, and plenty of them there were, for she rejoiced sincerely in the meeting, as Guy was pleased, and a home face was a welcome sight.

'I have your letters in my knapsack; I will unpack them as soon as we get to the hotel. I thought it safer not to send them in search of you again, as we were to meet so soon.'

'Certainly. Are there many?'

'One for each of you, both from Hollywell. I was very sorry to have engrossed them; but not knowing you were so near, I only gave my surname.'

'It was lucky for us,' said Guy, 'otherwise we could not have traced you. We saw your name at Altdorf, and have been trying to come up with you ever since.'

'I am glad we have met. What accounts have you from home?'

'Excellent,' said Amy; 'Charlie is uncommonly well, he has been out of doors a great deal, and has even dined out several times.'

'I am very glad.'

'You know he has been improving ever since his great illness.'

'You would be surprised to see how much better he moves,' said Guy; 'he helps himself so much more.'

'Can he set his foot to the ground?'

'No,' said Amy, 'there is no hope of that; but he is more active, because his general health is improved; he can sleep and eat more.'

'I always thought exertion would do more for him than anything else.'

Amabel was vexed, for she thought exertion depended more on health, than health on exertion; besides, she thought Philip ought to take some blame to himself for the disaster on the stairs. She made no answer, and Guy asked what Philip had been doing to-day.

'Walking over the hills from Como. Do you always travel in this fashion, "impedimentis relictis"?'

'Not exactly,' said Guy; 'the "impedimenta" are, some at Varenna, some at the inn with Arnaud.'

'So you have Arnaud with you?'

'Yes, and Anne Trower,' said Amy, for her maid was a Stylehurst person, who had lived at Hollywell ever since she had been fit for service. 'She was greatly pleased to hear we were going to meet the captain.'

'We amuse ourselves with thinking how she gets on with Arnaud,' said Guy. 'Their introduction took place only two days before we were married, since which, they have had one continued tete-a-tete, which must have been droll at first.'

'More so at last,' said Amy. 'At first Anne thought Mr. Arnaud so fine a gentleman, that she hardly dared to speak to him. I believe nothing awed her so much as his extreme courtesy; but lately he has been quite fatherly to her, and took her to dine at his sister's chalet, where I would have given something to see her. She tells me he wants her to admire the country, but she does not like the snow, and misses our beautiful clover-fields very much.'

'Stylehurst ought to have been better training for mountains,' said Philip.

They were fast losing the stiffness of first meeting. Philip could not but acknowledge to himself that Amy was looking very well, and so happy that Guy must be fulfilling the condition on which he was to be borne with. However, these were early days, and of course Guy must be kind to her at least in the honeymoon, before the wear and tear of life began. They both looked so young, that having advised them to wait four years, he was ready to charge them with youthfulness, if not as a fault, at least as a folly; indeed, the state of his own affairs made him inclined to think it a foible, almost a want of patience, in any one to marry before thirty. It was a conflict of feeling. Guy was so cordial and good-humoured, that he could not help being almost gained; but, on the other hand, he had always thought Guy's manners eminently agreeable; and as happiness always made people good-humoured, this was no reason for relying on him. Besides, the present ease and openness of manner might only result from security.

Other circumstances combined, more than the captain imagined, in what is popularly called putting him out. He had always been hitherto on equal terms with Guy; indeed, had rather the superiority at Hollywell, from his age and assumption of character, but here Sir Guy was somebody, the captain nobody, and even the advantage of age was lost, now that Guy was married and head of a family, while Philip was a stray young man and his guest. Far above such considerations as he thought himself, and deeming them only the tokens of the mammon worship of the time, Philip, nevertheless, did not like to be secondary to one to whom he had always been preferred; and this, and perhaps the being half ashamed of it, made him something more approaching to cross than ever before; but now and then, the persevering amiability of both would soften him, and restore him to his most gracious mood.

He gave them their letters when they reached the inn, feeling as if he had a better right than they, to one which was in Laura's writing, and when left in solitary possession of the sitting-room– a very pleasant one, with windows opening on the terrace just above the water– paced up and down, chafing at his own perplexity of feeling.

Presently they came back; Guy sat down to continue their joint journal-like letter to Charles, while Amabel made an orderly arrangement of their properties, making the most of their few books, and taking out her work as if she had been at home. Philip looked at the books.

'Have you a "Childe Harold" here?' said he. 'I want to look at something in it.'

'No, we have not.'

'Guy, you never forget poetry; I dare say you can help me out with those stanzas about the mists in the valley.'

'I have never read it,' said Guy. 'Don't you remember warning me against Byron?'

'You did not think that was for life! Besides,' he continued, feeling this reply inconsistent with his contempt for Guy's youth, 'that applied to his perversions of human passions, not to his descriptions of scenery.'

'I think,' said Guy, looking up from his letter, 'I should be more unwilling to take a man like that to interpret nature than anything else, except Scripture. It is more profane to attempt it.'

'I see what you mean,' said Amabel, thoughtfully.

'More than I do,' said Philip. 'I never supposed you would take my advice "au pied de la lettre",' he had almost added, 'perversely.'

'I have felt my obligations for that caution ever since I have come to some knowledge of what Byron was,' said Guy.

'The fascination of his "Giaour" heroes has an evil influence on some minds,' said Philip. 'I think you do well to avoid it. The half truth, resulting from its being the effect of self-contemplation, makes it more dangerous.'

'True,' said Guy, though he little knew how much he owed to having attended to that caution, for who could have told where the mastery might have been in the period of fearful conflict with his passions, if he had been feeding his imagination with the contemplation of revenge, dark hatred, and malice, and identifying himself with Byron's brooding and lowering heroes!

'But,' continued Philip, 'I cannot see why you should shun the fine descriptions which are almost classical– the Bridge of Sighs, the Gladiator.'

'He may describe the gladiator as much as he pleases,' said Guy; 'indeed there is something noble in that indignant line–

Butchered to make a Roman holiday;

but that is not like his meddling with these mountains or the sea.'

'Fine description is the point in both. You are over-drawing.'

'My notion is this,' said Guy,– 'there is danger in listening to a man who is sure to misunderstand the voice of nature,– danger, lest by filling our ears with the wrong voice we should close them to the true one. I should think there was a great chance of being led to stop short at the material beauty, or worse, to link human passions with the glories of nature, and so distort, defile, profane them.'

'You have never read the poem, so you cannot judge,' said Philip, thinking this extremely fanciful and ultra-fastidious. 'Your rule would exclude all descriptive poetry, unless it was written by angels, I suppose?'

'No; by men with minds in the right direction.'

'Very little you would leave us.'

'I don't think so,' said Amabel. 'Almost all the poetry we really care about was written by such men.'

'Shakspeare, for instance?'

'No one can doubt of the bent of his mind from the whole strain of his writings,' said Guy. 'So again with Spenser; and as to Milton, though his religion was not quite the right sort, no one can pretend to say he had it not. Wordsworth, Scott– '

'Scott?' said Philip.

'Including the descriptions of scenery in his novels,' said Amy, 'where, I am sure, there is the spirit and the beauty.'

'Or rather, the spirit is the beauty,' said Guy.

'There is a good deal in what you say,' answered Philip, who would not lay himself open to the accusation of being uncandid, 'but you will forgive me for thinking it rather too deep an explanation of the grounds of not making Childe Harold a hand-book for Italy, like other people.'

Amabel thought this so dogged and provoking, that she was out of patience; but Guy only laughed, and said, 'Rather so, considering that the fact was that we never thought of it.'

There were times when, as Philip had once said, good temper annoyed him more than anything, and perhaps he was unconsciously disappointed at having lost his old power of fretting and irritating Guy, and watching him champ the bit, so as to justify his own opinion of him. Every proceeding of his cousins seemed to give him annoyance, more especially their being at home together, and Guy's seeming to belong more to Hollywell than himself. He sat by, with a book, and watched them, as Guy asked for Laura's letter, and Amy came to look over his half-finished answer, laughing over it, and giving her commands and messages, looking so full of playfulness and happiness, as she stood with one hand on the back of her husband's chair, and the other holding the letter, and Guy watching her amused face, and answering her remarks with lively words and bright smiles. 'People who looked no deeper than the surface would, say, what a well-matched pair,' thought Philip; 'and no doubt they were very happy, poor young things, if it would but last.' Here Guy turned, and asked him a question about the line of perpetual snow, so much in his own style, that he was almost ready to accuse them of laughing at him. Next came what hurt him most of all, as they talked over Charles's letter, and a few words passed about Laura, and the admiration of some person she had met at Allonby. The whole world was welcome to admire her: nothing could injure his hold on her heart, and no joke of Charles could shake his confidence; but it was hard that he should be forced to hear such things, and ask no questions, for they evidently thought him occupied with his book, and did not intend him to listen. The next thing they said, however, obliged him to show that he was attending, for it was about her being better.

'Who? Laura!' he said, in a tone that, in spite of himself, had a startled sound. 'You did not say she had been ill?'

'No, she has not,' said Amy. 'Dr. Mayerne said there was nothing really the matter: but she has been worried and out of spirits lately; and mamma thought it would be good for her to go out more.'

Philip would not let himself sigh, in spite of the oppressing consciousness of having brought the cloud over her, and of his own inability to do aught but leave her to endure it in silence and patience. Alas! for how long! Obliged, meanwhile, to see these young creatures, placed, by the mere factitious circumstance of wealth, in possession of happiness which they had not had time either to earn or to appreciate. He thought it shallow, because of their mirth and gaiety, as if they were only seeking food for laughter, finding it in mistakes, for which he was ready to despise them.

Arnaud had brought rather antiquated notions to the renewal of his office as a courier: his mind had hardly opened to railroads and steamers, and changes had come over hotels since his time. Guy and Amabel, both young and healthy, caring little about bad dinners, and unwilling to tease the old man by complaints, or alterations of his arrangements, had troubled themselves little about the matter; took things as they found them, ate dry bread when the cookery was bad, walked if the road was 'shocking'; went away the sooner, if the inns were 'intolerable'; made merry over every inconvenience, and turned it into an excellent story for Charles. They did not even distress themselves about sights which they had missed seeing.

Philip thought all this very foolish and absurd, showing that they were unfit to take care of themselves, and that Guy was neglectful of his wife's comforts: in short, establishing his original opinion of their youth and folly.

So passed the first evening; perhaps the worst because, besides what he had heard about Laura, he had been somewhat over-fatigued by various hot days' walks.

Certain it is, that next morning he was not nearly so much inclined to be displeased with them for laughing, when, in speaking to Anne, he inadvertently called her mistress Miss Amabel.

'Never mind,' said Amy, as Anne departed– and he looked disconcerted, as a precise man always does when catching himself in a mistake– 'Anne is used to it, Guy is always doing it, and puzzles poor Arnaud sorely by sending him for Miss Amabel's parasol.'

'And the other day,' said Guy, 'when Thorndale's brother, at Munich, inquired after Lady Morville, I had to consider who she was.'

'Oh! you saw Thorndale's brother, did you?'

'Yes; he was very obliging. Guy had to go to him about our passports: and when he found who we were, he brought his wife to call on us, and asked us to an evening party.'

'Did you go?'

'Guy thought we must, and it was very entertaining. We had a curious adventure there. In the morning, we had been looking at those beautiful windows of the great church, when I turned round, and saw a gentleman– an Englishman– gazing with all his might at Guy. We met again in the evening, and presently Mr. Thorndale came and told us it was Mr. Shene.'

'Shene, the painter?'

'Yes. He had been very much struck with Guy's face: it was exactly what he wanted for a picture he was about, and he wished of all things just to be allowed to make a sketch.'

'Did you submit?'

'Yes' said Guy; 'and we were rewarded. I never saw a more agreeable person, or one who gave so entirely the impression of genius. The next day he took us through the gallery, and showed us all that was worth admiring.'

'And in what character is he to make you appear?'

'That is the strange part of it,' said Amabel. 'Don't you remember how Guy once puzzled us by choosing Sir Galahad for his favourite hero? It is that very Sir Galahad, when he kneels to adore the Saint Greal.'

'Mr. Shene said he had long been dreaming over it, and at last, as he saw Guy's face looking upwards, it struck him that it was just what he wanted: it would be worth anything to him to catch the expression.'

'I wonder what I was looking like!' ejaculated Guy.

'Did he take you as yourself, or as Sir Galahad?'

'As myself, happily.'

'How did he succeed?'

'Amy likes it; but decidedly I should never have known myself.'

'Ah,' said his wife—

'Could some fay the giftie gie us,
To see ourselves as others see us.'

'As far as the sun-burnt visage is concerned, the glass does that every morning.'

'Yes, but you don't look at yourself exactly as you do at a painted window,' said Amy, in her demure way.

'I cannot think how you found time for sitting,' said Philip.

'O, it is quite a little thing, a mere sketch, done in two evenings and half an hour in the morning. He promises it to me when he has done with Sir Galahad,' said Amy.

'Two— three evenings. You must have been a long time at Munich.'

'A fortnight,' said Guy, 'there is a great deal to see there.'

Philip did not quite understand this, nor did he think it very satisfactory that they should thus have lingered in a gay town, but he meant to make the best of them to-day, and returned to his usual fashion of patronizing and laying down the law. They were so used to this that they did not care about it; indeed, they had reckoned on it as the most amiable conduct to be expected on his part.

The day was chiefly spent in an excursion on the lake, landing at the most beautiful spots, walking a little way and admiring, or while in the boat, smoothly moving over the deep blue waters, gaining lovely views of the banks, and talking over the book with which their acquaintance had begun, "I Promessi Sposi". Never did tourists spend a more serene and pleasant day.

On comparing notes as to their plans, it appeared that each party had about a week or ten days to spare; the captain before he must embark for Corfu, and Sir Guy and Lady Morville before the time they had fixed for returning home. Guy proposed to go together somewhere, spare the post-office further blunders, and get the Signor Capitano to be their interpreter. Philip thought it would be an excellent thing for his young cousins for him to take charge of them, and show them how people ought to travel; so out came his little pocket map, marked with his route, before he left Ireland, whereas they seemed to have no fixed object, but to be always going 'somewhere.' It appeared that they had thought of Venice, but were easily diverted from it by his design of coasting the eastern bank of the Lago di Como, and so across the Stelvio into the Tyrol, all together as far as Botzen, whence Philip would turn southward by the mountain paths, while they would proceed to Innsbruck on their return home.

Amabel was especially pleased to stay a little longer on the banks of the lake, and to trace out more of Lucia's haunts; and if she secretly thought it would have been pleasanter without a third person, she was gratified to see how much Guy's manner had softened Philip's injustice and distrust, making everything so smooth and satisfactory, that at the end of the day, she told her husband that she thought his experiment had not failed.

She was making the breakfast the next morning, when the captain came into the room, and she told him Guy was gone to settle their plans with Arnaud. After lingering a little by the window, Philip turned, and with more abruptness than was usual with him, said–

'You don't think there is any cause of anxiety about Laura?'

'No; certainly not!' said Amy, surprised. 'She has not been looking well lately, but Dr. Mayerne says it is nothing, and you know'– she blushed and looked down– 'there were many things to make this a trying time.'

'Is she quite strong? Can she do as much as usual?'

'She does more than ever: mamma is only afraid of her overworking herself, but she never allows that she is tired. She goes to school three days in the week, besides walking to East-hill on Thursday, to help in the singing; and she is getting dreadfully learned. Guy gave her his old mathematical books, and Charlie always calls her Miss Parabola.'

Philip was silent, knowing too well why she sought to stifle care in employment; and feeling embittered against the whole world, against her father, against his own circumstances, against the happiness of others; nay, perhaps, against the Providence which had made him what he was.

Presently Guy came in, and the first thing he said was, 'I am afraid we must give up our plan.'

'How?' exclaimed both Philip and Amy.

'I have just heard that there is a fever at Sondrio, and all that neighbourhood, and every one says it would be very foolish to expose ourselves to it.'

'What shall we do instead?' said Amy.

'I told Arnaud we would let him know in an hour's time; I thought of Venice.'

'Venice, oh, yes, delightful.'

'What do you say, Philip?' said Guy.

'I say that I cannot see any occasion for our being frightened out of our original determination. If a fever prevails among the half-starved peasantry, it need not affect well-fed healthy persons, merely passing through the country.'

'You see we could hardly manage without sleeping there,' said Guy: 'we must sleep either at Colico, or at Madonna. Now Colico, they say, is a most unhealthy place at this time of year, and Madonna is the very heart of the fever– Sondrio not much better. I don't see how it is to be safely done; and though very likely we might not catch the fever, I don't see any use in trying.'

'That is making yourself a slave to the fear of infection.'

'I don't know what purpose would be answered by running the risk,' said Guy.

'If you chose to give it so dignified a name as a risk,' said Philip.

'I don't, then,' said Guy, smiling. 'I should not care if there was any reason for going there, but, as there is not, I shall face Mr. Edmonstone better if I don't run Amy into any more chances of mischief.'

'Is Amy grateful for the care,' said Philip, 'after all her wishes for the eastern bank?'

'Amy is a good wife,' said Guy. 'For Venice, then. I'll ring for Arnaud. You will come with us, won't you, Philip?'

'No, I thank you; I always intended to see the Valtelline, and an epidemic among the peasantry does not seem to me to be sufficient to deter.'

'O Philip, you surely will not?' said Amy.

'My mind is made up, Amy, thank you.'

'I wish you would be persuaded,' said Guy. 'I should like particularly to have you to lionize us there; and I don't fancy your running into danger.'

The argument lasted long. Philip by no means approved of Venice, especially after the long loitering at Munich, thinking that in both places there was danger of Guy's being led into mischief by his musical connections. Therefore he did his best, for Amabel's sake, to turn them from their purpose, persuaded in his own mind that the fever was a mere bugbear, raised up by Arnaud; and, perhaps, in his full health and strength, almost regarding illness itself as a foible, far more the dread of it. He argued, therefore, in his most provoking strain, becoming more vexatious as the former annoyance was revived at finding the impossibility of making Guy swerve from his purpose, while additional mists of suspicion arose before him, making him imagine that the whole objection was caused by Guy's dislike to submit to him, and a fit of impatience of which Amy was the victim; nay, that his cousin wanted to escape from his surveillance, and follow the beat of his inclinations; and the whole heap of prejudices and half-refuted accusations resumed their full ascendancy. Never had his manner been more vexatious, though without departing from the coolness which always characterized it; but all the time, Guy, while firm and unmoved in purpose, kept his temper perfectly, and apparently without effort. Even Amabel glowed with indignation, at the assumption with which he was striving to put her husband down, though she rejoiced to see its entire failure: for some sensible argument, or some gay, lively, good-humoured reply, was the utmost he could elicit. Guy did not seem to be in the least irritated or ruffled by the very behaviour which used to cause him so many struggles. Having once seriously said that he did not think it right to run into danger, without adequate cause, he held his position with so much ease, that he could afford to be playful, and laugh at his own dread of infection, his changeableness, and credulity. Never had temper been more entirely subdued; for surely if he could bear this, he need never fear himself again.

So passed the hour; and Amabel was heartily glad when the debate was closed by Arnaud's coming for orders. Guy went with him; Amabel began to collect her goods; and Philip, after a few moments' reflection, spoke in the half-compassionate, half-patronizing manner with which he used, now and then, to let fall a few crumbs of counsel or commendation for silly little Amy.

'Well, Amy, you yielded very amiably, and that is the only way. You will always find it best to submit.'

He got no further in his intended warning against the dissipations of Venice, for her eyes were fixed on him at first with a look of extreme wonder. Then her face assumed an expression of dignity, and gently, but gravely, she said, 'I think you forget to whom you are speaking.'

The gentlemanlike instinct made him reply, 'I beg your pardon'— and there he stopped, as much taken by surprise as if a dove had flown in his face. He actually was confused; for in very truth, he had, after a fashion, forgotten that she was Lady Morville, not the cousin Amy with whom Guy's character might be freely discussed. He had often presumed as far with his aunt; but she, though always turning the conversation, had never given him a rebuff. Amabel had not done; and in her soft voice, firmly, though not angrily, she spoke on. 'One thing I wish to say, because we shall never speak on this subject again, and I was always afraid of you before. You have always misunderstood him, I might almost say, chosen to misunderstand him. You have tried his temper more than any one, and never appreciated the struggles that have subdued it. It is not because I am his wife that I say this— indeed I am not sure it becomes me to say it; yet I cannot bear that you should not be told of it, because you think he acts out of enmity to you. You little know how your friendship has been his first desire— how he has striven for it— how, after all you have done and written, he defended you with all his might when those at home were angry— how he sought you out on purpose to try to be real cordial friends'

Philip's face had grown rigid, and chiefly at the words, 'those at home were angry.' 'It is not I that prevent that friendship,' said he: 'it is his own want of openness. My opinion has never changed.'

'No; I know it has never changed' said Amy, in a tone of sorrowful displeasure. 'Whenever it does, you will be sorry you have judged him so harshly.'

She left the room, and Philip held her in higher esteem. He saw there was spirit and substance beneath that soft girlish exterior, and hoped she would better be able to endure the troubles which her precipitate marriage was likely to cause her; but as to her husband, his combined fickleness and obstinacy had only become more apparent than ever— fickleness in forsaking his purpose, obstinacy in adherence to his own will.

Displeased and contemptuous, Philip was not softened by Guy's freedom and openness of manner and desire to help him as far as their roads lay together. He was gracious only to Lady Morville, whom he treated with kindness, intended to show that he was pleased with her for a reproof which became her position well, though it could not hurt him. Perhaps she thought this amiability especially insufferable: for when she arrived at Varenna her chief thought was that here they should be free of him.

'Come, Philip,' said Guy, at that last moment, 'I wish you would think better of it after all, and come with us to Milan.'

'Thank you, my mind is made up.'

'Well, mind you don't catch the fever: for I don't want the trouble of nursing you.'

'Thank you; I hope to require no such services of my friends,' said Philip, with a proud stem air, implying, 'I don't want you.'

'Good-bye, then,' said Guy. Then remembering his promise to Laura, he added, 'I wish we could have seen more of you. They will be glad to hear of you at Hollywell. You have had one warm friend there all along.'

He was touched for a moment by this kind speech, and his tone was less grave and dignified. 'Remember me to them when you write,' he answered, 'and tell Laura she must not wear herself out with her studies. Good-bye, Amy, I hope you will have a pleasant journey.'

The farewells were exchanged and the carriage drove off. 'Poor little Amy!' said Philip to himself, 'how she is improved. He has a sweet little wife in her. The fates have conspired to crown him with all man can desire, and little marvel if he should abuse his advantages. Poor little Amy! I have less hope than ever, since even her evident wishes could not bend his determination in this trifle; but she is a good little creature, happy in her blindness. May it long continue! It is my uncle and aunt who are to be blamed.'

He set himself to ascend the mountain path, and they looked back, watching the firm vigorous steps with which he climbed the hill side, then stood to wave his hand to Amabel looking a perfect specimen of health and activity.

'Just like himself,' said Amy, drawing so long a breath that Guy smiled, but did not speak.

'Are you much vexed?' said she.

'I don't feel as if I had made the most of my opportunities.'

'Then if you have not, I can tell you who has. What do you think of his beginning to give me a lecture how to behave to you?'

'Did he think you wanted it very much?'

'I don't know: for of course I could not let him go on.'

Guy was so much diverted at the idea of her wanting a lecture on wife-like deportment, that he had no time to be angry at the impertinence, and he made her laugh also by his view that was all force of habit.

'Now, Guido– good Cavaliere Guido– do grant me one satisfaction,' said she, coaxingly. 'Only say you are very glad he is gone his own way.'

On the contrary, I am sorry he is running his head into a fever,' said Guy, pretending to be provoking.

'I don't want you to be glad of that, I only want you to be glad he is not sitting here towering over us.' Guy smiled, and began to whistle–

'Cock up your beaver, and cock it fu' sprush!'

CHAPTER 31

And turned the thistles of a curse
To types beneficent.
– WORDSWORTH

It was about three weeks after the rendezvous at Bellagio, that Sir Guy and Lady Morville arrived at Vicenza, on their way from Venice. They were in the midst of breakfast when Arnaud entered, saying,–

'It was well, Sir Guy, that you changed your intention of visiting the Valtelline with Captain Morville.'

'What! Have you heard anything of him?'

'I fear that his temerity has caused him to suffer. I have just heard that an Englishman of your name is severely ill at Recoara.'

'Where?'

'At "la badia di Recoara". It is what in English we call a watering-place, on the mountains to the north, where the Vicentini do go in summer for "fraicheur", but they have all returned in the last two days for fear of the infection.'

'I'll go and make inquiries' said Guy, rising in haste. Returning in a quarter of an hour, he said,– 'It is true. It can be no other than poor Philip. I have seen his doctor, an Italian, who, when he saw our name written, said it was the same. He calls it "una febbre molto grave".'

'Very heavy! Did he only know the name in writing?'

'Only from seeing it on his passport. He has been unable to give any directions.'

'How dreadfully ill he must be! And alone! What shall we do? You won't think of leaving me behind you, whatever you do?' exclaimed Amabel, imploringly.

'It is at no great distance, and– '

'O, don't say that. Only take me with you. I will try to bear it, if you don't think it right; but it will be very hard.'

Her eyes were full of tears, but she struggled to repress them, and was silent in suspense as she saw him considering.

'My poor Amy!' said he, presently; 'I believe the anxiety would be worse for you if I were to leave you here.'

'Oh, thank you!' exclaimed she.

'You will have nothing to do with the nursing. No, I don't think there is much risk; so we will go together.'

'Thank you! thank you! and perhaps I may be of some use. But is it very infectious?'

'I hope not: caught at Colico, and imported to a fresh place. I should think there was little fear of its spreading. However, we must soon be off: I am afraid he is very ill, and almost deserted. In the first place, I had better send an express to the Consul at Venice, to ask him to recommend us a doctor, for I have not much faith in this Italian.'

They were soon on the way to Recoara, a road bordered on one side by high rocks, on the other by a little river flowing down a valley, shut in by mountains. The valley gradually contracted in the ascent, till it became a ravine, and further on a mere crevice marked by the thick growth of the chestnut-trees; but before this greater narrowing, they saw the roofs of the houses in the little town. The sun shone clear, the air had grown fresh as they mounted higher; Amabel could hardly imagine sickness and sorrow in so fair a spot, and turned to her husband to say so, but he was deep in thought, and she would not disturb him.

The town was built on the bank of the stream, and very much shut in by the steep crags, which seemed almost to overhang the inn, to which they drove, auguring favourably of the place from its fresh, clean aspect.

Guy hastened to the patient; while Amabel was conducted to a room with a polished floor, and very little furniture, and there waited anxiously until he returned. There was a flush on his face, and almost before he spoke, he leant far out of the window to try to catch a breath of air.

'We must find another room for him directly,' said he. 'He cannot possibly exist where he is— a little den— such an atmosphere of fever— enough to knock one down! Will you have one got ready for him?'

'Directly,' said Amabel, ringing. 'How is he?'

'He is in a stupor; it is not sleep. He is frightfully ill, I never felt anything like the heat of his skin. But that stifling hole would account for much; very likely he may revive, when we get him into a better atmosphere. No one has attended to him properly. It is a terrible thing to be ill in a foreign country without a friend!'

Arnaud came, and Amabel sent for the hostess, while Guy returned to his charge. Little care had been taken for the solitary traveller on foot, too ill to exact attention, and whose presence drove away custom; but when his case was taken up by a Milord Inglese, the people of the inn were ready to do their utmost to cause their neglect to be forgotten, and everything was at the disposal of the Signora. The rooms were many, but very small, and the best she could contrive was to choose three rooms on the lower floor, rather larger than the rest, and opening into each other, as well as into the passage, so that it was possible to produce a thorough draught. Under her superintendence, Anne made the apartment look comfortable, and almost English, and sending word that all was ready, she proceeded to establish herself in the corresponding rooms on the floor above.

Philip was perfectly unconscious when he was carried to his new room. His illness had continued about a week, and had been aggravated first by his incredulous and determined resistance of it, and then by the neglect with which he had been treated. It was fearful to see how his great strength had been cut down, as there he lay with scarcely a sign of life, except his gasping, labouring breath. Guy stood over him, let the air blow in from the open window, sprinkled his face with vinegar, and moistened his lips, longing for the physician, for whom, however, he knew he must wait many hours. Perplexed, ignorant of the proper treatment, fearing to do harm, and extremely anxious, he still was almost rejoiced: for there was no one to whom he was so glad to do a service, and a hope arose of full reconciliation.

The patient was somewhat revived by the fresh air, he breathed more freely, moved, and made a murmuring sound, as if striving painfully for a word.

'"Da bere",' at last he said; and if Guy had not known its meaning, it would have been plain from the gasping, parched manner in which it was uttered.

'Some water?' said Guy, holding it to his lips, and on hearing the English, Philip opened his eyes, and, as he drank, gazed with a heavy sort of wonder. 'Is that enough? Do you like some on your forehead?'

'Thank you.'

'Is that more comfortable? We only heard to-day you were ill.'

He turned away restlessly, as if hardly glad to see Guy, and not awake to the circumstances, in a dull, feverish oppression of the senses. Delirium soon came on, or, more properly, delusion. He was distressed by thinking himself deserted, and struggling to speak Italian, and when Guy replied in English, though the native tongue seemed to fall kindly on his ear, yet, to Guy's great grief, the old dislike appeared to prevent all comfort in his presence, though he could not repel his attentions. At night the wandering increased, till it became unintelligible raving, and strength was required to keep him in bed.

Amabel seldom saw her husband this evening. He once came up to see her, when she made him drink some coffee, but he soon went, telling her he should wait up, and begging her to go to rest quietly, as she looked pale and tired. Thc night was a terrible one, and morning only brought insensibility. The physician arrived, a sharp-looking Frenchman, who pronounced it to be a very severe and dangerous case, more violent than usual in malaria fever, and with more affection of the brain. Guy was glad to be set to do something, instead of standing by in inaction; but ice and blisters were applied without effect, and they were told that it was likely to be long before the fever abated.

Day after day passed without improvement, and with few gleams of consciousness, and even these were not free from wandering; they were only intervals in the violent ravings, or the incoherent murmurs, and were never clear from some torturing fancy that he was alone and ill at Broadstone, and neither the Edmonstones nor his brother-officers would come to him, or else that he was detained from Stylehurst. 'Home' was the word oftenest on his lips. 'I would not go home,' the only expression that could sometimes be distinctly heard. He was obliged to depend on Guy as the only Englishman at hand; but whenever he recognized him, the traces of repugnance were evident, and in his clearer intervals, he always showed a preference for Arnaud's attendance. Still Guy persevered indefatigably, sitting up with him every night, and showing himself an invaluable nurse, with his tender hand, modulated voice, quick eye, and quiet activity. His whole soul was engrossed: he never appeared to think of himself, or to be sensible of fatigue; but was only absorbed in the one thought of his patient's comfort! He seldom came to Amabel except at meals, and now and then for a short visit to her sitting-room to report on Philip's condition. If he could spare a little more time when Philip was in a state of stupor, she used to try to persuade him to take some rest; and if it was late, or in the heat of noon, she could sometimes get him, as a favour to her, to lie down on the sofa, and let her read to him; but it did not often end in sleep, and he usually preferred taking her out into the fresh air, and wandering about among the chestnut-trees and green hillocks higher up in the ravine.

Very precious were these walks, with the quiet grave talk that the scene and the circumstances inspired— when he would tell the thoughts that had occupied him in his night-watches, and they shared the subdued and deep reflection suited to this period of apprehension. These were her happiest times, but they were few and uncertain. She had in the meantime to wait, to watch, and hope alone, though she had plenty of employment; for besides writing constant bulletins, all preparations for the sickroom fell to her share. She had to send for or devise substitutes for all the conveniences that were far from coming readily to hand in a remote Italian inn— to give orders, send commissions to Vicenza, or even to Venice, and to do a good deal, with Anne's' assistance, by her own manual labour. Guy said she did more for Philip outside his room than he did inside, and often declared how entirely at a loss he should have been if she had not been there, with her ready resources, and, above all, with her sweet presence, making the short intervals he spent out of the sick chamber so much more than repose, such refreshment at the time, and in remembrance.

Thus it had continued for more than a fortnight, when one evening as the French physician was departing, he told Guy that he would not fail to come the next night, as he saw every reason to expect a crisis. Guy sat intently marking every alteration in the worn, flushed, suffering face that rested helplessly on the pillows, and every unconscious movement of the wasted, nerveless limbs stretched out in pain and helplessness, contrasting his present state with what he was when last they parted, in the full pride of health, vigour, and intellect. He dwelt on all that had passed between them from the first, the strange ancestral enmity that nothing had as yet overcome, the misunderstandings, the prejudices, the character whose faultlessness he had always revered, and the repeated failure of all attempts to be friends, as if his own impatience and passion had borne fruit in the merited distrust of the man whom of all others he respected, and whom he would fain love as a brother. He earnestly hoped that so valuable a life might be spared; but if that might not be, his fervent wish was, that at least a few parting words of goodwill and reconciliation might be granted to be his comfort in remembrance.

So mused Guy during the night, as he watched the heavy doze between sleep and stupor, and tried to catch the low, indistinct mutterings that now and then seemed to ask for something. Towards morning Philip awoke more fully, and as Guy was feeling his pulse, he faintly asked,–

'How many?' while his eyes had more of their usual expression.

'I cannot count,' returned Guy; 'but it is less than in the evening. Some drink?'

Philip took some, then making an effort to look round, said,– 'What day is it?'

'Saturday morning, the 23rd of August.'

'I have been ill a long time!'

'You have indeed, full three weeks; but you are better to-night.'

He was silent for some moments; then, collecting himself, and looking fixedly at Guy, he said, in his own steady voice, though very feeble,– 'I suppose, humanly speaking, it is an even chance between life and death?'

'Yes,' said Guy, firmly, the low sweet tones of his voice full of tenderness. 'You are very ill; but not without hope.' Then, after a pause, during which Philip looked thoughtful, but calm, he added,– 'I have tried to bring a clergyman here, but I could not succeed. Would you like me to read to you?'

'Thank you-presently– but I have something to say. Some more water;– thank you.' Then, after pausing, 'Guy, you have thought I judged you harshly; I meant to act for the best.'

'Don't think of that,' said Guy, with a rush of joy at hearing the words of reconciliation he had yearned for so long.

'And now you have been most kind. If I live, you shall see that I am sensible of it;' and he feebly moved his hand to his cousin, who pressed it, hardly less happy than on the day he stood before Mrs. Edmonstone in the dressing-room. Presently, Philip went on. 'My sister has my will. My love to her, and to– to– to poor Laura.' His voice suddenly failed; and while Guy was again moistening his lips, he gathered strength, and said,– 'You and

Amy will do what you can for her. Do not let the blow come suddenly. Ah! you do not know. We have been engaged this long time.'

Guy did not exclaim, but Philip saw his amazement. 'It was very wrong; it was not her fault,' he added. 'I can't tell you now; but if I live all shall be told. If not, you will be kind to her?'

'Indeed we will.'

'Poor Laura!' again said Philip, in a much weaker voice, and after lying still a little longer, he faintly whispered,– 'Read to me.'

Guy read till he fell into a doze, which lasted till Arnaud came in the morning, and Guy went up to his wife.

'Amy,' said he, entering with a quiet bright look, 'he has spoken to me according to my wish.'

'Then it is all right,' said Amabel, answering his look with one as calm and sweet. 'Is he better?'

'Not materially; his pulse is still very high; but there was a gleam of perfect consciousness; he spoke calmly and clearly, fully understanding his situation. Come what will, it is a thing to be infinitely thankful for! I am very glad! Now for our morning reading.'

As soon as it was over, and when Guy had satisfied himself that the patient was still quiet, they sat down to breakfast. Guy considered a little while, and said,–

'I have been very much surprised. Had you any idea of an attachment between him and Laura?'

'I know she is very fond of him, and she has always been his favourite. What? Has he been in love with her all this time, poor fellow?'

'He says they are engaged.'

'Laura? Our sister! Oh, Guy, impossible! He must have been wandering.'

'I could have almost thought so; but his whole manner forbade me to think there was any delusion. He was too weak to explain; but he said it was not her fault, and was overcome when speaking of her. He begged us to spare her from suddenly hearing of his death. He was as calm and reasonable as I am at this moment. No, Amy, it was not delirium.'

'I don't know how to believe it!' said Amabel. 'It is so impossible for Laura, and for him too. Don't you know how, sometimes in fevers, people take a delusion, and are quite rational about everything else, and that, too; if only it was true; and don't you think it very likely, that if he really has been in love with her all this time, (how much he must have gone through!) he may fancy he has been secretly engaged, and reproach himself?'

'I cannot tell,' said Guy; 'there was a reality in his manner of speaking that refuses to let me disbelieve him. Surely it cannot be one of the horrors of death that we should be left to reproach ourselves with the fancied sins we have been prone to, as well as with our real ones. Then'– and he rose, and walked about the room– 'if so, more than ever, in the hour of death, good Lord, deliver us!'

Amabel was silent, and presently he sat down, saying,– 'Well, time will show!'

'I cannot think it' said Amy. 'Laura! How could she help telling mamma!' And as Guy smiled at the recollection of their own simultaneous coming to mamma, she added,– 'Not only because it was right, but for the comfort of it.'

'But, Amy, do you remember what I told you of poor Laura's fears, and what she said to me, on our wedding-day?'

'Poor Laura!' said Amy. 'Yet– ' She paused, and Guy presently said,–

'Well, I won't believe it, if I can possibly help it. I can't afford to lose my faith in my sister's perfection, or Philip's, especially now. But I must go; I have loitered too long, and Arnaud ought to go to his breakfast.'

Amabel sat long over the remains of her breakfast. She did not puzzle herself over Philip's confession, for she would not admit it without confirmation; and she could not think of his misdoings, even those of which she was certain, on the day when his life was hanging in the balance. All she could bear to recollect was his excellence; nay, in the tenderness of her heart, she nearly made out that she had always been very fond of him, overlooking that even before Guy came to Hollywell, she had always regarded him with more awe than liking, been disinclined to his good advice, shrunk from his condescension, and regularly enjoyed Charles's quizzing of him. All this, and all the subsequent injuries were forgotten, and she believed, as sincerely as her husband, that Philip had been free from any unkind intention. But she chiefly dwelt on her own Guy, especially that last speech, so unlike some of whom she had heard, who were rather glad to find a flaw in a faultless model, if only to obtain a fellow-feeling for it.

'Yes,' thought she, 'he might look far without finding anything better than himself, though he won't believe it. If ever he could make me angry, it will be by treating me as if I was better than he. Such nonsense! But I suppose his goodness would not be such if he was conscious of it, so I must be content with him as he is. I can't be so unwifelike after all; for I am sure nothing makes me feel so small and foolish as that humility of his! Come, I must see about some dinner for the French doctor.'

She set to work on her housewifery cares; but when these were despatched, it was hard to begin anything else on such a day of suspense, when she was living on reports from the sick room. The delirium had returned, more violent than ever; and as she sat at her open window she often heard the disconnected words. She could do nothing but listen– she could neither read nor draw, and even letter-writing failed her to-day, for it seemed cruel to send a letter to his sister, and if Philip was not under a delusion, it was still worse to write to Hollywell; it made her shudder to think of the misery she might have inflicted in the former letters, where she had not spared the detail of her worst fears and conjectures, and by no means softened the account, as she had done to his sister.

Late in the afternoon the physician came, and she heard of his being quieter; indeed, there were no sounds below. It grew dark; Arnaud brought lights, and told her Captain Morville had sunk into stupor. After another long space, the doctor came to take some coffee, and said the fever was lessening, but that strength was going with it, and if "le malade" was saved, it would be owing to the care and attention of "le chevalier".

Of Guy she saw no more that evening. The last bulletin was pencilled by him on a strip of paper, and sent to her at eleven at night:

'Pulse almost nothing; deadly faintness; doctor does not give him up; it may be many hours: don't sit up; you shall hear when there is anything decisive.'

Amy submitted, and slowly put herself to bed, because she thought Guy would not like to find her up; but she had little sleep, and that was dreamy, full of the same anxieties as her waking moments, and perhaps making the night seem longer than if she had been awake the whole time.

At last she started from a somewhat sounder doze than usual, and saw it was becoming light, the white summits of the mountains were beginning to show themselves, and there was twilight in the room. Just then she heard a light, cautious tread in the passage; the lock of Guy's dressing-room was gently, slowly turned. It was over then! Life or death? Her heart beat as she heard her husband's step in the next room, and her suspense would let her call out nothing but– 'I am not asleep!'

Guy came forward, and stood still, while she looked up to the outline of his figure against the window. With a kind of effort he said, with forced calmness– 'He'll do now! and came to the bedside. His face was wet with tears, and her eyes were over-flowing. After a few moments he murmured a few low words of deep thanksgivings, and again there was a silence.

'He is asleep quietly and comfortably,' said Guy, presently, 'and his pulse is steadier. The faintness and sinking have been dreadful; the doctor has been sitting with his hand on his pulse, telling me when to put the cordial into his mouth. Twice I thought him all but gone; and till within the last hour, I did not think he could have revived; but now, the doctor says we may almost consider the danger as over.'

'Oh, how glad I am! Was he sensible? Could he speak?'

'Sensible at least when not fainting; but too weak to speak, or often, to look up. When he did though, it was very kindly, very pleasantly. And now! This is joy coming in the morning, Amy!'

'I wonder if you are happier now than after the shipwreck,' said Amy, after a silence.

'How can you ask? The shipwreck was a gleam, the first ray that came to cheer me in those penance hours, when I was cut off from all; and now, oh, Amy! I cannot enter into it. Such richness and fullness of blessing showered on me, more than I ever dared to wish for or dream of, both in the present and future hopes. It seems more than can belong to man, at least to me, so unlike what I have deserved, that I can hardly believe it. It must be sent as a great trial.'

Amabel thought this so beautiful, that she could not answer; and he presently gave her some further particulars. He went back in spite of her entreaties that he would afford himself a little rest, saying that the doctor was obliged to go away, and Philip still needed the most careful watching. Amy could not sleep any more, but lay musing over that ever-brightening goodness which had lately at all times almost startled her from its very unearthliness.

CHAPTER 32

Sure all things wear a heavenly dress,
Which sanctifies their loveliness,
Types of that endless resting day,
When we shall be as changed as they.
– HYMN FOR SUNDAY

From that time there was little more cause for anxiety. Philip was, indeed, exceedingly reduced, unable to turn in bed, to lift his head, or to speak except now and then a feeble whisper; but the fever was entirely gone, and his excellent constitution began rapidly to repair its ravages. Day by day, almost hour by hour, he was rallying, spending most of his time profitably in sleep, and looking very contented in his short intervals of waking. These became each day rather longer, his voice became stronger, and he made more remarks and inquiries. His first care, when able to take heed of what did not concern his immediate comfort, was that Colonel Deane should be written to, as his leave of absence was expired; but he said not a word about Hollywell, and Amabel therefore hoped her surmise was right, that his confession had been prompted by a delirious fancy, though Guy thought something was implied by his silence respecting the very persons of whom it would have been natural to have talked.

He was very patient of his weakness and dependence, always thankful and willing to be pleased, and all that had been unpleasant in his manner to Guy was entirely gone. He liked to be waited on by him, and received his attentions without laborious gratitude, just in the way partly affectionate, partly matter of course, that was most agreeable; showing himself considerate of his fatigue, though without any of his old domineering advice.

One evening Guy was writing, when Philip, who had been lying still, as if asleep, asked, 'Are you writing to Hollywell?'

'Yes, to Charlotte; but there is no hurry, it won't go till tomorrow. Have you any message?

'No, thank you.'

Guy fancied he sighed; and there was a long silence, at the end of which he asked, 'Guy, have I said anything about Laura?'

'Yes,' said Guy, putting down the pen.

'I thought so; but I could not remember,' said Philip, turning round, and settling himself for conversation, with much of his ordinary deliberate preparation; 'I hope it was not when I had no command of myself?'

'No, you were seldom intelligible, you were generally trying to speak Italian, or else talking about Stylehurst. The only time you mentioned her was the night before the worst.'

'I recollect,' said Philip. 'I will not draw back from the resolution I then made, though I did not know whether I had spoken it, let the consequences be what they may. The worst is, that they will fall the most severely on her: and her implicit reliance on me was her only error.'

His voice was very low, and so full of painful feeling that Guy doubted whether to let him enter on such a subject at present; but remembering the relief of free confession, he thought it best to allow him to proceed, only now and then putting in some note of sympathy or of interrogation, in word or gesture.

'I must explain,' said Philip, 'that you may see how little blame can be imputed to her. It was that summer, three years ago, the first after you came. I had always been her chief friend. I saw, or thought I saw, cause for putting her on her guard. The result has shown that the danger was imaginary; but no matter– I thought it real. In the course of the conversation, more of my true sentiments were avowed than I was aware of; she was very young, and before we, either of us, knew what we were doing, it had been equivalent to a declaration. Well! I do not speak to excuse the concealment, but to show you my motive. If it had been known, there would have been great displeasure and disturbance; I should have been banished; and though time might have softened matters, we should both have had a great deal to go through. Heaven knows what it may be now! And, Guy,' he added, breaking off with trembling eagerness, 'when did you hear from Hollywell? Do you know how she has borne the news of my illness?'

'We have heard since they knew of it,' said Guy; 'the letter was from Mrs. Edmonstone to Amy; but she did not mention Laura.'

'She has great strength; she would endure anything rather than give way; but how can she have borne the anxiety and silence? You are sure my aunt does not mention her?'

'Certain. I will ask Amy for the letter, if you like.'

'No, do not go; I must finish, since I have begun. We did not speak of an engagement; it was little more than an avowal of preference; I doubt whether she understood what it amounted to, and I desired her to be silent. I deceived myself all along, by declaring she was free; and I had never asked for her promise; but those things will not do when we see death face to face, and a resolve made at such a moment must be kept, let it bring what it may.'

'True.'

'She will be relieved; she wished it to be known; but I thought it best to wait for my promotion– the only chance of our being able to marry. However, it shall be put into her father's hands as soon as I can hold a pen. All I wish is, that she should not have to bear the brunt of his anger.'

'He is too kind and good-natured to keep his displeasure long.'

'If it would only light on the right head, instead of on the head of the nearest. You say she was harassed and out of spirits. I wish you were at home; Amy would comfort her and soften them.'

'We hope to go back as soon as you are in travelling condition. If you will come home with us, you will be at hand when Mr. Edmonstone is ready to forgive, as I am sure he soon will be. No one ever was so glad to forget his displeasure.'

'Yes; it will be over by the time I meet him, for she will have borne it all. There is the worst! But I will not put off the writing, as soon as I have the power. Every day the concealment continues is a further offence.'

'And present suffering is an especial earnest and hope of forgiveness,' said Guy. 'I have no doubt that much may be done to make Mr. Edmonstone think well of it.'

'If any suffering of mine would spare hers!' sighed Philip. 'You cannot estimate the difficulties in our way. You know nothing of poverty,– the bar it is to everything; almost a positive offence in itself!'

'This is only tiring yourself with talking,' said Guy, perceiving how Philip's bodily weakness was making him fall into a desponding strain. 'You must make haste to get well, and come home with us, and I think we shall find it no such bad case after all. There's Amy's fortune to begin with, only waiting for such an occasion. No, I can't have you answer; you have talked, quite long enough.'

Philip was in a state of feebleness that made him willing to avoid the trouble of thinking, by simply believing what he was told, 'that it was no bad case.' He was relieved by having confessed, though to the person whom, a few weeks back, he would have thought the last to whom he could have made such a communication, over whom he had striven to assume superiority, and therefore before whom he could have least borne to humble himself– nay, whose own love he had lately traversed with an arrogance that was rendered positively absurd by this conduct of his own. Nevertheless, he had not shrunk from the confession. His had been real repentance, so far as he perceived his faults; and he would have scorned to avail himself of the certainty of Guy's silence on what he had said at the time of his extreme danger. He had resolved to speak, and had found neither an accuser nor a judge, not even one consciously returning good for evil, but a friend with honest, simple, straightforward kindness, doing the best for him in his power, and dreading nothing so much as hurting his feelings. It was not the way in which Philip himself could have received such a confidence.

As soon as Guy could leave him, he went up to his wife. 'Amy,' said he, rather sadly, 'we have had it out. It is too true.'

Her first exclamation surprised him: 'Then Charlie really is the cleverest person in the world.'

'How? Had he any suspicion?'

'Not that I know of; but, more than once, lately, I have been alarmed by recollecting how he once said that poor Laura was so much too wise for her age, that Nature would some day take her revenge, and make her do something very foolish. But has Philip told you all about it?'

'Yes; explained it all very kindly. It must have cost him a great deal; but he spoke openly and nobly. It is the beginning of a full confession to your father.'

'So, it is true!' exclaimed Amabel, as if she heard it for the first time. 'How shocked mamma will be! I don't know how to think it possible! And poor Laura! Imagine what she must have gone through, for you know I never spared the worst accounts. Do tell me all.'

Guy told what he had just heard, and she was indignant.

'I can't be as angry with him as I should like,' said she, 'now that he is sorry and ill; but it was a great deal too bad! I can't think how he could look any of us in the face, far less expect to rule us all, and interfere with you!'

'I see I never appreciated the temptations of poverty,' said Guy, thoughtfully. 'I have often thought of those of wealth, but never of poverty.'

'I wish you would not excuse him. I don't mind your doing it about ourselves, because, though he made you unhappy, he could not make you do wrong. Ah! I know what you mean; but that was over after the first minute; and he only made you better for all his persecution; but I don't know how to pardon his making poor Laura so miserable, and leading her to do what was not right. Poor, dear girl! no wonder she looked so worn and unhappy! I cannot help being angry with him, indeed, Guy!' said she, her eyes full of tears.

'The best pleading is his own repentance, Amy. I don't think you can be very unrelenting when you see how subdued and how altered he is. You know you are to make him a visit to-morrow, now the doctor says all fear of infection is over.'

'I shall be thinking of poor Laura the whole time.'

'And how she would like to see him in his present state? What shall you do if I bring him home to Redclyffe? Shall you go to Hollywell, to comfort Laura?'

'I shall wait till you send me. Besides, how can you invite company till we know whether we have a roof over our house or not? What is he doing now?'

'As usual, he has an unlimited capacity for sleep.'

'I wish you had. I don't think you have slept two hours together since you left off sitting up.'

'I am beginning to think it a popular delusion. I do just as well without it.'

'So you say; but Mr. Shene would never have taken such a fancy to you, if you always had such purple lines as those under your eyes. Look! Is that a face for Sir Galahad, or Sir Guy, or any of the Round Table? Come, I wish you would lie down, and be read to sleep.'

'I should like a walk much better. It is very cool and bright. Will you come?'

They walked for some time, talking over the conduct of Philip and Laura. Amabel seemed quite oppressed by the thought of such a burthen of concealment. She said she did not know what she should have done in her own troubles without mamma and Charlie; and she could not imagine Laura's keeping silence through the time of Philip's danger; more especially as she recollected how appalling some of her bulletins had been. The only satisfaction was in casting as much of the blame on him as possible.

'You know he never would let her read novels; and I do believe that was the reason she did not understand what it meant.'

'I think there is a good deal in that,' said Guy, laughing, 'though Charlie would say it is a very novel excuse for a young lady falling imprudently in love.'

'I do believe, if it was any one but Laura, Charlie would be very glad of it. He always fully saw through Philip's supercilious shell.'

'Amy!'

'No; let me go on, Guy, for you must allow that it was much worse in such a grave, grand, unromantic person, who makes a point of thinking before he speaks, than if it had been a hasty, hand-over-head man like Maurice de Courcy, who might have got into a scrape without knowing it.

'That must have made the struggle to confess all the more painful; and a most free, noble, open-hearted confession it was.'

They tried to recollect all that had passed during that summer, and to guess against whom he had wished to warn her; but so far were they from divining the truth, that they agreed it must either have been Maurice, or some other wild Irishman.

Next, they considered what was to be done. Philip must manage his confession his own way; but they had it in their power greatly to soften matters; and there was no fear that, after the first shock, Mr. Edmonstone would insist on the engagement being broken off, Philip should come to recover his health at Redclyffe, where he would be ready to meet the first advance towards forgiveness,– and Amabel thought it would soon be made. Papa's anger was sharp, but soon over; he was very fond of Philip, and delighted in a love affair, but she was afraid mamma would not get over it so soon, for she would be excessively hurt and grieved. 'And when I was naughty,' said Amy, 'nothing ever made me so sorry as mamma's kindness.'

Guy launched out into more schemes for facilitating their marriage than ever he had made for himself; and the walk ended with extensive castle building on Philip's account, in the course of which Amy was obliged to become much less displeased. Guy told her, in the evening, that she would have been still more softened if she could have heard him talk about Stylehurst and his father. Guy had always wished to hear him speak of the Archdeacon, though they had never been on terms to enter on such a subject. And now Philip had been much pleased by Guy's account of his walks to Stylehurst, and taken pleasure in telling which were his old haunts, making out where Guy had been, and describing his father's ways.

The next day was Sunday, and Amabel was to pay her cousin a visit. Guy was very eager about it, saying it was like a stage in his recovery; and though the thought of her mother and Laura could not be laid aside, she would not say a word to damp her husband's pleasure in the anticipation. It seemed as if Guy, wanting to bestow all he could upon his cousin in gratitude for his newly-accorded friendship, thought the sight of his little wife the very best thing he had to give.

It was a beautiful day, early in September, with a little autumnal freshness in the mountain breezes that they enjoyed exceedingly. Philip's convalescence, and their own escape, might be considered as so far decided, that they might look back on the peril as past. Amabel felt how much cause there was for thankfulness; and, after all, Philip was not half as bad now as when he was maintaining his system of concealment; he had made a great effort, and was about to do his best by way of reparation; but it was so new to her to pity him, that she did not know how to begin.

She tried to make the day seem as Sunday-like as she could, by putting on her white muslin dress and white ribbons, with Charles's hair bracelet, and a brooch of beautiful silver workmanship, which Guy had bought for her at Milan, the only ornament he had ever given to her. She sat at her window, watching the groups of Italians in their holiday costume, and dwelling on the strange thoughts that had passed through her mind often before in her lonely Sundays in this foreign land, thinking much of her old home and East-hill Church, wondering whether the letter had yet arrived which was to free them from anxiety, and losing herself in a maze of uncomfortable marvels about Laura.

'Now, then,' at length said Guy, entering, 'I only hope he has not knocked himself up with his preparations, for he would make such a setting to rights, that I told him I could almost fancy he expected the queen instead of only Dame Amabel Morville.'

He led her down, opened the door, and playfully announced, 'Lady Morville! I have done it right this time. Here she is'!

She had of course expected to see Philip much altered, but she was startled by the extent of the change; for being naturally fair and high-coloured, he was a person on whom the traces of illness were particularly visible. The colour was totally gone, even from his lips; his cheeks were sunken, his brow looked broader and more massive from the thinness of his face and the loss of his hair, and his eyes themselves appeared unlike what they used to be in the hollows round them. He seemed tranquil, and comfortable, but so wan, weak, and subdued, and so different from himself, that she was very much shocked, as smiling and holding out a hand, where the white skin seemed hardly to cover the bone and blue vein, he said, in a tone, slow, feeble, and languid, though cheerful,–

'Good morning, Amy. You see Guy was right, after all. I am sorry to have made your wedding tour end so unpleasantly.'

'Nay, most pleasantly, since you are better,' said Amabel, laughing, because she was almost ready to cry, and her displeasure went straight out of her head.

'Are you doing the honours of my room, Guy?' said Philip, raising his head from the pillow, with a becoming shade of his ceremonious courtesy. 'Give her a chair.'

Amy smiled and thanked him, while he lay gazing at her as a sick person is apt to do at a flower, or the first pretty enlivening object from which he is able to derive enjoyment, and as if he could not help expressing the feeling, he said–

'Is that your wedding-dress, Amy?'

'Oh, no; that was all lace and finery.'

'You look so nice and bridal– '

'There's a compliment that such an old wife ought to make the most of, Amy,' said Guy, looking at her with a certain proud satisfaction in Philip's admiration. 'It is high time to leave off calling you a bride, after your splendid appearance at the party at Munich, in all your whiteness and orange-flowers.'

'That was quite enough of it,' said Amy, smiling.

'Not at all,' said Philip; 'you have all your troubles in the visiting line to come, when you go home.'

'Ah! you know the people, and will be a great help to us,' said Amy, and Guy was much pleased to hear her taking a voluntary share in the invitation, knowing as he did that she only half liked it.

'Thank you; we shall see,' replied Philip.

'Yes; we shall see when you are fit for the journey, and it will not be long before we can begin, by short stages. You have got on wonderfully in the last few days. How do you think he is looking, Amy?' finished Guy, with an air of triumph, that was rather amusing, considering what a pale skeleton face he was regarding with so much satisfaction.

'I dare say he is looking much mended,' said Amy; 'but you must not expect me to see it.'

'You can't get a compliment for me, Guy,' said Philip. 'I was a good deal surprised when Arnaud brought me the glass this morning.'

'It is a pity you did not see yourself a week ago,' said Guy, shaking his head drolly.

'It is certain, as the French doctor says, that monsieur has a very vigorous constitution.'

'Charles says, having a good constitution is only another name for undergoing every possible malady,' said Amy.

'Rather good' said Guy; 'for I certainly find it answer very well to have none at all.'

'Haven't you?' said Amy, rather startled.

'Or how do you know?' said Philip; 'especially as you never were ill.'

'It is a dictum of old Walters, the Moorworth doctor, the last time I had anything to do with him, when I was a small child. I suppose I remembered it for its oracular sound, and because I was not intended to listen. He was talking over with Markham some illness I had just got through, and wound up with, "He may be healthy and active now; but he has no constitution, there is a tendency to low fever, and if he meets with any severe illness, it will go hard with him."'

'How glad I am I did not know that before' cried Amy.

'Did you remember it when you came here?' said Philip.

'Yes,' said Guy, not in the least conscious of the impression his words made on the others. 'By the bye, Philip, I wish you would tell us how you fared after we parted, and how you came here.'

'I went on according to my former plan,' said Philip, 'walking through the Valtelline, and coming down by a mountain path. I was not well at Bolzano, but I thought it only fatigue, which a Sunday's rest would remove, so on I went for the next two days, in spite of pain in head and limbs.'

'Not walking!' said Amy.

'Yes, walking. I thought it was stiffness from mountain climbing, and that I could walk it off; but I never wish to go through anything like what I did the last day, between the up and downs of that mountain path, and the dazzle of the snow and heat of the sun. I meant to have reached Vicenza, but I must have been quite knocked up when I arrived here, though I cannot tell. My head grew so confused, that my dread, all the way, was that I should forget my Italian; I can just remember conning a phrase over and over again, lest I should lose it. I suppose I was able to speak when I came here, but the last thing I remember was feeling very ill in some room, different from this, quite alone, and with a horror of dying deserted. The next is a confused recollection of the relief of hearing English again, and seeing my excellent nurse here.'

There was a little more talk, but a little was enough for Philip's feeble voice, and Guy soon told him he was tired, and ordered in his broth. He begged that Amy would stay, and it was permitted on condition that he would not talk, Guy even cutting short a quotation of,– 'As Juno had been sick and he her dieter,'– appropriate to the excellence of the broths, which Amabel and her maid, thanks to their experience of Charles's fastidious tastes, managed to devise and execute, in spite of bad materials. It was no small merit in Guy to stop the compliment, considering how edified he had been by his wife's unexpected ingenuity, and what a comical account he had written of it to her mother, such, as Amy told him, deserved to be published in a book of good advice to young ladies, to show what they might come to if they behaved well. However, she was glad to have ocular demonstration of the success of the cookery, which she had feared might turn out uneatable; and her gentle feelings towards Philip were touched, by seeing one wont to be full of independence and self-assertion, now meek and helpless, requiring to be lifted, and propped up with pillows, and depending entirely and thankfully upon Guy.

When he had been settled and made comfortable, they read the service; and she thought her husband's tones had never been so sweet as now, modulated to the pitch best suited to the sickroom, and with the peculiarly beautiful expression he always gave such reading. It was the lesson from Jeremiah, on the different destiny of Josiah and his sons, and he read that verse, 'Weep ye not for the dead, neither bemoan him, but weep sore for him that goeth away; for he shall return no more, nor see his native country;' with so remarkable a melancholy and beauty in his voice, that she could hardly refrain from tears, and it also greatly struck Philip, who had been so near 'returning no more, neither seeing his native country.'

When the reading was over, and they were leaving him to rest, while they went to dinner, he said, as he wished Amy good-bye, 'Till now I never discovered the practical advantage of such a voice as Guy's. There never was such a one for a sick-room. Last week, I could not bear any one else to speak at all; and even now, no one else could have read so that I could like it.'

'Your voice; yes,' said Amy, after they had returned to their own sitting-room. 'I want to hear it very much. I wonder when you will sing to me again.'

'Not till he has recovered strength to bear the infliction with firmness,' said Guy; 'but, Amy, I'll tell you what we will do, if you are sure it is good for you. He will have a good long sleep, and we will have a walk on the green hillocks.'

Accordingly they wandered in the cool of the evening on the grassy slopes under the chestnut-trees, making it a Sunday walk, calm, bright and meditative, without many words, but those deep and grave, 'such as their walks had been before they were married,' as Amabel said.

'Better,' he answered.

A silence, broken by her asking, 'Do you recollect your melancholy definition of happiness, years ago?'

'What was it?'

'Gleams from another world, too soon eclipsed or forfeited. It made me sad then. Do you hold to it now?'

'Don't you?'

'I want to know what you would say now?'

'Gleams from another world, brightening as it gets nearer.'

Amabel repeated–

Ever the richest, tenderest glow,
Sets round the autumnal sun;
But their sight fails, no heart may know
The bliss when life is done.

'Old age,' she added; 'that seems very far off.'

'Each day is a step,' he answered, and then came a silence while both were thinking deeply.

They sat down to rest under a tree, the mountains before them with heavy dark clouds hanging on their sides, and the white crowns clear against the blue sky, a perfect stillness on all around, and the red glow of an Italian sunset just fading away.

'There is only one thing wanting,' said Amy. 'You may sing now. You are far from Philip's hearing. Suppose we chant this afternoon's psalms.'

It was the fifth day of the month, and the psalms seemed especially suitable to their thoughts. Before the 29th was finished, it was beginning to grow dark. There were a few pale flashes of lightning in the mountains, and at the words 'The voice of the Lord shaketh the wilderness,' a low but solemn peal of thunder came as an accompaniment.

'The Lord shall give his people the blessing of peace.'

The full sweet melody died away, but the echo caught it up and answered like the chant of a spirit in the distance– 'The blessing of peace.'

The effect was too solemn and mysterious to be disturbed by word or remark. Guy drew her arm into his, and they turned homewards.

They had some distance to walk, and night had closed in before they reached the village, but was only more lovely. The thunder rolled solemnly among the hills, but the young moon shone in marvellous whiteness on the snowy crowns, casting fantastic shadows from the crags, while whole showers of fire-flies were falling on them from the trees, floating and glancing in the shade.

'It is a pity to go in,' said Amy. But Arnaud did not seem to be of the same opinion: he came out to meet them very anxiously, expostulating on the dangers of the autumnal dew; and Guy owned that though it had been the most wonderful and delightful evening he had ever known, he was rather fatigued.

CHAPTER 33

From darkness here and dreariness,
We ask not full repose.
– CHRISTIAN YEAR

It seemed as if the fatigue which Guy had undergone was going to make itself felt at last, for he had a slight headache the next morning, and seemed dull and weary. Both he and Amabel sat for some time with Philip, and when she went away to write her letters, Philip began discussing a plan which had occurred to him of offering himself as chief of the constabulary force in the county where Redclyffe was situated. It was an office which would suit him very well, and opened a new hope of his marriage, and he proceeded to reckon on Lord Thorndale's interest, counting up all the magistrates he knew, and talking them over with Guy, who, however, did not know enough of his own neighbourhood to be of much use; and when he came up-stairs a little after, said he was vexed at having been so stupid. He was afraid he had seemed unkind and indifferent. But the truth was that he was so heavy and drowsy, that he had actually fallen twice into a doze while Philip was talking.

'Of course,' said Amy, 'gentle sleep will take her revenge at last for your calling her a popular delusion. Lie down, let her have her own way, and you will be good for something by and by.'

He took her advice, slept for a couple of hours, and awoke a good deal refreshed, so that though his head still ached, he was able to attend as usual to Philip in the evening.

He did not waken the next morning till so late, that he sprung up in consternation, and began to dress in haste to go to Philip; but presently he came back from his dressing-room with a hasty uncertain step, and threw himself down on the bed. Amabel came to his side in an instant, much frightened at his paleness, but he spoke directly. 'Only a fit of giddiness– it is going off;' and he raised himself, but was obliged to lie down again directly.

'You had better keep quiet' said she. 'Is it your headache?'

'It is aching,' said Guy, and she put her hand over it.

'How hot and throbbing!' said she. 'You must have caught cold in that walk. No, don't try to move; it is only making it worse.'

'I must go to Philip,' he answered, starting up; but this brought on such a sensation of dizziness and faintness, that he sunk back on the pillow.

'No; it is of no use to fight against it,' said Amy, as soon as he was a little better. 'Never mind Philip, I'll go to him. You must keep quiet, and I will get you a cup of hot tea.'

As he lay still, she had the comfort of seeing him somewhat revived, but he listened to her persuasions not to attempt to move. It was later than she had expected, and she found that breakfast was laid out in the next room. She brought him some tea; but he did not seem inclined to lift his head to drink it; and begged her to go at once to Philip, fearing he must be thinking himself strangely forgotten, and giving her many directions about the way he liked to be waited on at breakfast.

Very much surprised was Philip to see her instead, of her husband, and greatly concerned to hear that Guy was not well.

'Over-fatigue,' said he. 'He could not but feel the effects of such long-continued exertion.' Then, after an interval, during which he had begun breakfast, with many apologies for letting her wait on him, he said, with some breaks, 'Never was there such a nurse as he, Amy; I have felt much more than I can express, especially now. You will never have to complain of my harsh judgment again!'

'It is too much for you to talk of these things,' said Amabel, moved by the trembling of his feeble voice, but too anxious to return to her husband to like to wait even to hear that Philip's opinion had altered. It required much self-command not to hurry, even by manner, her cousin's tardy, languid movements; but she had been well trained by Charles in waiting on sick breakfasts.

When at length she was able to escape, she found that Guy had undressed, and gone to bed again. He said he was more comfortable, and desired her to go and take her own breakfast before coming back to him, and she obeyed as well as she could, but very soon was again with him. He looked flushed and oppressed, and when she put her cool hand across his forehead, she was frightened at the increased throbbing of his temples.

'Amy,' said he, looking steadily at her, 'this is the fever.'

Without answering, she drew his hand into hers, and felt his pulse, which did indeed plainly respond fever. Each knew that the other was recollecting what he had said, on Sunday, of the doctor's prediction, and Amy knew he was thinking of death; but all that passed was a proposal to send at once for the French physician. Amabel wrote her note with steadiness, derived from the very force of the shock. She could not think; she did not know whether she feared or hoped. To act from one moment to another was all she attempted, and it was well that her imagination did not open to be appalled at her own situation— so young, alone with the charge of two sick men in a foreign country; her cousin, indeed, recovering, but helpless, and not even in a state to afford her counsel; her husband sickening for this frightful fever, and with more than ordinary cause for apprehension, even without the doctor's prophecy, when she thought of his slight frame, and excitable temperament, and that though never as yet tried by a day's illness, he certainly had more spirit than strength, while all the fatigue he had been undergoing was likely to tell upon him now. She did not look forward, she did not look round; she did not hope or fear; she trusted, and did her best for each, as she was wanted, trying not to make herself useless to both, by showing that she wished to be in two places at once.

It was a day sufficiently distressing in itself had there been no further apprehension, for there was the restlessness of illness, working on a character too active and energetic to acquiesce without a trial in the certainty that there was no remedy for present discomfort. There was no impatience nor rebellion against the illness itself, but a wish to try one after another the things that had been effective in relieving Philip during his recovery. At the same time, he could not bear that Amabel should do anything to tire herself, and was very anxious that Philip should not be neglected. He tossed from one side to the other in burning oppression or cold chills; Amy saw him looking wistful, suggested something by way of alleviation, then found he had been wishing for it, but refraining from asking in order to spare her, and that he was sorry when she procured it. Again and again this happened; she smoothed the coverings, and shook up the pillow: he would thank her, look at her anxiously, beg her not to exert herself, but soon grew restless, and the whole was repeated.

At last, as she was trying to arrange the coverings, he exclaimed,–

'I see how it is. This is impatience. Now, I will not stir for an hour,' and as he made the resolution, he smiled at treating himself so like a child. His power of self-restraint came to his aid, and long before the hour was over he had fallen asleep.

This was a relief; yet that oppressed, flushed, discomposed slumber, and heavy breathing only confirmed her fears that the fever had gained full possession of him. She had not the heart to write such tidings, at least till the physician should have made them too certain, nor could she even bear to use the word 'feverish,' in her answers to the anxious inquiries Philip made whenever she went into his room, though when he averted his face with a heavy sigh, she knew his conclusion was the same as her own.

The opinion of the physician was the only thing wanting to bring home the certainty, and that fell on her like lead in the evening; with one comfort, however, that he thought it a less severe case than the former one. It was a great relief, too, that there was no wandering of mind, only the extreme drowsiness and oppression; and when Guy was roused by the doctor's visit, he was as clear and collected as possible, making inquiries and remarks, and speaking in a particularly calm and quiet manner. As soon as the doctor was gone, he looked up to Amabel, saying, with his own smile, only very dim,–

'It would be of no use, and it would not be true, to say I had rather you did not nurse me. The doctor hopes there is not much danger of infection, and it is too late for precautions.'

'I am very glad,' said Amy.

'But you must be wise, and not hurt yourself. Will you promise me not to sit up?'

'It is very kind of you to tell me nothing worse,' said she, with a sad submissiveness.

He smiled again. 'I am very sorry for you,' he said, looking very tenderly at her. 'To have us both on your hands at once! But it comes straight from Heaven, that is one comfort, and you made up your mind to such things when you took me.'

Sadness in his eye, a sweet smile on his lip, and serenity on his brow, joined with the fevered cheek, the air of lassitude, and the panting, oppressed breath, there was a strange, melancholy beauty about him; and while Amy felt an impulse of ardent, clinging affection to one so precious to her, there was joined with it a sort of awe and veneration for one who so spoke, looked, and felt. She hung over him, and sprinkled him with Eau-de-Cologne; then as his hair teased him by falling into his eyes, he asked her to cut the front lock off. There was something sad in doing this, for that 'tumble-down wave,' as Charlotte called it, was rather a favourite of Amy's; it always seemed to have so much sympathy with his moods, and it was as if parting with it was resigning him to a long illness. However, it was too troublesome not to go, and he looked amused at the care with which she folded up the glossy, brown wave, and treasured it in her dressing-case, then she read to him a few verses of a psalm, and he soon fell into another doze.

There was little more of event, day after day. The fever never ran as high as in Philip's case, and there was no delirium. There was almost constant torpor, but when for any short space he was thoroughly awakened, his mind was perfectly clear, though he spoke little, and then only on the subject immediately presented to him. There he lay for one quiet hour after another, while Amy sat by him, with as little consciousness of time as he had himself, looking neither forward nor backward, only to the present, to give him drink, bathe his face and hands, arrange his pillows, or read or repeat some soothing verse. It always was a surprise when meal times summoned her to attend to Philip, when she was asked for the letters for the post, when evening twilight gathered in, or when she had to leave the night-watch to Arnaud, and go to bed in the adjoining room.

This was a great trial, but he would not allow her to sit up; and her own sense showed her that if this was to be a long illness, it would not do to waste her strength. She knew he was quiet at night, and her trustful temper so calmed and supported her, that she was able to sleep, and thus was not as liable to be overworked as might have been feared, and as Philip thought she must be.

She always appeared in his room with her sweet face mournful and anxious, but never ruffled, or with any air of haste or discomfiture, desirous as she was to return to her husband; for, though he frequently sent her to take care of herself or of Philip, she knew that while she was away he always grew more restless and uncomfortable, and his look of relief at her re-entrance said as much to her as a hundred complaints of her absence would have done.

Philip was in the meantime sorely tried by being forced to be entirely inactive and dependent, while he saw Amabel in such need of assistance; and so far from being able to requite Guy's care, he could only look on himself as the cause of their distress, and an addition to it– a burthen instead of a help. If he had been told a little while ago what would be the present state of things, he would almost have laughed the speaker to scorn. He would never have thought a child as competent as Amy to the sole management of two sick persons, and he not able either to advise or cheer her. Yet he could not see anything went wrong that depended on her. His comforts were so cared for, that he was often sorry she should have troubled herself about them; and though he could have little of her company, he never was allowed to feel himself deserted. Anne, Arnaud, the old Italian nurse, or Amy herself, were easily summoned, and gave him full care and attention.

He was, however, necessarily a good deal alone; and though his cousin's books were at his disposal, eyes and head were too weak for reading, and he was left a prey to his own thoughts. His great comfort was, that Guy was less ill than he had been himself, and that there was no present danger; otherwise, he could never have endured the conviction that all had been caused by his own imprudence. Imprudence! Philip was brought very low to own that such a word applied to him, yet it would have been well for him had that been the chief burthen on his mind. Was it only an ordinary service of friendship and kindred that Guy had, at the peril of his own life, rendered him? Was it not a positive return of good for evil? Yes, evil! He now called that evil, or at least harshness and hastiness in judgment, which he had hitherto deemed true friendship and consideration for Guy and Amy. Every feeling of distrust and jealousy had been gradually softening since his recovery began; gratitude had done much, and dismay at Guy's illness did more. It would have been noble and generous in Guy to act as he had done, had Philip's surmises been correct, and this he began to doubt, though it was his only justification, and even to wish to lose it. He had rather believe Guy blameless. He would do so, if possible; and he resolved, on the first opportunity, to beg him to give him one last assurance that all was right, and implicitly believe him. But how was it possible again to assume to be a ruler and judge over Guy after it was known how egregiously he himself had erred? There was shame, sorrow, self-humiliation, and anxiety wherever he turned, and it was no wonder that depression of spirits retarded his recovery.

It was not till the tenth day after Guy's illness had begun that Philip was able to be dressed, and to come into the next room, where Amabel had promised to dine with him. As he lay on the sofa, she thought he looked even more ill than in bed, the change from his former appearance being rendered more visible, and his great height making him look the more thin. He was apparently exhausted with the exertion of dressing, for he was very silent all dinner-time, though Amabel could have better talked to-day than for some time past, since Guy had had some refreshing sleep, was decidedly less feverish, seemed better for nourishing food, and said that he wanted nothing but a puff of Redclyffe wind to make him well. He was pleased to hear of Philip's step in recovery, and altogether, Amy was cheered and happy.

She left her cousin as soon as dinner was over, and did not come to him again for nearly an hour and a half. She was then surprised to find him finishing a letter, resting his head on one hand, and looking wan, weary, and very unhappy.

'Have you come to letter writing?'

'Yes,' he answered, in a worn, dejected tone, 'I must ask you to direct this, I can't make it legible,'

No wonder, so much did his hand tremble, as he held out the envelope.

'To your sister?' she asked.

'No; to yours. I never wrote to her before. There's one enclosed to your father, to tell all.'

'I am glad you have done it,' answered Amy, in a quiet tone of sincere congratulation. 'You will be better now it is off your mind. But how tired you are. You must go back to bed. Shall I call Arnaud?'

'I must rest first'— and his voice failing, he laid back on the sofa, closed his eyes, turned ashy pale, and became so faint that she could not leave him, and was obliged to apply every restorative within reach before she could bring him back to a state of tolerable comfort.

The next minute her work was nearly undone, when Anne came in to ask for the letters for the post. 'Shall I send yours?' asked Amy.

He muttered an assent. But when she looked back to him after speaking to Anne, she saw a tremulous, almost convulsed working of the closed eyes and mouth, while the thin hands were clenched together with a force contrasting with the helpless manner in which they had hung a moment before. She guessed at the intensity of anguish it mast cost a temper so proud, a heart of so strong a mould, and feelings so deep, to take the first irrevocable step in self-humiliation, giving up into the hands of others the engagement that had hitherto been the cherished treasure of his life; and above all, in exposing Laura to bear the brunt of the penalty of the fault into which he had led her. 'Oh, for Guy to comfort him,' thought she, feeling herself entirely incompetent, dreading to intrude on his feelings, yet thinking it unkind to go away without one sympathizing word when he was in such distress.

'You will be glad, in time,' at last she said. He made no answer.

She held the stimulants to him again, and tried to arrange him more comfortably.

'Thank you,' at last he said. 'How is Guy?'

'He has just had another nice quiet sleep, and is quite refreshed.'

'That is a blessing, at least. But does not he want you? I have been keeping you a long time?'

'Thank you, as he is awake, I should like to go back. You are better now.'

'Yes, while I don't move.'

'Don't try. I'll send Arnaud, and as soon as you can, you had better go to bed again.'

Guy was still awake, and able to hear what she had to tell him about Philip.

'Poor fellow!' said he. 'We must try to soften it.'

'Shall I write?' said Amy. 'Mamma will be pleased to hear of his having told you, and they must be sorry for him, when they hear how much the letter cost him.'

'Ah! they will not guess at half his sorrow.'

'I will write to papa, and send it after the other letters, so that he may read it before he hears of Philip's.'

'Poor Laura!' said Guy. 'Could not you write a note to her too? I want her to be told that I am very sorry, if I ever gave her pain by speaking thoughtlessly of him.'

'Nay,' said Amy, smiling, 'you have not much to reproach yourself with in that way. It was I that always abused him.'

'You can never do so again.'

'No, I don't think I can, now I have seen his sorrow.'

Amabel was quite in spirits, as she brought her writing to his bed-side, and read her sentences to him as she composed the letter to her father, while he suggested and approved. It was a treat indeed to have him able to consult with her once more, and he looked so much relieved and so much better, that she felt as if it was the beginning of real improvement, though still his pulse was fast, and the fever, though lessened, was not gone.

The letter was almost as much his as her own, and he ended his dictation thus: 'Say that I am sure that if I get better we may make arrangements for their marriage.'

Then, as Amy was finishing the letter with her hopes of his amendment, he added, speaking to her, and not dictating– 'If not,'– she shrank and shivered, but did not exclaim, for he looked so calm and happy that she did not like to interrupt him– 'If not, you know, it will be very easy to put the money matters to rights, whatever may happen.'

CHAPTER 34

Sir,
It is your fault I have loved Posthumus;
You bred him as my playfellow; and he is
A man worth any woman, over-buys me
Almost the sum he pays.
– CYMBELINE

The first tidings of Philip's illness arrived at Hollywell one morning at breakfast, and were thus announced by Charles–

'There! So he has been and gone and done it.'

'What? Who? Not Guy?'

'Here has the Captain gone and caught a regular bad fever, in some malaria hole; delirious, and all that sort of thing, and of course our wise brother and sister must needs go and nurse him, by way of a pretty little interlude in their wedding tour!'

Laura's voice alone was unheard in the chorus of inquiry. She sat cold, stiff, and silent, devouring with her ears each reply, that fell like a death-blow, while she was mechanically continuing the occupations of breakfast. When all was told, she hurried to her own room, but the want of sympathy was becoming intolerable. If Amabel had been at home, she must have told her all. There was no one else; and the misery to be endured in silence was dreadful. Her dearest– her whole joy and hope– suffering, dying, and to hear all round her speaking of him with kindness, indeed, but what to her seemed indifference; blaming him for wilfulness, saying he had drawn it on himself,– it seemed to drive her wild. She conjured up pictures of his sufferings, and dreaded Guy's inexperience, the want of medical advice, imagining everything that was terrible. Her idol, to whom her whole soul was devoted, was passing from her, and no one pitied her; while the latent consciousness of disobedience debarred her from gaining solace from the only true source. All was blank desolation– a wild agony, untempered by resignation, uncheered by prayer; for though she did pray, it was without trust, without hope, while her wretchedness was rendered more overwhelming by her efforts to conceal it. These were so far ineffectual that no one could help perceiving that she was extremely unhappy, but then all the family knew she was very fond of Philip, and neither her mother nor brother could be surprised at her distress, though it certainly appeared to them excessive. Mrs. Edmonstone was very sorry for her, and very affectionate and considerate; but Laura was too much absorbed, in her own feelings to perceive or to be grateful for her kindness; and as each day brought a no better report, her despair became so engrossing that she could not attempt any employment. She wandered in the garden, sat in dreamy fits of silence in the house, and at last, after receiving one of the worst accounts, sat up in her dressing-gown the whole of one night, in one dull, heavy, motionless trance of misery.

She recollected that she must act her part, dressed in the morning and came down; but her looks were ghastly; she tasted no food, and as soon as possible left the breakfast-room. Her mother was going in quest of her when old nurse came with an anxious face to say,– 'Ma'am, I am afraid Miss Edmonstone must be very ill, or something. Do you know, ma'am, her bed has not been slept in all night?'

'You don't say so, nurse!'

'Yes, ma'am, Jane told me so, and I went to look myself. Poor child, she is half distracted about Master Philip, and no wonder, for they were always together; but I thought you ought to know, ma'am, for she will make herself ill, to a certainty.'

'I am going to see about her this moment, nurse,' said Mrs. Edmonstone; and presently she found Laura wandering up and down the shady walk, in the restlessness of her despair.

'Laura, dearest,' said she, putting her arm round her, 'I cannot bear to see you so unhappy.'

Laura did not answer; for though solitude was oppressive, every one's presence was a burthen.

'I cannot think it right to give way thus,' continued her mother. 'Did you really sit up all night, my poor child?'

'I don't know. They did so with him!'

'My dear, this will never do. You are making yourself seriously unwell.'

'I wish– I wish I was ill; I wish I was dying!' broke from Laura, almost unconsciously, in a hoarse, inward voice.

'My dear! You don't know what you are saying. You forget that this self-abandonment, and extravagant grief would be wrong in any one; and, if nothing else, the display is unbecoming in you.'

Laura's over-wrought feelings could bear no more, and in a tone which, though too vehement to be addressed to a parent, had in it an agony which almost excused it, by showing how unable she was to restrain herself, she broke forth:– – 'Unbecoming! Who has a right to grieve for him but me?– his own, his chosen,– the only one who can love him, or understand him. Her voice died away in a sob, though without tears.

Her mother heard the words, but did not take in their full meaning; and, believing that Laura's undeveloped affection had led her to this uncontrolled grief, she spoke again, with coldness, intended to rouse her to a sense that she was compromising her womanly dignity.

'Take care, Laura; a woman has no right to speak in such a manner of a man who has given her no reason to believe in his preference of her.'

'Preference! It is his love!– his love! His whole heart! The one thing that was precious to me in this world! Preference! You little guess what we have felt for each other!'

'Laura!' Mrs. Edmonstone stood still, overpowered. 'What do you mean?' She could not put the question more plainly.

'What have I done?' cried Laura. 'I have betrayed him!' she answered herself in a tone of despair, as she hid her face in her hands; 'betrayed him when he is dying!'

Her mother was too much shocked to speak in the soft reluctant manner in which she was wont to reprove.

'Laura,' said she, 'I must understand this. What has passed between you and Philip?'

Laura only replied by a flood of tears, ungovernable from the exhaustion of sleeplessness and want of food. Mrs. Edmonstone's kindness returned; she soothed her, begged her to control herself, and at length brought her into the house, and up to the dressing-room, where she sank on the sofa, weeping violently. It was the reaction of the long restraint she had been exercising on herself, and the silence she had been maintaining. She was not feeling the humiliation, her own acknowledgement of disobedience, but of the horror of being forced to reveal the secret he had left in her charge.

Long did she weep, breaking out more piteously at each attempt of her mother to lead her to explain. Poor Mrs. Edmonstone was alarmed and perplexed beyond measure; this half confession had so overthrown all her ideas that she was ready to apprehend everything most improbable, and almost expected to hear of a private marriage. Her presence seemed only to make Laura worse, and at length she said,– 'I shall leave you for half an hour, in hopes that by that time you may have recovered yourself, and be able to give the explanation which I require.'

She went into her own room, and waited, with her eyes on her watch, a prey to every strange alarm and anticipation, grievously hurt at this want of confidence, and wounded, where she least expected it, by both daughter and nephew. She thought, guessed, recollected, wondered, tormented herself, and at the last of the thirty minutes, hastily opened the door into the dressing-room. Laura sat as before, crouched up in the corner of the wide sofa; and when she raised her face, at her mother's entrance, it was bewildered rather than embarrassed.

'Well, Laura?' She waited unanswered; and the wretchedness of the look so touched her, that, kissing her, she said, 'Surely, my dear, you need not be afraid to tell me anything?'

Laura did not respond to the kindness, but asked, looking perplexed, 'What have I said? Have I told it?'

'What you have given me reason to believe,' said Mrs. Edmonstone, trying to bring herself to speak it explicitly, 'that you think Philip is attached to you. You do not deny it. Let me know on what terms you stand.'

Without looking up, she murmured, 'If you would not force it from me at such a time.'

'Laura, it is for your own good. You are wretched now, my poor child; why not relieve yourself by telling all? If you have not acted openly, can you have any comfort till you have confessed? It may be a painful effort, but relief will come afterwards.'

'I have nothing to confess,' said Laura. 'There is no such thing as you think.'

'No engagement?'

'No.'

'Then what am I to understand by your exclamations?'

'It is no engagement,' repeated Laura. 'He would never have asked that without papa's consent. We are only bound by our own hearts.'

'And you have a secret understanding with him?'

'We have never written to each other; we have never dreamed of any intercourse that could be called clandestine. He would scorn it. He waited only for his promotion to declare it to papa.'

'And how long has it been declared to you?'

'Ever since the first summer Guy was here.'

'Three years!' exclaimed her mother. 'You have kept this from me three years! O Laura!'

'It was of no use to speak!' said Laura, faintly.

If she had looked up, she would have seen those words, 'no use,' cut her mother more deeply than all; but there was only coldness in the tone of the answer, 'No use to inform your parents, before you pledged your affections!'

'Indeed, mamma,' said Laura, 'I was sure that you knew his worth.'

'Worth! when he was teaching you to live in a course of insincerity? Your father will be deeply hurt.'

'Papa! Oh, you must not tell him! Now, I have betrayed him, indeed! Oh, my weakness!' and another paroxysm of tears came on.

'Laura, you seem to think you owe nothing to any one but Philip. You forget you are a daughter! that you have been keeping up a system of disobedience and concealment, of which I could not have believed a child of mine could be capable. O Laura, how you have abused our confidence!'

Laura was touched by the sorrow of her tone; and, throwing her arms round her neck, sobbed out, 'You will forgive me, only forgive him!'

Mrs. Edmonstone was softened in a moment. 'Forgive you, my poor child! You have been very unhappy!' and she kissed her, with many tears.

'Must you tell papa?' whispered Laura.

'Judge for yourself, Laura. Could I know such a thing, and hide it from him?'

Laura ceased, seeing her determined, and yielded to her pity, allowing herself to be nursed as she required, so exhausted was she. She was laid on the sofa, and made comfortable with pillows, in her mother's gentlest way. When Mrs. Edmonstone was called away, Laura held her dress, saying, 'You are kind to me, but you must forgive him. Say you have forgiven him, mamma, dearest!'

'My dear, in the grave all things are forgiven.'

She could not help saying so; but, feeling as if she had been cruel, she added, 'I mean, while he is so ill, we cannot enter on such a matter. I am very sorry for you,' proceeded she, still arranging for Laura's ease; then kissing her, hoped she would sleep, and left her.

Sympathy was a matter of necessity to Mrs. Edmonstone; and as her husband was out, she went at once to Charles, with a countenance so disturbed, that he feared some worse tidings had come from Italy.

'No, no, nothing of that sort; it is poor Laura.'

'Eh?' said Charles, with a significant though anxious look, that caused her to exclaim,–

'Surely you had no suspicion!'

Charlotte, who was reading in the window, trembled lest she should be seen, and sent away.

'I suspected poor Laura had parted with her heart. But what do you mean? What has happened?'

'Could you have guessed? but first remember how ill he is; don't be violent, Charlie. Could you have guessed that they have been engaged, ever since the summer we first remarked them?'

She had expected a great storm; but Charles only observed, very coolly, 'Oh! it is come out at last!'

'You don't mean that you knew it?'

'No, indeed, you don't think they would choose me for their confidant!'

'Not exactly,' said Mrs. Edmonstone, with the odd sort of laugh with which even the most sensitive people, in the height of their troubles, reply to anything ludicrous; 'but really,' she continued, 'every idea of mine is so turned upside-down, that I don't know what to think of anybody.'

'We always knew Laura to be his slave and automaton. He is so infallible in her eyes, that no doubt she thought her silence an act of praiseworthy resolution.'

'She was a mere child, poor dear,' said her mother; 'only eighteen! Yet Amy was but a year older last summer. How unlike! She must have known what she was doing.'

'Not with her senses surrendered to him, without volition of her own. I wonder by what magnetism he allowed her to tell?'

'She has gone through a great deal, poor child, and I am afraid there is much more for her to suffer, whether he recovers or not.'

'He will recover' said Charles, with the decided manner in which people prophesy the restoration of those they dislike, probably from a feeling that they must not die, till there is more charity in their opinion of them.

'Your father will be so grieved.'

'Well, I suppose we must begin to make the best of it,' said Charles. 'She has been as good as married to him these four years, for any use she has been to us; it has been only the name of the thing, so he had better– '

'My dear Charlie, what are you talking of? You don't imagine they can marry?'

'They will some time or other, for assuredly neither will marry any one else. You will see if Guy does not take up the cause, and return Philip's meddling– which, by the bye, is now shown to have been more preposterous still– by setting their affairs in order for them.'

'Dear Guy, it is a comfort not to have been deceived in him!'

'Except when you believed Philip,' said Charles.

'Could anything have been more different?' proceeded Mrs. Edmonstone; 'yet the two girls had the same training.'

'With an important exception,' said Charles; 'Laura is Philip's pupil, Amy mine; and I think her little ladyship is the best turned out of hand.'

'How shocked Amy will be! If she was but here, it would be much better, for she always had more of Laura's confidence than I. Oh, Charlie, there has been the error!' and Mrs. Edmonstone's eyes were full of tears. 'What fearful mistake have I made to miss my daughter's confidence!'

'You must not ask me, mother,' said Charles, face and voice full of affectionate emotion. 'I know too well that I have been exacting and selfish, taking too much advantage of your anxieties for me, and that if you were not enough with my sisters when they were young girls, it was my fault as much as my misfortune. But, after all, it has not hurt Amy in the least; nor do I think it will hurt Charlotte.'

Charlotte did not venture to give way to her desire to kiss her mother, and thank Charles, lest she should be exiled as an intruder.

'And,' proceeded Charles, serious, though somewhat roguish, 'I suspect that no attention would have made much difference. You were always too young, and Laura too much addicted to the physical sciences to get on together.'

'A weak, silly mother, sighed Mrs. Edmonstone.

This was too much for Charlotte, who sprang forward, and flung her arms round her neck, sobbing out,–

'Mamma! dear mamma! don't say such horrid things! No one is half so wise or so good,– I am sure Guy thinks so too!'

At the same time Bustle, perceiving a commotion, made a leap, planted his fore-feet on Mrs. Edmonstone's lap, wagging his tail vehemently, and trying to lick her face. It was not in human nature not to laugh; and Mrs. Edmonstone did so as heartily as either of the young ones; indeed, Charlotte was the first to resume her gravity, not being sure of her ground, and being hurt at her impulse of affection being thus reduced to the absurd. She began to apologize,–

'Dear mamma, I could not help it. I thought you knew I wad in the room.'

'My dear child,' and her mother kissed her warmly, 'I don't want to hide anything from you. You are my only home-daughter now.' Then recollecting her prudence, she proceeded,– 'You are old enough to understand the distress this insincerity of poor Laura's has occasioned,– and now that Amy is gone, we must look to you to comfort us.'

Did ever maiden of fourteen feel more honoured, and obliged to be very good and wise than Charlotte, as she knelt by her mother's side? Happily tact was coming with advancing years, and she did not attempt to mingle in the conversation, which was resumed by Charles observing that the strangest part of the affair was the incompatibility of so novelish and imprudent a proceeding with the cautious, thoughtful character of both parties. It was, he said, analogous to a pentagon flirting with a hexagon; whereas Guy, a knight of the Round Table, in name and nature, and Amy, with her little superstitions, had been attached in the most matter-of-fact, hum-drum way, and were in a course of living very happy ever after, for which nature could never have designed them. Mrs. Edmonstone smiled, sighed, hoped they were prudent, and wondered whether camphor and chloride of lime were attainable at Recoara.

Laura came down no more that day, for she was worn out with agitation, and it was a relief to be sufficiently unwell to be excused facing her father and Charles. She had little hope that Charlotte had not heard all; but she might seem to believe her ignorant, and could, therefore, endure her waiting on her, with an elaborate kindness and compassion, and tip-toe silence, far beyond the deserts of her slight indisposition.

In the evening, Charles and his mother broke the tidings to Mr. Edmonstone as gently as they could, Charles feeling bound to be the cool, thinking head in the family. Of course Mr. Edmonstone stormed, vowed that he could not have believed it, then veered round, and said he could have predicted it from the first. It was all mamma's fault for letting him be so intimate with the girls– how was a poor lad to be expected not to fall in love? Next he broke into great wrath at the abuse of his confidence, then at the interference with Guy, then at the intolerable presumption of Philip's thinking of Laura. He would soon let him know what he thought of it! When reminded of Philip's present condition, he muttered an Irish imprecation on the fever for interfering with his anger, and abused the 'romantic folly' that had carried Guy to nurse him at Recoara. He was not so much displeased with Laura; in fact he thought all young ladies always ready to be fallen in love with, and hardly accountable for what their lovers might make them do, and he pitied her heartily, when he heard of her sitting up all night. Anything of extravagance in love met with sympathy from him, and there was no effort in his hearty forgiveness of her. He vowed that she should give the fellow up, and had she been present, would have tried to make her do so at a moment's warning; but in process of time he was convinced that he must not persecute her while Philip was in extremity, and though, like Charles, he scorned the notion of his death, and, as if it was an additional crime, pronounced him to be as strong as a horse, he was quite ready to put off all proceedings till his recovery, being glad to defer the evil day of making her cry.

So when Laura ventured out, she met with nothing harsh; indeed, but for the sorrowful kindness of her family towards her, she could hardly have guessed that they knew her secret.

Her heart leapt when Amabel's letter was silently handed to her, and she saw the news of Philip's amendment, but a sickening feeling succeeded, that soon all forbearance would be at an end, and he must hear that her weakness had betrayed his secret. For the present, however, nothing was said, and she continued in silent dread of what each day might bring forth, till one afternoon, when the letters had been fetched from Broadstone, Mrs. Edmonstone, with an exclamation of dismay, read aloud:–

'Recoara, September 8th.

'DEAREST MAMMA,– Don't be very much frightened when I tell you that Guy has caught the fever. He has been ailing since Sunday, and yesterday became quite ill; but we hope it will not be so severe an illness as Philip's was. He sleeps a great deal, and is in no pain, quite sensible when he is awake. Arnaud is very useful, and so is Anne; and he is so quiet at night, that he wants no one but Arnaud, and will not let me sit up with him. Philip is better.

'Your most affectionate,

'A.F.M.'

The reading was followed by a dead silence, then Mr. Edmonstone said he had always known how it would be, and what would poor Amy do?

Mrs. Edmonstone was too unhappy to answer, for she could see no means of helping them. Mr. Edmonstone was of no use in a sick-room, and she had never thought it possible to leave Charles. It did not even occur to her that she could do so till Charles himself suggested that she must go to Amy.

'Can you spare me?' said she, as if it was a new light.

'Why not? Who can be thought of but Amy? She ought not to be a day longer without you.'

'Dr. Mayerne would look in on you,' said she, considering, 'and Laura can manage for you.'

'Oh, I shall do very well. Do you think I could bear to keep you from her?'

'Some one must go,' said Mrs. Edmonstone, 'and even if I could think of letting Laura run the risk, this unhappy affair about Philip puts her going out of the question.'

'No one but you can go, said Charles; 'it is of no use to talk of anything else.'

It was settled that if the next account was not more favourable, Mr. and Mrs. Edmonstone should set off for Recoara. Laura heard, in consternation at the thought of her father's meeting Philip, still weak and unwell, without her, and perhaps with Guy too ill to be consulted. And oh! what would Philip think of her? Her weakness had disclosed his secret, and sunk her beneath him, and he must hear it from others. She felt as if she could have thrown herself at her mother's feet as she implored her to forbear, to spare him, to spare her. Her mother pitied her incoherent distress, but it did not make her feel more in charity with Philip. She would not promise that the subject should, not be discussed, but she tried to reassure Laura by saying that nothing should be done that could retard his recovery.

With this Laura was obliged to content herself; and early the second morning, after the letter arrived, she watched the departure of her father and mother.

She had expected to find the care of Charles very anxious work, but she prospered beyond her hopes. He was very kind and considerate, and both he and Charlotte were so sobered by anxiety, that there was no fear of their spirits overpowering her.

Mary Ross used to come almost every afternoon to inquire. One day she found Charles alone, crutching himself slowly along the terrace, and she thought nothing showed the forlorn state of the family so much as to see him out of doors with no one for a prop.

'Mary! Just as I wanted you!'

'What account?' said she, taking the place of one of the crutches.

'Excellent; the fever and drowsiness seem to be going off. It must have been a light attack, and the elders will hardly come in time for mamma to have any nursing. So there's Guy pretty well off one's mind.'

'And Amy?'

'This was such a long letter, and so cheerful, that she must be all right. What I wanted to speak to you about was Laura. You know the state of things. Well, the captain— I wish he was not so sorry, it deprives one of the satisfaction of abusing him— the captain, it seems, was brought to his senses by his illness, confessed all to Guy, and now has written to tell the whole truth to my father.'

'Has he? That is a great relief!'

'Not that I have seen his letter; Laura ran away with it, and has not said a word of it. I know it from one to papa from Amy, trying to make the best of it, and telling how thoroughly he is cut up. She says he all but fainted after writing. Fancy that poor little thing with a great man, six foot one, fainting away on her hands!'

'I thought he was pretty well again.'

'He must be to have written at all, and a pretty tolerably bitter pill it must have been to set about it. What a thing for him to have had to tell Guy, of all people— I do enjoy that! So, of course, Guy takes up his cause, and sends a message, that is worth anything, as showing he is himself better, though in any one else it would be a proof of delirium. My two brothers-in-law might sit for a picture of the contrast.'

'Then you think Mr. Edmonstone will consent?'

'To be sure; we shall have him coming home, saying—

It is a fine thing to be father in-law
To a very magnificent three-tailed bashaw.

He will never hold out against Guy and Amy, and Philip will soon set up a patent revolver, to be turned by the little god of love on the newest scientific principles.'

'Where is Laura?' said Mary, smiling.

'I turned her out to walk with Charlotte, and I want some counsel, as mamma says I know nothing of lovers.'

'Because I know so much?'

'You know feminine nature I want to know what is the best thing to do for Laura. Poor thing! I can't bear to see her look so wretched, worrying herself with care of me. I have done the best I could by taking Charlotte's lessons, and sending her out to mope alone, as she likes best; but I wish you would tell me how to manage her.'

'I know nothing better for her than waiting on you.'

'That's hard,' said Charles, 'that having made the world dance attendance on me for my pleasure, I must now do it for theirs. But what do you think about telling her of this letter, or showing it, remembering that not a word about her troubles has passed between us?'

'By all means tell her. You must judge about showing it, but I should think the opening for talking to her on the subject a great gain.'

'Should you? What, thinking as I do of the man? Should I not be between the horns of a dilemma if I had to speak the honest truth, yet not hurt her feelings?'

'She has been so long shut up from sympathy, that any proof of kindness must be a comfort.'

'Well, I should like to do her some good, but it will be a mercy, if she does not make me fall foul of Philip! I can get up a little Christian charity, when my father or Charlotte rave at him, but I can't stand hearing him praised. I take the opportunity of saying so while I can, for I expect he will come home as her betrothed, and then we shall not be able to say one word.'

'No, I dare say he will be so altered and subdued that you will not be so disposed to rail. This confession is a grand thing. Good-bye I must get back to church. Poor Laura! how busy she has been about her sketch there lately.'

'Yes, she has been eager about finishing it ever since Guy began to be ill. Good-bye. Wish me well through my part of confidant to-night. It is much against the grain, though I would give something to cheer up my poor sister.'

'I am sure you would,' thought Mary to herself, as she looked back at him: 'what a quantity of kind, right feeling there in under that odd, dry manner, that strives to appear to love nothing but a joke.'

As soon as Charlotte was gone to bed, Charles, in accordance with his determination, said to Laura,–

'Have you any fancy for seeing Amy's letter?'

'Thank you;' and, without speaking, Laura took it. He forbore to watch her expression as she read. When she had finished, her face was fixed in silent unhappiness.

'He has been suffering a great deal, I am sure,' said Charles, kindly. It was the first voluntary word of compassion towards Philip that Laura had heard, and it was as grateful as unexpected. Her face softened, and tears gushed from her eyes as she said,–

'You do not know how much. There he is grieving for me! thinking they will be angry with me, and hurting himself with that! Oh! if this had but come before they set off!'

'Guy and Amy will tell them of his having written.'

'Dear, dear Guy and Amy! He speaks so earnestly of their kindness. I don't fear it so much now he and Guy understand each other.'

Recollecting her love, Charles refrained, only saying, 'You can rely on their doing everything to make it better.'

'I can hardly bear to think of what we owe to them,' said Laura. 'How glad I am that Amy was there after he wrote, when he was so much overcome! Amy has written me such a very kind note; I think you must see that– it is so like her own dear self.'

She gave it to him, and he read:–

'MY DEAREST,– I never could tell you before how we have grieved for you ever since we knew it. I am so sorry I wrote such dreadful accounts; and Guy says he wants to ask your pardon, if he ever said anything that pained you about Philip. I understand all your unhappiness now, my poor dear; but it will be better now it is known. Don't be reserved, with Charlie, pray; for if he sees you are unhappy, he will be so very kind. I have just seen Philip again, and found him rested and better. He is only anxious about you; but I tell him I know you will be glad it is told.

'Your most affectionate sister,

'A. F. M.'

'Laura' said Charles, finishing the letter, 'Amy gives you very good advice, as far as I am concerned. I do want to be of as much use to you as I can– I mean as kind.'

'I know– I know; thank you,' said Laura, struggling with her tears. 'You have been– you are; but– '

'Ay,' thought Charles, 'I see, she won't be satisfied, if my kindness includes her alone. What will my honesty let me say to please her? Oh! I know.– You must not expect me to say that Philip has, behaved properly, Laura, nothing but being in love could justify such a delusion; but I do say that there is greatness of mind in his confessing it, especially at a time when he could put it off, and is so unequal to agitation.'

It was the absence of any tone of satire that made this speech come home to Laura as it was meant. There was no grudging in the praise, and she answered, in a very low, broken voice,–

'You will think so still more when you see this note, which he sent open, inside mine, to be given to papa when I had told my own story. Oh, his considerateness for me!'

She gave it to him. The address, 'C. Edmonstone, Esq.,' was a mere scrawl, and within the writing was very trembling and weak. Charles remarked it, and she answered by saying that her own letter began in his own strong hand, but failed and grew shaky at the end, as if from fatigue and agitation. The words were few, brief, and simple, very unlike his usual manner of letter-writing.

'MY DEAR UNCLE,– My conduct has been unjustifiable– I feel it. Do not visit it on Laura– I alone should suffer. I entreat your pardon, and my aunt's, and leave all to you. I will write more at length. Be kind to her.– Yours affectionately,

'PH. M.'

'Poor Philip!' said Charles, really very much touched. From that moment, Laura no longer felt completely isolated, and deprived of sympathy. She sat by Charles till late that night, and told him the whole history of her engagement, much relieved by the outpouring of her long-hidden griefs, and comforted by his kindness, though he could not absolutely refrain from words and gestures of censure. It was as strange that Charles should be the first person to whom Laura told this history, as that Guy should have been Philip's first confidant.

CHAPTER 35

There is a Rock, and nigh at hand,
A shadow in a weary land,
Who in that stricken Rock hath rest,
Finds water gushing from its breast.
– NEALE

In the meantime the days passed at Recoara without much change for the better or worse. After the first week, Guy's fever had diminished; his pulse was lower, the drowsiness ceased, and it seemed as if there was nothing to prevent absolute recovery. But though each morning seemed to bring improvement, it never lasted; the fever, though not high, could never be entirely reduced, and strength was perceptibly wasting, in spite of every means of keeping it up.

There was not much positive suffering, very little even of headache, and he was cheerful, though speaking little, because he was told not to excite or exhaust himself. Languor and lassitude were the chief causes of discomfort; and as his strength failed, there came fits of exhaustion and oppression that tried him severely. At first, these were easily removed by stimulants; but remedies seemed to lose their effect, and the sinking was almost death-like.

'I think I could bear acute pain better!' he said one day; and more than once the sigh broke from him almost unconsciously,– 'Oh for one breath of Redclyffe sea-wind!' Indeed, it seemed as if the close air of the shut-in-valley, at the end of a long hot day was almost enough to overwhelm him, weak as he had become. Every morning, when Amabel let in the fresh breeze at the window, she predicted it would be a cool day, and do him good; every afternoon the wind abated, the sun shone full in, the room was stifling, the faintness came on, and after a few vain attempts at relieving it, Guy sighed that there was nothing for it but quiet, and Amy was obliged to acquiesce. As the sun set, the breeze sprung up, it became cooler, he fell asleep, awoke revived, was comfortable all the evening, and Amy left him at eleven or twelve, with hopes of his having a good night.

It seemed to her as if ages had passed in this way, when one evening two letters were brought in.

'From mamma!' said she; 'and this one,' holding it up, 'is for you. It must have been hunting us everywhere. How many different directions!'

'From Markham,' said Guy. 'It must be the letter we were waiting for.'

The letter to tell them Redclyffe was ready to receive them! Amabel put it down with a strange sensation, and opened her mother's. With a start of joy she exclaimed–

'They are coming– mamma and papa!'

'Then all is right!'

'If we do not receive a much better account,' read Amy, 'we shall set off early on Wednesday, and hope to be with you not long after you receive this letter.'

'Oh I am so glad! I wonder how Charlie gets on without her.'

'It is a great comfort,' said Guy.

'Now you will see what a nurse mamma is!'

'Now you will be properly cared for.'

'How nice it will be! She will take care of you all night, and never be tired, and devise everything I am too stupid for, and make you so comfortable!'

'Nay, no one could do that better than you, Amy. But it is joy indeed— to see mamma again— to know you are safe with her. Everything comes to make it easy!' The last words were spoken very low; and she did not disturb him by saying anything till he asked about the rest of the letter, and desired her to read Markham's to him.

This cost her some pain, for it had been written in ignorance of even Philip's illness, and detailed triumphantly the preparations at Redclyffe, hinting that they must send timely notice of their return, or they would disappoint the tenantry, who intended grand doings, and concluding with a short lecture on the inexpediency of lingering in foreign parts.

'Poor Markham,' said Guy.

She understood; but these things did not come on her like a shock now, for he had been saying them more or less ever since the beginning of his illness; and fully occupied as she was, she never opened her mind to the future. After a long silence, Guy said—

'I am very sorry for him. I have been making Arnaud write to him for me.'

'Oh, have you?'

'It was better for you not to do it, Arnaud has written for me at night. You will send it, Amy, and another to my poor uncle.'

'Very well,' said she, as he looked at her.

'I have told Markham,' said he presently, 'to send you my desk. There are all sorts of things in it, just as I threw them in when I cleared out my rooms at Oxford. I had rather nobody but you saw some of them. There is nothing of any importance, so you may look at them when you please, or not at all.'

She gazed at him without answering. If there had been any struggle to retain him, it would have been repressed by his calmness; but the thought had not come on her suddenly, it was more like an inevitable fate seen at first at a distance, and gradually advancing upon her. She had never fastened on the hope of his recovery, and it had dwindled in an almost imperceptible manner. She kept watch over him, and followed his thoughts, without stretching her mind to suppose herself living without him; and was supported by the forgetfulness of self, which gave her no time to realize her feelings.

'I should like to have seen Redclyffe bay again,' said Guy, after a space. 'Now that mamma is coming, that is the one thing. I suppose I had set my heart on it, for it comes back to me how I reckoned on standing on that rock with you, feeling the wind, hearing the surge, looking at the meeting of earth and sky, and the train of sunlight.' He spoke slowly, pausing between each recollection,– 'You will see it some day,' he added. 'But I must give it up; it is earth after all, and looking back.'

Through the evening, he seemed to be dwelling on thoughts of his own, and only spoke to tell her of some message to friends at Redclyffe, or Hollywell, to mention little Marianne Dixon, or some other charge that he wished to leave. She thought he had mentioned almost every one with whom he had had any interchange of kindness at either of his homes, even to old nurse at Hollywell, remembering them all with quiet pleasure. At half-past eleven, he sent her to bed, and she went submissively, cheered by thinking him likely to sleep.

As soon as she could conscientiously call the night over, she returned to him, and was received with one of the sweet, sunny, happy looks that had always been his peculiar charm, and, of late, had acquired an expression almost startling from their very beauty and radiance. It was hardly to be termed a smile, for there was very little, if any, movement of the lips, it was more like the reflection of some glory upon the whole countenance.

'You have had a good night?' she said.

'I have had my wish, I have seen Redclyffe;' then, seeing her look startled, 'Of course, it was a sort of wandering; but I never quite lost the consciousness of being here, and it was very delightful. I saw the waves, each touched with light,– the foam– the sea-birds, floating in shade and light,– the trees– the Shag– the sky– oh! such a glory as I never knew– themselves– but so intensely glorious!'

'I am glad' said Amabel, with a strange participation of the delight it had given him.

'I don't understand such goodness!' he continued. 'As if it were not enough to look to heaven beyond, to have this longing gratified, which I thought I ought to conquer. Oh, Amy! is not that being Fatherly!'

'Yes, indeed.'

'Now after that, and with mamma's coming (for you will have her if I don't see her), I have but one wish unfulfilled.'

'Ah! a clergyman.'

'Yes, but if that is withheld, I must believe it is rightly ordered. We must think of that Sunday at Stylehurst and Christmas-day, and that last time at Munich.'

'Oh, I am so glad we stayed at Munich for that!'

'Those were times, indeed! and many more. Yes; I have been a great deal too much favoured already, and now to be allowed to die just as I should have chosen– '

He broke off to take what Amabel was preparing for him, and she felt his pulse. There was fever still, which probably supplied the place of strength, for he said he was very comfortable, and his eyes were as bright as ever; but the beats were weak and fluttering, and a thrill crossed her that it might be near; but she must attend to him, and could not think.

When it was time for her to go down to breakfast with Philip, Guy said, 'Do you think Philip could come to me to-day? I want much to speak to him.'

'I am sure he could.'

'Then pray ask him to come, if it will not tire him very much.'

Philip had, the last two mornings, risen in time to breakfast with Amabel, in the room adjoining his own; he was still very weak, and attempted no more than crossing the room, and sitting in the balcony to enjoy the evening air. He had felt the heat of the weather severely, and had been a good deal thrown back by his fatigue and agitation the day he wrote the letter, while also anxiety for Guy was retarding his progress, though he only heard the best side of his condition. Besides all this, his repentance both for his conduct with regard to Laura and the hard measure he had dealt to Guy was pressing on him increasingly; and the warm feelings, hardened and soured by early disappointment, regained their force, and grew into a love and admiration that made it still more horrible to perceive that he had acted ungenerously towards his cousin.

When he heard of Guy's desire to see him, he was pleased, said he was quite able to walk up-stairs, had been thinking of offering to help her by sitting with him, and was very glad to hear he was well enough to wish for a visit. She saw she must prepare him for what the conversation was likely to be.

'He is very anxious to see you,' she said. 'He is wishing to set all in order. And if he does speak about– about dying, will you be so kind as not to contradict him?'

'There is no danger?' cried Philip, startling, with a sort of agony. 'He is no worse? You said the fever was lower.'

'He is rather better, I think; but he wishes so much to have everything arranged, that I am sure it will be better for him to have it off his mind. So, will you bear it, please, Philip?' ended she, with an imploring look, that reminded him of her childhood.

'How do you bear it?' he asked.

'I don't know– I can't vex him.'

Philip said no more, and only asked when he should come.

'In an hour's time, perhaps, or whenever he was ready,' she said, 'for he could rest in the sitting-room before coming in to Guy.'

He found mounting the stairs harder than he had expected, and, with aching knees and gasping breath, at length reached the sitting-room, where Amabel was ready to pity him, and made him rest on the sofa till he had fully recovered. She then conducted him in; and his first glance gave him infinite relief, for he saw far less change than was still apparent in himself. Guy's face was at all times too thin to be capable of losing much of its form, and as he was liable to be very much tanned, the brown, fixed on his face by the sunshine of his journey had not gone off, and a slight flush on his cheeks gave him his ordinary colouring; his beautiful hazel eyes were more brilliant than ever; and though the hand he held out was hot and wasted, Philip could not think him nearly as ill as he had been himself, and was ready to let him talk as he pleased. He was reassured, too, by his bright smile, and the strength of his voice, as he spoke a few playful words of welcome and congratulation. Amy set a chair, and with a look to remind Philip to be cautious, glided into her own room, leaving the door open, so as to see and hear all that passed, for they were not fit to be left absolutely alone together.

Philip sat down; and after a little pause Guy began:

'There were a few things I wanted to say, in case you should be my successor at Redclyffe.'

A horror came over Philip; but he saw Amy writing at her little table, and felt obliged to refrain.

'I don't think of directing you,' said Guy, 'You will make a far better landlord than I; but one or two things I should like.'

'Anything you wish!'

'Old Markham. He has old-world notions and prejudices, but his soul is in the family and estate. His heart will be half broken, for me, and if he loses his occupation, he will be miserable. Will you bear with him, and be patient while he lives, even if he is cross and absurd in his objections, and jealous of all that is not me?'

'Yes– yes– if– '

'Thank you. Then there is Coombe Prior. I took Wellwood's pay on myself. Will you? And I should like him to have the living. Then there is the school to be built; and I thought of enclosing that bit of waste, to make gardens for the people; but that you'll do much better. Well; don't you remember when you were at Redclyffe last year' (Philip winced) 'telling Markham that bit of green by Sally's gate ought to be taken into the park? I hope you won't do that, for it is the only place the people have to turn out their cows and donkeys. And you won't cut them off from the steps from the Cove, for it saves the old people from being late for church? Thank you. As to the rest, it is pleasant to think it will be in such hands if— '

That 'if' gave Philip some comfort, though it did not mean what he fancied. He thought of Guy's recovery; Guy referred to the possibility of Amabel's guardianship.

'Amy has a list of the old people who have had so much a week, or their cottages rent-free,' said Guy. 'If it comes to you, you will not let them feel the difference? And don't turn off the old keeper Brown; he is of no use, but it would kill him. And Ben Robinson, who was so brave in the shipwreck, a little notice now and then would keep him straight. Will you tell him I hope he will never forget that morning-service after the wreck? He may be glad to think of it when he is as I am now. You tell him, for he will mind more what comes from a man.'

All this had been spoken with pauses for recollection, and for Philip's signs of assent. Amabel came to give him some cordial; and as soon as she had retreated he went on:—

'My poor uncle; I have written— that is, caused Arnaud to write to him. I hope this may sober him; but one great favour I have to ask of you. I can't leave him money, it would only be a temptation; but will you keep an eye on him, and let Amy rely on you to tell her when to help him I can't ask any one else, and she cannot do it for herself; but you would do it well. A little kindness might save him; and you don't know how generous a character it is, run to waste. Will you undertake this?'

'To be sure I will!'

'Thank you very much. You will judge rightly; but he has delicate feelings. Yes, really; and take care you don't run against them.'

Another silence followed; after which Guy said, smiling with his natural playfulness, 'One thing more. You are the lawyer of the family, and I want a legal opinion. I have been making Arnaud write my will. I have wished Miss Wellwood of St. Mildred's to have some money for a sisterhood she wants to establish. Now, should I leave it to herself or name trustees?'

Philip heard as if a flash of light was blinding him, and he interrupted, with an exclamation:—

'Tell me one thing! Was that the thousand pounds?'

'Yes. I was not at liberty to— '

He stopped, for he was unheard. At the first word Philip had sunk on his knees, hiding his face on the bed-clothes, in an agony of self-abasement, before the goodness he had been relentlessly persecuting.

'It was that?' he said, in a sort of stifled sob. 'Oh, can you forgive me?'

He could not look up; but he felt Guy's hand touch his head, and heard him say, 'That was done long ago. Even as you pardoned my fierce rage against you, which I trust is forgiven above. It has been repented!'

As he spoke there was a knock at the door, and, with the instinctive dread of being found in his present posture, Philip sprang to his feet. Amabel went to the door, and was told that the physician was down-stairs with two gentlemen; and a card was given her, on which she read the name of an English clergyman.

'There, again!' said Guy. 'Everything comes to me. Now it is all quite right.'

Amabel was to go and speak to them, and Guy would see Mr. Morris, the clergyman, as soon as the physician had made his visit. 'You must not go down,' he then said to Philip. 'You will wait in the sitting-room, won't you? We shall want you again, you know,' and his calm brightness was a contrast to Philip's troubled look. 'All is clear between us now,' he added, as Philip turned away.

Long ago, letters had been written to Venice, begging that if an English clergyman should travel that way he might be told how earnestly his presence was requested; this was the first who had answered the summons. He was a very young man, much out of health, and travelling under the care of a brother, who was in great dread of his doing anything to injure himself. Amabel soon perceived that, though kind and right-minded, he could not help them, except as far as his office was concerned. He was very shy, only just in priest's orders; he told her he had never had this office to perform before, and seemed almost to expect her to direct him; while his brother was so afraid of his over-exerting himself, that she could not hope he would take charge of Philip.

However, after the physician had seen Guy, she brought Mr. Morris to him, and came forward, or remained in her room, according as she was wanted. She thought her husband's face was at each moment acquiring more unearthly beauty, and feeling with him, she was raised above thought or sensation of personal sorrow.

When the first part of the service was over, and she exchanged a few words, out of Guy's hearing, with Mr. Morris, he said to her, as from the very fullness of his heart, 'One longs to humble oneself to him. How it puts one to shame to hear such repentance with such a confession!'

The time came when Philip was wanted. Amabel had called in Anne and the clergyman's brother, and went to fetch her cousin. He was where she had left him in the sitting-room, his face hidden in his arms, crossed on the table, the whole man crushed, bowed down, overwhelmed with remorse.

'We are ready. Come, Philip.'

'I cannot; I am not worthy,' he answered, not looking up.

'Nay, you are surely in no uncharitableness with him now,' said she, gently.

A shudder expressed his no.

'And if you are sorry— that is repentance— more fit now than ever— Won't you come? Would you grieve him now?'

'You take it on yourself, then,' said Philip, almost sharply, raising his haggard face.

She did not shrink, and answered, 'A broken and contrite heart, O God, Thou wilt not despise.'

It was a drop of balm, a softening drop. He rose, and trembling from head to foot, from the excess of his agitation, followed her into Guy's room.

The rite was over, and stillness succeeded the low tones, while all knelt in their places. Amabel arose first, for Guy, though serene, looked greatly exhausted, and as she sprinkled him with vinegar, the others stood up. Guy looked for Philip, and held out his hand. Whether it was his gentle force, or of Philip's own accord Amabel could not tell; but as he lay with that look of perfect peace and love, Philip bent down over him and kissed his forehead.

'Thank you!' he faintly whispered. 'Good night. God bless you and my sister.'

Philip went, and he added to Amy, 'Poor fellow! It will be worse for him than for you. You must take care of him.'

She hardly heard the last words, for his head sunk on one side in a deathlike faintness, the room was cleared of all but herself, and Anne fetched the physician at once.

At length it passed off, and Guy slept. The doctor felt his pulse, and she asked his opinion of it. Very low and unequal, she was told: his strength was failing, and there seemed to be no power of rallying it, but they must do their best to support him with cordials, according to the state of his pulse. The physician could not remain all night himself, but would come as soon as he could on the following day.

Amabel hardly knew when it was that he went away; the two Mr. Morrises went to the other hotel; and she made her evening visit to Philip. It was all like a dream, which she could afterwards scarcely remember, till night had come on, and for the first time she found herself allowed to keep watch over her husband.

He had slept quietly for some time, when she roused him to give him some wine, as she was desired to do constantly. He smiled, and said, 'Is no one here but you?'

'No one.'

'My own sweet wife, my Verena, as you have always been. We have been very happy together.'

'Indeed we have,' said she, a look of suffering crossing her face, as she thought of their unclouded happiness. 'It will not be so long before we meet again.'

'A few months, perhaps'– said Amabel, in a stifled voice, 'like your mother– '

'No, don't wish that, Amy. You would not wish it to have no mother.'

'You will pray– ' She could say no more, but struggled for calmness.

'Yes,' he answered, 'I trust you to it and to mamma for comfort. And Charlie– I shall not rob him any longer. I only borrowed you for a little while,' he added, smiling. 'In a little while we shall meet. Years and months seem alike now. I am sorry to cause you so much grief, my Amy, but it is all as it should be, and we have been very happy.'

Amy listened, her eyes intently fixed on him, unable to repress her agitation, except by silence. After some little time, he spoke again. 'My love to Charlie– and Laura– and Charlotte, my brother and sisters. How kindly they have made me one of them! I need not ask Charlotte to take care of Bustle, and your father will ride Deloraine. My love to him, and earnest thanks, for you above all, Amy. And dear mamma! I must look now to meeting her in a brighter world; but tell her how I have felt all her kindness since I first came in my strangeness and grief. How kind she was! how she helped me and led me, and made me know what a mother was. Amy, it will not hurt you to hear it was your likeness to her that first taught me to love you. I have been so very happy, I don't understand it.'

He was again silent, as in contemplation, and Amabel's overcoming emotion had been calmed and chastened down again, now that it was no longer herself that was spoken of. Both were still, and he seemed to sleep a little. When next he spoke, it was to ask if she could repeat their old favourite lines in "Sintram". They came to her lips, and she repeated them in a low, steady voice.

When death, is coming near,
And thy heart shrinks in fear,
    And thy limbs fail,
Then raise thy hands and pray
To Him who smooths the way
    Through the dark vale.

Seest thou the eastern dawn!
Hear'st thou, in the red morn,
    The angel's song?
Oh! lift thy drooping head,
Thou, who in gloom and dread
    Hast lain so long.

Death comes to set thee free,

Oh! meet him cheerily,
  As thy true friend
And all thy fears shall cease,
And In eternal peace
  Thy penance end.

'In eternal peace,' repeated Guy; 'I did not think it would have been so soon. I can't think where the battle has been. I never thought my life could be so bright. It was a foolish longing, when first I was ill, for the cool waves of Redclyffe bay and that shipwreck excitement, if I was to die. This is far better. Read me a psalm, Amy, "Out of the deep."'

There was something in his perfect happiness that would not let her grieve, though a dull heavy sense of consternation was growing on her. So it went on through the night– not a long, nor a dreary one– but more like a dream. He dozed and woke, said a few tranquil words, and listened to some prayer, psalm, or verse, then slept again, apparently without suffering, except when he tried to take the cordials, and this he did with such increasing difficulty, that she hardly knew how to bear to cause him so much pain, though it was the last lingering hope. He strove to swallow them, each time with the mechanical 'Thank you,' so affecting when thus spoken; but at last he came to, 'It is of no use; I cannot.'

Then she knew all hope was gone, and sat still, watching him. The darkness lessened, and twilight came. He slept, but his breath grew short, and unequal; and as she wiped the moisture on his brow, she knew it was the death-damp.

Morning light came on– the church bell rang out matins– the white hills were tipped with rosy light. His pulse was almost gone– his hand was cold. At last he opened his eyes. 'Amy! he said, as if bewildered, or in pain.

'Here, dearest!'

'I don't see.'

At that moment the sun was rising, and the light streamed in at the open window, and over the bed; but it was "another dawn than ours" that he beheld as his most beautiful of all smiles beamed over his face, and he said, 'Glory in the Highest!– peace– goodwill'– A struggle for breath gave an instant's look of pain, then he whispered so that she could but just hear– 'The last prayer.' She read the Commendatory Prayer. She knew not the exact moment, but even as she said 'Amen' she perceived it was over. The soul was with Him with whom dwell the spirits of just men made perfect; and there lay the earthly part with a smile on the face. She closed the dark fringed eyelids– saw him look more beautiful than in sleep– then, laying her face down on the bed, she knelt on. She took no heed of time, no heed of aught that was earthly. How long she knelt she never knew, but she was roused by Anne's voice in a frightened sob– 'My lady, my lady– come away! Oh, Miss Amabel, you should not be here.'

She lifted her head, and Anne afterwards told Mary Ross, 'she should never forget how my lady looked. It was not grief: it was as if she had been a little way with her husband, and was just called back.'

She rose– looked at his face again– saw Arnaud was at hand– let Anne lead her into the next room, and shut the door.

CHAPTER 36

The matron who alone has stood
When not a prop seemed left below,
The first lorn hour of widowhood,
Yet, cheered and cheering all the while,
With sad but unaffected, smile.
– CHRISTIAN YEAR

The four months' wife was a widow before she was twenty-one, and there she sat in her loneliness, her maid weeping, seeking in vain for something to say that might comfort her, and struck with fear at seeing her thus composed. It might be said that she had not yet realized her situation, but the truth was, perhaps, that she was in the midst of the true realities. She felt that her Guy was perfectly happy– happy beyond thought or comparison– and she was so accustomed to rejoice with him, that her mind had not yet opened to understand that his joy left her mourning and desolate.

Thus she remained motionless for some minutes, till she was startled by a sound of weeping– those fearful overpowering sobs, so terrible in a strong man forced to give way.

'Philip!' thought she; and withal Guy's words returned– 'It will be worse for him than for you. Take care of him.'

'I must go to him,' said she at once.

She took up a purple prayer-book that she had unconsciously brought in her hand from Guy's bed, and walked down-stairs, without pausing to think what she should say or do, or remembering how she would naturally have shrunk from the sight of violent grief.

Philip had retired to his own room the night before, overwhelmed by the first full view of the extent of the injuries he had inflicted, the first perception that pride and malevolence had been the true source of his prejudice and misconceptions, and for the first time conscious of the long-fostered conceit that had been his bane from boyhood. All had flashed on him with the discovery of the true purpose of the demand which he thought had justified his persecution. He saw the glory of Guy's character and the part he had acted,– the scales of self-admiration fell from his eyes, and he knew both himself and his cousin.

His sole comfort was in hope for the future, and in devising how his brotherly affection should for the rest of his life testify his altered mind, and atone for past ill-will. This alone kept him from being completely crushed,– for he by no means imagined how near the end was, and the physician, willing to spare himself pain, left him in hopes, though knowing how it would be. He slept but little, and was very languid in the morning; but he rose as soon as Arnaud came to him, in order not to occupy Arnaud's time, as well as to be ready in case Guy should send for him again, auguring well from hearing that there was nothing stirring above, hoping this was a sign that Guy was asleep. So hoped the two servants for a long time, but at length, growing alarmed, after many consultations, they resolved to knock at the door, and learn what was the state of things.

Philip likewise was full of anxiety, and coming to his room door to listen for intelligence, it was the "e morto" of the passing Italians that first revealed to him the truth. Guy dead, Amy widowed, himself the cause– he who had said he would never be answerable for the death of this young man.

Truly had Guy's threat, that he would make him repent, been fulfilled. He tottered back to his couch, and sank down, in a burst of anguish that swept away all the self-control that had once been his pride. There Amabel found him stretched, face downwards, quivering and convulsed by frightful sobs.

'Don't– don't, Philip,' said she, in her gentle voice. 'Don't cry so terribly!'

Without looking up, he made a gesture with his hand, as if to drive her away. 'Don't come here to reproach me!' he muttered.

'No, no; don't speak so. I want you to hear me; I have something for you from him. If you would only listen, I want to tell you how happy and comfortable it was.' She took a chair and sat down by him, relieved on perceiving that the sobs grew a little less violent.

'It was very peaceful, very happy,' repeated she. 'We ought to be very glad.'

He turned round, and glanced at her for a moment; but he could not bear to see her quiet face. 'You don't know what you say,' he gasped. 'No; take care of yourself, don't trouble yourself for such as me!'

'I must; he desired me,' said Amabel. 'You will be happier, indeed, Philip, if you would only think what glory it is, and that he is all safe, and has won the victory, and will have no more of those hard, hard struggles, and bitter repentance. It has been such a night, that it seems wrong to be sorry.'

'Did you say he spoke of me again?'

'Yes; here is his Prayer-book. Your father gave it to him, and he meant to have told you about it himself, only he could not talk yesterday evening, and could not part with it till– '

Amy broke off by opening the worn purple cover, and showing the name, in the Archdeacon's writing. 'He's very fond of it,' she said; 'it is the one he always uses.' (Alas! she had not learnt to speak of him in the past tense.)

Philip held out his hand, but the agony of grief returned the next moment. 'My father, my father! He would have done him justice. If he had lived, this would never have been!'

'That is over, you do him justice now,' said Amy. 'You did, indeed you did, make him quite happy. He said so, again and again. I never saw him so happy as when you began to get better. I don't think any one ever had so much happiness and it never ceased, it was all quiet, and peace, and joy, till it brightened quite into perfect day— and the angel's song! Don't you remember yesterday, how clear and sweet his voice came out in that? and it was the last thing almost he said. I believe'— she lowered her voice— 'I believe he finished it among them.'

The earnest placid voice, speaking thus, in calmness and simplicity, could not fail in soothing him; but he was so shaken and exhausted, that she had great difficulty in restoring him. After a time, he lay perfectly still on the sofa, and she was sitting by, relieved by the tranquillity, when there was a knock at the door, and Arnaud came in, and stood hesitating, as if he hardly knew how to begin. The present fear of agitating her charge helped her now, when obliged to turn her thoughts to the subjects on which she knew Arnaud was come. She went to the door, and spoke low, hoping her cousin might not hear or understand.

'How soon must it be?'

'My lady, to-morrow,' said Arnaud, looking down. 'They say that so it must be; and the priest consents to have it in the churchyard here. The brother of the clergyman is here, and would know if your ladyship would wish— '

'I will speak to him,' said Amabel, reluctant to send such messages through servants.

'Let me,' said Philip, who understood what was going on, and was of course impelled to spare her as much as possible.

'Thank you' said she, 'if you are able!'

'Oh, yes; I'll go at once!'

'Stop,' said she, as he was setting forth; 'you don't know what you are going to say.'

He put his hand to his head in confusion.

'He wished to be buried here,' said Amabel, 'and— '

But this renewal of the assurance of the death was too much; and covering his face with his hands, he sank back in another paroxysm of violent sobs. Amabel could not leave him.

'Ask Mr. Morris to be so good as to wait, and I will come directly,' said she, then returned to her task of comfort till she again saw Philip lying, with suspended faculties, in the repose of complete exhaustion.

She then went to Mr. Morris, with a look and tone of composure that almost startled him, thanking him for his assistance in the arrangements. The funeral was to be at sunrise the next day, before the villagers began to keep the feast of St. Michael, and the rest was to be settled by Arnaud and Mr.

Morris. He then said, somewhat reluctantly, that his brother had desired to know whether Lady Morville wished to see him to-day, and begged to be sent for; but Amy plainly perceived that he thought it very undesirable for his brother to have any duties to perform to-day. She questioned herself whether she might not ask him to read to her, and whether it might be better for Philip; but she thought she ought not to ask what might injure him merely for her own comfort; and, besides, Philip was entirely incapable of self-command, and it would not be acting fairly to expose him to the chance of discovering to a stranger, feelings that he would ordinarily guard so scrupulously.

She therefore gratefully refused the offer, and Mr. Morris very nearly thanked her for doing so. He took his leave, and she knew she must return to her post; but first she indulged herself with one brief visit to the room where all her cares and duties had lately centred. A look– a thought– a prayer. The beauteous expression there fixed was a help, as it had ever been in life and she went back again cheered and sustained.

Throughout that day she attended on her cousin, whose bodily indisposition required as much care as his mind needed soothing. She talked to him, read to him, tried to set him the example of taking food, took thought for him as if he was the chief sufferer, as if it was the natural thing for her to do, working in the strength her husband had left her, and for him who had been his chief object of care. She had no time to herself, except the few moments that she allowed herself now and then to spend in gazing at the dear face that was still her comfort and joy; until, at last, late in the evening, she succeeded in reading Philip to sleep. Then, as she sat in the dim candle-light, with everything in silence, a sense of desolation came upon her, and she knew that she was alone.

At that moment a carriage thundered at the door, and she remembered for the first time that she was expecting her father and mother. She softly left the room and closed the door; and finding Anne in the nest room, sent her down.

'Meet mamma, Anne,' said she; 'tell her I am quite well. Bring them here.'

They entered; and there stood Amabel, her face a little flushed, just like, only calmer, the daughter they had parted with on her bridal day, four months ago. She held up her hand as a sign of silence, and said,– 'Hush! don't wake Philip.'

Mr. Edmonstone was almost angry, and actually began an impatient exclamation, but broke it off with a sob, caught her in his arms, kissed her, and then buried his face in his handkerchief. Mrs. Edmonstone, still aghast at the tidings they had met at Vicenza, and alarmed at her unnatural composure, embraced her; held her for some moments, then looked anxiously to see her weep. But there was not a tear, and her voice was itself, though low and weak, as, while her father began pacing up and down, she repeated,–

'Pray don't, papa; Philip has been so ill all day.'

'Philip– pshaw!' said Mr. Edmonstone, hastily. 'How are you, yourself, my poor darling?'

'Quite well, thank you,' said Amy. 'There is a room ready for you.'

Mrs. Edmonstone was extremely alarmed, sure that this was a grief too deep for outward tokens, and had no peace till she had made Amabel consent to come up with her, and go at once to bed. To this she agreed, after she had rung for Arnaud, and stood with him in the corridor, to desire him to go at once to Captain Morville, as softly as he could, and when he waked, to say Mr. and Mrs. Edmonstone were come, but she thought he had better not see them to-night; to tell him from her that she wished him good night, and hoped he would, sleep quietly. 'And, Arnaud, take care you do not let him know the hour tomorrow. Perhaps, as he is so tired, he may sleep till afterwards.'

Mrs. Edmonstone was very impatient of this colloquy, and glad when Amabel ended it, and led the way up-stairs. She entered her little room, then quietly opened another door, and Mrs. Edmonstone found herself standing by the bed, where that which was mortal lay, with its face bright with the impress of immortality.

The shock was great, for he was indeed as a son to her; but her fears for Amabel would not leave room for any other thought.

'Is not he beautiful?' said Amy, with a smile like his own.

'My dear, my dear, you ought not to be here,' said Mrs. Edmonstone, trying to lead her away.

'If you would let me say my prayers here!' said she, submissively.

'I think not. I don't know how to refuse, if it would be a comfort,' said Mrs. Edmonstone, much distressed, 'but I can't think it right. The danger is greater after. And surely, my poor dear child, you have a reason for not risking yourself!'

'Go, mamma, I ought not to have brought you here; I forgot about infection,' said Amabel, with the tranquillity which her mother had hoped to shake by her allusion. 'I am coming.'

She took up Guy's watch and a book from the table by the bed-side, and came back to her sleeping-room. She wound up the watch, and then allowed her mother to undress her, answering all her inquiries about her health in a gentle, indifferent, matter-of-fact way. She said little of Guy, but that little was without agitation, and in due time she lay down in bed. Still, whenever Mrs. Edmonstone looked at her, there was no sleep in her eyes, and at last she persuaded her to leave her, on the plea that being watched made her more wakeful, as she did not like to see mamma sitting up.

Almost as soon as it was light, Mrs. Edmonstone returned, and was positively frightened, for there stood Amabel, dressed in her white muslin, her white bonnet, and her deep lace wedding-veil. All her glossy hair was hidden away, and her face was placid as ever, though there was a red spot on each cheek. She saw her mother's alarm, and reassured her by speaking calmly.

'You know I have nothing else but colours; I should like to wear this, if you will let me.'

'But, dearest, you must not– cannot go.'

'It is very near. We often walked there together. I would not if I thought it would hurt me, but I wish it very much indeed. At home by Michaelmas!'

Mrs. Edmonstone yielded, though her mind misgave her, comforted by hoping for the much-desired tears. But Amabel, who used to cry so easily for a trifle, had now not a tear. Her grief was as yet too deep, or perhaps more truly sorrow and mourning had not begun while the influence of her husband's spirit was about her still.

It was time to set forth, and the small party of mourners met in the long corridor. Mr. Edmonstone would have given his daughter his arm, but she said–

'I beg your pardon, dear papa, I don't think I can;' and she walked alone and firmly.

It was a strange sight that English funeral, so far from England. The bearers were Italian peasants. There was a sheet thrown over the coffin instead of a pall, and this, with the white dress of the young widow, gave the effect of the emblematic whiteness of a child's funeral; and the impression was heightened by the floating curling white clouds of vapour rising in strange shrouded shadowy forms, like spirit mourners, from the narrow ravines round the grave-yard, and the snowy mountains shining in the morning light against the sky.

Gliding almost like one of those white wreaths of mist, Amabel walked alone, tearless and calm, her head bent down, and her long veil falling round her in full light folds, as when it had caught the purple light on her wedding-day. Her parents were close behind, weeping more for the living than the dead, though Guy had a fast hold of their hearts; and his own mother could scarce have loved him better than Mrs. Edmonstone did. Lastly, were Anne and Arnaud, sincere mourners, especially Arnaud, who had loved and cherished his young master from childhood.

They went to the strangers' corner of the grave-yard, for, of course the church did not open to a member of another communion of the visible church; but around them were the hills in which he had read many a meaning, and which had echoed a response to his last chant with the promise of the blessing of peace.

The blessing of peace came in the precious English burial-service, as they laid him to rest in the earth, beneath the spreading chestnut-tree, rendered a home by those words of his Mother Church– the mother who had guided each of his steps in his orphaned life. It was a distant grave, far from his home and kindred, but in a hallowed spot, and a most fair one; and there might his mortal frame meetly rest till the day when he should rise, while from their ancestral tombs should likewise awaken the forefathers whose sins were indeed visited on him in his early death; but, thanks to Him who giveth the victory, in death without the sting.

Amabel, in obedience to a sign from her mother, sat on a root of the tree while the Lesson was read, and afterwards she moved forward and stood at the edge of the grave, her hands tightly clasped, and her head somewhat raised, as if her spirit was following her husband to his repose above, rather than to his earthly resting-place.

The service was ended, and she was taking a last long gaze, while her mother, in the utmost anxiety, was striving to make up her mind to draw her away, when suddenly a tall gaunt figure was among them– his face ghastly pale, and full of despair and bewilderment– his step uncertain– his dress disordered.

Amabel turned, went up to him, laid her hand on his arm, and said, softly, and quietly looking up in his face, 'It is over now, Philip; you had better come home.'

Not attempting to withstand her, he obeyed as if it was his only instinct. It was like some vision of a guiding, succouring spirit, as she moved on, slowly gliding in her white draperies. Mrs. Edmonstone watched her in unspeakable awe and amazement, almost overpowering her anxieties. It seemed as impossible that the one should be Amy as that the other should be Philip, her gentle little clinging daughter, or her proud, imperturbable, self-reliant nephew.

But it was Amy's own face, when they entered the corridor and she turned back her veil, showing her flushed and heated cheeks, at the same time opening Philip's door and saying, 'Now you must rest, for you ought not to have come out. Lie down, and let mamma read to you.'

Mrs. Edmonstone was reluctant, but Amy looked up earnestly and said, 'Yes, dear mamma, I should like to be alone a little while.'

She then conducted her father to the sitting-room up-stairs.

'I will give you the papers,' she said; and leaving him, returned immediately.

'This is his will,' she said. 'You will tell me if there is anything I must do at once. Here is a letter to Mr. Markham, and another to Mr. Dixon, if you will be so kind as to write and enclose them. Thank you, dear papa.'

She drew a blotting-book towards him, saw that there was ink and pen, and left him too much appalled at her ways to say anything.

His task was less hard than the one she had set her mother. Strong excitement had carried Philip to the grave-yard as soon as he learnt what was passing. He could hardly return even with Arnaud's support, and he had only just reached the sofa before he fell into a fainting-fit.

It was long before he gave any sign of returning life, and when he opened his eyes and saw Mrs. Edmonstone, he closed them almost immediately, as if unable to meet her look. It was easier to treat him in his swoon than afterwards. She knew nothing of his repentance and confession; she only knew he had abused her confidence, led Laura to act insincerely, and been the cause of Guy's death. She did not know how bitterly he accused himself, and though she could not but see he was miserable, she could by no means fathom his wretchedness, nor guess that her very presence made him conscious how far he was fallen. He was so ill that she could not manifest her displeasure, nor show anything but solicitude for his relief; but her kindness was entirely to his condition, not to himself; and perceiving this, while he thought his confession had been received, greatly aggravated his distress, though he owned within himself that he well deserved it.

She found that he was in no state for being read to; he was completely exhausted, and suffering from violent headache. So when she could conscientiously say that to be left quiet was the best thing for him, she went to her daughter.

Amabel was lying on her bed, her Bible open by her; not exactly reading, but as if she was now and then finding a verse and dwelling on it. Gentle and serene she looked; but would she never weep? would those quiet blue eyes be always sleepless and tearless?

She asked anxiously for Philip, and throughout the day he seemed to be her care. She did not try to get up and go to him, but she was continually begging her mother to see about him. It was a harassing day for poor Mrs. Edmonstone. She would have been glad to have sat by Amabel all the time, writing to Charles, or hearing her talk. Amy had much to say, for she wished to make her mother share the perfect peace and thankfulness that had been breathed upon her during those last hours with her husband, and she liked to tell the circumstances of his illness and his precious sayings, to one who would treasure them almost like herself. She spoke with her face turned away, so as not to see her mother's tears, but her mild voice unwavering, as if secure in the happiness of these recollections. This was the only comfort of Mrs. Edmonstone's day, but when she heard her husband's boots creaking in the corridor, it was a sure sign that he was in some perplexity, and that she must go and help him to write a letter, or make some arrangement. Philip, too, needed attention; but excellent nurse as Mrs.

Edmonstone was, she only made him worse. The more he felt she was his kind aunt still, the more he saw how he had wounded her, and that her pardon was an effort. The fond, spontaneous, unreserved affection— almost petting— which he had well-nigh dared to contemn, was gone; her manner was only that of a considerate nurse. Much as he longed for a word of Laura, he did not dare to lead to it,— indeed, he was so far from speaking to her of any subject which touched him, that he did not presume even to inquire for Amabel, he only heard of her through Arnaud.

At night sheer exhaustion worked its own cure; he slept soundly, and awoke in the morning revived. He heard from Arnaud that Lady Morville was pretty well, but had not slept; and presently Mrs. Edmonstone came in and took pains to make him comfortable, but with an involuntary dryness of manner. She told him his uncle would come to see him as soon as he was up, if he felt equal to talking over some business. Philip's brain reeled with dismay and consternation, for it flashed on him that he was heir of Redclyffe. He must profit by the death he had caused; he had slain, and he must take possession of the lands which, with loathing and horror, he remembered that he had almost coveted. Nothing more was wanting. There was little consolation in remembering that the inheritance would clear away all difficulties in the way of his marriage. He had sinned; wealth did not alter his fault, and his spirit could not brook that if spurned in poverty, he should be received for his riches. He honoured his aunt for being cold and reserved, and could not bear the idea of seeing his uncle ready to meet him half-way.

After the first shock he became anxious to have the meeting over, know the worst, and hear on what ground he stood with Laura. As soon as he was dressed, he sent a message to announce that he was ready, and lay on the sofa awaiting his uncle's arrival, as patiently as he could. Mr. Edmonstone, meantime, was screwing up his courage— not that he meant to say a word of Laura,— Philip was too unwell to be told his opinion of him, but now he had ceased to rely on his nephew, he began to dread him and his overbearing ways; and besides he had a perfect horror of witnessing agitation.

At last he came, and Philip rose to meet him with a feeling of shame and inferiority most new to him.

'Don't, don't, I beg,' said Mr. Edmonstone, with what was meant for dignity. 'Lie still; you had much better. My stars! how ill you look!' he exclaimed, startled by Philip's altered face and figure. 'You have had a sharpish touch; but you are better, eh?'

'Yes, thank you.'

'Well; I thought I had better come and speak to you, if you felt up to it. Here is— here is— I hope it is all right and legal; but that you can tell better than I; and you are concerned in it anyhow. Here is poor Guy's will, which we thought you had better look over, if you liked, and felt equal, eh?'

'Thank you,' said Philip, holding out his hand; but Mr. Edmonstone withheld it, trying his patience by an endless quantity of discursive half-sentences, apparently without connection with each other, about disappointment, and hopes, and being sorry, and prospects, and its 'being an unpleasant thing,' and 'best not raise his expectations:' during all which time Philip, expecting to hear of Laura, and his heart beating so fast as to renew the sensation of faintness, waited in vain, and strove to gather the meaning, and find out whether he was forgiven, almost doubting whether the confusion was in his own mind or in his uncle's words. However, at last the meaning bolted out in one comprehensive sentence, when Mr. Edmonstone thought he had sufficiently prepared him for his disappointment,– 'Poor Amy is to be confined in the spring.'

There Mr. Edmonstone stopped short, very much afraid of the effect; but Philip raised himself, his face brightened, as if he was greatly relieved, and from his heart he exclaimed, 'Thank Heaven!'

'That's right! that is very well said!' answered Mr. Edmonstone, very much pleased. 'It would be a pity it should go out of the old line after all; and it's a very generous thing in you to say so.'

'Oh no!' said Philip, shrinking into himself at even such praise as this.

'Well, well,' said his uncle, 'you will see he has thought of you, be it how it may. There! I only hope it is right; though it does seem rather queer, appointing poor little Amy executor rather than me. If I had but been here in time! But 'twas Heaven's will; and so– It does not signify, after all, if it is not quite formal. We understand each other.'

The will was on a sheet of letter-paper, in Arnaud's stiff French handwriting; it was witnessed by the two Mr. Morrises, and signed on the 27th of September, in very frail and feeble characters. Amabel and Markham were the executors, and Amabel was to be sole guardian, in case of the birth of a child. If it was a son, £10,000 was left to Philip himself; if not, he was to have all the plate, furniture, &c., of Redclyffe, with the exception of whatever Lady Morville might choose for herself.

Philip scarcely regarded the legacy (though it smoothed away his chief difficulties) as more than another of those ill-requited benefits which were weighing him to the earth. He read on to a sentence which reproached him so acutely, that he would willingly have hidden from it, as he had done from Guy's countenance. It was the bequest of £5000 to Elizabeth Wellwood. Sebastian Dixon's debts were to be paid off; £1000 was left to Marianne Dixon, and the rest of the personal property was to be Amabel's.

He gave back the paper, with only the words 'Thank you.' He did not feel as if it was for him to speak; and Mr. Edmonstone hesitated, made an attempt at congratulating him, broke down, and asked if it was properly drawn up. He glanced at the beginning and end, said it was quite correct, and laid his head down, as if the examination had been a great deal of trouble.

'And what do you think of Amy's being under age?' fidgeted on Mr. Edmonstone. 'How is she to act, poor dear! Shall I act for her?'

'She will soon be of age,' said Philip, wearily.

'In January, poor darling. Who would have thought how it would have been with her? I little thought, last May– but, holloa! what have I been at?' cried he, jumping up in a great fright, as Philip, so weak as to be overcome by the least agitation, changed countenance, covered his face with his hands, and turned away with a suppressed sob. 'I didn't mean it, I am sure! Here! mamma!'

'No, no,' said Philip, recovering, and sitting up; 'don't call her, I beg. There is nothing the matter.'

Mr. Edmonstone obeyed, but he was too much afraid of causing a renewal of agitation to continue the conversation; and after walking about the room a little while, and shaking it more than Philip could well bear, he went away to write his letters.

In the meantime, Amabel had been spending her morning in the same quiet way as the former day. She wrote part of a letter to Laura, and walked to the graveyard, rather against her mother's wish; but she was so good and obedient, it was impossible to thwart her, though Mrs. Edmonstone was surprised at her proposal to join her father and Philip at tea. 'Do you like it, my dear?'

'He told me to take care of him,' said Amabel.

'I cannot feel that he deserves you should worry yourself about him,' said Mrs. Edmonstone. 'If you knew all– '

'I do know all, mamma,– if you mean about Laura. Surely you must forgive. Think how he repents. What, have you not had his letter? Then how did you know?'

'I learned it from Laura herself. Her trouble at his illness revealed it. Do you say he has written?'

'Yes, mamma; he told Guy all about it, and was very sorry, and wrote as soon as he was able. Guy sent you a long message. He was so anxious about it.'

Amabel showed more eagerness to understand the state of the case, than she had about anything else. She urged that Philip should be spoken to, as soon as possible, saying the suspense must be grievous, and dwelling on his repentance. Mrs. Edmonstone promised to speak to papa, and this satisfied her; but she held her resolution of meeting Philip that evening, looking on him as a charge left her by her husband, and conscious that, as she alone understood how deep was his sorrow, she could make the time spent with her parents less embarrassing.

Her presence always soothed him, and regard for her kept her father quiet; so that the evening passed off very well. Mrs. Edmonstone waited on both; and, in Amy's presence, was better able to resume her usual manner towards her nephew, and he sat wondering at the placidity of Amy's pale face. Her hair was smoothed back, and she wore a cap,— the loss of her long shady curls helping to mark the change from the bright days of her girlhood; but the mournfulness of her countenance did not mar the purity and serenity that had always been its great characteristic; and in the faint sweet smile with which she received a kind word or attention, there was a likeness to that peculiar and beautiful expression of her husband's, so as, in spite of the great difference of feature and colouring, to give her a resemblance to him.

All this day had been spent by Mr. Edmonstone in a fret to get away from Recoara, and his wife was hardly less desirous to leave it than himself, for she could have no peace or comfort about Amabel, till she had her safely at home. Still she dreaded proposing the departure, and even more the departure itself; and, in spite of Mr. Edmonstone's impatience, she let her alone till she had her mourning; but when, after two days of hard work, Anne had nearly managed to complete it, she made up her mind to tell her daughter that they ought to set out.

Amabel replied by mentioning Philip. She deemed him a sort of trust, and had been reposing in the thought of making him a reason for lingering in the scene where the brightness of her life had departed from her. Mrs. Edmonstone would not allow that she ought to remain for his sake, and told her it was her duty to resolve to leave the place. She said, 'Yes, but for him;' and it ended in Mrs. Edmonstone going, without telling her, to inform him that she thought Amy ought to be at home as soon as possible; but that it was difficult to prevail on her, because she thought him as yet not well enough to be left. He was, of course, shocked at being thus considered, and as soon as he next saw Amabel, told her, with great earnestness, that he could not bear to see her remaining there on his account; that he was almost well, and meant to leave Recoara very soon; the journey was very easy, the sea voyage would be the best thing for him, and he should be glad to get to the regimental doctor at Corfu.

Amabel sighed, and knew she ought to be convinced. The very pain it gave her to lose sight of that green, grave, the chestnut-tree, and the white mountain; to leave the rooms and passages which still, to her ears, were haunted by Guy's hushed step and voice, and to part with the window where she used each wakeful night to retrace his profile as he had stood pausing before telling her of his exceeding happiness; that very pain made her think that opposition would be selfish. She must go some time or other, and it was foolish to defer the struggle; she must not detain her parents in an infected place, nor keep her mother from Charles. She therefore consented, and let them do what they pleased,– only insisting on Arnaud's being left with Philip.

Philip did not think this necessary, but yielded, when she urged it as a relief to her own mind; and Arnaud, though unwilling, and used to his own way, could make no objection when she asked it as a personal favour. Arnaud was, at his own earnest wish, to continue in her service; and, as soon as Philip was able to embark, was to follow her to Hollywell.

All this time nothing passed about Laura. Amabel asked several times whether papa had spoken, but was always answered, 'Not yet;' and at last Mrs. Edmonstone, after vainly trying to persuade him, was obliged to give it up. The truth was, he could not begin; he was afraid of his nephew, and so unused to assume superiority over him that he did not know what to do, and found all kinds of reasons for avoiding the embarrassing scene. Since Philip still must be dealt with cautiously, better not enter on the subject at all. When reminded that the suspense was worse than anything, he said, no one could tell how things would, turn out, and grew angry with his wife for wishing him to make up a shameful affair like that, when poor Guy had not been dead a week, and he had been the death of him; but it was just like mamma, she always spoilt him. He had a great mind to vow never to consent to his daughter's marrying such an overbearing, pragmatical fellow; she ought to be ashamed of even thinking of him, when he was no better than her brother's murderer.

After this tirade, Mrs. Edmonstone might well feel obliged to tell Amabel, that papa must not be pressed any further; and, of course, if he would not speak, she could not (nor did she wish it).

'Then, mamma,' said Amabel, with the air of decision that had lately grown on her, 'I must tell him. I beg your pardon,' she added, imploringly; 'but indeed I must. It is hard on him not to hear that you had not his letter, and that Laura has told. I know Guy would wish me, so don't be displeased, dear mamma.'

'I can't be displeased with anything you do.'

'And you give me leave?'

'To be sure I do,– leave to do anything but hurt yourself.'

'And would it be wrong for me to offer to write to him? No one else will, and it will be sad for him not to hear. It cannot be wrong, can it?' said she, as the fingers of her right hand squeezed her wedding-ring, a habit she had taken up of late.

'Certainly not, my poor darling. Do just as you think fit. I am sorry for him, for I am sure he is in great trouble, and I should like him to be comforted– if he can. But, Amy, you must not ask me to do it. He has disappointed me too much.'

Mrs. Edmonstone left the room in tears.

Amabel went up to the window, looked long at the chestnut-tree, then up into the sky, sat down, and leant her forehead on her hand in meditation, until she rose up, cheered and sustained, as if she had been holding council with her husband.

She did not over-estimate Philip's sufferings from suspense and anxiety. He had not heard a word of Laura; how she had borne his illness, nor how much displeasure his confession had brought upon her; nor could he learn what hope there was that his repentance was accepted. He did not venture to ask; for after engaging to leave all to them, could he intrude his own concerns on them at such a time? It was but a twelvemonth since he had saddened and shadowed Guy's short life and love with the very suffering from uncertainty that he found so hard to bear. As he remembered this, he had a sort of fierce satisfaction in enduring this retributive justice; though there were moods when he felt the torture so acutely, that it seemed to him as if his brain would turn if he saw them depart, and was left behind to this distracting doubt.

The day had come, on which they were to take their first stage, as far as Vicenza, and his last hopes were fading. He tried to lose the sense of misery by bestirring himself in the preparations; but he was too weak, and Mrs. Edmonstone, insisting on his attempting no more, sent him back: to his own sitting-room.

Presently there was a knock, and in came Amabel, dressed, for the first time, in her weeds, the blackness and width of her sweeping crape making her young face look smaller and paler, while she held in her hand some leaves of chestnut, that showed where she had been. She smiled a little as she came in, saying, 'I am come to you for a little quiet, out of the bustle of packing up. I want you to do something for me.'

'Anything for you.'

'It is what you will like to do,' said she, with that smile, 'for it is more for him than for me. Could you, without teasing yourself, put that into Latin for me, by and by? I think it should be in Latin, as it is in a foreign country.'

She gave him a paper in her own writing.

GUY MORVILLE, OF REDCLYFFE, ENGLAND. DIED THE EVE OF ST. MICHAEL AND ALL ANGELS, 18– AGED 21 1/2. I BELIEVE IN THE COMMUNION OF SAINTS.

'Will you be so kind as to give it to Arnaud when it is done?' she continued; 'he will send it to the man who is making the cross. I think the kind people here will respect it.'

'Yes,' said Philip,' it is soon done, and thank you for letting me do it. But, Amy, I would not alter your choice; yet there is one that seems to me more applicable "Greater love hath no man– "'

'I know what you mean,' said Amy; 'but that has so high a meaning that he could not bear it to be applied to him.'

'Or rather, what right have I to quote it?' said Philip, bitterly. 'His friend! No, Amy; you should rather choose, "If thine enemy thirst, give him drink; for in so doing thou shalt heap coals of fire on his head." I am sure they are burning on mine,' and he pressed his hand on his forehead.

'Don't say such things. We both know that, at the worst of times, he looked on you as a sincere friend.'

Philip groaned, and she thought it best to go on to something else. 'I like this best,' she said. 'It will be nice to think of far away. I should like, too, for these Italians to see the stranger has the same creed as themselves.'

After a moment's pause, during which he looked at the paper, he said, 'Amy, I have one thing to ask of you. Will you write my name in the Prayer-book?'

'That I will,' said she, and Philip drew it from under the sofa cushion, and began putting together his pocket gold pen. While he was doing this, she said, 'Will you write to me sometimes? I shall be so anxious to know how you get on.'

'Yes, thank you,' said he; with a sigh, as if he would fain have said more.

She paused; then said, abruptly, 'Do you know they never had your letter?'

'Ha! Good heavens!' cried he, starting up in consternation; 'then they don't know it!'

'They do. Sit down, Philip, and hear. I wanted to tell you about it. They know it. Poor Laura was so unhappy when you were ill, that mamma made it out from her.'

He obeyed the hand that invited him back to his seat, and turned his face earnestly towards her. He must let her be his comforter, though a moment before his mind would have revolted at troubling the newly-made widow with his love affairs. Amabel told him, as fully and clearly as she could, how the truth had come out, how gently Laura had been dealt with, how Charles had been trying to soften his father, and papa had not said one angry word to her.

'They forgive her. Oh, Amy, thanks indeed! You have taken away one of the heaviest burdens. I am glad, indeed, that she spoke first. For my own part, I see through all their kindness and consideration how they regard me.'

'They know how sorry you are, and that you wrote to tell all,' said Amabel. 'They forgive, indeed they do; but they cannot bear to speak about it just yet.'

'If you forgive, Amy,' said he, in a husky voice, 'I may hope for pardon from any.'

'Hush! don't say that. You have been so kind, all this time, and we have felt together so much, that no one could help forgetting anything that went before. Then you will write to me; and will you tell me how to direct to you?'

'You will write to me?' cried Philip, brightening for a moment with glad surprise. 'Oh, Amy, you will quite overpower me with your goodness!– The coals of fire,' he finished, sinking his voice, and again pressing his hand to his brow.

'You must not speak so, Philip,' then looking at him, 'Is your head aching?'

'Not so much aching as– ' he paused, and exclaimed, as if carried away in spite of himself, 'almost bursting with the thoughts of– of you, Amy,– of him whom I knew too late,– wilfully misunderstood, envied, persecuted; who,– oh! Amy, Amy, if you could guess at the anguish of but one of my thoughts, you would know what the first murderer meant when he said, "My punishment is greater than I can bear."'

'I can't say don't think,' said Amy, in her sweet, calm tone; 'for I have seen how happy repentance made him, but I know it must be dreadful. I suppose the worse it is at the time, the better it must be afterwards. And I am sure this Prayer-book'– she had her hand on it all the time, as if it was a pleasure to her to touch it again– 'must be a comfort to you. Did you not see that he made me give it to you to use that day, when, if ever, there was pardon and peace– '

'I remember,' said Philip, in a low, grave, heartfelt tone; and as she took the pen, and was writing his name below the old inscription, he added, 'And the date, Amy, and– yes,' as he saw her write 'From G. M.'– 'but put from A. F. M. too. Thank you! One thing more;' he hesitated, and spoke very low, 'You must write in it what you said when you came to fetch me that day,– "A broken"'–

As she finished writing, Mrs. Edmonstone came in. 'My Amy, all is ready. We must go. Good-bye, Philip,' said she, in the tone of one so eager for departure as to fancy farewells would hasten it. However, she was not more eager than Mr. Edmonstone, who rushed in to hurry them on, shaking hands cordially with Philip, and telling him to make haste and recover his good looks. Amabel held out her hand. She would fain have said something cheering, but the power failed her. A deep colour came into her cheeks; she drew her thick black veil over her face, and turned away.

Philip came down-stairs with them, saw her enter the carriage followed by her mother, Mr. Edmonstone outside. He remembered the gay smile with which he last saw her seated in that carriage, and the active figure that had sprung after her; he thought of the kind bright eyes that had pleaded with him for the last time, and recollected the suspicions and the pride with which he had plumed himself on his rejection, and thrown away the last chance.

Should he ever see Amabel again? He groaned and went back to the deserted rooms.

CHAPTER 37

And see
If aught of sprightly, fresh, or free,
With the calm sweetness may compare
Of the pale form half slumbering there.
Therefore this one dear couch about
We linger hour by hour:
The love that each to each we bear,
All treasures of enduring care,
Into her lap we pour.
– LYRA INNOCENTUM

The brother and sisters, left at home together, had been a very sad and silent party, unable to attempt comforting each other. Charlotte's grief was wild and ungovernable; breaking out into fits of sobbing, and attending to nothing till she was abashed first by a reproof from Mr. Ross, and next by the description of Amabel's conduct; when she grew ashamed and set herself to atone, by double care, for her neglect of Charles's comforts.

Charles, however, wanted her little. He had rather be let alone. After one exclamation of, 'My poor Amy!' he said not a word of lamentation, but lay hour after hour without speaking, dwelling on the happy days he had spent with Guy,– companion, friend, brother,– the first beam that had brightened his existence, and taught him to make it no longer cheerless; musing on the brilliant promise that had been cut off; remembering his hopes for his most beloved sister, and feeling his sorrow with imagining hers. It was his first grief, and a very deep one. He seemed to have no comfort but in Mr. Ross, who contrived to come to him every day, and would tell him how fully he shared his affection and admiration for Guy, how he had marvelled at his whole character, as it had shown itself more especially at the time of his marriage, when his chastened temper had been the more remarkable in so young a man, with the world opening on him so brightly. As to the promise lost, that, indeed, Mr. Ross owned, and pleased Charles by saying how he had hoped to watch its fulfilment; but he spoke of its having been, in truth, no blight, only that those fair blossoms were removed where nothing could check their full development or mar their beauty. 'The hope in earthly furrows sown, would ripen in the sky;' Charles groaned, saying it was hard not to see it, and they might speak as they would, but that would not comfort him in thinking of his sister. What was his sorrow to hers? But Mr. Ross had strong trust in Amabel's depth and calm resignation. He said her spirit of yielding would support her, that as in drowning or falling, struggling is fatal, when quietness saves, so it would be with her: and that even in this greatest of all trials she would rise instead of being crushed, with all that was good and beautiful in her purified and refined. Charles heard, strove to believe and be consoled, and brought out his letters, trying, with voice breaking down, to show Mr. Ross how truly he had judged of Amy, then listened with a kind of pleasure to the reports of the homely but touching laments of all the village.

Laura did not, like her brother and sister, seek for consolation from Mr. Ross or Mary. She went on her own way, saying little, fulfilling her household cares, writing all the letters that nobody else would write, providing for Charles's ease, and looking thoroughly cast down and wretched, but saying nothing; conscious that her brother and sister did not believe her affection for Guy equal to theirs; and Charles was too much dejected, and too much displeased with Philip, to try to console her.

It was a relief to hear, at length, that the travellers had landed, and would be at home in the evening, not till late, wrote Mrs. Edmonstone, because she thought it best for Amabel to go at once to her room, her own old room, for she particularly wished not to be moved from it.

The evening had long closed in; poor Bustle had been shut up in Charlotte's room, and the three sat together round the fire, unable to guess how they should meet her, and thinking how they had lately been looking forward to greeting their bride, as they used proudly to call her. Charles dwelt on that talk on the green, and his 'when shall we three meet again?' and spoke not a word; Laura tried to read; and Charlotte heard false alarms of wheels; but all were so still, that when the wheels really came, they were heard all down the turnpike road, and along the lane, before they sounded on the gravel drive.

Laura and Charlotte ran into the hall, Charles reached his crutches, but his hands shook so much that he could not adjust them, and was obliged to sit down, rising the next minute as the black figures entered together. Amy's sweet face was pressed to his, but neither spoke. That agitated 'My dear, dear Charlie!' was his mother's, as she threw her arms around him, with redoubled kisses and streaming tears; and there was a trembling tone in his father's 'Well, Charlie boy, how have you got on without us?'

They sat down, Charles with his sister beside him, and holding a hand steadier than his own, but hot and feverish to the touch. He leant forward to look at her face, and, as if in answer, she turned it on him. It was the old face, paler and thinner, and the eyelids had a hard reddened look, from want of sleep: but Charles, like his mother at first, was almost awed by the melancholy serenity of the expression. 'Have you been quite well?' she asked, in a voice which sounded strangely familiar, in its fond, low tones.

'Yes, quite.'

There was a pause, followed by an interchange of question and answer between the others, on the journey, and on various little home circumstances. Presently Mrs. Edmonstone said Amy had better come up-stairs.

'I have not seen Bustle,' said Amy, looking at Charlotte.

'He is in my room,' faltered Charlotte.

'I should like to see him.'

Charlotte hastened away, glad to wipe her tears when outside the door. Poor Bustle had been watching for his master ever since his departure, and hearing the sounds of arrival, was wild to escape from his prison. He rushed out the moment the door was open, and was scratching to be let into the drawing-room before Charlotte could come up with him. He dashed in, laid his head on Amabel's knee, and wagged his tail for welcome; gave the same greeting to Mr. and Mrs. Edmonstone, but only for a moment, for he ran restlessly seeking round the room, came to the door, and by his wistful looks made Charlotte let him out. She followed him, and dropping on her knees as soon as she was outside, pressed her forehead to his glossy black head, whispered that it was of no use, he would never come back. The dog burst from her, and the next moment was smelling and wagging his tail at a portmanteau, which he knew as well as she did, and she could hardly refrain from a great outburst of sobbing as she thought what joy its arrival had hitherto been.

Suddenly Bustle bounded away, and as Charlotte stood trying to compose herself enough to return to the drawing-room, she heard the poor fellow whining to be let in at Guy's bed-room door. At the same time the drawing-room door opened, and anxious that Amy should neither see nor hear him, she ran after him, admitted him, and shut herself in with him in the dark, where, with her hands in his long silky curls, and sitting on the ground, she sobbed over him as long as he would submit to her caresses.

Amabel meantime returned to her room, and looked round on its well-known aspect with a sad smile, as she thought of the prayer with which she had quitted it on her bridal day, and did not feel as if it had been unanswered; for surely the hand of a Father had been with her to support her through her great affliction.

Though she said she was very well, her mother made her go to bed at once, and Laura attended on her with a sort of frightened, respectful tenderness, hardly able to bear her looks of gratitude. The first time the two sisters were alone, Amabel said, 'Philip is much better.'

Laura, who was settling some things on the table, started back and coloured, then, unable to resist the desire of hearing of him, looked earnestly at her sister.

'He is gone to Corfu,' continued Amabel. 'He only kept Arnaud three days after we were gone, and Arnaud overtook us at Geneva, saying his strength had improved wonderfully. Will you give me my basket? I should like to read you a piece of a note he sent me.'

Laura brought it, and Amabel, holding her hand, looked up at her face, which she vainly tried to keep in order. 'Dearest, I have been very sorry for you, and so has Guy.'

'Amy!' and Laura found herself giving way to her tears, in spite of all her previous exhortations to Charlotte, about self-control; 'my own, own sister!' To have Amy at home was an unspeakable comfort.

'Papa and mamma were both as kind as possible to Philip,' continued Amabel; 'but they could not bear to enter on that. So I told him you had told all, and he was very glad.'

'He was not displeased at my betraying him?' exclaimed Laura. 'Oh, no! he was glad; he said it was a great relief, for he was very anxious about you, Laura. He has been so kind to me,' said Amabel, so earnestly, that Laura received another comfort, that of knowing that her sister's indignation against him had all passed by. 'Now I will read you what he says. You see his writing is quite itself again.'

But Laura observed that Amabel only held towards her the 'Lady Morville' on the outside, keeping the note to herself, and reading, 'I have continued to gain strength since you went; so that there is no further need of detaining Arnaud. I have twice been out of doors, and am convinced that I am equal to the journey; indeed, it is hardly possible for me to endure remaining here any longer.' She read no more, but folded it up, saying, 'I had rather no one saw the rest. He makes himself so unhappy about that unfortunate going to Sondrio, that he says what is only painful to hear. I am glad he is able to join his regiment, for a change will be the best thing for him.'

She laid her head on the pillow as if she had done with the subject, and Laura did not venture to pursue it, but went down to hear her mother's account of her.

Mrs. Edmonstone was feeling it a great comfort to have her son to talk to again, and availed herself of it to tell him of Philip, while Laura was absent, and then to return to speak of Amy on Laura's re-entrance. She said, all through the journey, Amy had been as passive and tranquil as possible, chiefly leaning back in the carriage in silence, excepting that when they finally left the view of the snowy mountains, she gazed after them as long as the least faint cloud-like summit was visible. Still she could not sleep, except that now and then she dozed a little in the carriage, but at night she heard every hour strike in turn, and lay awake through all, nor had she shed one tear since her mother had joined her. Mrs. Edmonstone's anxiety was very great, for she said she knew Amy must pay for that unnatural calmness, and the longer it was before it broke down, the worse it would be for her. However, she was at home, that was one thing to be thankful for, and happen what might, it could not be as distressing as if it had been abroad.

Another night of 'calm unrest,' and Amabel rose in the morning, at her usual hour, to put on the garments of her widowhood, where she had last stood as a bride. Charles was actually startled by her entering the dressing-room, just as she used to do, before breakfast, to read with him, and her voice was as steady as ever. She breakfasted with the family, and came up afterwards with Laura, to unpack her dressing-case, and take out the little treasures that she and her husband had enjoyed buying in the continental towns, as presents for the home party.

All this, for which she had previously prepared herself, she underwent as quietly as possible; but something unexpected came on her. Charlotte, trying to pet and comfort her in every possible way, brought in all the best flowers still lingering in the garden, and among them a last blossom of the Noisette rose, the same of which Guy had been twisting a spray, while he first told her of his love.

It was too much. It recalled his perfect health and vigour, his light activity, and enjoyment of life, and something came on her of the sensation we feel for an insect, one moment full of joyous vitality, the next, crushed and still. She had hitherto thought of his feverish thirst and fainting weariness being at rest, and felt the relief, or else followed his spirit to its repose, and rejoiced; but now the whole scene brought back what he once was; his youthful, agile frame, his eyes dancing in light, his bounding step, his gay whistle, the strong hand that had upheld her on the precipice, the sure foot that had carried aid to the drowning sailors, the arm that was to have been her stay for life, all came on her in contrast with– death! The thought swept over her, carrying away every other, and she burst into tears.

The tears would have their course; she could not restrain them when once they began, and her struggles to check them only brought an increase of them. Her sobs grew so violent that Laura, much alarmed, made a sign to Charlotte to fetch her mother; and Mrs. Edmonstone, coming in haste, found it was indeed the beginning of a frightful hysterical attack. The bodily frame had been overwrought to obey the mental firmness and composure, and now nature asserted her rights; the hysterics returned again and again, and when it seemed as if exhaustion had at length produced quiet, the opening of a door, or a sound in the distance, would renew all again.

It was not till night had closed in that Mrs. Edmonstone was at all satisfied about her, and had at length the comfort of seeing her fall into a sound deep sleep; such an unbroken dreamless sleep as had scarcely visited her since she first went to Recoara. Even this sleep did not restore her; she became very unwell, and both Dr. Mayerne and her mother insisted on her avoiding the least exertion or agitation. She was quite submissive, only begging earnestly to be allowed to see Mr. Ross, saying she knew it would do her good rather than harm, and promising to let him leave her the instant she found it too much for her; and though Mrs. Edmonstone was reluctant and afraid, they agreed that as she was so reasonable and docile, she ought to be allowed to judge for herself.

She begged that he might come after church on All Saints' day. He came, and after his first greeting of peace, Mrs. Edmonstone signed to him to read at once, instead of speaking to her. The beautiful lesson for the day overcame Mrs. Edmonstone so much that she was obliged to go out of Amabel's sight, but as the words were read, Amy's face recovered once more the serenity that had been swept away by the sight of the flowers. Peace had returned, and when the calm every-day words of the service were over, she held out her hand to Mr. Ross, and said, 'Thank you, that was very nice. Now talk to me.'

It was a difficult request, but Mr. Ross understood her, and talked to her as she sought, in a gentle, deep, high strain of hope and faith, very calm and soothing, and with a fatherly kindness that was very pleasant from him who had baptized her, taught her, and whom she had last seen blessing her and her husband. It ended by her looking up to him when it was time for him to go, and saying, 'Thank you. You will come again when you have time, I hope. My love to dear Mary, I should like to see her soon, but I knew you would do me more good than anybody, and know better how it feels.'

Mr. Ross knew she meant that he must better understand her loss, because he was a widower, and was greatly touched, though he only answered by a blessing, a farewell, and a promise to come very soon to see her again.

Amabel was right, the peace which he had recalled, and the power of resignation that had returned, had a better effect on her than all her mother's precautions; she began to improve, and in a few days more was able to leave her bed, and lie on the sofa in the dressing-room, though she was still so weak and languid that this was as much as she could attempt. Any exertion was to be carefully guarded against, and her tears now flowed so easily, that she was obliged to keep a check on them lest they might again overpower her. Mr. Ross came again and again, and she was able to tell him much of the grounds for her great happiness in Guy, hear how entirely he had understood him, and be assured that she had done right, and not taken an undue responsibility on herself by the argument she had used to summon Philip, that last evening. She had begun to make herself uneasy about this; for she said she believed she was thinking of nothing but Guy, and had acted on impulse; and she was very glad Mr. Ross did not think it wrong, while

Mr. Ross meanwhile was thinking how fears and repentance mingle with the purest sweetest, holiest deeds.

She was able now to take pleasure in seeing Mary Ross; she wrote to Philip at Corfu, and sent for Markham to begin to settle the executor's business. Poor Markham! the Edmonstones thought he looked ten years older when he arrived, and after his inquiry for Lady Morville, his grunt almost amounted to a sob. The first thing he did was to give Mrs. Edmonstone a note, and a little box sent from Mrs. Ashford. The note was to say that Mrs. Ashford had intended for her wedding present, a little cross made out of part of the wood of the wreck, which she now thought it beat to send to Mrs. Edmonstone, that she might judge whether Lady Morville would like to see it.

Mrs. Edmonstone's judgment was to carry it at once to Amabel, and she was right, for the pleasure she took in it was indescribable. She fondled it, set it up by her on her little table, made Charlotte put it in different places that she might see what point of view suited it best, had it given back to her, held it in her hands caressingly, and said she must write at once to Mrs. Ashford to thank her for understanding her so well. There was scarcely one of the mourners to be pitied more than Markham, for the love he had set on Sir Guy had been intense, compounded of feudal affection, devoted admiration, and paternal care– and that he, the very flower of the whole race, should thus have been cut down in the full blossom of his youth and hopes, was almost more than the old man could bear or understand. It was a great sorrow, too, that he should be buried so far away from his forefathers; and the hearing it was by his own desire, did not satisfy him, he sighed over it still, and seemed to derive a shade of comfort only when he was told there was to be a tablet in Redclyffe church to the memory of Guy, sixth baronet.

In the evening Markham became very confidential with Charles; telling him about the grievous mourning and lamentation at Redclyffe, when the bells rung a knell instead of greeting the young master and his bride, and how there was scarcely one in the parish that did not feel as if they had lost a son or a brother. He also told more and more of Sir Guy's excellence, and talked of fears of his own, especially last Christmas; that the boy was too unlike other people, too good to live; and lastly, he indulged in a little abuse of Captain Morville, which did Charles's heart good, at the same time as it amused him to think how Markham would recollect it, when he came to hear of Laura's engagement.

In the course of the next day, Markham had his conference with Lady Morville in the dressing-room, and brought her two or three precious parcels, which he would not, for the world, have given into any other hands. He could hardly bear to look at her in her widow's cap, and behaved to her with a manner varying between his deference and respect to the Lady of

Redclyffe, and his fatherly fondness for the wife of 'his boy.' As to her legal powers, he would have thought them foolishly bestowed, if they had been conferred by any one save his own Sir Guy, and he began by not much liking to act with her; but he found her so clear-headed, that he was much surprised to find a woman could have so much good sense, and began to look forward with some satisfaction to being her prime minister. They understood each other very well; Amabel's good sense and way of attending to the one matter in hand, kept her from puzzling and alarming herself by thinking she had more to do than she could ever understand or accomplish; she knew it was Guy's work, and a charge he had given her,– a great proof of his confidence,– and she did all that was required of her very well, so that matters were put in train to be completed when she should be of age, in the course of the next January.

When Markham left her she was glad to be alone, and to open her parcels. There was nothing here to make her hysterical, for she was going to contemplate the living soul, and felt almost, as if it was again being alone with her husband. There were his most prized and used books, covered with marks and written notes; there was Laura's drawing of Sintram, which had lived with him in his rooms at Oxford; there was a roll of music, and there was his desk. The first thing when she opened it was a rough piece of spar, wrapped in paper, on which was written, 'M. A. D., Sept. 18.' She remembered what he had told her of little Marianne's gift. The next thing made her heart thrill, for it was a slip of pencilling in her own writing, 'Little things, on little wings, bear little souls to heaven.'

Her own letters tied up together, those few that she had written in the short time they were separated just before their marriage! Could that be only six months ago? A great bundle of Charles's and of Mrs. Edmonstone's; those she might like to read another time, but not now. Many other papers letters signed S. B. Dixon, which she threw aside, notes of lectures, and memoranda, only precious for the handwriting; but when she came to the lower division; she found it full of verses, almost all the poetry he had ever written.

There were the classical translations that used to make him inaccurate, a scrap of a very boyish epic about King Arthur, beginning with a storm at Tintagel, sundry half ballads, the verses he was suspected of, and never would show, that first summer at Hollywell, and a very touching vision of his fair young mother. Except a translation or two, some words written to suit their favourite airs (a thing that used to seem to come as easily to him as singing to a bird), and a few lively mock heroic accounts of walks or parties, which had all been public property, there was no more that she could believe to have been composed till last year, for he was more disposed to versify in sorrow than in joy. There were a good many written during his loneliness, for his reflections had a tendency to flow into verse, and pouring them out thus had been a great solace. The lines were often imperfect and irregular, but not one that was not deep, pure, and genuine, and here and there scattered with passages of exquisite beauty and harmony, and full of power and grace. No one could have looked at them without owning in them the marks of a thorough poet, but this was not what the wife was seeking, and when she perceived it, though it made her face beam with a sort of satisfied pride, it was a secondary thing. She was studying not his intellect, but his soul; she did not care whether he would have been a poet, what she looked for was the record of the sufferings and struggles of the sad six months when his character was established, strengthened, and settled.

She found it. There was much to which she alone had the clue, too deep, and too obscurely hinted, to be understood at a glance. She met with such evidence of suffering as made her shudder and weep, tokens of the dark thoughts that had gathered round him, of the manful spirit of penitence and patience that had been his stay, and of the gleams that lighted his darkest hours, and showed he had never been quite forsaken. Now and then came a reference which brought home what he had told her; how the thought of his Verena had cheered him when he dared not hope she would be restored. Best of all were the lines written when the radiance of Christmas was, once for all, dispersing the gloom, and the vision opening on him, which he was now realizing. In reading them, she felt the same marvellous sympathy of subdued wondering joy in the victory of which she had partaken as she knelt beside his death-bed. These were the last. He had been too happy for poetry, except one or two scraps in Switzerland, and these had been hers from the time she had detected them.

No wonder Amabel almost lived on those papers! It would not be too much to say she was very happy in her own way when alone with them; the desk on a chair by her sofa. They were too sacred for any one else; she did not for many weeks show one even to her mother; but to her they were like a renewal of his presence, soothing the craving after him that had been growing on her ever since the first few days when his sustaining power had not passed away. As she sorted them, and made out their dates, finding fresh stores of meaning at each fresh perusal she learnt through them, as well as through her own trial, so patiently borne, to enter into his character even more fully than when he was in her sight. Mrs. Edmonstone, who had at first been inclined to dread her constant dwelling on them, soon perceived that they were her great aids through this sad winter.

She had much pleasure in receiving the portrait, which was sent her by Mr. Shene. It was a day or two before she could resolve to look at it, or feel that she could do so calmly. It was an unfinished sketch, taken more with a view to the future picture than to the likeness; but Guy's was a face to be better represented by being somewhat idealized, than by copying merely the material form of the features. An ordinary artist might have made him like a Morville, but Mr. Shene had shown all that art could convey of his individual self, with almost one of his unearthly looks. The beautiful eyes, with somewhat of their peculiar lightsomeness, the flexible look of the lip, the upward pose of the head, the set of that lock of hair that used to wave in the wind, the animated position, 'just ready for a start,' as Charles used to call it, were recalled as far as was in the power of chalk and crayon, but so as to remind Amabel of him more as one belonging to heaven than to earth. The picture used to be on her mantel-shelf all night, the shipwreck cross before it, and Sintram and Redclyffe on each side; and she brought it into the dressing-room with her in the morning, setting it up opposite to the sofa, before settling herself.

Her days were much alike. She felt far from well, or capable of exertion, and was glad it was thought right to keep her entirely upstairs; she only wished to spare her mother anxiety, by being submissive to her care, in case these cares should be the last for her. She did not dwell on the future, nor ask herself whether she looked for life or death. Guy had bidden her not desire the last, and she believed she did not form a wish; but there was repose to her in the belief that she ought not to conceal from herself that there was more than ordinary risk, and that it was right to complete all her affairs in this world, and she was silent when her mother tried to interest her in prospects that might cheer her; as if afraid to fasten on them, and finding more peace in entire submission, than in feeding herself on hope that must be coupled with fear.

Christmas-day was not allowed to pass without being a festival for her, in her quiet room, where she lay, full of musings on his lonely Christmas night last year, his verses folded among her precious books, and the real joy of the season more within her grasp than in the turmoil of last year. She was not afraid now to let herself fancy his voice in the Angel's Song, and the rainbow was shining on her cloud.

CHAPTER 38

The coldness from my heart is gone,
But still the weight is there,
And thoughts which I abhor will come
To tempt me to despair.
– SOUTHEY

Amabel's one anxiety was for Philip. For a long time nothing was heard of him at Hollywell, and she began to fear that he might have been less fit to take care of himself than he had persuaded her to believe. When at length tidings reached them, it was through the De Courcys. 'Poor Morville,' wrote Maurice, 'had been carried ashore at Corfu, in the stupor of a second attack of fever. He had been in extreme danger for some time, and though now on the mend, was still unable to give any account of himself.'

In effect, it was a relapse of the former disease, chiefly affecting the brain, and his impatience to leave Recoara, and free himself from Arnaud, had been a symptom of its approach, though it fortunately did not absolutely overpower him till after he had embarked for Corfu, and was in the way to be tended with the greatest solicitude. Long after the fever was subdued, and his strength returning, his mind was astray, and even when torturing delusions ceased, and he resumed the perception of surrounding objects, memory and reflection wavered in dizzy confusion, more distressing than either his bodily weakness, or the perpetual pain in his head, which no remedy could relieve.

The first date to which he could afterwards recur, though for more than a week he had apparently been fully himself, was a time when he was sitting in an easy-chair by the window, obliged to avert his heavy eyes from the dazzling waters of the Corcyran bay, where Ulysses' transformed ship gleamed in the sunshine, and the rich purple hills of Albania sloped upwards in the distance. James Thorndale was, as usual, with him, and was explaining that there had been a consultation between the doctor and the colonel, and they had decided that as there was not much chance of restoring his health in that climate in the spring.

'Spring!' he interrupted, with surprise and eagerness, 'Is it spring?'

'Hardly– except that there is no winter here. This is the 8th of January.'

He let his head fall on his hand again, and listened with indifference when told he was to be sent to England at once, under the care of his servant, Bolton, and Mr. Thorndale himself, who was resolved to see him safe in his sister's hands. He made no objection; he had become used to be passive, and one place was much the same to him as another; so he merely assented, without a question about the arrangements. Presently, however, he looked up, and inquired for his letters. Though he had done so before, the request had always been evaded, until now he spoke in a manner which decided his friend on giving him all except one with broad black edges, and Broadstone post-mark; the effect of which, it was thought, might be very injurious to his shattered nerves and spirits.

However, he turned over the other letters without interest, just glancing languidly through them, looked disappointed, and exclaimed—

'None from Hollywell! Has nothing been heard from them? Thorndale, I insist on knowing whether De Courcy has heard anything of Lady Morville.'

'He has heard of her arrival in England.'

'My sister mentions that— more than two months ago— I can hardly believe she has not written, if she was able. She promised, yet how can I expect— ' then interrupting himself, he added, authoritatively, 'Thorndale, is there no letter for me? I see there is. Let me have it.'

His friend could not but comply, and had no reason to regret having done so; for after reading it twice, though he sighed deeply, and the tears were in his eyes, he was more calm and less oppressed than he had been at any time since his arrival in Corfu. He was unable to write, but Colonel Deane had undertaken to write to Mrs. Henley to announce his coming; and as the cause of his silence must be known at Hollywell, he resolved to let Amabel's letter wait for a reply till his arrival in England.

It was on a chilly day in February that Mrs. Henley drove to the station to meet her brother, looking forward with a sister's satisfaction to nursing his recovery, and feeling (for she had a heart, after all) as if it was a renewal of the days, which she regarded with a tenderness mixed with contempt, when all was confidence between the brother and sister, the days of nonsense and romance. She hoped that now poor Philip, who had acted hastily on his romance, and ruined his own prospects for her sake in his boyish days, had a chance of having it all made up to him, and reigning at Redclyffe according to her darling wish.

As she anxiously watched the arrival of the train, she recognized Mr. Thorndale, whom she had known in his school-days as Philip's protege— but could that be her brother? It was his height, indeed; but his slow weary step as he crossed the platform, and left the care of his baggage to others, was so unlike his prompt, independent air, that she could hardly believe it to be himself, till, with his friend, he actually advanced to the carriage, and then she saw far deeper traces of illness than she was prepared for. A confusion of words took place; greetings on one hand, and partings on the other, for James Thorndale was going on by the train, and made only a few minutes' halt in which to assure Mrs. Henley that though the landing and the journey had knocked up his patient to-day, he was much better since leaving Corfu, and to beg Philip to write as soon as possible. The bell rang, he rushed back, and was whirled away.

'Then you are better,' said Mrs. Henley, anxiously surveying her brother. 'You are sadly altered! You must let us take good care of you.'

'Thank you! I knew you would be ready to receive me, though I fear I am not very good company.'

'Say no more, my dearest brother. You know both Dr. Henley and myself have made it our first object that our house should be your home.'

'Thank you.'

'This salubrious air must benefit you,' she added. 'How thin you are! Are you very much fatigued?'

'Rather,' said Philip, who was leaning back wearily; but the next moment he exclaimed, 'What do you hear from Hollywell?'

'There is no news yet.'

'Do you know how she is? When did you hear of her?'

'About a week ago; when she wrote to inquire for you.'

'She did? What did she say of herself?'

'Nothing particular, poor little thing; I believe she is always on the sofa. My aunt would like nothing so well as making a great fuss about her.'

'Have you any objection to show me her letter?' said Philip, unable to bear hearing Amabel thus spoken of, yet desirous to learn all he could respecting her.

'I have not preserved it,' was the answer. 'My correspondence is so extensive that there would be no limit to the accumulation if I did not destroy the trivial letters.'

There was a sudden flush on Philip's pale face that caused his sister to pause in her measured, self-satisfied speech, and ask if he was in pain.

'No,' he replied, shortly, and Margaret pondered on his strange manner, little guessing what profanation her mention of Amabel's letter had seemed to him, or how it jarred on him to hear this exaggerated likeness of his own self-complacent speeches.

She was much shocked and grieved to see him so much more unwell than she had expected. He was unfit for anything but to go to bed on his arrival. Dr. Henley said the system had received a severe shock, and it would be long before the effects would be shaken off; but that there was no fear but his health would be completely restored if he would give himself entire rest.

There was no danger that Margaret would not lavish care enough on her brother. She waited on him in his room all the next day, bringing him everything he could want, and trying to make him come down-stairs, for she thought sitting alone there very bad for his spirits; but he said he had a letter to write, and very curious she was to know why he was so long doing it, and why he did not tell her to whom it was addressed. However, she saw when it was put into the post-bag, that it was for Lady Morville.

At last, too late to see any of the visitors who had called to inquire, when the evening had long closed in, she had the satisfaction of seeing Philip enter the drawing-room, and settling him in the most comfortable of her easy-chairs on one side of the fire to wait till the Doctor returned for dinner. The whole apartment was most luxurious, spacious, and richly furnished; the fire, in its brilliant steel setting, glancing on all around, and illuminating her own stately presence, and rich glace silk, as she sat opposite her brother cutting open the leaves of one of the books of the club over which she presided. She felt that this was something like attaining one of the objects for which she used to say and think she married,– namely, to be able to receive her brother in a comfortable home. If only he would but look more like himself.

'Do you like a cushion for your head, Philip? Is it better?'

'Better since morning, thank you.'

'Did those headaches come on before your second illness?'

'I can't distinctly remember.'

'Ah! I cannot think how the Edmonstones could leave you. I shall always blame them for that relapse.'

'It had nothing to do with it. Their remaining was impossible.'

'On Amabel's account? No, poor thing, I don't blame her, for she must have been quite helpless; but it was exactly like my aunt, to have but one idea at a time. Charles used to be the idol, and now it is Amy, I suppose.'

'If anything could have made it more intolerable for me, it would have been detaining them there for my sake, at such a time.'

'Ah! I felt a great deal for you. You must have been very sorry for that poor little Amy. She was very kind in writing while you were ill. How did she contrive, poor child? I suppose you took all the head work for her?'

'I? I was nothing but a burden.'

'Were you still so very ill?' said Margaret, tenderly. 'I am sure you must have been neglected.'

'Would that I had!' muttered Philip, so low that she did not catch the words. Then aloud,– 'No care could have been greater than was taken for me. It was as if no one had been ill but myself, and the whole thought of every one had been for me.'

'Then Amabel managed well, poor thing! We do sometimes see those weak soft characters– '

'Sister!' he interrupted.'

'Have not you told me so yourself?'

'I was a fool, or worse,' said he, in a tone of suffering. 'No words can describe what she proved herself.'

'Self-possessed? energetic?' asked Mrs. Henley, with whom those were the first of qualities; and as her brother paused from repugnance to speak of Amabel to one so little capable of comprehending her, she proceeded: 'No doubt she did the best she could, but she must have been quite inexperienced. It was a very young thing in the poor youth to make her executrix. I wonder the will was valid; but I suppose you took care of that.'

'I did nothing.'

'Did you see it?'

'My uncle showed it to me.'

'Then you can tell me what I want to hear, for no one has told me anything. I suppose my uncle is to be guardian?'

'No; Lady Morville.'

'You don't mean it? Most lover-like indeed. That poor girl to manage that great property? Everything left to her!' said Mrs. Henley, continuing her catechism in spite of the unwillingness of his replies. 'Were there any legacies? I know of Miss Wellwood's.'

'That to Dixon's daughter, and my own,' he answered.

'Yours? How was it that I never heard of it? What is it?'

'Ten thousand,' said Philip, sadly.

'I am delighted to hear it!' cried Margaret. 'Very proper of Sir Guy– very proper indeed, poor youth. It is well thought of to soften the disappointment.'

Philip started forward. 'Disappointment!' exclaimed he, with horror.

'You need not look as if I wished to commit murder,' said his sister, smiling. 'Have you forgotten that it depends on whether it is a son or daughter?'

His dismay was not lessened. 'Do you mean to say that this is to come on me if the child is a daughter?'

'Ah! you were so young when the entail was made, that you knew nothing of it. Female heirs were expressly excluded. There was some aunt whom old Sir Guy passed over, and settled the property on my father and you, failing his own male heirs.'

'No one would take advantage of such a chance,' said Philip.

'Do not make any rash resolutions, my dear brother, whatever you do,' said Margaret. 'You have still the same fresh romantic generous spirit of self-sacrifice that is generally so soon worn out, but you must not let it allow you– '

'Enough of this,' said Philip, hastily, for every word was a dagger.

'Ah! you are right not to dwell on the uncertainty. I am almost sorry I told you,' said Margaret. 'Tell me about Miss Wellwood's legacy,' she continued, desirous of changing the subject. 'I want to know the truth of it, for every one is talking of it.''How comes the world to know of it?'

'There have been reports ever since his death, and now it has been paid, whatever it is, on Lady Morville's coming of age. Do you know what it is? The last story I was told was, that it was £20,000, to found a convent to pray for his grand– '

'Five thousand for her hospital,' interrupted Philip. 'Sister!' he added; speaking with effort, 'it was for that hospital that he made the request for which we persecuted him.'

'Ah! I thought so, I could have told you so!' cried Margaret, triumphant in her sagacity, but astonished, as her brother started up and stood looking at her, as if he could hardly resolve to give credit to her words.

'You– thought– so,' he repeated slowly.

'I guessed it from the first. He was always with that set, and I thought it a very bad thing for him; but as it was only a guess, it was not worth while to mention it: besides, the cheque seemed full evidence. It was the general course, not the individual action.'

'If you thought so, why not mention it to me? Oh! sister, what would you not have spared me!'

'I might have done so if it had appeared that it might lead to his exculpation, but you were so fully convinced that his whole course confirmed the suspicions, that a mere vague idea was not worth dwelling on. Your general opinion, of him satisfied me.'

'I cannot blame you,' was all his reply, as he sat down again, with his face averted from the light.

And Mrs. Henley was doubtful whether he meant that she had been judicious! She spoke again, unconscious of the agony each word inflicted.

'Poor youth! we were mistaken in those facts, and of course, all is forgiven and forgotten now; but he certainly had a tremendous temper. I shall never forget that exhibition. Perhaps poor Amabel is saved much unhappiness.'

'Once for all,' said Philip, sternly, 'let me never hear you speak of him thus. We were both blind to a greatness of soul and purity of heart that we shall never meet again. Yours was only prejudice; mine I must call by a darker name. Remember, that he and his wife are only to be spoken of with reverence.'

He composed himself to silence; and Margaret, after looking at him for some moments in wonder, began in a sort of exculpatory tone:

'Of course we owe him a great deal of gratitude. It was very kind and proper to come to you when you were ill, and his death must have been a terrible shock. He was a fine young man; amiable, very attractive in manner.'

'No more!' muttered Philip.

'That, you always said of him,' continued she, not hearing, 'but you have no need to reproach yourself. You always acted the part of a true friend, did full justice to his many good qualities, and only sought his real good.'

'Every word you speak is the bitterest satire on me,' said Philip, goaded into rousing himself for a moment. 'Say no more, unless you would drive me distracted!'

Margaret was obliged to be silent, and marvel, while her brother sat motionless, leaning back in his chair, till Dr. Henley came in; and after a few words to him, went on talking to his wife, till dinner was announced. Philip went with them into the dining-room, but had scarcely sat down before he said he could not stay, and returned to the drawing-room sofa. He said he only wanted quiet and darkness, and sent his sister and her husband back to their dinner.

'What has he been doing?' said the Doctor; 'here is his pulse up to a hundred again. How can he have raised it?'

'He only came down an hour ago, and has been sitting still ever since.'

'Talking?'

'Yes; and there, perhaps, I was rather imprudent. I did not know he could so little bear to hear poor Sir Guy's name mentioned; and, besides, he did not know, till I told him, that he had so much chance of Redclyffe. He did not know the entail excluded daughters.'

'Did he not! That accounts for it. I should like to see the man who could hear coolly that he was so near such a property. This suspense is unlucky just now; very much against him. You must turn his thoughts from it as much as possible.'

All the next day, Mrs. Henley wondered why her brother's spirits were so much depressed, resisting every attempt to amuse or cheer them; but, on the third, she thought some light was thrown on the matter. She was at breakfast with the Doctor when the post came in, and there was a black-edged letter for Captain Morville, evidently from Amabel. She took it up at once to his room. He stretched out his hand for it eagerly, but laid it down, and would not open it while she was in the room. The instant she was gone, however, he broke the seal and read:—

'Hollywell, February 20th.

'MY DEAR PHILIP,— Thank you much for writing to me. It was a great comfort to see your writing again, and to hear of your being safe in our own country. We had been very anxious about you, though we did not hear of your illness till the worst was over. I am very glad you are at St. Mildred's, for I am sure Margaret must be very careful of you, and Stylehurst air must be good for you. Every one here is well; Charles growing almost active, and looking better than I ever saw him. I wish I could tell you how nice and quiet a winter it has been; it has been a great blessing to me in every way, so many things have come to me to enjoy. Mr. Ross has come to me every Sunday, and often in the week, and has been so very kind. I think talking to him will be a great pleasure to you when you are here again. You will like to hear that Mr. Shene has sent me the picture, and the pleasure it gives me increases every day. Indeed, I am so well off in every way, that you must not grieve yourself about me, though I thank you very much for what you say. Laura reads to me all the evening from dinner to tea. I am much better than I was in the winter, and am enjoying the soft spring air from the open window, making it seem as if it was much later in the year. 'Good-bye, my dear cousin; may God bless and comfort you. Remember, that after all, it was God's will, not your doing; and therefore, as he said himself, all is as it should be, and so it will surely be.

'Your affectionate cousin,
'AMABEL F. MORVILLE.'

Childishly simple as this letter might be called, with its set of facts without comment, and the very commonplace words of consolation, it spoke volumes to Philip of the spirit in which it was written— resignation, pardon, soothing, and a desire that her farewell, perhaps her last, should carry with it a token of her perfect forgiveness. Everything from Amabel did him good; and he was so perceptibly better, that his sister exclaimed, when she was next alone with Dr. Henley, 'I understand it all, poor fellow; I thought long ago, he had some secret attachment; and now I see it was to Amabel Edmonstone.'

'To Lady Morville?'

'Yes. You know how constantly he was at Hollywell, my aunt so fond of him? I don't suppose Amy knew of it; and, of course, she could not be blamed for accepting such an offer as Sir Guy's; besides, she never had much opinion of her own.'

'How? No bad speculation for him. She must have a handsome jointure; but what are your grounds?'

'Everything. Don't you remember he would not go to the marriage? He mentions her almost like a saint; can't hear her name from any one else— keeps her letter to open alone, is more revived by it than anything else. Ah! depend upon it, it was to avoid her, poor fellow, that he refused to go to Venice with them.'

'Their going to nurse him is not as if Sir Guy suspected it.'

'I don't suppose he did, nor Amy either. No one ever had so much power over himself.'

Philip would not have thanked his sister for her surmise, but it was so far in his favour that it made her avoid the subject, and he was thus spared from hearing much of Amabel or of Redclyffe. It was bad enough without this. Sometimes in nursery tales, a naughty child, under the care of a fairy, is chained to an exaggeration of himself and his own faults, and rendered a slave to this hateful self. The infliction he underwent in his sister's house was somewhat analogous, for Mrs. Henley's whole character, and especially her complacent speeches, were a strong resemblance of his own in the days he most regretted. He had ever since her marriage regarded her as a man looks at a fallen idol, but never had her alteration been so clear to him, as he had not spent much time with her, making her short visits, and passing the chief of each day at Stylehurst. Now, he was almost entirely at her mercy, and her unvarying kindness to him caused her deterioration to pain him all the more; while each self-assertion, or harsh judgment, sounded on his ear like a repetition of his worst and most hateful presumption. She little guessed what she made him endure, for he had resumed his wonted stoicism of demeanour, though the hardened crust that had once grown over his feelings had been roughly torn away, leaving an extreme soreness and tenderness to which an acute pang was given whenever he was reminded, not only of his injuries to Guy, but of the pride and secret envy that had been their root.

At the same time he disappointed her by his continued reserve and depression. The confidence she had forfeited was never to be restored, and she was the last person to know how incapable she was of receiving it, or how low she had sunk in her self-exaltation.

He was soon able to resume the hours of the family, but was still far from well; suffering from languor, pain in the head, want of sleep and appetite; and an evening feverishness. He was unequal to deep reading, and was in no frame for light books; he could not walk far, and his sister's literary coteries, which he had always despised, were at present beyond his powers of endurance. She hoped that society would divert his thoughts and raise his spirits, and arranged her parties with a view to him; but he never could stay long in the room, and Dr. Henley, who, though proud of his wife and her talents, had little pleasure in her learned circle, used to aid and abet his escape.

Thus Philip got through the hours as best he might, idly turning the pages of new club-books, wandering on the hills till he tired himself, sitting down to rest in the damp air, coming home chilled and fatigued, and lying on the sofa with his eyes shut, to avoid conversation, all the evening. Neither strength, energy, nor intellect would, serve him for more; and this, with the load and the stings of a profound repentance, formed his history through the next fortnight.

He used often to stand gazing at the slowly-rising walls of Miss Wellwood's buildings, and the only time he exerted himself in his old way to put down any folly in conversation, was when he silenced some of the nonsense talked about her, and evinced his own entire approval of her proceedings.

CHAPTER 39

Beneath a tapering ash-tree's shade
Three graves are by each other laid.
Around the very place doth brood
A strange and holy quietude.
– BAPTISTERY

Late on the afternoon of the 6th of March, Mary Ross entered by the half-opened front door at Hollywell, just as Charles appeared slowly descending the stairs.

'Well! how is she?' asked Mary eagerly.

'Poor little dear!' he answered, with a sigh; 'she looks very nice and comfortable.'

'What, you have seen her?'

'I am at this moment leaving her room.'

'She is going on well, I hope?'

'Perfectly well. There is one comfort at least,' said Charles, drawing himself down the last step.

'Dear Amy! And the babe– did you see it?'

'Yes; the little creature was lying by her, and she put her hand on it, and gave one of those smiles that are so terribly like his; but I could not have spoken about it for the world. Such fools we be!' concluded Charles, with an attempt at a smile.

'It is healthy?'

'All a babe ought to be, they say, all that could be expected of it, except the not being of the right sort, and if Amy does not mind that, I don't know who should,' and Charles deposited himself on the sofa, heaving a deep sigh, intended to pass for the conclusion of the exertion.

'Then you think she is not disappointed?'

'Certainly not. The first thing she said when she was told it was a girl, was, "I am so glad!" and she does seem very happy with it, poor little thing! In fact, mamma thinks she had so little expected that it would go well with herself, or with it, that now it is all like a surprise.'

There was a silence, first broken by Charles saying, 'You must be content with me– I can't send for anyone. Bustle has taken papa and Charlotte for a walk, and Laura is on guard over Amy, for we have made mamma go and lie down. It was high time, after sitting up two nights, and meaning to sit up a third.'

'Has she really– can she bear it?'

'Yes; I am afraid I have trained her in sitting up, and Amy and all of us know that anxiety hurts her more than fatigue. She would only lie awake worrying herself, instead of sitting peaceably by the fire, holding the baby, or watching Amy, and having a quiet cry when she is asleep. For, after all, it is very sad!' Charles was trying to brave his feelings, but did not succeed very well. 'Yesterday morning I was properly frightened. I came into the dressing-room, and found mamma crying so, that I fully believed it was all wrong, but she was just coming to tell us, and was only overcome by thinking of not having him to call first, and how happy he would have been.'

'And the dear Amy herself!'

'I can't tell. She is a wonderful person for keeping herself composed when she ought. I see she has his picture in full view, but she says not a word, except that mamma saw her to-day, when she thought no one was looking, fondling the little thing, and whispering to it– "Guy's baby!" and "Guy's little messenger!"' Charles gave up the struggle, and fairly cried, but in a moment rallying his usual tone, he went on, half laughing,– 'To be sure, what a morsel of a creature it is! It is awful to see anything so small calling itself a specimen of humanity!'

'It is your first acquaintance with infant humanity, I suppose? Pray, did you ever see a baby?'

'Not to look at. In fact, Mary, I consider it a proof of your being a rational woman that you have not asked me whether it is pretty.'

'I thought you no judge of the article.'

'No, it was not to inspect it that Amy sent for me; though after all it was for a business I would almost as soon undertake, a thing I would not do for any other living creature.'

'Then I know what it is. To write some kind message to Captain Morville. Just like the dear Amy!'

'Just like her, and like no one else, except– Of course my father wrote him an official communication yesterday, very short; but the fact must have made it sweet enough, savage as we all were towards him, as there was no one else to be savage to, unless it might be poor Miss Morville, who is the chief loser by being of the feminine gender,' said Charles, again braving what he was pleased to call sentimentality. 'Well, by and by, my lady wants to know if any one has written to "poor Philip," as she will call him, and, by no means contented by hearing papa had, she sends to ask me to come to her when I came in from wheeling in the garden; and receives me with a request that I would write and tell him how well she is, and how glad, and so on. There's a piece of work for me!'

'Luckily you are not quite so savage as you pretend, either to him, or your poor little niece.'

'Whew! I should not care whether she was niece or nephew but for him; at least not much, as long as she comforted Amy; but to see him at Redclyffe, and be obliged to make much of him at the same time, is more than I can very well bear; though I may as well swallow it as best I can, for she will have me do it, as well as on Laura's account. Amy believes, you know, that he will think the inheritance a great misfortune; but that is only a proof that she is more amiable than any one else.'

'I should think he would not rejoice.'

'Not exactly; but I have no fear that he will not console himself by thinking of the good he will do with it. I have no doubt that he was thoroughly cut up, and I could even go the length of believing that distress of mind helped to bring on the relapse, but it is some time ago. And as to his breaking his heart after the first ten minutes at finding himself what he has all his life desired to be, in a situation where the full influence of his talents may be felt,' said Charles, with a shade of imitation of his measured tones, 'why that, no one but silly little Amy would ever dream of.'

'Well, I dare say you will grow merciful as you write.'

'No, that is not the way to let my indignation ooze out at my fingers' ends. I shall begin by writing to condole with Markham. Poor man! what a state he must be in; all the more pitiable because he evidently had entirely forgotten that there could ever be a creature of the less worthy gender born to the house of Morville; so it will take him quite by surprise. What will he do, and how will he ever forgive Mrs. Ashford, who, I see in the paper, has a son whom nobody wants, as if for the express purpose of insulting Markham's feelings! Well-a-day! I should have liked to have had the sound of Sir Guy Morville still in my ears, and yet I don't know that I could have endured its being applied to a little senseless baby! And, after all, we are the gainers; for it would have been a forlorn thing to have seen Amy go off to reign queen-mother at Redclyffe,– and most notably well would she have reigned, with that clear little head. I vow 'tis a talent thrown away! However, I can't grumble. She is much happier without greatness thrust on her, and for my own part, I have my home-sister all to myself, with no rival but that small woman– and how she will pet her!'

'And how you will! What a spoiling uncle you will be! But now, having heard you reason yourself into philosophy, I'll leave you to write. We were so anxious, that I could not help coming. I am so glad that little one thrives! I should like to leave my love for Amy, if you'll remember it.'

'The rarity of such a message from you may enable me. I was lying here alone, and received the collected love of five Harpers to convey up-stairs, all which I forgot; though in its transit by Arnaud and his French, it had become "that they made their friendships to my lady and Mrs. Edmonstone."'

Charles had not talked so like himself for months; and Mary felt that Amabel's child, if she had disappointed some expectations, had come like a spring blossom, to cheer Hollywell, after its long winter of sorrow and anxiety. She seemed to have already been received as a messenger to comfort them for the loss, greatest of all to her, poor child, though she would never know how great. Next Mary wondered what kind of letter Charles would indite, and guessed it would be all the kinder for the outpouring he had made to her, the only person with whom he ventured to indulge in a comfortable abuse of Philip, since his good sense taught him that, ending as affairs must, it was the only wise way to make the best of it, with father, mother, and Charlotte, all quite sufficiently disposed to regard Philip with aversion without his help.

Philip was at breakfast with the Henleys, on the following morning, a Sunday,– or rather, sitting at the breakfast-table, when the letters were brought in. Mrs. Henley, pretending to be occupied with her own, had an eager, watchful eye on her brother, as one was placed before him. She knew Mr. Edmonstone's writing, but was restrained from exclaiming by her involuntary deference for her brother. He flushed deep red one moment, then turned deadly pale, his hand, when first he raised it, trembled, but then became firm, as if controlled by the force of his resolution. He broke the black seal, drew out the letter, paused another instant, unfolded it, glanced at it, pushed his chair from the table, and hastened to me door.

'Tell me, tell me, Philip, what is it?' she exclaimed, rising to follow him.

He turned round, threw the letter on the table, and with a sign that forbade her to come with him, left the room.

'Poor fellow! how he feels it! That poor young creature!' said she, catching up the letter for explanation.

'Ha! No! Listen to this, Dr. Henley. Why, he must have read it wrong!'

'Hollywell, March 5th.

'DEAR PHILIP,– I have to announce to you that Lady Morville was safely confined this morning with a daughter. I shall be ready to send all the papers and accounts of the Redclyffe estate to any place you may appoint as soon as she is sufficiently recovered to transact business. Both she and the infant are as well as can be expected.

– Yours sincerely,

'C. EDMONSTONE.'

'A daughter!' cried Dr. Henley. 'Well, my dear, I congratulate you! It is as fine a property as any in the kingdom. We shall see him pick up strength now.'

'I must go and find him. He surely has mistaken!' said Margaret, hastening in search of him; but he was not to be found, and she saw him no more till she found him in the seat at church.

She hardly waited to be in the churchyard, after the service, before she said, 'Surely you mistook the letter!'

'No, I did not.'

'You saw that she is doing well, and it is a girl.'

'I– '

'And will you not let me congratulate you?'

She was interrupted by some acquaintance; but when she looked round he was nowhere to be seen, and she was obliged to be content with telling every one the news. One or two of her many tame gentlemen came home with her to luncheon, and she had the satisfaction of dilating on the grandeur of Redclyffe. Her brother was not in the drawing-room, but answered when she knocked at his door.

'Luncheon is ready. Will you come down?'

'Is any one there?'

'Mr. Brown and Walter Maitland. Shall I send you anything, or do you like to come down?'

'I'll come, thank you,' said he, thus secured from a tete-a-tete.

'Had you better come? Is not your head too bad?'

'It will not be better for staying here; I'll come.'

She went down, telling her visitors that, since his illness, her brother always suffered so much from excitement that he was too unwell to have derived much pleasure from the tidings: and when he appeared his air corresponded with her account, for his looks were of the gravest and sternest. He received the congratulations of the gentlemen without the shadow of a smile, and made them think him the haughtiest and most dignified landed proprietor in England.

Mrs. Henley advised strongly against his going to church, but without effect, and losing him in the crowd coming out, saw him no more till just before dinner-time. He had steeled himself to endure all that she and the Doctor could inflict on him that evening, and he had a hope of persuading Amabel that it would be only doing justice to her child to let him restore her father's inheritance, which had come to him through circumstances that could not have been foreseen. He was determined to do nothing like an act of possession of Redclyffe till he had implored her to accept the offer; and it was a great relief thus to keep it in doubt a little longer, and not absolutely feel himself profiting by Guy's death and sitting in his seat. Not a word, however, must be said to let his sister guess at his resolution, and he must let her torture him in the meantime. He was vexed at having been startled into betraying his suffering, and was humiliated at the thought of the change from that iron imperturbability, compounded of strength, pride, and coldness in which he had once gloried.

Dr. Henley met him with a shake of the hand, and hearty exclamation:–

'I congratulate you, Sir Philip Morville.'

'No; that is spared me,' was his answer.

'Hem! The baronetcy?'

'Yes,' said Margaret, 'I thought you knew that only goes to the direct heir of old Sir Hugh. But you must drop the "captain" at least. You will sell out at once?'

He patiently endured the conversation on the extent and beauty of Redclyffe, wearing all the time a stern, resolute aspect, that his sister knew to betoken great unhappiness. She earnestly wished to understand him, but at last, seeing how much her conversation increased his headache, she desisted, and left him to all the repose his thoughts could give him. He was very much concerned at the tone of the note from his uncle, as if it was intended to show that all connection with the family was to be broken off. He supposed it had been concerted with some one; with Charles, most likely,– Charles, who had judged him too truly, and with his attachment to Guy, and aversion to himself, was doubtless strengthening his father's displeasure, all the more for this hateful wealth. And Laura? What did she feel?

Monday morning brought another letter. At first, he was struck with the dread of evil tidings of Amabel or her babe, especially when he recognized Charles's straggling handwriting; and, resolved not to be again betrayed, he carried it up to read in his own room before his sister had noticed it. He could hardly resolve to open it, for surely Charles would not write to him without necessity; and what, save sorrow, could cause that necessity? He saw that his wretchedness might be even more complete! At length he read it, and could hardly believe his own eyes as he saw cheering words, in a friendly style of interest and kindliness such as he would never have expected from Charles, more especially now.

'Hollywell, March 6th.

'MY DEAR PHILIP,– I believe my father wrote to you in haste yesterday, but I am sure you will be anxious for further accounts, and when there is good news there is satisfaction in conveying it. I know you will be glad to hear our affairs are very prosperous; and Amy, whom I have just been visiting, is said by the authorities to be going on as well as possible. She begs me to tell you of her welfare, and to assure you that she is particularly pleased to have a daughter; or, perhaps, it will be more satisfactory to have her own words. "You must tell him how well I am, Charlie, and how very glad. And tell him that he must not vex himself about her being a girl, for that is my great pleasure; and I do believe, the very thing I should have chosen if I had set to work to wish." You know Amy never said a word but in all sincerity, so you must trust her, and I add my testimony that she is in placid spirits, and may well be glad to escape the cares of Redclyffe. My father says he desired Markham to write to you on the business matters. I hope the sea-breezes may do you good. All the party here are well; but I see little of them now, all the interest of the house is upstairs.

– Your affectionate,

'C. M, EDMONSTONE.

P. S. The baby is very small, but so plump and healthy, that no one attempts to be uneasy about her.'

Never did letter come in better time to raise a desponding heart. Of Amabel's forgiveness he was already certain; but that she should have made Charles his friend was a wonder beyond all others. It gave him more hope for the future than he had yet been able to entertain, and showed him that the former note was no studied renunciation of him, but only an ebullition of Mr. Edmonstone's disappointment.

It gave him spirit enough to undertake what he had long been meditating, but without energy to set about it– an expedition to Stylehurst. Hitherto it had been his first walk on coming to St. Mildred's, but now the distance across the moor was far beyond his powers; and even that length of ride was a great enterprise. It was much further by the carriage road, and his sister never liked going there. He had never failed to visit his old home till last year, and he felt almost glad that he had not carried his thoughts, at that time, to his father's grave. It was strange that, with so many more important burdens on his mind, it had been this apparent trivial omission, this slight to Stylehurst, that, in both his illnesses, had been the most frequently recurring idea that had tormented him in his delirium. So deeply, securely fixed is the love of the home of childhood in men of his mould, in whom it is perhaps the most deeply rooted of all affections.

Without telling his sister his intention, he hired a horse, and pursued the familiar moorland tracks. He passed South Moor Farm; it gave him too great a pang to look at it; he rode on across the hills where he used to walk with his sisters, and looked down into narrow valleys where he had often wandered with his fishing-rod, lost in musings on plans for attaining distinction, and seeing himself the greatest man of his day. Little had he then guessed the misery which would place him in the way to the coveted elevation, or how he would loathe it when it lay within his grasp.

There were the trees round the vicarage, the church spire, the cottages, whose old rough aspect, he knew so well, the whole scene, once 'redolent of joy and youth:' but how unable to breathe on him a second spring! He put up his horse at the village inn, and went to make his first call on Susan, the old clerk's wife, and one of the persons in all the world who loved him best. He knocked, opened the door, and saw her, startled from her tea-drinking, looking at him as a stranger.

'Bless us! It beant never Master Philip!' she exclaimed, her head shaking very fast, as she recognized his voice. 'Why, sir, what a turn you give me! How bad you be looking, to be sure!'

He sat down and talked with her, with feelings of comfort. Tidings of Sir Guy's death had reached the old woman, and she was much grieved for the nice, cheerful-spoken young gentleman, whom she well remembered; for she, like almost every one who had ever had any intercourse with him, had an impression left of him, as of something winning, engaging, brightening, like a sunbeam. It was a refreshment to meet with one who would lament him for his own sake, and had no congratulations for Philip himself; and the 'Sure, sure, it must have been very bad for you,' with which old Susan heard of the circumstances, carried more of the comfort of genuine sympathy than all his sister's attempts at condolence.

She told him how often Sir Guy had been at Stylehurst, how he had talked to her about the archdeacon; and especially she remembered his helping her husband one day when he found him trimming the ash over the archdeacon's grave. He used to come very often to church there, more in the latter part of his stay; there was one Sunday– it was the one before Michaelmas– he was there all day, walking in the churchyard, and sitting in the porch between services.

'The Sunday before Michaelmas!' thought Philip, the very time when he had been most earnest in driving his uncle to persecute, and delighting himself in having triumphed over Guy at last, and obtained tangible demonstration of his own foresight, and his cousin's vindictive spirit. What had he been throwing away? Where had, in truth, been the hostile spirit?

He took the key of the church, and walked thither alone, standing for several minutes by the three graves, with a sensation as if his father was demanding of him an account of the boy he had watched, and brought to his ancestral home, and cared for through his orphaned childhood. But for the prayer-book, the pledge that there had been peace at the last, how could he have borne it?

Here was the paved path he had trodden in early childhood, holding his mother's hand, where, at each recurring vacation during his school days, he had walked between his admiring sisters, in the consciousness that he was the pride of his family and of all the parish. Of his family? Did he not remember his return home for the last time before that when he was summoned thither by his father's death? He had come with a whole freight of prizes, and letters full of praises; and as he stood, in expectation of the expression of delighted satisfaction, his father laid his hand on his trophy, the pile of books, saying, gravely,– ' All this would I give, Philip, for one evidence of humility of mind.'

It had been his father's one reproof. He had thought it unjust and unreasonable, and turned away impatiently to be caressed and admired by Margaret. His real feelings had been told to her, because she flattered them and shared them, he had been reserved and guarded with the father who would have perceived and repressed that ambition and the self-sufficiency which he himself had never known to exist, nor regarded as aught but sober truth. It had been his bane, that he had been always too sensible to betray outwardly his self-conceit, in any form that could lead to its being noticed.

He opened the church door, closed it behind him, and locked himself in.

He came up to the communion rail, where he had knelt for the first time twelve years ago, confident in himself, and unconscious of the fears with which his father's voice was trembling in the intensity of his prayer for one in whom there was no tangible evil, and whom others thought a pattern of all that could be desired by the fondest hopes.

He knelt down, with bowed head, and hands clasped. Assuredly, if his father could have beheld him then, it would have been with rejoicing. He would not have sorrowed that robust frame was wasted, and great strength brought low; that the noble features were worn, the healthful cheek pale, and the powerful intellect clouded and weakened; he would hardly have mourned for the cruel grief and suffering, such would have been his joy that the humble, penitent, obedient heart had been won at last. Above all, he would have rejoiced that the words that most soothed that wounded spirit were,– 'A broken and contrite heart, O God, Thou wilt not despise.'

There was solace in that solemn silence; the throbs of head and heart were stilled in the calm around. It was as if the influences of the prayers breathed for him by his father, and the forgiveness and loving spirit there won by Guy, had been waiting for him there till he came to take them up, for thenceforth the bitterest of his despair was over, and he could receive each token of Amabel's forgiveness, not as heaped coals of fire, but as an earnest of forgiveness sealed in heaven.

The worst was over, and though he still had much to suffer, he was becoming open to receive comfort; the blank dark remorse in which he had been living began to lighten, and the tone of his mind to return.

He spoke more cheerfully to Susan when he restored the key; but she had been so shocked at his appearance, that when, the next day, a report reached her that Mr. Philip was now a grand gentleman, and very rich, she answered,–

'Well, if it be so, I am glad of it, but he said never a word of it to me, and it is my belief he would give all the money as ever was coined, to have the poor young gentleman back again. Depend upon it, he hates the very sound of it.'

At the cost of several sheets of paper, Philip at length completed a letter to Mr. Edmonstone, which, when he had sent it, made his suspense more painful.

'St. Mildred's, March 12th.

'MY DEAR MR. Edmonstone,– It is with a full sense of the unfitness of intruding such a subject upon you in the present state of the family, that I again address you on the same topic as that on which I wrote to you from Italy, at the first moment at which I have felt it possible to ask your attention. I was then too ill to be able to express my contrition for all that has passed; in fact, I doubt whether it was even then so deep as at present, since every succeeding week has but added to my sense of the impropriety of my conduct, and my earnest desire for pardon. I can hardly venture at such a time to ask anything further, but I must add that my sentiments towards your daughter are unaltered, and can never cease but with my life, and though I know I have rendered myself unworthy of her, and my health, both mental and bodily, is far from being re-established, I cannot help laying my feelings before you, and entreating that you will put an end to the suspense which has endured for so many months, by telling me to hope that I have not for ever forfeited your consent to my attachment. At least, I trust to your kindness for telling me on what terms I am for the present to stand with your family. I am glad to hear such favourable reports of Lady Morville, and with all my heart I thank Charles for his letter.

'Yours ever affectionately,

'P. H. MORVILLE.'

He ardently watched for a reply. He could not endure the idea of receiving it where Margaret's eyes could scan the emotion he could now only conceal by a visible rigidity of demeanour, and he daily went himself to the post-office, but in vain. He received nothing but business letters, and among them one from Markham, with as much defiance and dislike in its style as could be shown, in a perfectly formal, proper letter. Till he had referred to Lady Morville, he would not make any demonstration towards Redclyffe, and evaded all his sister's questions as to what he was doing about it, and when he should take measures for leaving the army, or obtaining a renewal of the baronetcy.

Anxiety made him look daily more wretchedly haggard; the Doctor was at fault, Mrs. Henley looked sagacious, while his manner became so dry and repellent that visitors went away moralizing on the absurdity of "nouveaux riches" taking so much state on them.

He wondered how soon he might venture to write to Amabel, on whom alone he could depend; but he felt it a sort of profanity to disturb her.

He had nearly given up his visits to the post in despair, when one morning he beheld what never failed to bring some soothing influence, namely, the fair pointed characters he had not dared to hope for. He walked quickly into the promenade, sat down, and read:–

'Hollywell, March 22nd.

'MY DEAR PHILIP,– Papa does not answer your letter, because he says speaking is better than writing, and we hope you are well enough to come to us before Sunday week. I hope to take our dear little girl to be christened on that day, and I want you to be so kind as to be her godfather. I ask it of you, not only in my own name, but in her father's, for I am sure it is what he would choose. Her Aunt Laura and Mary Ross are to be her godmothers, I hope you will not think me very foolish and fanciful for naming her Mary Verena, in remembrance of our old readings of Sintram. She is a very healthy, quiet creature, and I am getting on very well. I am writing from the dressing-room, and I expect to be down-stairs in a few days. If you do not dislike it very much, could you be so kind as to call upon Miss Wellwood, and pay little Marianne Dixon's quarter for me? It is £10, and it will save trouble if you would do it; besides that, I should like to hear of her and the little girl. I am sorry to hear you are not better,– perhaps coming here may do you good.– Four o'clock. I have been keeping my letter in hopes of persuading papa to put in a note, but he says he had rather send a message that he is quite ready to forgive and forget, and it will be best to talk it over when you come."

'Your affectionate cousin,

'A. F. MORVILLE.'

It was well he was not under his sister's eye, for he could not read this letter calmly, and he was obliged to take several turns along the walk before he could recover his composure enough to appear in the breakfast-room, where he found his sister alone, dealing her letters into separate packets of important and unimportant.

'Good morning, Philip. Dr. Henley is obliged to go to Bramshaw this morning, and has had an early breakfast. Have you been out?'

'Yes, it is very fine– I mean it will be– the haze is clearing.'

Margaret saw that he was unusually agitated, and not by grief; applied herself to tea-making, and hoped his walk had given him an appetite; but there seemed little chance of this so long were his pauses between each morsel, and so often did he lean back in his chair.

'I am going to leave you on– on Friday,' he said at length, abruptly.

'Oh, are you going to Redclyffe?'

'No; to Hollywell. Lady Morville wishes me to be her little girl's sponsor; I shall go to London on Friday, and on, the next day.'

'I am glad they have asked you. Does she write herself? Is she pretty well?'

'Yes; she is to go down-stairs in a day or two.'

'I am rejoiced that she is recovering so well. Do you know whether she is in tolerable spirits?'

'She writes cheerfully.'

'How many years is it since I saw her? She was quite a child, but very sweet-tempered and attentive to poor Charles,' said Mrs. Henley, feeling most amiably disposed towards her future sister-in-law.

'Just so. Her gentleness and sweet temper were always beautiful; and she has shown herself under her trials what it would be presumptuous to praise.'

Margaret had no doubt now, and thought he was ready for more open sympathy.

'You must let me congratulate you now on this unexpected dawn of hope, after your long trial, my dear brother. It is a sort of unconscious encouragement you could hardly hope for.'

'I did not know you knew anything of it,' said Philip.

'Ah! my dear brother, you betrayed yourself. You need not be disconcerted; only a sister could see the real cause of your want of spirits. Your manner at each mention of her, your anxiety, coupled with your resolute avoidance of her— '

'Of whom? Do you know what you are talking of, sister!' said Philip, sternly.

'Of Amabel, of course.'

Philip rose, perfectly awful in his height and indignation.

'Sister!' he said— paused, and began again. 'I have been attached to Laura Edmonstone for years past, and Lady Morville knows it.'

'To Laura!' cried Mrs. Henley, in amaze. 'Are you engaged?' and, as he was hardly prepared to answer, she continued, 'If you have not gone too far to recede, only consider before you take any rash step. You come into this property without ready money, you will find endless claims, and if you marry at once, and without fortune, you will never be clear from difficulties.'

'I have considered,' he replied, with cold loftiness that would have silenced any one, not of the same determined mould.

'You are positively committed, then!' she said, much vexed. 'Oh, Philip! I did not think you would have married for mere beauty.'

'I can hear no more discussion on this point,' answered Philip, in the serious, calm tone that showed so much power over himself and every one else.

It put Margaret to silence, though she was excessively disappointed to find him thus involved just at his outset, when he might have married so much more advantageously. She was sorry, too, that she had shown her opinion so plainly, since it was to be, and hurt his feelings just as he seemed to be thawing. She would fain have learned more; but he was completely shut up within himself, and never opened again to her. She had never before so grated on every delicate feeling in his mind; and he only remained at her house because in his present state of health, he hardly knew where to bestow himself till it was time for him to go to Hollywell.

He went to call on Miss Wellwood, to whom his name was no slight recommendation, and she met him eagerly, asking after Lady Morville, who, she said, had twice written to her most kindly about little Marianne.

It was a very pleasant visit, and a great relief. He looked at the plans, heard the fresh arrangements, admired, was interested, and took pleasure in having something to tell Amabel. He asked for Marianne, and heard that she was one of the best of children— amiable, well-disposed, only almost too sensitive. Miss Wellwood said it was remarkable how deep an impression Sir Guy had made upon her, and how affectionately she remembered his kindness; and her distress at hearing of his death had been far beyond what such a child could have been supposed to feel, both in violence and in duration.

Philip asked to see her, knowing it would please Amabel, and in she came— a long, thin, nine-year-old child, just grown into the encumbering shyness, that is by no means one of the graces of "la vieillesse de l'enfance".

He wished to be kind and encouraging; but melancholy, added to his natural stateliness, made him very formidable; and poor Marianne was capable of nothing beyond 'yes' or 'no.'

He told her he was going to see Lady Morville and her little girl, whereat she eagerly raised her eyes, then shrank in affright at anything so tall, and so unlike Sir Guy. He said the baby was to be christened next Sunday, and Miss Wellwood helped him out by asking the name.

'Mary,' he said, for he was by no means inclined to explain the Verena, though he knew not half what it conveyed to Amabel.

Lastly, he asked if Marianne had any message; when she hung down her head, and whispered to Miss Wellwood, what proved to be 'My love to dear little cousin Mary.'

He promised to deliver it, and departed, wishing he could more easily unbend.

CHAPTER 40

Blest, though every tear that falls
Doth in its silence of past sorrow tell,
And makes a meeting seem most like a dear farewell.
– WORDSWORTH

On Saturday afternoon, about half-past five, Philip Morville found himself driving up to the well-known front door of Hollywell. At the door he heard that every one was out excepting Lady Morville, who never came down till the evening, save for a drive in the carriage.

He entered the drawing-room, and gazed on the scene where he had spent so many happy hours, only darkened by that one evil spot, that had grown till it not only poisoned his own mind, but cast a gloom over that bright home.

All was as usual. Charles's sofa, little table, books, and inkstand, the work-boxes on the table, the newspaper in Mr. Edmonstone's old folds. Only the piano was closed, and an accumulation of books on the hinge told how long it had been so; and the plants in the bay window were brown and dry, not as when they were Amabel's cherished nurslings. He remembered Amabel's laughing face and abundant curls, when she carried in the camellia, and thought how little he guessed then that he should be the destroyer of the happiness of her young life. How should he meet her– a widow in her father's house– or look at her fatherless child? He wondered how he had borne to come thither at all, and shrank at the thought that this very evening, in a few hours, he must see her.

The outer door opened, there was a soft step, and Amabel stood before him, pale, quiet, and with a smile of welcome. Her bands of hair looked glossy under her widow's cap, and the deep black of her dress was relieved by the white robes of the babe that lay on her arm. She held out her hand, and he pressed it in silence.

'I thought you would like just to see baby,' said she, in a voice something like apology.

He held out his arms to take it, for which Amy was by no means prepared. She was not quite happy even in trusting it in her sister's arms, and she supposed he had never before touched an infant. But that was all nonsense, and she would not vex him with showing any reluctance; so she laid the little one on his arm, and saw his great hand holding it most carefully, but the next moment he turned abruptly from her. Poor silly little Amy, her heart beat not a little till he turned back, restored the babe, and while he walked hastily to the window, she saw that two large tear-drops had fallen on the white folds of its mantle. She did not speak; she guessed how much he must feel in thus holding Guy's child, and, besides, her own tears would now flow so easily that she must be on her guard. She sat down, settled the little one on her knee, and gave him time to recover himself.

Presently he came and stood by her saying, in a most decided tone, 'Amabel, you must let me do this child justice.'

She looked up, wondering what he could mean.

'I will not delay in taking steps for restoring her inheritance,' said he, hoping by determination to overpower Amabel, and make her believe it a settled and a right thing.

'O Philip, you are not thinking of that!'

'It is to be done.'

'You would not be so unkind to this poor little girl,' said Amy, with a persuasive smile, partaking of her old playfulness, adding, very much in earnest, 'Pray put it out of your head directly, for it would be very wrong.'

The nurse knocked at the door to fetch the baby, as Amabel had desired. When this interruption was over, Philip came and sat down opposite to her, and began with his most decided manner:—

'You must listen to me, Amy, and not allow any scruples to prevent you from permitting your child to be restored to her just rights. You must see that the estate has come to me by circumstances such that no honest man can be justified in retaining it. The entail was made to exclude females, only because of the old Lady Granard. It is your duty to consent.'

'The property has always gone in the male line,' replied Amabel.

'There never was such a state of things. Old Sir Guy could never have thought of entailing it away from his own descendant on a distant cousin. It would be wrong of me to profit by these unforeseen contingencies, and you ought not, in justice to your child, to object.'

He spoke so forcibly and decidedly that he thought he must have prevailed. But not one whit convinced, Amabel answered, in her own gentle voice, but beginning with a business-like argument:— 'Such a possibility was contemplated. It was all provided for in the marriage settlements. Indeed, I am afraid that, as it is, she will be a great deal too rich. Besides, Philip, I am sure this is exactly what Guy would have chosen,' and the tears rose in her eyes. 'The first thing that came into my head when she was born, was, that it was just what he wished, that I should have her for myself, and that you should take care of Redclyffe. I am certain now that he hoped it would be so. I know— indeed I do— that he took great pleasure in thinking of its being in your hands, and of your going on with all he began. You can't have forgotten how much he left in your charge? If you were to give it up, it would be against his desire; and with that knowledge, how could I suffer it? Then think what a misfortune to her, poor little thing, to be a great heiress, and how very bad for Redclyffe to have no better a manager than me! Oh, Philip, can you not see it is best as it is, and just as he wished?'

He almost groaned– 'If you could guess what a burden it is.'

'Ah! but you must carry it, not throw it down on such hands as mine and that tiny baby's,' said she, smiling.

'It would have been the same if it had been a boy.'

'Yes; then I must have done the best I could, and there would have been an end to look to, but I am so glad to be spared. And you are so fit for it, and will make it turn to so much use to every one.'

'I don't feel as if I should ever be of use to any one,' said Philip, in a tone of complete dejection.

'Your head is aching,' said she, kindly.

'It always does, more or less,' replied he, resting it on his hand.

'I am so sorry. Has it been so ever since you were ill? But you are better? You look better than when I saw you last.'

'I am better on the whole, but I doubt whether I shall ever be as strong as I used to be. That ought to make me hesitate, even if– ' then came a pause, while he put his hand over his face, and seemed struggling with irrepressible emotion; and after all he was obliged to take two walks to the window before he could recover composure, and could ask in a voice which he tried to make calm and steady, though his face was deeply flushed– 'Amy, how is Laura?'

'She is very well,' answered Amabel. 'Only you must not be taken by surprise if you see her looking thinner.'

'And she has trusted– she has endured through all?' said he, with inquiring earnestness.

'O yes!'

'And they– your father and mother– can forgive?'

'They do– they have. But, Philip, it was one of the things I came down to say to you. I don't think you must expect papa to begin about it himself. You know he does not like awkwardness, though he will be very glad when once it is done, and ready to meet you half way.' He did not answer, and after a silence Amabel added, 'Laura is out of doors. She and Charlotte take very long walks.'

'And is she really strong and well, or is it that excited overdoing of employment that I first set her upon?' he asked, anxiously.

'She is perfectly well, and to be busy has been a great help to her,' said Amabel. 'It was a great comfort that we did not know how ill you had been at Corfu, till the worst was over. Eveleen only mentioned it when you were better. I was very anxious, for I had some fears from the note that you sent by Arnaud. I am very glad to see you safe here, for I have felt all along that we forsook you; but I could not help it.'

'I am very glad you did not stay. The worst of all would have been that you should have run any risk.'

'There is the carriage,' said Amy. 'Mamma and Charlie have been to Broadstone. They thought they might meet you by the late train.'

Philip's colour rose. He stood up— sat down; then rising once more, leant on the mantel-piece, scarcely knowing how to face either of them— his aunt, with her well-merited displeasure, and Charles, who when he parted with him had accused him so justly— Charles, who had seen through him and had been treated with scorn.

A few moments, and Charles came in, leaning on his mother. They both shook hands, exclaimed at finding Amabel downstairs, and Mrs. Edmonstone asked after Philip's health in her would-be cordial manner. The two ladies then went up-stairs together, and thus ended that conference, in which both parties had shown rare magnanimity, of which they were perfectly unconscious; and perhaps the most remarkable part of all was that Philip quietly gave up the great renunciation and so-called sacrifice, with which he had been feeding his hopes, at the simple bidding of the gentle-spoken Amabel— not even telling her that he resigned it. He kept the possessions which he abhorred, and gave up the renunciation he had longed to make, and in this lay the true sacrifice, the greater because the world would think him the gainer.

When the mother and daughter were gone, the cousins were silent, Philip resting his elbow on the mantel-shelf and his head on his hand, and Charles sitting at the end of the sofa, warming first one hand, then the other, while he looked up to the altered face, and perceived in it grief and humiliation almost as plainly as illness. His keen eyes read that the sorrow was indeed more deeply rooted than he had hitherto believed, and that Amabel's pity had not been wasted; and he was also struck by the change from the great personal strength that used to make nothing of lifting his whole weight.

'I am sorry to see you so pulled down,' said he. 'We must try if we can doctor you better than they did at St. Mildred's. Are you getting on, do you think?'

He had hardly ever spoken to Philip, so entirely without either bitterness or sarcasm, and his manner hardly seemed like that of the same person.

'Thank you, I am growing stronger; but as long as I cannot get rid of this headache, I am good for nothing.'

'You have had a long spell of illness indeed,' said Charles. 'You can't expect to shake off two fevers in no time. Now all the anxiety is over, you will brighten like this house.'

'But tell me, what is thought of Amabel? Is she as well as she ought to be?'

'Yes, quite, they say— has recovered her strength very fast, and is in just the right spirits. She was churched yesterday, and was not the worse for it. It was a trial, for she had not been to East-hill since— since last May.'

'It is a blessing, indeed,' said Philip, earnestly.

'She has been so very happy with the baby,' said Charles. 'You hear what its name is to be?'

'Yes, she told me in her letter.'

'To avoid having to tell you here, I suppose. Mary is for common wear, Verena is for ourselves. She asked if it would be too foolish to give such a name, and mamma said the only question was, whether she would like indifferent people to ask the reason of it.'

Philip lapsed into thought, and presently said, abruptly, 'When last we parted you told me I was malignant. You were right.'

'Shake hands!' was all Charles's reply, and no more was said till Charles rose, saying it was time to dress. Philip was about to help him, but he answered, 'No, thank you, I am above trusting to anything but my own crutches now; I am proud to show you what feats I can perform.'

Charles certainly did get on with less difficulty than heretofore, but it was more because he wanted to spare Philip fatigue than because he disdained assistance, that he chose to go alone. Moreover, he did what he had never done for any one before— he actually hopped the whole length of the passage, beyond his own door to do the honours of Philip's room, and took a degree of pains for his comfort that seemed too marvellous to be true in one who had hitherto only lived to be attended on.

By the time he had settled Philip, the rest of the party had come home, and he found himself wanted in the dressing-room, to help his mother to encourage his father to enter on the conversation with Philip in the evening, for poor Mr. Edmonstone was in such a worry and perplexity, that the whole space till the dinner-bell rang was insufficient to console him in. Laura, meanwhile, was with Amabel, who was trying to cheer her fluttering spirits and nerves, which, after having been so long harassed, gave way entirely at the moment of meeting Philip again. How would he regard her after her weakness in betraying him for want of self-command? Might he not be wishing to be free of one who had so disappointed him, and only persisting in the engagement from a sense of honour! The confidence in his affection, which had hitherto sustained her, was failing; and not all Amabel could say would reassure her. No one could judge of him but herself, his words were so cautious, and he had so much command over himself, that nobody could guess. Of course he felt bound to her; but if she saw one trace of his being only influenced by honour and pity, she would release him, and he should never see the struggle.

She had worked herself up into almost a certainty that so it would be, and Amabel was afraid she would not be fit to go down to dinner; but the sound of the bell, and the necessity of moving, seemed to restore the habit of external composure in a moment. She settled her countenance, and left the room.

Charlotte, meantime, had been dressing alone, and raging against Philip, declaring she could never bear to speak to him, and that if she was Amy she would never have chosen him for a godfather. And to think of his marrying just like a good hero in a book, and living very happy ever after! To be sure she was sorry for poor Laura; but it was all very wrong, and now they would be rewarded! How could Charlie be so provoking as to talk about his sorrow! She hoped he was sorry; and as to his illness, it served him right.

All this Charlotte communicated to Bustle; but Bustle had heard some mysterious noise, and insisted on going to investigate the cause; and Charlotte, finding her own domain dark and cold, and private conferences going on in Amabel's apartment and the dressing-room, was fain to follow him down-stairs, as soon as her toilet was complete, only hoping Philip would keep out of the way.

But, behold, there he was; and even Bustle was propitiated, for she found him, his nose on Philip's knee, looking up in his face, and wagging his tail, while Philip stroked and patted him, and could hardly bear the appealing expression of the eyes, that, always wistful, now seemed to every one to be looking for his master.

To see this attention to Bustle won Charlotte over in a moment. 'How are you, Philip? Good dog, dear old Bustle!' came in a breath, and they were both making much of the dog, when she amicably asked if he had seen the baby, and became eager in telling about the christening.

The dinner-bell brought every one down but Amabel. The trembling hands of Philip and Laura met for a moment, and they were in the dining-room.

Diligently and dutifully did Charles and Mrs. Edmonstone keep up the conversation; the latter about her shopping, the former about the acquaintances who had come to speak to him as he sat in the carriage. As soon as possible, Mrs. Edmonstone left the dining-room, then Laura flew up again to the dressing-room, sank down on a footstool by Amabel's side, and exclaiming, 'O Amy, he is looking so ill!' burst into a flood of tears.

The change had been a shock for which Laura had not been prepared. Amy, who had seen him look so much worse, had not thought of it, and it overcame Laura more than all her anxieties, lest his love should be forfeited. She sobbed inconsolably over the alteration, and it was long before Amabel could get her to hear that his face was much less thin now, and that he was altogether much stronger; it was fatigue and anxiety to-night, and to-morrow he would be better. Laura proceeded to brood over her belief that his altered demeanour, his settled melancholy, his not seeking her eye, his cold shake of the hand, all arose from the diminution of his love, and his dislike to be encumbered with a weak, foolish wife, with whom he had entangled himself when he deemed her worthy of him. She dwelt on all this in silence, as she sat at her sister's feet, and Amy left her to think, only now and then giving some caress to her hair or cheek, and at each touch the desolate waste of life that poor Laura was unfolding before herself was rendered less dreary by the thought, 'I have my sister still, and she knows sorrow too.' Then she half envied Amy, who had lost her dearest by death, and held his heart fast to the last; not, like herself, doomed to see the love decay for which she had endured so long– decay at the very moment when the suspense was over.

Laura might justly have envied Amabel, though for another reason; it was because in her cup there was no poison of her own infusing.

There she stayed till Charlotte came to summon her to tea, saying the gentlemen, except Charles, were still in the dining-room.

They had remained sitting over the fire for a considerable space, waiting for each other to begin, Mr. Edmonstone irresolute, Philip striving to master his feelings, and to prevent increasing pain and confusion from making him forget what he intended, to say. At last, Mr. Edmonstone started up, pulled out his keys, took a candle, and said, 'Come to the study– I'll give you the Redclyffe papers.'

'Thank you,' said Philip, also rising, but only because he could not sit while his uncle stood. 'Not to-night, if you please. I could not attend to them.'

'What, your head? Eh?'

'Partly. Besides, there is another subject on which I hope you will set me at rest before I can enter on any other.'

'Yes– yes– I know,' said Mr. Edmonstone, moving uneasily.

'I am perfectly conscious how deeply I have offended.'

Mr. Edmonstone could not endure the apology.

'Well, well,' he broke in nervously, 'I know all that, and it can't be helped. Say no more about it. Young people will be foolish, and I have been young and in love myself.'

That Captain Morville should live to be thankful for being forgiven in consideration of Mr. Edmonstone's having been young!

'May I then consider myself as pardoned, and as having obtained your sanction?'

'Yes, yes, yes; and I hope it will cheer poor Laura up again a little. Four years has it gone on? Constancy, indeed! and it is time it should be rewarded. We little thought what you were up to, so grave and demure as you both were. So you won't have the papers to-night? I can't say you do look fit for business. Perhaps Laura may suit you better– eh, Philip?'

Love-making was such a charming sight to Mr. Edmonstone, that having once begun to look on Philip and Laura as a pair of lovers, he could not help being delighted, and forgetting, as well as forgiving, all that had been wrong.

They did not, however, exactly answer his ideas; Laura did not once look up, and Philip, instead of going boldly to take the place next her, sat down, holding his hand to his forehead, as if too much overpowered by indisposition to think of anything else. Such was in great measure the case; he was very much fatigued with the journey, and these different agitating scenes had increased the pain in his head to a violent degree; besides which, feeling that his aunt still regarded him as she did at Recoara, he could not bear to make any demonstration towards Laura before her, lest she might think it a sort of triumphant disregard of her just displeasure.

Poor Laura saw in it both severe suffering and dislike to her; and the more she understood from her father's manner what had passed in the other room, the more she honoured him for the sacrifice he was making of himself.

Mrs. Edmonstone waited on the headache with painful attention, but they all felt that the only thing to be done for the two poor things was to let them come to an explanation; so Charlotte was sent to bed, her mother went up to Amy, Charles carried off his father to the study, and they found themselves alone.

Laura held down her face, and struggled to make her palpitating heart and dry tongue suffer her to begin the words to which she had wound herself up. Philip raised his hands from his eyes as the door shut, then rose up, and fixed them on Laura. She, too, looked up, as if to begin; their eyes met, and they understood all. He stepped towards her, and held out his hands. The next moment both hers were clasped in his– he had bent down and kissed her brow.

No words of explanation passed between them. Laura knew he was her own, and needed no assurance that her misgivings had been vain. There was a start of extreme joy, such as she had known twice before, but it could be only for a moment while he looked so wretchedly unwell. It did but give her the right to attend to him. The first thing she said was to beg him to lie down on the sofa; her only care was to make him comfortable with cushions, and he was too entirely worn out to say anything he had intended, capable only of giving himself up to the repose of knowing her entirely his own, and of having her to take care of him. There he lay on the sofa, with his eyes shut, and Laura's hand in his, while she sat beside him, neither of them speaking; and, excepting that she withdrew her hand, neither moved when the others returned.

Mrs. Edmonstone compassionated him, and showed a great deal of solicitude about him, trying hard to regard him as she used to do, yet unable to bring back the feeling, and therefore, do what she would, failing to wear its semblance.

Laura, sad, anxious, and restless, had no relief till she went to wish her sister good night. Amabel, who was already in bed, stretched out her hand with a sweet look, beaming with affection and congratulation.

'You don't want to be convinced now that all is right!' said she.

'His head is so dreadfully bad!' said Laura.

'Ah! it will get better now his mind is at rest.'

'If it will but do so!'

'And you know you must be happy to-morrow, because of baby.'

'My dear,' said Mrs. Edmonstone, coming in, 'I am sorry to prevent your talk, but Amy must not be kept awake. She must keep her strength for to-morrow.'

'Good night, then, dear, dear Laura. I am so glad your trouble is over, and you have him again!' whispered Amabel, with her parting kiss; and Laura went away, better able to hope, to pray, and to rest, than she could have thought possible when she left the drawing-room.

'Poor dear Laura,' said Mrs. Edmonstone, sighing; 'I hope he will soon be better.'

'Has it been very uncomfortable?'

'I can't say much for it, my dear. He was suffering terribly with his head, so that I should have been quite alarmed if he had not said it was apt to get worse in the evening; and she, poor thing, was only watching him. However, it is a comfort to have matters settled; and papa and Charlie are well pleased with him. But I must not keep you awake after driving Laura away. You are not over-tired to-night I hope, my dear?'

'Oh, no; only sleepy. Good night, dearest mamma.'

'Good night, my own Amy;' then, as Amy put back the coverings to show the little face nestled to sleep on her bosom, 'good night, you little darling! don't disturb your mamma. How comfortable you look! Good night, my dearest!'

Mrs. Edmonstone looked for a moment, while trying to check the tears that came at the thought of the night, one brief year ago, when she left Amy sleeping in the light of the Easter moon. Yet the sense of peace and serenity that had then given especial loveliness to the maiden's chamber on that night, was there still with the young widow. It was dim lamplight now that beamed on the portrait of her husband, casting on it the shade of the little wooden cross in front, while she was shaded by the white curtains drawn from her bed round the infant's little cot, so as to shut them both into the quiet twilight, where she lay with an expression of countenance that, though it was not sorrow, made Mrs. Edmonstone more ready to weep than if it had been; so with her last good night she left her.

And Amabel always liked to be shut in by herself, dearly as she loved them all, and mamma especially; there was always something pleasant in being able to return to her own world, to rest in the thoughts of her husband, and in the possession of the little unconscious creature that had come to inhabit that inner world of hers, the creature that was only his and hers.

She had from the first always felt herself less lonely when quite alone, before with his papers, and now with his child; and could Mrs. Edmonstone have seen her face, she would have wept and wondered more, as Amy fondled and hushed her babe, whispering to it fond words which she could never have uttered in the presence of any one who could understand them, and which had much of her extreme youthfulness in them. Not one was so often repeated or so endearing as 'Guy's baby! Guy's own dear little girl!' It did not mean half so much when she called it her baby; and she loved to tell the little one that her father had been the best and the dearest, but he was gone away, and would she be contented to be loving and good with only her mother to take care of her, and tell her, as well as she could, what a father hers was, when she was old enough to know about him?

To-night, Amy told her much in that soft, solemn, murmuring tone, about what was to befall her to-morrow, and the great blessings to be given to her, and how the poor little fatherless one would be embraced in the arms of His mercy, and received by her great Father in heaven:— 'Ay, and brought nearer to your own papa, and know him in some inner way, and he will know his little child then, for you will be as good and pure and bright as he, and you will belong to the great communion of saints to-morrow, you precious little one, and be so much nearer to him as you will be so much better than I. Oh! baby, if we can but both endure to the end!'

With such half-uttered words, Amabel Morville slept the night before her babe's christening.

CHAPTER 41

A stranger's roof to hold thy head,
A stranger's foot thy grave to tread;
Desert and rock, and Alp and sea,
Spreading between thy home and thee.
– SEWELL

Mary Ross was eager for the first report from Hollywell the next morning, and had some difficulty in keeping her attention fixed on her class at school. Laura and Charlotte came in together in due time, and satisfied her so far as to tell her that Amy was very well.

'Is Captain Morville come?' thought Mary. 'No, I cannot guess by Laura's impressive face. Never mind, Charles will tell me all between services.'

The first thing she saw on coming out of school was the pony carriage, with Charles and Captain Morville himself. Charlotte, who was all excitement, had time to say, while her sister was out of hearing,–

'It is all made up now, Mary, and I really am very sorry for Philip.'

It was fortunate that Mary understood the amiable meaning this speech was intended to convey, and she began to enter into its grounds in the short conference after church, when she saw the alteration in the whole expression of countenance.

'Yes,' said Charles, who as usual remained at the vicarage during the two services, and who perceived what passed in her mind, 'if it is any satisfaction to you to have a good opinion of your fellow-sponsor, I assure you that I am converted to Amy's opinion. I do believe the black dog is off his back for good and all.'

'I never saw any one more changed,' said Mary.

'Regularly tamed,' said Charles. He is something more like his old self to-day than last night, and yet not much. He was perfectly overpowered then– so knocked up that there was no judging of him. To-day he has all his sedateness and scrupulous attention, but all like a shadow of former time– not a morsel of sententiousness, and seeming positively grateful to be treated in the old fashion.'

'He looks very thin and pale. Do you think him recovered?'

'A good way from it,' said Charles. 'He is pretty well to-day, comparatively, though that obstinate headache hangs about him. If this change last longer than that and his white looks, I shall not even grudge him the sponsorship Amy owed me.'

'Very magnanimous!' said Mary. 'Poor Laura! I am glad her suspense is over. I wondered to see her at school.'

'They are very sad and sober lovers, and it is the best way of not making themselves unbearable, considering– Well, that was a different matter. How little we should have believed it, if any one had told us last year what would be the state of affairs to-day. By the bye, Amy's godson is christened to-day.'

'Who?'

'Didn't you hear that the Ashfords managed to get Amy asked if she would dislike their calling their boy by that name we shall never hear again, and she was very much pleased, and made offer in her own pretty way to be godmother. I wonder how Markham endures it! I believe he is nearly crazy. He wrote me word he should certainly have given up all concern with Redclyffe, but for the especial desire of– .What a state of mind he will be in, when he remembers how he has been abusing the captain to me!'

The afternoon was fresh and clear, and there was a spring brightness in the sunshine that Amabel took as a greeting to her little maiden, as she was carried along the churchyard path. Many an eye was bent on the mother and child, especially on the slight form, unseen since she had last walked down the aisle, her arm linked in her bridegroom's.

'Little Amy Edmonstone,' as they had scarcely learnt to cease from calling her, before she was among them again, the widowed Lady Morville; and with those kind looks of compassion for her, were joined many affectionate mourning thoughts of the young husband and father, lying far away in his foreign grave, and endeared by kindly remembrances to almost all present. There was much of pity for his unconscious infant, and tears were shed at the thought of what the wife must be suffering; but if the face could have been seen beneath the thick crape folds of her veil, it would have shown no tears– only a sweet, calm look of peace, and almost gladness.

The babe was on her knees when the time for the christening came; she was awake, and now and then making a little sound and as she was quieter with her than any one else, Amabel thought she might herself carry her to the font.

It was deep, grave happiness to stand there, with her child in her arms, and with an undefined sense that she was not alone as if in some manner her husband was present with her; praying with her prayers, and joining in offering up their treasure; when the babe was received into Mr. Ross's arms, and Amy, putting back her veil, gazed up with a wistful but serene look.

'To her life's end?' Therewith came a vision of the sunrise at Recoara, and the more glorious dawn that had shone in Guy's dying smile, and Amabel knew what would be her best prayer for his little Mary Verena, as she took her back, the drops glistening on her brow, her eyes open, and arms outspread. It was at that moment that Amabel was first thrilled with a look in her child that was like its father. She had earnestly and often sought a resemblance without being able honestly to own that she perceived any; but now, though she knew not in what it consisted, there was something in that baby face that recalled him more vividly than picture or memory.

'Lord, now lettest Thou Thy servant depart in peace.'

Those words seemed to come from her own heart. She had brought Guy's daughter to be baptized, and completed his work of pardon, and she had a yearning to be departing in peace, whither her sunshine was gone. But he had told her not to wish that his child should be motherless; she had to train her to be fit to meet him. The sunshine was past, but she had plenty to do in the shade, and it was for his sake. She would, therefore, be content to remain to fulfil her duties among the dear ones to whom he had trusted her for comfort, and with the sense of renewed communion with him that she had found in returning again to church.

So felt Amabel, as she entered into the calm that followed the one year in which she had passed through the great events of life, and known the chief joy and deepest grief that she could ever experience.

It was far otherwise with her sister. Laura's term of trouble seemed to be ending, and the spring of life beginning to dawn on her.

Doubt and fear were past, she and Philip were secure of each other, he was pardoned, and they could be together without apprehension, or playing tricks with their consciences; but she had as yet scarcely been able to spend any time with him; and as Charles said, their ways were far more grave and less lover-like than would have seemed natural after their long separation.

In truth, romantic and uncalculating as their attachment was, they never had been lover-like. They had never had any fears or doubts; her surrender of her soul had been total, and every thought, feeling, and judgment had taken its colour from him as entirely as if she had been a wife of many years' standing. She never opened her mind to perceive that he had led her to act wrongly, and all her unhappiness had been from anxiety for him, not repentance on her own account; for so complete was her idolatry, that she entirely overlooked her failure in duty to her parents.

It took her by surprise when, as they set out together that evening to walk home from East-hill, he said, as soon as they were apart from the village—

'Laura, you have more to forgive than all.'

'Don't, speak so, Philip, pray don't. Do you think I would not have borne far more unhappiness willingly for your sake? Is it not all forgotten as if it had not been?'

'It is not unhappiness I meant,' he replied, 'though I cannot bear to think of what you have undergone. Unhappiness enough have I caused indeed. But I meant, that you have to forgive the advantage I took of your reliance on me to lead you into error, when you were too young to know what it amounted to.'

'It was not an engagement,' faltered Laura.

'Laura, don't, for mercy's sake, recall my own hateful sophistries,' exclaimed Philip, as if unable to control the pain it gave him; 'I have had enough of that from my sister;' then softening instantly: 'it was self-deceit; a deception first of myself, then of you. You had not experience enough to know whither I was leading you, till I had involved you; and when the sight of death showed me the fallacy of the salve to my conscience, I had nothing for it but to confess, and leave you to bear the consequences. O Laura! when I think of my conduct towards you, it seems even worse than that towards—towards your brother-in-law!'

His low, stern tone of bitter suffering and self-reproach was something new and frightful to Laura. She clung to his arm and tried to say— 'O, don't speak in that way! You know you meant the best. You could not help being mistaken.'

'If I did know any such thing, Laura! but the misery of perceiving that my imagined anxiety for his good,— his good, indeed! was but a cloak for my personal enmity— you can little guess it.'

Laura tried to say that appearances were against Guy, but he would not hear.

'If they were, I triumphed in them. I see now that a shade of honest desire to see him exculpated would have enabled me to find the clue. If I had gone to St. Mildred's at once— interrogated him as a friend— seen Wellwood—but dwelling on the ifs of the last two years can bring nothing but distraction,' he added, pausing suddenly.

'And remember,' said Laura, 'that dear Guy himself was always grateful to you. He always upheld that you acted for his good. Oh! the way he took it was the one comfort I had last year.'

'The acutest sting, and yet the only balm,' murmured Philip; 'see, Laura,' and he opened the first leaf of Guy's prayer-book, which he had been using at the christening.

A whispered 'Dear Guy!' was the best answer she could make, and the tears were in her eyes. 'He was so very kind to me, when he saw me that unhappy wedding-day.'

'Did Amy tell you his last words to me?'

'No,' said Laura.

'God bless you and my sister!' he repeated, so low that she could hardly hear.

'Amy left that for you to tell,' said Laura, as her tears streamed fast. How can we speak of her, Philip?'

'Only as an angel of pardon and peace!' he answered.

'I don't know how to tell you of all her kindness,' said Laura; 'half the bitterness of it seemed to be over when once she was in the house again, and, all the winter, going into her room was like going into some peaceful place where one must find comfort.'

'"Spirits of peace, where are ye" I could have said, when I saw her drive away at Recoara, and carry all good angels with her except those that could not but hover round that grave.'

'How very sad it must have been! Did– '

'Don't speak of it; don't ask me of it' said Philip, hastily. 'There is nothing in my mind but a tumult of horror and darkness that it is madness to remember. Tell me of yourself– tell me that you have not been hurt by all that I have brought on you.'

'Oh, no!' said Laura 'besides, that is all at an end.'

'All an end! Laura, I fear in joining your fate to mine, you will find care and grief by no means at an end. You must be content to marry a saddened, remorseful man, broken down in health and spirits, his whole life embittered by that fatal remembrance, forced to endure an inheritance that seems to have come like the prosperity of the wicked. Yet you are ready to take all this? Then, Laura, that precious, most precious love, that has endured through all, will be the one drop of comfort through the rest of my life.

She could but hear such words with thrills of rejoicing affection; and on they walked, Laura trembling and struck with sorrow at the depth of repentance he now and then disclosed, though not in the least able to fathom it, thinking it all his nobleness of mind, justifying him to herself, idolizing him too much to own he had ever been wrong; yet the innate power of tact and sympathy teaching her no longer to combat his self-reproaches, and repeat his former excuses, but rather to say something soothing and caressing, or put in some note of thankfulness and admiration of Amy and Guy. This was the best thing she could do for him, as she was not capable, like Amy, of acknowledging that his repentance was well-founded. She was a nurse, not a physician, to the wounded spirit; but a very good and gentle nurse she was, and the thorough enjoyment of her affection and sympathy, the opening into confidence, and the freedom from doubt and suspense, were comforts that were doing him good every hour.

The christening party consisted only of the Rosses, and Dr. Mayerne, who had joined them at East-hill church, and walked home with Mr. Edmonstone. They could not have been without him, so grateful were they for his kindness all through their anxious winter, and Mr. Edmonstone was well pleased to tell him on the way home that they might look to having a wedding in the family; it had been a very long attachment, constancy as good as a story, and he could all along have told what was the matter, when mamma was calling in the doctor to account for Laura's looking pale.

The doctor was not surprised at the news, for perhaps he, too, had had some private theory about those pale looks; but, knowing pretty well the sentiments Charles had entertained the winter before last, he was curious to find out how he regarded this engagement. Charles spoke of it in the most ready cordial way. 'Well, doctor, so you have heard our news! I flatter myself we have as tall and handsome a pair of lovers to exhibit here, as any in the United Kingdom, when we have fattened him a little into condition.'

'Never was there a better match,' said Dr. Mayerne. 'Made for each other all along. One could not see them without feeling it was the first chapter of a novel.'

When Mrs. Edmonstone came in, the doctor was a little taken aback. He thought her mind must be with poor Sir Guy, and was afraid the lovers had been in such haste as to pain Lady Morville; for there was a staidness and want of "epanchement du coeur" of answering that was very unlike her usual warm manner. At dinner, Mr. Edmonstone was in high spirits, delighted at Amy's recovery, happy to have a young man about the house again, charmed to see two lovers together, pleased that Laura should be mistress of Redclyffe, since it could not belong to Amy's child; altogether, as joyous as ever. His wife, being at ease about Amy, did her best to smile, and even laugh, though sad at heart all the time, as she missed the father from the christening feast, and thought how happy she had been in that far different reunion last year. It might be the same with Charles; but the outward effect was exhibited in lively nonsense; Charlotte's spirits were rising fast, and only Philip and Laura themselves were grave and silent, she, the more so, because she was disappointed to find that the one walk back from East-hill, much as he had enjoyed it, had greatly tired Philip. However, the others talked enough without them; and Mr. Edmonstone was very happy, drinking the health of Miss Morville, and himself carrying a bit of the christening cake to the mamma in the drawing-room.

There sat Amabel by the fire, knowing that from henceforth she must exert herself to take part in the cheerfulness of the house, and willing to join the external rejoicing in her child's christening, or at least not to damp it by remaining up-stairs. Yet any one but Mr. Edmonstone would have seen more sadness than pleasure in the sweet smile with which she met and thanked him; but they were cheerful tones in which she replied, and in her presence everything was hushed and gentle, subdued, yet not mournful. The spirit of that evening was only recognized after it was past, and then it ever grew fairer and sweeter in recollection, so as never to be forgotten by any of those who shared it.

CHAPTER 42

She was not changed when sorrow came,
  That awed the sternest men;
It rather seemed she kept her flame
  To comfort us till then.

But sorrow passed, and others smiled
  With happiness once more;
And she drew back the spirit mild
  She still had been before.
— S. R.

Philip's marriage could not take place at once. No one said, but every one felt, that it must not be talked of till the end of Amabel's first year of widowhood; and in the meantime Philip remained at Hollywell, gaining strength every day, making more progress in one week than he had done in six at St. Mildred's, finding that, as his strength returned, his mind and memory regained their tone, and he was as capable as ever of applying to business, and, above all, much settled and comforted by some long conversations with Mr. Ross.

Still he could not endure the thought of being at Redclyffe. The business connected with it was always performed with pain and dislike, and he shrank with suffering at every casual mention of his going thither. Mrs. Edmonstone began to wonder whether he could mean to linger at Hollywell all the summer, and Amabel had some fears that it would end in his neglecting Redclyffe, till a letter arrived from Lord Thorndale, saying that his brother, the member for Moorworth, had long been thinking of giving up his seat, and latterly had only waited in hopes that the succession at Redclyffe might come to Philip Morville. Moorworth was entirely under the Thorndale and Morville interest, and Lord Thorndale wrote to propose that Philip should come forward at once, inviting him to Thorndale instead of going to his own empty house.

To be in parliament had been one of the favourite visions of Philip's youth, and for that very reason he hesitated, taking it as one of the strange fulfilments of his desires that had become punishments. He could not but feel that as this unhappy load of wealth had descended on him, he was bound to make it as beneficial as he could to others, and not seeking for rest or luxury, to stand in the gap where every good man and true was needed. But still he dreaded his old love of distinction. He disliked a London life for Laura, and he thought that, precarious as his health had become, it might expose her to much anxiety, since he was determined that if he undertook it at all, he would never be an idle member.

It ended in his referring the decision to Laura, who, disliking London, fearful for his health, eager for his glory, and reluctant to keep back such a champion from the battle, was much perplexed, only desirous to say what he wished, yet not able to make out what that might be. She carried her doubts to Charles and Amabel, who both pronounced that the thought of going to Redclyffe seemed far worse for him than any degree of employment– that occupation of the mind was the best thing for his spirits; and ended by recommending that Dr. Mayerne should be consulted.

He was of the same opinion. He said a man could hardly have two fevers following, and one of them upon the brain, without having reason to remember them. That his constitution had been seriously weakened, and there was an excitability of brain and nerves which made care requisite; but depression of spirits was the chief thing to guard against, and a London life, provided he did not overwork himself, was better for him than solitude at Redclyffe.

Accordingly Philip went to Thorndale, and was returned for Moorworth without opposition. Markham sent his nephew to transact business with him at Thorndale, for he could not bear to meet him himself, and while there was any prospect of his coming to Redclyffe, walked about in paroxysms of grunting and ill-humour. The report that Mr. Morville was engaged to the other Miss Edmonstone did but render him more furious, for he regarded it as a sort of outrage to Lady Morville's feelings that a courtship should be carried on in the house with her. She was at present the object of all his devoted affection for the family, and he would not believe, but that she had been as much disappointed at the birth of her daughter, as he was himself. He would not say one word against Mr. Morville, but looked and growled enough to make Mr. Ashford afraid that the new squire would find him very troublesome.

The Ashfords were in a state of mind themselves to think that Mr. Morville ought to be everything excellent to make up for succeeding Sir Guy; but having a very high opinion of him to begin with, they were very sorry to find all Redclyffe set against him. In common with the parish, they were very anxious for the first report of his arrival and at length he came. James Thorndale, as before, drove him thither, coming to the Ashfords while he was busy with Markham. He would not go up to the Park, he only went through some necessary business with Markham, and then walked down to the Cove, afterwards sitting for about ten minutes in Mrs. Ashford's drawing-room.

The result of the visit was that old James Robinson reported that the new squire took on as much about poor Sir Guy as any one could do, and turned as pale as if he had been going into a swoon, when he spoke his name and gave Ben his message. And as to poor Ben, the old man said, he regularly did cry like a child, and small blame to him, to hear that Sir Guy had took thought of him at such a time and so far away; and he verily believed Ben could never take again to his bad ways, after such a message as that.

Markham was gruff with the Robinsons for some time after and was even heard to mutter something about worshipping the rising sun, an act of idolatry of which he could not be accused, since it was in the most grudging manner that he allowed, that Mr. Morville's sole anxiety seemed to be to continue all Sir Guy had undertaken; while Mrs. Ashford, on the other hand was much affected by the account her cousin James had been giving her of the grief that he had suffered at Sir Guy's death, his long illness, his loss of spirits, the reluctance he had shown to come here at all, and his present unconquerable dread of going to the Park.

He was soon after in London, where, as far as could be judged in such early days, he seemed likely to distinguish himself according to the fondest hopes that Margaret or Laura could ever have entertained. Laura was only afraid he was overworking himself, especially as, having at present little command of ready money, he lived in a small lodging, kept no horse, and did not enter into society; but she was reassured when he came to Hollywell for a day or two at Whitsuntide, not having indeed regained flesh or colour, but appearing quite well, in better spirits, and very eager about political affairs.

All would have been right that summer, but that, as Philip observed, the first evening of his arrival, Amabel was not looking as well as she had done at the time of the christening. She had, just after it, tried her strength and spirits too much, and had ever since been not exactly unwell, but sad and weary, more dejected than ever before, unable to bear the sight of flowers or the sound of music, and evidently suffering much under the recurrence of the season, which had been that of her great happiness— the summer sunshine, the long evenings, the nightingale's songs. She was fatigued by the most trifling exertion, and seemed able to take interest in nothing but her baby, and a young widow in the village, who was in a decline; and though she was willing to do all that was asked of her, it was in a weary, melancholy manner, as if she had no peace but in being allowed to sit alone, drooping over her child.

From society she especially shrunk, avoiding every chance of meeting visitors, and distressed and harassed when her father brought home some of his casual dinner guests, and was vexed not to see her come into the drawing-room in the evening. If she did make the effort of coming, to please him, she was so sure to be the worse for it, that her mother would keep her up-stairs the next time, and try to prevent her from knowing that her father was put out, and declared it was nonsense to expect poor Amy to get up her spirits, while she never saw a living soul, and only sat moping in the dressing-room.

A large dinner-party did not interfere with her, for even he could not expect her to appear at it, and one of these he gave during Philip's visit, for the pleasure of exhibiting such company as the M.P. for Moorworth. After dinner, Charlotte told Mary Ross to go and see Amy. Not finding her in the dressing-room, she knocked at her own door. 'Come in,' answered the low soft voice; and in the window, overhung by the long shoots of the roses, Amabel's close cap and small head were seen against the deep-blue evening sky, as she sat in the summer twilight, her little one asleep in her cot.

'Thank you for coming,' said she. 'I thought you would not mind sitting here with baby and me. I have sent Anne out walking.'

'How pretty she looks!' said Mary, stooping over the infant. 'Sleep is giving her quite a colour; and how fast she grows!'

'Poor little woman!' said Amy, sighing.

'Tired, Amy?' said Mary, sitting down, and taking up the little lambswool shoe, that Amy had been knitting.

'N– no, thank you,' said Amy, with another sigh.

'I am afraid you are. You have been walking to Alice Lamsden's again.'

'I don't think that tires me. Indeed, I believe the truth is,' and her voice sounded especially sad in the subdued tone in which she spoke, that she might not disturb the child, 'I am not so much tired with what I do, which is little enough, as of the long, long life that is before me.'

Mary's heart was full, but she did not show her thought otherwise than by a look towards the babe.

'Yes, poor little darling,' said Amabel, 'I know there is double quantity to be done for her, but I am so sorry for her, when I think she must grow up without knowing him.'

'She has you, though,' Mary could not help saying, as she felt that Amabel was superior to all save her husband.

Perhaps Amy did not hear; she went up to the cot, and went on:– 'If he had but once seen her, if she had but had one kiss, one touch that I could tell her of by and by, it would not seem as if she was so very fatherless. Oh no, baby, I must wait, that you may know something about, him; for no one else can tell you so well what he was, though I can't tell much!' She presently returned to her seat. 'No, I don't believe I really wish I was like poor Alice,' said she; 'I hope not; I am sure I don't for her sake. But, Mary, I never knew till I was well again how much I had reckoned on dying when she was born. I did not think I was wishing it, but it seemed likely, and I was obliged to arrange things in case of it. Then somehow, as he came back last spring, after that sad winter, it seemed as if this spring, though he would not come back to me, I might be going to him.'

'But then she comforted you.'

'Yes, that she did, my precious one; I was so glad of her, it was a sort of having him again, and so it is still sometimes, and will be more so, I dare say. I am very thankful for her, indeed I am; and I hope I am not repining, for it does not signify after all, in the end, if I am weary and lonely sometimes. I wish I was sure it was not wrong. I know I don't wish to alter things.'

'No, I am sure you don't.'

'Ah!' said Amabel, smiling, 'it is only the old, silly little Amy that does feel such a heart-aching and longing for one glance of his eye, or touch of his hand, or sound of his foot in the passage. Oh, Mary, the worst of all is to wake up, after dreaming I have heard his voice. There is nothing for it but to take our baby and hold her very tight.'

'Dearest Amy! But you are not blaming yourself for these feelings. It might be wrong to indulge them and foster them; but while you struggle with them, they can't in themselves be wrong.'

'I hope not,' said Amabel pausing to think. 'Yes, I have "the joy" at the bottom still; I know it is all quite right, and it came straight from heaven, as he said. I can get happy very often when I am by myself, or at church, with him; it is only when I miss his bright outside and can't think myself into the inner part, that it is so forlorn and dreary. I can do pretty well alone. Only I wish I could help being so troublesome and disagreeable to everybody' said Amy, concluding in a matter-of-fact tone.

'My dear!' said Mary, almost laughing.

'It is so stupid of me to be always poorly, and making mamma anxious when there's nothing the matter with me. And I know I am a check on them down-stairs— papa, and Charlotte, and all— they are very kind, considerate, and yet'— she paused— 'and it is a naughty feeling; but when I feel all those dear kind eyes watching me always, and wanting me to be happy, it is rather oppressive, especially when I can't; but if I try not to disappoint them, I do make such a bad hand of it, and am sure to break down afterwards, and that grieves mamma all the more.'

'It will be better when this time of year is over,' said Mary.

'Perhaps, yes. He always seemed to belong to summer days, and to come with them. Well, I suppose trials always come in a different shape from what one expects; for I used to think I could bear all the doom with him, but, I did not know it would be without him, and yet that is the best. Oh, baby!'

'I should not have come to disturb her.'

'No— never mind; she never settles fairly to sleep till we are shut in by ourselves. Hush! hush, darling— No? Will nothing do but being taken up?

Well, then, there! Come, and show your godmamma what a black fringe those little wakeful eyes are getting.'

And when Mary went down it was with the conviction that those black eyelashes, too marked to be very pretty in so young a babe, were more of a comfort to Amabel than anything she could say.

The evening wore on, and at length Laura came into her sister's room. She looked fagged and harassed, the old face she used to wear in the time of disguise and secrecy, Amabel asked if it had been a tiresome party.

'Yes— no— I don't know. Just like others,' said Laura.

'You are tired, at any rate,' said Amabel. 'You took too long a ride with Philip. I saw you come in very late.'

'I am not in the least tired, thank you.'

'Then he is,' said Amabel. 'I hope he has not one of his headaches again.'

'No,' said Laura, still in a dissatisfied, uncomfortable tone.

'No? Dear Laura, I am sure there is something wrong;' and with a little more of her winning, pleading kindness, she drew from Laura that Philip had told her she idolized him. He had told her so very gently and kindly, but he had said she idolized him in a manner that was neither good for herself nor him; and he went on to blame himself for it, which was what she could not bear. It had been rankling in her mind ever since that he had found fault with her for loving him so well, and it had made her very unhappy. She could not love him less, and how should she please him? She had much rather he had blamed her than himself.

'I think I see what he means' said Amy, thoughtfully. 'He has grown afraid of himself, and afraid of being admired now.'

'But how am I to help that, Amy?' said Laura, with tears in her eyes: 'he cannot help being the first, the very first of all with me— '

'No, no,' said Amy, quickly, 'not the very first, or what would you do if you were to be— like me? Don't turn away, dear Laura; I don't think I over could bear this at all, if dear Guy had not kept it always before my eyes from the very first that we were to look to something else besides each other.'

'Of course I meant the first earthly thing,' said Laura; but it was not heartfelt— she knew she ought, therefore she thought she did.

'And so,' proceeded Amy, 'I think if that other is first, it would make you have some other standard of right besides himself, then you would be a stay and help to him. I think that is what he means.'

'Amy! let me ask you,' said Laura, a little entreatingly, yet as if she must needs put the question— 'surely, you never thought Guy had faults?'

Her colour deepened. 'Yes, Laura,' she answered, firmly. 'I could not have understood his repentance if I had not thought so. And, dear Laura, if you will forgive me for saying it, it would be much better for yourself and Philip if you would see the truth.'

'I thought you forgave him,' murmured Laura.

'Oh, Laura! but does not that word "forgive" imply something? I could not have done anything to comfort him that day, if I had not believed he had something to be comforted for. It can't be pleasant to him to see you think his repentance vain.'

'It is noble and great.'

'But if it was not real, it would be thrown away. Besides, dear Laura, do let me say this for once. If you would but understand that you let him lead you into what was not right, and be really sorry for that, and show mamma that you are, I do think it would all begin much more happily when you are married.'

'I could never have told, till I was obliged to betray myself,' said Laura. 'You know, Amy, it was no engagement. We never wrote to each other, we had but one walk; it was no business of his to speak till he could hope for papa's consent to our marriage. It would have been all confusion if he had told, and that would have been only that we had always loved each other with all our hearts, which every one knew before.'

'Yet, Laura, it was what preyed on him when he thought he was dying.'

'Because it was the only thing like a fault he could think of,' said Laura, excited by this shade of blame to defend him vehemently– 'because his scruples are high and noble and generous.'

She spoke so eagerly, that the baby's voice again broke on the conversation, and she was obliged to go away; but though her idolatry was complete, it did not seem to give full satisfaction or repose. As to Philip, though his love for her was unchanged, it now and then was felt, though not owned by him, that she was not fully a helpmeet, only a 'Self'; not such a 'Self' as he had left at St. Mildred's, but still reflecting on him his former character, instead of aiding him to a new one.

CHAPTER 43

> But nature to its inmost part
> Faith had refined; and to her heart
> A peaceful cradle given,
> Calm as the dew drops free to rest
> Within a breeze-fanned rose's breast
> Till it exhales to heaven.
> – WORDSWORTH

It had long been a promise that Mr. Edmonstone should take Charlotte to visit her grandmamma, in Ireland. They would have gone last autumn, but for Guy's illness, and now Aunt Charlotte wrote to hasten the performance of the project. Lady Mabel was very anxious to see them, she said; and having grown much more infirm of late, seemed to think it would be the last meeting with her son. She talked so much of Mrs. Edmonstone and Laura, that it was plain that she wished extremely for a visit from them, though she did not like to ask it, in the present state of the family.

A special invitation was sent to Bustle; indeed, Charles said Charlotte could not have gone without his permission, for he reigned like a tyrant over her, evidently believing her created for no purpose but to wait on him, and take him to walk.

Laura was a great favourite at the cottage of Kilcoran, and felt she ought to offer to go. Philip fully agreed, and held out home hopes of following as soon as the session, was over, and he had been to Redclyffe about some business that had been deferred too long.

And now it appeared that Mr. Edmonstone had a great desire to take his wife, and she herself said, that under any other circumstances she should have been very desirous of going. She had not been to Ireland for fifteen years, and was sorry to have seen so little of her mother-in-law; and now that it had been proved that Charles could exist without her, she would not have hesitated to leave him, but for Amabel's state of health and spirits, which made going from home out of the question.

Charles and Amabel did not think so. It was not to be endured, that when grandmamma wished for her, she should stay at home for them without real necessity; besides, the fatigue, anxiety, and sorrow she had undergone of late, had told on her, and had made her alter perceptibly, from being remarkably fresh and youthful, to be somewhat aged; and the change to a new scene, where she could not be distressing herself at every failure in cheerfulness of poor Amy's, was just the thing to do her good.

Amabel was not afraid of the sole charge of Charles or of the baby, for she had been taught but too well to manage for herself, she understood

Charles very well, and had too much quiet good sense to be fanciful about her very healthy baby. Though she was inexperienced, with old nurse hard by, and Dr. Mayerne at Broadstone, there was no fear of her not having good counsel enough. She was glad to be of some use, by enabling her mother to leave Charles, and her only fear was of being dull company for him; but as he was so kind as to bear it, she would do her best, and perhaps their neighbours would come and enliven him sometimes.

Charles threw his influence into the same scale. His affectionate observation had shown him that it oppressed Amabel's spirits to be the object of such constant solicitude, and he was convinced it would be better for her, both to have some necessary occupation and to be free from that perpetual mournful watching of her mother's that caused her to make the efforts to be cheerful which did her more harm than anything else.

To let her alone to look and speak as she pleased without the fear of paining and disappointing those she loved, keep the house quiet, and give her the employment of household cares and attending on himself, was, he thought, the best thing for her; and he was full of eagerness and pleasure at the very notion of being of service to her, if only by being good for nothing but to be waited on. He thought privately that the spring of his mother's mind had been so much injured by the grief she had herself suffered for 'her son Guy,' her cruel disappointment in Laura, and the way in which she threw herself into all Amy's affliction, that there was a general depression in her way of observing and attending Amy, which did further harm; and that to change the current of her thoughts, and bring her home refreshed and inspirited, would be the beginning of improvement in all. Or, as he expressed it to Dr. Mayerne, 'We shall set off on a new tack.'

His counsel and Mr. Edmonstone's wishes at length decided mamma, on condition that Mary Ross and Dr. Mayerne would promise to write on alternate weeks a full report, moral and physical, as Charles called it. So in due time the goods were packed, Mrs. Edmonstone cried heartily over the baby, advised Amabel endlessly about her, and finally looked back through her tears, as she drove away, to see Charles nodding and waving his hand at the bay-window, and Amabel standing with her parting smile and good-bye on the steps.

The reports, moral and physical, proved that Charles had judged wisely. Amabel was less languid as she had more cause for exertion, and seemed relieved by the absence of noise and hurry, spending more time down-stairs, and appearing less weary in the evening. She still avoided the garden, but she began to like short drives with her brother in the pony-carriage, when he drove on in silence, and let her lean back and gaze up into the sky, or into the far distance, undisturbed. Now and then he would be rejoiced by a bright, genuine smile, perfectly refreshing, at some of the pretty ways of the babe, a small but plump and lively creature, beginning to grasp with her hands, laugh and gaze about with eyes that gave promise of the peculiar colour and brilliancy of her father's. Amabel was afraid she might be tempted into giving Charles too much of the little lady's society; but he was very fond of her, regarding her with an odd mixture of curiosity and amusement, much entertained with watching what he called her unaccountable manners, and greatly flattered when he could succeed in attracting her notice. Indeed, the first time she looked full at him with a smile on the verge of a laugh, it completely overcame him, by the indescribably forcible manner in which it suddenly recalled the face which had always shone on him like a sunbeam. Above all, it was worth anything to see the looks she awoke in her mother, for which he must have loved her, even had she not been Guy's child.

In the evening, especially on Sunday, Amabel would sometimes talk to him as she had never yet been able to do, about her last summer's journey, and her stay at Recoara, and his way of listening and answering had in it something that gave her great pleasure; while, on his side, he deemed each fresh word of Guy's a sort of treasure for which to be grateful to her. The brother and sister were a great help and happiness to each other; Amabel found herself restored to Charles, as Guy had liked to think of her, and Charles felt as if the old childish fancies were fulfilled, in which he and Amy were always to keep house together. He was not in the least dull; and though his good-natured visitors in the morning were welcome, and received with plenty of his gay lively talk, he did not by any means stand in need of the compassion they felt for him, and could have done very well without them; while the evenings alone with Amy had in them something so pleasant that they were almost better than those when Mr. Ross and Mary came to tea. He wrote word to his mother that she might be quite at ease about them, and he thought Amy would get through the anniversaries of September better while the house was quiet, so that she need not think of trying to hurry home.

He was glad to have done so, for the letters, which scarcely missed a day in being written by his mother and Charlotte, seemed to show that their stay was likely to be long. Lady Mabel was more broken than they had expected, and claimed a long visit, as she was sure it would be their last, while the Kilcoran party had taken possession of Laura and Charlotte, as if they never meant to let them go. Charlotte wrote her brother very full and very droll accounts of the Iricisms around her which she enjoyed thoroughly, and Charles, declaring he never expected to see little Charlotte come out in the character of the facetious correspondent, used to send Mary Ross into fits of laughing by what he read to her. Mr. Fielder, the tutor, wrote Charlotte, was very nearly equal to Eveleen's description of him, but very particularly agreeable, in fact, the only man who had any conversation, whom she had seen since she had been at Kilcoran.

'Imagine,' said Charles, 'the impertinent little puss setting up for intellectual conversation, forsooth!'

'That's what comes of living with good company,' said Mary.

The brother and sister used sometimes to drive to Broadstone to fetch their letters by the second post.

'Charlotte, of course,' said Charles, as he opened one. 'My Lady Morville, what's yours?'

'Only Mr. Markham,' said Amabel, 'about the winding up of our business together, I suppose. What does Charlotte say?'

'Charlotte is in a fit of impudence, for which she deserves chastisement,' said Charles, unable to help laughing, as he read,–

'Our last event was a call from the fidus Achates, who, it seems, can no longer wander up and down the Mediterranean without his pius Aeneas, and so has left the army, and got a diplomatic appointment somewhere in Germany. Lord Kilcoran has asked him to come and stay here, and Mabel and I are quite sure he comes for a purpose. Of course he has chosen this time, in order that he may be able to have his companion before his eyes, as a model for courtship, and I wish I had you to help me look on whenever Philip comes, as that laugh I must enjoy alone with Bustle. However, when Philip will come we cannot think, for we have heard nothing of him this age, not even Laura, and she is beginning to look very anxious about him. Do tell us if you know anything about him. The last letter was when parliament was prorogued, and he was going to Redclyffe, at least three weeks ago.'

'I wonder if Mr. Markham mentions him,' said Amabel, hastily unfolding her letter, which was, as she expected, about the executors' business, but glancing on to the end, she exclaimed,–

'Ah! here it is. Listen, Charlie. "Mr. Morville has been here for the last few weeks, and is, I fear, very unwell. He has been entirely confined to the house, almost ever since his arrival, by violent headache, which has completely disabled him from attending to business; but he will not call in any advice. I make a point of going to see him every day, though I believe my presence is anything but acceptable, as in his present state of health and spirits, I cannot think it right that he should be left to servants." Poor fellow! Redclyffe has been too much for him.'

'Over-worked, I suppose,' said Charles. 'I thought he was coming it pretty strong these last few weeks.'

'Not even writing to Laura! How very bad he must be! I will write at once to ask Mr. Markham for more particulars.'

She did so, and on the third day they drove again to fetch the answer. It was a much worse account. Mr. Morville was, said Markham, suffering dreadfully from headache, and lay on the sofa all day, almost unable to speak or move, but resolved against having medical advice, though his own treatment of himself did not at all succeed in relieving him. There was extreme depression of spirits, and an unwillingness to see any one. He had positively refused to admit either Lord Thorndale or Mr. Ashford, and would hardly bear to see Markham himself, who, indeed, only forced his presence on him from thinking it unfit to leave him entirely to the servants, and would be much relieved if some of Mr. Morville's friends were present to free him from the responsibility.

'Hem!' said Charles. 'I can't say it sounds comfortable.'

'It is just as I feared!' said Amy. 'Great excitability of brain and nerve, Dr. Mayerne said. All the danger of a brain fever again! Poor Laura! What is to be done?'

Charles was silent.

'It is for want of some one to talk to him,' said Amabel. 'I know how he broods over his sad recollections, and Redclyffe must make it so much worse. If mamma and Laura were but at home to go to him, it might save him, and it would be fearful for him to have another illness, reduced as he is. How I wish he was here!'

'He cannot come, I suppose,' said Charles, 'or he would be in Ireland.'

'Yes. How well Guy knew when he said it would be worse for him than for me! How I wish I could do something now to make up for running away from him in Italy. If I was but at Redclyffe!'

'Do you really wish it?' said Charles, surprised.

'Yes, if I could do him any good.'

'Would you go there?'

'If I had but papa or mamma to go with me.'

'Do you think I should do as well?'

'Charlie!'

'If you think there would be any use in it, and choose to take the trouble of lugging me about the country, I don't see why you should not.'

'Oh! Charlie, how very, kind! How thankful poor Laura will be to you! I do believe it will save him!' cried Amabel, eagerly.

'But, Amy,'– he paused– 'shall you like to see Redclyffe?'

'Oh! that is no matter,' said she, quickly. 'I had rather see after Philip than anything. I told you how he was made my charge, you know. And Laura! Only will it not be too tiring for you?'

'I can't see how it should hurt me. But I forget, what is to be done about your daughter?'

'I don't know what harm it could do her,' said Amy, considering. 'Mrs. Gresham brought a baby of only three months old from Scotland the other day, and she is six. It surely cannot hurt her, but we will ask Dr. Mayerne.'

'Mamma will never forgive us if we don't take the doctor into our councils.'

'Arnaud can manage for us. We would sleep in London, and go on by an early train, and we can take our— I mean my— carriage, for the journey after the railroad. It would not be too much for you. How soon could we go?'

'The sooner the better,' said Charles. 'If we are to do him any good, it must be speedily, or it will be a case of shutting the stable-door. Why not to-morrow?'

The project was thoroughly discussed that evening, but still with the feeling as if it could not be real, and when they parted at night they said,— 'We will see how the scheme looks in the morning.'

Charles was still wondering whether it was a dream, when the first thing he heard in the court below his window was—

'Here, William, here's a note from my lady for you to take to Dr. Mayerne.'

'They be none of them ill?' answered William's voice.

'O no; my lady has been up this hour, and Mr. Charles has rung his bell. Stop, William, my lady said you were to call at Harris's and bring home a "Bradshaw".'

Reality, indeed, thought Charles, marvelling at his sister, and his elastic spirits throwing him into the project with a sort of enjoyment, partaking of the pleasure of being of use, the spirit of enterprise, and the 'fun' of starting independently on an expedition unknown to all the family.

He met Amabel with a smile that showed both were determined. He undertook to announce the plan to his mother, and she said she would write to tell Mr. Markham that as far as could be reckoned on two such frail people, they would be at Redclyffe the next evening, and he must use his own discretion about giving Mr. Morville the note which she enclosed.

Dr. Mayerne came in time for breakfast, and the letter from Markham was at once given to him.

'A baddish state of things, eh, doctor!' said Charles. 'Well, what do you think this lady proposes? To set off forthwith, both of us, to take charge of him. What do you think of that, Dr. Mayerne?'

'I should say it was the only chance for him,' said the doctor, looking only at the latter. 'Spirits and health reacting on each other, I see it plain enough. Over-worked in parliament, doing nothing in moderation, going down to that gloomy old place, dreaming away by himself, going just the right way to work himself into another attack on the brain, and then he is done for. I don't know that you could do a wiser thing than go to him, for he is no more fit to tell what is good for him than a child.' So spoke the doctor, thinking only of the patient till looking up at the pair he was dismissing to such a charge, the helpless, crippled Charles, unable to cross the room without crutches, and Amabel, her delicate face and fragile figure in her widow's mourning, looking like a thing to be pitied and nursed with the tenderest care, with that young child, too, he broke off and said– 'But you don't mean you are in earnest?'

'Never more so in our lives,' said Charles; on which Dr. Mayerne looked so wonderingly and inquiringly at Amabel, that she answered,–

'Yes that we are, if you think it safe for Charles and baby.'

'Is there no one else to go? What's become of his sister?'

'That would never do,' said Charles, 'that is not the question;' and he detailed their plan.

'Well, I don't see why it should not succeed,' said the doctor, 'or how you can any of you damage yourselves.'

'And baby?' said Amy.

'What should happen to her, do you think?' said the doctor with his kind, reassuring roughness. 'Unless you leave her behind in the carriage, I don't see what harm she could come to, and even then, if you direct her properly, she will come safe to hand.' Amabel smiled, and saying she would fetch her to be inspected, ran up-stairs with the light nimble step of former days.

'There goes one of the smallest editions of the wonders of the world!' said Charles, covering a sigh with a smile. 'You don't think it will do her any harm?'

'Not if she wishes it. I have long thought a change, a break, would be the best thing for her– poor child!– I should have sent her to the sea-side if you had been more movable, and if I had not seen every fuss about her made it worse.'

'That's what I call being a reasonable and valuable doctor,' said Charles. 'If you had routed the poor little thing out to the sea, she would have only pined the more. But suppose the captain turns out too bad for her management, for old Markham seems in a proper taking?'

'Hem! No, I don't expect it is come to that.'

'Be that as it may, I have a head, if nothing else, and some one is wanted. I'll write to you according as we find Philip.'

The doctor was wanted for another private interview, in which to assure Amabel that there was no danger for Charles, and then, after promising to come to Redclyffe if there was occasion, and engaging to write and tell Mrs. Edmonstone they had his consent, he departed to meet them by and by at the station, and put Charles into the carriage.

A very busy morning followed; Amabel arranged household affairs as befitted the vice-queen; took care that Charles's comforts were provided for; wrote many a note; herself took down Guy's picture, and laid it in her box, before Anne commenced her packing; and lastly, walked down to the village to take leave of Alice Lamsden.

Just as the last hues of sunset were fading, on the following evening, Lady Morville and Charles Edmonstone were passing from the moor into the wooded valley of Redclyffe. Since leaving Moorworth not a word had passed. Charles sat earnestly watching his sister; though there was too much crape in the way for him to see her face, and she was perfectly still, so that all he could judge by was the close, rigid clasping together of the hands, resting on the sleeping infant's white mantle. Each spot recalled to him some description of Guy's, the church-tower, the school with the two large new windows, the park wall, the rising ground within. What was she feeling? He did not dare to address her, till, at the lodge-gate, he exclaimed– 'There's Markham;' and, at the same time, was conscious of a feeling between hope and fear, that this might after all be a fool's errand, and a wonder how they and the master of the house would meet if it turned out that they had taken fright without cause.

At his exclamation, Amy leant forward, and beckoned. Markham came up to the window, and after the greeting on each side, walked along with his hand on the door, as the carriage slowly mounted the steep hill, answering her questions: 'How is he?'

'No better. He has been putting on leeches, and made himself so giddy, that yesterday he could hardly stand.'

'And they have not relieved him?'

'Not in the least. I am glad you are come, for it has been an absurd way of going on.'

'Is he up?'

'Yes; on the sofa in the library.'

'Did you give him my note? Does he expect us?'

'No, I went to see about telling him this morning, but found him so low and silent, I thought it was better not. He has not opened a letter this week, and he might have refused to see you, as he did Lord Thorndale. Besides, I didn't know how he would take my writing about him, though if you had not written, I believe I should have let Mrs. Henley know by this time.'

'There is an escape for him,' murmured Charles to his sister.

'We have done the best in our power to receive you' proceeded Markham; 'I hope you will find it comfortable, Lady Morville, but– '

'Thank you, I am not afraid,' said Amy, smiling a little. Markham's eye was on the little white bundle in her lap, but he did not speak of it, and went on with explanations about Mrs. Drew and Bolton and the sitting-room, and tea being ready.

Charles saw the great red pile of building rise dark, gloomy, and haunted-looking before them. The house that should have been Amabel's! Guy's own beloved home! How could she bear it? But she was eagerly asking Markham how Philip should be informed of their arrival, and Markham was looking perplexed, and saying, that to drive under the gateway, into the paved court, would make a thundering sound, that he dreaded for Mr. Morville. Could Mr. Charles Edmonstone cross the court on foot? Charles was ready to do so; the carriage stopped, Amabel gave the baby to Anne, saw Arnaud help Charles out; and turning to Markham, said, 'I had better go to him at once. Arnaud will show my brother the way.'

'The sitting-room, Arnaud' said Markham, and walked on fast with her, while Charles thought how strange to see her thus pass the threshold of her husband's house, come thither to relieve and comfort his enemy.

She entered the dark-oak hall. On one side the light shone cheerfully from the sitting-room, the other doors were all shut. Markham hesitated, and stood reluctant.

'Yes, you had better tell him I am here,' said she, in the voice, so gentle, that no one perceived its resolution.

Markham knocked at one of the high heavy doors, and softly opened it. Amabel stood behind it, and looked into the room, more than half dark, without a fire, and very large, gloomy, and cheerless, in the gray autumn twilight, that just enabled her to see the white pillows on the sofa, and Philip's figure stretched out on it. Markham advanced and stood doubtful for an instant, then in extremity, began– 'Hem! Lady Morville is come, and– '

Without further delay she came forward, saying– 'How are you, Philip?'

He neither moved nor seemed surprised, he only said, 'So you are come to heap more coals on my head.'

A thrill of terror came over her, but she did not show it, as she said, 'I am sorry to find you so poorly.'

It seemed as if before he had taken her presence for a dream; for, entirely roused, he exclaimed, in a tone of great surprise, 'Is it you, Amy?' Then sitting up, 'Why? When did you come here?'

'Just now. We were afraid you were ill, we heard a bad account of you, so we have taken you by storm: Charles, your goddaughter, and I, are come to pay you a visit.'

'Charles! Charles here?' cried Philip, starting up. 'Where is he?'

'Coming in,' said Amy; and Philip, intent only on hospitality, hastened into the hall, and met him at the door, gave him his arm and conducted him where the inviting light guided them to the sitting-room. The full brightness of lamp and fire showed the ashy paleness of his face; his hair, rumpled with lying on the sofa, had, on the temples, acquired a noticeable tint of gray, his whole countenance bore traces of terrible suffering; and Amabel thought that even at Recoara she had never seen him look more wretchedly ill.

'How did you come?' he asked. 'It was very kind. I hope you will be comfortable.'

'We have taken good care of ourselves,' said Amy. 'I wrote to Mr. Markham, for I thought you were not well enough to be worried with preparations. We ought to beg your pardon for breaking on you so unceremoniously.'

'If any one should be at home here– ' said Philip, earnestly;– then interrupting himself, he shaded his eyes from the light, 'I don't know how to make you welcome enough. When did you set off?'

'Yesterday afternoon,' said Charles; 'we slept in London, and came on to-day.'

'Have you dined?' said Philip, looking perplexed to know where the dinner could come from.

'Yes; at K– – , thank you.'

'What will you have? I'll ring for Mrs. Drew.'

'No, thank you; don't tease yourself. Mrs. Drew will take care of us. Never mind; but how bad your head is!' said Amabel, as he sat down on the sofa, leaning his elbow on his knee, and pressing his hand very hard on his forehead. 'You must lie down and keep quiet, and never mind us. We only want a little tea. I am just going to take off my bonnet, and see what they have done with baby, and then I'll come down. Pray lie still till then. Mind he does, Charlie.'

They thought she was gone; but the next moment there she was with the two pillows from the library sofa, putting them under Philip's head, and making him comfortable; while he, overpowered by a fresh access of headache, had neither will nor power to object. She rang, asked for Mrs. Drew, and went.

Philip lay, with closed eyes, as if in severe pain: and Charles, afraid to disturb him, sat feeling as if it was a dream. That he, with Amy and her child, should be in Guy's home, so differently from their old plans, so very differently from the way she should have arrived. He looked round the room, and everywhere knew what Guy's taste had prepared for his bride– piano, books, prints, similarities to Hollywell, all with a fresh new bridal effect, inexpressibly melancholy. They brought a thought of the bright eye, sweet voice, light step, and merry whistle; and as he said to himself 'gone for ever,' he could have hated Philip, but for the sight of his haggard features, gray hairs, and the deep lines which, at seven-and-twenty, sorrow had traced on his brow. At length Philip turned and looked up.

'Charles,' he said, 'I trust you have not let her run any risk.'

'No: we got Dr. Mayerne's permission.'

'It is like all the rest,' said Philip, closing his eyes again. Presently he asked: 'How did you know I was not well?'

'Markham said something in a business letter that alarmed Amy. She wrote to inquire, and on his second letter we thought we had better come and see after you ourselves.'

No more was said till Amabel returned. She had made some stay up-stairs, talking to Mrs. Drew, who was bewildered between surprise, joy, and grief; looking to see that all was comfortable in Charles's room, making arrangements for the child, and at last relieving herself by a short space of calm, to feel where she was, realize that this was Redclyffe, and whisper to her little girl that it was her father's own home. She knew it was the room he had destined for her; she tried, dark as it was, to see the view of which he had told her, and looked up, over the mantel-piece, at Muller's engraving of St. John. Perhaps that was the hardest time of all her trial, and she felt as if, without his child in her arms, she could never have held up under the sense of desolation that came over her, left behind, while he was in his true home. Left, she told herself, to finish the task he had begun, and to become fit to follow him. Was she not in the midst of fulfilling his last charge, that Philip should be taken, care of? It was no time for giving way, and here was his own little messenger of comfort looking up with her sleepy eyes to tell her so. Down she must go, and put off 'thinking herself into happiness' till the peaceful time of rest; and presently she softly re-entered the sitting-room, bringing to both its inmates in her very presence such solace as she little guessed, in her straightforward desire to nurse Philip, and take care Charles was not made uncomfortable.

That stately house had probably never, since its foundation, seen anything so home-like as Amabel making tea and waiting on her two companions; both she and Charles pleasing each other by enjoying the meal, and Philip giving his cup to be filled again and again, and wondering why one person's tea should taste so unlike another's.

He was not equal to conversation, and Charles and Amabel were both tired, so that tea was scarcely over before they parted for the night; and Amy, frightened at the bright and slipperiness of the dark-oak stairs, could not be at peace till she had seen Arnaud help Charles safely up them, and made him promise not to come down without assistance in the morning.

She was in the sitting-room soon after nine next morning, and found breakfast on one table, and Charles writing a letter on the other.

'Well,' said he, as she kissed him, 'all right with you and little miss?'

'Quite, thank you. And are you rested?'

'Slept like a top; and what did you do? Did you sleep like a sensible woman?'

'Pretty well, and baby was very good. Have you heard anything of Philip?'

'Bolton thinks him rather better, and says he is getting up.'

'How long have you been up?'

'A long time. I told Arnaud to catch Markham when he came up, as he always does in a morning to see after Philip, and I have had a conference with him and Bolton, so that I can lay the case before Dr. Mayerne scientifically.'

'What do you think of it?'

'I think we came at the right time. He has been getting more and more into work in London, taking no exercise, and so was pretty well knocked up when he came here; and this place finished it. He tried to attend to business about the property, but it always ended in his head growing so bad, he had to leave all to Markham, who, by the way, has been thoroughly propitiated by his anxiety for him. Then he gave up entirely; has not been out of doors, written a note, nor seen a creature the last fortnight, but there he has lain by himself in the library, given up to all manner of dismal thoughts without a break.'

'How dreadful!' said Annabel, with tears in her eyes. 'Then he would not see Mr. Ashford? Surely, he could have done something for him.'

'I'll tell you what,' said Charles, lowering his voice,' from what Bolton says, I think he had a dread of worse than brain fever.'

She shuddered, and was paler, but did not speak.

'I believe,' continued Charles, 'that it is one half nervous and the oppression of this place, and the other half, the over-straining of a head that was already in a ticklish condition. I don't think there was any real danger of more than such a fever as he had at Corfu, which would probably have been the death of him; but I think he dreaded still worse, and that his horror of seeing any one, or writing to Laura, arose from not knowing how far he could control his words.'

'O! I am glad we came,' repeated Amabel, pressing her hands together.

'He has been doctoring himself,' proceeded Charles; 'and probably has kept off the fever by strong measures, but, of course, the more he reduced his strength, the greater advantage he gave to what was simply low spirits. He must have had a terrible time of it, and where it would have ended I cannot guess, but it seems to me that most likely, now that he is once roused, he will come right again.'

Just as Charles had finished speaking, he came down, looking extremely ill, weak, and suffering; but calmed, and resting on that entire dependence on Amabel which had sprung up at Recoara.

She would not let him go back to his gloomy library, but made him lie on the sofa in the sitting-room, and sat there herself, as she thought a little quiet conversation between her and Charles would be the best thing for him. She wrote to Laura, and he sent a message, for he could not yet attempt to write; and Charles wrote reports to his mother and Dr. Mayerne; a little talk now and then going on about family matters.

Amabel asked Philip if he knew that Mr. Thorndale was at Kilcoran.

'Yes,' he said, 'he believed there was a letter from him, but his eyes had ached too much of late to read.'

Mrs. Ashford sent in to ask whether Lady Morville would like to see her. Amabel's face flushed, and she proposed going to her in the library; but Philip, disliking Amy's absence more than the sight of a visitor, begged she might come to the sitting-room.

The Ashfords had been surprised beyond measure at the tidings that Lady Morville had actually come to Redclyffe, and had been very slow to believe it; but when convinced by Markham's own testimony, Mrs. Ashford's first idea had been to go and see if she could be any help to the poor young thing in that great desolate house, whither Mrs. Ashford had not been since, just a year ago, Markham had conducted her to admire his preparations. There was much anxiety, too, about Mr. Morville, of whose condition, Markham had been making a great mystery, and on her return, Mr. Ashford was very eager for her report.

Mr. Morville, she said, did look and seem very far from well, but Lady Morville had told her they hoped it was chiefly from over fatigue, and that rest would soon restore him. Lady Morville herself was a fragile delicate creature, very sweet looking, but so gentle and shrinking, apparently, that it gave the impression of her having no character at all, not what Mrs. Ashford would have expected Sir Guy to choose. She had spoken very little, and the chief of the conversation had been sustained by her brother.

'I was very much taken with that young Mr. Edmonstone,' said Mrs. Ashford; 'he is about three-and-twenty, sadly crippled, but with such a pleasing, animated face, and so extremely agreeable and sensible, I do not wonder at Sir Guy's enthusiastic way of talking of him. I could almost fancy it was admiration of the brother transferred to the sister.'

'Then after all you are disappointed in her, and don't lament, like Markham, that she is not mistress here?'

'No: I won't say I am disappointed; she is a very sweet creature. O yes, very! but far too soft and helpless for such a charge as this property, unless she had her father or brother to help her. But I must tell you that she took me to see her baby, a nice little lively thing, poor little dear! and when we were alone, she spoke rather more, begged me to send her godson to see her, thanked me for coming, but crying stopped her from saying more. I could grow very fond of her. No, I don't wonder at him, for there is a great charm in anything so soft and dependent.

Decidedly, Mary Ross had been right when she said, that except Sir Guy, there was no one so difficult to know as Amy.

In the afternoon, Charles insisted on Amabel's going out for fresh air and exercise, and she liked the idea of a solitary wandering; but Philip, to her surprise, offered to come with her, and she was too glad to see him exert himself, to regret the musings she had hoped for; so out they went, after opening the window to give Charles what he called an airing, and he said, that in addition he should 'hirple about a little to explore the ground-floor of the house.'

'We must contrive some way for him to drive out,' said Philip, as he crossed the court with Amabel; 'and you too. There is no walk here, but up hill or down.'

Up-hill they went, along the path leading up the green slope, from which the salt wind blew refreshingly. In a few minutes, Amabel found herself on a spot which thrilled her all over.

There lay before her Guy's own Redclyffe bay; the waves lifting their crests and breaking, the surge resounding, the sea-birds skimming round, the Shag Rock dark and rugged, the scene which seemed above all the centre of his home affections, which he had so longed to show her, that it had cost him an effort on his death-bed to resign the hope; the leaping waves that he said he would not change for the white-headed mountains. And now he was lying among those southern mountains, and she stood in the spot where he had loved to think of seeing her; and with Philip by her side. His sea, his own dear sea, the vision of which had cheered, his last day, like the face of a dear old friend; his sea, rippling and glancing on, unknowing that the eyes that had loved it so well would gaze on it no more; the wind that he had longed for to cool his fevered brow, the rock which had been like a playmate in his boyhood, and where he had perilled his life, and rescued so many. It was one of the seasons when a whole gush of fresh perceptions of his feelings, like a new meeting with himself, would come on her, her best of joys; and there she stood, gazing fixedly, her black veil fluttering in the wind, and her hands pressed close together, till Philip, little knowing what the sight was to her, shivered, saying it was very cold and windy, and without hesitation she turned away, feeling that now Redclyffe was precious indeed.

She brought her mind back to listen, while Philip was considering of means of taking Charles out of doors; he supposed there might be some vehicle about the place; but he thought there was no horse. Very unlike was this to the exact Philip. The great range of stables was before them, where the Morvilles had been wont to lodge their horses as sumptuously as themselves, and Amabel proposed to go and see what they could find; but nothing was there but emptiness, till they came to a pony in one stall, a goat in another, and one wheelbarrow in the coach-house.

On leaving it, under the long-sheltered sunny wall, they came in sight of a meeting between the baby taking the air in Anne's arms, and Markham, who had been hovering about all day, anxious to know how matters were going on. His back was towards them, so that he was unconscious of their approach, and they saw how he spoke to Anne, looked fixedly at the child, made her laugh, and finally took her in his arms, as he had so often carried her father, studying earnestly her little face. As soon as he saw them coming, he hastily gave her back to Anne, as if ashamed to be thus caught, but he was obliged to grunt and put his hand up to his shaggy eyelashes, before he could answer Amabel's greeting.

He could hardly believe his eyes, that here was Mr. Morville, who yesterday was scarcely able to raise his head from the pillow, and could attend to nothing. He could not think what Lady Morville had done to him, when he heard him inquiring and making arrangements about sending for a pony carriage, appearing thoroughly roused, and the dread of being seen or spoken to entirely passed away, Markham was greatly rejoiced, for Mr. Morville's illness, helplessness, and dependence upon himself, had softened and won him to regard him kindly as nothing else would have done; and his heart was entirely gained when, after they had wished him good-bye, he saw Philip and Amabel walk on, overtake Anne, Amy take the baby and hold her up to Philip, who looked at her with the same earnest interest. From thenceforward Markham knew that Redclyffe was nothing but a burden to Mr. Morville, and he could bear to see it in his possession since like himself, he seemed to regard Sir Guy's daughter like a disinherited princess.

This short walk fatigued Philip thoroughly. He slept till dinner-time, and when he awoke said it was the first refreshing dreamless sleep he had had for weeks. His head was much better, and at dinner he had something like an appetite.

It was altogether a day of refreshment, and so were the ensuing ones. Each day Philip became stronger, and resumed more of his usual habits. From writing a few lines in Amabel's daily letter to Laura, he proceeded to filling the envelope, and from being put to sleep by Charles's reading, to reading aloud the whole evening himself. The pony carriage was set up, and he drove Charles out every day, Amabel being then released from attending him, and free to enjoy herself in her own way in rambles about the house and park, and discoveries of the old haunts she knew so well by description.

She early found her way to Guy's own room, where she would walk up and down with her child in her arms, talking to her, and holding up to her, to be admired, the treasures of his boyhood, that Mrs. Drew delighted to keep in order. One day, when alone in the sitting-room, she thought of trying the piano he had chosen for her. It was locked, but the key was on her own split-ring, where he had put it for her the day he returned from London. She opened it, and it so happened, that the first note she struck reminded her of one of the peculiarly sweet and deep tones of Guy's voice. It was like awaking its echo again, and as it died away, she hid her face and wept. But from that time the first thing she did when her brother and cousin were out, was always to bring down her little girl, and play to her, watching how she enjoyed the music.

Little Mary prospered in the sea air, gained colour, took to springing and laughing; and her intelligent lively way of looking about brought out continually more likeness to her father. Amabel herself was no longer drooping and pining, her step grew light and elastic, a shade of pink returned to her cheek, and the length of walk she could take was wonderful, considering her weakness in the summer. Every day she stood on the cliff and looked at 'Guy's sea,' before setting out to visit the cottages, and hear the fond rough recollections of Sir Guy, or to wander far away into the woods or on the moor, and find the way to the places he had loved. One day, when Philip and Charles came in from a drive, they overtook her in the court, her cloak over her arm, her crape limp with spray, her cheeks brightened to a rosy glow by the wind, and a real smile as she looked up to them. When Charles was on his sofa, she stooped over him and whispered, 'James and Ben Robinson have taken me out to the Shag!'

She saw Mr. Wellwood, and heard a good account of Coombe Prior. She made great friends with the Ashfords, especially little Lucy and the baby. She delighted in visits to the cottages, and Charles every day wondered where was the drooping dejection that she could not shake off at home. She would have said that in Guy's own home, 'the joy' had come to her, no longer in fitful gleams and held by an effort for a moment, but steadily brightening. She missed him indeed, but the power of finding rest in looking forward to meeting him, the pleasure of dwelling on the days he had been with her, and the satisfaction of doing his work for the present, had made a happiness for her, and still in him, quiet, grave, and subdued, but happiness likely to bloom more and more brightly throughout her life. The anniversary of his death was indeed a day of tears, but the tears were blessed ones, and she was more full of the feeling that had sustained her on that morning, than she had been through all the year before.

Charles and Philip, meanwhile, proceeded excellently together, each very anxious for the comfort of the other. Philip was a good deal overwhelmed at first by the quantity of business on his hands, and setting about it while his head was still weak, would have seriously hurt himself again, if Charles had not come to his help, worked with a thorough good will, great clearness and acuteness, and surprised Philip by his cleverness and perseverance. He was elated at being of so much use; and begged to be considered for the future as Philip's private secretary, to which the only objection was, that his handwriting was as bad as Philip's was good; but it was an arrangement so much to the benefit of both parties, that it was gladly made. Philip was very grateful for such valuable assistance; and Charles amused himself with triumphing in his importance, when he should sit in state on his sofa at

Hollywell, surrounded with blue-books, getting up the statistics for some magnificent speech of the honourable member for Moorworth.

In the meantime, Charles and Amabel saw no immediate prospect of their party returning from Ireland, and thought it best to remain at Redclyffe, since Philip had so much to do there; and besides, events were occurring at Kilcoran which would have prevented his visit, even without his illness.

One of the first drives that Charles and Philip took, after the latter was equal to any exertion, was to Thorndale. There Charles was much amused by the manner in which Philip was received, and he himself, for his sake; and as he said to Amabel on his return, there was no question now, that the blame of spoiling Philip did not solely rest at Hollywell.

Finding only Lady Thorndale at home, and hearing that Lord Thorndale was in the grounds, Philip went out to look for him, leaving Charles on the sofa, under her ladyship's care. Charles, with a little exaggeration, professed that he had never been so flattered in his whole life, as he was by the compliments that reflected on him as the future brother-in-law of Philip; and that he had really begun to think even Laura not half sensible enough of her own happiness. Lady Thorndale afterwards proceeded to inquiries about the De Courcy family, especially Lady Eveleen; and Charles, enlightened by Charlotte, took delight in giving a brilliant description of his cousin's charms, for which he was rewarded by very plain intimations of the purpose for which her son James was gone to Kilcoran.

On talking the visit over, as they drove home, Charles asked Philip if he had guessed at his friend's intentions. 'Yes,' he answered.

'Then you never took the credit of it. Why did you not tell us?'

'I knew it from himself, in confidence.'

'Oh!' said Charles, amusing himself with the notion of the young man's dutifully asking the permission of his companion, unshaken in allegiance though the staff might be broken, and the book drowned deeper than did ever plummet sound. Philip spoke no more, and Charles would ask no more, for Philip's own affairs of the kind were not such as to encourage talking of other people's. No explanation was needed why he should now promote an attachment which he had strongly disapproved while James Thorndale was still in the army.

A day or two after, however, came a letter from Charlotte, bringing further news, at which Charles was so amazed, that he could not help communicating it at once to his companions.

'So! Eveleen won't have him!'

'What?' exclaimed both.

'You don't mean that she has refused Thorndale?' said Philip.

'Even so!' said Charles. 'Charlotte says he is gone. "Poor Mr. Thorndale left us this morning, after a day of private conferences, in which he seems to have had no satisfaction, for his resolute dignity and determination to be agreeable all the evening were"— ahem— "were great. Mabel cannot get at any of the real reasons from Eveleen, though I think I could help her, but I can't tell you."'

'Charlotte means mischief.' said Charles, as he concluded.

'I am very sorry!' said Philip. 'I did think Lady Eveleen would have been able to estimate Thorndale. It will be a great disappointment— the inclination has been of long standing. Poor Thorndale!'

'It would have been a very good thing for Eva,' said Amabel. 'Mr. Thorndale is such a sensible man.'

'And I thought his steady sense just what was wanting to bring out all her good qualities that are running to waste in that irregular home,' said Philip. 'What can have possessed her?'

'Ay! something must have possessed her,' said Charles. 'Eva was always ready to be fallen in love with on the shortest notice, and if there was not something prior in her imagination, Thorndale would not have had much difficulty. By the bye, depend upon it, 'tis the tutor.'

Philip looked a little startled, but instantly reassuring himself, said,—

'George Fielder! Impossible! You have never seen him!'

'Ah! don't you remember her description!' said Amy, in a low voice, rather sadly.

The very reason, Amy,' said Charles; 'it showed that he had attracted her fancy.'

Philip smiled a little incredulously.

'Ay!' said Charles, 'you may smile, but you handsome men can little appreciate the attractiveness of an interesting ugliness. It is the way to be looked at in the end. Mark my words, it is the tutor.'

'I hope not!' said Philip, as if shaken in his confidence. 'Any way it is a bad affair. I am very much concerned for Thorndale.'

So sincerely concerned, that his head began to ache in the midst of some writing. He was obliged to leave it to Charles to finish, and go out to walk with Amy.

Amabel came in before him, and began to talk to Charles about his great vexation at his friend's disappointment.

'I am almost sorry you threw out that hint about Mr. Fielder,' said she. 'Don't you remember how he was recommended?'

'Ah! I had forgotten it was Philip's doing; a bit of his spirit of opposition,' said Charles. 'Were not the boys to have gone to Coombe Prior?'

'Yes' said Amabel, 'that is the thing that seems to have made him so unhappy about it. I am sure I hope it is not true,' she added, considering, 'for, Charlie, you must know that Guy had an impression against him.'

'Had he?' said Charles, anxiously.

'It was only an impression, nothing he could accuse him of, or mention to Lord Kilcoran. He would have told no one but me, but he had seen something of him at Oxford, and thought him full of conversation, very clever, only not the sort of talk he liked.' 'I don't like that. Charlotte concurs in testifying to his agreeableness; and in the dearth of intellect, I should not wonder at Eva's taking up with him. He would be a straw to the drowning. It looks dangerous.'

They were very anxious for further intelligence, but received none, except that Philip had a letter from his friend, on which his only comment was a deep sigh, and 'Poor Thorndale! She little knows what she has thrown away!' Letters from Kilcoran became rare; Laura scarcely wrote at all to Philip, and though Mrs. Edmonstone wrote as usual, she did not notice the subject; while Charlotte's gravity and constraint, when she did achieve a letter to Charles, were in such contrast to her usual free and would-be satirical style, that such eyes as her brother's could hardly fail to see that something was on her mind.

So it went on week after week, Charles and Amabel wondering when they should ever have any notice to go home, and what their family could be doing in Ireland. October had given place to November, and more than a week of November had passed, and here they still were, without anything like real tidings.

At last came a letter from Mrs. Edmonstone, which Amabel could not read without one little cry of surprise and dismay, and then had some difficulty in announcing its contents to Philip.

'Kilcoran, Nov. 8th.

'My Dearest Amy,— You will be extremely surprised at what I have to tell you, and no less grieved. It has been a most unpleasant, disgraceful business from beginning to end, and the only comfort in it to us is the great discretion and firmness that Charlotte has shown. I had better, however, begin at the beginning, and tell you the history as far as I understand it myself. You know that Mr. James Thorndale has been here, and perhaps you know it was for the purpose of making an offer to Eveleen. Every one was much surprised at her refusing him, and still more when, after much prevarication, it came out that the true motive was her attachment to Mr. Fielder, the tutor. It appeared that they had been secretly engaged for some weeks, ever since they had perceived Mr. Thorndale's intentions, and not, as it was in poor Laura's case, an unavowed attachment, but an absolute engagement. And fancy Eva justifying it by Laura's example! There was of course great anger and confusion. Lord Kilcoran was furious, poor Lady Kilcoran had nervous attacks, the gentleman was dismissed from the house, and supposed to be gone to England, Eva shed abundance of tears, but after a great deal of vehemence she appeared subdued and submissive. We were all very sorry for her, as there is much that is very agreeable and likely to attract her in Mr. Fielder, and she always had too much mind to be wasted in such a life as she leads here. It seemed as if Laura was a comfort to her, and Lady Kilcoran was very anxious we should stay as long as possible. This was all about three weeks or a month ago; Eva was recovering her spirits, and I was just beginning a letter to tell you we hoped to be at home in another week, when Charlotte came into my room in great distress to tell me that Eveleen and Mr. Fielder were on the verge of a run-away marriage. Charlotte had been coming back alone from a visit to grandmamma, and going down a path out of the direct way to recall Bustle, who had run on, she said, as if he scented mischief, came, to her great astonishment, on Eveleen walking arm-in-arm with Mr. Fielder! Charlie will fancy how Charlotte looked at them! They shuffled, and tried to explain it away, but Charlotte was too acute for them, or rather, she held steadily to "be that as it may, Lord Kilcoran ought to know it." They tried to frighten her with the horrors of betraying secrets, but she said none had been confided to her, and mamma would judge. They tried to persuade her it was the way of all lovers, and appealed to Laura s example, but there little Charlotte was less to be shaken than on any point. "I did not think them worthy to hear their names," she said to me, "but I told them, that I had seen that the truest and deepest of love had a horror of all that was like wrong, and as to Philip and Laura, they little knew what they had suffered; besides, theirs was not half so bad." I verily believe these were the very words she used to them. At last Eva threw herself on her mercy, and begged so vehemently that she would only wait another day, that she suspected, and, with sharpness very like Charlie's, forced from Eva that they were to marry the next morning. Then she said it would be a great deal better that they should abuse her and call her a spy than do what they would repent of all their lives; she begged Eva's pardon, and cried so much that Eva was in hopes she would relent, and then came straight to me, very unhappy, and not in the least triumphant in her discovery. You can guess what a dreadful afternoon we had, I don't think any one was more miserable than poor Charlotte, who stayed shut up in my room all day, dreading the sight of any one, and expecting to be universally called a traitor. The end was, that after much storming, Lord Kilcoran, finding Eveleen determined, and anxious to save her the discredit of an elopement, has agreed to receive Mr. Fielder, and they are to be married from this house on the 6th of December, though what they are to live upon no one can guess. The Kilcorans are very anxious to put the best face on the matter possible, and have persuaded us, for the sake of the family, to stay for the wedding; indeed, poor Lady Kilcoran is so completely overcome, that I hardly like to leave her till this is over. How unpleasant the state of things in the house is no one can imagine, and very, very glad shall I be to get back to Hollywell and my Amy and Charlie. Dearest Amy,

'Your most affectionate.

'L. EDMONSTONE.'

The news was at length told, and Philip was indeed thunder-struck at this fresh consequence of his interference. It threatened at first to overthrow his scarcely recovered spirits, and but for the presence of his guests, it seemed as if it might have brought on a renewal of the state from which they had restored him.

'Yes,' said Charles to Amy, when they talked it over alone, 'It seems as if good people could do wrong with less impunity than others. It is rather like the saying about fools and angels. Light-minded people see the sin, but not the repentance, so they imitate the one without being capable of the other. Here are Philip and Laura finishing off like the end of a novel, fortune and all, and setting a very bad example to the world in general.'

'As the world cannot see below the surface,' said Amy, 'how distressed Laura, must be! You see, mamma does not say one word about her.'

Philip had not much peace till he had written to Mr. Thorndale, who was going at once to Germany, not liking to return home to meet the condolences. Mrs. Edmonstone had nearly the whole correspondence of the family on her hands; for neither of her daughters liked to write, and she gave the description of the various uncomfortable scenes that took place. Lord de Courcy's stern and enduring displeasure, and his father's fast subsiding violence; Lady Kilcoran's distress, and the younger girls' excitement and amusement; but she said she thought the very proper and serious way in which Charlotte viewed it, would keep it from doing them much harm, provided, as was much to be feared, Lord Kilcoran did not end by keeping the pair always at home, living upon him till Mr. Fielder could get a situation. In fact, it was difficult to know what other means there were of providing for them.

At last the wedding took place, and Mrs. Edmonstone wrote a letter, divided between indignation at the foolish display that had attended it, and satisfaction at being able at length to fix the day for the meeting at Hollywell. No one could guess how she longed to be at home again, and to be once more with Charlie.

Nor were Charles and Amabel less ready to go home, though they could both truly say that they had much enjoyed their stay at Redclyffe. Philip was to come with them, and it was privately agreed that he should return to Redclyffe no more till he could bring Laura with him. Amabel had talked of her sister to Mrs. Ashford, and done much to smooth the way; and even on the last day or two, held a few consultations with Philip, as to the arrangements that Laura would like. One thing, however, she must ask for her own pleasure. 'Philip,' said she, 'you must let me have this piano.'

His answer was by look and gesture.

'And I want very much to ask a question, Philip. Will you tell me which is Sir Hugh's picture?'

'You have been sitting opposite to it every day at dinner.'

'That!' exclaimed Amy. 'From what I heard, I fully expected to have known Sir Hugh's in a moment, and I often looked at that one, but I never could see more likeness than there is in almost all the pictures about the house.'

She went at once to study it again, and wondered more.

'I have seen him sometimes look like it; but it is not at all the strong likeness I expected.'

Philip stood silently gazing, and certainly the countenance he recalled, pleading with him to desist from his wilfulness, and bending over him in his sickness, was far unlike in expression to the fiery youth before him. In a few moments more, Amabel had run up-stairs, and brought down Mr. Shene's portrait. There was proved to be more resemblance than either of them had at first sight credited. The form of the forehead, nose, and short upper lip were identical, so were the sharply-defined black eyebrows, the colour of the eyes; and the way of standing in both had a curious similarity; but the expression was so entirely different, that strict comparison alone proved, that Guy's animated, contemplative, and most winning countenance, was in its original lineaments entirely the same with that of his ancestor. Although Sir Hugh's was then far from unprepossessing, and bore as yet no trace of his unholy passions, it bought to Amabel's mind the shudder with which Guy had mentioned his likeness to that picture, and seemed to show her the nature he had tamed.

Philip, meanwhile, after one glance at Mr. Shene's portrait, which he had not before seen, had turned away, and stood leaning against the window-frame. When Amy had finished her silent comparison, and was going to take her treasure back, he looked up, and said, 'Do you dislike leaving that with me for a few minutes?'

'Keep it as long as you like,' said she, going at once, and she saw him no more till nearly an hour after; when, as she was coming out of her own room, he met her, and gave it into her hands, saying nothing except a smothered 'Thank you;' but his eyelids were so swollen and heavy, that Charles feared his head was bad again, while Amy was glad to perceive that he had had the comfort of tears.

Every one was sorry to wish Lady Morville and her brother good-bye, only consoling themselves with hoping that their sister might be like them; and as to little Mary, the attention paid to her was so devoted and universal, that her mamma thought it very well she should receive the first ardour of it while she was too young to have her head turned.

They again slept a night in London, and in the morning Philip took Charles for a drive through the places he had heard of, and was much edified by actually beholding. They were safely at home the same evening, and on the following, the Hollywell party was once more complete, gathered round Charles's sofa in a confusion of welcomes and greetings.

Mrs. Edmonstone could hardly believe her eyes, so much had Charles's countenance lost its invalid look, and his movements were so much more active; Amabel, too, though still white and thin, had a life in her eye and an air of health most unlike her languor and depression.

Every one looked well and happy but Laura, and she had a worn, faded, harassed aspect, which was not cheered even by Philip's presence; indeed, she seemed almost to shrink from speaking to him. She was the only silent one of the party that evening, as they gathered round the dinner or tea-table, or sat divided into threes or pairs, talking over the subjects that would not do to be discussed in public. Charlotte generally niched into Amy's old corner by Charles, hearing about Redclyffe, or telling about Ireland. Mrs. Edmonstone and Amy on the opposite sides of the ottoman, their heads meeting over the central cushion, talking in low, fond, inaudible tones; Mr. Edmonstone going in and out of the room, and joining himself to one or other group, telling and hearing news, and sometimes breaking up the pairs; and then Mrs. Edmonstone came to congratulate Charles on Amy's improved looks, or Charlotte pressed up close to Amy to tell her about grandmamma. For Charlotte could not talk about Eveleen, she had been so uncomfortable at the part she had had to act, that all the commendation she received was only like pain and shame, and her mother was by no means dissatisfied that it should be so, since a degree of forwardness had been her chief cause of anxiety in Charlotte; and it now appeared that without losing her high spirit and uncompromising sense of right, her sixteenth year was bringing with it feminine reserve.

Laura lingered late in Amabel's room, and when her mother had wished them good night, and left them together, she exclaimed, 'Oh, Amy! I am so glad to be come back to you. I have been so very miserable!'

'But you see he is quite well,' said Amy. 'We think him looking better than in the summer.'

'O yes! Oh, Amy, what have you not done? If you could guess the relief of hearing you were with him, after that suspense!' But as if losing that subject in one she was still more eager about, 'What did he think of me?'

'My dear,' said Amabel, 'I don't think I am the right person to tell you that.'

'You saw how it struck him when he heard of my share in it.'

'Yours? Mamma never mentioned you.'

'Always kind!' said Laura. 'Oh, Amy! what will you think of me when I tell I knew poor Eva's secret all the time? What could I do, when Eva pleaded my own case? It was very different, but she would not see it, and I felt as if I was guilty of all. Oh, how I envied Charlotte.'

'Dear Laura, no wonder you were unhappy!'

'Nothing hitherto has been equal to it! said Laura. 'There was the misery of his silence, and the anxiety that you, dearest, freed me from, then no sooner was that over than this was confided to me. Think what I felt when Eva put me in mind of a time when I argued in favour of some such concealment in a novel! No, you can never guess what I went through, knowing that he would think me weak, blameable, unworthy!'

'Nay, he blames himself too much to blame you.'

'No, that he must not do! It was my fault from the beginning. If I had but gone at once to mamma!'

'Oh, I am so glad!' exclaimed Amy, suddenly.

'Glad?"

'I mean,' said Amy, looking down, 'now you have said that, I am sure you will be happier.'

'Happier, now I feel and see how I have lowered myself even in his sight?' said Laura, drooping her head and hiding her face in her hands, as she went on in so low a tone that Amy could hardly hear her. 'I know it all now. He loves me still, as he must whatever he has once taken, into that deep, deep heart of his: he will always; but he cannot have that honouring, trusting, confiding love that– you enjoyed and deserved, Amy– that he would have had if I had cared first for what became me. If I had only at first told mamma, he would not even have been blamed; he would have been spared half this suffering and self-reproach; he would have loved me more; Eva might not have been led astray, at least she could not have laid it to my charge,– and I could lift up my head,' she finished, as she hung it almost to her knees.

Her sister raised the head, laid it on her own bosom, and kissed, the cheeks and brow again and again. 'Dearest, dearest Laura, I am so sorry for you; but I am sure you must feel freer and happier now you know it all, and see the truth.'

'I don't know!' said Laura, sadly.

'And at least you will be better able to comfort him.'

'No, no, I shall only add to his self-reproach. He will see more plainly what a wretched weak creature he fancied had firmness and discretion. Oh, what a broken reed I have been to him!'

'There is strength and comfort for us all to lean upon,' said Amy. 'But you ought to go to bed. Shall I read to you, Laura? you are so tired, I should like to come and read you to sleep.'

Laura was not given to concealments; that fatal one had been her only insincerity, and she never thought of doing otherwise than telling the whole of her conduct in Ireland to Philip. She sat alone with him the next morning, explained all, and entreated his pardon, humiliating herself so much, that he could not bear to hear her.

'It was the fault of our whole lifetime, Laura,' said he, recovering himself, when a few agitated words had passed on either side. 'I taught you to take my dictum for law, and abused your trusty and perverted all the best and most precious qualities. It is I who stand first to bear the blame, and would that I could bear all the suffering! But as it is, Laura, we must look to enduring the consequence all our lives, and give each other what support we may.'

Laura could hardly brook his self-accusation, but she could no longer argue the point; and there was far more peace and truth before them than when she believed him infallible, and therefore justified herself for all she had done in blind obedience to him.

CHAPTER 44

Thus souls by nature pitched too high,
  By sufferings plunged too low,
Meet in the church's middle sky,
  Halfway 'twixt joy and woe;

To practise there the soothing lay,
  That sorrow best relieves,
Thankful for all God takes away,
  Humbled by all He gives.
    – CHRISTIAN YEAR

One Afternoon, late in April, Charles opened the dressing-room door, and paused a moment, smiling. There sat Amabel on the floor before the fire, her hand stretched out, playfully holding back the little one, who, with scanty, flossy, silken curls, hazel eyes and jet-black lashes, plump, mottled arms, and tiny tottering feet, stood crowing and shouting in exulting laughter, having just made a triumphant clutch at her mamma's hair, and pulled down all the light, shining locks, while under their shade the reddening, smiling face recalled the Amy of days long gone by.

'That's right! cried Charles, delighted, 'pull it all down. Out with mamma's own curls again!'

'No, I can never wear my curls again,' said Amy, so mournfully, that he was sorry he had referred to them; and perceiving this, she smiled sweetly, and pulling a tress to its full length, showed how much too short it was for anything but being put plainly under the cap, to which she restored it.

'Is Mrs. Henley come?' she asked.

'As large as life, and that is saying a good deal. She would make two of Philip. As tall and twice as broad. I thought Juno herself was advancing on me from the station.'

'How did you get on with her?'

'Famously; I told her all about everything, and how the affair is to be really quiet, which she had never believed. She could hardly believe my word, when I told her there was to be absolutely no one but ourselves and Mary Ross. She supposed it was for your sake, and I did not tell her it was for their own. It really was providential that the Kilcoran folk disgusted my father with grand weddings, for Philip never could endure one.'

'Oh, Miss Mischief, there goes my hair again! You know Philip is exceedingly worried about Mr. Fielder. Lord Kilcoran has been writing to ask him to find him a situation.'

'That is an article they will be seeking all the rest of their lives,' said Charles. 'A man is done for when he begins to look for a situation! Yes, those Fielders will be a drag on Philip and Laura for ever; for they don't quite like to cast them off, feeling as he does that he led to her getting into the scrape, by recommending him; and poor Laura thinking she set the example.'

'I wish Eva was away from home,' said Amy, 'for Aunt Charlotte's accounts of her vex Laura so much.'

'Ay! trying to eat her cake and have it, expecting to be Mr. Fielder's wife, and reign as the earl's daughter all the same. Poor thing! the day they get the situation will be a sad one for her. She does not know what poortith cauld will be like.'

'Poor Eva!' said Amy. 'I dare say she will shine and be all the better for trouble. There is much that is so very nice in her.'

'Ay, if she has not spoilt it all by this time,— as that creature is doing with your hair! You little monkey, what have you to say to me?'

'Only to wish you good night. Come, baby, we must go to Anne. Good night, Uncle Charles.'

Just as Amabel had borne off her little girl, Mrs. Edmonstone and Charlotte came in, after conducting Mrs. Henley to her room. Charlotte made a face of wonder and dismay, and Mrs. Edmonstone asked where Amy was.

'She carried the baby to the nursery just before you came. I wish you had seen her. The little thing had pulled down her hair and made her look so pretty and like herself.'

'How well her spirits keep up! She has been running up and down stairs all day, helping about everything. Well! we little thought how things would turn out.'

'And that after all Amy would be the home-bird,' said Charles. 'I don't feel as if it was wrong to rejoice in having her in this sweet, shady brightness, as she is now.'

'Do you know whether she means to go to church to-morrow? I don't like to ask.'

'Nor I.'

'I know she does,' said Charlotte. 'She told me so.'

'I hope it will not be too much for her! Dear Amy.'

'She would say it was wrong to have our heads fuller of her than of our bride,' said Charles.

'Poor Laura!' said Mrs. Edmonstone. 'I am glad it is all right at last. They have both gone through a great deal.'

'And not in vain,' added Charles. 'Philip is— '

'Oh, I say not a word against him!' cried Mrs. Edmonstone. 'He is most excellent; he will be very distinguished,– he will make her very happy. Yes.'

'In fact,' said Charles, 'he is made to be one of the first in this world, and to be first by being above it; and the only reason we are almost discontented is, that we compare him with one who was too good for this world.'

'It is not only that.'

'Ah! you did not see him at Redclyffe, or you would do more than simply forgiving him as a Christian.'

'I am very sorry for him.'

'That is not quite enough,' said Charles, smiling, with a mischievous air, though fully in earnest. 'Is it, Charlotte? She must take him home to her mamma's own heart.'

'No, no, that is asking too much, Charlie,' said Mrs. Edmonstone. 'Only one ever was– ' then breaking off– 'and I can never think of Philip as I used to do.'

'I like him much better now,' said Charlotte.

'For my part,' said Charles, 'I never liked him– nay, that's too mild, I could not abide him, I rebelled against him, heart, soul, and taste. If it had not been for Guy, his fashion of goodness would have made me into an extract of gall and wormwood, at the very time you admired him, and yet a great deal of it was genuine. But it is only now that I have liked him. Nay, I look up to him, I think him positively noble and grand, and when I see proofs of his being entirely repentant, I perceive he is a thorough great man. If I had not seen one greater, I should follow his young man's example and take him for my hero model.'

'As if you wanted a hero model,' whispered Charlotte, in a tone between caressing and impertinence.

'I've had one!' returned Charles, also aside.

'Yes,' said Mrs. Edmonstone, going on with her own thoughts, 'unless there had been a great fund of real goodness, he would never have felt it so deeply. Indeed, even when I best liked Philip, I never thought him capable of such repentance as he has shown.'

'If mamma wants to like him very much,' said Charlotte, 'I think she has only to look at our other company.'

'Ay!' said Charles, 'we want no more explanation of the tone of the "Thank you," with which he answered the offer to invite his sister.'

'One comfort is, she can't stay long. She has got a committee meeting for the Ladies' Literary and Scientific Association, and must go home for it the day after to-morrow,' said Charlotte.

'If you are very good, perhaps she will give you a ticket, Charlotte,' said her brother, 'and another for Bustle.'

Mrs. Henley was, meanwhile, highly satisfied with the impression she thought she was making on her aunt's family, especially on Charles and Charlotte. The latter she patronized, to her extreme though suppressed indignation, as a clever, promising girl; the former, she discovered to be a very superior young man, a most valuable assistant to her brother in his business, and her self-complacency prevented her from finding out how he was playing her off, whenever neither Philip nor Laura were at hand to be hurt by it.

She thought Laura a fine-looking person, like her own family, and fit to be an excellent lady of the house; and in spite of the want of fortune, she perceived that her brother's choice had been far better than if he had married that poor pale little Amabel, go silent and quiet that she never could make a figure anywhere, and had nothing like the substantive character that her brother must have in a wife.

Could Mrs. Henley have looked behind the scenes she would have marvelled.

'One kiss for mamma; and one for papa,' was Amy's half-uttered morning greeting, as she lifted from her cot her little one, with cheeks flushed by sleep. Morning and evening Amy spoke those words, and was happy in the double kiss that Mary had learnt to connect with them; happy too in holding her up to the picture, and saying 'papa,' so that his child might never recollect a time when he had not been a familiar and beloved idea.

A little play with the merry child, then came Anne to take her away; and with a suppressed sigh, Amabel dressed for the first time without her weeds, which she had promised to leave off on Laura's wedding-day.

'No, I will not sigh!' then she thought, 'it does not put me further from him. He would be more glad than any one this day, and so I must show some sign of gladness.'

So she put on such a dress as would be hers for life— black silk, and face cap over her still plain hair, then with real pleasure she put on Charles's bracelet, and the silver brooch, which she had last worn the evening when the echoes of Recoara had answered Guy's last chant. Soon she was visiting Laura, cheering her, soothing her agitation, helping her to dress in her bridal array, much plainer than Amy's own had been, for it had been the especial wish of both herself and Philip that their wedding should be as quiet and unlike Guy's as possible. Then Amabel was running down-stairs to see that all was right, thinking the breakfast-table looked dull and forlorn, and calling Charlotte to help her to make it appear a little more festal, with the aid of some flowers. Charlotte wondered to see that she had forgotten how she shunned flowers last summer, for there she was flitting from one old familiar plant to another in search of the choicest, arranging little bouquets with her own peculiar grace and taste, and putting them by each person's place, in readiness to receive them.

It was as if no one else could smile that morning, except Mr. Edmonstone, who was so pleased to see her looking cheerful, in her altered dress, that he kissed her repeatedly, and confidentially told Mrs. Henley that his little Amy was a regular darling, the sweetest girl in the world, poor dear, except Laura.

Mrs. Henley, in the richest of all silks, looked magnificent and superior. Mrs. Edmonstone had tears in her eyes, and attended to every one softly and kindly, without a word; Charlotte was grave, helpful, and thoughtful; Charles watching every one, and intent on making things smooth; Laura looked fixed in the forced composure which she had long ago learnt, and Philip,– it was late before he appeared at all, and when he came down, there was nothing so plainly written on his face as headache.

It was so severe that the most merciful thing was to send him to lie on the sofa in the dressing-room. Amabel said she would fetch him some camphor, and disappeared, while Laura sat still with her forced composure. Her father fidgeted, only restrained by her presence from expressing his fears that Philip was too unwell for the marriage to take place to-day, and Charles talked cheerfully of the great improvement in his general health, saying this was but a chance thing, and that on the whole he might be considered as quite restored.

Mrs. Henley listened and answered, but could not comprehend the state of things. Breakfast was over, when she heard Amabel speaking to Laura in the ante-room.

'It will go off soon. Here is a cup of hot coffee for you to take him. I'll call you when it is time to go.'

Amabel and Charlotte were very busy looking after Laura's packing up, and putting all that was wanted into the carriage, in which the pair were to set off at once from church, without returning to Hollywell.

At the last moment she went to warn Philip it was time to go, if he meant to walk to church alone, the best thing for his head.

'It is better,' said Laura, somewhat comforted.

'Much better for your bathing it, thank you,' said Philip, rising; then, turning to Amy,– 'Do I wish you good-bye now?'

'No, I shall see you at church, unless you don't like to have my blackness there.'

'Would we not have our guardian angel, Laura?' said Philip.

'You know *he* would have been there,' said Amy. 'No one would have been more glad, so thank you for letting me come.'

'Thank you for coming,' said Laura, earnestly. 'It is a comfort.'

They left her, and she stood a few minutes to enjoy the solitude, and to look from the window at her little girl, whom she had sent out with Anne. She was just about to open the window to call to her, and make her look up with one of her merry shouts of 'Mamma!' when Philip came out at the garden-door, and was crossing the lawn. Mary was very fond of him, flattered by the attention of the tallest person in the house, and she stretched her arms, and gave a cry of summons. Amabel watched him turn instantly, take her from her nurse, and hold her in a close embrace, whilst her little round arms met round his neck. She was unwilling to be restored to Anne, and when he left she looked up in his face, and unprompted, held up to him the primroses and violets in her hand.

Those flowers were in his coat when Amabel saw him again at church, and she knew that this spontaneous proof of affection from Guy's little unconscious child was more precious to him than all the kindnesses she could bestow.

Little space was there for musing, for it was high time to set off for church. Mary Ross met the party at the wicket of the churchyard, took Charles on her arm, and by look and sign inquired for Amy.

'Bright outwardly,' he answered, 'and I think so inwardly. Nothing does her so much good as to represent him. Did you wonder to see her?'

'No' said Mary. 'I thought she would come. It is the crowning point of his forgiveness.'

'Such forgiveness that she has forgotten there is anything to forgive,' said Charles.

Philip Morville and Laura Edmonstone stood before Mr. Ross. It was not such a wedding as the last. There was more personal beauty, but no such air of freshness, youth, and peace. He was, indeed, a very fine-looking man, his countenance more noble than it had ever been, though pale and not only betraying the present suffering of the throbbing, burning brow, but with the appearance of a care-worn, harassed man, looking more as if his age was five-and-thirty than eight-and-twenty. And she, in her plain white muslin and quiet bonnet, was hardly bridal-looking in dress, and so it was with her face, still beautiful and brilliant in complexion, but with the weight of care permanent on it, and all the shades of feeling concealed by a fixed command of countenance, unable, however, to hide the oppression of dejection and anxiety.

Yet to the eyes that only beheld the surface, there was nothing but prosperity and happiness in a marriage between a pair who had loved so long and devotedly, and after going through so much for each other's sake, were united at length, with wealth, honour, and distinction before them. His health was re-established, and the last spring had proved that his talents would place him in such a position as had been the very object of his highest hopes. Was not everything here for which the fondest and most aspiring wishes could seek? Yet for the very reason that there was sadness at almost every heart, not one tear was shed. Mrs. Edmonstone's thoughts were less engrossed with the bride than with the young slender figure in black, standing in her own drooping way, her head bent down, and the fingers of her right hand clasping tight her wedding-ring, through her white glove.

The service was over. Laura hung round her mother's neck in an ardent embrace.

'Your pardon! O, mamma, I see it all now!'

Poor thing! she had too much failed in a daughter's part to go forth from her home with the clear, loving, hopeful heart her sister had carried from it! Mrs. Edmonstone's kiss was a full answer, however, a kiss unlike what it had been with all her efforts for many and many a month.

'Amy, pray that it may not be visited!' were the last words breathed to her sister, as they were pressed in each other's arms.

Philip scarcely spoke, only met their kindnesses with grateful gestures and looks, and brief replies, and the parting was hastened that he might as soon as possible be at rest. His only voluntary speech was as he bade farewell to Amabel,–

'My sister now!'

'And his brother,' she answered. 'Good-bye!'

As soon as Amabel was alone in the carriage with Charles, she leant back, and gave way to a flood of tears.

'Amy, has it been too much?'

'No,' she said, recovering herself; 'but I am so glad! It was his chief desire. Now everything he wished is fulfilled.'

'And you are free of your great charge. He has been a considerable care to you, but now he is safe on Laura's hands, and well and satisfactory; so you have no care but your daughter, and we settle into our home life.'

Amabel smiled.

'Amy, I do wish I was sure you are happy.'

'Yes, dear Charlie, indeed I am. You are all so very kind to me, and it is a blessing, indeed, that my own dear home can open to take in me and baby. You know he liked giving me back to you.'

'And it is happiness, not only thinking it ought to be! Don't let me tease you, Amy, don't answer if you had rather not.'

'Thank you, Charlie, it is happiness. It must be when I remember how very happy he used to be, and there can be nothing to spoil it. When I see how all the duties of his station worry and perplex Philip, I am glad he was spared from it, and had all his freshness and brightness his whole life. It beams out on me more now, and it was such perfect happiness while I had him here, and it is such a pleasure and honour to be called by his name;

besides, there is baby. Oh! Charlie, I must be happy— I am; do believe it! Indeed, you know I have you and mamma and all too. And, Charlie, I think he made you all precious to me over again by the way he loved you all, and sent me back, to you especially. Yes, Charlie, you must not fancy I grieve. I am very happy, for he is, and all I have is made bright and precious by him.'

'Yes,' said he, looking at her, as the colour had come into her face, and she looked perfectly lovely with eager, sincere happiness; one of her husband's sweetest looks reflected on her face; altogether, such a picture of youth, joy, and love, as had not been displayed by the bride that morning. 'Amy, I don't believe anything could make you long unhappy!'

'Nothing but my own fault. Nothing else can part me from him,' she whispered almost to herself.

'Yes; no one else had such a power of making happy,' said Charles, thoughtfully. 'Amy, I really don't know whether even you owe as much to your husband as I do. You were good for something before, but when I look back on what I was when first he came, I know that his leading, unconscious as it was, brought out the stifled good in me. What a wretch I should have been; what a misery to myself and to you all by this time, and now, I verily believe, that since he let in the sunlight from heaven on me, I am better off than if I had as many legs as other people.'

'Better off?'

'Yes. Nobody else lives in such an atmosphere of petting, and has so little to plague them. Nobody else has such a "mamma," to say nothing of silly little Amy, or Charlotte, or Miss Morville. And as to being of no use, which I used to pine about— why, when the member for Moorworth governs the country, I mean to govern him.'

'I am sure you are of wonderful use to every one,' said Amabel; 'neither Philip nor papa could get on without you to do their writing for them. Besides, I want you to help me when baby grows older.'

'Is that the laudable result of that great book on education I saw you reading the other day?' said Charles. 'Why don't you borrow a few hints from Mrs. Henley?'

Amy's clear, playful laugh was just what it used to be.

'It is all settled, then, that you go on with us! Not that I ever thought you were going to do anything so absurd as to set up for yourself, you silly little woman: but it seems to be considered right to come to a formal settlement about such a grand personage as my Lady Morville.'

'Yes; it was better to come to an understanding,' said Amabel. 'It was better that papa should make up his mind to see that I can't turn into a young lady again. You see Charlotte will go out with him and be the Miss Edmonstone for company, and he is so proud of her liveliness and— how pretty she is growing— so that will keep him from being vexed. So now you see I can go on my own way, attend to baby, and take Laura's business about the school, and keep out of the way of company, so that it is very nice and comfortable. It is the very thing that Guy wished!'

Amabel's life is here pretty well shown. That of Philip and Laura may be guessed at. He was a distinguished man, one of the most honoured and respected in the country, admired for his talents and excellence, and regarded universally as highly prosperous and fortunate, the pride of all who had any connection with him. Yet it was a harassed, anxious life, with little of repose or relief; and Laura spent her time between watching him and tending his health, and in the cares and representation befitting her station, with little space for domestic pleasure and home comfort, knowing her children more intimately through her sister's observation than through her own.

Perfect and devoted as ever was their love, and they were thought most admirable and happy people. There was some wonder at his being a grave, melancholy man, when he had all before him so richly to enjoy, contrary to every probability when he began life. Still there was one who never could understand why others should think him stern and severe, and why even his own children should look up to him with love that partook of distant awe and respect, one to whom he never was otherwise than indulgent, nay, almost reverential, in the gentleness of his kindness, and that was Mary Verena Morville.

THE END

DETAILED HISTORICAL CONTEXT

THE HEIR OF REDCLYFFE

During the period this book was originally written, the world was a very different place. The events of the time produced an impact on the authorship, style and content of this work. In order for you the reader to better appreciate and connect with this book, it is therefore important to have some context on world events during this timeframe. To this end, we have included a detailed events calendar for the 19th century for your reference.

INTRODUCTION

The 19th century was a fascinating and significant period of development for Western literature because it provided the Foundation for the future development and emergence of contemporary literary traditions and styles. The Romantic, Symbolist, and Realist movements, as well as many social and economic conditions that dominated the 20th century, had their origins and ancestors in the 19th century, according to additional research.

ACTIVITIES AND LITERATURE

Romanticism

In the 19th century, Romanticism emerged as a new approach with a contrasting emphasis on emotion and the irrational. In contrast, the 18th century was considered the age of logic, reason, and intelligence. Romanticism emphasized the singular, the subjective, the mystic, the emotional, and the inner life. It had its origins in the German Sturm und Drang ("Stress and Storm") movement of the late 18th century, whose prominent members included Goethe and Friedrich Schiller. It impacted music, art, literature, and even architecture.

Rousseau

His emphasis on the individual and the value of inspiration influenced the Preromantic and Romantic movements, as well as the Age of Enlightenment and certain aspects of the French Revolution.

Earliest Romantic poets

The 1798 publication of Lyrical Ballads by the English Romantic poets William Wordsworth and Samuel Taylor Coleridge is regarded as the movement's forerunner in the late 18th and early 19th centuries. As evidenced by the works of Pushkin in Russia, Ugo Foscolo and Giacomo Leopardi in Italy, José de Espronceda in Spain, and Giacomo Leopardi, the Romantic poetry movement spread across Europe and beyond.

Romanticism in the U.S.

The historical adventure novels of James Fenimore Cooper, the occult and mystical writings of Edgar Allan Poe, Walt Whitman's poetry, and the transcendentalist writings of Emerson and Henry David Thoreau are examples of the Romantic movement's influence and growth in America.

Poets of the Second Generation of Romanticism

To determine the "truth" of things, the Romantics relied on people's emotions, which were derived from and exemplified by contact with nature and the primal self, rather than logical inquiry. These perspectives are exemplified by the works of the second-generation Romantic poets John Keats, Lord Byron, and Percy Bysshe Shelley.

The Post-Romantic Movement

Parnassianism

The French poets Théophile Gautier and Charles Baudelaire provide examples of Parnassianism in their works. With its emphasis on aesthetics and the concept of art for art's sake, Parnassianism is a continuation of early Romantic perspectives. The philosophical views of Schopenhauer also had an impact. Devotees sought to move away from the Romantic movement's exaggerated passion and sentimentality in favor of a more controlled, formal approach to their fascination with exotic and ancient themes.

Signification and Impressionism

Claude Monet and other Paris-based artists aided the development of impressionism in France at the end of the 19th century, which was first evident in painting and then in music. Impressionism was a painting movement that attempted to depict the visual world as accurately as possible by utilizing the various qualities of light and color as perceived and experienced by humans.

Symbolism can be understood as a shift away from naturalism and realism toward a harsher, more accurate representation of the world that emphasizes the ordinary over the extraordinary. Through the use of imagery, symbolist poetry, as practiced by poets such as Gustave Kahn and Ezra Pound, aimed to "evoke" rather than "depict" or "describe" such a novel.

Beginning in the late 18th century with Horace Walpole's The Castle of Otranto (1765) and Ann Radcliffe's The Mysteries of Udolpho, this was a popular subgenre of European Romantic literature. It was referred to as "gothic" as a result of the prevalence of Gothic architecture in the early works of this genre. The concept that the protagonists' present lives are haunted by their pasts distinguishes this story from other supernatural or ghost tales. Frankenstein by Mary Shelley, Bride of Lammermoor by Walter Scott, The Devil's Elixirs by E.T.A. Hoffmann, Wuthering Heights by Emily Bront, The Strange Case of Dr. Jekyll and Mr. Hyde by Robert Louis Stevenson, and Dracula by Bram Stoker are well-known and cherished 19th-century gothic novels. In addition to Bleak House and Great Expectations by Charles Dickens, other well-known Victorian works influenced by the Gothic tradition are Bleak House and Great Expectations.

Common Philosephy

Deutsch Idealism

Members of this school of thought included Arthur Schopenhauer, who, in contrast to Georg Wilhelm Friedrich Hegel, argued for a return to Kantian transcendentalism, Johann Gottlieb Fichte, who developed Kantian metaphysics and promoted the concept of a self that is a "self-producing and changing process," Georg Wilhelm Friedrich Hegel, whose writings emphasized the significance of the historical thinking process in which the spirit conceives of itself, and Georg Wilhelm Friedrich Hegel.

Marxism

A school of thought that Karl Marx and Friedrich Engels founded and advanced. The Communist Manifesto (1848) laid the groundwork for the modern communist movement by predicting that capitalism would eventually self-destruct and be replaced by socialism and then communism.

Positivism

Authentic knowledge, according to empiricist philosophical theory, is either true by definition or positive, i.e., an a posteriori fact determined by reason and logic derived from sensory experience, as opposed to instinct or theology. This theory was first articulated and described by August Comte.

Societal Evolution

Social Darwinism seeks to apply biological concepts of natural selection and survival of the fittest, such as those described in Charles Darwin's On the Origin of Species. Francis Galton was one of the proponents, arguing that mental aptitudes were inherited similarly to physical ones and that it was best to prevent overbreeding among the "less fit" members of society. Francis Spencer and Herbert Spencer supported the concept, which they advocated in their 1860 book The Social Organism, which compared society to a living organism that changes and develops in a similar manner.

Effects on Society, Commerce, and Politics

Industrial Reformation

The Industrial Revolution, a period of significant social, political, and economic upheaval and change that occurred between the late 18th century and the years 1820 to 1840, involved the transition from largely manual production methods to mechanical manufacturing methods, particularly in the fields of textiles, steam power, iron making, and the invention of machine tools. Prior to industrialization, the European economy was supported by agriculture. Simultaneously, fundamental political, scientific, and religious beliefs were being dismantled entirely.

As a result of this mechanization, a substantial number of people moved from rural villages to urban areas, resulting in a substantial rise in population and the formation of new, larger cities. New technology paved the way for factories, a horrifying and dehumanizing form of labor that included child labor, and a capitalist lifestyle. As described in 1844 works such as Friedrich Engels' The Condition of the Working Class in England, cities were unable to accommodate the sudden increase in population, resulting in overcrowded slums and terrible living conditions.

The Cry of the Children by Elizabeth Barrett Browning, Tess of the D'Urbervilles by Thomas Hardy, and works by author and philosopher Thomas Carlyle all foresaw the danger these inhumane practices and the profit-driven, materialistic ideals of the "mechanical age" posed to society.

Influential Works of Nonfiction and the Sciences

Victorian efforts to comprehend and classify the natural world had a significant impact on scientific theory and understanding throughout the 19th century. The revolutionary concept of evolution that Charles Darwin advanced in his writings, such as the well-known On the Origin of Species (1859), would have a profound and far-reaching effect because it contradicted many of the preconceived notions and religious beliefs of the time.

The French Revolution: A History, published in 1837, and On Heroes, Hero-Worship, and the Heroic in History, published in 1841, were two additional influential nonfiction works of the period that influenced political thought in the middle of the 19th century.

Significant Historical Occasions

The Treaty of Amiens and the Acts of Union

The Acts of Union, which united Britain and Ireland to form the United Kingdom, were passed in 1800, following periods of unpredictability and disorder caused by the French Revolution and the Irish Rebellion in the late 18th century.

The Second Coalition French Revolutionary War ended with the signing of the Treaty of Amiens, which also promised to end disputes between France and the United Kingdom. However, the effect was short-lived, as the Napoleonic Wars began three years later.

US enlargement

With their newly-won independence, the United States decided in 1803 to acquire the land known as the Louisiana Purchase in order to expand their control over the Mississippi River and double their size. Native Americans inhabit a sizeable portion of the land acquired from the French First Republic for fifteen million dollars.

American Revolutionary War

Admiral Nelson soundly defeated the French and Spanish armies at the Battle of Trafalgar, establishing the nation's dominance over the oceans, thwarting Napoleon's plans to invade England. In 1805, Napoleon had previously defeated the Russian and Austrian armies.

Napoleon's former reputation as an unbeatable general was shattered during the invasion of Russia, when up to 380,000 French soldiers perished. In 1814, the French king's defeat in the War of the Sixth Coalition led to his abdication and exile to Elba.

The British and Russian empires' expansion

Britain expanded its overseas territories in Canada, Australia, South Africa, and Africa, while Russia expanded its sphere of influence to include Central Asia and the Caucasus following the defeat of France. The British East India Company was dissolved as a result of the 1857 Indian Rebellion, a significant rebellion against its rule. Later, the British Raj was established, with the British Crown governing directly.

Opium warfare

By the middle of the nineteenth century, China was experiencing severe opium problems as a result of the opening of trade with the West and the illegal opium trade orchestrated by British businessmen seeking to profit at the trade ports. The First Opium War and the Treaty of Nanking, which allowed the drug trade to continue and resulted in British control of Hong Kong, were precipitated by Britain's opposition to the emperor's attempt to ban the sale of opium on the basis of free trade principles.

In 1856, the second Opium War, in which the French and British joined forces, was fought violently against the backdrop of the Taiping Rebellion. As a result of the 1860 Convention of Peking, which legalized the opium trade and required the handover of additional territories, the Qing dynasty was overthrown in the early 19th century.

The 1848 Revolutions

The 1848 Revolutions, also known as the Springtime of the Nations, refer to a series of political upheavals that occurred virtually simultaneously throughout Europe and the rest of the world at this time. The primary objectives of these uprisings were the overthrow of the previous monarchies and the installation of free-nation governments.

In an effort to establish a liberal government and liberate Italy from Austrian rule, Italian nationalists orchestrated revolts in Sicily and the Italian peninsula's republics. Following the suppression of the campagne des banquets, a bloody uprising against the monarchy that resulted in the overthrow of King Louis Philippe, the French February Revolution took place in Paris. Other nations, such as Germany, Denmark, Hungary, Galicia, Sweden, and Switzerland, also experienced revolutions against the Habsburg Monarchy.

Abolition of slavery and abolitionist efforts

The United States prohibited the transatlantic slave trade in 1808, and the Slavery Abolition Act of 1833 made slavery illegal throughout the British Empire. The abolitionist movement triumphed in the nineteenth century. In the United States, abolitionism persisted until the end of the Civil War in 1865, which prompted the Thirteenth Amendment to the Constitution, which officially abolished slavery.

Suffrage movement for women

The Seneca Falls Convention in the United States and the National Women's Rights Convention in 1850 made the call for universal women's suffrage louder and more forceful during the 1840s. In 1839, both The Equality of the Sexes and the Condition of Women by Sarah Grimké and Margaret Fuller's influential feminist book Woman in the Nineteenth Century were published.

After suffragist attempts to obtain the right to vote failed in the early 1870s, a prolonged and persistent campaign for a constitutional amendment on women's rights and for suffrage in every state was launched. Wyoming was the first state to grant women the right to vote in 1869. Following Wyoming's failure, a prolonged and persistent campaign for a constitutional amendment on women's rights and for suffrage in every state was launched. Wyoming was the first state to grant women the franchise in 1869. In 1880, Emmeline Pankhurst joined and assisted in leading the British suffragette movement.

This concludes the historical context.

Thank you for your interest in our publications. Please don't forget to check out our other books at Vintage Bookworks and leave a review if you enjoyed this book.

Made in the USA
Coppell, TX
25 May 2024

32767303R10301